WOLFMOTHER
PUBLISHING LLC

ALMA, MICHIGAN
UNITED STATES
COPYRIGHT © 2025 BY AMY QUILLEN

Book cover by Wolfmother Publishing LLC.
**First edition, 2025.**

# The Lemon Ladies

## By Amy Quillen

This novel is dedicated to the fiercest beast in North America—the mighty Midwestern Mama Bear, in all her various shades.

May your cubs make the world a safer and kinder place for all of us.

...and to **Liam.**

# Chapters

# Chapter 1

# Hot Shot

**M**ateo plastered his body to the wall of his family's dining room, as close to the door as possible. Taking slow, deep breaths he reminded himself he could leave any time he wanted to. He wasn't trapped. He was safe. The twenty-five people crammed into his house were his relatives.

The air was humid with body heat and steam from a boiling pot of potatoes. He took a long sip of orange soda from a red plastic cup.

Smoldering turkey juices spilled in the oven.

Coffee brewing.

People laughing over a game of *La Loteria*.

Too close. Too loud. Too much.

Glass shattered in the 30-gallon trash can he was attempting to hide behind. He jumped with a whimper.

"Sorry kid. Didn't mean to startle you…" his aunt, Sofia, stood with a freshly opened bottle of wine in one hand, and an unlit cigarette and lighter in the other. An empty wine bottle lay broken in the bottom of the trash can. "Can I get around you? I need to step outside. Your dad has a *lot* of goddamn cousins. Two bottles won't be enough to get through this night."

Mateo stood unresponsive and hyperventilating, eyes wide and staring at the oblivious horde of out-of-town relatives snacking on baby carrots and summer sausage.

Sofia snapped her fingers in front of his face. "Holy shit, you're still doing that? You're sixteen!"

She sighed while rolling her eyes, grabbed him by the elbow, and led him through the sliding doors to the backyard patio.

The only light was the moon and a soft glow from the kitchen window. Cool November air felt good on Mateo's face as consciousness returned to his body, leading him out of The Dark Place.

Sofia gestured for him to sit in a cedar Adirondack chair, but he wasn't all the way Home yet. He was still with the moon, luminous overhead.

"Are you kidding me, *sobrino?*" She took the red plastic cup from his clenched hands and dumped his soda on the leaf-coated lawn. Sofia then refilled it to the brim from her bottle of wine.

"Fine, you don't have to sit down, but I am." She passed him back the cup, then tossed her sister's decorative *Thankful, Grateful, Blessed* throw pillows from the patio furniture across the yard. "I've been cleaning nasty hotel rooms all day. This is only my third bottle of wine, you're lucky I'm sharing." Sofia settled into the chair intending to stay there until the cold forced her inside or the booze ran out, whichever came first.

Mateo returned to Earth and took a small sip of wine. Bitter and dry, it hit his tongue like a magic potion and snapped him fully into his body once more. He'd only ever tried a stolen craft beer from his dad's work cooler; this was a very different experience. Mateo climbed into the low reclining chair across from his aunt, trying not to spill the red liquid from his cracked plastic cup.

With narrowed eyes, his aunt pointed at him while the tip of her menthol cigarette burned orange in the dim moonlight. "It's been ten years. You need to figure this shit out."

He was used to his family questioning his claustrophobia. He tried to pretend it was better, but in truth, he was only avoiding his triggers-crowds, small spaces, and the dark. His parents spent years taking him to CBT and trying different types of benzos. When he became a teenager, the doctor encouraged him to try antidepressants instead. He explained that

Benzodiazepines- Valium, Xanax, Ativan- are addictive and easily abused. His parents immediately stopped the medication. Mateo didn't mind; none of it worked anyway, it just made him tired. His best medicine was avoidance- of his triggers *and* his parents.

"I'm fine." He gulped his drink. "It's like you said, Dad's got a lot of goddamn cousins."

Sofia glared at him. "What's with the devil horn hoodie? Are you one of those 'sad boi emo kids' now?" Her words were slurring. She sat back in the chair to stop the world from spinning.

"I'm not an emo...Christ, Auntie." Mateo pointed at the name on the front of his hoodie. "It's my favorite band, Set it Off. They're coming to St. Louis in a few months."

Sofia took a long drag of her cigarette. "Hmph. So, are you *going* to the concert? D'you manage to make friends and shit despite being a fuckin' weirdo?"

Mateo managed a small laugh. He couldn't remember the last time someone in his family asked him about his interests instead of the status of his "condition". "Yeah, I have a group of friends. We're trying to get enough money for tickets before they sell out."

"I thought you were working for that creepy old farmer selling shit at the farmer's market." Sofia glugged straight from the bottle, then looked off into the night sky.

"Yeah, I am...he's a cheap bastard though. Hey...do you think you could loan me a couple hundred dollars?" He pleaded as a last-ditch attempt to his favorite relative. "I can pay you back after I get Christmas cash from Dad's family."

Sofia gave a short, cynical laugh. "Money isn't what it used to be for me, Mateenio."

Mateo would normally cringe at the use of his childhood nickname, but tonight he found it comforting. "Oh, right...I forgot."

Silence hung in the air, mixing with the smoke from her nearly extinguished cigarette. Sofia took a pack of menthols from her pocket and expertly lit the end of the fresh stick with the stub of the other. "Normally I would. Jay's family kicked me out of our house and I'm living in a hotel. I clean rooms for a reduced rate. His family took everything except the Mustang. Bastards only let me have it 'cuz that's where he died."

Mateo sipped from his cup. "I'm sorry, Auntie. I really liked Jason."

"Me too…" Sofia pointed her glowing cigarette again. "He was one cool motherfucker, wasn't he?"

Mateo nodded. "Sofia…Mom and Dad won't tell me what happened."

"I know. They told me not to tell you, so don't ask." She said flatly.

Mateo didn't say anything. Sofia inhaled with a heave and released a deep, boozy breath that Mateo could smell from five feet away.

"Someone fuckin' killed him is what happened." She said, finally.

Confused, Mateo said, "…but I don't remember there being any detectives or anything. I don't understand."

"Yeah 'cuz everyone's saying he did it to himself." She flicked her cigarette a little too hard and knocked off the hot end. Mateo waited for her to relight it with a pack of hotel matches

"The only thing wrong with him that night is he had a toothache. Are you sure you want to hear about this *nino?*"

Mateo nodded.

Sophia took a deep breath and began. "Alright then… Jason has a toothache. He headed out to the pharmacy to get some numbing ointment until he could go to the dentist in the morning. On the way, he was going to pay his sister rent. When his parents died, they split the estate, so we've been paying rent to buy out her share for the last three years.

"Two hours go by, and he's still not home. Not answering his phone, and his sister hadn't seen him. Now it's getting dark and I'm worried, calling hospitals and checking police reports online. Nothing. Then I remembered we enabled location sharing on our phones, and it says he's out in the woods on his family's property.

"It's fuckin' weird, right? He'd just got the Mustang polished and detailed, there was no way in hell he'd drive it back there. It's all dirt trails and overgrown trees. By this time it's getting late and dark, so I called your dad and he picked me up in his work truck.

"We go out there, following the little dot on my phone. We find the Mustang, still running, blasting 'The Wizard' by Black Sabbath of all fuckin' songs. And there he is in the driver's seat, slumped over dead with a needle in his arm."

Mateo's mouth hung open in shock. "I didn't know…I didn't know Jay did that kind of stuff."

"He doesn't!" Sofia shouted into the night. "I mean, he *didn't.*" she sniffed. "He'd been clean for ten years. Someone gave him a hot shot. To the cops, and everyone else, he's just an addict that relapsed and OD'd on bad heroine. But they don't know Jason. That man *loved* his 'boring sober life', as he called it. Work, grilling, tv, sleep, his Mustang, and Olive Garden once a week are all it took to make him happy. Before getting sober, he lived his whole life in the fast lane, and it nearly destroyed him. He would *never* go back to that."

Sofia hurled the now-empty wine bottle across the yard where it landed on the pile of throw pillows.

Mateo was afraid to push too far, but he had to know. "What's a hot shot?"

Sofia took a long drag of her cigarette and shook her head in disbelief. "What kind of fuckin' sixteen-year-old are you? You don't know shit about what's goin' on in the world, do you?"

Mateo shrugged, unoffended.

Sofia rolled her eyes, collected herself, and sat up straight. "It's when someone kills another person by giving them drugs laced with other shit to make it strong enough to kill them. Jay's hot shot had heroin and benzos in it.

"Benzos?" Mateo's stomach turned.

"Yeah, kid. It's a slippery slope when you get on that stuff. Plus, you can't trust nothin' people give you anymore. It's all laced with fenty or whatever other poison is out there."

At this point Sofia had angry tears in her eyes, and so did Mateo. After a brief silence she said, "Mateenio…look at me."

He sat up and gave her his full attention.

Her glazed-over eyes were pleading with him. "That's why you gotta figure out a way to cope with your problems that doesn't kill you or make you seem like some kind of weirdo at family functions."

Frustration flooded his body: at his family, at himself, at his condition, at his past. "But how?! How do *you* manage it? How does *anyone* manage it?"

Sofia fell back into the chair sloppily, laughing at the question. "I don't know about other people, but if you look in the glove compartment of the Mustang I'll show you how I cope. It might help you, too."

She pulled the keys from her coat and clumsily threw them on the ground near Mateo. He picked them up and ran his thumb over the engraved white image of a Mustang on the key, then trotted across the damp dark leaves of a scarlet maple, and through the fence gate to the front of his house. He found Jason's red Mustang parked on the lawn, crushing his mother's treasured 'double knock-out' pink roses. He wasn't going to hear the end of that tomorrow.

Jason once told Mateo that this Mustang wasn't just *red*. It's *true red*- just slightly orange with no hint of cherry color. Every time he saw it, he thought of the Hot Wheels cars he played with as a kid, and he told Jay as much. He laughed and said kids told him that all the time. The next time they met up to grill at his house, he gave Mateo a Matchbox version of his exact Mustang in *true red*. "Now you have one, too." He'd said. Mateo kept the car on his desk and remembered Jason every time he saw it.

When Mateo opened the wide, heavy door of the Mustang, the first thing he noticed was the smell. When Jason drove it, the Mustang somehow always maintained that 'new car' smell. Now, it had a smell he couldn't place. It wasn't death, as some part of his brain expected…it was a chemical. He knew it couldn't be cigarettes. There's no way Sofia would smoke in Jason's car. He would come back as a ghost and haunt her for disrespecting his Queen.

Mateo sat in the cold leather seat, gripping the steering wheel. Jay had promised to let him drive it around the block after he got his full driver's license, but he passed away before that happened. Mateo felt around in the dim overhead light for the latch to the glove compartment. It was locked, and the key Sofia gave him was a fob.

He opened the center console to look for a key and was immediately hit with what could only be the source of the chemical smell in the car. A crumpled blue rag was inside. Mateo lifted it out and noticed it smelled sweet, but maybe like nail polish remover. Jay would be pissed if he knew Sofia was doing her nails in his car. He threw the rag out the open door.

He pulled out a stack of papers-car insurance, a speeding ticket (Sofia's, not Jay's), and an unlabeled, but unsealed envelope. Mateo opened it and removed the paper inside. It was yellowed, coffee-stained, and ink-smeared on the outside. When he unfolded the paper, he realized he was looking at a hand-drawn map. It illustrated a road leading to a cave entrance, and an elaborately detailed cave system. It was titled, "The Cheese Caves".

Mateo laughed and stuffed it in his pocket. He felt around blindly inside the console until his fingers landed on a small, metal, key-shaped object. "Yes!" he whispered to himself as he snatched it up and then shoved all the papers back into the console. He unlocked the glove box and there, gleaming in the tiny bulb light was a six-shooter pistol, next to a tiny sandwich bag decorated with snowmen, rolled up like a burrito.

He assumed the way his aunt "dealt with life" was with whatever was in the plastic bag and not the gun. He removed the bag from the compartment and unrolled it to reveal three fat joints. He rolled his eyes, left the gun, locked the glove box, and then the Mustang. As he walked towards the house, his mother opened the front door.

"Junior, is that you?" she asked.

"Yeah," he yelled from the dark. "I'm just getting something for Tia Sofia."

"Did she park on my roses?!" she shrieked into the night.

Mateo kept a straight face as he walked past her on the porch toward the backyard. "No, *Madre*, they're fine. She just missed them."

His mother scowled. "She better hope she did."

Mateo speed-walked around the corner and locked the gate behind him. Sofia was slumped to one side, lazily scrolling on her phone. "Why does Stephanie keep tagging me trying to get me to buy candles? I'm broke, sweetheart. Block. Oh, hey Mattie. Did you get the stuff?" she asked with renewed vigor.

He held up the keys to the Mustang. "I'm keeping hold of these until morning."

"Okay, fine. Did you find my stuff?" she asked again.

He held up the snowman bag. "I assume you mean this and not the pistol?"

"What?" a sudden realization surfaced in Sofia's inebriated brain. "Oh shit. I forgot about that. Jay had people try to carjack him a few times, twice when we went camping in upstate New York. New Yorkers are *nuts*. I forgot the gun was in there."

Mateo tossed the bag of joints to Sofia. "I thought you told me not to do drugs." He raised his eyebrows in jest.

"Marijuana is not a drug. It's a plant." She removed a joint from the bag. "Besides, it's from a dispensary, so I know it's safe. Don't go buying 'project weed' even though it's cheaper!" Sofia puffed furiously as she tried to light it. "First of all, it's always stank weed AND usually mixed with other shit. You never know if it's fenty or catnip. It's like playing Russian roulette. Grow it yourself, or buy it in a legit shop, homie."

Mateo didn't acknowledge her unnecessary advice or her hilarious use of the word *homie*. Rather, he watched her puff away as smoke encircled her head like a wreath. He couldn't help but think she looked like the middle-aged Latino version of the advice-doling caterpillar from *Alice in Wonderland*.

"Auntie, why would someone give Jason a hot shot?"

She took a moment to process her response. "Well, usually people are given a hot shot because they owe their dealer so much money they can't pay it back. They reach the end of the road, and the dealer takes them out in retaliation. Kind of uses them as an example, I guess. But I was with Jason every day. He doesn't owe anybody a damned thing, not even Capital One. I haven't seen that man high on anything besides Bojangles fried chicken in ten years."

"So, why then?" Mateo pressed.

Sofia was beginning to drift and reclined lazily in the Adirondack chair. "Sometimes people get a hot shot for knowing too much, like a police informant. *Una rata*, you know? But all that man did was work, eat, and sleep. He was boring as fuck."

Mateo shook her foot as her head began to slump. "Auntie, wake up! So why, then? Why do you think someone did it?"

She scoffed. "Everyone thinks I'm crazy, that Jason is just some addict that overdosed. Open and shut. Case closed. I knew Jay better than anyone, and I think he saw something he shouldn't. He didn't do that hot shot willingly. Someone did it *to him*. I just don't know what *puta madre* did it and why."

Sofia drifted off, Mateo watching as the joint in her fingers smoldered away and filled the air with skunk-smelling smoke. Jason was pretty much his "common law" uncle. Losing him devastated his aunt in every way, not just from his death. They weren't married, even after all these years, so his sister inherited everything, including Jason's share of the family estate. He wondered if that had something to do with Jason's death, but he'd never known Jay's family. He never talked about them either.

He shook his aunt awake again. "Hey! You're wasting your pot."

She sat up and brushed the ashes off her coat. "Shit."

"Hey…I just want you to know I don't think you're crazy. I don't think Jason would do that to himself, either." He paused a moment and pulled the map out of his pocket. Mateo opened it and held it up close to Sofia's drunk eyes so she could see clearly. "I found this in the Mustang, do you think this has something to do with it?"

She snatched it from him, laughed, and didn't seem surprised by Mateo's mysterious discovery. "Look at you, playing detective! No, Mateenio. That's just a map of the Cheese Caves. Out on Jay's family's property. We used to party there during the winter as teenagers. It's like 50 degrees all year. I haven't been out there in like ten years. Jay and I got old, fat, and lazy. It's too much work for a good time and a slice of cheese. I can get that at home."

Mateo shook his head. "Wait, what? Are you saying there's real cheese in this cave? Are you serious?"

His aunt began to nod again. "Sofia! Don't pass out! What is this?!"

She growled and rolled her head from side to side. "Ugh! Fine! You're so annoying, Mateo!"

She sat up slightly. "After this, you're going to leave me alone, right?"

"Sure, whatever, *Tia.*"

"It's stupid Springfield folklore. Apparently, back in the eighties, the government had like, a billion pounds of cheese for some reason, and nowhere to put it. So, they paid "rent" to people with limestone caves on their property to store it until it could be used. I guess they had so much it started to go bad or something and the government never came back for a lot of it. The caves on Jason's family's land were abandoned. Last I knew the cheese is still in there. Back in the day I even ate some, but I'm classy like that. Good ol' reliable government cheese." She gave a few shallow chuckles and slipped into sleep almost instantly, as her chuckles turned to gentle snores. Mateo knew he wouldn't get any more answers tonight.

For a few minutes, he watched his aunt sleeping peacefully. Drool began to form in the corners of her mouth. He removed his favorite demon-horned Set it Off hoodie, and laid it across his aunt, carefully tucking the hood, with horned side down, under her head like a pillow.

He took the ashy joint from her fingers and smoked it down to a nub. He felt his body relax and his anxious thoughts lessen. He snatched the Cheese Cave map from his aunt's grip, flicked away the blunt, and then using an overturned terra cotta pot to step on, climbed into his bedroom window.

# Chapter 2

## The Cheese Caves

"You want to steal old cheese…from a cave…and then sell it to hipsters so we can go to the concert?"

Five teenagers gawked at the sixth, with a range of expressions on their faces: confusion, curiosity, disinterest, fear, concern.

"Bro, are you okay?" Theo asked in disbelief. "You've been watching too many urban legend videos. That shit's not real. I shouldn't have to tell you this." He scanned the board game shop to make sure no one was listening, then laid a few *Magic the Gathering* cards on his playmat and nervously sipped at his boba tea.

"Yeah, for real, Mateo." Said Trix from the next table down where they took turns laying cards, mumbling actions, and turning the damage counter die as Ash scowled in silence at another obvious loss. "Dude don't start acting weird in this shop too or we'll get kicked out and have nowhere to play. I live on the north side. I can't afford gas to drive all the way to Nixa for Friday Night Magic."

Mateo mumbled *untap, upkeep, draw* before pulling from his deck of cards and said a little too loudly, "Guys, hear me out. I know it sounds stupid, but there really is cheese in the limestone caves."

All five teenagers stopped playing and side-eyed the shop owner, who was busy stocking the latest *Ticket to Ride* expansion, appearing unconcerned with their conversation. Mateo lowered his voice and gestured for them to come sit with him. Eyes rolling, they brought their folding chairs to the center table and pretended to negotiate trades.

When everyone was settled, Mateo began whispering fervently. "So back in the seventies, there was a dairy shortage in the United States. Milk and cheese were super expensive. So, when Jimmy Carter became president, he gave billions of dollars to the dairy industry."

"I'm listening."

"I hate history."

"Did anyone ever tell you how beautiful your eyes are, Mateo?" asked Theo with a smirk, from directly across the table.

"Only you, asshole." Mateo sighed with frustration. "Can you please just listen for a minute?"

They quieted down to allow Mateo to speak, occasionally shuffling their decks or slipping newly purchased cards into protective plastic sleeves.

"Thank you," Mateo said indignantly, then sat back in his chair and took a sip of his chocolate drink as he collected his thoughts. "So...after all this money is pumped into the dairy industry, farmers started producing like crazy. Or, rather, their cows did. There was so much milk that the government had to start buying it from the farmers. They turned it into cheese, butter, and dry milk to give to poor people."

Trix nodded in understanding and picked at their blue nail polish. "Stepdad Number Two told me that the best grilled cheese sandwich you can eat is made with government cheese. Apparently, it melts just right or something. He says they don't give it out anymore though."

"He's right." Said Mateo. "Most people think it's all gone."

Theo grumbled. "Ugh, now I'm hungry for a grilled cheese sandwich. I'm training so much that I eat constantly. Alex did this super illegal rabbit punch to some guy who stole his girlfriend...*POW* right in the back of the head. He got kicked off the team so I'm carrying the hopes and dreams of the entire boxing gym now, *I guess.* Hey Mattie, what are you drinking?"

Mateo shrugged. "A Dark Elf. Chocolate milk, chocolate syrup, and espresso. It's pretty good if you don't like the taste of coffee."

Theo stood up and pushed out of his chair. "Aww, hell yeah, that sounds perfect. I'm gonna get one from the café."

Oliver grabbed him by his muscley shoulder. "I need to get home and study, He-man. Let Mateo finish telling us about his ridiculous side quest."

Mateo continued. "So, they turn all this milk into cheese, but they were running out of refrigerators to put it in, and electricity was super expensive. People kept telling the president 'Hey, why don't you just dump the milk in the ocean? That's the cheapest way to get rid of it.' Then the president was like, 'Nah dude, that is *wasteful* and people in America are starving, we gotta save it.'

That's when somebody figured out that Missouri is full of limestone caves that stay 45 degrees *all the time*…the perfect temperature for cheese."

"Wait…" said Ash, as he packed his cards into a deck box covered in *Set it Off* stickers. "Who was the president that did all this?"

Mateo shrugged, not seeing why it mattered. "Well, it started with Carter, but Reagan is the one that had to get rid of it."

Ash flipped the lid shut on his deck box with a snap. "Man, fuck Reagan. I've got two gay dads. I'm not getting involved with anything he did."

The store owner coughed and glanced their way. Ash looked down sheepishly, not wanting to get kicked out of the only remaining card shop in Springfield that would have them.

"No, I don't want to trade *Rhystic Study* for *Llanowar Wastes*, Ashton." Esme feigned a trade in an attempt to reassure the store owner that they weren't, in fact, hooligans. "What kind of crap is this?" She tossed some loose cards across the table to Ash, who responded by rolling his eyes.

"Ez! Stop throwing cards!" demanded Theo, highly offended.

"Yeah, those aren't even sleeved, you heathen!" scolded Trix.

"Jeesh. They're just Lands, nerds." Esme pouted as she collected her cards and put them in pink sleeves with a fairy on the back.

"Noob mistake. We've taught you better than that." Mateo scowled, momentarily distracted by this cardinal *Magic the Gathering* sin. "Anyway, Ash- this has nothing to do with Reagan. It's about us being able to go to the concert, buy some t-shirts, eat some pulled pork nachos at Fitz's, and not run out of gas in the middle of Mark Twain Forest on the way home!" Mateo pleaded to his friends.

"Mattie…" Esme asked gently as she put away her remaining cards. "I can see this is important to you, but I'm just not understanding- how is this going to get us money? Hasn't all the cheese already gone bad? Who would actually buy it?"

Mateo threw up his arms in frustration. "If you guys focus for two seconds, I can tell you. Is everyone ready now? Do you have your *listening ears* on?" He then spoke to them in a baby voice. "Alright children, *Hocus Pocus*-"

Trix gave a huge grin revealing rainbow banded braces. "*Time to focus!*"

Theo, Oliver, Ash, and Esme groaned and crossed their arms but sat back in the chairs silently. Mrs. Ross had repeated that phrase to them often in the first grade when they all met in her class.

"So, in the eighties…" Mateo pressed forward despite his friends' scowls. "The government started paying people with caves to store the cheese, and all the country's excess dairy got shipped to Missouri."

"Wait…" interrupted Oliver. "You're not talking about breaking into the Springfield Underground, are you? I worked a temp job there last summer stocking pre-made coffee drinks *for a company I can't mention*. That place is locked down like Fort Knox. You can't just walk in there. All the big brand food companies use the caves to store products- mac and cheese, ketchup, butter. When you're hired at The Vaults, you don't even know who you're working for until you get there. You're not allowed to tell anyone what you see, either."

"Why, though?" asked Esme, perplexed.

"They don't say." Said Oliver. "It's all super secretive and they only hire temps, so no single person knows a whole lot about the place. They don't advertise what businesses use The Underground, and all the companies are sectioned off from each other. I only know about the other places because I met some people who worked in those departments on my lunch break."

"I know why they don't want you to tell anyone what you see," deduced Ash. "It's because if people knew their food was stored in a limestone cave under the meth capital of the United States—AKA Springfield, Missouri—they would lose their damned minds. Granola moms would riot in the streets."

Mateo nodded. "You're probably right, Ash. The government stopped using The Vaults in the nineties from what I understand. They said all the cheese was used up in food programs and public school lunches. The thing is…" Mateo geared up for his grand finale. "The government didn't just use The Vaults. They paid people with large caves on *private* land, too. There were so many caves that the government forgot some and never came back for the products."

He shifted in his seat. "I'm not talking about breaking into The Vaults. I know of a private cave that's been abandoned…and even better- I have a map."

Mateo pulled his aunt Sofia's map from his pocket and slapped it down dramatically on the table. His friends considered it in silence. "Well?" asked Mateo expectantly.

"Aren't you afraid of the dark?" asked Theo.

"…and small spaces." Added Trix.

Mateo blushed in embarrassment. "Well, I thought maybe you guys could go get it."

"What!" They whisper-yelled.

"So, you're telling me you want us to pull off your silly little cheese quest on our own, like your personal rabble of goblin cheese thieves?!" demanded Esme.

"No! You're not my minions. It helps all of us. I thought I could drive the getaway car." Mateo said matter-of-factly.

"You don't even have a car, Mateo!" said Oliver.

"Your dad does." He pointed out.

"Oh, come on…" Oliver was beside himself. "Alright. Since we've already gone off the rails on the crazy train, what happens when we find the cave?"

Mateo pointed to the northeast portion of the map in what appeared to be a large clearing. "You guys use the map to find the cheese. My aunt says it's right here. She hasn't been there in ten years though, so she says the entrance may be hard to find." Mateo rushed his last sentence, "Also, she says it's haunted by some boys that got lost in the cave back in the fifties and were never found…"

Ash grabbed his bag and stood up to leave. "Nope. You almost lost me at Reagan. You definitely lost me at ghosts of missing children."

"Don't leave!" Mateo pleaded with his friends. "Listen…last week I was working at the farmer's market with Mr. Archer, that cranky old corn farmer. The booth across from us was selling artisan cheese for like twenty dollars a pound. And they sold out even before the market closed! Each of those government cheese blocks is five pounds. If you each carry out two blocks, that's a thousand dollars!"

After a moment of silence, Ash and Oliver exchanged looks and shrugged, not knowing what to say.

"That would be great and all, but how are you going to sell government cheese at a farmer's market?" Oliver asked with skepticism in his voice.

"See, that's where I'm useful. I'll repackage it in half-pound blocks and put a fancy sticker on it." Mateo said. "Mr. Archer won't give a shit if I sell at his booth. I'm the one helping him buy all his corn from Walmart at three a.m. on market day because he can't compete with the Amish. He won't ask questions, I promise."

Trix spoke up. "Is the cheese any good after being in a cave for that long?"

"From what I understand, cheese gets better with age, like wine. It gets sharper and has more funk. I read a book last weekend called *Cheese, Sex, Death*, and it said when cheese is moldy you can just cut that part off and still eat it." Mateo explained.

Trix laughed. "Well, I don't mind spelunking for cheese in a haunted cave for a thousand dollars." They gave Mateo a small hug. "I gotta go babysit. Let me know when, okay?"

The group watched Trix, formerly Bellatrix, leave. It was their first school year fully nonbinary, and they seemed happier than ever. Even the idea of caving for cheese didn't bring Trix down. The group always felt relieved to see them happy after last year's suicide scare.

"Is there actually spelunking involved?" asked Oliver. "I don't feel confident in my ability to spelunk. Can someone please define spelunk? What shoes and equipment do I need?"

"I can't do it tonight," Esme said. "But I'm off work at six tomorrow."

"Are we *really* doing this?" asked Theo as he shoved his huge biceps through the straps of his comically small backpack.

Oliver shrugged. "I guess it's worth a shot. I'll borrow my dad's car and come get you guys after Esme finishes her shift at Sonic."

Mateo grinned, "It's going to work. I swear."

"I hope you're right. Okay, are we done? Can I get my Dark Elf now?" Theo rushed off without waiting for a response to the small café that generated most of the income for Bear's Den Boardgames.

"You kids want to order something?" asked the owner/manager/clerk/stocker/barista from behind a stack of recently unpacked board games.

"Yeah, man. I'm starving." whined Theo. "Can I get a large Dark Elf with whipped cream and a half dozen mixed donuts?"

Esme patted Theo on the back and said, "Aww, Theo it's so nice of you to finally buy *us* snacks for a change."

"What are you talking about?" he asked. "The donuts are for me."

Esme scowled.

"Fine. I'd like a *dozen* mixed donuts, please."

The clerk packed the donuts in two separate bags, at Theo's request—six for him in one bag, and six for his friends to share in the other. As he stood in front of the register taking a long gulp of his chocolatey drink, the clerk passed Theo the bags, then the change and said:

"You guys know all that cheese is gonna be bad, right?"

# Chapter 3

# Mighty Midwestern Mama Bear

**$214,200.08**

Emily furrowed her brow, then withdrew her debit card and forty dollars in cash. She knew most people would be thrilled to have that amount in their bank account, but her heart still skipped a beat every time she saw it. After paying off her house, that was all she had left to raise and educate two children…and if she's careful, have enough left to live on for a few years. The numbers didn't add up. Harper is only six. College will be astronomical by the time she graduates._

Emily closed the window, fastened her seatbelt, and turned down the radio. She took four deep breaths, then held to the count of four just like they taught her in grief counseling. Anxiety subsided as she reminded herself that she was in a better position than most spouses would be. The money bought her time, at least.

"You guys want some Sonic?" she asked the passengers in the back seat.

"Oh yeah, baby! Can I get a Route 44 Big Red? I'm so thirsty..." Harper dramatically fainted over the side of her booster seat.

"No way, kiddo." said Emily. "44 ounces of soda and you're guaranteed to turn into a tiny demon. How about some water with lemon?"

"…and mozzarella sticks with extra granch?" pleaded Harper.

Emily pulled into the restaurant parking lot and carefully maneuvered her red minivan into the drive-in booth. "Harper, it's *ranch*, no 'guh' sound. And yes, you can have mozzarella sticks with extra *ranch.*"

Emily hated correcting her youngest daughter when she said *granch*. She wanted the baby talk to last forever. She wanted Disney movies playing on a loop. She wanted her daughter to fall asleep in "the big bed" every night despite having her own princess-themed bedroom. She wanted Harper to eat everything with *granch*. To never grow up. To never leave.

She shifted the van into park and put down the window. An ancient Great Pyrenees rose like the dead from her resting place on the floor, nose twitching at the smell of burgers before she even opened her eyes. Emily pushed the big red button on the speaker, and a voice crackled from the speakers. "Welcome to Sonic, what can I get you today?"

"Hi there," Emily barked over the noise of the radios and idling car engines. "I need a four-piece mozzarella stick with double granch, I mean ranch, a small water with lemon, a Route 44 Sprite Zero with diet mango and peach flavor..." A cold, wet nose touched her arm. Big brown eyes from her longest and most loyal friend stared back. "...and a small vanilla cone in a dish."

No response came from the speaker, but a total flashed across the screen, and she paid with her card. After about fifteen minutes, an arm thrust a steaming paper bag through the open window.

"Esme!" Emily laughed "How did you know it was us?"

"You order the same thing nearly every day I'm working. I swear, no one eats as much fried cheese and ranch dressing as my family." Her eldest daughter walked to the passenger side of the van, while her youngest gleefully inhaled her favorite food dipped in her *second* favorite food.

Esme climbed in the back seat and laid a generously filled dish of vanilla ice cream on the floor in front of their polar bear passenger. She scratched under her chin. "How is Miss Ziggy Stardust today?" Ziggy gave Esme a small lick on the cheek before being distracted by the bacon grease on her shirt. Then she raised her paw and sat it on Esme's shoulder while staring her in the eyes, as if asking how her day was going. "Goofy girl." She laughed and moved to the front seat next to her mother.

"Why aren't you wearing your roller skates today, hun?"

"Because I don't feel like it, Mom." Esme huffed. "I am not a dancing monkey. We aren't required to perform on skates. We just get better tips if we do."

"I'd watch your tone with me, or you won't get a tip for sure." Emily raised an eyebrow.

Esme engaged her mom in a silent battle of wills. Emily cracked first, reached into her purse, and handed her daughter the forty dollars she withdrew from the ATM earlier.

"Thank you for your patronage. Can I stay over at Trix's place tonight after work? We want to have a game night." Esme asked her mother.

"Sure. We're going to be busy tonight anyway." She looked in the rearview mirror. "Aren't we, girly? Tell your sister what we're doing."

"BUNNY YOGA!" Harper shouted through a mouthful of cheese.

"…since when do you do yoga, Mom? And what the heck is bunny yoga?" Esme gave a surprised laugh.

"Bunny yoga is..I guess yoga…with bunnies. You're supposed to be able to pet them while they climb on you. I don't really know. My therapist suggested it. It's out at Rosewood Farm." Said Emily.

"That sounds kind of fun. Let me know if you go again." Emily reached in the backseat to give Harper a high five. "I gotta get back to work. See you guys tomorrow."

"See ya, kiddo. Love you." Emily waved at her daughter who was already outside the van, straightening her condiment belt.

"Love you too. Be careful, Jodie was driving out there and hit a deer, totaled her car." Warned Esme.

"Yup it's that time of year. They're eating the corn. Anyhoo, I'm gonna head out. I have an interview for nursing school at OTC. They said I could bring your sister." Emily said.

"I'm sorry I forgot! Good luck mom! And remember…you're not too old. You're not even forty yet." smiled Esme.

"Thanks…see you tomorrow."

Emily and Harper made a pit stop at home to drop off Ziggy and change into what Harper considered "Mom's fancy clothes" -a knee knee-length black skirt, pink blouse to compliment her blue eyes, and low black heels. She double-checked her purse to make sure she had the letters of recommendation and drove to Springfield Community College for an admission interview to nursing school.

"Wow, Mom, this place is huge!" said Harper as they walked up the stairs into the large, brick health sciences building.

"It sure is…there's a lot of people too." *A lot of young people*, Emily thought. She felt good about her outfit before she left, but as she passed a group of twenty-year-olds with long hair and small waists, she couldn't help but feel insecure. She tucked the streak of gray hair that her husband loved so much behind her ear. She untucked her shirt ever so slightly to disguise her somewhat jiggly post-two-babies-belly.

She introduced herself at the check-in desk. "Hello, I'm Emily Sharp. I have an interview at four with Ms. Trent. She said I could bring my daughter."

Harper took a mint from a candy bowl. "Yes, and I promise to be very very very very VERY quiet."

The secretary smiled. "I'm sure you will. Have a seat, Becky will come get you both in a few minutes."

Emily read the latest *Pete the Cat* story to Harper while they waited.

"Mrs. Sharp?" A tall woman with curly black hair propped the door open.

Emily stood up and gave the best smile she could muster. "That's me."

"Great! I'm Rebecca Trent, I'll be doing your nursing program interview today." She turned to Harper, "And you must be…?"

"Harper Sharp, ma'am. It is a pleasure to make your acquaintance." She curtseyed with an imaginary skirt.

Rebecca grinned at the formality. "If you both follow me, we'll interview in my office. My granddaughter left a coloring book and crayons behind when she visited me for lunch last week. You're welcome to use them, Harper."

"Thank you, Mrs. Trent. I will color most excellently." Harper followed her mother down the long hallway with her best version of a princess stride.

Rebecca Trent's office was not what Emily had expected. She imagined an interrogation of sorts, a cold room with folding chairs and a clipboard. Instead, she entered an office with flowered wallpaper, cushy armchairs, and a large walnut desk. A bouquet of roses by the window added extra warmth.

"Those roses are beautiful, Ms. Trent." Observed Emily.

Rebecca smiled. "Aren't they? Yesterday was my 25th wedding anniversary, they were a gift from my husband. We went to dinner at Fuji. Have you been there?"

"No, can't say I have." Said Emily.

"The chef makes the food right at your table. They made an onion volcano and lit it on fire. The chef cooked a piece of shrimp and tossed it to my husband, and it hit him right in the face!" she laughed. "Delicious plum wine, though."

"That place sounds awesome!" exclaimed Harper.

"It is." Rebecca gestured to a chair with a small table that had a Disney-themed coloring book and a box of neon crayons. "Harper, you can sit right over there while I get to know your mom better. It won't take long."

Harper skipped over to the table and got to work. Emily took a seat in the purple armchair in front of Rebecca's desk. She withdrew the letters of recommendation from her purse and handed them to Rebeccas as she settled into her seat and pulled a notebook from a drawer. "I was told to bring two letters of recommendation. The first is from Karma Kats. It's a cat rescue I volunteer at twice a month with my children. It's mostly cleaning, but I also help take care of the sick and injured when they're short-staffed."

Rebecca put on a pair of pink reading glasses and studied the letter. "It says here that you demonstrate exceptional compassion when treating the rescue animals, and you have been a reliable and helpful volunteer. You help educate potential adoptees and find the best pet for their household." She looked up at Emily from the paper. "Is this that place where you pay ten bucks and get to play with a room full of cats?"

"Yes, it is. The owner is brilliant. The visiting room allows people to get to know the cats before they commit to any of them. Even if they don't adopt, it's a lot of fun. Some people go there as a form of animal therapy." Explained Emily. "And of course, the admission fee goes a long way to support the needs of the facility."

"I see." Said Rebecca. "I should take my granddaughter there. She loves cats. Hey Harper! Do you think my granddaughter would like it there? She's eight years old."

Harper looked up from her coloring page of Cinderella. "Oh yeah, it's tons of fun. Just don't let Jackson climb on you. He pees on people. Jackson is the black and white one that runs on the big wheel."

"Noted." Said Rebecca with a chuckle.

Emily cleared her throat. "The second letter is from Sheila Evans. She's a hospice nurse at Everyday Angels…she helped me get my CNA training at the hospital so that I could be my husband's caregiver."

Rebecca took her time reading the letter of recommendation. When she finished, she gently sat it down on her desk. "Emily, I'm so sorry for your loss."

Even after two years, she couldn't bring herself to say anything except "Thank you." Any other response poked at a dam of grief ready to burst.

"She says that you were a dedicated caregiver to your husband. You were quick to learn about his medications and needs. She says you are exceptionally compassionate and empathetic to the needs of others, and that you set your own fears aside to be an excellent nurse's aide to your spouse and mother to two children during his cancer treatment. She also says you exhibit a strength she has seen in few women…" her eyes flicked to Harper, and she lowered her voice, "…expecting the passing of their spouse, especially as a mother of young children. She believes you have the heart and strength to be a registered nurse in any specialty of nursing, but especially hospice care."

Silence filled the room, as Emily looked at her hands. She had read the letter five times. She knew what it said, yet somehow, having a stranger read it back to her made her husband's passing feel more real.

"Emily, I'd like to move on to the interview questions." Rebecca folded the recommendation letters and put them in her desk drawer. "Sheila Evans says she believes you will make an excellent hospice nurse. If you become licensed, is that your preferred specialty? If not, what would it be?"

Emily to a deep breath to center herself. "I don't believe I would like to work in hospice care. I'm not sure what specialty I would choose. I am open-minded and hope that my potential education at OTC will give me the opportunity to try different areas of expertise."

"It certainly would. With two major hospitals in Springfield, there are never enough nurses. We crank them out as fast as we can," Rebecca laughed "but we also want the best of the best healthcare professionals graduating from our school. Nursing students are put on rotation at different departments during their training. There are many opportunities you can explore."

"That sounds great." Said Emily.

"Next question…why did you choose OTC for your education?" asked Rebecca.

"Well, two reasons. The first is affordability. I have a daughter preparing for college next year, so I'll be paying tuition for two."

Rebecca nodded in understanding.

"The second reason is the flexible class schedules. I was able to take online and night classes to meet the prerequisite courses for nursing school." Said Emily.

"Emily, are you aware of how intense nursing school classes are? You will be in class or training from eight in the morning until five in the evening. There are no alternative times." Rebecca explained delicately.

"I am. Harper starts kindergarten in August. My older daughter agreed to pick her up from school and babysit on the days I have class… potentially…if I'm admitted." Stammered Emily.

"Okay…I just wanted to be sure. Next question." Rebecca looked down at the apparent list of questions in her notebook and asked: "What is your dream job?"

Emily thought for a moment, settling upon an honest answer. "Truthfully, my dream job is not nursing. My dream job is to be a stay-at-home parent. Realistically that is not an option for me anymore. My choice to become a nurse is based on practicality: nursing is a high-paying, in-demand career with longevity and growth potential. People admired the way I cared for my husband for over three years before he passed, and I believe healthcare is a career field I have a natural gift for."

"Well, that is the most honest response to that question I have ever received. For most candidates, nursing is 'all they've ever dreamt of doing ever since they were young'." She laughed. "I guess I don't have to ask my next question: Why do you want to become a nurse?"

Emily exhaled a sigh of relief. Apparently, her response didn't blow the interview.

"I've held you two ladies hostage long enough, so I only have one more question." Said Rebecca.

Emily straightened her back, ready for a whopper as the grand finale.

"Do you prefer to work with others to complete a project, or do you prefer to work on your own?" she asked with a raised eyebrow.

Emily was used to doing everything alone. She was estranged from her family and her in-laws. Max even named his pub "The Black Sheep Tavern" in honor of their rebellion from their abusive families. The only people they could ever count on for anything were each other. Their relationship motto was always *us against the world*.

"I have another honest answer for you Ms. Trent- I don't know what it's like to accomplish something as a team. I've never had the opportunity. I've needed to handle just about everything on my own since I was sixteen. So, I suppose I could say I'm *comfortable* doing things on my own, but I would love to be surrounded by ambitious, helpful, knowledgeable professionals. I feel I could easily be a team player with the right people, but if needed I can easily excel independently." Emily went all in.

"I appreciate how frank you've been with your answers to my interview questions. It was refreshing." Said Rebecca.

"Thanks." Replied Emily.

"Just so you know, I have sixty candidates to interview and we are only admitting twenty-five this semester. If you are not chosen this term, we encourage you to apply the next. Just because we pass on someone it does not mean the weren't qualified. We simply admit the most exceptional candidate in that pool, in terms of grades, references and what we feel is the best temperament for the nursing profession." After Rebecca explained this, she stood from her chair and extended her hand to Emily.

Emily shook her hand and said, "I understand. Thank you for

considering me. It was nice to meet you."

"You, too. I hope to see you in the halls someday soon. In a few weeks, you'll get a phone call and an email if you're accepted; a letter in the mail if we passed. It was nice to meet you Harper!"

"Nice to meet you too, Mrs. Trent. I made you this." Harper handed Rebecca a colored page of Cinderella with a white nurse's cap on. "It's just to show you how cool my mommy would look like a nurse."

Emily turned red from head to toe. "Alright Harper, time to go."

"It's a lovely picture. I'll put this on my wall." Said Rebecca, as she waved goodbye.

Emily barely said a word as they walked hand-in-hand through the parking lot to her van. *Did I do okay? Was I too honest? Am I too old? Should I have hired a babysitter for Harper?* Her mind rampaged out of control with self-doubt.

"Mommy, are you okay?" asked Harper, clearly unnerved by her mother's silence as she secured her in the booster seat.

"What?" Emily asked, then realized how weird she must have seemed to her daughter at that moment. She kissed Harper on the head. "Mommy is fine, I was just nervous. How about we go home and change into yoga pants for…"

"BUNNY YOGA!" shouted Harper. "That's right, girly. Let's go practice our downward-facing Ziggy Stardust!"

# Chapter 4

## Raising Gaybies

"**B**ig Daddy, I'm SORRY! The corn is just so damn high I couldn't see around the corner!"

Benny wailed into his cell phone with one hand, while using a football hold on a squirming baby rabbit with the other.

"First of all, *Benjamin*, I've asked you not to call me Big Daddy outside of the bedroom!" Chris scolded. "You may have been able to speak that way in New Orleans, but you are in the Ozarks now. If you keep waving your rainbow flag, soon you'll be hearing banjos. They're gonna paddle your ass down the River Styx!

"Who's speaking all *gay* now? You're the one talking about paddling asses!" Benny shouted.

The woman inspecting the front bumper of her minivan coughed to conceal a laugh.

Benny lowered his voice and shifted the rabbit in his arms as it began nibbling his finger. "I understand your concern…but people here aren't *that* bad."

"Yes, they are, you just haven't met them yet because I shelter you and the kids in a good neighborhood, and Ashton goes to a progressive private school. That's why I work 700 miles away for weeks at a time on an oil rig- so I can pay for nice things and know you are safe."

Benny sighed dramatically, then leaned down to peek at the twins who were fast asleep in their car seats. The front bumper of his crossover dangled in the road.

"What the hell are you doing out in farmland anyway?" Christopher demanded. "Please tell me you didn't buy any more chickens. The HOA only allows six. I'm not culling any roosters, it's your turn!"

Benny straightened his back as he spoke now, "Listen to me, Christopher! I am not your sheltered, declawed house cat. I have all my claws, *thankyouverymuch*. I can handle myself just fine. I keep the kids safe and happy and do my best to stay out of trouble. I didn't get chickens. I bought the Gaybies a rabbit."

Ten seconds of silence. "That is a terrible idea."

"They have to learn to be gentle and responsible from a young age!" Benny stated.

"They're two years old." his husband replied. "I hope you know they're going to be eating the rabbit's poop like they do your 'sunshine infused' organic raisins."

"Don't mock my raisins. It's my most saved recipe on Pinterest." Benny watched as police lights shone through a dust cloud on the road. "The police are here. Gotta go, hun."

"Yeah, I need to get back to work. Make sure you get the other driver's insurance info. I'm glad no one was hurt. Call you tonight."

"Ouch!" The rabbit bit Benny's finger and drops of blood fell to the ground. "Okay Chris, talk later."

The driver in the minivan approached Benny and handed him a copy of her insurance card. "You can take a picture with your phone if you want."

Benny shuffled the rabbit, insurance, and his phone. He held the rabbit out to the woman. "Would you mind, hun? I still need to get mine from the car."

"Sure, why not." She laughed and held the rabbit carefully, but it was clear she didn't know what she was doing. "Am I holding it right?"

"Honey, I have no idea. I've owned that rabbit for about fifteen minutes." Benny shrugged and trotted over to the passenger side of his vehicle and dug around for his insurance. When he looked up, he could see the deputy and the woman chatting and laughing like they knew each other.

"Here you go. I took a picture of yours already." Benny passed both insurance cards to the woman and noticed they were smeared with blood. "Oh lord, what is that?"

The deputy stepped closer to Benny to see where he was bleeding. "Are you hurt, sir? Dispatch told me there weren't any injuries, but I can call an ambulance."

Benny held his hands up and flipped them over. "It's okay, the rabbit bit me. I didn't realize it was so deep…shit." For lack of better options, he pressed a corner of his shirt against the bite to slow the bleeding.

"Oh, don't ruin your shirt!" said the minivan mom. "I have a first aid kit. I can fix you up." She passed the rabbit to the deputy. "Rocky, would you mind?"

"Emily, you can't call me that when I'm working." The deputy scolded.

"You're right. I'm sorry *Sherriff's Deputy Rocky.*" Emily ran off to the hatch of her vehicle and pulled out a red, square first aid kit. "Would you mind coming over here? It will be easier if I can lay out my kit."

"Deputy Rocky, ma'am, would you mind keeping an eye on my babies for a moment? They're asleep in the back seat." Benny didn't wait for a response and ran off to get his finger patched.

Isabella huffed, and looked at the rabbit squirming in her arms. "It's *Lieutenant Kentworth*, actually. I got promoted."

Benny took a seat in Emily's minivan while she went to work cleaning his wound. "I'm Ben, by the way. Did I hear your name is Emily? Ouch!"

"Sorry…I should have warned you before I used the alcohol." She apologized. "Yup, I'm Emily."

A little girl turned around in the front seat to look at Benny. "Hello, Ben! My name is Harper!"

"Nice to meet you, Harper. I'm sorry about our accident. Looks like you two were headed for yoga." Benny nodded at the yoga mats on the floor of the van.

Emily finished wrapping the bandage around Benny's finger. "Ironically, we are on our way to bunny yoga."

Benny laughed. "It's a good thing it's not with my rabbit."

"Did you get that out at Rosewood Farm? That's where we are headed." Emily asked.

"I sure did. It's a pet for my gaybies...er, I mean babies." Benny remembered his promise to Christopher to be careful where he waves his rainbow flag.

"I can't believe they slept through the crash. Well, your finger is all fixed up. Let's go talk to Rocky. Be right back, Harper." Emily said as she closed the van doors.

"Can I listen to Taylor Swift?" Harper asked with her fingers crossed.

"Sure." Emily turned to Benny and whispered, "as long as I'm not in there! I like Taylor Swift as much as anyone, but that girl is obsessed. If I hear *Shake it Off* one more time..."

Benny smiled. She didn't seem bothered too much by the accident.

Lieutenant Kentworth handed Benny his rabbit. "Emily, your vehicle is alright to drive?"

"Yup, just cosmetic. I think we'll even make it to bunny yoga in time."

*I never miss a beat, I'm lightning on my feet* blasted from inside the van.

Emily groaned but smiled and waved at Harper who bounced to the music in the front seat.

"Benjamin, I took the liberty of calling you a tow service since your vehicle is obviously not safe." The Lieutenant gestured at the bumper dangling on the ground and the caved-in wheel wall. "Unfortunately, they can't get out here for two hours."

"Are you serious? I have babies! And a rabbit!" Benny was nearly in tears.

"You can't be out here alone with your twins for two hours." Said Emily. "How about you, the babies, and your rabbit come with us to bunny yoga? There will be snacks and drinks. Other people with kids, too. It ends around the time you're expecting a tow truck, and we can drop you off on our way home. I'll even wait with you if the truck's not there yet."

"That sounds like a great idea, Emily!" said Lieutenant Kentworth. Her scanner started blasting. "Excuse me for a minute."

"That's a very kind offer…especially after I hit your van." Benny seemed taken aback by the gesture.

"Well, as they say-*kindness is doing what you can, where you are, with what you have.* I try to be a good human when the opportunity arises." Said Emily.

Benny had a feeling this woman didn't own a banjo. "Can you help me with the car seats?"

After the still-sleeping babies were buckled in safely, and the rabbit was in its crate, the deputy approached. "It looks like everything is under control here. I'm not going to cite anyone since it appears to be an accident. You need to be careful this time of year- you can't see around corners because of the corn."

"And the deer." Added Emily.

"Exactly. Well, I better go. I've got a trespassing call not far from here, so I need to figure out where these kids are at. Stay safe!" Lieutenant Kentworth climbed into her dirty patrol car and disappeared into a cloud of dust just as the sun began to set.

"Alright! Let's go do some bunny yoga…and I *really* need to pee." Emily danced a little.

Benny laughed. Midwestern women certainly weren't the self-serving, flamboyant party animals he was used to meeting in New Orleans. This must be what Christopher called "Midwest Nice"-polite, down to earth, friendly. "Ozarkers" must be a different breed.

Rosewood farm set upon a lush, green hill surrounded by corn fields and an apple orchard. A parking lot in front of a red barn was filling quickly filling up with eco-smart vehicles driven by women in brightly colored yoga pants, who laughed and greeted each other with hugs.

"Great, huggers…" Emily mumbled.

"You don't know anyone here?" asked Benny

"Nope, it's my first time. I've never even been to a yoga class before." Said Emily as she maneuvered into the parking lot.

"Well, as long as you're wearing underwear, you'll be fine. Those leggings look kind of thin." Benny observed.

"You think so? Damnit." Said Emily.

"Don't worry about it, girl. I've seen my share of coochie coo in yoga, it happens to everyone. You never know until you're in bridge pose all stretched out showing the goods to your neighbor. Also, don't be embarrassed if you fart, they literally have a position called *wind pose*." Benny advised.

"Are you going to join in?" Emily asked.

"Yeah, might as well. Unless the twins start raising hell." Benny sighed. "It's been a long-ass day."

They unloaded Harper and gave her the rabbit to carry inside. The twins were now awake and making raspberries at each other. Benny and Emily each took one, and a diaper bag.

"My goodness, Ben. Your boys look like little cherubs with their curly blonde hair! What cuties!" exclaimed Emily as she hoisted a little one on her hip in a way only an experienced mom would do.

"Yeah, they're both biologically mine. That one is Finn; this one is Liam. My husband and I mixed the embryos from both of us with our surrogate. The two that finally took were mine. Guess the best dad won!" He smoothed back Liam's hair and kissed him gently. "We waited so long for these guys…so don't you drop him!"

Emily laughed. "Luckily, I'm not in the habit of dropping babies. Do you wanna go see bunnies, Finn?" He giggled and tried to grab Emily's nose.

The group followed signs with a picture of a rabbit to an octagon-shaped barn they used as an event venue, primarily for weddings. It was beautifully renovated inside, with glossy wood floors and tall ceilings, and handmade antler chandeliers dangled down just above their heads, emitting a soothing light.

"Welcome, new friends." Said a voice like wind chimes behind them. They turned around to see a barefoot goddess of a woman, nearly six feet tall with shiny black hair down to her waist in an ornate French braid. She held a clipboard in her hand. "I'm Dahlia, and I'll be your yoga guide tonight. May I have your names for check-in?"

"Emily and Harper Sharp. This is Ben and his twin boys…we got into a little fender bender on the way here and he's waiting for a tow truck. Is it okay if they join us?" Emily asked.

"Absolutely. We had a few last-minute cancellations. We have a volunteer in the baby-gated area in the corner if you'd like someone to watch your little ones so you're free to participate. We have a couple of our gentlest rabbits over there, and the volunteer is very attentive…I would know, she's my grandmother." Dahlia gave an exaggerated wink-smile.

"That sounds great, but first I need somewhere to change their diapers," Benny said.

"Of course! The bathrooms are on your left, and both the men's and women's bathrooms have changing stations. I hate it when dads have to change their baby on their lap, you know? I appreciate that the Rosewoods thought of that little detail in their venue." Chatted Dahlia.

Emily squirmed and passed Finn to Benny. "Yes, that's great. If you'll excuse me… I'll help in just a minute."

Ten minutes later, Emily returned, shaking the water off her hands. "Thanks for waiting. Alright, give me one of the angels and a diaper. Harper, do you need to go before we start?"

Harper trotted off to the women's restroom as Benny passed Emily a diaper and Finn. He was awestruck at the ease with which Emily took charge of another person's child, making it seem like the most normal thing in the world to swoop a stranger's family under her wing.

After the babies were changed, they brought them to Dahlia's grandmother. There was only a little girl in the "daycare" area, and both she and the grandmother were overjoyed to have two adorable babies to entertain. The little girl immediately showed them a rabbit in a box, "Look, babies! This is Biscuit!" The twins squealed with excitement.

"Don't worry, I've got eighteen grandchildren. Your little ones are safe with me! Go have fun." Dahlia's grandmother said, waving them off.

Benny positioned himself within the eye-line of Finn and Liam on a loaner yoga mat next to where Emily and Harper sat cross-legged. They were attempting to copy the mudra hand positions of a man a few rows ahead.

"You don't have to do that," Benny whispered, sitting on his knees and stretching his lanky arms up towards the ceiling. "it's called a mudra. It helps focus the energy, but it's not necessary. It's all fluffy floo floo."

Dahlia took her position at the front of the classroom, and tinkling meditation music played on the audio system. "Welcome, everyone. Before we release the bunnies, we need to share a few rules with you. Afterward, my helper Eric will pass out the liability waivers."

Benny raised an eyebrow at Emily. She shrugged, not knowing why they'd need one either.

"As I take you on a beginner yoga journey this evening, these delightful bunnies will sniff, hop, climb over, and run around you. Please be careful where you step, but feel free to reach out and touch them. Here are a few rules to keep all of us from getting hurt:

First, don't let them eat your yoga mat, the foam is bad for them. Rabbits explore their environment by chewing, which is why you may have noticed we taped all electrical cords up the wall and out of their reach.

Next, don't dangle them in front of you with their feet hanging in the air or they will kick and scratch you in the face.

On that note, please understand that rabbits have a very fragile spine, so please don't drop them.

And finally, if a bunny in your area has an accident, wave a hand at Eric and he will clean it up expeditiously."

Eric nodded.

"We would like to thank all of you for being here. The money you paid for this experience goes directly to Bluebell Bunny Sanctuary to help rescued rabbits be rehabilitated and find forever homes." Several women clapped in appreciation.

"Eric, will you now pass out the waivers and lettuce?" Dahlia retreated to a meditation cushion and sat in full lotus pose while chanting *ONG NAMO GURU DEV NAMO* quietly to herself.

After Eric collected the signed liability waivers and exchanged them for romaine lettuce, he walked the perimeter of the room releasing rabbits from their cages, allowing them to wander the room at their leisure.

Dahlia rose from her cushion and took her place on a mat at the front of the class. "We will begin our practice on our bellies. Let's warm up with some baby cobras."

Benny immediately placed his hands on the floor and lifted his chest off the ground like a snake. Emily and Harper watched him and followed suit.

"Now, I would like you to hold this position and tilt your neck side to side. One…two…three. Four. Great. Now, rise into full cobra." Instructed Dahlia. The class pushed up their torso so only their hips were on the ground. As Benny tilted his head, he noticed Eric open his rabbit's cage and let it free into the yoga class.

"Oh no! Eric, babe! That's my rabbit!" He loudly whispered. The rabbit skittered out of the cage to the center of the room. Eric shrugged and moved to the front of the room where he was already being flagged down to clean up some "organic raisins".

"Well at least it can't escape." Emily pointed out. "Also, you get to see what your bunny is like with people."

"Oooh, Ben, can I pet your bunny?" Harper asked.

"Sure, if you can find it…" He scanned the room as he tilted his head in cobra pose. Between the blur of fifteen rabbits and half-naked bodies, it was impossible to see where his young rabbit was.

"Now, please lower to the ground and push back into child's pose. Feel free to place a piece of lettuce in your hand, and pet any of these benevolent creatures if they choose to approach you. Stay here for eight breaths." Dahlia spoke serenely to the class as she slid her bottom to her heels and stretched out her arms on the floor in front of her.

A gray and white Holland Lop approached Harper and tickled her hand with its whiskers as it chewed at the piece of romaine. Harper giggled uncontrollably.

In front of Emily, an enormous brown Flemish Giant climbed on the back of an elderly man. His wife left her mat to get her cellphone to take a picture, which started an avalanche of others doing the same.

"As you move about the class, please try to keep the noise to a minimum," warned Dahlia. "We don't want to frighten our little visitors."

As people returned to their mats, Dahlia continued the class. "Now, slowly transition to downward facing dog, by first going to tabletop position. Then, peel your bottom up to the sky. Allow your head to hang, and slowly rock it back and forth. The rush of blood will re-oxygenate your brain. Remember to belly-breathe."

"Ben, look underneath you! Isn't that your rabbit? The little cream-colored one with short ears, right?" Emily pointed with her left foot.

Ben looked between his arms as his head hung upside down. "Shit, there you are! It's cute, isn't it?"

"Super cute!" Exclaimed Harper, who had given up on yoga, and was instead feeding a piece of lettuce to a white rabbit with pink eyes.

"It's called a *Netherland Dwarf.* It won't get much bigger than tha-AAAAHHHT! Oh Sweet baby Jesus GET IT OFF!" Benny wailed.

Emily dove into action to get the rabbit before Benny collapsed his downward dog pose.

"It's got your pinky toe and won't let go! Eric! How do I get a rabbit to let go?" Emily shouted across the room. Eric ignored her and cleaned up more poop.

Benny was crying as tears dripped to the floor. "Emily you have about ten seconds before I fling that rabbit across the room. Don't make me do it."

Emily cupped both hands around the rabbit and blew hard in its face. It blinked and released Benny's toe. He collapsed on his side.

Blood pooled on the mat as it dripped to the floor. "Oh my God…it bit my toe off!"

Emily moved in for a closer look. "Actually, it looks like it's just the tip."

"THAT'S WHAT THEY ALL SAY!" Benny cried.

The class went silent. Eric finally came to their aid, passing Emily a paper towel while he used another to wipe up the blood. "There's a first aid kit in the women's bathroom." He said.

"Harper, why don't you stay here and have fun…I'm going to help Ben again." Emily smirked, "Alright soldier, let's go stitch up another battle wound."

She helped Benny to his feet as tears poured down his face. Using Emily for stability, he hopped with her to the women's bathroom leaving a trail of bloody footprints behind. Emily found the first aid kit in the cabinet under the seat, as Benny took a seat in the handicap stall and sat on the toilet. Emily started by rinsing his foot with sterile water. "Let's see what we're dealing with…"

Benny pulled four feet of toilet paper from the roll, dabbed his eyes and blew his nose. "At least it's a women's bathroom. I can't even *imagine* what filth I'd be stepping in if this was the men's bathroom."

"Hmm, it looks like the skin is still attached, but I can see the fat pad which means you need stitches. I'll fold it over and bandage it until you can go to urgent care. I forgot to ask, where's your husband? Can't he come pick you up?" It finally dawned on Emily that Benny had mentioned his husband earlier.

"Christopher's in Louisiana. He's an engineer on an oil rig not far from New Orleans and not due back until next week…you got any Tylenol in there?" Benny winced.

"Let's see…here ya go." Emily passed him the tablets. He tossed them in his mouth and gestured for the bottle of sterile water.

Emily's sports bra suddenly lit up and started playing "Enter Sandman" by Metallica. She pulled her cell phone out of her bra.

"That is *not* the ringtone I expected you to have." Benny teased.

"What *did* you expect? To be fair, you barely know me." Emily grinned, then looked at the caller ID and her face fell. "…it's the Sherriff's department. Do you think it's about your tow?"

Benny squinted at her. "Why would the police care that a rabbit ate my toe?"

The phone continued to buzz. "No, Ben, the tow truck."

"Oh, that. Wouldn't they call me, not you?" he said.

Emily answered. "Hello, this is Emily… Yes, Esme is my daughter…

is she okay?" Panic filled her voice, but the answer made her suddenly relax. "Okay then, so what happened? *Arrested!* For what?... I see. I'll be there as soon as I can."

Emily's teeth were clenched, and her face was red hot. "My older daughter has apparently been arrested, and I need to pick her up from the station. Your tow should be here in about thirty minutes...but now you're injured...two babies and a rabbit. Fuck it, Esme can sit her ass at the station... wait, after they tow your car, how are you getting home? They can't fit all of you in the tow truck... Okay, how about this..."

Her plans were cut short when Benny's pocket started vibrating. He gave Emily an arched eyebrow and pulled out his phone. "...it's the Sherriff's department."

Emily and Benny exchanged confused looks.

"Hello?" Benny answered. "Yes, this is Benjamin Sanders...Ashton is my stepson. His father is working out of town...he was arrested for trespassing?"

Emily gasped and covered her mouth, eyes wide.

Benny shook his head in disbelief. "Yes, I'll be there as soon as I can... officer, is he there with someone named Esme?... I see...and *four* others. Okay, I'll be there soon. Bye."

He ended the call, and they stared at each other.


"Emily, it appears our teenagers know each other," said Benny "and they're both in a hell of a lot of trouble."

# Chapter 5

## Stars and Shadows Ain't Good to See By

"What about a Lotus Field Combo deck?" Esme asked from the back seat of Oliver's dad's twenty-year-old Buick LeSabre.

Mateo frowned at her in the rearview mirror. "Gross, you're not becoming a blue player, are you?"

Theo reached across Esme to push the release button in front of her, smothering her face in his enormous shoulder. "Holy shit! Is that an ashtray? I've heard there used to be ashtrays in cars, but I didn't know they were in the back seat, too! That must mean this is…" Theo pulls out a cylinder with a glowing orange coil on the end. "A lighter! That's so badass. If there would've been lighters in the back seat of cars when I was a kid, I probably would have set my seat on fire."

Esme uses both hands to shove Theo's meaty body off her. "Get off me, you ogre!"

Trix chimed in from the middle front. They were the only person short enough to sit there and not block the rearview mirror. "Ez, the only person who will tell you a blue deck doesn't suck is a blue deck player. And they don't have a lot of friends."

"Lotus Field seems so powerful, what's so bad about it?" asked Esme.

"Let me put it this way," said Oliver from next to Esme, "a game against a blue player is pretty much like watching someone play solitaire. Their whole strategy is to not allow their opponent the chance to play any cards. Does that sound very fun?"

Esme deflated. "…I guess not."

"Yeah, you don't want to be that guy," Theo said as he returned the extinguished lighter to its heating port.

Esme scowled.

"Oops, sorry. You don't want to be that *girl*." Theo corrected himself.

Trix coughed.

"Fine! You don't want to be that *player*. I'm sorry guys, I really *am* trying to be inclusive. Wait...am I allowed to say 'guys'?" Theo earnestly asked.

Trix laughed. "It's fine, Teddy. You're such a goon." They pointed at a barely visible trail off the main road. "Mattie, slow down. I think that's it."

The deeply rutted trail led across a fallow cornfield to a thick tree line. Mateo slowed down the LeSabre to allow a truck to pass, waited for it to be out of eyesight, then drove down a slight incline and into the field.

As the slowly navigated the path, all that could be heard were thumps and cries of pain as the teenagers hit their heads on the low ceiling like a game of whack a mole. Mateo stuck his head out the window to make sure he had the wheels in the ancient ruts. The earth was cracked from the blazing Missouri sun and littered with old corn stalks. He felt his heart rate begin to rise and pushed away the memories. *Not now.* He thought. *I can't do this now.* "Hey, Ash, can you roll down your window? I need some air."

Ash took an assessing look at Mateo. His pale face and wide, flicking eyes meant Mateo was close to having an episode. "Stop the car, Mattie. Let me drive."

Mateo inhaled deeply with his head out the window as they approached the tree line. "No, no. I'm fine. I swear."

"You're gonna get your head knocked off by a tree branch. Stop the car now." Ash commanded with an authoritative tone he'd never heard from him before. He stopped the car.

No one said a word as the two changed seats. Ashton adjusted the mirrors and turned off the radio. "Put your seatbelts on, I don't know what we're driving into."

After ten minutes of helping Theo adjust his belt to fit him, Oliver pleaded, "Ash, please be careful with my dad's car. I know it's super old, but it was in my grandma's garage for twenty years. It only has five thousand old lady miles."

"Chill out. I have my license, Oliver. I only had to retake the test twice, unlike you." Ash scowled, offended at the assumption he would be careless.

"Mateo, get your face in the car and use the map to navigate."

Mateo knew navigating was meant to be a distraction, but he grabbed the map off the floor anyway. "I guess you just follow the trail about a quarter mile. It says there's a wet weather creek we may need to cross, but it hasn't rained in a while."

Ash shifted the car into drive with a clunk and slowly began to creep into the dense forest. Immediately, the setting sun was blocked, and they were plunged into dim green darkness. Ashton turned on the headlights.

"Is that a good idea? What if someone sees the lights?" asked Trix.

Ashton shrugged. "If I don't use them, there's no way I can see where I'm going."

No air flowed between the trees, and it became increasingly humid in the car. With all the windows down, they quickly became swarmed by mosquitoes and inundated them with the sweet smell of invasive honeysuckle. The land had obviously been left unmanaged for many years.

Something slowly slid across the roof of the Bonneville. "Oh my god, was that a snake hanging from the tree?"

"I think it's Kudzu." Said Trix. "You know, 'The Vine that Ate the South'...now it's moved north and is eating the Midwest because of climate change. It will literally kill every native plant around it. They're smothered and starved of nutrients. When my grandpa was sick, he let his property in Michigan go...in two years Kudzu managed to kill a 100-year-old Blue Spruce tree in his back yard, and it fell on his house. The Stepdads, Mom, and I went up there to help clean up during spring break. Even between the three of us it took two weeks to untangle the vines, cut up the tree, and kill the Kudzu. More than likely it will all grow back again. It's *so* difficult to get rid of."

"Thanks, Captain Planet." Said Theo. "It looked like a snake to me. My motto when I'm trail running is this: every vine is a snake until proven otherwise. I think that strategy should be applied to our little adventure, too."

"We're going into a cave." Reminded Ashton. "I'd be more worried about black bears. Or mountain lions. Or meth labs."

"We'd get more money selling meth than cheese." Joked Esme.

Oliver started digging through a military-style tactical backpack he cradled on his lap. "Okay, so I have a couple of flashlights and some of those cheap headlamps on elastic bands. A first aid kit, some food…"

"You'll be in there an hour, tops. You don't need food." Said Mateo optimistically.

"Yeah," said Ashton as he navigated around a curve "If we get lost, we can just eat Mateo's cheese."

Ashton slowed to a stop. Ahead of them was a clearing where what little sunlight left illuminated a waist-high meadow of beard grass and milkweeds. A gray limestone mound rose beyond. Small trees grew from the cracks between layers of stone, and drippled of water seeped from others. Like the rest of the forest, Kudzu had taken hold of any and every natural structure it could wrap around.

"Oh man…" groaned Trix. "It's going to be impossible to find the entrance, and it's already getting dark. Are you sure you all want to do this?"

"We already came all this way…" pleaded Mateo to his friends, with a tone of uncertainty.

"I suppose it doesn't really matter if it gets dark," Ash gestured to the pink and orange sky above them. "it's going to be dark in the cave anyway."

No one responded, they simply unclicked their seatbelts and piled out of the overloaded Buick. The group walked through the prairie, scanning the ground as they went for potential hazards.

Theo let out a high-pitched squeal. "Big black snake! Big black snake!"

Everyone froze except Theo who bolted to the rock formation.

"It's okay, guys." Said Oliver. "It's just a rat snake. They're huge but not venomous."

"It's hissing at me!" shrieked Mateo.

"Just back up slowly. It's a warning. I find them in our chicken coop all the time." He took his own advice and walked slowly backward towards the mapped location of the cave entrance. "They usually just eat eggs, but sometimes they'll try to eat a chicken, and I'll find one with a wet head. It won't hurt you,"

The group surrendered to Oliver's sage advice for a lack of other options and retreated backward, occasionally looking over their shoulders for logs or more snakes, until at last their backs felt cold wet stone.

They collectively exhaled a sigh of relief, as Mateo opened the Cheese Cave map and compared the drawing to the overgrown, rocky hillside in front of them. "It says the entrance is behind a tree called a *chinquapin oak.*"

"No way!" said Trix. "Chinquapin oaks are pretty rare around here; I've always wanted to forage some of the acorns from that tree…they're supposed to be really sweet."

"Great," replied Ashton, handing them a flashlight. "Since you know what we're looking for, we'll follow you."

Trix scanned the area near the limestone. "They like to grow near limestone…but they aren't very shade tolerant so I'm going to assume it's not near the tree line…there!" They pointed with their flashlight. "That must be it!"

Trix ran over and began examining the leaves. "This is definitely an oak…see the serrated edges? Shiny top, pale underside…and look, acorns!" Trix began picking through the acorns littered on the ground and collecting the ones without wormholes.

"Great, thanks Trix. Enjoy your tree." Teased Theo. "Alright gang, I'd like to be home before eleven. I've got cardio tomorrow. Barf." He started tugging vines away from the rock wall, and the others followed suit.

After fifteen minutes, they still hadn't found the entrance, so Trix joined them.

"Nice of you to stop foraging nuts to help us." Griped Ash. "Why are my eyes so itchy?"

"Yeah, me too." Said Oliver. "Maybe I'm allergic to Kudzu."

Trix came closer with a flashlight. "Oh no…that's not Kudzu. It's poison ivy."

Everyone stopped what they were doing and pawed at their eyes.

"Stop!" commanded Trix. "You'll make it worse! Use water or something."

Mateo emerged from the dark, a huge smile of white teeth appearing before the rest of him. "Guys! I found it! We were looking too high. It's on the ground right over there, with a grate covering it. It's not locked."

Through watering eyes, they stumbled over to where Mateo had pulled up a four-foot rusty grate that had been laid over the cave opening. They peered into the hole, their headlamps revealing natural limestone steps, worn smooth over time and slick with water that steadily seeped from seams between sedimentary layers in the walls. No more could be seen beyond the steps without going inside.

Ash knelt and looked around. "I don't see anything. Are you sure this is the right place? This entrance is like four feet wide, there's no way they got truckloads of cheese in through here."

Mateo considered Ash's point. "Well, I assume there's another entrance, but this is how my Aunt Sofia and Jason got in. I read that cave systems like this can go on for miles." He passed Ash the map. "Stick to the map. No wandering off."

Ash took the map in one hand and braced himself to climb down with the other. "Are you sure you don't want to come with us?"

Mateo looked at his friends, already red-eyed and muddy before they even entered the cave. He felt like a coward. He swallowed, took a step towards the cave entrance and stood there for a moment as if to follow Ash into the dark hole. His hands began shaking uncontrollably. He stepped back and fell into Esme.

She turned him around, saw the fear in his eyes, and hugged him. "It's okay Mattie. We have a map, and it won't take long. Before you know it, we will be a thousand dollars richer and crowd surfing at the concert."

He silently nodded and watched as his closest friends disappeared one by one into the depths of the earth.


The first thing they noticed was the temperature drop.

"Wow, it really does stay fifty degrees down here." Theo zipped up his *Mighty Mick's Boxing Gym* hoodie

They gathered around Ashton with the open map. "Looks like we just follow the path until we reach a fork and go right. There's no scale for distance so…I guess let's just find out."

The path, at first, could accommodate two people walking side by side. It quickly narrowed and they were forced to walk sideways single file. Oliver held his tactical bag on top of his head. "Do you think the whole cave is like this? This bag is heavy."

"It will do you good to build some upper body strength. I could use another sparring partner." Theo grinned at Oliver, who was struggling under the weight of their supplies next to him.

"No thanks," Oliver growled. "I'm a pacifist. I use my intelligence and diplomacy to get things done. Not my fists."

Theo plucked the bag from on top of Oliver's head like it was a daisy behind his ear and carried it with one hand. "So, was it your brains or diplomacy that decided to bring a fifty-pound backpack on this short spelunking adventure?"

"…I may have over-prepared. Hey, look!" Oliver pointed to the walls as he crab-walked through the tunnel. "There's writing on here!"

Theo squinted in the dim light of his headlamp. "*Sam Clemens March 9th, 1851.* Who's Sam Clemens?"

Oliver examined the signature. "Probably some other homeschooled nerd whose mom insisted he learn Spencerian penmanship so he could '*read the Emancipation Proclamation in Abe's handwriting*'."

"…how is that more useful than punching?" Theo asked.

"It's not." Oliver admitted.

"Homeschooled kids are so weird." Teased Theo.

"Well, this is my first human interaction in months, I'm bound to have social deficits. You know, this cave reminds me a lot of my average school day, locked in a basement with a Bible…" smirked Oliver.

"Didn't your mom just take all six of you on a 'field trip' to Silver Dollar City in Branson last week? I'm pretty sure riding roller coasters doesn't count as science." Said Esme

"Um, actually…" Oliver feigned pushing glasses up his nose. "We learned about kinetic and potential energy. I also learned how to make apple butter. Oh, and I learned not to eat an entire red velvet funnel cake and a nacho Tater Twist before riding the Electro Spin."

"Mmm…Tater Twists." Theo fantasized.

"It's not much further!" Shouted Ash from the front. "I'm pretty sure I see where it branches out."

"Wow, there has to be hundreds of signatures on the walls!" pointed out Esme. "I don't see many past the 1990's but there's some as far back as the 1820's."

"Hold up! It can't be." Trix said. "There's one that says *Jesse James, Sept. 22nd, 1879.*"

The group stopped moving and tried to turn around to face the opposite wall. Trix's smaller frame had allowed them to move through the tunnel without needing to walk sideways.

Oliver shined his flashlight on the signature. "It looks legit. Do you think it's *the* Jesse James?"

"My dad is *really* obsessed with the Civil War. I remember him telling me that Confederate sympathizers used to hide supplies in caves." Theo said, passing Oliver's backpack to Esme so he could get a closer look. "Jesse James served in the Confederate army. Supposedly he knew where all these cache caves were, so that's where he would hide out when the law was after him. There's like ten caves in Missouri called The Jesse James Cave."

Theo, Oliver, and Trix began scanning the walls for other notable names. Ash yelled from up ahead, "Come on already! The first branch is up here!"

Theo took a picture of the Jessy James signature with his phone. "I can't wait to show my dad. He will shit his pants."

"Teddy, you idiot. You can't tell your dad we were here." Trix scoffed.

"Damn, you're right. It's still cool though." he shoved his phone in his pocket and scooted sideways to catch up with Ash and Esme.

They emerged from the tunnel with sighs of relief into a much larger area with two clearly defined pathways to the left and right.

Esme dropped Oliver's bag to the ground and did a few side stretches. "Anyone thought about how much it's going to suck to carry the cheese back through that tunnel?"

They groaned at the realization…and were answered with a cacophony of squeaks.

Slowly, they looked up, and dangling from the grooves in the ceiling were hundreds of brown bats, some with wings outstretched, preparing to drop and take flight.

Esme inhaled, about to scream. Ash knew it was coming, grabbed her close to him, and put his hand over her mouth. He whispered, "If you scream, you'll scare them, and they'll all come flying at us!"

She exhaled through her nose, collected herself, and nodded. Ash removed his hand and motioned for his friends to follow him to the right, careful to keep his headlamp pointed down. The others followed suit, walking until certain they were far enough away from the bats so as not to disturb them.

Ashton stopped and took the map out of the front pouch of his hoodie. "I think this arrow means the path starts to go down. It doesn't seem as narrow as the first one." The group marched forward, continuing around the spiraling and steadily declining path. Their heavy breathing and dripping water were the only sound echoing in the chamber.

THUMP. "Son of a bitch!" moaned Oliver laying face first on the gravelly ground.

"Oliver said a swear! I'm telling his mom!" Theo laughed as he offered his hand to pull him off the ground. "Watch where you're going, bro."

He stood up, dusting his pants and picking gravel out of his hands. "I tripped on something. Look out, Trix."

Trix, who brought up the rear of the party, surveyed the ground with their headlamp as they approached. "It's a net. You know, like for butterflies… weird."

The strange discovery made the others uneasy, and they looked around the cavern they were passing through. "There's a box over there. Is this where the cheese is?" Esme asked Ash.

"According to the map, we're only halfway," Ash answered, then took the initiative to do what they all were too afraid to do: open the box.

What surprised Ash about the shoe box, is it wasn't *old*. It was barely dusty. He picked it up and shook it. Definitely something inside. The group surrounded him to combine their headlights. Ash flipped open the lid.

"Oh my God, bats!" squeaked Esme.

"Chill, Ez. They're dead." Theo scolded before she had a chance to scream.

"…so are those." Oliver pointed to their feet.

Littered on the ground surrounding them were at least two dozen dead bats. "Guys. Why are they headless?" Esme whispered, barely even able to say the words.

"Let me see that box, Ash." Trix demanded as they snatched it from his hands. Trix pulled a blue glitter gel pen from their pocket and gently used it to examine the bats. "These are Indiana Bats. They're a threatened species, and it's super illegal to kill them. They need really specific cave conditions to live in, so they are only in a few caves in the Midwest. Just the fact that they are here is incredible. Why the fuck is someone killing them?"

"…I think I might know." Oliver said, unable to take his eyes off the furry headless creatures at his feet. "I went on a mission trip with my church to Bolivia last year. We were helping out at this medical rehabilitation center… one of the kids there had epilepsy. While I was there, his parents brought a live bat into his room, cut off its head, and made him drink the blood."

"Are you serious?!" said Esme.

"Yeah. The American doctor I was with was losing his mind, trying to explain to the parents that this wasn't safe. The nurse said a lot of cultures in South America believe bat blood can cure the uncurable, so it's something they deal with all the time…anyway, what if somebody is doing that here?"

Trix continued to examine the box of bats. "These bats still have their heads. No evidence of white nose syndrome…clearly there are no wind turbines or pesticides down here…they probably suffocated or died of stress. What kind of monster would do this?" Trix's face glowed red hot with anger.

"Yeah, they're actually pretty cute close up…all brown and fuzzy with mouse ears." Said Esme, getting brave enough to take a closer look.

"They've got tiny eyes and a little pink pig nose. Kind of like your mom, Ash." Theo grinned and turned around. "Ash, where the hell are you?"

"Over here." He said from across the room. He was crouched, with something in his hand. "You might want to see this."

He held up his flashlight to reveal a glass bottle of amber liquid, with a dead bat settled on the bottom like a worm in a bottle of Mezcal. "It smells like booze."

"Put it down, Ash." Said Oliver. "Trix, forget about the bats. Let's get the cheese and get out of here."

They all nodded in agreement and continued through the winding passageway. Ash stopped just as the path began to narrow to a single-file corridor again. "After we get through here is something called 'The Shakehole', then on the other side is the cheese storage. Almost there."

After fifty feet of squeezing through passage, they emerged into another large cavern. Jagged spikes hung from the ceiling dripping water onto their heads.

"I can never remember…" Theo said, deep in thought as he considered the ceiling. "Are those stalactites or stalagmites?"

They all turned to Trix. "What, so I'm supposed to know everything about nature?"

"Yes." They all said in unison.

"Hey Trix, what do you call a group of bats?" Ezme asked sarcastically.

"A cloud." Replied Trix reflexively, sounding a little Hermione Granger-y.

Theo smirked at them.

"Oh, fine." Trix huffed. "Stalactites are on the ceiling. Stalagmites are on the ground. The 'T' in stalactites can be remembered as 'top'. The 'G' in stalagmites can be remembered as 'ground'. Stalactites are jagged and pointy. Stalagmites are rounded."

"Thank you, Park Ranger Trix. Please, continue the tour of this very creepy cave." Gestured Theo down the path.

"Those *stalagmites* are huge!" said Esme. "Can I check it out real quick?"

Ash shrugged. "Might as well. I have no intention of doing this shit again, guess we should take in the sights."

"Whoa!" Esme exclaimed. "There's a huge hole over here!"

"Guess we know what a shakehole is now." Said Oliver. "Do you think it's like a sinkhole or something?"

The group peered around the stalagmites. "There's a hole in the middle, with water running down. I don't think sinkholes have an opening."

"Hmph." Said Ash. "That's cool and all, but can we keep it moving? We've been down here at least an hour. Mateo's probably freaking out up there alone."

"Yeah, let's go." Esme agreed. "I have the opening shift tomorrow and it's half-price Super Sonic Burrito Day. It'll be busy."

They followed the path around the shakehole buffered by stalagmites. "Hey Ez, if I stop by, will you give me a free burrito?" asked Theo.

"Sorry, bud. My manager watches us like a hawk for that kind of thing. However…I can sneak a few onion rings in your tater tots." Esme winked.

"You better." Said Theo.

Oliver made it his duty to illuminate the cave floor with his single high-powered flashlight for hazards after tripping over the net. "Hey, stop walking for a minute. There are some animal tracks or something her."

"Those look like dog pawprints." Observed Theo.

"I don't think so…" said Oliver. "It looks like a cat. The bottom pad is all wavy."

"Big cat." Gulped Esme. "How did it get in if the entrance is gated off?"

"There is definitely another entrance. There's no way cheese was hauled through here." Said Trix. "I'm assuming this is a mountain lion…and it has another way in."

"Come on, guys." Said Ash. "Quit playing detective let's just get out of here and hope we don't find it."

After about 100 feet of winding pathways, the air felt colder as they emerged into an enormous room lined with rusted steel shelves eight feet high bolted to the limestone walls. Dusty cardboard boxes lined the shelves with what could only be the cheese. Yellowed bags of dried milk were stacked up on the bottom of every shelf.

"Finally!" exclaimed Ash. "Let's check it out!"

They each ran to a different shelf and began lifting the lids off dusty boxes.

"Gross!" said Trix. "This one is moldy. Like *really* moldy."

"My box has a dead mouse in it." Said Esme.

"This cheese is all shriveled up like Ash's mom's--"

"Shut up, Theo!" said Ash. "Guys…I don't think any of this is salvageable but keep looking. Even just a few would help us out."

They pawed through boxes, tossing lids and bad cheese into a heap in the center of the room. "Maybe we can sell some of the other stuff. What is this, dried milk? Does anyone even use that anymore?"

Theo pawed through a leaning tower of sacks on the floor. They tipped to the back of the shelf with a thud. "Whoops…what the heck is that?"

Near the bottom of the stack, an ivory grip of a silver firearm stuck out between the bags. Theo pulled it out gingerly. "It can't be…I'm going to cry. I swear to God I'm about to cry right now."

"Is that a GUN?" asked Trix in disbelief.

"Not just any gun…this is a Le Mat Revolver…also known as a Grape Shot Revolver. With an ivory grip…" Theo wiped a tear from his eye. "It's like…the holy grail of civil war firearms. 9 rounds. Muzzle loaded, but it has two barrels."

"What, really?" said Oliver, rushing over to take a closer look.

"Yeah. See that switch on the hammer? If you push it down, it moves from the main barrel to the shotgun barrel below it."

"No way!" Oliver held out his hand. "Let me see it."

Theo hesitated. "Fine, but you have to give it back. Finders keepers. My dad will die when I show him this."

"Theo, I already told you this: you *can't* tell your dad we were down here. You can't show him the gun. Besides, should we really be stealing things like this from the cave?" said Trix.

"What, cheese is okay, but not something actually valuable? Guys, forget the cheese. If we sell this gun, we could get at least double what we would selling cheese to hipsters. Let's sell this instead." Theo beamed, snatched the gun away from Oliver, and without waiting for approval, shoved the gun in the pocket of his cargo shorts with the barrel sticking out. "Let's search the rest of the room for cool shit."

They stood around the heap of moldy cheese, collectively realizing it was a lost cause, and dispersed among the cavern.

"I found a lot of old beer bottles." Said Trix.

"Look at this ancient pack of Marlboros. Probably from the eighties." Said Oliver, tossing it in the cheese heap.

"I found a weird bone." Said Esme. "It kind of looks like a tooth…but if it's a tooth, it's huge."

"Hmm." Said Ash. "Might as well keep it and see what it is later."

"Who just called me Bellatrix?" asked Trix with their eyes furrowed. "That's not my name anymore."

Esme and Ash exchanged glances. "It wasn't us." Said Esme.

Ash went over to where Theo was clearing bags of dried milk off shelves looking for more treasure. "Any luck?"

"Nah. Did see a cool salamander though. It was orange with black spots. It had a really long tail." Theo pulled his hood over his head and tucked his hands in his sleeves. "Man, I thought it's supposed to be warm down here, but I can see my breath. Maybe we should get going."

Ash laughed. "Yeah, the way your stomach is growling, we better get out of here before you eat the moldy cheese and die of listeria."

"What? I'm not hungry." Theo gave Ash a quizzical look. "You literally picked me up from Jose Loco's. I drank two horchatas and ate a smothered burrito the size of my arm…I might have to poop soon though."

Ash looked around in confusion, certain he heard growling, and began walking back slowly to the rest of the group.

"Hey Ez!" Theo shouted, his voice echoing off the limestone walls. "Gimme your flashlight, I'm gonna run back to that shakehole."

Esme huffed. "Are you serious?"

"Yes," said Theo, dancing side to side. "I need to poop."

Ash approached, looking over his shoulder. "Oliver, get over here!"

"What's up?" asked Oliver, sensing the tension in Ash's voice.

"I need to poop." Squirmed Theo.

"We need to go. Something weird is going on down here. Forget the cheese. We'll sell the gun." Ash straightened his headlamp and tightened the straps on his backpack.

"Yeah, I want to leave too." Said Esme. "I wasn't going to say anything because it seemed stupid…I *swear* I felt someone grab my hand."

The group exchanged uneasy glances. Theo rocked on his heels. "Fine we'll go, but can we wait just one minute? Esmerelda Sharp, give me your flashlight *right now* or I will never speak to you again."

"Fine, if you can't hold it." Esme passed a travel pack of tissues from her denim jacket pocket and the flashlight to Theo, just as the light slowly faded and went out.

"Dang." Said Oliver. "I just put those batteries in. It's okay, I have more."

Oliver knelt on the ground, digging through his tactical bag. "Can you guys come closer; my headlamp is too dim. I can't see."

They stepped around Oliver in a circle, and one by one, their headlamps flickered and went out until they were swallowed in the damp darkness.

Mateo sat against the chinquapin oak, waiting to hear the loud chatter from his best friends echoing out of the hole in the ground.

He bounced acorns off boulders.

He tapped his phone to check the time.

He fidgeted with the car keys in his lap and looked at the keepsake keychain photo of Oliver's family on a Disney Cruise. He'd never been on a cruise and wondered if he would feel claustrophobic on a boat he couldn't escape for five days. He decided he probably wouldn't like it, even if Mickey Mouse was there. Nowhere to escape unless he jumped overboard.

He checked his phone again. Almost eight. The sun was only a smudge of red through the trees. In the distance, coyotes howled with call and response. One behind Mateo, probably in the field. One beyond the stone hill, somewhere in the forest. He became increasingly uneasy as the howls sounded closer. Were they circling him?

He tried to remember what you're supposed to do with coyotes. *It's definitely not play dead. "Hazing" seemed like the right choice...be loud, make yourself big, throw stuff.* He stood up and searched below the oak tree for a big stick to use as a staff. A few yards away was a knotted Osage Orange tree. He gathered the lumpy green prehistoric fruit the size of softballs in his shirt and piled them at his outpost under the oak. He'd been hit in the face by these plenty of times playing with his cousins, they could hurt a coyote. His dad told him no animals eat them; it was the main food source for mammoths during the Ice Age. The Osage tribe used the wood to make prized hunting bows. His dad had one hanging in his office- a trade for fixing an old Native American guy's toilet on the reservation when his family briefly lived in Oklahoma.

Nearly two hours, and no sign of his friends. Even if Mateo was brave enough to go look for them, they took all the flashlights. He began to wonder what would happen if they didn't come out. How could he get help? He'd have to admit what they were doing, and they'd probably go to jail. But what if they're hurt? Juvie and fines are better than dead.

The howls were closer now. Mateo stood and began to pace in front of the cave entrance carrying a lumpy fruit and his makeshift staff.

The stars were visible now. *It's been way too long. Something is wrong.*

He took out his phone and typed 9-1-1 on the keypad. "Sorry guys…" he whispered to himself.

Before he hit the call button, the brush in the forest to his left began to move.

"No, no, no, no, no." He whined as he held out his stick and backed up against the tree. His chest heaved. *Stand your ground. Don't run or it will chase you. Animals sense fear.*

Mateo's eyes flicked to the LeSabre on the other side of the field. He dropped his "weapons" and bolted like a bullet from a gun to the car just as he heard gurgling wheezes and hisses from the dark. *That is not a coyote.* He heaved open the passenger door and slid across the leather to the driver's seat. After pushing down the lock, Mateo surveyed the field, waiting for whatever was out there to show itself in the moonlight.

He breathed heavily, searching the car interior for some sort of weapon. He wished he was in Jason's Mustang instead of *Youth Pastor of the Year's* Buick. He tossed a #1 Homeschool Dad travel mug in the backseat out of frustration. There was absolutely nothing to help him.

"Please, please, please make whatever it is go away." He closed his eyes and prayed, not knowing to who. He opened his eyes and in front of him hung a rosary on the rear view mirror. Frantically, he unraveled the beads it and put it over his neck. "Please God…Jesus…Mary, Peter…um Paul? Bring my friends back."

He picked up the phone and hit *call.*

"Um. Hi, so…I was out near Highway 110 and I saw a big group of kids going into the woods on private property. It looked like they were about to start trouble, so you probably want to send a whole bunch of people out there to break up the party or whatever they are doing. Yeah, it's just past that big yellow farmhouse. The cops can probably see the tire tracks through the field. Okay, gotta go, bye."

Mateo hung up before they asked his name. He started the car, pulled it into reverse, and adjusted it so the headlights pointed across the field. In the headlights, two beady eyes were following Mateo's trail through the field. He laid on the horn.

"Get out of here!" He yelled as loud as he could. "Go!"

The creature jumped, turned tail, and skittered on clumsy feet back to where it came.

"...a possum? A fucking *possum?*" Mateo groaned. He had already called the cops. He had to try and get his friends out so they could leave before they got caught.

He left the car running and sprinted through the tall grass and back to the cave opening. He got on his hands and knees and screamed into the hole. "Guys, forget the cheese! Get out here now! If you can hear me, say something!"

He waited. No response. He tugged at his hair and stood up, pacing again in front of the entrance. He had no choice. He had to go in there.

He ran back to the Bonneville, to retrieve the only light he had-his cell phone. He turned on the flashlight feature and sent a group text to his friends in case there was any chance they had reception in the cave:

*I'm coming to get you. Cops on the way. I hope you're alright. I think I remember the map, I'll try to mark my path.*

He looked up just as shadows began to move in the headlights.

"Guys? Is that you?" He ran towards them. He could see they were dirty and seemed tired. They weren't carrying any cheese. He ran closer.

"Hey, hurry up! The cops are coming, we need to leave now! I'm going to go cover up the entrance, so they don't find it." Mateo said as he ran past his friends.

They didn't reply.

He threw the grate over the hole, some brush, and a few Osage Oranges for good measure, then sprinted to his friends who had nearly reached the car.

"Hey, slow down a minute! Are you guys okay?" he asked. They didn't turn around and kept walking. "Why are you walking in V formation? I suppose I *did* send you on a wild goose chase."

Mateo was hoping for a laugh from his lame joke to break the ice. They didn't even turn to look at him. *They must be mad at me for making them go down there.*

He ran in front of his friends, where Ash took the lead. "Stop walking, Ash! Just get in the car! I don't care about the cheese, I'm just glad you're okay. We need to get out of here before the cops come!"

Mateo put his hands on Ash's chest to stop him from moving. Finally, Ash locked eyes with Mateo.

They were black with rage.

"What the hell?" Mateo stepped back. Ashton's eyes fell to the rosary on Mateo's neck. His mouth contorted in a sneer, and he growled.

Theo stepped forward, grabbed Mateo under the arms, and threw him onto the LeSabre, leaving a teenager-sized dent in the hood. He gasped attempting to catch his breath, then rolled off, watching his friends leave him behind as they walked down the rutted path.

"Please. Wait." he begged. "I know you're mad, but you're really overreacting. Just get in the car and we can talk about it on the way home."

Mateo hobbled over to Theo, certain he had a broken rib. "Theo, I'm not even mad you threw me into the car. Hell, I probably deserve it for asking you to go down there. But I'm not hurt, I'm fine. Let's just go home, okay?"

The group stopped and turned to Mateo in unison. Theo grabbed him by the shirt, grunted, and pulled him close. *Did he just...smell me?*


Theo thrust Mateo back, cocked his arm, twisted his hips, and landed a cross hook to Mateo's face in a way only a professionally trained boxer hitting well below his weight could.

Mateo swayed, darkness filling his vision. He felt his body hit the hard Missouri clay, and the last thing he saw was the flashing of red and blue lights.

# Chapter 6
## Eye of the Tiger (Mom)

"**S**he kicked me in the dick!"

The sheriff's deputy and principal exchanged looks with raised eyebrows.

Principal Spencer addressed the boy holding an ice pack between his legs, and another over a swelling black eye. "Son, I realize you've been hurt but can you please watch the language?"

The deputy knelt in front of eleven-year-old Isabella. "Miss Gallows, is this true? Did you kick him in the, er, groin?" His badge caught the fluorescent lighting. Deputy Kentworth smelled like coffee and cheap aftershave.

Isabella moved the icepack from her also swelling left eye, to her throbbing jaw. She looked the law enforcement officer square in the face. "Yeah, I did. He deserved it."

Silence. More raised eyebrows and sideways glances passed between the adults. Principal Spencer spoke after clearing his throat. "So, I'm left to conclude that after you kicked him, a fight began?"

Tears were swimming down the cheeks of the hefty twelve-year-old boy as he spat words from bloody lips. "I punched her in the face and knocked her clear to the ground!"

The sheriff scowled at him.

"...but it was self-defense! She started it!"

"No, I didn't." Isabella fixed her eyes on a Star Wars poster in the nurse's office from the 1970's *Parents of Earth-Are your Children Fully Immunized?* She felt dizzy. "Richard started it. He said I don't have a winter coat because my mom is too busy spending all our money at the bar trying to find me a new daddy. I said I don't wear a coat because I don't want to."

"Okay, and then?" asked Principal Spencer.

"Well," said Isabella, "I kicked him in the dick."

Deputy Kentworth stifled a laugh with a cough and briefly turned away from the middle schooler's interrogation.

"Richard," Principal Spencer addressed the young man, "would you please tell us what happened next?"

"Yeah, well, she's a maniac for starters! After she kicked me, I punched her in the face, and she fell to the ground. I thought it was over...but she got right back up and punched *me* in the face. So, I hit her again! She fell and got back up AGAIN. This time she got me in the mouth, real hard too...man, I think one of my front teeth is loose..." He began wiggling every tooth in his mouth in succession.

"This kind of violence is absolutely inexcusable," said Principal Spencer. "Please excuse Deputy Kentworth and me while we discuss our next steps." The adults stepped into the hallway, Principal Spencer keeping eyes on the two students the entire time through the tiny glass window in the door.

They returned ten minutes later, stern glares in place. Isabella noticed a slight smirk threatening to break the sheriff deputy's formal veneer.

"Fighting on school grounds is strictly forbidden," Principal Spencer informed them. "Therefore, you are both suspended for a week. This incident will be noted in your academic records. Richard, we've called your parents and they are waiting for you in the lobby. We've recommended they take you to the emergency room for a more thorough examination than our school nurse can provide. You may go."

Richard snatched his backpack from under his seat, and mumbled "Finally.", then flung open the door and left to meet his parents.

"Deputy Kentworth, thank you for your assistance in this matter. I think I can handle it from here." The deputy nodded and they shook hands.

Before leaving, Deputy Kentworth turned to Isabella and said, "Hey, Rocky. If you're gonna eat lightnin' and crap thunder...make sure it's off school grounds, okay?"

"...what?" Isabella asked in confusion. The deputy chuckled and left.

The principal pulled up a chair in front of Isabella and gave a pat on the arm before he sighed and said, "We tried calling your mother. No answer. Is there anyone else that can come get you?"

Isabella knew no one would come. Even if they managed to reach a relative, she doubted they would even remember her name. "No. It's just me and my mom."

"Alright. I'll have Julie at the front desk keep trying. You hang out here for a bit, I'm sure we will reach her soon." The principal stuck his hand in his pocket and pulled out a Hershey bar. "I always keep one of these in my pocket to eat when I'm having a bad day. I think you need it more than I do." He gave a small smile as he left the nurse's office, leaving her alone to ice her swelling purple face.

An hour passed. The candy bar was eaten. Isabella was tired and wanted to go home. She knew her mother probably wouldn't stroll in until at least midnight, so she grabbed her bag, left the school through a side door, and began the two-mile walk home.

Snow began to fall, big fat flakes that stuck to your clothes and hair, and gently coat the ground. If she hadn't been shivering so violently, she would have been more inclined to appreciate how beautiful it made the normally dirty neighborhood look. The pristine white snow hid the cigarette butts and trash, the dead grass, the flattened fox squirrels. It insulated the street and sounded wonderfully quiet.

Red and blue lights flashed behind her as a police vehicle approached. *Great*, she thought. *They're going to drag me back to school.*

"Hey, Rocky! They let you go home, or are you truant?" Deputy Kentworth yelled out his window. Isabella stopped as he pulled up next to her. "You really don't like wearing a coat? Even in the snow? Wow, you are a fighter aren't you?"

"I don't have a coat," Isabella admitted through chattering teeth.

The deputy pursed his lips. "I figured. Hey, I'm on my way home. My daughter is about your size, but she lives with her mom now in California. She left a ton of winter clothes here that I just boxed up to take to Goodwill. You want to hop in and warm up? I live around the corner so we can stop by and throw them in the trunk and then give you a ride back to your place."

Isabella said nothing. Between the black eye, swollen jaw, chattering teeth, and trembling body she didn't trust herself to speak. She just walked to the passenger side of the car and got in.

"Good choice. Alright, let's get this heat blasting." Deputy Kentworth fiddled with the knobs and warm air blasted from the vents. She sat back in the seat, saying nothing, as he drove away from the curb, down a few blocks, and turned the corner to a quiet street.

The deputy's house was small, and a little shabby, but neatly groomed on the outside. An rusty truck sat in the driveway, and a big chocolate lab barked in the window.

"You stay here and keep warm; I'm going to open the garage and grab those boxes." The Deputy loaded four overflowing boxes of clothes into the trunk. She could see snow boots and puffy coats, colorful sweaters, and acid-washed jeans. She'd always wanted a pair of those.

He shook the snow from his flat brim hat before climbing back inside the toasty patrol car. "It's that time of year it gets dark early! I'm glad I found you, kids shouldn't be walking around here at night. Not that you couldn't handle yourself, Rocky. You *are* a little hypothermic though. That gives your opponent an advantage."

Isabella managed a small smile. "If you think the neighborhood's dangerous, why do you live here? Don't you have a good job? You could live someplace better if you wanted to, unlike me."

"Well, that's a great question." He put the car in reverse and began backing out of the driveway. "First thing is…law enforcement officers don't make as much money as you think. We do the work because we love it and want to make a positive difference in our community."

He pulled out to the street. "Alright kid, where are we going?"

"East Monroe Terrace. The dump on the corner." Isabella grumbled.

"Hmm." Deputy Kentworth was quiet for a minute, then continued. "The second reason I live here is because I grew up here. I inherited my parent's house, and the taxes are cheap. Some of my childhood friends still live here…well, the ones that didn't get into drugs, anyway. A lot of times, just having an officer living in a neighborhood is enough to keep it safe. People are less likely to commit a crime when they see a cop car sitting in the driveway. My neighbors and I look out for each other, which is important in places like this."

"Makes sense. They don't do that on my block."

Isabella unbuckled her seatbelt as they pulled into her driveway. All the lights were off. As predicted, her mother wasn't home. Deputy Kentworth helped unload the boxes and sat them on the slanted wooden porch. "I can bring them inside on my own," Isabella said "…my place is kind of a mess right now. You'd probably trip or something."

"Sure thing, Rocky. Anyway, I better get home and feed Butkus. Stay out of trouble so you don't have to see me again." He winked and made his way back to the patrol car.

Before he shut his door, Isabella remembered he had just given her an entire winter wardrobe and yelled, "Thanks for the clothes, Deputy Kentworth! I really appreciate it…"

"No problem." He waved and headed home to his dog.

That night, Isabella opened the boxes and laid all the clothes out on her mattress. She had never owned this many outfits in her life. In addition to the coats and boots, there were sneakers, sweatpants, an unopened package of socks with a Christmas tag still on it (To Olivia, Love Dad), and even a green dress with poofy sleeves. If she had to get punched in the face for the stars to align and bring her this wardrobe, it was worth it.

Then to her delight, at the bottom of the box were five training bras-one for each school day. She'd been developing early, but her mom refused to accept this fact. She kept saying "Not yet. Those are itty bitty titties. You can wait." She felt relieved that she wouldn't have to work so hard to conceal her chest anymore.

Isabella heard the uneven thumps of her drunk mother up the creaky front porch. The doorknob jiggled and she heard the door burst open. There was a crash of furniture hitting the scratched and dingy hardwood floor, and Isabella knew she must have knocked over the small table by the front door where they left their keys.

"Son of a bitch!" her mother growled, and she heard the table smash into the wall.

*She must not have found a "date". It's going to be one of those nights.* Isabella crammed her new clothes back in the box as fast as she could and attempted to shove the box under the bed, but it was too tall. She threw her tattered baby blanket over it just as her mother stormed into her room.

"*You* should be asleep! You have school tomorrow." Her mother gurgled. She was wearing torn jeans, and a black lace top over a black bra. Isabella cringed. She was a grown woman dressed like a nineteen-year-old at a rave. Her waist-length bleached blonde hair was disheveled and frizzy. Her overboard makeup was smeared. *She looks like she crawled out of a dumpster.*

Isabella dropped her head. She knew the best thing to do was stay out of her way until she slept the drunk or drugs off. "I was just getting ready for bed, Mom. Do you want a sandwich before I go to sleep?"

"Fine." She surrendered her rage at the table and flopped onto Isabella's bed.

*Great, guess I'm sleeping in the recliner tonight.*

Isabella left her mom and went into the kitchen to make some kind of sandwich to put her mom to sleep. In the bread box, she found two pieces of edge bread. *If I flip the edge to the inside she won't even notice.* She opened the fridge. No lettuce. A black spotted tomato. Spicy mustard, but no mayo. She opened the sliding drawers. One slice of ham and some Velveeta. Good enough.

She assembled the sandwich-edge bread facing inside, spicy mustard, single slice of ham, a thin-as-possible slice of squishy Velveeta, and one quarter of a roma tomato without the spots. Then she opened the silverware drawer, took out a knife, sliced the sandwich in half, and then reached way in the back of the drawer for a bottle of Benadryl tablets. She crushed four tablets with the back of her mom's coffee spoon, lifted the top slice of bread on each half, and sprinkled it on.

When Isabella entered her room, holding her mother's "sleepy time sandwich" on a napkin, she found her mother sitting on her bed holding a training bra with a look of utter disgust on her face.

"What is *this?*" she sneered.

Isabella cooly replied, "It's a bra. Here's your sandwich, Mom. You seem tired."

Her mother slapped the sandwich out of her hand, and spicy brown mustard splattered on the old blue carpet. "What does a girl like you need a bra like this for?"

"Mom, that's a normal training bra." Isabella pleaded. "I'm getting bullied in the girl's locker room during gym. I really need it, *please.*" Isabella reached for it, and her mother snapped it away.

"Where'd you get it from, eh? Did you steal it?" her mother asked, her voice dripping venom.

"No! I wouldn't do that!" Isabella said.

Her mom cocked her head. "Cuz if you're going to steal, I can think of a lot better things you can grab than bras."

"What?" Isabella gawked at her mother in disbelief. "I'm not going to steal things for you! I didn't steal it! Someone *gave* it to me!"

Isabella lunged at her mother to grab the bra from her hands, and she shoved her back hard. Isabella tripped on the box of clothes and fell hard on her back.

"*What is this*?!" the blanket had fallen off the box during Isabella's tumble. "You have an entire *box* of nice clothes? Well, now I *know* you didn't steal it." Her mother reached inside the box and pulled out the green dress with poofy sleeves. "This is pretty...I think it will fit *me.*"

"No!" Isabella shouted; rage filled her body as if she summoned it from the core of the earth. She felt it trembling through her feet, legs, stomach, face. "That is *mine.* It was given to *me.*" Isabella reached to grab it, and her mother snatched it back like she had with the bra.

"No, no, no. What's yours is mine until you leave this house." Her mother shook her finger. "Do you have yourself a sugar daddy, Little Miss Fancy? Did you do a favor for a *man* to get these clothes?"

"No!" the hot magma that coursed through her veins was now filling her arms. "I'm *eleven.*" Isabella's jaw was clenched, and her feet rooted to the ground like a tree.

Her mother stood up. "Yes, you're eleven…almost twelve." She took Isabella's face in one red-clawed hand. "Maybe I *should* accept you are becoming a woman now…and as a woman, I could teach you ways to get things from men. Wouldn't you like to make some *money*, sweetie? You and I could buy *lots* of new clothes…get our nails done…go out to dinner at places with *cloth* napkins…"

"No!" Isabella's hands were trembling so badly that she balled them into fists as she squirmed out of her mother's grip. "I'm not a whore! I'm not YOU!"

"What did you say to me, you little *bitch*?! Her mother lunged at her with outstretched hands towards her throat.

Isabella stood still until her mother was within reach, twisted her hips, and landed a punch to her jaw with the full force of her weight behind it.

Her mother stood stunned with her hand on her face. The hit, it appeared, had sobered her up. She walked over to their landline phone and picked up the receiver. "I'm done with you, little girl. You don't want to be me, eh? Well, how about I put you through the foster system just like my parents did!" she punched 9-1-1 into the glowing yellow lights. "Look me up in ten years so I can see just how *different* you are from me!"

Isabella's hands relaxed. She ran into her room, locked the door, and shoved a broken dining room chair she used to hold her CD player under the knob. She grabbed two old backpacks from her closet and began filling them with clothes. She left out winter boots and a coat, then began changing into the pair of acid-washed jeans, the training bra her mother threw on the floor, a purple sweater made of sparkly yarn, and new wooly socks.

She could hear her mother speaking loudly to the emergency operator through the thin walls. "My daughter is out of control. She just hit me in the face. I can't do this anymore. Send CPS, I want to voluntarily surrender her. No, I don't need an ambulance."

Isabella put on the winter boots and laced them up tight, then the puffy coat. She hefted one backpack on each shoulder. *I'd rather live on the streets than go to foster care* she thought as she thrust open the drafty cracked window of her bedroom. She tossed the bags in the bushes below and landed on top of them with a soft thud. Her mom had stopped talking, so CPS was probably already on the way. She crept around the corner of the house, checked for passing cars, and ran down the street toward the nearest bus stop. When she was close enough to see the enclosed glass booth, she slowed to catch her breath and heard barking approaching quickly.

*Did CPS send dogs after me?* Isabella looked around for a place to hide when she saw a big brown dog barreling at her, with a loose blue leash trailing behind.

"Rocky! Stop running!" a man's voice yelled from the dark. "Me and Butkus are too old for this!"

The big brown dog ran until he reached Isabella, then sat down dutifully and barked, waiting patiently until his owner caught up. Deputy Kentworth appeared under the streetlamp, and bent over trying to catch his breath. He was wearing gray sweatpants and a maroon-colored SMSU sweatshirt with a huge logo of a bear. Butkus barked again.

"Okay, maybe *he's* not too old, but I am." He laughed.

"What are you doing? How did you find me?" Isabella scowled, peeking over his shoulder to see who else was coming.

"Well, first of all, I didn't find you. Butkus did. I was almost to your house, and he saw you dart out from the bushes and ripped the leash right outta my hands like he was chasing a fox squirrel." Deputy Kentworth said as he leaned against the lamp post, nursing a stitch in his side.

Isabella adjusted the backpacks she carried on either shoulder. "Why were you coming over to my house?"

"To see if you're alright." He tried to get an assessment of her condition in the light of the streetlamp. "I was up late watching Letterman and heard a domestic dispute come across the scanner...I remembered your address. Your face has had such a busy day it's hard to tell if you have new bruises. Are you hurt?"

Isabella was done defending her mom. "My back hurts. She threw me on the ground. She said she wanted me to become a prostitute and then tried to choke me. So, I punched her in the face."

His face hardened. "Is that so?"

Isabella nodded. Butkus sniffed her hand, then tried to flip it up to encourage her to pet him.

"I heard CPS is on the way to your house, Isabella. Do you know what that means?" Deputy Kentworth asked.

"That I'm going into foster care," Isabella said flatly.

"Is that why you're running away?" he asked.

She nodded and obliged Butkus with a scratch on the head.

"Now that I've found you, I can't let you run away. If you do, I'll have to send Butkus after you." He gave Isabella a small smile as Butkus licked the spicy mustard from her fingernails.

"What's going to happen to me?" Isabella asked as silent tears slipped down her cheeks.


"Honestly, I don't know." Said Deputy Kentworth. "But I'll do my best to help. Let's go, Slugger."

Isabella begrudgingly followed Deputy Kentworth and Butkus around the corner where she could see lights flashing from two police cars in her driveway. A shiny black Toyota was parked on the street. Her mother sat with a woman on the porch stoop signing paperwork.

"Officer Phillips, I believe I have someone you need to talk to." Two officers turned around and approached Deputy Kentworth. The woman on the porch looked up, and quickly began wrapping up whatever she was doing with Isabella's mother.

Officer Phillips knelt in front of Isabella. "Hi there. I'm told you and your mom had some trouble getting along tonight. Do you think you can hang out here for a little bit while we sort this out?"

Isabella nodded and then looked over at Deputy Kentworth. "I'll stay with her, Paul."

The woman took a clipboard from Isabella's mom, just as a cab pulled up. Her mother went inside, got her purse and climbed into the cab without even a glance in Isabella's direction. They all watched as she left.

"Hello, Isabella." Said the woman. "My name is Melanie. Is it okay if we step inside your house while we talk so we can stay warm?"

"It's not much warmer in there," Isabella shrugged. "But sure."

Isabella led Melanie and Deputy Kentworth inside her ragged house. The obvious melee had left it even worse than usual-broken table, clothes, and "sleeptime sandwich" parts were strewn around.

"Okay." Melanie hugged the clipboard to her chest. "My job is to make sure children have all the essential things they need to live a healthy life. Your mom called us because she feels like it would be in your best interest to live somewhere else. Do you understand?"

Isabella nodded. As she took in the hovel around her, contrasted by Melanie's shiny black heels and tidy haircut, she began to wonder if a foster home-or even a group home-could be as bad as this.

"First, I'd like to understand a bit about your life. Do you have a bedroom?" Melanie asked.

Isabella pointed behind her, and Melanie peeked inside. "It's pretty cold in here. Is that your only blanket?"

"I have my baby blanket, too. It's down there." Isabella gestured towards the holey polyester blanket with threadbare satin edging and a faded print of a giraffe. "My window has a crack in it, so usually I just sleep in my clothes."

Melanie nodded and scribbled on her clipboard. "Speaking of clothes, can I see your closet?"

Isabella pulled the cheap folding door open. "You can look but I don't have any clothes in there. It's just some of my mom's old stuff in boxes. I've got a few things in my dresser."

"I see you have quite a few nice things here on the floor…" Melanie pointed out.

Deputy Kentworth cleared his throat. "Actually, I just gave her those. Some stuff my daughter left behind. There was an incident at school today because she didn't have a coat…that's how we met, right Rocky?"

Isabella nodded, and Melanie said "Thank you, Deputy Kentworth. I'd like to talk to you about that in a minute. First, Isabella, can you show me your kitchen? I'd like to see what kind of food you like to eat."

"We don't have any food I like to eat…we don't really even have food." Said Isabella.

Deputy Kentworth opened the fridge. "Are you telling me your favorite food isn't a mustard and moldy tomato salad…with a side of pickle juice?"

Isabella managed a small smile, and Deputy Kentworth gave her a wink. "You know, all this talk of delicious food has got me and Butkus *really* hungry. I think I'm going to run up to McDonald's while you and Melanie talk. Do you want anything?"

Isabella shrugged. "Well…what do they have? I've never been to McDonald's."

Deputy Kentworth's eyes widened. "You've never been to…BUTKUS! You hear that? Isabella has never had McDonald's. I think we better get a forty-piece nugget meal and a couple of chocolate milkshakes"

Butkus barked in approval from the porch.

"Okay, fine…" Deputy Kentworth said as he walked outside. "Large fries, too."

After the deputy left, Melanie sat with Isabella on her mom's tattered faux suede sofa. Isabella fussed with the holes made by misplaced cigarettes.

"You're old enough to understand…this isn't how children are supposed to live, right?" Melanie asked delicately.

"Yes, I understand."

"Children should have food to eat, warm clothes, a warm bed…and most importantly, they should feel safe at home and school. Do you feel that you have

that?" Melanie continued.

"No, I don't. I've never felt safe in my entire life." Isabella stuck her finger all the way through the cigarette hole and started pulling out yellow foam.

"I am going to place you with an emergency foster for a few days until we can find a more permanent solution. I promise I will do my best to make sure you have everything you need, okay?" Melanie placed a warm hand on Isabella's shoulder.

"Alright."

"What I'd like you to do now, is take this trash bag," Melanie handed Isabella a thick black construction bag. "Fill it with your things. Unfortunately, you can't take more than that, but your permanent foster will help you buy new things soon."

Isabella nodded and Melanie stepped outside to speak to the officers preparing to leave. She shook the bag open and tossed in both her backpacks, then went into her room. There was nothing she wanted, except the clothes Deputy Kentworth gave her. After the bag was half full, she picked up her ragged baby blanket. It looked like Swiss cheese and smelled like cigarettes, but it was all she had from her childhood. *Should I keep it for the memories?*

She dropped it in an empty box and closed the lid.

*I don't want to remember.*

The jingle of dog tags let Isabella know that Butkus had returned. She dragged the big black bag of clothes into the living room. Butkus had settled himself in her mother's recliner/bed as Deputy Kentworth moved overflowing ashtrays and celebrity gossip magazines off the coffee table. He sat down a drink carrier with four milkshakes and began unpacking French fries and boxes of chicken nuggets.

"I brought Melanie a vanilla milkshake…she struck me as a vanilla kind of person. Anyway, she passed, so it looks like Butkus gets two. Unless you want it…?"

Isabella shook her head no. "One is probably enough for me."

"Alright, then. Here you go, friend." Deputy Kentworth positioned the milkshake between his dog's paws on the chair, and Butkus went to work right away, expertly burying his snout in the cup. "What kind of sauce do you like? I'm a sweet and sour guy myself, but most people like ranch."

"Sweet and sour." Said Isabella.

He tossed her three dipping cups and placed a box with ten chicken nuggets and large fries in front of her. "Eat one of those nuggets fresh and tell me that's not the best thing you've ever eaten."

She took one and dipped it in the sauce. The crust crunched as she bit down, and the inside exploded with chicken juice.

Deputy Kentworth's mouth was also stuffed with food. "Guf, hunf?"

Isabella nodded enthusiastically in agreement.

Melanie appeared in the doorway. "Deputy, may I speak with you briefly?"

He placed his shake on the table and turned to Isabella "Don't give Butkus any fries, no matter how many times he asks. It makes him fart."

Isabella giggled as Deputy Kentworth and Melanie walked out to her car. Through the window, she could see them talking and signing papers. By the time they came back inside, Isabella had eaten all ten nuggets and a large fry. She and Butkus slurped up the remaining drops of their milkshakes.

Melanie took a seat on the sofa arm. "Now I kind of wish I would have taken that shake Deputy Kentworth offered. Is it just me, or does McDonald's taste better after midnight?"

Isabella sat down the shake and waited quietly for Melanie to tell her where she was about to end up.

"So, we've arranged an emergency foster for you through the weekend-possibly a week-until we can find a home to place you in. Your mother has surrendered her parental rights. I'm so sorry, Isabella." Melanie said.

"It's okay. She sucks anyway." Isabella stood up and brushed nugget crumbs off her shirt, then tied her trash bag shut. "I'm ready to go."

"Great. Fortunately…you don't have to go very far. Deputy Kentworth is going to be your emergency foster, and he tells me he lives a few blocks away." Melanie smiled.

"…you'd do that?" Isabella asked Deputy Kentworth who appeared in the doorway.

"Yeah, sure." He waved his hand at her. "It's no big deal. Like I told you, my daughter is out in California and I've got an extra bedroom and everything."

Melanie led them out the door, locking it behind her, then slipped the key under the frayed doormat. "I'm going to follow you over there and do a quick check to make sure Deputy Kenworth's home is adequate for you, okay?"

They loaded her belongings in the trunk of Melanie's car, and she sat in the back with Butkus laid across her lap. When they pulled into his driveway, Melanie said, "Isabella, why don't you stay here for a few minutes while I take a look at the home."

"Sure." Isabella was feeling drowsy due to the late hour and her stomach full of food. She leaned her head against the window as Butkus kept her warm and closed her eyes.     She realized she should feel sad. Her mother had just abandoned her and tossed her to the curb like yesterday's trash. Why did she feel so…relieved?

"Isabella, wake up." Melanie was gently shaking her knee.

Her eyes fluttered open, and for a moment she looked around and didn't know where she was.

"I think you'll be very comfortable here for the time being. Usually, emergency placements aren't this easy…kids end up sleeping on a cot at an already full foster home. Mr. Kentworth already brought your things inside. Why don't you and Butkus go get some rest? I'll call tomorrow afternoon to see how you're doing." Melanie helped Isabella out of the car, as Butkus trotted over to a box shrub, peed, and then ran up the stairs to where Deputy Kentworth held the door open.

She staggered from the car and up the stairs as the deputy waved goodbye. Isabella was led into a cozy living room with a big tv, and two leather recliners with a dog bed in between them. Butkus immediately collapsed in his bed, and began to whimper in his sleep as if he were chasing a rabbit.

"Well, this is the living room. I can show you the rest of the house tomorrow. I'll just show you where you'll be sleeping for now. Olivia's bedroom and a bathroom are downstairs. I finished the basement a few years ago, so it's pretty nice." Deputy Kenworth led the way down some carpeted stairs and flipped on a light to the biggest bedroom she'd ever seen. It was nearly the size of the entire top floor. A green canopy bed was centered on a wall covered in posters of celebrities from *Girl Talk* magazine.

"The bathroom is right through here…it's ocean-themed. Olivia loves the beach…which is why she lives with her mom. Beaches in Missouri kind of suck, huh? Plus, you never know if you're going to get hit by an alligator gar or sucked up by a two-hundred-pound catfish!" He made a slurping sound, laughed, and opened the cabinet under the sink. He pulled out shampoo, conditioner, a bar of soap, two blue towels, and a stack of washcloths. "I'll leave these on the counter for when you need a shower."

"...do you have a toothbrush? I forgot mine." Isabella hated to ask for things from someone who'd already been so generous.

"Sure do." He opened a drawer and placed a new pink toothbrush, a tube of toothpaste, and some floss on the counter. "Don't forget to floss. Flossing is just as important as brushing."

"...thanks." She said.

Deputy Kentworth led her through the bedroom. "There's the bed, obviously. The sheets are clean. There's a TV over there on the dresser...clicker is on the nightstand by the bed. I don't know what all Olivia left behind...she's probably not coming back for it, so use whatever. She's a bit older than you, so you probably won't find any toys. Do you play with toys?"

"Not really." She said. "I do read books, though."

"Yes! Now that I can provide." Deputy Kentworth flipped on a light switch further in the basement. "Olivia has a reading nook."

Three neon-colored beanbags were lumped together on the floor in front of a massive bookshelf. Deputy Kentworth gestured to the bottom shelf. "She's got every *Baby Sitters Club* book in the series. I joined a mail order book club thing, so every time one comes out, they just send it to the house...I also started buying her *Goosebumps* books, so she's got most of those too."

The love Deputy Kentworth had for his daughter was evident in every part of this room. *Is this what it's like to have a normal parent?* "That's great." Isabella mumbled.

"There are movies on the top few shelves, too. We have one of those combo VHS/DVD players so you can watch anything...I've got cable TV too, had them run it downstairs for Olivia..." Deputy Kentworth trailed off as Isabella's attention was taken by something else.

She pointed across the room to the only dusty corner in the basement, near the boiler. "...is that yours?"

He led her over and pulled the chain on a bare overhead lightbulb. "Yup. Bronze Medal in heavyweight boxing."

"You went to the Olympics? That must have been so cool." Isabella stepped closer to get a better look at the framed medal.

"It was. I competed against the best fighters in the world and earned the privilege to stand on that podium." He pointed to a photo of three young men with medals around their necks. "I paid for it though…I messed up my left shoulder pretty bad and couldn't compete anymore. Fortunately, my shooting arm is my right! So, I started working in law enforcement."

"That sucks," Isabella said as she picked up a pair of dusty black boxing gloves from the floor.

"It doesn't suck. It's just…different. Most fighters have very short careers. The human body can only take so much punishment, ya know?" He wiped some dust off the top of a punching bag suspended from a beam in the ceiling. Isabella put her hands inside the boxing gloves and punched them together.

Deputy Kentworth watched her carefully for a moment.

"Alright, Rocky. Listen up. In this house, I only have one rule-don't feed Butkus French fries."

Isabella laughed. "Got it."

Deputy Kentworth stepped up to the boxing bag hanging from the ceiling, and using his finger, drew a happy face in the dust. "And I also have one *suggestion…*"

She punched the air with the oversized gloves. "Okay, what's that?"

"…if you ever feel like hitting someone again, hit the bag instead."


Six Years Later

"Coach!"

The boxer groaned on the floor of the ring, clutching his groin and writhing in pain.

"Sanchez!" David barked as he climbed into the ring. "She already warned you twice to cool it. We are *sparring* not *fighting*. If I didn't know any better, I'd think you were trying to damage my best fighter before she has a chance to make it to the Olympic trials!"

Isabella bounced on the balls of her feet, trying to resist the urge to do more than knee his dick into his stomach. "He got in close and kept hitting me in the ribs. Going way too hard. Fuckin' asshole."

She spat her bloody mouthguard at him.

"I saw it, Roc-…Izzy." David put his hand on her shoulder in reassurance and then leaned over her opponent hunched over in pain on the mat. He put a finger in Sanchez's face. "Not only is she a woman, but she is well below your weight class. The only reason she's fighting *you* is because she's already beat every female fighter in southwest Missouri. Get out of this gym, and never come back."

Sanchez sat up, panting in pain, embarrassment, and anger. "It's not your gym, Deputy Dickhead."

"Hey! It's *Captain* Dickhead!" said David, in mock defense.

"You can't kick me out, *Captain* Dickhead." Sanchez whipped his spit-covered mouthguard in David's direction.

"Yeah, well, *I* fuckin' can." Said a gravelly voice behind him. "Punks like you are a dime a dozen. Get your shit and get out. If you want to beat up a woman, I just finished fuckin' your mother in the alleyway. You might be able to land a few shots despite your weak ass uppercut."

Sanchez stood up and immediately shifted gears. "Big Hefty…I didn't know you were here. I'm sorry, man. Don't kick me out…if you do, I won't be allowed to fight anywhere else."

Big Hefty lit his cigar. "That's right. You won't. Get the fuck out. Leave your gear as payment for wasting my time and I won't break your scrawny ass legs."

When pleading didn't work, Sanchez switched to intimidation. "Your old ass can't even get up in the ring anymore. You don't scare me. I'm staying."

The gym grew deadly silent, like wild birds sensing a tornado. Isabella and David climbed out of the ring and retreated toward the locker rooms. They'd only seen what was about to happen once before and didn't want to witness it despite Sanchez's bad attitude.

Big Hefty rubbed his hand on his round, shirtless, black belly like a Magic 8 Ball, deep in thought. He took a long drag of his cigar and exhaled smoke through the corners of his mouth.

"Boy…if I wasn't higher than giraffe pussy, you'd be dead right now."

Six of the biggest men in the gym unwrapped their gloves, gave Big Hefty a nod, and climbed into the ring with Sanchez.

"Patrons!" Bellowed Big Hefty. "Class is dismissed. Get the fuck out."

The remaining fighters scattered towards the exits without removing their gear or emptying their lockers. As the last one left, Big Hefty's sugar baby drew the shades and locked the doors.

On the drive home from Heavy Hitters Boxing Club, Isabella stared out the window of David's old pickup, watching traffic flash by. She wondered what was happening to Sanchez.

"Should I feel bad, David?" she asked her adoptive dad.

"Absolutely not," David said without taking his eyes off the road. "Everyone knows the rules at Big Hefty's place. It's *his* rules. Sanchez went too far. Hefty and I see your talent, and with the right training, you'll go far… potentially making him- and you- a lot of money."

Isabella rubbed her swollen knuckles. "Is that why all the men try to pulverize me during spars?"

"Maybe." David shrugged his shoulders. "Everyone wants Hefty on their side. He's got money, connections, and experience. You're his favorite, and you're a seventeen-year-old female. There are men at that gym who spend their entire careers trying to impress Big Hefty, and he doesn't even glance at them. He saw the champion in *you* right away. So did I."

"I'm grateful to you both…but I don't know if I can do this. No women are willing to fight me anymore, and the men are too big and aggressive. Rather than sparring to train me, they are sparring to *hurt* me and prove something to themselves. Or Big Hefty." Isabella said.

"I know." David said. "I'll figure something out. You're going to the Olympic Team Trials."

She huffed. "It's in ten weeks. I'm not ready."

"You will be, I promise," David said as they pulled into the driveway of the small home they shared with their geriatric brown labrador retriever. He could no longer climb up to the window to bark, but he always recognized the rumble of David's old Chevy and whimpered at the door.

"Did you pick up Tiger Balm yesterday?" Isabella asked as she unlocked the door.

"It's in your bathroom," David said. "Hey there Butkus, wanna go outside?"

Butkus didn't wait to be led, he shoved his way between Isabella and David, down the stairs, and shuffled through the yard to pee on his favorite bush.

"I told you he can still run," David said.

"That's not running," Isabella said as she dropped her gym bag just inside the door.

"You know better than to leave that there." He pointed at the bag. Isabella grumbled, picked it up, and stomped downstairs towards her room. "And it doesn't matter if Butkus can't run, or walk, or bark. I'll carry him outside if I need to…he'll meet his Maker when *he* wants to."

"I'm going to bed!" she yelled from the basement.

David brewed a pot of coffee and sat down at the kitchen table with a small black book of contacts. He found a number and dialed into his cordless phone.

"Hi Jess. It's David. Yeah, I know…it's been a long time. I should have checked in on you guys… Izzy's doing great, honor roll and everything. How's Tyler doing?…he already graduated? Jeesh I'm sorry I forgot. I'm going to send him a gift this week. So is he going to college or what?…mmhmm. Is he working?…yeah, grocery stores don't pay a lot. Is he still boxing over at Rooster's place?…I bet he's grown a lot since I last saw him. 6 feet, huh. I'm actually looking for an assistant for a few months to help me train Isabella for the Olympic trials, do you think he'd be interested? I'll give him a thousand dollars, and free room and board. I'll even drive to Tulsa to pick him up…Yeah, of course. Have him call me tomorrow. Love you too. Bye."

"Rocky, wake up."

"Ugh. I told you not to call me that anymore."

David shook her foot harder. "Wake up. I have to drop you off at school early. I'm going to Tulsa."

"Gross, why are you going to Tulsa?" Isabella sat up on her elbows. "There's better casinos near Joplin."

"I'm picking up your new sparring partner." He said, grinning as he presented his idea like a Christmas gift.

"Seriously? Please tell me it's a girl." Isabella said.

David leaned his head to the side. "Well…no. It's my nephew, Tyler. He's a few years older than you. I spent some time training him in middle school, but then my sister moved to Tulsa. I haven't seen him in a while. From what I remember, he was a fast learner and a pretty nice kid. He doesn't have any skin in the game other than being my assistant, so we shouldn't have any issues with ego."

Isabella pursed her lips. "How big is he?"

"He said six feet even, about 175 lean muscle. Just a few inches taller than you."

"Fine…now go away so I can get dressed. Maybe make me some bacon or something." Isabella said.

"The best I can do is microwaved bacon and black coffee. You've got fifteen minutes." David winked.

"Ugh, sometimes I hate you and your endless enthusiasm for problem-solving." She shouted after him as he went upstairs.

Thirty minutes later, David dropped Isabella in front of the school and began his three-hour trip to Tulsa from Springfield. Isabella planned to take a cab home in the afternoon in case he was running late.

At 3:30 she checked the front parking lot and he wasn't there. Rather than take a cab, she decided to run a few miles on the school track before going home. By five p.m. she had run four miles, and the school was nearly empty of staff and students. Sticky with sweat, she went to the locker room to change before calling a cab on the pay phone. Just as she was about to remove her sports bra, she heard the squeaking wheels of a cart behind her.

"Whoa, sorry. Didn't know anybody was in here. I'm just collecting towels for Mrs. Heart. You know, part-time job to pay for gas and Doritos, right?" The boy laughed. Isabella turned around.

"I'll be done in ten minutes. Maybe go do the guy's locker room first?"

"Sure..." the blond-haired boy studied her face. "You look familiar. Everybody calls you Rocky, right?"

"It's Isabella. You probably remember me because I punched you in the face in middle school." She scowled.

A sideways grin formed on his face but didn't touch his eyes. "As I recall, I got a few in too."

"Can you just leave, please?" Isabella asked calmly. She'd fought enough grown men to know how to keep her cool when situations were tense.

"You know, you really should be thanking me..." Rich leaned with his elbow on the handle of the cart. "From what I've heard, things turned out pretty well for you after our little altercation. Your whore of a mother threw you out...you got adopted by the deputy that came to the school...he taught you how to fight..."

"I don't need to thank you for shit. You're a worthless, insecure bully." Isabella spat.

He smiled sweetly. "Isabella...I've changed. I am not a bully. Just about everyone loves me now...I bet if you gave me a chance, you might like me too."

"Doubtful." Isabella started putting her running shoes back on and closing her locker. *I'll shower at home. This guy probably has a hole drilled in the wall to watch me.*

"So, Isabella, tell me about yourself. Is it true you are trying out for the Olympics? It's kind of an honor to know I'm the first person you ever punched." Rich had dimples on his cheeks, bright blue eyes, and shoulder-length curly hair. She hated that her childhood bully turned out to be so handsome.

"I need to catch a cab. Can you please move your cart so I can get out?" Isabella stood with her head held high, and her gym bag over her shoulder. *I'm not a scared little girl anymore. I'm safe because I'm strong. I can take him down if I need to.*

He touched her arm gently. "How about…I let you out if you give me your number…and let me take you on a date."

"Sure." Said Isabella. "Do you have a pen and paper?"

"Yeah!" Rich enthusiastically dug in his pocket and pulled out a mechanical pencil and a folded-up page of calculus homework. "I swear, you'll change your mind about me."

Isabella scribbled on the paper, folded it, and handed it back to him. Then she swung her gym bag as hard as she could into his head and shoved him into the wall so she could fit between him and the cart. As Isabella ran up the stairs into the gymnasium, she heard him yell:

"Nice. Fuck you too, Rocky!"


David still wasn't home by the time Isabella arrived in the cab. She let Butkus outside, refilled his food and water, and opened the fridge door to find something for dinner. Inside were three steaks wrapped in white paper labeled "GRILL ME IZZY" written in black marker.

"Of course…" she sighed, then went into the backyard to heat up the grill. Just as she lit the pilot, she heard car doors shut, and Butkus barking at the door.

"I'm out here!" she yelled inside.

"We arrived just in time. If Izzy grilled our steaks, they'll be charcoaled hockey pucks." David told their guest.

"Well, then why did you tell me to grill them?!" Isabella yelled back.

"You were a last resort. I hoped to be home in time to do it myself. Why don't you come in and make a salad before you blow up the house?" said David from the kitchen.

Isabella turned off the burners and went inside to make a salad and greet her new sparring partner.

Tyler was sat on the floor, scratching Butkus's belly to make his leg kick. Three duffle bags were piled next to him. When Isabella walked into the room, he stopped scratching the dog and tried to speak but the words stuck in his throat. He stood up, brushed the dog hair off his jeans, and removed his white cowboy which he sat on the arm of the recliner. He took his time, then extended his hand to Isabella. "I'm Tyler. I look forward to working with you." In a few beats, he was able to turn on a professionalism which almost made Isabella think she imagined his initial awkwardness.

"…thanks. I promise not to beat you up too bad." Isabella joked.

"I've been helping my buddy break some wild horses he adopted from the Bureau of Land Management…getting punched in the face by you will probably feel like a vacation!" Tyler smiled, and for some reason, Isabella blushed. His skin was bronze from the sun, and she could see his muscles under his Brooks & Dunn shirt. Not bulky, so he was probably fast. Most female boxers are built that way, too. Isabella wondered how Tyler would like living in Springfield, where the vibe was a mix of urban and hillbilly, as opposed to country.

"I convinced him to leave his boots at home. There won't be much time for *boot scootin' boogie* after today. The three of us have a lot of work to do." Said David, in between whacks with a meat tenderizer.

"Do you want some help Uncle Dave?" he asked.

"Oh, no. Dinner will be ready in about thirty minutes. In the meantime, Izzy can show you to the guest bedroom. You can unpack or shower. You might call your mom to tell her we made it…if I call her, I won't be able to get off the phone for hours. As it was, we were three hours late because she had to tell me all the family gossip…" David mumbled to himself as he chopped a cucumber for the salad.

Izzy led him down the hallway to a small room next to the bathroom. "You'll have to share a bathroom with David. His room's across the hall. I'm downstairs if you need anything. Oh, make sure you lock your window at night…it's not the best neighborhood. Also, shut your door or Butkus will climb in your bed, and he farts all night. I keep telling David to stop giving him milkshakes, but he doesn't listen."

Isabella smiled. Tyler looked at the floor. "Will do. Guess I'll start unpacking then."

She retreated to the kitchen, finished the salad, and set the dinner table while David seared the steaks outside.

When the three of them were settled at the table with their sizzling steaks in front of them, David explained their training routine for the next ten weeks-four a.m. wakeup to train at Heavy Hitters before Isabella went to school. After school, she comes home and sleeps until David's patrol shift ends at six. Then it's back to the gym until nine. Eat, sleep, and breathe boxing until the day they leave for Louisiana.

"Hell, by the time we're done training Isabella, I might be able to try out for the Olympics too!" Tyler joked.

"Speaking of that…what ever happened to your training, kid?" David asked. "Weren't you able to find a coach in Tulsa?"

He swallowed a gulp of sweet tea. "Well, I could have, but I didn't. I love to box, and still go to the club to work out…but I don't have the fire in me to go pro. You really gotta want it, ya know? I have other things I'd like to do."

"Oh yeah? Like what?" Isabella asked.

David raised an eyebrow. Isabella had always been a 'lone wolf', and generally wasn't interested in what other people were doing.

"I'd like to go to college and study history…then maybe work in a museum or teach. I love how history repeats itself- when you understand the past, you can help plan the future…avoid making the same mistakes." Tyler said.

"Huh. Teaching is a noble profession. It pays about as well as my "noble profession" in law enforcement." David chuckled. "We're living the dream, aren't we Izzy?"

"It's a pretty good life to me," Isabella said.

David was silent for a moment, and his eyes misted over. He patted Isabella on the hand.

Tyler cleared his throat, expertly transitioning the conversation to a topic less emotionally loaded. "Yeah, so after I'm done helping here, I'm traveling to Peru to study the Inca Empire. Have either of you ever been to South America?"

"Nope," said Isabella. "I haven't even been to South Carolina."

"I see. Well, you're not missing much in South Carolina…just crowded beaches, overpriced seafood, and condos as far as the eye can see. The part of the state that isn't on the coast is just…swamp." Tyler laughed.

David watched them converse with a smirk on his face.

"Alright, folks. Let's clear the table and get to bed." Said David. "We've got an early morning."

By 4:30 a.m. the next morning, the three of them were loaded in the Chevy with their gym bags, travel mugs of black coffee, and water bottles. Big Hefty gave David a key to use the gym before they officially opened at six, so they had the place to themselves. Tyler and Isabella warmed up with drills on the bag, and after thirty minutes David blew the whistle and told them to get in the ring.

"What happened here?" Tyler asked. "It looks like a damned murder scene."

In the center of the ring was a two-foot wide red stain. The edges around it had faded the blue boxing ring white, as if someone unsuccessfully tried to clean it with bleach. A trail of red drag marks led out from the center of the ring to the edge.

Isabella gave Tyler a look that meant *don't ask questions.* "Don't piss off Big Hefty."

"Who's Big Hefty?" Tyler asked.

"Trust me, you'll know. Now glove up, cowboy. It's time to make me a champion." Isabella grinned, popped in her mouthguard, and slipped on her 16-ounce sparring gloves.

The two of them sparred, doing catches and counters, combos and blocks. Tyler let Isabella lead the session as David called out commands from outside the ring.

"1-2-3 catch and counter," David yelled. "Good. Keep it up."

David smelled Big Hefty's cherry Swisher Sweet cigar before he saw him.

"Got yourself a new guy, Dave?" asked Big Hefty, watching the session.

"He's my nephew from Oklahoma, here as a favor to me." Said David.

Hefty nodded. "They're a good match. He's big enough to challenge her, but not enough to hurt her. Doesn't seem like an egotistical show-off like the rest of these pricks."

"Izzy seems to like him, too, which is a feat in itself…" David chuckled.

"You think she can make it in Lafayette?" Hefty squinted, assessing David for any sign of doubt.

"Not only do I think she can make the team, but I also think she can win it." David blew his whistle, and Isabella and Tyler dropped their gloves. "Hit the showers. Tyler, you can drop her off at school in my truck and head home. My partner's going to pick me up in the patrol car."

After they showered and dressed, it was nearly eight am and Tyler began the short drive to Isabella's high school. "Turn left here?" he asked.

"Yup. Just a few miles down this road. The school's on the right." Isabella chugged a Gatorade.

Tyler snuck a glance at her while they were stopped in traffic. "So, is this what you do *all* the time? What do you do with friends?"

"I don't have any friends." She scoffed. "Friends are a waste of time."

Tyler seemed taken aback, and unsure how to respond. "You're seventeen…you're telling me you don't hang out with friends or go on dates?"

"Yes, that's exactly what I'm telling you." Said Isabella. "Most people suck. I'm focused on boxing and school. David and Butkus are enough for me."

"So you don't have a boyfriend?" Tyler asked coyly.

"Most guys are scared of me. I like it that way." Isabella remembered her encounter with Rich in the girl's locker room. "It keeps the creeps away."

"I get the feeling you just haven't met the right people yet," Tyler said.

"Maybe you're right, Tyler." Isabella shoved her Gatorade into the side pouch of her backpack. "Or maybe love and friendship are simply manipulation. Everyone wants something for themselves."

"Do you feel that way about David?" he asked as he slowed to a stop in front of the school.

"No. He's the only exception." Isabella replied.

"And what about me, Izzy? What do you think I want?" Tyler asked.

She thought for a moment. "Isn't David paying you?"

He didn't respond. Isabella opened the creaky truck door, jumped out, and slammed it shut.

"Be here at 3:15." She said through the open window. "And bring Butkus. It's his ice cream day."

For the next three weeks, Tyler and Isabella trained six hours a day. Tyler wasn't used to the demanding workout routine, and it was starting to wear on him. In between sparring sessions, he approached his uncle.

"Hey, Uncle Dave...can I talk to you a minute?" he asked.

"Sure, kid. It's loud in here, let's step out back." David led Tyler through the emergency exit into the alley behind the building.

"What's going on?" he asked with concern.

"It's hard to say this...but I've gotta be honest. Izzy is a straight up savage-which is awesome and all-but I just can't keep up. My body is all beat to hell, and I need a few recovery days. Is there anyone else who can practice with her a bit?" Tyler asked.

David sighed. "You know what, I owe you an apology Tyler. I've asked a lot of you, and you haven't complained once. Go home. Izzy can work the bag for a few days while you recover."

"Thanks, Uncle David." Tyler sighed in relief. "My shoulders are so tight I can barely lift my arms."

David tossed Tyler the keys to his truck. "Feed Butkus, will ya? I'll drop Izzy off before work. There's some Advil and tiger balm in the bathroom cabinet. Rent a few movies and get some rest."

When David came back inside the gym without Tyler, Izzy stopped jumping rope. "Where's Tyler?"

"It took three weeks, but you finally broke him." David teased.

"He lasted longer than the rest of 'em!" Big Hefty yelled from across the room. "Don't let that one get away."

Isabella's face fell, and her heart sank. "He went back to Tulsa? He didn't even say goodbye."

"Relax, Rocky." Said David as he poured coffee into a Styrofoam cup. "He's just taking a few days off. He's at home."

"Oh."

*Why do I care?* thought Isabella. *Sparring partners are practically a revolving door for me. I barely know him.*

She picked up her jump rope, practiced footwork, and then--as David always preached--ended with abs. On the way home, they grabbed a pizza for Tyler and a couple of new releases from the video rental store as a thank you. Considering the beatings he'd been taking, it probably wasn't enough.

Butkus announced her arrival just as Tyler was leaving the bathroom with a towel around his waist. "Oh, hey Izzy...look, I'm really sorry, but I just need a few days and I'll be right back at it with you. I know you don't have long to train...I wouldn't hold you up unless I absolutely had to."

Isabella set the pizza on the table. Butkus perched underneath, his nose twitching at the smell of hot pepperoni. "Don't be sorry, Tyler. I've never had a sparring partner last as long as you."

"...really?" he asked, as his guilt appeared to lessen.

"Yeah. I've had guys way bigger than you, and more experienced, only last a week or two. I'm grateful you're only taking a few days off instead of hitching up a horse and riding off in the sunset to Oklahoma." Isabella gestured at the pizza. "Are you hungry?"

"Always. I don't think I've ever been as hungry as I have been since I got here. I probably burn ten thousand calories a day." Tyle grabbed two plates from the kitchen. "I don't know how you do it."

Isabella took a plate from Tyler, loaded it with two slices, and sat it on the floor for Butkus. "Unfortunately, I can't have pizza right now. Gotta eat clean."

"Oh yeah. I forgot." Tyler grabbed three slices for himself and caught Isabella's eyes flick down to his towel. "Oops, I suppose I should go put some pants on before I eat."

Tyler handed her his plate while he ran back to the guestroom and put on a pair of athletic shorts. He came back and grabbed the plate from her hands, collapsed into David's recliner, and shoved half a slice into his mouth.

"I wouldn't get too comfortable," Isabella said. "There's a Chiefs game tonight. David's going to kick you out of his chair as soon as he gets home."

"Ugh, you're right." Tyler pushed his legs in to bring the recliner upright. "What movies did you rent?"

"I have *Fight Club* and *Austin Powers: The Spy Who Shagged Me.*" She held up a DVD in each hand. "Which one? You can watch downstairs if you want."

"Easy choice, I've had enough fighting." He pointed at her right hand. "Austin Powers."

Isabella tossed him the movie without a word, began rifling through her gym bag, and pulled out a Gatorade. Tyler's eyes never left her.

"You're not going to watch with me, are you?" he asked, barely concealing a hint of disappointment.

Isabella sighed and looked up. "I can't…I need a shower and sleep. Can't seem to get enough of either." She sniffed her armpit and gave a forced laugh in an attempt to soften the obvious blow.

"Yeah, I get it." He stood up and wiped pizza crust crumbs off his sculpted bare chest. "Guess I just miss hanging out with my friends back in Tulsa…but I'll be seeing them soon enough, right? In a month you'll be on the Olympic Team and won't need me anymore." Tyler pulled a sherpa blanket off the back of the chair and wrapped it around his shoulders. "Before I know it, wild horses will be bustin' my ass again instead of *you* bustin' my face."

Tyler walked past her, into the kitchen and took two of David's beers from the fridge without any suggestion of shame or guilt, slammed the door, and stomped downstairs.

Isabella knew she often pushed her sparring partners to their breaking points despite all of them knowing full well what they were getting themselves into. Like a revolving door, they came and went, so she never bothered getting emotionally invested in any of them. If she lost Tyler at this point, she'd likely be stuck with someone bigger *or* weaker than her. Neither would help her train properly. She knew she was on thin ice with the only person who could help her make the team. She left her gym bag in the middle of the dining room floor and followed Tyler downstairs.

She found Tyler dragging a bean bag from her reading nook to the floor in front of her bedroom TV. He looked up when she turned on her bedside lamp. "I see Uncle Dave is still obsessed with the Rocky movies," he gestured with his head to the top shelf of Isabella's bookcase. "Seriously, how many copies of each one does he need?"

"That's because he keeps wearing out his old copies but can't bear to throw them out," Isabella smirked as she started pulling cotton lavender pajamas from her dresser.

Tyler flopped down in the beanbag and turned on the TV with the remote. "DVDs would last longer than VHS."

"True…Dave's not much of a fan of technology. We still don't have internet at the house…it's so annoying." Isabella stood over Tyler who was attempting to burrow his large body into the same hot-pink beanbag Isabella had read *James and the Giant Peach* at twelve years old. "Ty…you don't have to sit on the floor. I'm going to take a salt bath to soak my shoulders, and it'll probably be a while. Just use my bed."

His eyes flashed to the stairs as if expecting David to rush down and object to even the thought of a man in his precious girl's bed. "Uh…are you sure?"

Isabella rolled her eyes. "It's fine, you're just watching a movie, Ty."

"Alright, cool." He laughed, grabbed both beers and the remote, and rolled out of the beanbag while Isabella went into the bathroom. "Thanks, Izzy. I'm kind of big for a beanbag."

As Isabella was about to close the bathroom door, she peeked out and said: "He shouldn't be home for a while…but if you hear Butkus barking, move to the beanbag. It ll save us both some drama."

"Got it." Tyler gave her finger guns as the first beer began to loosen him up and he popped the top on his second.

"…and hide the beer." Isabella raised an eyebrow at him, then shut the door.

After a few minutes, Tyler heard the bathtub running and he pushed play on the remote. He moved lacey throw pillows around attempting to get comfortable, and ultimately decided the best use for them was on the floor. He pulled back the covers of Isabella's bed and laid his head on one of her overstuffed feather-filled pillows. A whiff of her vanilla-scented shampoo puffed from the pillow into his face. He recognized the smell from when he locked her arms against her in a clinch so she could practice shoving or spinning out. Tyler covered himself with Isabella's heavy flowered comforter and began dozing off before he even through the previews for upcoming films.

His eyes fluttered open at the sound of the phone next to the bed ringing. He picked it up. "Hello?" he coughed "I mean…Kentworth residence, this is Tyler."

"Did I catch you sleeping, kid? Where's Izzy?" David laughed.

"Uh, she's in the bathtub, I think. I was watching a movie." Tyler sat up, and paused it just as Austin Powers began shouting '*Do I make you horny, baby?*'

"Alright, well leave her a note or tell her I need to pull a double shift tonight. Someone called in sick, and I won't be off until seven tomorrow morning. Can you drive her to the gym at four?"

"Yeah, sure. No problem." Tyler agreed.

"And don't drink my beer." Said David.

Tyler gulped. "Uh…yeah, no, I won't."

"You already did, didn't you?" David asked with amusement.

Tyler didn't know what to say.

"Guess I'll be home around seven *thirty*. I'll need to grab more beer. Make sure you guys let Butkus out before you go to sleep."

"I will." Tyler squeaked.

"See you tomorrow, Chief." The phone clicked on David's end, so Tyler hung up the phone and rubbed the sleep from his eyes as the bathroom door clicked open.

Isabella was detangling her wet hair with a large toothed comb and peeked around the corner. "Was that Dave?"

"Yeah…he's working a double shift, I guess. He wants us to take Butkus outside and not drink his beer." Tyler grimaced.

"I told you, dummy!" She threw the comb at him. "He counts his beers and has just enough to get him through until payday."

"It's been a rough week…" Tyler immediately flipped the blankets off and began climbing out of her bed. "Anyway, guess I'll go upstairs. I'll drive you to the gym in the morning,"

"Tyler…" Isabella stood at the foot of the bed, taking in the dark circles under his eyes, and a fresh bruise she hadn't noticed earlier beginning to darken on his jaw. "Stay there, finish the movie. I'll take the dog out."

"…I feel like shit." He collapsed back into the bed.

"Well, you look like shit too." Isabella covered him with her blanket whistled for Butkus who was snoring upside down in the unoccupied beanbag and took him outside to do his business. She returned twenty minutes later with the box of remaining pizza, four of David's post-work beers, a bottle of Tylenol, and a bottle of Aleve. She clumsily plopped all of it in the middle of the bed.

"Move over, this is my favorite side of the bed. It's by the lamp." She commanded.

"Wait…what?" Tyler was trying to understand what was happening. "Dave said not to drink his beer!"

"We're already in trouble. In for a penny, in for a pound." Isabella shoved at Tyler to move to the other side of the bed.

"Ouch! Stop, you brute! Haven't you hurt me enough already?" he scooched sideways in obvious agony. "I'm trying to move around all this shit you threw in the bed with my achy, broken body."

"Such a whiner…" Isabella joked as she climbed under the blankets and Tyler stared at her in disbelief.

"I can't eat all this pizza…or drink all this beer." Tyler gestured at the greasy box between them.

Isabella flipped open the lid and pulled out the biggest slice. "That's good because you're sharing with me. Check out that cheese pull, eh?"

He watched her dangle the cheese and drop it into her mouth. "What about your training diet?"

"I think we both deserve a night off, don't you?" Isabella passed Tyler a slice.

Tyler sheepishly took it from her hands and took a small bite, confused by Isabella's uncharacteristically easygoing behavior. As long as he had known her, she always had her fists up-even energetically. "So…do you want me to turn the TV off or something so you can sleep?"

"No." She flicked the aluminum beer top open. "I'm going to watch a movie with you. Tonight, I am just a normal person doing normal person things."

"You couldn't be normal if you tried." He teased with a smile, as he restarted the movie.

Isabella shrugged. "At least I'm trying. We're not watching *Fight Club*, are we? I can turn off my punchy brain once in a while."

"Alright, if you say so, Rocky." Tyler couldn't hide the way his face lit up as he situated himself next to her on the bed and the movie began. Isabella felt her cheeks turn red.

She reached for the bottles of pain reliever to take his eyes away from studying her face, "Okay, so an old boxer's trick is to take Tylenol and Aleve at the same time. Two of each. They work differently, the Aleve helps with inflammation, and the Tylenol with pain. Just don't do it all the time. Only when you really need it. It's not good for your kidneys." She passed him the pills and her beer.

Tyler swallowed them without a second thought. "If you say so, Rocky."

By halfway through the film, they had finished all four beers and the remaining pizza. Tyler's pain was finally managed, and he sunk deeper and deeper into the bed until he was no longer sitting up, but lying on his side, watching the movie through half-open eyes. It was Isabella's turn to study *his* face.

"How did you get the bruise on your jaw?" Isabella asked.

"Oh, that? Bar fight. You should see the other guy." He mumbled.

"You know what I mean…" she reached over to his face and gently traced her fingers along the bruise. Stubble scratched under her nails. "When did I do that? I didn't think I was hitting that hard during sparring."

Tyler gave a weak laugh. "Oh, you definitely are. The whole point of me being here is so you can get stronger while beating up on me, isn't it? I try not to complain."

Isabella brushed some of his tousled hair out of his face to inspect it. She noticed His breathing became faster and shallower. "You must really want to go to Peru."

His eyes followed her hands as she touched his hair. "I do…I can't wait to visit Lake Titicaca…the Uros people live on islands made of totara reeds. Most tourists want to see Machu Picchu, which is amazing…but there's so much more in Peru. Rainbow Mountain, the Nazca Lines. My boxing days are done after this. I want to make it to college before my brain gets rattled much more. Try to take it easy on me, champ."

Isabella smiled. "I can't make any promises…"

"Have you ever thought about doing anything other than boxing?" Tyler asked as Isabella pulled her hand away.

"Hmm…not really." She said. "Ever since I saw Dave's medal and put that dusty glove on my hand…it's all I've ever wanted to do."

Tyler nodded. "That's why you'll be a champion. You have the fire. You need to be obsessed with excellence."

Isabella held his gaze. "What about you? Are you obsessed with excellence?"

"No," he laughed. "I'm obsessed with adventure, and too easily distracted by llamas to be excellent."

The air felt electric as they both inched nearer to each other. "I think you're pretty excellent." Said Isabella quietly.

"Yes, I'm an excellent punching bag." He whispered.

"No," Isabella leaned in close enough for them to feel each other's hot breath. "You're so much more than that."

Just as when they sparred, he let her lead and felt her lips touch his. He surrendered to the fantasy he never thought would happen as it became a reality. He told himself he only thought about her so much because of all the time they spent together, watching, assessing, grappling. They ate together, lived in the same house, picked up groceries, and ran laps around the block... every day for the last month. He was always thinking about her, what it would be like to be with her...and not just *be* with her. To have her in his life beyond the ten weeks of training.

Tyler remembered that soon she would be training with the Olympic Team-he knew she could make the trials in Louisiana. He would probably only ever see her again on television, while she spent the next year in Australia.

His hands had found their way to her waist and were caressing the soft, bare skin under her pajamas. Their kisses were becoming deeper now, and her tongue passed through both their lips and searched for his tongue. Every second felt like a runaway train picking up speed.

Australia. She's going to Australia. She'll have no use for you in a few weeks.

Tyler pulled his hands and mouth away from Isabella as if he were touching fire. "I can't...you're leaving..."

Isabella looked rejected. "What? This doesn't need to be a big thing, Tyler. I thought we were just having fun."

Tyler looked away. "To me, it wouldn't be just fun."

Understanding dawned in Isabella's eyes. She didn't have enough experience with men to realize Tyler had feelings for her. "I'm sorry...I didn't know you liked me in that way."

"Yeah, well, I do..." he reached for her hand, and ran his thumb across her swollen and purple knuckles. "Which is why I think I should leave tomorrow."

Isabella sat up straight. "No! I don't want you to leave…I like you that way, too."

Tyler leaned in and gently kissed her mouth. "In that case, I think I should leave tonight."

"You said you love adventure! Come with me to Louisiana, and we can visit New Orleans after the trials. We could walk around all those creepy cemeteries and eat crawfish!" she pleaded.

He smiled. "And after that, you'll fly to the other side of the world, where you'll find some hot Australian surfer bro to keep you company."

"I don't want a surfer!" Isabella grabbed his arm as he flipped the blankets back. "Come with me to Australia! You can help me train."

He pulled his arm away and climbed out of her bed. "You're already too good at fighting for me to help train you."

"Tyler…please don't go. Come with me to Australia…even if it just means you carry my gear and keep me company." Isabella climbed across the bed and stood up, towering above him like the goddess Athena. Lamplight glowed behind her chiseled body. Her hair was loose and wild. Her eyes were misty with tears. To Tyler, she had never looked more vulnerable, or more beautiful. Isabella reached down to him. "I just want to be with you."

He put his broad hands under her arms to help her down, but instead of landing on her feet, she slid down his arms, hooking her own around his neck and then wrapped her legs around his waist.

The feeling of the warmth between her legs against his body was the end of his admirable resolve to leave. He kissed her neck and slid his hands down to cradle her firm bottom, one hand on each cheek. Isabella moaned in his ear and Tyler felt his heart beating out of his chest. *Leave now, she's going to break your heart. Get out while you can.*

Isabella wrapped herself tighter around him, and slid one of her hands from his neck, down his chest, to the space between where their hips met and into Tyler's shorts.

He was a dead man.

He tossed her on the bed and pawed at her pajama bottoms, became distracted, and ran his hand up her shirt to cup and gently squeezed her breasts as Isabella kissed furiously at every piece of his skin she could reach- his ear, neck, shoulder. She wiggled out of her pajama bottoms and panties, and using her feet, tugged at his loose gym shorts while Tyler lay on top of her, stroking her hair as he gently sucked and nibbled her nipples.

When his shorts made it just far enough down his thighs, he traced her warmth and entered her. They moaned in each other's ears, the sound only muffled between deep kisses.

Round one was over as fast as it began and ended with a double knockout.

The rematch, however, went the distance.

Isabella awoke to the phone ringing. She groggily picked up the receiver from her bedside table.

"…hello?"

"Why aren't you at the gym?" David demanded.

"…what? What time is it?" Isabella sat up, disoriented.

"It's eight o'clock. Tyler was supposed to drive you here at four!" David reminded her.

"Oh, shit. We must have overslept. I'm sorry, we'll be there as soon as we can." Isabella ran her fingers through her hair and began scanning the floor for her clothes.

"Alright, but you two better bring Krispy Kreme or I'm going to be *really* mad." Said David.

Isabella sighed. "Okay, fine. It's not fair I have to buy you fresh donuts I can't even eat."

"Hey, Rocky…how many beers do I have left?" David chuckled and the line went silent.

Isabella hung up and grabbed her underwear off the floor. The waistband was torn. "Tyler, wake up, we're late! Can you take Butkus out while I get dressed?"

Silence.

The other side of the bed was empty.

"Tyler?" she called into the room. Her stomach turned.

She ran out of her room and upstairs naked. She smelled coffee brewing.

"Tyler, you should have woken me up! Dave's losing his mind!"

The kitchen was empty except for Butkus who was eating from a freshly filled bowl of food. Isabella's gym bag was packed and on the table. The truck keys were next to it. She unzipped her bag- inside were two cold Gatorades and a stuffed toy llama.

"NO! Damnit, Tyler! No!" Isabella cried as she collapsed to the floor. Butkus ran over to her, licking her face and sniffing her hair.


She arrived at the gym an hour later, juggling a dozen donuts, her gym bag, and equipment.

Dave rushed over to her and grabbed the box of donuts. "Gotta save the most important things first. Where's your squire? Parking the steed?"

Isabella tossed her bag on a bench. "Tyler's gone. Is Sanchez still around?"

David was quiet for a moment and decided from the look of Isabella's swollen red eyes that now was not a good time to ask about Tyler. "He's missing a few teeth, but he should be healed enough to fight. I'll call Big Hefty and see if he can get Sanchez over here."

Isabella nodded and started jumping rope. "Let's go to the Olympics, Captain Kentworth."


David wiped his brow with the back of his arm. "For fuck's sake, don't they have air conditioning in this building? After being in Louisiana, I will never complain about the humidity in the Ozarks again. You doing alright, Rocky? You look pale, take my water."

Like David, sweat poured down Isabella's forehead as she waited with the rest of the Women's Boxing Olympic team hopefuls in a long hallway. They were told this was the first round of eliminations but were instructed to leave their gear in the locker rooms.

Isabella took her coach's water and guzzled it. Immediately she was hit with a wave of nausea. She felt dizzy and grabbed David's arm to steady herself. "I think I'm gonna be sick."

David dropped his information booklet and complimentary tote bag of *2000 Summer Olympics* merchandise and put a hand on each of her shoulders. "Nope, no, no, no. You *will not* vomit on my lucky 'Go Rocky Go' shirt signed by Sylvester Stallone. It's disrespectful to the champion. Look at me, Izzy."

Her chest heaved up and down as she stared wide-eyed at her mentor. Several coaches looked her way, and Isabella heard another fighter not-quite whisper *She's never gonna make it if she can't handle this.* Isabella willed her stomach to cooperate. She focused on David's shirt. *Go, Rocky Go. If he can make it out of the gutter to become a champion, I can too. I wish Tyler was here. I know if he was here, I could get it together.*

Isabella's stomach cramps subsided, and her breathing slowed. David gave her a quick hug and whispered. "Eye of the tiger, kid. You've got this. I'm here for you."

They had been waiting in the hallway with the other fighters and coaches for nearly half an hour and leaned against the painted concrete block wall. David caught the attention of the coach next to them.

"Hey, do you know what we're doing here? We were told not to bring gear." David asked.

The coach shrugged. "No idea. This is our first time at the trials."

David huffed and wiped his brow again.

"Hey, David…" Isabella tried to sound casual like she was just making chitchat. "Did you ever find out what happened to Tyler? What did your sister say?"

He furrowed his brows at her and chose his words carefully. "My sister said he came home and packed a few bags. She drove him to the airport, and he flew to South America."

Isabella didn't act surprised. "Oh yeah. He mentioned Peru. Did she say when he's coming back to Tulsa?"

"Well, from what I understand, he's not." Said David. "Apparently he's trying to find work, then go to the University of Lima. My sister mentioned trying to convince him to come home for Christmas."

Isabella nodded nonchalantly. "So, are we going to Tulsa for Christmas this year?"

David grinned. "Do you *want* to go to Tulsa for Christmas this year?"

Isabella blushed.

The sound of heels and a squeaking cart echoed down the hallway as the competitors grew quiet. A woman in a pantsuit and another in scrubs stopped halfway down the hallway.

"Welcome, fighters! My name is Jessica Radford, and I'm one of the coordinators for the 2000 Women's Olympic Boxing trials. This," Jessica gestured to the woman in scrubs, "is my assistant Nicole."

Nicole nodded and began removing the cover from her cart.

"The first round of elimination is simple: pee in a cup." Jessica pointed at the plastic cups, all labeled with a competitor's name and birthdate.

"Each of you will take your cup into the restroom and pee into the cup *in front of Nicole.* You will then return your cup to the cart, and we will test it in front of all of you. We know how hard all of you have worked to be here, and we want the competition to be as fair as possible. We do not allow performance-enhancing drugs on our team. We also believe in full transparency- your tests will be performed in front of you to ensure you feel comfortable that the results have not been tampered with.

"That said: if anyone wishes to leave before the tests are performed, please do so now." Jessica raised her eyebrows and looked up and down the hall. She locked eyes with a heavyweight competitor and evaluated her huge biceps.

The fighter scowled and glanced at her coach. "Fuckin' bitch." she spat at Jessica, and stomped down the hallway, flinging the closest exit door open with so much force it didn't close correctly afterward.

The remaining competitors exchanged looks to see if anyone else would leave.

Jessica seemed unbothered by the outburst. "Alright then, get in line, grab a cup. When you're done, give Nicole your cup and sit on the floor in the hallway while we wait for the rest! I know you all are anxious to get in the ring- this won't take long!"

Twenty or so female Olympic hopefuls formed a line leading into the bathroom. Isabella took her turn peeing in front of Nicole- a welcome relief after nearly an hour of waiting in the hallway after chugging two bottles of water. She returned to David and sat down next to him.

"I wish I could pee in a cup right now…my bladder isn't what it used to be." He hit Isabella with his elbow. "You take any steroids I don't know about, Izzy?"

Isabella laughed. "Yeah, right. We spend all our money on donuts for you and McDonald's for Butkus. I can't afford to be enhanced."

"You don't need to be." David put his arm around Isabella like he did when they first met. Isabella let him squeeze her tight.

"Stop, David!" Isabella giggled.

The bathroom door slammed shut as Nicole pushed the cart full of cups containing varied shades of yellow liquid into the hallway.

"Okay, let's get this show on the road!" said Jessica.

Nicole grabbed a random cup and said. "Autumn Haywood."

She used a disposable plastic dropper, dipped it in the cup, and dropped the urine onto several different test strips.

"It takes several minutes to process the tests, so we are going to do a few at a time. Erin Briar, and Stephanie Lock. These are yours."

Jessica used a new dropper for each set of strips. Jessica peeked over and whispered to Nicole.

"Autumn Haywood, qualified. Go to the gym at the end of the hallway. Erin Briar…looks like you are also clean." Said Jessica.

Erin and her coach happily rushed towards the gym.

"Stephanie Lock…you are positive for marijuana use. We've decided not to disqualify you, but don't do it again. You'll be required to test daily until you leave or make the team. Understood?" asked Jessica.

Stephanie and her coach exhaled dramatically. "Yes."

Jessica nodded. "Next up we have, April Rains? Not the best name for a fighter, is it?"

April shrugged, and some of the women gave good natured laughs as Nicole went to work on the urine samples.

"Isabella Gallows and Reba Trent."

David made an audible "Yes!" and whispered to Isabella "I need to stop by the restroom before we go to the gym. There's no way I can last another two hours."

Isabella rolled her eyes.

"April Rains…disqualified for cocaine." Said Jessica sternly.

A few competitors gasped. April Rains and her coach silently exited down the hallway opposite the gym.

Nicole and Jessica didn't even notice but were instead whispering over one of the samples. *Give it a few more minutes.*

"Reba Trent, clear. Isabella Gallows, your sample needs a few more minutes." Said Jessica with a reassuring smile.

Isabella shrugged. "…okay."

David gave her a questioning look.

"I'm not on drugs, David. Calm down." Isabella shook her head.

"Lisa Smith, Chloe Haverson. Your samples are next." Said Jessica.

She looked over at Isabella. "Isabella Gallows, unfortunately, you are disqualified."

Isabella flew to her feet and rushed over to see the test. "What? I don't do drugs!"

"Do the test again in front of us!" David objected. "Izzy doesn't do drugs!"

Nicole and Jessica frowned.

"You are correct. The test shows Isabella doesn't do drugs." Said Jessica.

Confusion flooded Isabella's face. "I don't understand! Why am I disqualified?"

Jessica sighed. "Honey…you're pregnant."

"I think I work harder now than before I retired." Said David, holding out a chubby, drooling baby to Isabella before she even made it fully through the door.

Isabella kissed him on the top of his blonde curls. He looked more and more like his dad every day. "Hello, Teddy Bear! Maybe Pops can hold on for just *one freakin' second* so I can take my backpack off."

David sat him on the floor, and he immediately bolted for Butkus's tale. "The dog and I need a nap. Also, his diaper is loaded."

Isabella groaned. "Great, thanks. Speaking of loaded…we start firearms training tomorrow. Any advice from my wise, retired, law-enforcement sage?"

"Yeah, avoid using them. Spend more time studying less-lethal defensive practices. Diplomacy first. If that fails, you could probably knock someone out with a 1-2 punch if you started practicing again."

Isabella swooped up Theodore with one arm on the floor and flipped him over to change his diaper. He responded with giggles as drool bubbles dripped from the corner of his mouth. "Dave, I told you I don't want to box anymore. I'm a mom now…I can't put in the long hours needed to win championships. And the only way boxers make money is by winning."

Dave flopped in his favorite chair, kicked up the footrest, and cracked a beer. "Fine. But don't be surprised if I've got Teddy punching the bag as soon as he can walk. He's my last hope to coach somebody to gold. I'm getting too old for this shit."

After Theodore's diaper was changed, Isabella blew raspberries on his tummy until he was paralyzed in uncontrollable fits of giggles long enough for her to wrangle him into fuzzy pajamas. "Are you sure you're up to watching him until he's old enough for school? I'm sure I could figure something out if it's too much."

David scoffed. "I ain't dead yet, missy. I'm just complaining. Besides, he's the happiest damn baby I've ever seen. We're doing too good of a job raising him, he'll never be angry enough to make a good boxer."

Isabella laughed. "True. Hey, have you seen his llama? I'm going to put him to bed."

Dave reached into the cracks of his chair and pulled out a long-necked gray lump wearing a multicolored scarf. "Is this thing it?"

Theodore grunted and held out his hands, making grabbing motions in the air.

"Well, I guess so!" Dave handed the baby his toy and kissed him on the forehead. "Goodnight, Champ. I'm sure we will see each other bright and early again…"

Isabella smiled at David. "Did I ever tell you how grateful I am for you?"

"No. You're incredibly ungrateful. You never bring coffee with my Krispy Kreme. And you don't buy Boston Cremes." He winked.


After Isabella rocked Teddy to sleep in the nursery-their former guest room where Tyler slept-she tiptoed out and gently shut the door. She could hear David talking on the phone on the patio.

"I appreciate the heads up. So, did you tell him? …yeah, that's for the best. I'll let her know. Thanks, Judy. I'll let you know how it goes."

Isabella was standing in the doorway when David turned around. The blood was drained from her face.

"It's him, isn't it?" she asked.

David took a deep breath, bracing himself for what was sure to be a long night. "He's back in Tulsa…or at least he *was*. My sister said no one had heard from him in almost a year and a half, not even his friends. He showed up on her doorstep and told her his visa expired so he had to come back for a while."

Isabella gulped and uncontrollable tears flowed down her cheeks.

Dave went to her and wrapped his arms around her as she buried her head in his salt-and-pepper beard. It smelled like Budweiser and the same cheap aftershave he was wearing when she first met him at eleven years old in Principal Spencer's office. "Hey, it's going to be okay. Tyler is a good guy. He needs to know."

"His mom didn't tell him?" she pulled back, shocked.

"She didn't get a chance. He asked about your Olympic trials...when Judy said you didn't go to Australia and were still living in Springfield, he asked for her car keys and ran out the door. We are all assuming he's on his way, that's why she called. So you had some warning..." David shrugged.

"Wait..." panic made the blood rush back into Isabella's face. "He's on his way here...*now?*"

"Yeah, I guess so." Said David.

"How far away is Tulsa? When did he leave?" demanded Isabella.

"Judy said he left about an hour ago, and it's around three from Tulsa to Springfield..." David scratched at his beard. "It's not a big deal, just relax, kid."

"This is a very big deal!" Isabella ran into the kitchen and downstairs to her childhood bedroom. She peeled off her sweaty cadet uniform, showered, blow-dried and straightened her hair, and applied light makeup. She didn't want to go full face...she's not even supposed to know he's coming. She tore through her closet trying to find something to wear that was the middle ground between *exhausted mom/college student* and *at the club looking for a hookup.* Her club clothes didn't fit anymore anyway, so she settled on her newest pair of jeans and a light blue sweater. Just as she finished dressing, she heard Butkus bark like he always does when someone pulls in the driveway. She took a deep breath and slowly walked upstairs, listening as David greeted his nephew.

"Tyler! What a surprise, it's been so long! I think your mom was getting ready to send a search party into the Andes Mountains to find you."

"Yeah…there aren't a lot of phones where I was living." She heard Tyler say.

"Not a lot of barbers apparently, either!" David joked. They were laughing as Isabella walked around the corner and into the living room. Everyone fell silent as Isabella and Tyler looked at each other across a chasm of intense life experiences that had separated them for over a year and a half.

Tyler was slim and strong, but without the muscle definition he had when they boxed together. His skin was bronzed from the South American sun, and he'd allowed his hair to grow to his shoulders. It was curly and white-blonde, just like his son's. Seeing the resemblance briefly took her breath away.

"Tyler," Isabella said through tight lips. She was afraid if she said too much that the emotions she'd stuffed deep down in her heart for the sake of her son would spill out in a flood. "It's been a long time."

He looked uncomfortable. "I know…it's good to see you." Tyler stepped awkwardly towards Isabella and gave her a light hug. He felt her shaking but didn't mention it.

David clapped his hands together to break the ice. "So, the Chiefs game is about to start, and me and Butkus promised my buddy Frank we'd watch with him. We were just about to head out. Wish I could visit with you longer, Tyler. Are you going to be in town for a few days? Maybe we could go fishing out at Stockton Lake."

"I don't know actually…I'm so used to living day by day, I forget to plan things out sometimes. Do you still have that guest room? Maybe I could stay here a few days." Tyler suggested.

Isabella looked at David with panic in her eyes.

David gave her a small nod to let her know he had it under control. "Actually, Tyler, we have a guest staying with us at the moment, but if you don't mind sleeping in a recliner you're welcome to stay as long as you like."

"That would be great, Uncle Dave." He glanced at Isabella. "I mean, as long as I'm not intruding on Isabella or your other guest."

Isabella giggled nervously. "Oh no it's fine with me. No problem at all."

"Cool," said Tyler. "what about your other guest though? Your place is kind of small I don't want to impose too much."

Dave laughed while Isabella looked horrified. "Oh, no, our guest won't mind at all! He's a real nice guy, my next boxing prodigy. Izzy likes him a lot too. I'm sure you'll get along." David gave Isabella a wink, grabbed the dog leash from the hook by the door, and whistled for Butkus. "Come on, dog. Let's go eat some chicken wings."

David left and shut the door quickly behind him before Isabella could respond or ask him to stay. Tyler was quiet and looking at his feet.

"Do you want a beer?" Isabella asked.

"Will Dave get mad?" Tyler joked.

She took two from the fridge. "Nah, he's mellowed out in his old age. It helps I pay some of the bills around here now, so he has a bigger beer budget."

"I see." Said Tyler as he twisted open the top of his glass bottle. "So, what kind of work are you doing?"

"Security at Bass Pro Shop. It's mostly shoplifting. Pretty boring." Isabella struggled to open the twist cap. "How did you do this with your bare hands?"

He reached out for her to hand him the bottle. He effortlessly twisted it off and handed it back. "My hands are really calloused. Do you remember the Uros people I told you about? They live on islands made of totara reeds. I lived with them for a little while, and the islands need to be rebuilt constantly. The reeds at the bottom will rot away, so you have to keep weaving in new stuff. It's a lot of work."

"Wow, you finally made it to Peru. What made you come back to Tulsa?" Isabella asked.

"My visa expired. When I got to the airport, I checked my email, and it was just bombed with messages from my family and friends. I didn't realize people were so worried about me…didn't see any from you though." He fished for an emotional reaction.

"Yeah…I figured you didn't want to hear from me. Also, I've been busy." Isabella gulped her beer.

"You've been busy doing *what* exactly? Have you been busy with your mysterious houseguest?" Tyler pried.

Isabella looked up at him. "Yes, actually, I have."

Tyler frowned. "I knew you'd meet an Australian guy…"

"I didn't go to Australia." Isabella whispered.

"That's what my mom said. I didn't believe her though…I had to find out for myself." He said. "What happened?"

Isabella leaned back in the chair, exhausted from the emotional burden she'd been carrying for eighteen months.

"I was disqualified." She said without further explanation. "Why did you leave?"

Shame filled his eyes, and he looked away. "You were better off without me. I didn't want to mess up your chances of going to the Olympics."

Isabella couldn't help but laugh. "Yeah, well, you did anyway."

"Izzy, I didn't mean to hurt you. I wanted to help you…and I didn't want to get hurt either. There's no way you would have time or energy for me while you were at the Olympics." Tyler pleaded. "Please don't hate me, Isabella."

Silent tears ran down Isabella's face. "I don't hate you, Tyler. I never did. I loved you."

Tyler reached out to hold her hand. He ran his thumb across her knuckles. They were soft and smooth now, rather than bruised and swollen. "Did you stop boxing because of me?"

Isabella squeezed his hand. "Not exactly…stay here…I need to show you something."

She rose from her chair and disappeared down the hallway. Tyler heard a door open, and then close. She came back into the room carrying a cherub-faced, sleeping child…with long, white-blond curls.

Tyler froze, and Isabella stayed silent as she gently bounced the sleeping baby in her arms, allowing him to process what he was seeing.

He stood up slowly and touched a lock of the baby's hair. "Is he… mine?"

"His name is Theodore Tyler Kentworth. I was allowed to name him Kentworth because it's my adoptive father's last name…since you weren't here. We call him Teddy." Isabella carefully handed him over to Tyler.

He held him so still like a statue that Isabella wasn't sure Tyler was breathing. Teddy stirred as a tear fell on his button nose.

"Isabella…I'm so sorry. I'm sorry you couldn't compete in the Olympics. I'm sorry you went through this alone. I just don't know what else to say right now…" Tyler choked as he spoke.

"Don't be sorry…I wasn't alone. David retired and is helping me raise him. I'm working, going to college, and the police academy. I want to be a sheriff's deputy like him. I don't really miss boxing…Teddy fills my heart with so much love I don't have that kind of fight in me anymore. I just want to make him proud… keep him safe and fed. I want him to know he's loved. Everything I never knew as a kid…at least until David came around. My life is good--so is Teddy's." Isabella gently took Theodore from Tyler's arms before he passed out. "You don't have to stick around unless you want to."

Without hesitation, he said, "I want to."

Isabella was surprised at the conviction in his voice. "Oh, okay. That's great…but you can sleep on it if you want to. Maybe you *should*, you know?"

"I don't need to sleep on it." Tyler wrapped his long arms around Isabella and Teddy. "You are all I've thought about since the day we met. I've climbed mountains in the Andes, swam in the Amazon River, and slept on a reed raft under the stars…no matter what I did, where I was in the world, or how exhausted I made myself…being with you was always the first thing I thought of in the morning, and the last thing I thought of at night. It's all I want."

"…what are you saying, Tyler?" Isabella asked.

"I'm saying I want to be with you forever. I want to marry you. I want to be a good dad to Teddy…" Tyler's voice croaked as he held back tears. "I don't care if we're young. We can figure this out."

"What about Peru? What about the University of Lima?" Isabella felt his determination to be with her and her son was too good to be true.

"I'll go to school here, in Springfield. They need teachers everywhere."

Tyler smiled and put his finger in Teddy's tiny, chubby palm. "And once a year, we'll take a vacation to Peru. I can put Theodore in one of those baby backpacks…we'll hike to Machu Picchu together and watch the sun rise through the mist."

"…that sounds wonderful. But are you willing to give up all your adventures to live a boring life as a teacher, a dad…and a husband?" Isabella didn't want to get her hopes too high without knowing Tyler understood what he was sacrificing.

"Being with you…and Teddy…will *still* be an adventure. Just not the one I planned."

Tyler and Isabella smiled at each other with tears in their eyes, and at long last, kissed…

…just as the front door opened and Butkus rushed in between their legs.

"Well, that was fast!" proclaimed David as he hung up his coat and kicked off his shoes. "When's the wedding?"

\*\*\*

Isabella sat in the front seat of the cruiser talking into her cell phone.

"I'll be home soon, I'm just wrapping up with a fender bender. One of the drivers is an old friend from high school…yeah, everyone is fine I'm just waiting to hear back on a tow truck before I leave. Hold on a sec, Ty."

She put the cell phone down in the passenger seat and picked up the mic from the scanner. "This is Lieutenant Kentworth, copy."

*Are you near West Bypass? We've got a trespassing report of a group of teenagers on some farmland. We need a few cars to patrol the area and locate them.*

"Copy. Send me the last reported location."

She climbed out of her patrol car to say goodbye to Emily and give the other driver towing information and ran back to her phone call which had been on hold for ten minutes.

Isabella picked it up as she buckled her seatbelt. "Sorry that took so long…I'm probably going to miss dinner. I have a trespassing call. Why don't you order Chinese? Get me some Springfield Cashew and Crab Rangoon… no, I haven't heard from Theo, I thought he was with you…yeah, he's probably playing Magic at that new shop in Nixa…just get him a double order of Mongolian Beef with fried rice and pork eggrolls…because that's what he *always* gets. If he complains, give him mine and I'll eat his. *Everyone* loves Springfield Cashew, he'll eat it. Don't give him my Crab Rangoon though…oh, hey I gotta go… Love you too."

Isabella looped back to the highway to the location where dispatch took the call. It was getting dark, but she could still make out fresh tire treads off the road just past the farmhouse the caller described. She could see in her headlights that the tracks led across a corn field and into the forest. She picked up the mic to her radio.

"This is Lieutenant Kentworth. I've found where the trespassers entered the property. Their exact location and number are unknown. Requesting backup. My car can't get back there."

*Affirmative.*

While she waited, she called Theo. It went straight to voicemail.

"Theo, I'm going to be late tonight, but Dad bought Chinese. If I get home before you do, I'm going to eat your dinner. Consider yourself warned. Also, remember you are running with Pops tomorrow. He's got the Bigwheeler all shined and ready. Love you, Bye."

Isabella's Captain arrived in a large SUV, better suited for the rutted pathway into the woods than Isabella's sedan. She climbed in the backseat.

"Good evening, Captain Andrews. Lieutenant Smith. I'm sure you're both missing a lovely dinner to break up a teenage party in the woods as well?" Isabella laughed.

"My wife was making calzones." Grumbled Captain Andrews.

"I don't have a wife. The only thing I'm missing out on is a Hungry Man frozen dinner." Lieutenant Smith laughed.

"Okay, then why don't you handle this call on your own, and Captain and I can go home?" Joked Isabella.

Lieutenant Smith gripped the ceiling handles as Captain Andrews maneuvered his vehicle through the field. "No way. Those woods look creepy as hell. I'll probably get killed by the Ozark Howler."

"Pfft." Captain Andrew scoffed. "That's a bunch of bullshit. There's no such thing as an Ozark Howler, but it never fails, at least once a year we get a call from someone convinced they saw it. *Help me, there's a devil cat with antlers trying to eat my corgi.* It's probably just a mangey coyote or a mountain lion."

The SUV bounced through the woods, kudzu dragging across the hood. Their eyes swept the forest for lights as they drove. Isabella rolled down her window to listen for music or voices to guide them to the trespasser's location.

"So, I met this woman on *Plenty of Fish…*" said Lieutenant Smith.

"Oh no, not one of these stories again!" protested Isabella.

"I keep telling you, Smith." Scolded Captain Andrews "You've gotta stop using the free services. Suck it up and pay for professional matching. Otherwise, you get all kinds of weirdos. I met my wife on a paid dating site, and we've been happily married for six years. Plus, she's a hell of a cook. I put that on my profile- I like women who know how to cook. Boom. Matched with a woman who can make a calzone."

"Guys, that's not what I'm saying, but thanks for the advice I guess… anyway… I met this woman who wants to go on a date to Missouri State Penitentiary in Jeff City to do a ghost tour. You know, because I'm in law enforcement. Either of you been there? I don't really like spooky shit. I deal with enough weird stuff at work." Smith shook off a shiver.

"Hell, no." spat Captain Andrews. "I paid my dues as a prison guard in my younger days. The evil that goes on in places like that lives in the walls. It never leaves. I think that's why I try to avoid sending people to prison if I can help it. I wasn't the same after working as a guard. I can't imagine what it's like as an inmate living there. They don't usually leave prison better than they went in. If they leave at all."

"MO State Pen has been closed for what, twenty years?" Isabella asked.

"That's what I read online." Said Lieutenant Smith, "*Operating for 168 years, it's dubbed 'The Bloodiest 47 Acres in America'.*"

"My husband is a history teacher. He's always wanted to go there." Said

Isabella. "Back in the eighties they were digging to make a rec yard and found some buried prison cells from the 1840's. I'm sure if we go, we'll probably spend more time in the museum than looking for ghosts."

"Did you see that, Cap?" asked Andrews. "Looks like taillights reflecting up ahead."

"Yup. There's someone back here." The captain got quiet and approached the vehicle slowly.

"I count five." Said Lieutenant Smith.

"No, it's six." Isabella pointed. "There's someone on the ground."

"Well, we found them." Captain Andrews slowed his SUV to a stop a safe distance away and turned on his red and blue lights, but not the sirens. "Looks like we've got a fight at the very least."

Lieutenant Andrews called dispatch. "Barb, we found them. Go ahead and send backup and an ambulance. We've got six teenagers, one is down. No obvious weapons. Send someone out to the property owner's place to let them know what's going on. I doubt the kids are here with permission but ask anyway."

"Copy, Smith." Barb's voice crackled.

"Looks like it's just the three of us for now...let's get them on the ground and cuffed." Directed Captain Andrews. "We'll each take two. Kentworth, check the vitals of the one on the ground. If he's breathing, cuff him until the EMTs get here just to be safe."

"Got it, sir." Said Isabella.

They opened their doors in unison, hands on weapons, but not pulled.

"This is the Greene County Sherriff's department. You are trespassing on private property. Get on the ground so we can talk." The enormous Captain Andrews' voice boomed and echoed in the quiet forest. As a former Navy SEAL, even his verbal commands were intimidating-almost everyone obeyed. Very slowly, four of the trespassers lowered themselves to the ground. "Now put your hands on your head."

The fifth teenager, well over six feet tall with hulking muscles, stood hunched over a dark-haired boy on the ground like a predator guarding its prey. A pool of blood collected around his victim's head.

"Hey! Big guy!" Bellowed Captain Andrews with the tone of an impatient parent. "I *said* get down on the ground."

The teenager didn't respond, and a quick glance to his left was a subtle gesture to Rocky that there was potential for resistance. Isabella and Lieutenant Smith spread out on either flank, preparing for the worst. Meth is almost always a possibility in the Ozarks, and since users don't feel pain, they are unnaturally strong and unconcerned about their own self-preservation. Tasers usually don't work, and situations involving meth are dangerous for everyone involved.

"I need to check his vitals. Step back!" Isabella said as she inched closer to the boys, trying to assess if anyone was under the influence. Maybe the boy on the ground was an overdose. She tried to remember if she had Narcan in her belt.

The shoulders of the enormous teenager seemed to twitch, and he turned to face her.

She gasped in shock, and then her face went stone cold. "Get on the ground, NOW."

He blinked rapidly and fell to his knees, then flopped on his stomach in the dirt.

The deputies breathed a sigh of relief at avoiding a more elevated confrontation. They began cuffing everyone on the ground. Isabella approached the unconscious boy and checked his pulse, not taking her eyes off the others. "He's alive, but he's lying on one of his arms. I'd rather not cuff him in case of a head injury."

"That's fine." Agreed Captain Andrews. "We'll keep eyes on him in case he wakes up."

"I'll cuff the big one." She said pulling out two pairs of cuffs and linking them together to account for the boy's large frame.

"You sure? It looks like he knocked that kid out cold. I can get him." Deputy Andrews offered.

"I'm sure," Isabella said. "He's my son."

# Chapter 7

## Library Magick

"Why is *The Adventures Huckleberry Finn* in the restricted section? Isn't that a children's classic?" Charlotte juggled a stack of *The Magic Treehouse* series into one arm to take the tattered book from the librarian.

"Well…" the librarian fidgeted with her black pentagram necklace and her eyes flicked to Charlotte's silver cross. "Have you read *Huckleberry Finn?*"

Charlotte blushed in embarrassment. She'd always been insecure when it came to her lack of formal education. She did her best to bridge the gaps made from a troubled youth by being a voracious reader, but every now and then a topic would sneak in and remind her she missed something. "…um, well, I didn't read a lot of classics as a child. My daughter's homeschool literature curriculum listed it as required reading. I thought I could read it out loud to her and we could learn together."

"No!" the librarian exclaimed loud enough to trigger a warning cough from one of her nearby coworkers reshelving DVDs. She lowered her voice. "…I mean, I *highly* suggest you don't read it out loud…or maybe you could, but read it by yourself first, and then maybe change some elements, or um, wording?"

Charlotte squinted at the woman's nametag. "What do you mean… Gemma? Why would I need to change such a renowned book?"

"Look, I'm not trying to get political with you, but I will be honest. There's problematic language throughout the book…in particular, the "N" word, which a lot of parents, teachers…and students…feel uncomfortable reading." Gemma shrugged. "That's why it's in the restricted section. We've got 'book banners' breathing down our necks, threatening to defund the library system for allowing kids access to literature that they deem as having 'inappropriate themes or language'."

"I had no idea *Huckleberry Finn* used that word…but wasn't that culturally appropriate for Mark Twain's time?" Charlotte asked with genuine interest.

"…it was. Despite *Huckleberry Finn* using that language so often, it *is* an antiracist book that was considered progressive for the early 1800's. There's a heavy theme of slavery…it's usually difficult for young, modern children to understand. Also, Huck Finn is *quite* mean to Jim which makes people uncomfortable. Some teachers I've spoken to substitute the N-word for the word *slave*…but still, my opinion is it shouldn't be read earlier than high school. Older children have a broader perspective and understanding of America's history." Gemma took a deep breath and smoothed down the loose hairs of her purple bob cut. "Sorry, went on a bit of a tangent there. Librarians, *am I right?*"

Charlotte laughed. "No, it's great. I love discussing literature. I appreciate your help." She handed *The Adventures of Huckleberry Finn* back to Gemma. "I think I'm going to wait a few years before we tackle Mark Twain's work."

Gemma took the book from Charlotte. "Are there any other books I can help you find?" She peered over Charlotte's shoulder into the children's section. A herd of dark-haired and unnaturally well-dressed, clean children ran around playing with toys and puzzles. "I see you've got quite a gang with you today."

Charlotte looked back and gave a tired smile. "Yup. That's my five youngest. I have a teenager also…all homeschooled."

"Wow. I don't know how you do it. I only have one, and my husbands and I are always exhausted." Gemma said.

Husbands? Charlotte thought she must have misheard. "…they definitely have me outnumbered, one to seven."

"Hell, we outnumber our kid three to one, and she-I mean, they- were practically feral in elementary school!" Gemma laughed.

Charlotte knew now she didn't mishear. *She must be one of those…what are they called? Poly-somethings.* She shook it out of her mind before she started asking herself questions about how it all worked-otherwise she'd be up all night falling down internet rabbit holes. "Gemma, do you have David Grann's latest book yet? It's about a shipwreck in South America, but the name of it slipped my mind."

"*The Wager* is fantastic! Actually…I was the last person to check it out and returned it this morning. It's right over there on the 'New Releases' shelf." Gemma pointed behind Charlotte.

"Okay, thanks! Have a good day." Charlotte turned to leave and felt a tap on her arm.

"Hold on one sec!" Gemma ripped a flier off one of the bookshelves. "You should come to our book club. We read a lot of the popular new releases…That's why we call it *The Basic B Book Club*… hey, they're popular for a reason, right? It's 7 o'clock on Saturdays. Maybe your huzz can watch the kiddos?"

Charlotte took the flier and put it in the cover of one of her books. "Yeah, hopefully! I only have one, ya know!"

Gemma smiled, then became distracted by a phone vibrating in her pocket. She looked at the caller ID and frowned. "It was nice meeting you. I have to take this call. Hope I see you this weekend!"

Charlotte watched as the librarian rushed off into a public meeting room and shut the door. After finding *The Wager* she plopped it on her stack and proceeded to the children's area to collect her offspring.

"Alright, Littles. Time to go! Let's check out our books and get Braum's! Who wants a frozen yogurt twist?"

"Me! Me! Me!" the baby birds chirped.

They all flocked to the front desk and Charlotte plopped her stack of books and library card on the counter. "Can I buy one of those tote bags?"

The short, gray-haired librarian laughed. "Like you do every week?"

"I know, I know. I always forget to bring one with me." Charlotte opened her purse and began digging around for the loose five-dollar bill she kept in case the Tooth Fairy made a surprise visit. Between the five youngest, someone lost a tooth every other day. She removed her van keys, a banana, a juice pouch, a dog biscuit, and her cell phone, and placed it on the counter. The librarian waited patiently as Charlotte's children wiggled and giggled until she finally handed over a wrinkled five-dollar bill.

She piled the books into the tote bag, then the dog biscuit, juice pouch, banana, and keys into her purse. As she reached for her cell phone, she saw the screen glow with an incoming call.

*Greene County Sherriff's Dept.*

Her heart leaped into her throat. She grabbed her bags and ushered her children away from the front desk to the restrooms. "Quick, quick. Everyone, use the potty before we go! Mommy will be right here waiting!"

She watched them scatter into the restroom stalls and answered the phone.

"Hello?"

*Is this Charlotte Campbell?*

"Yes it is. Is everything okay?"

*We're calling to notify you that we have your vehicle in impound. Just to confirm, do you own a 1992 Buick LeSabre?*

"That's my husband's car! Is he okay? Why is it in impound?"

*We haven't been able to reach your husband. Do you have a seventeen-year-old son named Oliver?*

"Yes! Oh, Jesus! Please tell me my baby boy is alive!"

*…Ma'am, your son is being held at Greene County jail for trespassing. He hasn't been arrested but can only be released to a legal guardian.*

"…WHAT?" Charlotte took a deep breath and growled, "I'll be there in fifteen minutes."


"Hold hands! Everyone hold hands in the parking lot!" Charlotte shrieked at her five young children as they piled out of her white Ford Transit-

affectionately called *the homeschooler van* in the Ozarks. It was usually bought after your fourth child in eight years, and only when you're completely sure *this homeschooling "experiment"* was here to stay. These vans are usually found in libraries, parks, zoos, museums, and movie theaters…all in the middle of the day, in the middle of the week. That is when homeschoolers reign supreme and have the entire world to themselves.

Today, Charlotte's little homeschoolers were going to have a different sort of field trip.

"Mommy. Where are we? I want ice cream." Asked five-year-old Gabriel as Charlotte guided him up the concrete steps of the Greene County Sheriff's Department.

"Well, we need to pick up your brother, Oliver." Said Charlotte, as she attempted to hide the shrill of anxiety in her voice.

"Mom!" called eight-year-old Megan from the rear where she was keeping 4-year-old Tristan from running astray. "If we're picking up Oliver, does that mean I can't sit in the front seat anymore? I never get to sit in the front seat when we go out!"

"Oh, no, sweetie," Charlotte responded. "Your brother will be sitting *all the way* in the back today."

"It's super bouncy back there!" giggled Tristan. "It makes my tummy bubbly."

*Oliver is lucky he's not walking home.* Charlotte whipped open the door to the lobby and held it open as her children filed in. When at last listen Tristan stopped pushing the automatic door button, the curious children took in their surroundings.

"Mom why are there so many police here?" asked six-year-old Caleb.

"…because sometimes police take people here who've broken the law, Caleb." Said Charlotte as she scanned the lobby for enough benches to seat everyone without being too close to any unsavory characters.

"Hey, look!" Pointed seven-year-old Rosilynn. "That cop has some dirty guy in handcuffs. Maybe they are taking him for a bath."

"Wait…if Oliver is here…" the wheels turned in Caleb's mind. "Did Ollie break the law?!"

All five mouths went silent. All five sets of eyes snapped to their mother eagerly awaiting the answer.

Charlotte sighed and knelt in front of them. "Listen…I don't know what's going on yet, we are here to find out. What I need you all to do right now is go sit on those wooden benches by the window and silently pray to Jesus to help your brother with whatever is troubling his heart. And I'd like you to pray for me and your dad so that we can continue to straighten the little arrows God has given us- that's you all and Oliver. Remember, Dad and I are the bows that launch you into the world. Pray that when we let you fly, your paths will be straight towards the target God has planned for you."

"Yes, Mommy." Charlotte's children whispered and sat down quietly.

The receptionist cleared her throat. "Ma'am, can I help all of you? I wasn't aware of any student visitors this afternoon."

Charlotte approached the receptionist and said sheepishly, "Um, we aren't here as visitors. I received a call saying my son Oliver is here and I need to pick him up."

Realization dawned across her face. "Oh, I see. You're part of that group. Wait here for a moment and I'll be right back."

The receptionist disappeared into a back office. Charlotte's children were sitting quietly watching squirrels chasing each other outside the window. She held the silver cross around her neck in her right hand.

*"Like arrows in the hands of a warrior are children born in one's youth. Blessed is the man whose quiver is full of them."* Charlotte whispered scripture to herself.

"Dear Lord," she prayed, "I want my children to make an impact on your kingdom. Please give me the wisdom to teach them and train them so that they may launch into the world to make a difference for you. In Jesus' name, amen."

"Mrs. Campbell?" the receptionist said, as she gestured to an older man with a limp approaching them. "This is retired Captain Kentworth. He's kindly offered to give your children a private tour of the Sherrif's Office while we process Oliver if you're comfortable with that."

Captain Kentworth held out his hand to shake Charlotte's. "They're not runners, are they?" He winked and gave an easy smile that put her mind at ease.

"They usually listen quite well. They shouldn't give you any trouble." Charlotte assured him.

"Well, I may not have my gun and badge anymore, but I still have my taser!" Deputy Kentworth laughed as he hobbled over to the children using a cane. They were looking at each other with wide, frightened eyes.

"Mrs. Campbell, if you follow me, I'll take you to the room with the rest of the parents." The receptionist said.

"What do you mean, *the rest of the parents?*" Charlotte asked, perplexed.

"It's probably best we talk in private." She said, nodding at the children behind her. The oldest two were listening intently.

Captain Kentworth motioned for the kids to stand up and follow him. "Have any of you ever eaten Krispy Kreme donuts? They've got some in the break room. Don't drink the coffee though, the department always uses the cheap crap you get at bad hotels."

Charlotte's five children dutifully followed the old man, and she waited until she couldn't hear his voice anymore before leaving. *"Did you kids know that if you drive by Krispy Kreme and the red sign in the window is on, it means they just made a fresh batch of donuts and they'll give you one for free…make sure you bug your mom about it…they're best when they're fresh…"*

She walked down the narrow hallway past interrogation rooms and offices to a large conference room at the back of the building. An enormous man with a booming voice pointed to a folding chair next to a man and woman each holding a twin baby. "Mrs. Campbell, you are the last to arrive, so we will go ahead and get started."

Her son was not in the room. Beyond the people holding the twins was a female Sheriff's Deputy, and Charlotte caught a glimpse of purple hair on the other side of her.

*It can't be…*

The woman turned her head as Charlotte sat down and they both went wide-eyed with surprise. It was Gemma, the librarian. *What in the world is going on?*

"My name is Captain Andrews. I would like to begin first by saying *your children are not under arrest. They are not being charged with a crime.* This is a meeting to inform all of you, as a group, that your teenagers have been getting into some trouble. It has become apparent to us that none of you really know each other or who your kids are hanging out with. We hope that you all can work together as parents to figure out what they're up to because honestly, they've been pretty uncooperative. I hope you can all set these youth on the straight-and-narrow…" He emphasized the words with spittle, "… and I don't ever have to see them again. Are we clear?"

The clearly confused parents nodded.

"Good.

"This evening, we received a call about a group of teenagers seen trespassing on private farmland off Farm Road 110. Tracks were identified by Lieutenant Kentworth, who called for backup. We followed the tracks into forested land where we found six teenagers engaged in what we presumed to be a fight. One of the males was unconscious and bleeding. He was able to be revived, and his parent transported him to urgent care. He has declined to press charges; however, I would encourage you to smooth things over with his parents.

We contacted the owners of the property, they stated your children were *not* on the property with permission. She declined to press charges as well.

"We did *not* find drugs, alcohol, weapons, etc. on any of them. They have refused to explain what they were doing out there, and we can't force them to tell us. As far as we know there wasn't any property vandalism or theft. The only crime they committed was being weird on someone else's property.

"As I've said, your children are not *technically* in trouble, well, at least not with us!" Captain Andrews chuckled, the parents did not. "However, I would like to *invite* your teenagers to join us on the department's annual James River Clean Up Day."

Another deputy passed a flier to each of the parents with the date, time, and location.

"I figure since your kids like being in the woods so much, they might as well help out their community. What do you think, parents?" Captain

Andrews raised a bushy eyebrow at them.

Nods and murmurs of agreement came from all the parents- *why did they give one to the female deputy?* Charlotte's confusion deepened. She'd never even met any of these people before except for the brief encounter with the librarian. It was clear that their children were being encouraged to do the river cleanup in exchange for the deputies going easy on them.

It felt like a fair exchange to Charlotte.

"Can I see Oliver now, please?" Charlotte asked impatiently.

"Yes Ma'am." Captain Andrews nodded to Lieutenant Smith, who opened a side door of the conference room. "You're all free to go, just sign them out at the front."

The first boy out was tall and slim. He wore a beanie and a gray and black striped sweater that was caked in red clay earth. He had dark circles under his eyes and walked slowly up to the man holding one of the babies. He stood up and took the second baby from the woman and expertly held one on each hip.

"Ashton, your father is going to lose his *gawd.damned.mind* when he gets home!" The man scolded with a deep southern drawl. "He will never leave me alone with you again!"

The boy said nothing as they left the room.

The woman next to Charlotte and the female deputy stood up as a hulking blond boy and a girl with curly hair filled with twigs entered. The mothers turned to each other and whispered. Charlotte couldn't help but eavesdrop.

*Rocky, I had no idea our kids knew each other.*

*Neither did I. I'm sorry this happened, Emily. Here's my number in case you figure out what's going on.*

The deputy slipped her a folded pink index card. They gave each other a quick hug, and their children also exited the room silently. Charlotte found it strangely unnerving to watch.

Charlotte and Gemma were left alone in the room while Captain

Andrews took a phone call and Lieutenant Smith retrieved the remaining kids from holding.

"Fancy meeting you here..." joked Gemma awkwardly.

"...small world, I guess." Charlotte looked down at her hands, holding back tears. "My son's never been in trouble before. I have no idea what he could have been doing out there."

"Me neither. Trix told me they were having a game night." Gemma shrugged. The door flew open. Trix barely glanced at her mother and stormed for the exit. Gemma sprinted to catch up.

Finally, the door creaked open, and her eldest son peeked around at her sheepishly.

"Mom..."

When she saw him gaunt, dirty, and dazed, all anger left her body as she was flooded with maternal instincts. She rushed to him and brushed his muddy hair out of his eyes. "Are you okay Ollie?"

"I'm really tired...I don't know. I don't really know what happened. I think I dozed off in the holding cell, and then they told me you were here, and I could go home." Oliver's voice was weak and uncertain.

Charlotte studied him carefully. Maybe tonight wasn't the right time to unpack this. "Let's go home. Let's get you a shower and something to eat. I'll make an appointment with your doctor in the morning. Maybe we can have a family meeting with Pastor Sherwood?"

Oliver nodded with submission and followed his mother to the front desk where they were greeted with fits of laughter. Captain Kentworth was tossing stuffed dogs dressed in sheriff uniforms to each of Charlotte's children one by one.

"Alright Caleb, you get the last one, and he can jump super high. Are you ready?" Captain Kentworth asked.

"Yes, Captain!" Caleb squealed and held out his arms as Captain Kentworth tossed him the toy. They were all grinning ear to ear when they saw their mother.

"We took turns locking each other in a cell and got to turn the big key!" Megan said.

"And we got these cool sheriff's badges!" said Roselynn

"And popcorn!" said Tristan.

"And Krispie Kreme donuts!" Caleb exclaimed, jumping up and down.

"This has been the *best* field trip ever!" said Gabriel. "I'm so glad you're a criminal, Ollie!"

Charlotte closed her eyes for a moment and took a deep breath to center herself. "Captain Kentworth, thank you so much for your help with my children. Wait…isn't Kentworth one of the officers I just met?"

This was Captain Kentworth's turn to sigh. "Well, Lieutenant Kentworth is my daughter…and the big guy that was with your son is my grandson, Theo."

Charlotte put a hand on her mouth as the pieces came together…that means Lieutenant Kentworth had to detain her own *son?* "Oh. Wow…well, I've never actually met Theo or his parents before. Oliver doesn't usually do this sort of thing…"

Captain Kentworth nodded. "I understand. Your little ones are good kids… how do you keep them so *clean?*"


Charlotte smiled and the children waved goodbye to Captain Kentworth as he left with Isabella and Theo in an old, rumbling pickup truck. She signed a few forms, loaded her crew into the Transit (Oliver in the dreaded *way-back*), and drove home in silence as one by one her six little arrows drifted into an exhausted sleep.

# Chapter 8

## Tradwife

W hat is it called when a harmless phrase becomes something different...something derogatory?

*Semantic changes* are always occurring in the English language.

A *mouse* is still a harmless, gray rodent

...but it is also a device I use to control my desktop computer.

A *bookmark* is still my favorite piece of cardstock, hand-painted with purple wildflowers during a rainy June afternoon while a fat orange cat purred on my lap and spearmint tea steamed from a delicate teacup

...but it is also how I return to the website I check *never-more-than-once* daily, to soak in a stream of constant questions, comments-and so much hate.

It's hard to believe that being a *traditional wife* can inspire so much rage in women, and weirdly, sexual obsession and objectification from men. I enjoy my life of lavender cookies and gardening, of low heels and below-the-knee skirts. My husband goes to work, I bake fresh bread, steam mop the floors and tend to my hens. I pressure can twenty jars of pizza sauce made from fresh basil and Roma tomatoes I grew myself...and it feels like bliss. I'm so grateful for this life. I simply want to share it with the world. I want women who are interested in those things to have a community of support in a world that tells them they are too old-fashioned and anti-feminist.

My husband and I are both happy. We live comfortably and each brings to the relationship what we're good at. How is that something anti-feminist or sexual? To me, it seems like a beneficial partnership with neither of us bearing the burden of needing to be and do *everything*. I know our lifestyle isn't for everyone. Some people share duties and that's fine. I prefer my life this way. How is being a traditional wife anti-feminist if it is *my* choice? I am not abused or oppressed. I am happy, safe, and adored by my husband. I don't understand the hate, because I'm not hurting anyone.

To the women who have a problem with me, *I'm submitting to my husband.*

I'm not.

We are both doing what we want to do; together we benefit.

To the men who sexualize me, *I'm submitting to my husband.*

I'm not.

I dress ladylike because I want to, not because it's Nolan's fetish. I wear a skirt and heels and pearl earrings most days because *doing so makes me feel beautiful and girly.* I happen to like beautiful and girly things.

Now, I'm labeled a *tradwife.* Oppressing women. Stealing their husbands. Making working women and moms feel bad about themselves *apparently.* That was never my intention. I only ever wanted to use my blog to share the joy that can be found in making simple things beautiful and important. There is so much joy to be found in slowing down. I wake up in the morning and put on a pair of pearl earrings that were a gift from a dear friend, and every time I look in the mirror, I think of her and smile. A spritz of my husband's favorite perfume on my neck is enough to entice him to draw me in close for a hug. People overlook the everyday magic that adds up to create a beautiful life. Happiness is not limited to two weeks of vacation time per year and your birthday. It's everywhere, all the time. You just need eyes to see it and a heart to feel it.

I've done my time as the "sad girl". It was a constant whiplash after graduating college between corporate work, clubs, parties, one-night stands, and drunken snot bubble cries on the bathroom floor of a dirty apartment. I did that for ten years before I found my one true love.

Welbutrin XR.

It's a hell of a drug.

Before I got help, I never saw myself as a depressed person. I would have the occasional bad day, or maybe a few weeks after a breakup. Then I had a few months after my cat died. Suddenly, I looked in the mirror at the dark circles under my eyes. I thought about the 30 pounds I'd gained over the last year from my nightly bottle of wine I felt I needed just to forget long enough to fall asleep. I needed to forget the guys who never called, the insults from my boss, and the friends I lost as they married and had babies.

I was alone. Hollowed out by the artificiality of my life, the fleeting moments of happiness and thoroughly disgusted with myself, I couldn't even summon the energy after work to do the dishes. They piled up until I ran out of salad plates and wine glasses. Instead, I used the dish soap to fill the bathtub full of bubbles. One night I found myself drinking cheap red wine straight from the bottle in the bathtub with a one-pound block of extra-sharp Vermont white cheddar in my other hand. I ate every morsel of that delicious cheese, and then slit my wrists.

If there was a God, I hoped He would forgive me and let me see my cat again.

Momma was coming to be with you, Goose.

But I couldn't even get that right.

I didn't die. I passed out from the wine and woke up the next morning in a cold bathtub to pigeons cooing outside my bathroom window. My bloody arm had a crusted over not-deep-enough, wobbly wound from elbow crook to wrist. Empty, empty, empty. I felt the girl I once was wash down the drain with the bloody water. I really had died that night, just not physically. I died spiritually.

I flopped over the side of the bathtub like a fat walrus on a rock. I lay naked on my belly on the freezing cold tile, staring at my toilet. I wasn't thinking about my ex-friends and partners. I wasn't thinking about the promotion I was passed over for. I wasn't thinking about Goose.

All I could think about was what was directly in front of me: the underbelly of the toilet.

It was absolutely filthy.

Why hadn't I ever cleaned under there?

I sat up and opened the cabinet under the bathroom sink. I pulled out bleach cleaner and a roll of paper towels.

Naked, wet, hungover, and wounded, I cleaned my toilet like it's never been cleaned before. It still smelled kind of weird.

I opened a drawer in the vanity.

*Brent's toothbrush.*

For three months I'd been waiting for him to call me. To take me to dinner and sleep over. I hadn't been with anyone since him.

I sprayed bleach cleaner on his toothbrush and scrubbed the hinges on the toilet seat lid, and then the floor around the toilet. I moved the trash can and the plunger. I continued scrubbing the floor with Brent's toothbrush for an hour. When the floor shined like I'd never seen it before, I sat up on my knees and suddenly realized I was shivering. I was still naked, wet, and cold.

I went to my bedroom to put on clothes. Every drawer of my dresser was empty. A mountain of dirty clothes overflowed to the point where I couldn't even see the hamper in the pile. I opened the closet. The only items left hanging were club clothes that didn't fit anymore-skirts that barely covered my ass, a leather tank top that showed so much of my tits it couldn't even pass as a bra, let alone a shirt, and skimpy dresses that looked like lingerie.

I pulled out a pair of see-through, high-waist, mesh, sequined pants. I held them up to the dim morning light. Two enormous holes were ripped in the mesh- one under each ass cheek from when Brent tried to tear them apart when we fucked in the club bathroom the first time.

We'd known each other for two hours.

Hot, angry tears escaped my eyes without a sob. Calmly, I walked to my bedroom window, pulled up the blinds, and opened the window of my fourth-floor apartment. Pigeons squawked and flew off protesting as I threw the pants out the window, watching them flap, get caught in the wind, and land in a neighboring parking garage. I caught the attention of two men exiting their Mercedes on their way to the movie theatre.

"Whoa! Hey momma, how you doing?" one of them yelled while the other laughed in disbelief.

I was still naked, so I went back to the closet…and pulled out every single item I had ever worn to the club then chucked those out the window, too. As I was about to start throwing shoes, I heard a scratch and a thump on the window sill. Sitting on the ledge was a scruffy orange stray cat with a notched ear.

He looked like Goose, if Goose had been addicted to meth. Scrawny, yet bloated-- probably with worms--he had a bent tail, patches of missing fur, and scabs on his back. I approached him slowly, reaching my hand out to pet his head. His scarred pink nose sniffed at my torn arm and licked at the blood. He let me pet him, and then I wrapped my arms around the cat, pulled it into my apartment, and shut the window.

I wrapped myself in a blanket, and he followed me to the kitchen. I dug through my nearly empty cupboards finding two cans of albacore tuna. I opened both and sat on the living room sofa. The stray jumped on my lap and began to eat from one of the cans. I drank the tuna water from the other, then ate with my fingers. I sat with the cat, stroking his fur, for six hours.

"If you're going to live here, you'll need more than a can of tuna." I scratched under his scabby chin, then sighed, knowing I needed to go to the market. I didn't have any clean clothes, so I started a load of laundry. While I waited, I loaded the dishwasher. Then I made the bed, so the cat had a comfortable place to sleep while I was gone.

I didn't realize it at the time, but I had accomplished more in half a day than I had all week by being fully present in my needs--what was directly in front of me, not the past, not who I used to be.

I had no one. I *was* no one. Accepting this, I began to realize I was free…free to be anyone I wanted to be. If I could imagine my ideal life, what would it look like? How would I feel? What would bring me *joy?*

Peace. I wanted peace. Simplicity. Beauty. Love. I wanted to celebrate my husband's 40th birthday on a cruise ship to the Bahamas and come home sunburnt and pregnant. I wanted to celebrate Christmas Eve like they do in Norway, and exchange books and candy with close friends, then read all night in front of the fireplace. I wanted to complain about the HOA, and taxes, and grumble about *all the children's birthday parties we attend on the weekends*. Most of all, I want to be cherished and respected by the people in my life, because that's what I give in return.

I'm done being the throw-away girl with "fair weather" friends.

I'd rather be alone.

But I wasn't alone. I have a cat again. I named him Butterscotch.

I tried to kill myself, but I lived.

I realized my toilet was dirty, so I cleaned it.

I didn't have clothes, so I did laundry.

I went to the store to buy cat food, and I ended up buying food for me too—but no wine.

Tomorrow was a work day, but I had nothing to wear. On the way home I passed a vintage clothing store and went inside to buy something pretty, classy, and uncommon. Something that reflected the person *I wanted to be.*

That's where I met Miss Marigold. She changed my life forever.

When I entered her shop, I felt as though I walked through a time warp into the 1950's. An elderly woman in a jumpsuit--blue pants with shiny gold buttons and a blue polka dot sleeveless top--sat on a barstool angrily typing on a computer keyboard. At the chime of the door, she briefly looked up over the top of her horn-rimmed glasses.

"Hello dearie," she said. "I was just fixin' to close but I'm busy with this damned computer. You're welcome to look around. My name is Miss Marigold, let me know if you have any questions."

"…thank you."

The shop felt so…pretty, tidy, and wholesome. The shoes on the rack were shined, and all the shirts were pressed. The pleats in the skirts were sharply defined. Even Miss Marigold's silver hair was rolled and sprayed in a retro style above her shoulders. Not a hair was out of place.

My attention was drawn to a mannequin with a green and white plaid skirt that fell just below the knees; the top was a peachy yellow with short sleeves and a high collar with an enormous bow on the front. It felt so… cheerful. Could I pull it off?

"Buy it." Miss Marigold said, followed by a coughing fit.

I jumped. I didn't realize she'd been watching me. "I don't know if it would look alright on me."

"Well, grab it and go try it on. I *know* it will." Miss Marigold gestured with her head towards the dressing room and returned to grumbling at her computer.

I carefully took the dress off the mannequin, went into the dressing room, and removed my clothes. I refrained from judging my body in the full-length mirror. *We don't do that anymore. All love.* I slid the dress over my head, and it fit like a glove. I felt more like a woman in this outfit that didn't show my knees or my chest than I ever did in skimpy club clothing. How is that possible?

I didn't change out of the dress. I took my sweatpants and University of Missouri t-shirt and threw them in the trash can.

I approached the counter to pay for the vintage outfit, complete with Nike sneakers and a messy bun. I grinned at Miss Marigold "I'd like to buy this!"

She looked up from her computer scowling, but when she saw me, her face matched my joy. "Ahh, see I told you! Clothing *speaks* to me. It tells me who it's meant for. I'm so happy you found each other!" She winked.

"How much?" I asked.

"One twenty-five. However…" she tilted her head at me. "If you help me with my computer, I'll make it a hundred even."

I laughed. "I'll certainly try to help if I can. What's going on?" I assumed it was something with inventory. I'm fluent in spreadsheets and felt confident I could at least help a little.

"Come over here, deary." She waved me behind the counter. Her wrinkled fingers were manicured with glossy red nail polish. "How do I get this damned person off my newsfeed? We met at a Chamber of Commerce event, and she sells the weirdest shit. She's got enthusiasm, I'll give her that! Everything is *awesome* or *amazing*. Honey, that looks like some crap I'd make with my granddaughter on a Sunday afternoon while we watched SpongeBob. Give me a goddamned break."

I couldn't help but stifle a giggle. Here I was thinking she needed business help, and this eighty-year-old woman was asking me to teach her how to block someone on social media. "Well, Miss Marigold, you have a few options. You can "mute" this person which means you will still be connected but you won't see her updates. You can "unfriend" her which means you won't be connected anymore, but she could still contact you if she wants to. Or you can "block" her which means she can't contact you or see anything you post, and you can't see anything she posts."

Without hesitation, she said, "Block that bitch."

I cleared my throat. "Um, okay, sure. So just click on her page and then under her name is the option to block."

"Fantastic!" Miss Marigold clapped. "Tonight, after I close the shop, I am going to settle in my favorite chair with my laptop and a glass of wine and block about fifty other people."

"Glad I could help." I smiled at her. "One hundred then?"

"Yup. Cash or card?" she asked, but her eyes seemed to be assessing me.

"You know that dress really suits you. And you seem like a nice young lady. Are you interested in part-time work by chance?" she asked as if she was throwing spaghetti at a wall to see if it stuck.

I thought for a moment. "I might be...doing what?"

"Helping me at the shop. I need help with the social media crap, and my health isn't what it used to be. I could use a pretty young lady to help out on the weekends." Miss Marigold batted her heavily mascaraed eyelashes.

Normally I would have said *no way*. Weekends are for rebelling against the 9-5. That was "me time" ...for drinking, and parties and dates.

"Yes, I'll do it." I handed her my card to pay for the dress. She pushed it back to me.

"Nope, the dress is on the house." Miss Marigold said. "Come back and work for me on Fridays and Saturdays, and every Sunday, I will let you pick out any dress in the store you like as payment."

"That sounds wonderful!" I needed the distraction. I wasn't too worried about money, so being paid in dresses seemed like fun. "I'll see you Friday."

"Wait, before you leave, I forgot to ask your name, sweetie. I'm running out of pet names." Miss Marigold laughed.

"Oh, right! It's Lucy." I said.

"Lucy, darling. I look forward to seeing you on Friday. In the meantime," she pointed at the uncovered wounds on my arms. "You need to go see a doctor, okay? Ladies like us need to take care of their bodies and our spirits, don't we?"

I blushed in embarrassment, forgetting to conceal or wrap where I had obviously injured myself, and nodded. "I will. Thank you for the dress."

Miss Marigold followed me to the door and turned the sign from open to closed. "Bye now, Lucy. Take care."

I went home in my new dress, and then put away groceries. Butterscotch was curled in a bun on the bed, so I set up his new litter box, a drinking fountain, and a bowl of dry food. After a shower, I wrapped my arms in gauze wrap and called my doctor.

"Hi, this is Lucy Gladstone...I'd like to schedule an appointment with Dr. Morris as soon as possible. I need to talk to her about some issues with depression, and maybe get a referral to a therapist. Um, no, I'm not a danger to myself. Yes, I can do it tomorrow. Thanks."

The next day I saw my doctor, and the minute she saw my arms she chewed me out for not getting help sooner. I started on a high dose of antidepressants...they made me sick at first, with headaches and nausea. After a few weeks, I began to feel better, kind of like a fog was lifting and I was able to see clearly again. I went to therapy weekly and worked for Miss Marigold on weekends stocking, ironing, and managing her shop's social media.

I took Butterscotch to the vet-he was already neutered in a trap-neuter-release program, hence, the notched ear. He got his shots and was treated for parasites. I spoiled him with cat climbers and fuzzy mice, vitamins, and only the finest canned food. It only took a few months for his scabs to heal, his belly to fatten and his orange fur to become sleek. He looked like a different cat. I was beginning to think the same thing about myself, too.

Miss Marigold taught me how to do retro hairstyles, and what shoes go best with which style of dress. She taught me an easy way to tell real pearls from fake-real pearls are fastened off individually, so if the necklace breaks you don't lose all of them. On my birthday, she threw me a tea party and taught me

English etiquette from her time spent in London during fashion school- then gifted me the tea set she'd bought there. She never knew this, but this 83-year-old spitfire was the best, most genuine, and honest friend I'd ever had.

Piece by piece, the broken fragments of myself were put back together. The glue that held it in place was the new, ideal-for-me person I was becoming. I saw myself as a well-dressed woman with a clean toilet, a bowl full of organic seasonal fruit on the kitchen counter, and a sunny disposition. That is who I became.

I'd been working for Miss Marigold for nearly a year when she started asking me to open the store by myself on weekends. During midweek, I dropped by the shop to pick up my paycheck (well, dress) and found the store closed and Miss Marigold nowhere in sight. The neighboring record shopkeeper must have noticed my confusion and came out to speak to me.

"Hey there, Lucy. You lookin' for Goldie?" asked Reggie. He was a former jazz musician with a voice like butter. We listened to his backroom sessions with old bandmates through the thin mutual wall every Saturday night, and it was the highlight of my week.

"Yeah, I'm picking up a dress. Why is the shop closed?" I peeked through the window, expecting it to be some kind of prank- as far as I knew, Miss Marigold practically lived there and never missed an opportunity to display her carefully curated collection of vintage clothing and shoes.

Reggie screwed his face as if trying to decide if it was his place to tell me something. "Lucy…the only time this shop is open anymore is when you're here on the weekends. Gold's got stage 4 lung cancer and can't manage it anymore."

My heart skipped a beat. How…*why*…had she hidden it from me? Tears welled in my eyes. "Reggie…I didn't know."

He sighed. "I figured. I'm sorry, babygirl. I think she's in hospice care at home. She lives in that big blue Victorian house on Walnut."

"…the one that looks like a dollhouse?" Of course she does, I thought.

"That's the one. Make sure you go see her, no matter what she tells you. She ain't got much longer to bless the Earth with her timeless beauty." Reggie gave me a solemn look and retreated into his store.

I immediately drove to her impossible-to-miss home, and the door was answered by the man who is now my husband.

He was her hospice nurse.

I look back now and see with clarity: out of everything Miss Marigold ever gave me-which was generous-nothing was more valuable than this incredible man.

"Can I help you?" Nolan asked hastily as he opened the door. He was dressed in scrubs...that were soaking wet. He smelled like Miss Marigold's earthy-smelling purple shampoo for gray hair.

"Um...I'm a friend of Miss Marigold's. I help run her shop. I was wondering if I could speak to her." I asked politely.

"Well, that's up to her...but honestly, I could really use a hand if you have a minute. I'm trying to give her a shower, but she's not comfortable with me...as a man. Do you think you could talk to her? I mean, I do this for a living. I'm a professional. I've done this before." He shrugged.

"Sure, I'll help if I can."

Stepping into her home was like stepping into the home of a wealthy family from the 1880's. I would later find out that the home had never been *restored* to its original state, but rather *preserved*. It had been in Miss Marigold's family since it was built. Her mother was obsessed with caring for her home while her husband was away on business as a mineral baron. Victorian-era teddy bears sat on still-glossy wooden rocking horses in the foyer, heavy curtains framed the windows, and the wood floors gleamed wherever they peaked out from under ornate rugs. A spiral staircase led to the upstairs. The entire home was so stunning I was at a loss for words.

Seeming to understand my gawking silence, Nolan said "Incredible, huh? It's a shame she doesn't have a family to leave it to. It'll go to the state when she passes."

Passes.

"...how long does she have?" I asked, attempting to maintain my composure before speaking to my beloved Miss Marigold.

Nolan took a deep breath. "It's hard to tell. A few months at the most, but maybe as little as a few weeks."

I nodded and summoned my strength. "Please take me to see her."

Nolan led me to a lower lever bedroom. Miss Marigold sat in a chair wrapped in a bathrobe watching wild birds peck at a birdfeeder.

"Did you know deer are *opportunistic omnivores*, Lucy?" she asked without turning to look at me. "Yesterday a doe was out here eating seeds with the chickadees…then turned its head, snatched one up, and ate the damn thing! Can you believe it? Eighty-seven years on this planet and I never knew they did that shit. Seems like no matter how old we get, there's always something we don't know."

I walked across the room and kneeled at her feet. "Goldie…why didn't you tell me?"

She reached out and took my hand, then turned it over to show the scars on my wrist. "Because you're finally smiling, Lulu."

Her words hit me like an arrow in the heart. I felt her love; a love I had never known from anyone, especially my own family. Then I felt grief, knowing she was about to leave me. "I have you to thank for that."

Miss Marigold laughed. "I know! When we found each other, you were like a mangy kitten in the gutter wearing sweatpants." She gently touched the perfectly rolled curls in my blonde hair. "Now look at you, shining like the sun from the inside out. You're the prettiest thing to ever leave my shop. Don't you agree, Nolan?"

Miss Marigold gave Nolan a wink, and he quickly looked away blushing and stammering. "Yes…very beautiful. Miss Marigold…how about we try to get you in the shower? Maybe Lucy can help."

"You're the one I'm paying the big bucks, Nolan. Why are you making Lucy do your dirty work?" Miss Marigold scowled.

He laughed. "You're the one making it dirty work, Goldie. How about I make all of us dinner while you get cleaned up?"

Miss Marigold grumbled and slowly rose from her seat. "Fine…but for your information young man, I am fully aware that you are slipping fiber powder in my glass of milk every day. It's all frothy and weird. At least put a squirt of chocolate syrup in there or something."

Nolan laughed. "Understood. Lucy, her clothes and towels are in the bathroom there to your left. Good luck…"

I held out my arm to Miss Marigold and led her to the bathroom. "Why won't you let Nolan help you? He's a nurse. He's seen it all before."

She huffed and dropped her robe without a hint of shame. "First of all, Nolan is not a nurse yet. He's a *nurse's aide*. He's been helping me for six months, paying his way through college. I give him hell, but he's a good guy. That's the problem…he's too goddamn handsome. Reminds me of my first boyfriend…stirs up all those feelings and I don't want to think about him. Spent my whole damn life trying to forget that man and now here I am at the end with a nurse that could be his damned twin."

I laughed. "Alright, I understand. I'll get the water started."

With a quick snap, Miss Marigold unclipped her bra with one hand and let the 'ladies' roll out. "Let's do this, Lulu."


I visited Miss Marigold and Nolan every day for a week. Nolan lived upstairs in one of the bedrooms and attended nursing school classes four days a week. The remainder of his time was spent with Miss Marigold, but it was becoming apparent that she needed help the entire day rather than just early mornings and evenings. After caring for her for just one week, Miss Marigold asked me (and Butterscotch) to move into her home and help full-time. When I expressed concern that I couldn't manage my regular job and caretaking, she handed me an actual paycheck from the vintage clothing store. "Go ahead. Open it."

Confused, I opened the envelope. What should have been a couple of hundred dollars for twenty hours of work…was one hundred thousand dollars. "Goldie! What is this?"

She shrugged. "Well, by my calculations that's at least a year's worth of pay from your 9-5 job…and equivalent wages from the shop."

"More like two!" I exclaimed.

"Good. Now you can quit your job and help Nolan wash my hair. That man has no idea what he's doing, and I look ridiculous. He never gets all the shampoo out. My hair is turning purple!" She gestured at her hair, acting as if handing me a six-figure check was as big a deal as buying me an ice cream cone.

"Miss Marigold, I love helping you, but I have an apartment…and a cat." My confusion left me grasping at anything solid in my life to make sense of what was happening. There wasn't much.

"Well, why don't you use some of that money to break your lease? Take a few days to pack, and you and the cat can move in here," Miss Marigold raised her eyebrows as if it was the most obvious answer in the world.

"I couldn't impose on you! I…I…" I stammered.

"Dearie, look around you. This house is so big and lonely a week could pass and I wouldn't even know you're here. If you live with me…until the end…you could use some of that money I gave you for a down payment on a cute little home you *own*. You're too damn old to be living in an apartment. You deserve your own space. Grow some plants or something." She shrugged and slumped back. "Besides…almost a century on this planet, and you and Nolan are the only people I want here with me when I go."

"…that's something I don't understand. Don't you have family? You've barely known me or Nolan for a year."

"I don't have any family at all. I was an only child…besides…you remind me of my youth. And he reminds me of my first love. I like being reminded of those times…" She looked drowsy, and I helped her to the bed. Nolan appeared in the doorway.

"Is there a new tenant at Miss Marigold's Victorian Boarding House?" he smirked.

I took in his golden silhouette as the setting sun shone through the lightly shaded window. He really was handsome.

"I suppose so."

That night I gave my landlord notice that I was moving out. I began packing my apartment, and by the end of the week, Nolan and I were unpacking my belongings into the foyer of Miss Marigold's dollhouse. Butterscotch immediately made himself at home by curling up in her lap and watching reruns of *The Golden Girls* as Nolan and I did the heavy lifting.

The first few weeks at Miss Marigold's house were dare I say *fun*, despite the reason we were all together. We watched old movies and played ancient board games pulled out of dusty closets. We even made a game out of making dinner: each night we would reach into a rusty metal recipe box Miss Marigold had collected since the 1950's. Some were even older family recipes from the turn of the century. Out of all the decades, we dreaded making anything from the 1960's-why must everything be made with gelatin and canned meat?

It wasn't long before Miss Marigold wasn't able to stay awake through a game of backgammon, and even her mother's famous recipe for Victoria Sponge Cake began to go untouched. She dropped weight quickly, and Nolan and I took shifts sitting with her. There were nights when I watched Nolan gently cleaning her skin with wet wipes, changing her clothes, and helping her drink protein shakes with a straw…all I could think was *this is the most incredibly kind, gentle, and patient man I've ever met.* This was a man who would be gentle with a woman's heart and soul. This is the type of man that would make a loving father.

Nolan was a man a woman could grow old with.

"You love him, don't you?" Miss Marigold wheezed out in between coughs as I leaned her forward and gently rubbed her back as she worked through a cough.

"What?" I pulled my eyes away from him as I watched him set the dining room table in the other room. "We barely know each other, Goldie.'

"You're going to get married. I have a sense for these things. That's the gift God gave me…I know what fits people. Shoes, skirts, spouses…I just know." She burst into a low laugh. "I *see* you, Lulu."

I grinned, knowing that Miss Marigold had just shined a light on a corner of my heart I was trying to keep dim. The one that wanted the loving husband, the garden, the kids. "I don't know what you're talking about."

"Just promise me you'll name your first daughter after me." She smiled knowingly.

"Sure, Goldie. Whatever you say." I laughed and leaned her back against her pillows, secretly praying she was right.

Nolan and I spent long days together, caring for Miss Marigold, her home, and each other. I stayed up during the night and made him a lunch to take to nursing school when he left in the morning. He always brewed a strong pot of coffee with dinner to help me stay awake for the night shift. During the in-between times, we sat in the damp grass of her carefully tended backyard, looking at the stars and listening to cicadas. We got to know each other as friends, but it never went further. Once, I'd casually asked him during our nighttime chats if he was dating anyone. He said he wasn't interested in dating until he was done with school and established a career. He wanted to make sure he had something of value to offer a partner. I told him I felt he had plenty to offer.

That's when he told me about how he grew up poor and watched his mom struggle her whole life to put food on the table and pay for their tiny apartment. She worked so hard for what little they had, and he barely saw her. He didn't want that for his wife or children. Nolan said he didn't bother with casual dating and saw it as a distraction if he wasn't interested in anything serious until he finished school. Right then I knew…I *had* to marry this man, and the cheap and easy tactics the old version of me used to keep a guy around would not help me keep him. Only one thing would work on this spectacular unicorn: patience.

Miss Marigold held on for three more months. It was after one of our nightly chats, as we were about to change shifts, we found her no longer breathing in her bed. She had gently passed in her sleep. After the coroner took her away, Nolan held me in his arms as I cried until the sun rose. He carried me to my bed, and I slept for ten hours. I awoke to find him in the kitchen, opening a can of cat food for Butterscotch…and the dam of my love for him finally burst. He was up with me all night and still remembered my cat needed to eat. I rushed across the room, wrapped my arms around his neck, and kissed him in a way I never kissed a man before. It was gentle and passionate; full of hope for a future--our future. I felt with every fiber of my being that this kiss was just the beginning for us…and for someone so dedicated to finishing college before getting involved with a woman, Nolan dropped the cat food to the floor and kissed me back just the same.

What I didn't know then, is that Miss Marigold's death gave me my life back. She healed my damaged heart, and through her, I had finally found *my person.*

After she passed, Nolan and I were unsure if we were allowed to continue to live in Miss Marigold's house. We'd never signed a lease, and she never mentioned what would happen to her home upon her death. All she left for instructions was a single phone number written on a pink sticky note to her attorney's office. When Nolan called to ask what we should do, he told us that Miss Marigold had her affairs put in order before her death and that he would provide us with more information in a few weeks after his office had prepared the documents.

For those few weeks, we tried to find a new normal. Nolan went to class and spent the time he normally would have cared for Miss Marigold to study for his NCLEX. I re-opened Marigold's shop and continued to run it as if she were there behind the counter with me. Mostly, we waited in limbo to find out if we needed to find new homes.


Nolan and I sat nervously in the estate attorney's office. My leg bounced. Once again, my life was turned upside down. Where should I move? Should I buy a house like Goldie suggested? Maybe I should leave Springfield altogether. If I did, what about Nolan? Maybe it would be for the best if I left. He needed to focus on his career.

Nolan put his hand on my shaking leg, and I felt all the anxious thoughts leave my body down through my feet and into the earth. No. Nolan is my person. There is no one else I want, there is no one else for me. We are meant for each other. Even if he was not there yet--and at that time, I didn't know if he was--I would be patient. He is my *soul mate*. I turned to face him and smiled. His eyes lingered on my face and studied my lips. Was he thinking about our kiss?

"Mr. Murphy?" the attorney's paralegal gestured for him to enter the office hidden behind a heavy walnut door. "You're up first."

We both took a deep breath. Why were we being called in individually if this was just about tenancy?

Thirty minutes later, a visibly stunned Nolan exited the office with a folder of paperwork and a small box. He slowly sat in the seat next to me and I noticed his hands shaking.

"Nolan...are you okay? What happened?!" I asked, my anxiety returning a hundredfold.

"...Goldie...paid off all my student loans..." he stammered.

"Oh my God. Nolan! That's amazing and so generous of her! I

exclaimed. Of course she did, rest her soul.

"...and she set up a fund for me to get my bachelor's degree...and then a nurse practitioner...and enough money for living expenses so I don't have to work while I'm in school." His head was down, staring at the manilla envelope in his hands. Tears dropped and bled the ink where his name was written in Goldie's elaborate cursive.

I covered my mouth with my hand in disbelief at a loss for words, and he continued.

"Not only that...she set up a scholarship fund for nursing students for the next ten years, and made me the head of the selection committee."

"Nolan...that's incredible. *Goldie* is incredible. I'm so happy for you." I knew what this meant for him--he could spend more time focused on his studies and being human rather than an endless whirlwind of work-sleep-study-bike 3 miles-school-bike 3 miles and repeat every day. "...what about the house? Did he say if you need to move out?"

"The attorney said we can both stay there as long as we need to, without rent, as long as we maintain the property. All the taxes, landscaping, and regular maintenance is paid for indefinitely." He said.

"...that's great! But what happens after we move out?" I asked, confused.

"Honestly, I didn't ask. I don't know...maybe you can ask when it's your turn." Nolan wiped his eyes on his sleeve.

"I will." I pointed to the box in his lap. "What's in the box?"

He laughed. "It's the weirdest thing, she left me a woman's ring. It's an antique worth a fortune apparently, the attorney gave me appraisal documents. I don't know if she expects me to sell it or something."

I knew exactly what Goldie expected him to do with it. "Can I see it?"

He opened the ornately carved box. Inside was the most beautiful ring I'd ever seen. It had a gold octagon-shaped band, the head of which was box-shaped and coated in blue enamel. In the center was a purple-toned garnet nestled in a star of diamonds.

And someday it would be mine.

"If she was going to leave me an heirloom, I think that mahogany desk in the den would have made more sense." He chuckled.

"Yeah," I laughed. "You spend a lot of time there studying. It *would* have made more sense…but maybe hang on to the ring until you know for sure you want to sell it. You probably don't need the money right now anyway, right?"

"That's true, Lucy." He gingerly shut the lid. "Do you want me to hang around here while you talk to the lawyer, or do you want to meet up at The Dollhouse later?"

"We'll meet up later and I'll let you know how it goes. Do you want me to bring home Chinese?" I offered.

"That sounds great! Get Springfield Cashew Chicken…and Crab Rangoon." He smirked.

"Well, of course. No red-blooded Springfieldian would ever order anything else." I smiled at this local truth.

He winked and left to catch a cab home, probably to get a nap in before dinner.

"Lucy? He's ready for you now." The office assistant gestured for her to follow through the walnut door. I took a deep breath and walked into the attorney's office. It was overtly masculine. An imposing desk sat in the center of the room, where his chair rose slightly higher than the visitor's chair to shake my hand. He wore a two-thousand-dollar suit, smelled like sandalwood, and was bronzed from what I could only assume was weekend golf. Golf guys have a vibe. Miss Marigold didn't cheap out on her attorney.

"Lucy, it's nice to finally meet you. Goldie spoke so highly of you that I thought you were her daughter at first. I'm sorry for your loss." He gestured to the leather chair across from him. I sat and gripped my purse nervously in my lap.

"Thank you. She was very special to me." I stuffed down tears threatening to escape with the same resolve that I'd used so often lately to give Nolan space.

Instinctively, the attorney inched a box of tissues towards me. "I apologize for how long it took for us to process her final wishes…she made a few last-minute adjustments that made things more complicated."

"Oh really?" I wondered if she recently decided to pay for Nolan's education.

He nodded. "It's my understanding that you've been living at Goldie's home and it's unclear whether you need to move or not?"

"That's correct. We--Nolan and I--never signed a lease or anything." I said.

"Well, the good news is you can stay as long as you wish. However, she *did not* leave you the house. Not quite." He pointed at her with his pen as if I was expecting it.

"Oh! Of course not! I wasn't expecting…" I stammered.

"Lucy. Goldie has been very generous to you, which I'll get to in a moment, however, there's a caveat and it's related to the house." He was squinting at her with bushy black eyebrows furrowed together like a caterpillar.

"Um, okay?" I didn't know what to say.

"You may stay at what Nolan called *The Dollhouse* for as long as you need to. However, when you choose to move out, the home will technically become… *The Butterscotch Boarding House for Women and Children.* Quite a mouthful, isn't it? Essentially, Goldie has requested that half of her investments go towards making the home into a domestic abuse shelter. She wants you to oversee its operations…hire the appropriate personnel and put in maintenance requests. Victorian houses require an incredible amount of upkeep. In fact, Goldie instructed me to tell you that she didn't bestow you the house because it's too difficult to maintain and she wants you to find your own perfect home." He smiled sweetly. "What do you think?"

"I think I don't know anything about operating a women's shelter…I don't mean to sound ungrateful for her letting me stay there for free, but why me? Isn't there some sort of organization more qualified to take ownership?" I was flummoxed.

"Of course there are others more qualified than you. That's why Goldie left you enough funds to pay those people to help you. She believes you have the heart for it, and the rest can be figured out along the way. I'd also like to mention…there are certain *financial* incentives for overseeing the shelter."

I squirmed in my seat. I didn't want to appear greedy, but I couldn't spend all my time running a women's shelter, working, and eventually raising a family. "Such as?"

"Well, first of all, Goldie said you are to go through her entire home and keep anything you'd like. Many of the items in her home are antiques in extremely good condition so this is generous. Anything you don't want will be auctioned off and put into a fund for addiction rehabilitation services for any of the women at the boardinghouse that need it." He extracted a document from a folder with my name on it. "…and here's where it gets really fun."

"Wait…there's more?" I ask.

His eyes went wide. "Don't you know anything about Goldie? Her father went to California during the Gold Rush and came back a very wealthy man. He invested in mines, mills, and other businesses in southwest Missouri, becoming even wealthier. Goldie is an only child, and comes from old money… honey, you're about to inherit it all."

I scrunched up my face and pushed my chair back from the desk. This isn't real. I needed air. "No, you've made a mistake. She has to have someone else. A relative or old friend."

"Believe it or not, she doesn't. If she hadn't chosen you as an heir, her estate would have gone to the State of Missouri. Personally, I'd rather see you with it!" he chuckled.

"…how…how much?"

"After cashing out her investments and what is in her bank account, you'll inherit… a nearly new Mercedez Benz, a lovely cabin in Eureka Spring, Arkansas-Goldie let my family stay there for a week last summer, spectacular views- and…well, fifty million dollars."

The room spun. "…what?"

"Fifty million. Five zero. A cabin, and a car." He smiled and waited as the words sunk into my brain.

"I…I had no idea." I stammered.

"Oh! I almost forgot!" he pushed a button on an intercom. "Becka, can you bring me the paperwork for *la tienda?*" He laughed and turned his attention back to Lucy. "I'm learning to speak Spanish. Tomorrow I'm leaving for a vacation in Cabo San Lucas. Have you been?"

"...no...no." I blinked.

"Well, you can certainly go now!" he laughed.

Becka opened the door and handed the attorney a paperclipped stack of papers.

"Thanks, Beckers. Alright, so Goldie also left you her vintage clothing store. She says you can do what you like with it, but suggests you keep it open and give some of the women at the shelter temporary jobs. A lot of the women at these shelters are stay-at-home moms without work history, and it makes things difficult for them to start over. Goldie believed employing them could give a little boost, but she also stated it's okay if you would like to essentially sell it to the boarding house, and then hire someone to run it."

"Okay...well for now I still plan on working there. I like what I do." I said.

"Great! Well, that's all. Give your bank info to Ruby at the front desk and she'll do a wire transfer. You should have funds in a few days, but make sure you call your bank, so they know what's going on. Also, you'll need to sign a few things." The attorney stood, signally their business was concluded, then held out his hand. "Nice meeting you, Lucy. Call me up if you ever need an attorney, especially related to the estate. I've spent a lot of time on it, might be easier to have someone familiar with the situation to help out."

"Oh, yes...of course. Thanks." I shook his hand.

"Oh, hey, one last thing...if you ever want to sell that cabin, give me first dibs, alright?" he winked.

"Sure." I smiled, still in a daze, and fumbled for the bronze doorknob.

I walked through that door, and into my dream life.

Patiently, I lived as Nolan's friend and roommate for a year. I'd help him study, cook dinner, and keep up the Dollhouse. On weekends I opened the boutique and continued Miss Marigold's vintage legacy. When Nolan wasn't busy, we'd watch TV, eat pizza, and play board games. Neither of us had other friends, but we didn't mind. We got to know each other inside and out and discovered we both wanted similar things-a stable, comfortable home life. Reliable income. A family. Peace.

Everything we never knew as children.

I attended his graduation ceremony, and he gave me his honors sash as the person who helped him achieve his goals. I told him Goldie was the one who deserved it. Nolan agreed but said I made some pretty good flashcards of human anatomy. That day, I met his mother for the first time.

"I didn't know you had a girlfriend!" she said.

"I don't know if I do…" replied Nolan, giving me a sly grin.

My heart glowed, I stepped to him and wrapped my arms around his neck, whispering in his ear: "You definitely do."

Within a few weeks, he was hired to work the graveyard shift in the perpetually short-staffed emergency room at the largest hospital in southern Missouri. I never told him about my fifty-million-dollar inheritance or the cabin. Only the Mercedes and the store. He wanted so badly to be seen as the breadwinner. On our first anniversary, he asked me to marry him at the Ha Ha Tonka castle ruins overlooking Lake of the Ozarks. The puzzle pieces were coming together in my life so beautifully, if I thought too long about how much had changed for me in just three years it brought tears to my eyes. I had never felt more blessed.

We were married a few months later on a riverboat on Lake Taneycomo, then honeymooned in Florida, spending an entire week at Disney World. After we returned, we pooled our money from his savings and the boutique (padded with my inheritance-the income from the boutique barely paid the utility bills. Nolan didn't need to know that.) and purchased a large home in a gated community on a quarter of an acre of land. It had a tidy lawn and room for a large garden in the back. Our nearest neighbors were also new to the community-a gay couple from Louisiana with a teenage son and twin babies, so there wasn't a lot of pressure to conform to neighborly norms. We were both figuring out the trash days and grass length rules or where to install the new fence. Life was easy-breezy. Our home was cozy and updated, but painted in twenty different shades of gray which felt a bit sad. So, Nolan and I spent every weekend making that house our own with cheerful cottagecore and soft carpet. From the day we signed the deed to the house, we were eager to start a family. Being young and enthusiastic, we figured we'd get pregnant the first month we tried, so the first room we decorated was the nursery.

As our first year passed, I lovingly tended an elaborate English garden in our backyard. I watched longingly as our neighbor's twin babies learned to crawl in the bright green grass, then wobble on chubby bare feet until they could walk. In the summer I heard them giggle and splash in their tiny swimming. How could such a joyful sound make my heart ache in agony?

I just couldn't get pregnant.

"God dammit, Buttercup! Get your loud ass in the box!" I heard from the other side of the fence as I planted a variety of milkweeds for the monarchs. "Liam! No, get away from the barbeque grill! Oh, hell!"

I sat down the pot I was about to overturn, removed my gloves, and walked around the fence, carefully pushing open my neighbor's gate. "Ben? Is everything okay?"

Benny was cleaning one toddler's charcoal-blackened hands just as the other pulled open the door to a small chicken coop. A flood of feathers and yellow feet blew through the door, knocking the twin to the ground. He lay there silent for three full seconds in shock before inhaling as deeply as his little lungs could and letting out a long wail like a freight train. I sprang to action, shut the gate behind me to contain the chickens, and ran toward my neighbor's baby, swatting away chickens as I closed the distance between us. I scooped him up in my arms and started checking him for scrapes. I pulled a green leaf from his beautiful curly hair. Even with tears streaming down red cheeks, he looked like an angel. "It's okay, little guy. Let's go see Daddy."

Benny was trotting across the yard with the other twin on his hip, yelling at chickens as he went. "HELL, Dorthy! Get your big fluffy ass out of my way!" He was wearing cow-print tall rubber boots and had an enormous pair of kitchen shears in his pocket. I passed him his son who had already begun to calm down and was pawing at the dangly gemstone honeybee earrings I was wearing.

With a baby on each hip and his face flushed, he was distraught and nearly in tears. "Christopher's gone."

I'd only spoken to my neighbors a few times, and Christopher once. I wasn't sure if he was telling me their relationship was in trouble or if he was dead.

"Oh…I…uh…" I stammered, not knowing what to say.

"He's in New Orleans." Benny nodded quickly. "On the oil rig. He's been gone for three weeks. It's just me. All me. Every day…and night. I'm sorry if I smell. I can't remember the last time I showered."

So his husband was gone…*working*. "It's okay, Ben. Hey, why don't you let me hold the other little guy for a minute? Your arms must be tired."

He clumsily passed me the baby, then collapsed in the grass and put the other in his lap. "*Three* roosters."

"What?" I asked and sat down next to him with the other baby.

"I have the worst luck lately. *Three Goddamned Rooster Luck*. That's what I'm calling it. If things can go wrong, they will. I think I'm cursed." He yelled at the chicken with a much larger comb than the others, slowly inching its way toward us. It shook its feathers to appear larger, then thought better of making a challenge, and turned away from us. "The babies wanted some chicks when we visited the feed store a few weeks ago. The idiot kid running the brooders told me they were all females. This morning, they were *crowing*."

"Oh, no." I had looked into the HOA rules for chickens and was considering building a tiny replica coop of our home. "We're only allowed six hens…no roos."

"I know!" Benny dramatically pulled the kitchen shears out of his pocket. "I'm trying to take care of them before Christopher gets home tomorrow. He wouldn't even notice if I had more hens…but he'll know three goddamned roosters!"

I gestured at the kitchen shears. "Were you trying to…with kitchen shears?"

He nodded. "The internet says if they're sharp enough…and the chickens are young… I was just going to catch it and *snip*"

"Ben…" I squirmed. "That sounds kind of gruesome and I'm not sure it will work. Have you ever killed a chicken before?"

"No…" he shuddered as he breathed in and stifled tears. "I tried to cull our last rooster. At first, I wasn't going to kill him. I was going to try one of those rooster necklaces that stop them from crowing. One morning the little asshole chased me out of the coop and karate kicked me in the shin, and I knew that—" Ben covered Liam's ears. Lucy followed suit and covered Finn's. "-- little motherfucker needed to go. I cut the bottom off a bleach bottle and nailed it to the coop. I grabbed that punk ass bird by the feet…of course, he tried to bite me! So, I swung him back and forth…you know, to hypnotize him. Well, it worked! I put him headfirst into the bleach bottle so just his head stuck out. I was *so pissed off* as this bird. I pulled that knife out, and up to his neck, but I was shaking so bad I dropped it. As much as I hated this goddamn rooster, I couldn't do it."

"I completely understand. I've never killed anything either…but it's part of owning chickens." I nodded. "So, what happened to the rooster?"

Benny rolled his eyes. "Christopher came outside and saw me acting like a mess. He took the knife from my hands and told me to turn around…I will tell you; my husband is completely repulsed by chickens, refuses to touch them. Says they look like tiny evil dinosaurs. He told me when we got them, he didn't want anything to do with it including killing them. For him to cut that rooster's throat…was the kindest thing he's ever done for me. I swear to *God* I fell in love with him all over again when he did that. I just *can't* ask him to do it again…for THREE of them!"

I stood up and sat Benny's little boy on his feet. I took his hand and started walking him towards the patio. "How about this…let's get these little guys a snack, and some cartoons. Maybe you and I can figure out a better way to do this, okay? Maybe we can call a few farms and see if they want some free roosters."

Benny smiled and awkwardly stood up, stumbling in his big rubber boots. "What is with you midwestern women? Ya'll are so…*helpful.*"

I shrugged. "I've never left the Midwest. People aren't like this other places?"

He smirked. "No, hunny, they ain't. In New Orleans, it's safe to assume someone being helpful is about to pick your pockets or steal your car."

"That happens here, too." I pointed out.

He opened the door to the family room. The boys rampaged into a ball pit in front of the TV. "Well, maybe I've just been lucky to meet a few nice people this week…that's the only good luck I've had."

Heavy footsteps pounded down the stairs. "Oh, hey…good timing, Ash." Said Benny. "Lucy, this is my stepson, Ashton. I don't think you've met him yet…"

Ashton didn't make eye contact with either of us, just walked between us and out the back door, slamming it behind him.

Benny looked stunned, turned to me, and whispered, "I don't know what the fuck is wrong with that kid lately. I had to go pick his ass up at the police station for trespassing a few weeks ago-I don't know if I should tell his dad or not…"

I just raised my eyebrows and shrugged, knowing better than to get involved in family drama. "Do you want me to call Rosewood Farm and see if they want some roosters? You could check online pet listings while I do that."

Online we only found listings of people wanting to give roosters *away*, but I was able to reach someone at Rosewood Farm who agreed to take the roosters. Apparently, hawks were taking off with a lot of their free-range pullets, and they could use the protection.

"I found a farm that will take them! Do you have a travel crate we can use?" I asked

"Yup, it's in the storage room down the hall." Benny pointed. "Would you mind grabbing it? I'm going to ask Ashton if he can watch the babies while we catch the roosters."

Ben went outside to speak to his stepson, and after retrieving the crate I followed.

The first thing I saw was blood. It sprayed out from the spasming headless bodies of two roosters at my feet, droplets landing on my pristine pink and white sneakers.

Benny's stepson stood in front of us with a rooster positioned between his feet, squeezed tight and unable to move. He positioned a pair of limb loppers on either side of its neck, and with one quick motion, closed them hard, and the rooster's head rolled to the ground.

Benny stood pale with his hand on his chest in shock as blood spurted from the trembling body. "Ashton…" he exhaled.

"You wanted them dead, right? And you're too much of a pussy to do it?" The boy's pupils were wide, making the irises nearly black. I instinctively took a step back from the boy splattered in chicken blood.

"What do you want me to do with them, Benjamin?" he asked, cocking his head to one side. "Dinner maybe?"

He sputtered, clearly confused at this chain of events. "Ashton…you're a vegan."

He scowled at his stepfather menacingly, then threw the loppers across the yard at the rest of the flock, sending them scattering in a fit of squawks, then went back inside the house, leaving a trail of bloody footprints on the plush white carpet.

I stepped over the bird carcass and placed a gentle hand on Benny's shoulder. His stepson was visibly troubled, and Benny's life was made more difficult being left alone with twin toddlers for weeks at a time.

"Are you interested in being my nanny?" he asked, composing himself and straightening his back with a look of determination.

"Sure…if you need the help, I can do it once in a while." I sort of believed babies were contagious.

"Good. I need you right now. Let's pack the kids up…it's time for us to figure out what those kids were doing out in the cave last week. Whether it's drugs or *what the hell ever*— something going on. I'm getting to the bottom of this crazy bullshit once and for all."

And that is how I became a nanny to a gay dad of twins with an evil stepson.

It's easier than being a tradwife on the internet.

# Chapter 9
## The Legion?

### rawr.

*Bellatrix…I know you hear me, little rabbit.*

*Why are you running?*

*You know, you can't outrun yourself…because you take yourself wherever you go.*

*Why is it so difficult to accept the body God gave you, huh?*

*Do you really think God made a mistake?*

*It must be so difficult to look in the mirror and not be reflected back the person you think you are on the inside…to think you're so ugly and wrong…to think you are a boy…or is it girl? You can't even figure that out, can you? Pitiful.*

*Maybe the problem is you.*

*Maybe you're broken.*

*I bet God is so disappointed in His creation of you.*

*Maybe you should be thrown away.*

*The world would be better off without people like you.*

Trix had been running for four miles.

Normally, two miles was enough to keep the voices that had plagued them their entire life away, but lately, they'd grown louder. Like a drum, hateful thoughts pounded in their brain repeating every cruel thing anyone had ever said to them… the worst bully being themself. Self-hate had been creeping up like a dark cloud from the depths of hell, and was starting to obscure Trix's vision. The fog in their head stopped them from seeing the sun setting, or the road turning into one they didn't recognize.

Pound, pound, pound.

Heartbeat, pavement, heartbeat, pavement.

*Ugly. Wrong. Unworthy.*

Trix finally stopped when the burning in their lungs was so painful they nearly vomited. Their chest heaved for air as they bent over with their hands on their knees, when Trix finally noticed they were standing on wooden planks. Dark water from the James River rushed beneath their feet.

*"Too thick to drink, too thin to plow. The James River is only good for hiding bodies and noodling."*

Trix's grandfather would never take them swimming at the river, let alone noodling for man-sized catfish. He said the Kansas City mafia threw bodies in the James River because what wasn't eaten by the catfish was swallowed by the mud and never seen again. Almost all drownings were never recovered.

Trix walked to the rail of the bridge, gauging the distance to the water below. Fifty feet? Is that enough?

Trix climbed between the rusty iron railings and stuck her finger on a fishing hook that was tangled around the barrier. On the other side, they teetered on the heels of their feet, toes dangling over the edge.

Bullfrogs croaked.

Crickets chirped.

Music thumped from a vehicle in the distance.

*They'd never find your body.*

*Your parents would think you ran away.*

*They wouldn't have to explain you to anyone again.*

*They wouldn't have to defend you. They would be happier and eventually move on.*

*The world will continue to spin without you.*

*The bullfrogs will croak.*

*The crickets will…*

"Rawr!" a voice called behind Trix.

The glow of headlights lit shadows in the trees, illuminating the large yellow eyes of a barred owl not ten feet in front of Trix on a branch. Startled, they nearly slipped.

Car doors slammed shut. "Oh, shit…hey! Don't do it!"


*Don't respond.*

*They don't care about you.*

*They just want to say they *tried*.*

*Hurry up and get it over with.*


Soft footsteps approached.

"Go away!" Trix shouted, their shrill voice echoing as it bounced off the steel bridge and the rocks below.

The person stopped. "Uh…no?"

"Oh, for fuck's sake, Direpaw."

"Shrox, I work at Little Ceasar's, I'm not a goddamn crisis counselor. I don't know what I'm supposed to do here."

A large shadow crept over Trix, much larger than what a human's should be.

*Do it.*

*Do it now, freak.*

Trix took a deep breath and bent their knees...

Just as a strong pair of arms reached between the rail and wrapped around Trix's waist, pinning them in place.

"Shrox, quick, get her feet. Direpaw-take my head off! I already dropped one of my paws in the river!"

Paws? Momentarily distracted from their jump, Trix looked at the hands around their waist. Arms covered in white fur with black stripes. One human hand with black-painted fingernails, another with an enormous paw... with pink toe beans and short black claws. Two more arms shoved through the bottom rails and locked Trix's legs in place. This fur was long and white with silver strands throughout, sparkling like tinsel on a Christmas tree in the headlights. Rather than paws, these arms had long, tri-fingered raptor claws.

Shaken and confused, Trix tried to turn around. "What the...what the hell is this? Who the hell are you?"

A gray paw sat on her shoulder. "We're *friends*, trying to save your life!"

"Yeah!" said raptor-claws. "We've all been there, dude! It gets better!"

Trix tried to kick out of their grip, the arms squeezed tighter.

"I bet there are so many people who love you and would be really sad if you jumped off this bridge." Said gray-paws.

"Like your parents...or if your parents don't love you, Jesus probably does. Or maybe your cat...or grandma." Said toe-beans.

"Remember the semicolon..." pleaded raptor-claws. "your story isn't over! And neither is your life!"

"RAWR!" they all shouted in unison.

Trix stopped struggling. The voices in their head quieted. "Let me go."

"No." they all said, firmly.

"I'm not going to jump."

"Uh…we don't believe you." Said toes-beans.

"So, what, then? Are you going to just stand here all night and miss your costume party? Why the fuck do you care?" Trix spat into the night.

There was brief silence, while the good Samaritans considered their next move.

"I think we should take her with us." Said toe-beans.

"Ragekitten, are you suggesting we kidnap this troubled youth and expose her to the joy that can be found in a proper Furmeet?" asked gray-paws.

"That is precisely what I'm suggesting, Direpaw.

"Hell yeah!" said raptor-claws. "Lift her up and over on the count of three. One, two, three!"

Trix screamed and flailed in protest, as the three strangers lifted her small body up and over the rail. Tripping over their collective tails and costumed feet, all four fell into a heap on the bridge, but Ragekitten's hand never stopped gripping Trix's wrist.

"Holy shit! You're Furries!" Trix panicked, scraped at the ground, and tried to yank her arm free.

Raptor-claws shrugged. His headpiece was some sort of lizard with golden eyes and bushy brows. The snout was full of sharp teeth framed by a long, curly mustache. "Exactly…we're Furries. Why are you so fucking scared?"

"Because I don't want to be kidnapped by an anthropomorphic sex cult!" Trix bellowed.

"Okay, so, first of all, you were about to jump off a bridge into a dark, watery grave. I think an anthropomorphic sex cult sounds *way* more fun." Said raptor-claw-mustache-lizard.

"Shrox!" Ragekitten sat up to brace herself for more leverage if Trix bolted. "I don't think you're helping!"

"Fine." Shrox removed his headpiece and ran his fingers through curly black hair shining with sweat. He looked to be in his early twenties, and much more handsome than Trix expected a Furry to be. "The Furry fandom is not a sex cult."

Direpaw coughed. "Not usually, anyway."

"Every fandom has weirdos." Ragekitten tipped her head to one side to shake platinum blonde hair out of her face. Her cheeks were flushed pink from the scuffle. Trix and Ragekitten locked eyes for a moment, and a jolt of electricity sparked between them, quickly startling them both. "Being a Furry means being a part of an inclusive community of people who love animals and art."

"And sometimes weird fetishes." Said Direpaw, who still wore a headpiece of a gray and brown wolf.

"Direpaw!" scolded Ragekitten. "I can't speak for all Furries…just as I can't speak for the entirety of any group. All I can say is…*our* Furmeet is for fellowship, cosplay, and fun."

"I'm pretty sure Rosebloom and Bloodmoon are yiffing. Just sayin'." Said Direpaw, tapping his foot impatiently.

Shrox held out his hand to help Trix off the ground. "Is it okay if we kidnap you now?"

Without a word, Trix took his hand and stood up. Ragekitten led her to their car, never letting go of her arm, and made Trix sit in the backseat squished between her and Shrox.

"I don't need you opening the door and rolling down the freeway," Ragekitten said with a sly grin. She had dimples… on both cheeks. Trix felt her heart flutter.

Trix turned to Shrox. "So, what are you, anyway? Some kind of lizard angel?"

"God dammit!" Shrox tossed his hands up in frustration.

"Bro, I told you the wings aren't pointy enough. You look like some kind of mutant butterfly." Said Direpaw as he pulled into a Kum-n-Go convenience store. Earlier he had removed his head so he could fit in the car and like Shrox, appeared to be in his early twentie. Trix noticed a Missouri State Football shirt under his costume.

"Friend, I am a dragon. A subrace of Furry called a Scaley. We are the the lizardfold." Shrox swelled with pride. "I just need to fix my wings."

"I see…and you two are a cat and a wolf?" Trix asked the others.

"Yup. I used to be a Feathery-a bird race. A Eurasian Eagle Owl. It was too hard to get my feathers to stay on. I molted everywhere." Shrugged Rage kitten.

Direpaw climbed out of the front seat and leaned through the window. "Hey, since you guys have to watch the prisoner, what kind of pizza slice do you want? There was so much dog hair in that taco dip Talon made last week, I vowed to never eat anything at Furmeets again."

"Breakfast." Shrox and Ragekitten said in unison.

Direpaw nodded. "What about you?"

"Um, I'll have breakfast pizza too. I didn't know they served it this late." Trix said shyly.

"Yeah they serve it all night now because everyone loves it. Hey… we never asked your name." pointed out Ragekitten.

"It's Trix." They said.

when they assume their Fursona. They aren't judged in the way all of us are judged when we walk around in our fleshy meatsuits. They get to be something cute, fun…and free. The Fursuits…and the community…help people feel like they *belong*. That's all anyone wants."

Trix considered Ragekitten's words. Maybe that was worth more than money. Trix nodded.

"I get that."

Direpaw, Ragekitten and Shrox dropped off Trix in front of their home at four am the next morning, with the promise that Trix would text at least one of them every day until the next Furmeet to make sure they're still alive and well. Ragekitten promised to call every night after work.

Trix tripped over a sunflower solar light marking the pathway to the front door, and hobbled up the porch steps in their new fursuit, still not able to get the hang of the large rabbit feet. She carried the head upside down in one arm, inside of which were her paws, a giant felt carrot, her phone, and a foil-wrapped paper plate with a large slice of cherry pie-a gift from an overly-friendly Fur-croc. When she tugged on the door it was locked.

"Shit!" Trix didn't bring her keys when she left for her run. Everyone was awake at the time she was expected back. The stepdads would have her rabbit hide for being out so late.

Trix peeked through a small crack in the curtains. She could just barely make out the image of a video game on their seventy-inch TV.

Trix knocked. No answer.

She knocked louder. The video game paused, and hesitant steps approached the door. Stepdad Number 1, Eric, opened the door with a scowl.

"Trix, what the hell? Your mom's been losing her mind waiting for you to get home. I told her to go to bed and I'd wait for you." He had a Bluetooth headset around his neck, an Xbox controller in one hand, and rubbed his shirtless, hairy belly with the other.

"Sorry, Dad. I was with friends." Trix said flatly.

He pointed at the rabbit suit. "Well, are your friends Santa Clause and the Tooth Fairy? Because I called all your usual friends and none of them have heard from you in weeks. They're pretty upset about it, too."

Trix shifted uncomfortably. They'd been avoiding Theo, Esme, Ash, and Mateo since the night at the Cheese Caves. Mateo called them at least five times a day, and Trix never answered.

"Are you going to let me inside?" Trix said.

"Not until you tell me where you've been, young la…person." Eric still struggled at times to remember to change the way he addressed Trix. "And tell me why you're dressed like a rabbit."

Trix shrugged. "Why does it matter? I'm home *now*."

"Kid, I'm gonna level with you. You're seventeen, and when I was seventeen, I was doing way worse shit than dressing like a rabbit and coming home at four in the morning. I'm glad you're safe, but I'm not gonna get on your ass about it. However…your mother is really upset, and I need some wins. Mika detailed your mom's car today and he's making me look bad. I'd like to resolve this by telling your mom you lost track of time watching movies with a friend, and you're safe and sound in bed. I need some gold stars here, Trix. Help me be your mom's favorite dad."

Trix rolled their eyes. "If you must know, I was at a Furmeet."

He blinked at her. "You're a Furry?"

Trix shrugged inside her rabbit-suit shell. "Well…yeah, I guess so."

Eric sighed, hung his head, took a deep breath mumbling *Ididnotseethatcoming*.

He turned and yelled behind him. "Gemma! Mika…wake up! Our child joined an anthropomorphic sex cult, and I don't know what to do!"


## River Rocks


Oliver slammed the car door shut.

"Dad, I don't understand why I have to do the river cleanup. No one else is going."

Brent fiddled with the satellite radio until he landed on a contemporary Christian rock channel, a small attempt at connecting with his teenage son. "The sheriff's deputies said they wanted you to come help out as a condition of your release."

Oliver growled. "Dad! We weren't arrested, we were detained for a few hours! We don't have to do the river cleanup; it was just encouraged. I have summer AP classes I don't have time for this kind of thing! None of my friends are going!"

His father sighed, as he began the short drive to the James River. "Son, in this family we do the right thing, and we atone when we make mistakes. I'd also like to remind you that the correctness of our behavior is not measured by what everyone else is doing—even our closest friends. We must always ask ourselves…"

"…what would Jesus do?!" Oliver snarled.

"Exactly, Oliver." Replied his father tersely.

Oliver surrendered and closed his eyes attempting a cat nap. He'd been up past midnight every night for the last two weeks studying for two AP foreign language classes to hopefully secure a chance to study abroad and get as far away as possible from his parents.

It's not like they were *bad* parents. Oliver knew he shouldn't complain. They doted over all of their children, wanting them to have the Godliest education, be surrounded by the most virtuous people and to grow into successful adults who could spread the word of Jesus Christ from a position of leadership. Oliver had never missed a meal. He went to Florida once a year. His laundry was always folded, and his mother kissed him goodnight every single night of his life.

It was driving him insane.

At seventeen, most of his friends' parents had loosened the reins in anticipation of their children being on their own soon. Even his

Christian friends were allowed to date. Oliver's mother kept him so busy with his education, extracurriculars, work, and family outings that every minute of his day was scheduled. She'd probably faint if he mentioned any interest in dating.

Sometimes he wondered if she overloaded him on purpose.

As the oldest, Oliver knew his mom was worried about "messing up", especially given her lifestyle at his age. She had experienced what life was like with irresponsible parents and almost didn't survive her teenage years. If she hadn't met Dad in the ambulance while he was training to be an EMT, he would never have introduced her to the church, and she never would have gotten clean.

*I'm not like her.* Oliver thought. *Why can't she lighten up on me?*

"You stay up late, Ollie?" his dad poked him in the leg. "You just woke up!"

He grumbled. "Like I said, I have to study. Why can't we get coffee?"

"Oliver, you know better than that. God wants us to live healthy and happy lives, without any addictive substances. Health is our greatest wealth during our time on Earth."

Oliver turned towards the window and rolled his eyes. He'd seen plenty of churchgoers chugging coffee from a travel mug in their cars before going to Sunday service. Oliver himself bought a cappuccino every morning at the community college cafeteria that hosted summer AP classes for homeschoolers. He was pretty sure Jesus cared more about him being awake for AP Spanish than his daily bean water.

His father pulled off onto a dirt road lined with the vehicles of off-duty police officers gearing up in waders and work gloves. They wore t-shirts representing their districts. Captain Kentworth waved as they approached and limped over to their car with two buckets and long-handled grabbers.

He held out his hand to Oliver's dad. "You must be Brent; we spoke on the phone. You've got some real good kiddos. I had a lot of fun hanging out with them on their visit to the station!"

Brent gave a proud smile. "I appreciate you saying so, Captain Kentworth. We try to teach our kids that even though everyone makes mistakes, the truly great person at least tries to make it right."

Taking this cue from his father, he held out his hand to Captain Kentworth. "I'm happy to help out today, sir."

"Well, that's fantastic Oliver. Theo was supposed to meet me here, but he never showed. What about the rest of your gang?" Captain Kentworth asked with genuine interest.

"Honestly, I haven't spoken to any of them since that night in the station. Even Theo." Oliver shrugged.

"Humph." Said Captain Kentworth. "Well, at least you're here now, so let's get started, gentlemen! Here are a few buckets and grabbers. This part of the river can get kind of seedy so there's a lot of syringes and broken glass lying around. Be careful where you step and wear gloves. Also, watch out for snakes. Lots of cottonmouths and copperheads. There's plenty of trash for everyone, so just wander the shore for a few hours and we'll meet up back here. I'll be hanging back grilling burgers for everyone to eat when you're done. Sound good?"

Brent nodded and thanked the Captain, then they carefully traversed the sharp limestone rocks until reaching the waterline.

"Why do people swim here?" Oliver asked "Besides being dirty, there's no beach. You'll just trip on rocks and bust your head open."

"I agree. That's why we drive an hour to swim at Stockton Lake. You'll get tetanus…or worse…at the river." His dad laughed as he picked up a pair of gray underwear and dropped them in Oliver's bucket. "Here ya go Ollie. Seems about your size."

"Gross, dad."

Oliver looked up and saw a man in rubber waders walking down the shore waving at them.

"By golly, is that you, Brent?" the man shouted.

His dad laughed in elation and dropped his bucket and grabbers. "David Morrows? It can't be! I thought you moved to Arkansas!"

Oliver's dad rushed off to greet his apparent old friend, leaving Oliver alone to clean up the trash. Most of the officers headed downstream as a group, so he turned upstream towards the overpass. There was probably all kinds of weird stuff thrown off the bridge, he thought. At least it would make this interesting.

Beer bottles, milk jugs full of pee, used tampons.

Swollen diapers, plastic forks, cherry cigarillo wrappers.

Condoms, syringes, empty boxes of male enhancement pills.

*Humans are disgusting. No wonder the only animals out here are cottonmouth snakes.*

Oliver tried not to think about the stories behind the objects he picked up, but rather, attempted to remember both their Spanish and French names.

"Espuma de poliestireno… polystyrène… dentadura postiza?" Oliver laughed and plopped a set of fake teeth in his bucket. « Dentiers. »

"Hey, kid!" someone shouted from beneath the overpass.

Oliver knew enough about Springfield to know you stay the hell away from bridge people. He quickly turned to leave and started back to the safety of the group.

"Don't leave! Hey! Don't I know you from somewhere?" The person's voice echoed off the water and the steel beams.

*Come on, Oliver. Why are you so nervous?*

*Didn't Jesus teach you to love everyone unconditionally…even bridge people?*

*What if they just want to say hello?*

*Are you afraid your mother and father would be upset with you?*

*Or--heaven forbid--disappointed that you took an unnecessary risk?*

*It doesn't hurt to see what they want.*

*Maybe you'll make a new friend.*

*Maybe it will be someone who actually understands you.*


Oliver stopped and turned around, but didn't walk towards the voice. "What do you want?"

"Come here!"

"Not until you tell me what you want," Oliver shouted through the tangle of honeysuckle bushes obscuring his view of the person on the other side.

"You're Oliver, right? My dad knows your mom."

His curiosity began to pique. Who is this?

Oliver walked around the brush and saw three boys sitting around a bonfire. They appeared to be his age. One looked familiar.

"How'd you know my name?" Oliver asked.

"I told you, punk. My dad knows your mom." The boy patted the ground next to him. "Take a load off. Say hello. We don't bite."

He dropped his bucket and grabbers and cautiously approached the trio. Two were smoking…something. The boy who spoke to him wore black cargo shorts, dirty Converse, and a black shirt with a picture of a cat playing the drums that said "Heavy Meowtal". Oliver sat next to him. He left his wallet and phone in the car so it didn't get wet. It's not like they could rob him.

The boy chucked a black walnut into the fire. "My name's

Magnus."

"Magnus?" Oliver questioned without thinking.

"Yeah, I know it's weird." Said Magnus. "My dad's really into all that Norse shit. We've got a dog named Thor and a one-eyed cat named Odin. It's pretty cringe."

"How do you know my mom?" Oliver asked.

"Well, like I said, I don't, but my dad does. You probably don't remember me, but we went to the same Christian summer camp once." He said.

Magnus didn't strike Oliver as the Christian-summer-camp-sort. "Sorry…I don't remember you."

He hurled another walnut into the fire after the first one popped open and fizzled. "I'm not surprised. I was only there for a week. We were about twelve. I was in the same cabin as you. I think we were called—"

"The grasshoppers. Pretty lame." Oliver chuckled. "Yeah, my mom was the senior camp counselor for the girls that year."

"I know. She tried to talk the other counselors into letting me stay after I broke into the kitchens and ate all the chocolate bars for smores. I overheard her talking to them…she said she knew my dad and that if anyone needed to be at the camp it was me. That I would need God more than any kid there." The other two boys sniggered. Magnus charred another walnut.

Oliver watched him carefully. "I didn't know that. Who's your dad?"

Magnus raised an eyebrow. "Her ex-boyfriend from high school."

"…your dad is Ray?" Oliver remembered her mom mentioning him a few times when she spoke about her life before Dad and the church.

"Yeah. I know. He used to be a real piece of shit. He's not as bad now…still, I'd rather hang out under the bridge with these assholes than go home, ya know?" He tossed two walnuts in their direction.

"The guy with the septum ring is Scott. The one with the prematurely receding hairline is Nate."

"Fuck off, Magnus."

Oliver had unconsciously been digging a mote around himself in the thick brown river dirt he was sitting on. It was filled with water and made a small barrier between himself and Magnus. His jeans were getting wet, and he stood up to leave.

"Nice meeting you guys…and you again, Magnus." He brushed as much dirt as possible off his bottom. "I better get going."

Magnus stood up and gave Oliver a friendly smile. "Aww, come on, bro. You just sat down. What are you doing out here anyway?"

"River cleanup with the sheriff's department," Oliver said flatly as he turned to leave.

Magnus laughed. "You're still a goodie two shoes, aren't you?"

Oliver's eye twitched.

*You are, aren't you Oliver?*

*Have you \*ever\* done anything your parents wouldn't approve of?*

*Seventeen years old and never taken a sip of alcohol*

*A hit of a joint*

*Kissed a girl*

*Sucked a titty.*

*A shame, really.*

Oliver turned to them whip quick. "Actually, I was arrested for trespassing. They let me go as a condition of my release."

*That's not entirely true, is it Oliver?*

*Didn't you just tell your father you weren't arrested?*

*Look at you, all grown up and telling a lie to impress someone.*

*Not very Christian of you…*

*But it feels good, doesn't it?*

Magnus looked genuinely shocked. "Wait…what? I had you all wrong, I guess. Where'd you trespass?"

Oliver puffed his chest. "Me and some friends partied in a cave on private land and got caught. I got really fucked up that night. My parents were so pissed they had the DMV revoke my driver's license."

*So, you were "fucked up" that night?*

*Or…you don't remember anything at all until the cuffs were on?*

Scott and Nate stood up now, seeming to relax upon learning Oliver wasn't a complete square. Nate walked around the campfire to join the conversation. He was now wearing a green bandana on his head--it was obvious Magnus hit a nerve with the "receding hairline" comment.

"Man, you gotta be careful what you're using out there. I got so fucked up one time I don't remember what I did for three days. Woke up on some 45-year-old woman's dirty couch. I just grabbed my shit and left, you know?"

Magnus and Scott laughed at him, not with him

"Ever since then, I only get the good stuff." Nate continued. "That shit coming up to the States from the Mexican cartels will kill you." He reached into his pocket and pulled out a small plastic bag with what looked to be crushed ice.

As if on cue, Scott stepped forward and turned into a salesman. "This shit here is pure, American-made. I know the guy personally. Sixty bucks."

Oliver took a step back, realizing he had entangled himself deeper than intended. "Uh, sorry dude. I've got summer classes and really need to focus. I can't be eating Cheetos and falling asleep watching cartoons this week."

All three looked at each other and laughed.

"Bro…" said Magnus laying a hand on his shoulder. "If you need to focus, that's exactly what this does. You could stay awake for a week and be sharp as a tack. You'll have like Spidey-senses and shit."

*That doesn't sound so bad, does it Oliver?*

*There's no way you can pass your classes without more time and energy to study.*

*It's impossible.*

*You'll fail your exams and won't be able to study abroad.*

*You'll never get away from them.*

*You'll never be free.*

Oliver studied the bag. "What do I do with it?"

"You smoke it, dumbass." Said Nate, eager to pass the "dumbass trophy" to someone else, even momentarily.

"How? Do you roll it in paper or something?" Oliver's "bad-boy" veneer was cracking.

Magnus put his arm around Oliver, then pulled out a blackened glass pipe from his pocket. "You put it in a pipe. Heat the bottom with a lighter. Here, you can have mine. I need a new one anyway."

Oliver blinked at the dirty pipe Magnus had palmed him. Without looking up he said, "I don't have any money with me."

Scott and Nate exchanged a look, then deferred to Magnus who said: "Don't worry about it, man. Give me your cell number and you can send the money to us when you get home."

Scott nodded. "And if you like our product, you can hit us up again."

Voices were echoing towards the overpass and the cleanup crew approached.

"Shit!" said Magnus.

Nate shoved the bag deep into Oliver's back pocket.

Scott pointed at the pipe in Oliver's hand. "Put that in your pocket, idiot! Don't tell anyone you saw us!"

Before the group of law enforcement officers approached, the three boys had already scrambled up the rocky hillside and were out of sight hitchhiking down the road. Oliver kicked dirt over their fire, then quickly picked up his grabbers and bucket.

He then returned to the Greene County Sheriff's Department's annual river cleanup with a gram of the finest Ozark Mountain trailer park methamphetamine sixty dollars could buy stuffed in his back pocket.

## The Well-Timed Swoop of a Falcon

"Theo! That's the bell! Get off him!"

His father's hands landed hard on his shoulders, yanking Theo away from the corner of the ring where a bleeding teenager lay slumped against the ropes. Theo turned on his father and shoved him hard in the chest with his gloves.

"Get the fuck off me!"

Tyler inhaled to his full height--still not enough to tower over his enormous gorilla of a son--and squared his feet.

"Excuse me?" he snapped

Theo spat blood on the mat. "Get the fuck off me…*coach*."

Tyler tossed the white towel he had around his neck to the trainer wiping blood off the Puerto Rican teenager's face. "Why are you smother punching? Look at him! This is just a trial fight. You're gonna bust the kid up before he even has a shot at a title."

The smell of cigar smoke came closer as Theo hopped back and forth on the balls of his feet in the ring, scowling at *El Halcón* as he chugged water and attempted to stand.

"THEO! Get your Marvel-superhero-Thor-motherfucker-lookin-ass over here!"

Theo growled and stomped to the edge of the mat to face Big Hefty.

"What do you want?" he scowled.

"Bitch, don't you look at me like that." Big Hefty flicked the ashes of his cigar on the tile floor. Perspiration was forming on his shiny bald head. "Why are you trying to break my Puerto Rican?"

"If he can't put up a fight with me, he won't last in the ring. I don't think he's as good as everyone says he is." Theo lifted his chin in a show of confidence.

Big Hefty ignored Theo's show of arrogance and looked past him to his opponent.

"Falcon! You alright?"

Swiftly he stood and hopped back and forth. "All set, *Grande.*"

Now Big Hefty turned to Theo. "Listen up, kid. You are in my gym, funded by my money. So is he. I just dropped ten grand to bring him here and turn him into a champion. I didn't pay shit for you! Your momma practically dropped your ass on my lap at ten years old and told me to get you to the Olympics. Who do you think is gonna fund that?"

Theo crossed his arms. "Perfect Storm's pole dancing."

"BOY! You're lucky I can't get in that goddamn ring, or I'd knock your block for talkin' bout my girl like that! You know damn well she's past her prime. Barely pays the fuckin' light bill." Big Hefty threw his cigar at Theo, and it singed a hole in his shorts before falling to the mat. "Falcon, whoop this punk's ass. I've got a plate of warm brownies to eat."

Big Hefty stomped heavily to his office and slammed the door shut.

Tyler rushed to his son's ear and whispered. "You really know how to bite the hand that feeds, don't you? Let him hit you and end the fight. We'll talk about this at home."

Theo scowled and returned to the center of the ring. His father stayed close to referee the fight and intervene if needed. Falcon landed an uppercut on Theo's jaw, and he rolled his eyes up in the back of his head, trying to control his rage and well-trained instinct to return fire.

*Wow, that was a good hit, wasn't it Teddy Bear?*

*Did you mean to let him hit you so hard?*

*I don't think you did. He's got a lot of talent.*

*He's certainly a lot faster than you.*

*No wonder Big Hefty wants to train him.*

*He's ready to win matches already…*

*You still need work.*

Theo moved back a few steps in the ring, matching the bounce of his footsteps with the steam he blew out his nose. The Falcon approached cautiously, blood still pouring from his presumably broken nose. His eyes flicked to Theo's right side, a "tell" that he was about to land a kidney shot--and he did. Theo growled and bent over in pain but forced himself to stand. Tyler stood behind The Falcon and nodded at Theo as if telling him to let the newcomer end the fight.

*He doesn't think you can win this fight cleanly*

*You're too hot-headed*

*Too out of control.*

*Your father doesn't respect you*

*He probably doesn't even like you.*

*After all, you're the reason your mother ended her career…*

*Then you turned out to be \*such\* a disappointment.*

The Falcon moved close, and as Theo predicted, swung for a cross punch. Theo blocked it and landed an uppercut that caused The Falcon to sway on his feet.

"Theo! That's it! Match is over! Get your gloves off and grab your shit, we're going home." Tyler shouted at Theo's side.

The Falcon steadied himself and looked at Theo with the feral eyes of a man that said *this is over when one of us is on the mat.*

Silently, Theo accepted the challenge. Circling, they stared each other down like rival wolves assessing each other's abilities and injuries.

"I said the match is over! Don't make me drag you out of there, son!" Tyler shadowed his child who was completely lost to the darkness of his fury.

The Falcon drew back his fist, aiming a hook punch directly at Theo's left temple. Leaning back, he expertly dodged the move which brushed past his nose…

And landed on his father's jaw with a crunch.

Unprepared for the hit, his father crumpled to the mat unconscious.

*Can you believe the power in that hit?*

*Incredible.*

*A hit like that could kill a man.*

*Do you think your daddy is dead?*

*What are you going to do now?*

The pupils in Theo's eyes grew wide, and his body relaxed. The voices around him were filtered from his head. He didn't hear the cries to call an ambulance or to call his mother, Isabella. He stepped over the limp feet of his father and zeroed in on *El Hacon*. The Puerto Rican knew the gloves were off. He knew there would be more than one person leaving in an ambulance.

"*Lo siento*, Theo. Accident. Accident. Calm down." He held up his hands in surrender as he backed towards the ropes to exit the ring.

Theo lunged and grabbed him around the arms in a clinch, then slipped an arm around his neck and landed blow after blow to The Falcon's face. In a trance, he watched blood drip to the mat, and then a tooth.

He didn't hear the men shouting

Or Perfect Storm crying

Or Big Hefty saying *give me that motherfucking fire extinguisher.*

"Theodore! You terrifying psychopathic motherfucker you better drop that man right now!" Big Hefty stood in the ring panting behind him.

Theo landed another blow to The Falcon's nose, or what was left of it beneath the fleshy mass.

Big Hefty unloaded the contents of the fire extinguisher all over Theo's bare back and circled around to blast him in the face. Like a pit bull with its jaws locked on its victim, Theo couldn't let go. The icy white foam also blasted The Falcon in the face, which instantly turned pink with blood but momentarily brought him back to consciousness. As he fought to get away, Theo grabbed him as he attempted to stand and landed the most illegal move in boxing--a rabbit punch--to the back of his head. The Falcon fell limp and bleeding next to Tyler on the mat.

"Oh, you think you're bad, Theodore?" Big Hefty growled from behind him. "I'm about to show you how we fight in St. Louis."

Big Heavy drew back the now-empty fire extinguisher like he was about to hit a home run at a Cardinals game and landed it on the side of Theo's head.

A metallic gong rattled in his mind, followed by a voice:

*Have you heard of Sun-tzu, Theo?*

*He was a real fighter*

*Unlike you...*

*"The quality of decision is like the well-timed swoop of a falcon*

*which enables it to strike and destroy its victim.*
*Therefore the good fighter will be terrible in his onset,*

*and prompt in his decision."*

Theo's vision faded in and out. The last image he saw before surrendering to the darkness was Big Hefty towering over him, sweat dripping from his bald brown head to his forehead and down his crooked boxer's nose, saying:

"What the FUCK is wrong with you lately?"

## Sugar Skulls

The water in the cave was up to Mateo's knees.

*I'm not supposed to be here.*

Gone were his fears of the dark and enclosed spaces. There was something more important to be afraid of. He had to keep moving. There must be a way out.

The man followed. Mateo heard the splashes not far behind him. His back burned from where he'd been jolted with a cattle prod before escaping into a crack in the wall to an unknown end. Anywhere was better than with him. Mateo quickly accepted that unless he found a way to escape, he was going to die.

The man had the dead, black eyes you only hear about in horror stories. There's something visceral that happens inside the human brain when you see that switch flip in another person. They are the predator. You are the prey.

*Run, little rabbit. I will find you.*

How do rabbits survive in the wild? If they can't run, they try to blend in to their surroundings, stand very still, or hide.

*He'd smell me. I wore that perfume he said he liked.*

*He'd see me. I bought this red dress yesterday to impress him.*

Mateo took off the dress and scooped up whatever muck he could find, smearing it through his blond hair and over every bit of exposed porcelain skin. Then he swiftly walked along the walls of the corridor, franticly patting for a crevice to hide in. If the man passed by, maybe he could turn back and find his way out of the cave and get help.

His teeth were chattering so hard he thought he would bite his tongue off. He touched his mouth and when he brought back his hand it was stained red. Blood? No, lipstick. He tried to calm the tremors in his jaw from the cold that were sure to give him away, but the rest of his body was shaking from fear. The swish of knee-high water was approached, along with the ominous crackling of the cattle prod.

Mateo closed his eyes and prayed. *God please help me. Please, please!*

"You know, Mariah, if you would have kept your clothes on you wouldn't be so cold. Oh well…saves me the trouble." The man said.

He grabbed Mateo by the hair, and he screamed. "No! Please, No!"

The man dragged Mateo behind him through the water. When one patch of hair ripped out, he'd grab another. When Mateo screamed, he'd dunk his head underwater until just before he lost consciousness. After several turns through the cave, they increased elevation and reached a dry path.

The man stopped and held up his lantern for Mateo to see.

"Welcome to the Sugar Pit. Enjoy your stay."

The man pushed Mateo hard on the back, and he fell twenty feet into murky water. Trying to find his equilibrium, he grabbed at anything he could, finally finding a moss-covered branch. He pulled himself up and realized he could stand on the bottom and the water reached his waist.

"Did you make it?" The man asked with a jovial laugh.

Mateo groaned. His head pounded from where he hit it on the side of the wall on the way down.

Lantern light glowed down from above.

"Be sure to tell the girls I said hello."

In the dim light Mateo could see stacked neatly in a recessed shelf of the cave, a dozen or so human skulls.

…and the mossy branch in his hand was a human femur covered in rotten flesh.

Mateo awoke, rolled over, and vomited off the side of his bed onto the carpet.

The dreams started the night they visited the caves, and had grown more vivid, and gruesome. When it started, it was like watching a movie. Tonight was the first time he was actually in one of the women's bodies.

He wondered if any of the others were having the dreams, too. None of them would return his calls, so he assumed they were still mad. No one showed up for Friday Night Magic except him. Mateo was trying to accept that this could be the end of his longest friendships. He wished they never went to the Cheese Caves. He wished his friends would at least give him a chance to make it right.

Mateo wiped the vomit off his face with his bed sheet and grabbed the sketchbook he kept at the side of his bed. He flipped past all the gruesome drawings of the women he'd dreamt about to a blank page and wrote the name *Mariah*.

*Blonde hair. Red dress. Pale skin. Sugar pit?*

Underneath the keywords, he began to sketch a drawing of the sugar pit since he was inside Mariah's body and didn't know what she looked like. He drew the stack of skulls and the murky water from Mariah's perspective, and finally, he drew the femur covered in rotten flesh. He took less care with the shading, wanting to forget the dream… but for some reason, he felt it was important for him to keep track of what he saw so he kept recording his dreams. He closed the book with a shudder.

"Ugh. Hope I don't have that dream again…" Mateo grabbed the rosary and cross he kept hanging on his bedpost. It was Oliver's dad's, and he'd been wearing it the night they were caught trespassing. He put his hands together and began to pray: "God, as I've said all week, I don't know how to pray but just hear me out. Please keep me safe from all the creepy shit that's been happening to me. Please make the dreams stop. Please look out for my friends and tell them to talk to me again. In exchange, I will try to be a better human, in your image, yada yada. Amen."

He did the sign of the cross on his chest, and accidentally stuck his foot in vomit. He kissed the rosary. "P.S. …please help Mom show mercy on me when she finds out I stained the new white carpet in my room with Coco Puff vomit."

As Mateo brushed his teeth, he could see in the mirror how gaunt his face was looking. He wasn't sleeping well, and dark circles formed under his hollow eyes. He needed to get some sleep before his parents got worried. After getting dressed, he cleaned up the vomit on his carpet the best he could, then rode his bike downtown to talk to someone who might be able to help.

Scott and Nate were notorious for selling anything even remotely elicit. Even though cannabis had been legalized for recreational use in Missouri, it was still illegal for anyone under twenty-one to buy. He found them eating chilidogs at a booth outside Sonic. He wondered if Esme was working and circled the parking lot once to see if she was zipping around on roller skates before finally approaching Scott and Nate.

"Hey, guys," Mateo said, casually sitting between them at the table. Scott held up a finger for Mateo to hold on while he shoved the last bit of a mustard-covered foot-long chili dog in his mouth and swallowed.

"Mateo, right?" he wiped his face with a paper napkin.

"Yeah," Mateo nodded. "We took American History together."

"That class sucked. So much reading." He scowled. "I think the only reason Mr. Pine passed me is so he didn't have me in his class again."

"Yeah…" Mateo shifted in the seat uncomfortably and systematically cracked his knuckles, unsure how to phrase his question. Nate seemed to notice.

"So, Mateo, are you here on business…or something else?" Nate asked in between slurps of his cherry limeade.

"Business…I guess." Mateo raised an eyebrow.

"What kind of business?" Scott asked.

He hesitated, then spat out, "Edibles. I can't sleep, man."

"You look it, bro." teased Nate.

Scott picked up his backpack from the ground and dug to the bottom. "All I have left is chocolate-covered cherries from Las Vegas. Remember, West Coast cannabis is a whole different beast, don't take more than one or you'll be trippin' balls. Forty bucks for ten. It'll definitely help you sleep."

"Deal." Mateo reached into his pocket and pulled out some cash to hand it to him.

Nate shook his head *no*. "Under the napkin. My homie Scott is going to get up to use the bathroom, and he's going to leave his cup in the stall. You feel me?"

Mateo slipped the two twenties under a loose paper napkin. "Yeah, yeah. Of course I feel you."

Nate nodded, and Scott left. Five minutes later, Mateo went into the bathroom and found an apparently empty cup on top of a urinal. Inside, as promised, was a package of ten chocolate-covered cherries from a dispensary in Las Vegas. He put them in his backpack, and as he was leaving, saw Esme in a yellow Jeep parked by the trash bins. He slowly approached and saw she was making out with a man easily twice her age. His hand was up her shirt.

Surprisingly to Mateo, his first instinct was to pull the guy out of the Jeep and beat his ass. He took two steps forward, fists clenched, and then stopped himself.

*Why should I care what Esme does? She's nearly an adult. It's not like she's my girlfriend.*

"Esme!" Mateo yelled from a safe distance, to prevent the physical altercation his heart so desperately wanted.

She stopped dead and stared at him mouth agape. Once the man knew he was being watched, he panicked and put on his seatbelt. "I gotta go. Get out!"

"What about my money, asshole?" She turned on him.

"Just get out!" He demanded.

"Fine, I'll get out." She snatched his phone from the cup holder and jumped out of the vehicle. "Maybe I'll give your wife a call since I'm still on break."

The man's anger suddenly turned to whines. "No, no, no. Don't do that. Just give me my phone back. Here's the fifty I promised." He pulled out his wallet, plucked out a fifty-dollar bill, and tossed it out the window. Esme did not pick it up.

"Give me the rest of it." She demanded.

"…what?" he asked with confusion.

"Your phone is worth a lot more than the make out session you paid for. I want all the cash in your wallet. I know you have one seventy five. I also want the Best Buy gift card you got for being employee of the month." She held his phone in the air waiting for his reply.

The man's face flushed red. He pulled out the rest of his cash and the gift card and threw it out the window onto the pavement. Esme picked it up, shoved the cash in her bra, and handed the gift card to Mateo. Then she slowly and carefully handed him back his phone. He snatched it and threw the Jeep into reverse.

"Hustling little whore!" He shouted as he sped off through the parking lot.

Esme turned to Mateo and said nonchalantly "Hey, Mattie. What are you doing here?"

"I think that was my neighbor…" Mateo watched the Jeep peel out into traffic. "he's got like four kids."

"Not my problem." Esme straightened her shirt. It was much smaller than the one she usually wore.

"…what were you doing, Ez?" Mateo asked sheepishly.

"Making easy money, since the whole Cheese Cave fiasco didn't work out." She stuck up her nose and raised an eyebrow.

"I'm really sorry about that, Esme. You'd know how sorry I am if you'd answer my calls or texts." He pleaded.

"It doesn't matter. I'm not interested in going to the concert anyway. I think Lana Del Ray had it right…*Money, Power, Glory*." Esme pulled wads of cash from every pocket of her uniform, as well as a few slips of paper and business cards.

"…good day for tips, Ez? Didn't even have to wear roller skates." Mateo forced a laugh.

"Yeah, it turns out men are idiots. All I have to do is compliment them, show a little cleavage, call them sir…you know, make them feel important. I haven't got less than a twenty-dollar tip all day. Your neighbor offered me fifty bucks just to make out for fifteen minutes… who knew middle-aged men were so starved for affection?" Esme systematically sorted the dollar denominations, smoothing out the wrinkles in the bills on the edge of the table as she went.

Mateo was horrified. "So are you…um…are you…"

She rolled her eyes. "I'm not a prostitute."

"What's with the phone numbers?" Mateo pointed at the stack of business cards.

"Guys that want to take me on dates," Esme said matter-of-factly.

Mateo shifted from foot to foot, unsure how to phrase what he was about to say without being offensive. "Do you think…that they might have different ideas of what a date is than you do?"

"You know what, Mateo? I don't need to listen to you. Go play games and chase cave treasure. Some of us have to live in the real world." Esme gathered her cash in an organized stack, folded it, and put it in her apron.

"Esme…we've been friends a long time." He stepped towards her and grabbed her hand. "I care about you…and what you're doing seems dangerous."

She scoffed. "Coming from the guy who sent his friends into an unknown cave to bring him rotten cheese…that's rich." Esme pulled her hand away and sneered.

"Jeesh…Ez, you know it wasn't like that. Why are you so mad at me?" Mateo said.

"I don't have time for this…or you. Leave me alone." Esme unlocked the employee entrance door and slammed it behind her.

Mateo stood shocked, staring at the metal door feeling like he was stabbed with a stalagmite to the heart.

# *Chapter 10*

## *Hot Tamale*

**M**ateo Sr. watched patiently as his wife grunted her way through a set of barbell back squats in the basement of their 1970's ranch-style home. They bought it six months previously, and boxes, stacks of laminate flooring and drywall crowded the room. He spent his weekends expertly renovating their home for his beloved *reina*, and tomorrow he planned to finish the flooring.

The washer churned loudly on a load of towels.

"*Esposa...*why are you working out?" he asked loudly over the noise of the off-balance spin cycle.

She paused briefly at the lift, took a deep breath, and started another set of fifteen. "Don't you worry about it *papi*, I'm just trying to get my figure back, you know?"

His eyes began to mist. Summoning his courage, he took a deep breath, preparing to ask the question that festered in his mind for months. "You've been acting distant... and I want you to be honest with me. Are you planning to leave me?" Mateo asked barely above a whisper.

"If you keep on distracting me from my routine I might!" Stella growled.

"I'm serious. Are you planning to start stripping again?" He swallowed hard and his voice croaked. "You promised me when we got married you were done with that shit. I don't like other men looking at your titties, baby."

"Oh, for fuck's sake Mateo, I'm thirty-eight years old, five foot five, and two hundred and fifty pounds. The only person who wants to see me strip after three kids is *you*."

A door slammed loudly on the deep freezer and their oldest son stood behind them holding a box of frozen pizza rolls and a Mountain Dew. "Oh my God. Please…both of you shut up! And get away from my shit, Mom. Your big ass is going to break it."

Flames flashed in Stella's eyes. Mateo Junior and Senior both eyed the closest exit-- the stairs. She dropped the barbell with a hundred pounds worth of plates from shoulder height. It dented Mateo's new flooring.

"Excuse me, *hijo*? You can't possibly be speaking to your *madre* like that? Big ass? BIG ASS? I'll show you a big ass!" She turned around and twerked at both the men. "Huh? You like that? Is that big enough for you?" She slapped her cheeks together in her purple leopard print leggings before turning her attention to the squat rack. She catwalked over, then began sliding up and down rubbing the bars between her cheeks. "Oh yeah! You know, I'm *real* sweaty right now! This bar is nice and cold, feels so good between my hot buttcheeks!"

Junior fake vomited. "You're so nasty *puta*! You better clean my equipment! I'm going to my room." He slammed back the soda and threw the empty can at her.

"Yeah, you do that!" she yelled as her son stomped upstairs. "I better not see you in the kitchen when you start smelling my *empanadas*. I plan to eat them all myself!"

"Whatever…psycho." He grumbled from a distance.

As Stella composed herself, their three dogs barked upstairs, and the sound of nails clacking at full speed to the front door above them meant they had a visitor. "Fuck me…" Stella sighed. "I'll get it." She stomped upstairs to answer the door while Mateo Sr. inspected the damage to his floor.

The tiny mutts skittered and yipped and tore at the already destroyed vinyl blinds to look out the window. *"Vamos!"* she bellowed. As if sensing her energy, they scattered to different parts of the house. Stella flung open the door with a scowl on her face.

A group of women stood behind a well-dressed man carrying a toddler on her covered porch. They all sported small fake-ish smiles at first, and then their mouths and eyes dropped one by one. No one said a word, but the man stared intently into Stella's eyes.

"...well, what do you want?" she asked impatiently, looking from person to person trying to figure out who they were. One woman wore a huge gold cross on her neck. "Is this a church thing? I'm not religious. I mean, I believe in God, but I'm not going to give the church ten percent of what my husband makes every week, you know? I've got three kids, and I'd rather take them to Disneyland or some shit."

The man coughed and finally spoke. "No. No! Sorry, um, we are not a church group." He looked behind him. None of the women spoke or looked at Stella.

"Listen, I would love to tell you why we are here..." his Louisianan accent drawled "It's just that you got a big ol 'gater peeking out from your pond and I think it's scaring the ladies." Benny gave a small laugh and pointed at Stella's chest.

In her fit of rage...or while twerking...stomping up the stairs...or chasing away the dogs...one of her size G breasts had escaped from the too-small prison of her sports bra. Stella had stood in the doorway of her home hands on hips and scowling at these strangers with her titty out. *Good thing Mateo is downstairs*, she thought.

She grabbed a fleshy handful and stuffed it safely away. *"Qué vergüenza,"* Stella's cheeks flushed red. "My apologies, they're a lot to manage..." She shifted on her feet and crossed her arms. The other women finally began to make eye contact with her and mumbled weak greetings.

Benny smiled and shifted his fussy baby to the other hip. He felt the best way forward was to pretend the great escape never happened. "Look, sweetie, the reason we are here is because we want to talk about our kids. They got in trouble a few days ago, and from what we understand, your son

Mateo was with them. We are trying to figure out what's going on with all of them, do you have time for a quick chat?"

Stella's eyes narrowed. "What do you mean Mateo got in trouble?"

Isabella stepped forward. "Your name is Stella, right? You were listed as the guardian who took him home. I'm an off-duty sheriff's deputy. I helped bring them into the station...ironically my kid was also there."

It was clear the blood was boiling in Stella's face. Instinctually, Benny and the ladies took a single step back. She turned around and stormed into the house. A flurry of dogs rushed past her, outside through the legs of the visitors, and hid in the rose bushes. "Mateooooo! Where are you? Get out here now!"

A crash. A thud. A scrawny teenager with a backpack fell out of a window and took off running across the lawn and down the street. Stella shoved her way past Benny and through the women and stood on the lawn screaming, "Did you pay your Auntie to bail you out of jail? You little son of a bitch...she is just going to use it to buy pot! I AM GOING TO WHOOP YOUR ASS WHEN YOU COME HOME!" She took off a pink Croc and threw it down the street. "I'm not chasing you, you little bastard!"

He looked back, "Yeah cuz you can't run, fatty."

Benny and the rest of the group nodded at each other knowingly, taking this encounter as confirmation that Stella's son was also affected by the same issues as their children. They allowed Stella to huff for a few minutes before Charlotte stepped forward and gently put a hand on her shoulder. "I'm so sorry this happened, but that's why we are here. Ever since the night they got in trouble, our children have been mean and acting out of character."

Stella laughed. "Out of character? Honey, my son is *not* out of character. He always has been and always will be an *asshole*." She shook her head and whistled for the dogs. "Well, come inside. I'll make some daiquiris, and you can tell me what sort of hell our kids have been raising."

Stella motioned for the parents to follow her, and booped Finn's nose with a smile as she passed. She led them through a dated living room with brown dirty paneling and matted green-yellow carpet, then around the corner and into a stunning modern kitchen. Stainless steel appliances gleamed. Gray granite countertops mounted on pristine white cabinets. Woven baskets of limes, onions, and garlic hung from the ceiling. Stella began washing her hands in a farmhouse sink with a detachable sprayer that was over a foot deep.

"Stella, your kitchen is gorgeous!" Emily exclaimed, then smelled a vase of pink roses on the counter.

She dried her hands on a linen towel. "I know, right? My husband is a contractor. He's trying to start up his own company building houses. Right now, he is doing kitchen renovations while we are saving up capital. He's brilliant at what he does."

Mateo Sr. entered the kitchen with a big smile on his face upon overhearing the praise. He walked over to his wife, kissed her on the cheek, and said "*Estrella*, you didn't tell me you had friends." He held out his hand to shake Benny's.

"We're not friends. I don't have friends." Stella mumbled.

Benny laughed and shook Mateo's hand. "We're not friends *yet*."

As Mateo introduced himself, he explained that they do 'live and flips'--living in a house they are in the process of renovating before selling it for a profit.

"It's disruptive as all hell, you know?" Stella added. "There's always something being worked on, and our weekends are always spent on the house, but he can usually finish in about a year. Eventually, we'll make enough to hire a crew and don't have to live in the house while we flip it."

Mateo nodded. "Every big business starts small!"

Stella's tough exterior softened for just a moment as she watched her husband's enthusiasm for the work he's so proud of, and the hope in his eyes for an easier and more prosperous future. "Matty...these people are here because Junior got into trouble with the law. And he paid Sofia to bail him out."

Mateo's eyes widened. "Are...you...KIDDING ME?" He looked around at the group for an explanation.

"He was with our children as well. Apparently, they are friends and partners in mischief!" Charlotte giggled awkwardly.

Stella shrugged at Mateo. "Why don't I deal with it, okay? You've had a long week. Go watch the game and I'll fill you in later."

He sighed. "*O hijole*. Well, Stella is better suited for this sort of thing, so I'll let her handle it. It was really nice meeting all of you."

Lucy stepped forward to catch Mateo before he left, juggling Liam and then finally just setting him down to toddle around the dining room. "Excuse me, Mateo, before you leave can I get your business card? I've been thinking about renovating my kitchen, and maybe a few other areas of my home. Would you be interested in doing a consultation?"

Mateo beamed and grappled for his back pocket to extract a card from his wallet. "Of course!" He passed a card to Lucy. "I look forward to hearing from you and your husband."

With a wave at the group, he left the room and a few minutes later they heard the sound of a recliner kick out, a beer crack, and the roaring crowd of a Kansas City Chiefs game on the TV.

Stella brought out eight hurricane glasses and a blender. She passed a knife and four limes to Charlotte. "Stella, I see you put out eight glasses, but there are only six of us."

She placed a large bottle of white rum on the counter. "What, you think I'd forget about the babies?"

Charlotte's eyes grew wide.

"One is for Matty. Two are for me." Stella winked

"Oh…" Charlotte began sheepishly cutting lime wedges. "I see. Can you make mine a virgin? I'm driving."

Stella pulled a fresh container of strawberries from the fridge and rinsed it, then picked out two of the fattest and juiciest berries, cut the tops off, and handed one to each of the twins, who eagerly stuffed their faces. "What about you guys? Are you drinking?"

The group sat at the walnut dining room table watching Stella expertly throw ice, frozen strawberries, lemon and lime juice, sugar, and rum--without measuring--into an enormous blender.

"You really know your way around a daiquiri, Stella." Gemma observed.

Stella laughed. "Yeah, I used to be a bartender at a strip club. Part of the girls' pay was unlimited daiquiris. I never took advantage of that perk when I was a dancer though. It's hard enough to stay on the pole without being drunk, right? I don't know how they did it."

Sideways glances were exchanged as questions formed and were then interrupted by the blast of noise from the blender.

In the blink of an eye, eight glasses were filled with Sprite, then strawberry daiquiri mix, and a lime wedge. "Alright, let's go to the patio and get this party started. I'll drop one off to Matty and meet you out back, *amigas*. Okay?"

They grabbed their drinks in turn and headed through the sliding doors to a beautifully landscaped backyard. In the center of a circle of pavers was a fire pit and an outdoor pizza oven. Adirondack chairs and child-sized folding chairs surrounded it as if it were a place of worship. It was clearly a place their family enjoyed often.

"This is *not* what I expected to be doing this afternoon, but I've never been one to turn down free booze". Benny settled into a chair, took a sip of his daiquiri, and watched as the twins ran towards hummingbirds drinking from a brightly colored glass feeder. "A chance to put my feet up is rare these days too. Lucy, hunny, can you make sure they don't break that shit?"

Lucy sat down her drink after one sip. "How much am I getting paid, again?"

Stella emerged from the house a few minutes later, a drink in each hand, and settled next to Benny.

"How's the drinks? Normally it would be stronger but I'm pretty sure Junior drank some and filled it back up with water." Stella sipped from a fat straw.

"It's delicious!" they all agreed.

Stella looked over and saw Lucy herding the twins away from the bird feeder. "Oh, no. Don't put the babies in the grass. There's dog shit everywhere. Over there—"

"The trampoline?" asked Lucy hesitantly, looking to Benny for permission.

"Yeah," said Stella, waving her hand. "It's enclosed, they can't get out. Put them in there with some rubber balls. Zip it up. They'll be fine."

Lucy waited for Benny to object. Instead, he gave her a thumbs up and took another sip of his daiquiri.

"Alright," Stella sat up. "let's hear from Deputy Mom first. What did they do?"

All eyes turned to Isabella, who sat her daiquiri on the iron table between them.

"Well, I was called to a report of some teenagers possibly trespassing on private land. I found tracks leading through a cornfield into the forest, so I called my superior and we drove back.

"A cornfield?" Stella interrupted and sat up squinting her eyes in suspicion. "...and Mateo was there?"

Isabella flicked eyes to Benny. "Well, he was found with the others in the forest."

"Hmph." Isabella scowled. "Go on."

"When we arrived, Mateo was unconscious on the ground, evidently... my son hit him." Isabella looked down, unable to meet Stella's eyes.

It was Stella's turn to set down her drink. Isabella now had her full attention. "Well, that explains his face being busted up. He told me he fell off his bike."

"We spoke with the owner of the property...she believes they may have been looking for a cave on the property, but it's been closed up for safety. Mateo woke up in the ambulance and we took them all to the station. We spoke to who we thought was his mother..." Isabella gestured to Stella.

"That's my good-for-nothing sister, Sophia." Stella scowled.

Isabella squirmed under the heat of Stella's gaze despite being a law enforcement officer. "...she declined to press charges against my son...to which I'm very grateful."

Gemma spoke up to relieve Isabella from solely carrying the burden of parental guilt. "*All* of our children were behaving strangely the night we picked them up--"

"--and have been ever since," added Charlotte.

"They were dazed like they were on some kind of drug or something..." Emily pointed out. "That's why we're here. To see if you have any idea what's going on with all of our children. We don't even know where to start. We can't get anything out of them."

Stella pulled a pack of cigarettes and a lighter out of her sweaty sports bra, taking a moment to collect her thoughts while the rest stared at her expectantly.

"First of all, it seems unlikely Mateo would go anywhere near a cornfield…and a cave? No fuckin' way." Stella inhaled deeply on her cigarette.

The rest of the parents looked at each other not sure where this was going.

"Stella," said Benny in his smooth, disarming southern drawl, "we were all at the station. He was there. Why do you think he wouldn't be?"

She took a deep breath. "Because he fell in an old cistern when he was seven years old during Halloween in a corn maze. We didn't find him for three days. You can check the records if you want, deputy." Stella flicked her cigarette. "It wasn't even the search parties that found him…it was Bandito."

Upon hearing his name, a lanky white poodle came prancing from the bushes. "We were losing hope…everyone thought he was abducted and long gone. Out of desperation, we took the dogs out to the field…to see if they could smell him, you know? Bandito shot off like a bullet. We followed him to the far end of the maze, and he started barking at a pile of old stalks. We thought the worst. We expected a body. Then we heard crying. The hole was so small and covered up with debris… everyone missed it. Not Bandito." Stella scratched behind his ear. "This dog is special. He sees ghosts and shit, too."

Charlotte looked uncomfortable and chose to ignore the last part. "Stella…your son must have been very lucky. Aren't those cisterns usually filled with methane gas?"

Stella nodded. "Yup. Apparently, this one was really old…and shallow. But I wouldn't consider Mateo lucky. He's got claustrophobia because of it, been in therapy for ten years and it's still worse than ever, even though he tries to hide it from me. That's why I can tell you…my kid was *not* going in a damned cave."

Gemma sighed. "I don't understand. What were they all doing out there? Has Mateo been acting strange?"

"Hmm…" Stella considered the question. "He has been kind of cagey.

You know what? I think it's time I check his room."

She snuffed out her cigarette and looked around expectantly. "Well? Are you coming or not?"

Charlotte slowly shook her head no and said "Stella…that seems so invasive, I don't think it's our place to be there."

Stella laughed. "Are you kidding me, *amiga*? Rightfully raiding a teenager's bedroom is one of the few joys we have until they move the fuck out. This involves your kids, too, no? If there are no drugs, you have proof that Mateo had nothing to do with this. If he does have drugs…you can watch me beat his ass with a flip-flop."

Lucy stayed with the twins, climbing inside the trampoline and letting them bounce and tumble and kick her in the face.

Uncomfortable being an accomplice to raiding a stranger's child's bedroom, the parents hesitantly filed into the house. Stella seemed nonplussed.

"Who wants to take bets on what we find? I've got ten dollars on titty magazines." Stella said as she led the march through the kitchen.

"I'm pretty sure people use the internet now…," said Gemma. "If he's hanging out with my kid, I've got ten bucks on a full-body costume of an animal."

Stella turned to Gemma and squinted. "…what?", then seemed to decide she wasn't interested, and continued to the back of the main level of the home until they reached a door with a poster of a blonde woman with an eyeball on it. It said "Set it Off: Elsewhere"

Stella pointed at the poster. "Junior's into weird shit. But that's his normal weird shit. We're looking for extra weird shit." She jiggled the handle. It was locked.

"Damnit, Mateo!" she turned around and assessed Benny. "You look like somebody with a credit card. Let me borrow it."

Benny was so surprised at the request that he automatically extracted his wallet and handed it to her. Stella promptly went to work jimmying the lock. After a few jiggles, it popped open.

"Thanks…" Stella read the name on the credit card. "Benjamin."

Benny shoved the card back into his wallet. "…no problem, I guess?"

Stella walked around the room like a cat in a dirty litterbox. "What is that smell? Ugh!" She continued to sniff until she found a brown stain on the floor next to Mateo's bed. "His dad installed this carpet last month and he's already stained it. Boys will destroy every goddamn thing you own, I swear."

Charlotte stepped toward Stella and gestured at the bedpost. "I think that rosary is my husband's. It was hanging on the rearview mirror of his car… the one they used to trespass that night."

Stella removed it from the post and studied it in her hands. "A rosary? That is definitely weird. We're Catholic, but not religious… I don't think we've ever taken Mattie to church." Something suddenly softened in Stella, and for a moment she seemed genuinely worried. She returned the rosary to Charlotte, but Charlotte hung it back on the bed.

"Why don't you all check his dressers and the closet? I'll get the bathroom and around his bed." Stella instructed.

Hesitantly the others dug through Mateo's belongings while Stella inspected the bathroom and complained about the moldy wet towels on the floor. When Stella emerged, Charlotte held out a devil-horned hoodie she found in the closer. "What about this? It seems…Satanic."

Stella shook her head. "Normal weird."

Charlotte returned the hoodie to the closet, holding it with two fingers as if it were dripping with sin.

"What about this?" Benny pulled a short sword out of Mateo's underwear drawer. It looked sharp and was engraved with runes.

"Oh hey, a replica of Sting!" Gemma said cheerfully.

Again, Stella shook her head. "Nerd shit. Normal weird."

Isabella pulled a gallon storage bag out of the closet. Inside was something rolled in a paper towel. "My police nose thinks this might be something."

Stella snatched it from her and swiftly dumped the contents on Mateos bed. Carefully she unwrapped the paper towel bundle as the other stood near and watched.

Inside were the skulls of twenty-five different small animals.

"Oh, Jesus!" Charlotte crossed her chest. "Your son's a sociopath."

Stella did not appear insulted, but she did seem surprised by the contents. "Okay, *this* is extra weird shit."

"…Stella?" said Emily quietly. She was slowly leafing through the pages of a sketchbook on the bedside table. Her face was pale.

Stella took the book from Emily and her face also turned white. "What the hell is this? Murdered women? This last page…skulls and bones. Who is Mariah?"

"Mom? What are you doing in my room…with all these people?" Mateo's eyes were huge, and he looked ready to bolt when he saw Stella with the sketchbook in her hands.

Her reaction surprised everyone. She didn't yell. She gently sat the sketchbook on the bed and slowly approached her son with a soft smile. "Hey… Mateenio…" She walked slowly and wrapped an arm over his shoulder. "My friends were just leaving. *You* have an appointment with Dr. Montgomery today at the hospital. Why don't you put your bag down? We need to leave right now, okay?"

The others took the hint and quietly slipped out of the room. Emily was last to leave, and Stella grabbed her by the arm. "On your way out, give your phone number to Mattie Sr so we can talk later, and tell him to come back here please." Emily nodded. When she found Mateo, he sensed the urgency in her voice and jumped from his recliner. She wrote her number on a piece of junk mail and left it on the kitchen table before meeting the others outside.

Charlotte was in a tailspin.

"I've seen enough to know exactly what's happening! This is the hand of Satan and he is playing with our children like puppets!"

"Slow down, Charlie. Maybe the kids just got into magic mushrooms or something…let's not jump to Satan right out the gate, sweetie." said Benny, attempting to quell a religious meltdown.

"The skulls! The drawings! All our kids are angry and mean and dressing like animals—" Charlotte stammered.

"--actually only my kid is a Furry as far as I know." Pointed out Gemma.

"Mine *killed* some animals." Benny admitted. "My chickens."

The group fell silent as they considered the ridiculous possibility that their children were possessed.

Charlotte nodded in vindication. "Let's go to church."

# Chapter 11
## Take Me to Church

"Lucy! Get over here with those babies and be my beard!"

Benny gestured Lucy forward, who lingered in the back of the group at the bottom of the church stairs with a double stroller and an overloaded diaper bag. She'd been thrown in the deep end of nannying as Benny organized their parental detective agency but jumped to attention, and pushed the stroller up the wheelchair accessibility ramp to his side.

Benny paused as she handed him the diaper bag, and gently touched Lucy's perfectly rolled hair, which had staying in place despite spending the day hauling twins babies all over Springfield. "Lucy, I don't think I've properly appreciated how goddamn gorgeous you are. I am so proud to have you as my fake wife."

Lucy smiled and curtseyed. "You're not too bad looking yourself, husband."

"We make some adorable babies, too." He peeked in the stroller at his sons who were both asleep with milky spit bubbles in the corners of their mouths. "Let me know if my gay is showing, okay? Gemma! Put that necklace in your bra. I'd like to leave this church without being drawn and quartered."

Gemma scowled but removed her pentacle necklace and stuffed it down her black bra, she turned to Charlotte. "Are you seriously taking me--a *witch*-- into a Catholic church? And you want me to tell them what, exactly? That my nonbinary child is being possessed by a demon that compels them to dress like a rabbit?"

"Yes! We have to save our children's souls, Gemma!" Charlotte moved to the front of the pack and turned around to address them. "Catholics have a direct line to Mary, Mother of Jesus Christ. They have the most powerful faith and are therefore most capable of breaking demonic influence."

"...Charlie, what if our kids just got into drugs or something? The priests won't help." Emily pointed out.

Charlotte nodded. "Listen, I went on a deep dive into Father Gabriele Amorth's books. He's a famous exorcist and wrote all about possessions and demonic influences. If they are on drugs, that could be part of it! The symptoms you've all described sound like oppression...not to mention Mateo's drawings! We need help. I've known Father Ezra for nearly ten years. He has a duty to help all of God's children afflicted by sin!"

During Charlotte's impassioned speech, she didn't notice the door behind her opening. Behind her stood a confused man in his late thirties with ashy brown hair and the kind of light blue-green eyes that sparkle in the sun.

"Charlotte...is everything okay?" the priest tried to assess the situation by visually considering the group of people individually but seemed to lack a cohesive conclusion.

Charlotte jumped and turned to him, while the rest grew silent and clustered together behind her as if to protect themselves from judgment by this holy man. "Father Ezra! I need to speak to Bishop Vincent."

Sensing Charlotte's urgency and rising panic, he expertly met her with the opposite, and calmly stepping forward with a smile, he laid a hand on her shoulder. "Well, you lucked out because he's here today helping me plan this month's homily. Since my office is rather small--and I can see you brought some friends with you--why don't we go downstairs to the children's church and you can talk to me first so I can help you when we approach the Bishop?"

Charlotte nodded enthusiastically as tears welled in her eyes. The others followed as Father Ezra led them through the foyer. Gemma took the rear, with her arms cautiously out low at her sides as if sensing the energy and expecting flames of hell to shoot up from the hardwood floors and consume her.

They were led by Father Ezra to a door with a wooden sign of a lamb. "Unfortunately, the children's church isn't wheelchair or stroller accessible, so you'll have to carry the babies down. I hope to have the funds to remedy that soon...but it's an old church. There's always something else that takes priority." He gestured for the others to follow Charlotte and he waited for them to pass, giving each a reassuring smile. When Emily passed, they both stopped and considered each other for a moment.

"Do I know you, Father?" questioned Emily.

"You do look familiar! I'm not sure..." he laughed. "Maybe it will come to me. In the meantime, let's see if I can help all of you."

They maneuvered down a narrow, creaky staircase with old greenish carpet to the children's church. Benny and Lucy sat the twins in a corner of the room with a wooden playhouse that was a recreation of Noah's Ark. A stuffed toy Jesus stood at the helm like a sea captain. Benny smirked at Lucy as they helped pull plastic chairs to the center of the room, where they formed a circle on the alphabet rug.

Father Ezra positioned his chair next to Emily, but across from Charlotte. "Well, first things first: I'm Father Ezra, and it's nice to meet all of you. Charlotte, who did you bring with you today?"

She coughed and sat up straight attempting to collect herself. "These are the parents of my son Oliver's friends. We're just getting to know each other. That's Ben, Lucy--ehem...and their twins--"

"Liam and Finn," said Lucy, settling into her fake wife/mom roll with ease. Benny grinned.

"--Isabella...or should I say Lieutenant Kentworth?" Charlotte continued.

"Isabella's fine." She said as she gave Father Ezra a polite grin.

"And that's Gemma and Emily." Charlotte finished.

As she pointed to Emily, Father Ezra's eyes grew wide. "I remember you now."

She cocked her head and turned his face over in her mind. Those eyes looked so familiar, but she still couldn't place who he was.

Before Emily could respond, Charlotte spouted her words out like a steaming teakettle. "Father...I'm afraid our children are under a demonic influence."

Father Ezra pulled himself away from Emily and momentarily broke clergyman mode as he tried to process what Emily had said. "Wait...what?"

"Charlie, that's quite a concern. Demonic influence isn't like what you see in the movies...and it's often some other condition causing the person to--"

"No, it's demons! I know it! I feel it in my gut. The Holy Spirit is rolling inside of me telling me something is wrong." Charlotte tilted forward rocking on the edge of her plastic chair looking as if she were about to fall off and start praying on her knees.

Father Ezra tried to diffuse the situation. "Okay, Charlotte. It's okay. Why don't you tell me what's going on with Oliver?"

"He didn't show up for his AP finals!" Charlotte dropped this as if it were the most scandalous thing a child could've possibly done.

As if reading the priest's mind, the rest of the group looked at each other, and Isabella spoke up. "There's more to it Charlie, isn't there? Why don't you tell him the rest?"

Charlotte nodded. "Ever since our kids were found out in the woods, he's been acting strange...staying up late, losing weight, snapping at the family. These foreign language classes were so important to him--he wants to go to school abroad.

When Brent and I went to pick him up from his test, we brought the whole family. We just *knew* he passed because he'd studied so hard, and we wanted to surprise him by going out for fro-yo. When he didn't come out of the school, I went in to speak to the instructor and he said he never showed up for the exam and he hadn't received any homework from him for a week! His father and I went into full panic mode. First, checked where we dropped him off in the morning. We found him at the back of the building…with a couple of… well, *hooligans.*" Charlotte crossed her chest. "They ran off when they saw me… and Oliver…he was *high*. He wouldn't tell us what he used! Oliver Couldn't even *walk*. Brent practically carried him to the van. We brought him home, put him in bed, and started praying over him…"

Father Ezra listened very intently. "Go on, Charlotte. I am not here to judge you or Oliver. I want to help, and I've known Oliver for a long time. You're right. That doesn't seem like something he would do."

Tears streamed down her face. "Thank you…but when we prayed over him, he got so *angry*. He started cursing at us, calling me such foul names I can't repeat them. This is not my boy. This is *not* my boy!"

"I can understand why you would think this is the influence of Satan, but I have to say, all the things you describe could also be the result of whatever drug he's been taking." Compassion filled Father Ezra's eyes. "I'm more than willing to come to your home and perform a blessing on Oliver, but I would hesitate to call this demonic."

"He knew things he shouldn't." Charlotte hung her head to the ground. "About me…my past. The hateful things he said…no one else knew."

All eyes turned to Charlotte as she revealed this. Father Ezra raised an eyebrow.

"When we prayed over him…his eyes rolled back so far in his head they were white. Brent and I…I'm afraid to admit this but that night we locked him in his room while we figured out how to help him…the next day, Benny called." She turned to him.

Benny cleared his throat. "Look, you're about to hear a whole collective of crazy shit—*stuff*--about our kids. My oldest son is being a mean little *tatataille*, too. It's been ever since that night they were found in the woods. The last straw for me…he killed my chickens. Lopped their heads right off and tossed their bodies on the ground without a hint of remorse."

"Uh…okay. That…is certainly something." Said Father Ezra, who unconsciously began wringing his hands.

"Yeah, especially since he's a go…*sh darn* vegan!" Benny waved his hands dramatically. Lucy elbowed him and he quickly put them back in his lap. "Also, I swear this child has cursed me. I'm having the worst luck imaginable. If something can go wrong, it does. I got into a car accident. I got bit by a rabbit--twice. I tripped down the stairs, which is how I got \*this\* lovely lump on my head. And on and on."

"I see…" The wheels seemed to be turning in Father Ezra's mind. "And what about you, Emily? Your child was with them in the woods as well?"

She blushed red. "Um, yes. My daughter, Esme. She's been uncharacteristically mean and inconsiderate to others. Also…she's been dressing *provocatively*. It's out of the norm for her. I'm concerned because I found a huge stack of money in her dresser when I put her laundry away--way more than her usual tips from Sonic. She couldn't possibly be…"

Father Ezra held up his hand to stop her. "I understand. It's okay. We will get to the bottom of this together. And you? Gemma, right?"

Gemma squirmed under the holy light of Father Ezra, unsure how to frame her response. "Well, after we picked them up at the police station, Trix seemed really down for quite a few days. They wouldn't take calls from friends and barely came out of their room to visit with family. Trix struggled with depression before but we--her dads and I--thought it was under control. I recognized the signs that Trix was sinking--withdrawal, bad mood, not eating, not interested in things they usually do like Magic…the game! *Not* witchcraft!"

The priest gave a reassuring smile. "Believe it or not, I was a teenager once and actually played the game before I joined the church. So, beyond mood changes, did anything else occur with Trix?"

The room felt uncomfortable for Gemma, knowing she felt embarrassed to say. "I convinced Trix to go for a run. It's one of the ways they cope with anxiety. Trix left in the afternoon and didn't return until four the next morning…then came to the door…dressed in a fursuit."

Father Ezra furrowed his brows. "A what?"

"Full costume of a rabbit. Carrot and all."

Taking a beat, Father Ezra finally said, "Do you mean…like a Furry?"

The group tried to conceal smiles due to the seriousness of the situation but couldn't help being amused that this priest knew what a Furry was.

"Yeah." Gemma sunk into her chair.

"Being a Furry isn't in itself an indication of demonic influence. It's a legitimate hobby like Magic the Gathering, or anything else. Have they ever shown interest in this before that night?" he asked.

"No. Never. She-they-weren't with anyone they usually hang out with…they've been avoiding their old friends." Explained Gemma.

"I noticed you corrected your pronoun usage, is it correct for me to assume there are some gender changes here? Is that new?" Father Ezra did not appear to come from a judgmental place, but rather one of collecting facts.

Gemma shook her head no. "Trix is nonbinary. It's not a new identity. Fully embracing it last year improved their mental health dramatically. These current changes are so uncharacteristic. They're usually so bright and cheery. The weird part for me…they are completely *obsessed* with the Furry stuff. I got a notice from the bank that Trix overdrew their account…they paid a thousand dollars for the rabbit suit to someone named Gator Greg. And all day every day Trix is sewing and altering this thing, trying to make it perfect. I don't know what to do, it's like it's consumed their every thought."

Father Ezra nodded thoughtfully and gently turned to Isabella. "And what is the name of your child, Isabella?"

"Theo. He's a boxer…a prodigy, really. Training for the Olympics." Despite her worry, she couldn't hide the pride in her voice at that statement. "When we found the kids in the woods out on private property, he had punched one of the other kids--Mateo--hard enough to knock him out cold. When Theo's not in the ring, we call him Teddy Bear. He's not the type to be aggressive in everyday life, especially to his friends. If something bothers him, he banks it for the ring just like I taught him to do. Afterward, he wouldn't tell me why he did it."

"So, there was a fight between Theo and Mateo?" Father Ezra asked.

Isabella shrugged. "I don't know. Mateo's family declined to press charges, so I assumed it was a normal teenage boy scuffle. Until yesterday…" Isabella straightened her shirt attempting to compose herself.

The rest exchanged glances, as Isabella was about to reveal new information to them as well.

"Theo...nearly killed someone in the ring."

Gasps filled the room. Father Ezra sat up and focused his attention on Isabella. "Were you there? Did you see what he looked like as he hurt the person?"

"I wasn't there. My husband said he was being too aggressive and tried to take him out of the ring. There was a scuffle, and Tyler accidentally got his jaw broken by the guy Theo was fighting. From what the others in the gym said--my husband was knocked out-- he went into a blind rage, and they couldn't pull him off the other guy. Theo hit him on the back of the head; it's fighting dirty and he knows it. You can kill or paralyze someone with a rabbit punch. Theo...*normal Theo*...would never fight dirty, even at his worst." Isabella's eyes pleaded with the priest as if trying to convince him her son wasn't a bad person.

"Oh, Izzy. I'm so sorry!" Emily said. "Is everyone going to be okay?"

Isabella sighed. "Like I said, Tyler got a fractured jaw, but he's okay and recovering at home. He's been hit plenty in the ring and will be back to normal in a few months. Tyler...well, the owner of the gym had to hit him with a fire extinguisher across the side of the head to make him stop. He was released yesterday with a concussion and a black and blue face."

It was clear the priest was becoming very concerned by the collective behavior of the teenagers. "...and his opponent?"

"He may not make it." Isabella swallowed hard.

"Oh no..." said Gemma as she took a hand from her mouth. "Does that mean Theo could face charges?"

Isabella looked away in shame. "Normally in a boxing match, the fighters can't be charged for hurting someone unless it was clearly with intent to kill or maim...and let me put it this way--Big Hefty is a family friend who's trained three generations of Kentworth fighters. The other guy is here illegally *on his dime.* As far as everyone is concerned, it was an accident."

Uncomfortable glances were exchanged. The depth of what was happening seemed deeper when all the parents shared their stories together.

Father Ezra coughed. "Based on everything you've shared with me I can understand why all of you are considering demonic influence. I won't say for certainty that's what this is, but I want to start by saying I am more than willing to perform blessings on all of your children with the Bishop's help if he's willing. I have a few more questions before we speak with him. Isabella, you mentioned another boy, the one Theo knocked out when you arrested them. Why aren't Mateo's parents here?"

Benny spoke up to give Isabella a chance to compose herself. "We spoke with his mother, Stella. She says he hasn't been acting any differently, besides not sleeping. She found a bag of animal skulls in his closet, and a sketchbook next to his bed filled with drawings of women being murdered. And a cave."

The priest's eyes grew wide. "And where is Mateo now?"

"I spoke to Stella a few hours ago. She said they were taking him to the hospital. That's all I know." Said Emily.

The twins giggled as they dumped out a pile of blocks, babbling at each other as if they were conspiring in mischief.

"What can all of you tell me about the place where they trespassed?" he asked.

"I was the only one there," said Isabella. "It's an old trail through a cornfield and a forest. The owner said there is a cave on the property they may have been looking for, but it's been closed up. We don't think they actually found it though…"

"A cave like Mateo drew in his sketchbook?" pointed out Benny.

Clarity dawned on the group. Charlotte spoke up. "Do you think…they found the cave? Do you think something is in there?"

The steps creaked from across the room as Bishop Vincent descended. "Father Ezra, there you are. I didn't realize we had guests today, but when I saw the stroller by the stairs, I figured I'd find someone down here."

Father Ezra stood up and so did the others. "Bishop, I was just about to seek you out myself. This is one of the members of our church, Charlotte.

She stepped forward and shook his hand, then wiped mascara from under her eyes. The bishop noticed and began assessing the room. "Nice to meet you Charlotte."

"She's brought some friends to speak to us today." the priest gestured to the group. "They are not members of the church, but are the parents of some friends of her son, Oliver. Please, Bishop. Would you mind sitting with us for a moment?"

He nodded and gingerly sat in the chair, looking as if he'd just wandered into a bear's den.

"In short…Oliver--and his friends--are in need of a blessing. Or possibly more." Said Father Ezra.

Bishop Vincent scowled as if he sensed what he was being asked. "What are you asking me for? Surely you can't mean—"

"I've already screened them, Bishop." Interrupted Father Ezra. "I wouldn't approach you with this request if it didn't meet the criteria. It does… for multiple entities. A simple blessing by just one priest is probably not enough."

"The church doesn't do that anymore, Father. You know that." The bishop scoffed.

Father Ezra hardened his face. "They do in Italy. I've seen it performed during my studies in Europe. What these parents described is eerily similar to what I've seen."

The bishop looked down his nose at the priest. "Well in case you didn't notice, this isn't Europe. They're a superstitious bunch in Italy. In America, we know better. Ninety-nine percent of the time what parents think is a child possessed is ADHD, or a teenager who got into drugs and a bad crowd. Bad parenting is a more likely culprit in most circumstances than Satan!"

The room grew deadly quiet until Gemma stood up in her defiant witchy glory. "I'm not going to stand here and listen to this. I've done everything possible to raise a good human being! I would never in a million years be at this church standing in front of you if this situation wasn't so unbelievably strange, and Trix's behavior so unusual that I was desperate for any solution."

Gemma grabbed her black bat-shaped handbag from the wall and stomped up the stairs. The room was quiet as everyone listened to Gemma's Doc Martens stomp across the ceiling and the front door of the church slam shut.

Anger glowed in Father Ezra's normally kind eyes for the sake of the parents who sought his help. "I've known Charlotte and her son a long time. She and her husband are the best parents to their six children I have *ever* met. I worked for Emily and her husband many years ago, and they are good people, too. And from my brief time with the rest of these parents, I can tell they care deeply about the salvation of their children and do not want the will of Satan to take hold of their hearts!"

Bishop Vincent stood with an air implying that he had better things to do than listen to them. "If these parents wish for the salvation of their children, then the solution is simple. They must give their hearts to Jesus Christ and bring their children to mass every week. They should repent their sins. They should pray every morning and night and teach their children to live by the word of the Bible. That is the only protection against evil. Devilish behavior cannot grow in the hearts and minds of those who have given themselves to Jesus. It's ridiculous to assume every dysfunctional youth is possessed by the devil when the solution is a God-centered home. I will leave you all now with the wise words of Mother Teresa- "If you want to change the world, go home and love your family." I suggest you do that, and then attend mass this Sunday. Whatever troubles your homes will be fixed by God."

"Bishop—" Father Ezra stood to stop him.

He held out a hand at the Father as if repelling him with divinity. "Enough. If you will excuse me, I have a meeting."

With the swift swish of his robes, the bishop left as quickly as he arrived, leaving Father Ezra and the group in a confused stupor.

"I'm sorry. I didn't expect him to be so...unkind." Father Ezra said. "I will still help you the best I can despite the disapproval of my superior. I believe your children are experiencing signs of oppression. Maybe not full possession... but certainly some sort of influence. Demonic entities will chisel away at their victim's weaknesses until they can be fully claimed."

The father removed his own rosary beads and walked around the room removing various crosses from the walls and tables. He gave Charlotte, Isabella, and Emily one each. "Put it under their bed. Don't let them see it."

He then approached Benny and Lucy. "Taking the lives of animals seems advanced, I'd like you to take my rosary. I bless it every day. Hide it under his mattress." Then Father Ezra strode across the room and grabbed the stuffed toy of Jesus from the helm of Noah's Ark. "For the babies…just in case."

Lucy hugged the Jesus to her chest with wide eyes and nodded. "I hope these will lessen any demonic influence while I develop a strategy. It would be easier if I had someone more knowledgeable to help me, but since Bishop Vincent is unwilling I will do my best. I want to be clear--*this is not an exorcism.* Exorcisms require approval from the Church, and they seldom give it. I need as much information as possible about the events leading up to these changes. Do you think the parents of Mateo would be willing to speak to me?"

Emily pulled her phone from her bag to retrieve the number. "I have a text from Stella. They took Mateo to Willow Creek Hospital."

"Willow Creek? Where's that?" Benny asked.

"It's just outside of town…" said Lucy, her eyes telling Benny there was more to the story.

Father Ezra nodded in understanding. "It's a mental hospital."

# Chapter 12
## Willow Creek Hospital

Mateo Sr. and Stella tailed behind the ambulance carrying their protesting teenage son down a winding tree-lined driveway that led to a sprawling single-level hospital. A single level, in case anyone was tempted to jump out a window.

"How much do you think that ambulance ride cost?" Stella asked her husband as they parked in front of the building. The ambulance drove to the rear, where family isn't allowed, they were told.

Mateo Sr. pursed his lips in thought. "…three hundred?"

"Sounds right." Stella agreed. "I don't understand why they wouldn't just let us drive him here."

"Stella, like the doctor said it's for safety. They don't want him trying to jump out of the car while it's moving." Mateo said weakly. How much more could he and his wife do for Junior?

Stella cracked the window and lit a cigarette before they went inside. "He wouldn't do that."

Mateo Sr. removed the keys from the ignition and fidgeted with them. "We also didn't think he'd have a bag of animal skulls in his closet."

Stella took one deep puff of her barely lit cigarette and threw it out the window. "Let's go inside."

The long sidewalk led through a park-like lawn framed with small evergreen trees. They opened the first set of doors and entered a small room surrounded by windows. The next set of doors was locked. Stella looked around. She could see an empty waiting room, a water cooler, and a wall of small lockers. In the corner sat a table with a bottle of hand sanitizer and a mask. Above it was a camera.

"Hello?" Mateo Sr. waved at the camera. "Are you going to let us in? You have our kid in an ambulance."

A disheveled woman in scrubs shuffled to the door, unlocked and pushed it open. "Sorry about that. I was getting Mateo's paperwork ready. First, we will get you checked in, then you can take a seat."

They were led through the waiting room and around the corner to a small booth. "Go ahead and write your names down and then I'll need you to put your belongings in this tray." She slapped a tan plastic bedpan in front of them. "Wallet, watches, cell phones, hair clips, earrings, belts, bracelets, keys. Pretty much anything that can be stolen or used to cause harm to oneself or another…which is pretty much anything."

Stella and Mateo obeyed until she got to her wallet. "I don't want to leave my wallet around for anyone to take it."

The attendant gave an understanding smile. "Of course. All visitors are given a locker to use while they're here." She passed a small metal key to Mateo Sr. "…but you need to leave the key with me after you lock your items. Number ten, over there."

Stella reached down at her feet and put a plastic shopping bag of clothes on the counter. "What about Junior's things? They told me to bring clothes."

The attendant nodded. "I'll go through them to make sure everything is allowed while you place your items in the locker."

Mateo Sr. and Stella exchanged a glance. "Allowed?" Stella whispered. "It's sweatpants."

After they placed their items in the locker and returned the key to the attendant she said, "Okay so a lot of these items are not allowed. They can only have three days' worth of tops, bottoms, underwear and socks. Two sets of sleepwear. One jacket. One pair of slippers or clog-type shoes. Otherwise, we will supply them with grippy socks, but they have to wear them even outside in the courtyard."

"Alright," Stella was becoming testy, never being a person fond of rules and regulations. She kicked off her pink crocs and passed them across the counter. "Give him these. So what else can't he have?"

The attendant cautiously took the pink shoes and marked them on a sheet of paper. "Well, he can't have gym shorts." She shoved them back in the plastic bag.

"That's like 95% of a teenage boy's wardrobe, why not?" Stella barked.

The attendant cleared her throat. "Well, let me put it this way. This is a co-ed facility and sometimes the patients touch each other inappropriately."

Mateo Sr. blushed and mumbled something like *that's understandable.*

"Also, these sweatpants have a string. He can keep them if you allow me to cut it out, but they might be too big." The attendant picked up a small pair of scissors out of a lock box she had sitting next to her, evidently doing this regularly.

Stella shifted her weight to one foot. "Go for it. Otherwise, he'll be in his goddamn underwear. Is he allowed to wear those?"

She pulled out a neatly folded stack. "Only three. I'll allow you to choose which to keep. He *will* have access to a laundry facility during his stay."

Stella picked through the stack and chose the most colorful ones--cats with mustaches, chili peppers, Christmas reindeer. "Good luck getting him to do laundry."

She passed back the demon-horned Set It Off hoodie. "Nothing with zippers, hoods, or buttons. It needs to be a pullover."

"Why?" asked Mateo Sr.

The attendant finally realized Stella and Mateo Sr. were not experienced in the arena of adolescent mental health facilities. For most parents, this was a repeat occurrence. "You'd be surprised at how creative people can be when they want to hurt themselves. We are very strict in the adolescent ward."

Mateo and Stella deflated at the thought of their son in a place like this. The doctor said it was the best and fastest way for him to be evaluated and treated. "So…he has a couple of t-shirts, some underwear and socks? How long is he going to be here?"

"That's something that will be decided by the doctor. I have to keep these items behind the desk until after you are done with intake, due to the plastic bag and everything. However, tomorrow is visiting day so you can bring your son more clothing--no more than three days' worth, no strings, zippers, or hoods. Must be pants. Go ahead and sign this sheet acknowledging Mateo's belongings at check-in."

The attendant flipped the clipboard and passed it to Stella. She scribbled and returned it. "Now I have to wand you. Stand in the hallway with your arms out at your sides. It will only take a moment."

She exited and locked the booth, swiping Mateo Sr. head to toe first, and then Stella down to her bare feet. "Do I need to squat and cough, too?"

"Nope. That's only for female patients." Said the attendant with a straight face.

"I was only joking…" Stella said with raised eyebrows. A parental panic was slowly creeping into her mind. *What have I done? My boy doesn't belong here. He's never hurt anyone. How could I bring him to this place?* Typically cool, she felt her very old enemy, anxiety, creeping up. "Hey, where's the restroom?"

The attendant reached under the counter and pulled out a key fastened to a piece of wood, then handed it to Stella. "It's just past the lockers. You can have a seat in the waiting room after you're finished. Just drop the key off on your way to intake."

Matco Sr. busied himself filling a paper cup at the water cooler while Stella left to compose herself in the restroom. She opened the door, and the lights automatically came on. No switches. She sat on the toilet and put her head between her knees taking deep breaths. *It's the best thing for him. I've done everything I can. This is bigger than me. Bigger than his regular doctor. He's strong, he'll get through this. He needs help.*

Stella reached for toilet paper to wipe her eyes and found that the toilet paper had no roller--there was a small round cubby where the toilet paper (without a cardboard tube) was placed. *What the hell can a kid do with a toilet paper holder?* She tried not to play out scenarios and wiped her eyes. There was no trash can either. Just a paper bag on the floor.

She grabbed the key and stomped out of the bathroom to her husband. As soon as he saw her, he knew she was struggling. After twenty years of marriage, he was one of the few people who could read Stella's actual mood and intentions behind her typically callous exterior. He put his arms around her, and she laid her head on his chest.

"Was I too hard on him?" Stella asked. "Or not hard enough?"

Mateo thought for a moment. "I think we've done the best we could, and that Junior has a good heart…he went through something traumatic as a kid. Nobody would come out of that the same."

"Do you think he's traumatized enough to be a serial killer or something?" she asked.

"No, *mama*. No way. I don't know what those drawings are about. The doctors will help. He's spiky on the outside like a cactus to protect himself… inside is nothing but clear water. Just like his *madre*."

"Mateo…I'm pretty sure that's a myth. There's like…acid and shit inside that makes you throw up. Cactus juice is toxic."

"Are you Mateo's parents?" A woman asked from across the room. She was wearing a pantsuit, but a pair of black rubber clogs instead of heels. "Please come back with me to intake."

They were led down a dimly lit hallway past a series of heavy doors with digital keypads on them. Somewhere deeper in the building was a cacophony of raised voices, and someone issuing warnings to quiet down.

They stopped at a door different from the rest only in that it had faded decal of a yellow flower on it and the word "hope" written in cursive below. The woman first swiped her ID badge in the lock, and then entered a code. She opened the door and she said "My name is Jolene. I'm Mateo's intake nurse. Please take a seat."

The only thing in the room between the two locked doors on either side was a round table and four chairs with rounded edges. Mateo Sr. and the woman sat, but when Stella attempted to pull the chair out further to accommodate her size it wouldn't move. She tugged hard, and it *ever so slightly* moved an inch. Stella squeezed her round body into the space between the chair and table the best she could.

"Sorry about that…" Jolene said. "The table and chairs are weighted for safety. You, know, so they can't be thrown."

Stella looked to her husband for reassurance that they were doing the right thing, but his eyes were on the table. He had lined up the four fingers of his right hand into four fingernail-width scratches on the surface in front of him.

Jolene plopped an inch-thick folder on the table and two pens. "Right now, Mateo is being evaluated to determine his most urgent needs, and whether he is potentially aggressive, so we know which roommate to place him with. Fortunately, we have a smaller crowd right now--around 30 youth--and none of them are exceptionally difficult. It's my understanding your son isn't violent?"

Mateo Sr. snapped back to attention. "No, not at all."

"Okay...we don't typically take adolescents with major aggression issues. It's actually very difficult to find facilities that *do* in this area. At Willow Creek, most of our patients have issues with addiction, suicidal ideation, and depression. Mateo will be thoroughly evaluated during his time here and speak with a psychiatrist daily to determine his needs as we progress toward stabilization. The average stay is nine days. Does Mateo have health insurance?"

"Yes, and his brother made sure we met our out-of-pocket max last month when he broke his leg. Go ahead and give Mattie the king's treatment... just don't keep him past January!" Stella gave a weak smile, which Jolene returned.

"I'll need a copy of his insurance card and both your IDs so I can verify his coverage...but before we do that and begin paperwork there is one aspect of in-patient facility stays that I would like to explain to you both so you can understand and agree to our process." Said Jolene, as she began unclipping and sorting her stack of papers.

"Uh, okay...go on." Stella said.

"As I've mentioned, the average stay is nine days. I've seen a few kids go home in three--but that is a rarity. A lot of them stay longer, maybe a month or so. It depends on how responsive they are to treatment. After a month, if they are still not progressing, they will likely need extended care at a long-term facility." Jolene paused to make sure Mateo Sr. and Stella were still on board. "You agree so far?"

"Yeah...I mean, whatever Mattie needs." Said Stella.

"Okay, good." Jolene continued. "The most important thing we require parents to understand is this document here..." Jolene pushed a piece of paper and two pens toward them. "What it says is that once Mateo is admitted into

Willow Creek Hospital, *he cannot be released without doctor approval.* It's saying you agree that Mateo must stay until it is safe for him to leave; his release will only happen when it is determined by the medical staff that he is no longer a danger to himself or others. The reason we do this is because often parents become upset after a few days, usually with guilt or worry, and show up pounding on the doors at two in the morning demanding we release their child. Legally, we can't do that."

Stella sat back, looking at the paper like it was on fire. "I don't like the sound of that."

"I understand. No one does." Jolene said. "I want to stress that your child will be allowed to call you whenever they like--within reason, of course. You will be allowed one-hour visits twice a week. You are also allowed to write postal letters. There is no technology allowed here so no texting or email, but there is still contact. All of this is for everyone's own good. Mateo will be released with a medical evaluation and diagnosis, set up with a regular therapist and psychiatrist, and medication if needed. At Willow Creek Hospital, we teach coping tools and strategies for managing negative behavior. Does Mateo smoke or vape that you know of?"

"Not that I know of. Stella?" Mateo deferred to Stella.

"I don't think so...but who knows?" Stella shrugged.

"Well, if Mateo is honest with us, we even have a successful smoking and vape cessation program. A yoga teacher visits twice a week to teach the patients breathing techniques that mimic vaping. It can trick the brain into thinking it has a vape hit without actually taking one." Jolene swelled with pride as she shared this.

"That's great but Mattie doesn't vape. He's here because he has animal skulls in his closet and drawings of murdered women in a sketchbook." Stella said stone-faced.

"Oh," Jolene skimmed through the intake forms, evidently missing that piece of information about her son. "Well...the yoga techniques are just an example of the programs we have available here. My point is, Mateo is in expert hands, no matter the situation."

Stella and Mateo Sr. exchanged looks as if trying to decide if they should follow through. They sighed, both having exhausted all other ideas.

"Okay." Stella grabbed the pen, signed the form, and passed it to her husband. They returned it to Jolene with their IDs and insurance.

"Fantastic. I'm going to call the insurance company and make sure everything is square. And don't worry--after intake you'll be able to see Mateo and say goodbye, mmkay?" Jolene swooped up their cards and forms, then left the room locking it behind her. Stella noticed the door was dented just above the handle, in the perfect shape of a fist.

Jolene returned twenty minutes later with a warm smile. "Good news, you have indeed met your out-of-pocket max which means Mateo can get all the help he needs without financials getting in the way. Otherwise, our facility is two thousand dollars per day."

"What?" Mateo and Stella both exclaimed.

"...but like I said, you don't have to worry about it." Jolene flipped the first page of her stack and passed it to Stella. "This is just general information, but we will need to go over all of Mateo's medical history, his family mental health history, any traumas...things like that. I'll also explain some of our policies during Mateo's stay. This will take about thirty minutes, and at the end, we will allow you a few minutes privately with your son before we take him to his room for the evening."

Nearly an hour later, Stella finished filling out the forms, detailing Mateo's accident in the corn maze and subsequent anxiety and claustrophobia. She listed all the doctors, the treatments, and the medications that didn't help. The therapists. The prayer circles. There were even things she didn't share, like how she and Sofia once took him to a voodoo priest in New Orleans when he was too young to remember. The priest prayed over him but said "This boy is haunted," and left it at that. Stella's hand was cramped, and the cheap pen was running out of ink. Mateo Sr. nodded off in his chair, only opening his eyes when a signature was needed.

Finally, Jolene gave them a folder with their medical contract and the rules and regulations of Willow Creek Hospital. "That's it. If you'd like to see Mateo tomorrow during visiting hours, make sure to call and let them know you will be here so we can be appropriately staffed. Trish will bring Mateo in from that other door to say goodbye after I lock this one, okay?"

After Jolene left, Mateo Sr. stood up and stretched his arms over his head. "This place is intense. I hope Junior can handle it."

The door clicked open, and Mateo entered the room looking even thinner and gaunter under the fluorescent lighting. He rushed to his father and hugged him. "Dad, please! Please don't leave me here! I'm not crazy! I just can't sleep. I'm having all these nightmares. I just need help sleeping. Do you know how loud this place is? I've already seen two fights since I got here."

The aide stepped toward Mateo. "Mateo, you need to sit in the chair for everyone's safety. You can speak to your parents, and when they are ready to leave you can hug them…but for now, I need you to sit down. Then I will leave you alone."

Mateo looked into the faces of both his parents as if saying *how could you leave me here, this place is crazy, not me!* All three of them sat down, and when Trish was satisfied that all was calm, she nodded and left, locking the door behind her.

"Mateenio…" Stella reached across the table to hold his hands in hers. "I know you're struggling right now, and I want to help you…but some of this stuff is getting really scary. I don't know what to do anymore. We want you to be happy and to live a normal life, you know?"

Mateo Sr. nodded. "That's right, son. Normal kids don't have a collection of animal skulls in their closet. Serial killers do."

"Dad!" Mateo's dark eyes grew even wider. "I'm NOT a serial killer!"

Stella scowled at her husband, then smiled sweetly at her son. "We know, baby…but just in case, we want to have you tested."

Mateo slapped the table in frustration. "First of all, there's no test for serial killers! And the animal skulls are for Aunt Sofia!"

"You've always been terrible at gift giving." His dad mumbled.

"Mattie…you're not thinking clearly. Your auntie doesn't want animal bones." Stella spoke to him like a preschooler.

"They're from owl pellets, Mom. You know, biology class. We dissected them earlier this year, and I asked the other kids if I could have their skulls so I could paint them like Sugar Skulls and turn them into Christmas ornaments for Auntie. She loves dark shit like that. Why isn't she here, huh? She's watched enough serial killer documentaries to tell you I'm not one!" Mateo spat the truth at his parents.

Mateo Sr. let out a deep breath of relief. "Well, that explanation is weird as hell, but makes sense."

Stella nodded. "Normal weird."

Mateo Jr. agreed. "Normal weird."

"What about the sketchbook, huh? There's some fucked up shit in there." Stella's eyes burned into her sons.

"That's not me, mom." Mateo seemed to collapse from the inside out. "Ever since that night I got in trouble--I'm really sorry about that, by the way--I've been having these horrible vivid nightmares. They're always about women being murdered. It's not me though…it's like I'm just *watching*."

The door clicked open, and Trish stood there with a small cup of water and another with pills. "Alright, Mateo. Time for bedtime meds. You won't have any trouble sleeping tonight. Give your parents a hug."

Stella was still trying to understand what he was telling her, her eyebrows still furrowed deep in thought as her son hugged her tighter than he had since he was a little boy, his arms begging her not to abandon him. His father pulled him off after a look from Trish.

"Alright Mattie." He ruffled his son's head. "It's gonna be okay. We'll come visit tomorrow and bring you some better stuff to wear."

It was dark outside by the time Mateo Sr and Stella left Willow Creek Hospital. Mateo Sr. had been awake since four am working, so Stella drove home while he slept. Her phone rang through their SUV's Bluetooth. The caller ID said *St. Caspar's Catholic Church*. It was a local number, so she answered it on speakerphone.

"Hello?"

"Hello, I'm sorry to bother you this late in the evening. I'm Father Ezra at St. Caspar's Catholic Church, and I'd like to speak to Mateo's parents if they are available."

"This is his mom, Stella. Who gave you my number?"

"A woman named Emily Sharp; she and a group of parents approached me today about some concerns they have about their children."

"I *knew* it was a church thing! They lied to me!" Stella reached out to end the call.

"They have concerns that the behavior changes in your children could be…supernatural in nature."

Silence.

"Stella? Are you there? I'd like to help if I can, but I have a few questions about Mateo."

Mateo Sr., now awake, pulled the lever to bring his seat into an upright position. "This is his dad. What do you want to know?"

"*Papi, we don't know this person. He's probably just some hillbilly tent-preaching snake healer.*" Stella whispered.

"Actually, I'm a Catholic priest for the church Charlotte and her family attend. I've been there for nearly a decade. Your friends shared with me the behavior changes their own children expressed over the last few weeks, and to be frank…it checks a lot of boxes for demonic oppression by multiple entities. I witnessed something similar in Italy during my training. Has Mateo been acting strangely?" The priest waited patiently for either of the parents to respond.

"I just dropped him off at an in-patient mental health facility if that's any indicator of a behavior issue." Stella pulled into their driveway and left the vehicle running.

"He's not sleeping." Mateo Sr. told the priest. "He said he's having nightmares of women being murdered. And then he draws it in his sketchbook."

"I see. Has he been overly aggressive, cruel, sexual…anything like that?"

Stella and Mateo Sr. thought about it for a moment and admitted, "Not really. He seems bummed out his friends won't talk to him, and not sleeping is making him edgy…other than that he's pretty much the same."

"Would it be possible for me to see the drawings and to speak to Mateo personally?" Father Ezra asked.

"He has visiting hours tomorrow. You can meet us at Willow Creek

Hospital at noon." Said Mateo Sr., not waiting for Stella's approval.

"I'll be there."

Stella ended the call. "So, what, you think our son is possessed?"

"I don't know...this is all pretty weird, Stella."

"And how the hell did he get infected with a demon? What is doing, casting a summoning circle in a cornfield? The kid pretends to be asleep when we drive through farmland so he doesn't have to look at it" Stella barked in frustration.

"I think we need to figure out what those kids were doing in the woods that has them acting like lunatics. Talking to a priest can't hurt. We're technically Catholic, right?" Mateo Sr. said.

"Yes, just like I'm technically not a stripper anymore and haven't been to confession since 1997."

"When did he start making these drawings?" Father Ezra asked Stella as he slowly flipped through the pages in Mateo's sketchbook. They'd arrived early to bring extra clothes for Mateo--the finest elastic band sweatpants, plain t-shirts, and pullover sweatshirts Wal-mart had to offer.

"He said the nightmares started the night they were arrested." Stella was glad the waiting room at Willow Creek was empty.

"Catholics believe all forms of mysticism are demonic...if he doesn't know any of these people, this may be some type of clairvoyance or remote viewing. Either he's being shown something that's already happened...or yet to. But why would a demon show him this?" Father Ezra turned to the last page, the room with skulls. "Sugar pit?"

Mateo Sr. shrugged. "We're as clueless as everyone else."

The entrance doors to the hospital opened, and Father Ezra quickly closed the book and passed it back to Stella, who left to put it in the locker that held their keys and cell phones. A flustered, scowling woman entered carrying a paper bag and approached the check-in booth.

"My daughter, Christine, was checked in a few days ago. I need to drop off these clothes." She said.

The attendant gave her the usual check-in procedures and proceeded to empty the bag.

"Unfortunately, she can't have any of these bottoms." The attendant pushed them across the counter towards the woman.

"Why not? There are no strings. It's leggings. That's what she wears, she doesn't have anything else." The woman's energy rattled like an old window in a thunderstorm.

"I understand, but leggings are stretchy and can be used for self-harm. I'm sorry. We suggest basic sweatpants."

Christine's mother scoffed. "She's going to have to make do with what she has then. I can't miss work again to come back here."

"Okay. The local community often donates clothing for patients unable to provide their own. Everything else you brought is acceptable. We're about to start visiting hour, if you'd like I can squeeze you in so you can see her today." The attendant suggested cheerfully in an attempt to diffuse an obviously irritated woman.

"No, I'm good." She swept the pile of leggings in her arms. "I need to get back to work."

She turned on her heel and flung open the door, nearly colliding with a man carrying a party-size tray of cookies. He and his wife moved aside as the woman stormed through the entrance and down the sidewalk to her car. They approached the desk and set the large tray on the counter. "Big day! We're here to pick up Cailie Williams. These are for the staff to share."

"Oh my goodness! That's so kind of you!" said the attendant as she came around to bring them to the breakroom.

"We're just so grateful to all of you." said the mother. "She already seems like a different kid."

"It's been a long eighteen days, but we know she's been in good hands." Said the father.

The attendant smiled. "We love seeing our kiddos improve. Go ahead and take a seat, I'll drop these off and get you checked in with the financial coordinator and then we'll go get Cailie."

The parents exchanged a confused look.

"I thought they're billing insurance..." the woman whispered to her husband.

They sat down and waited, looking worried. Mateo and Stella watched them like a hawk, considering how their own situation might play out similarly in a week or two.

"Mr. and Mrs. Williams? Come on back." It was the same woman who did Mateo Jr.'s intake the day before.

Father Ezra held his rosary beads, closed his eyes, and silently prayed for God to give him strength and guidance on how to best help the families who trusted him to help their children.

Stella turned in her chair and pressed her ear against the wall of the waiting room that was shared with the outtake room. Mateo leaned back ever so slightly, not wanting to be quite as obvious as Stella with his eavesdropping.

*The total cost of your daughter's stay of 18 days is $36,000. We were able to negotiate that price down with your insurance company to $25,000. Your out-of-pocket maximum is $11,000 which you haven't met yet. How would you like to pay that today?*

Stella's eyes bulged out of her head. Even Father Ezra momentarily stopped praying and lifted his head.

*What do you mean? When she checked in, you said it was covered by our insurance. We don't have eleven thousand dollars!*

*In order to release your daughter today, you will need to provide payment for at minimum, twenty percent of your portion of the bill. When you receive the final bill after insurance pays out, we can negotiate a payment plan for the remainder.*

*So, what, you're just going to hold our daughter hostage as collateral until we pay up twenty percent? You can't do that!*

*Mr. Williams, I know you're upset, but that is our policy, and you agreed to it in your contract. Perhaps you and wife can find someone to help with that amount, or something to sell. If you return by 3 pm with $2200 she can be released today, however, after three we will have to charge for another day's stay so you'll need to account for that.*

A thud.

*Unlock the goddamn door!*

Slam.

The parents exited the hospital without their daughter, tears streaming down their cheeks.

Stella, Mateo Sr., and Father Ezra sat in worrisome silence as three more families checked in and waited to be brought into the cafeteria to visit their child.

"Okay, looks like you're it for today. If you follow me single file, I'll lead you to our visiting area." Said the attendant

They were led through echoing empty hallways. The building was square, and one side of the hallway was lined with windows overlooking a courtyard bordered by a walking track. In the center were concrete benches and a few rubber balls.

The visiting area turned out to be the cafeteria, post lunch. Silver trays were behind glass waiting to be filled at the next meal. On a large whiteboard was written: Dinner--Brats and Chips. Cherry cobbler.

Stella pointed at the sign. "Poor kid's gonna get nothing but midwestern food here…casseroles and sauerkraut. Bud Light and Faygo Rockin' Rye. Mattie's gonna be *begging* for my empanadas and horchata when he gets home."

Father Ezra pointed at a table in the far corner of the cafeteria, away from the other families. "Is that one okay?"

When they had dragged out the weighted chairs and all the families were seated, the teenage patients were escorted in by three attendants. Mateo rushed out of line to his mother looking like a thirsty man being offered a glass of water.

"Mom! Mom…please. I don't need to be here. Please take me home."

Stella gently pushed him off her and into a chair. "Mateenio, sit down. We have someone who wants to speak with you."

He looked like he wanted to bolt. "Holy shit, you brought a Catholic priest? What the hell, mom? Are you going to get me Baptized or something?"

"*Are* you Baptized, Mateo?" The priest cocked his head to one side.

Mateo looked at his mom. "...am I?"

Stella shrugged. "With you being a newborn and all, I was busy and never got around to it. I figured Jesus would understand and still let you into heaven."

"Son, it's good to see you." Mateo Sr. patted his arm. "Are they treating you alright here?"

Mateo kept side-eyeing the priest but finally spoke to his dad, "They're treating me fine...the food sucks though."

Stella peeked around to look at her husband. "Told you."

"Why is the priest here?" Mateo turned his attention to Father Ezra.

"You know what I don't understand..." Stella surveyed the room. "Is that out of thirty kids in this place, only four families are visiting."

"A lot of youth in places like this have troubled home lives," observed Father Ezra. "For many parents, this is a last resort. I imagine there's a lot of bad blood at times."

Mateo scoffed. "You wouldn't believe the stories I've heard in the last 24 hours." He lowered his voice. "That girl is over there is dating my seventeen-year-old roommate. She's fourteen and *pregnant*...with her *second* kid. Not my roommate's. Somebody else's. The first one she had at twelve was by her stepdad. He's in prison. I said to my roommate...bro, that girl has way too much going on *do not* get involved. Focus on yourself."

Stella scowled. "You better not be messing with girls here. You have more important things to do, Mateo."

"I know, Mom! Jeesh." He fiddled with a forgotten packet of salt on the table. "You know we can't have saltshakers here? Kids were snorting it. We're each allowed one packet of salt per meal. Anyway...I've been asked to be someone's boyfriend twice since I checked in. *Twice.*"

"And what did you tell these young ladies, Mateo?" Mateo Sr. asked sternly.

"Calm down, Dad. I told them I'm not interested in romantic relationships at this time because I have a lot of other stuff on my mind. Now it's even worse though because they apparently see me as a challenge and won't leave me alone. Girls are so weird." Mateo dumped out the salt on the table and absentmindedly began creating a ring with his fingers.

"Mateo…" said Father Ezra, watching him carefully. "I'd like to talk to you about your drawings, and I thought maybe you could tell me about how all this started."

At this point, Mateo fully absorbed the scene. He was wearing giant sweatpants and his mom's pink crocs in the cafeteria of a mental institution with his parents and a Catholic priest. Oh, and everyone thinks his only future goal is to become a serial killer.

"Fuck it…" he said under his breath.

"Mateo!" Scolded Stella. "You're speaking to a man of God can you at least try not to swear for f…please?"

Mateo sighed and decided it would be easier if he just forgot about his parents. Where he was. What other people thought. He would treat this as a confession. It was just him, God, and Father Ezra.

"Forgive me, Father, for I have sinned. It has been seventeen years since my last confession." Mateo stared straight ahead at Father Ezra.

"That's not normally how this is done…but go ahead. What is your sin, child of God?"

"Intent to commit theft." Mateo summoned his courage.

Father Ezra raised an eyebrow at Stella who shook her head like she had no idea.

"Long story short-- I found a map to a place called The Cheese Cave in my aunt's car. She said it was a cave the government used to store cheese and there was still some in there. I got this idea after working at the farmer's market that we could go into the cave and steal the cheese and sell it for money to go to a concert." He took a breath.

"You're a fuckin' idiot Mattie." Said Stella.

"…I think it's clever. Have you seen how much artisan cheese costs? I've had my eye on that block of habanero mango cheddar at Price Cutter but it's twenty bucks!" said Mateo Sr.

He ignored his parents and continued. "I knew I couldn't go in the cave…because I'm claustrophobic…so I asked my friends to go in, while I planned it out and drove the getaway car. I wish I hadn't. Now they won't talk to me. Theo even punched me in the face when they got out." Mateo hung his head and rubbed his jawbone, clearly his feelings hurt more than his nearly healed face.

Father Ezra raised his eyebrows as if he had an epiphany. "So, you didn't actually go into the cave?"

"No…and they were in there a really long time. I was getting worried and tried to go in to find them. I really did….but I chickened out. I called the cops on us, anonymously." Mateo shook his head. "I figured they wouldn't be mad at me that way. They'd think it was someone else."

Father Ezra thrummed his fingers on the table and looked from Stella to Mateo Sr. "If he didn't go inside, that could explain why he's not affected like the others. Do you consider yourself religious, Mateo? Do you pray often?"

Stella snickered, but Mateo answered. "Lately, I've been praying a lot. I suck at it…but I guess it makes me feel better."

The priest's eyes were glued to Mateo. "When did this start?"

His eyes started to grow wide. "That night."

For a moment the adults held their breath.

"Mom, what is this? Why is the priest here?" Mateo's hands started to twitch.

"Mateo," said Father Ezra. "I would like you to tell me what happened between the time your friends went in the cave and the time you were arrested."

"Okay…" he looked uncomfortable. "I waited outside for them, but I started hearing animals and shit. It's really creepy out there! I ran back to the car…I waited for like an hour and they still weren't out. I heard coyotes howling and got scared. Oliver's dad has one of those hanging in his car—", Mateo pointed at Father Ezra's rosary. "And I put it on my neck. I prayed for help."

"You put on a rosary and prayed?" Father Ezra looked as if he was ready to jump out of his skin.

"Yeah, for like…courage, you know? I ran out across the field and tried to go into the cave. I couldn't…so I called the police. Right after that, my friends came out and I was trying to get everyone in the car so we could get out of there before the cops arrived."

"Did they look any different? Any markings, etc.?" Father Ezra asked.

"They wouldn't listen to me. It's like they were in a daze, marching or something. I remember putting my hands on Theo's shoulders trying to stop him. He got really mad…then it was lights out for me. Woke up in an ambulance." Mateo rubbed his hands like he was cold. "They haven't talked to me since."

"This is your ten-minute warning, families! You can sign up to visit again in a few days." The attendant said.

"Mateo, quickly before I go, please tell me about your drawings," whispered Father Ezra.

Mattie nodded. "I dream nearly every night. It's different women every time, but the same man. I'm in the cave watching him torment and kill people. The last dream I had…I actually *became* the woman. I was in her body, hearing her thoughts. He threw me--her--in a hole full of skeletons. When I woke up, it felt like my head was splitting open and I threw up over the side of my bed."

"…that's what happened to my carpet…" whispered Stella.

"I am not the murderer. Some guy is. It's like I'm seeing through the eyes of the victims."

Father Ezra considered Mateo's words in silence.

"Mattie, that's creepy as hell." Said Mateo Sr.

"Mateo, I don't think you're being oppressed. We need to find out what's in that cave. Where is the map?" asked Father Ezra.

"Say your goodbyes, everyone!"

Mateo thought for a moment. "After I woke up in the ambulance, I saw the owner pick it up off the ground."

"Son, where is this place? Who's the owner?" asked Mateo Sr.

"…I don't know….Jason's sister I think….it's where they found him. You know, in the Mustang." Mateo looked ashamed.

"Oh, great!" said Mateo Sr., loud enough to draw unwanted attention to their table.

"That's right, GREAT. Thanks, Mattie." Said Stella sarcastically. "You have perfected the art of making bad things worse!"

"What do you mean?" asked Mateo, confused.

She stood up, turned her back on the three still sitting at the table, and stomped across the cafeteria, her flip-flops echoing down the silent hallway back to the waiting room.

Mateo Sr. shook his head, then gave Mateo a goodbye hug.

"Son, you stepped on the tail of Snake Oil Stephanie."

# Chapter 13

## Snake Oil Stephanie

"Please tell me we don't have to talk to Snake Oil Stephanie. I had to cite her for trespassing at the old bank last week and she tried to sell me hair rinse to stop my 'premature graying'," Isabella scoffed. "I wasn't going to ticket her until she did that."

"Are you sure we can't just ask her for the map?" asked Charlotte.

Gemma, Emily, and Isabella exchanged a look that said *no way*.

"Look," said Stella. "I don't know this woman, I've only heard about her. My sister says if they went to the trouble to close up that cave, they're hiding something. She also said not to go down there without a map. Some boys went exploring in there back in the sixties…never found 'em. It's a whole system of caves or some shit. There are other ways to get in but Sophia doesn't know where they are."

"Come on Charlie," said Isabella. "We went to the same high school. I know you heard the rumors about Stephanie…she's not the type of person you want to ask for favors. Her family has connections to some weird shit. She's always given me the creeps."

"Where's Benny?" Stella suddenly asked Lucy, realizing someone was missing as the rest of the moms assembled in a circle like a midwestern version of the Avengers. Gemma, Emily, and Charlotte were all in sweatpants, grass-stained sneakers, and hoodies with the names of local high schools; their hair all some variation of messy bun. Stella dressed like she was going on a date: black ankle boots, black leather pants, and a flowy pink blouse. Her hair was straightened, black with only a few strands of gray, and so sleek it almost flowed like water down the middle of her back. Every woman in the group envied it, and absentmindedly touched her own hair thinking the same thought: *maybe I should have tried harder tonight.*

"He's picking up his husband from the airport," said Lucy. "He says he'll join us after they get *reacquainted.* I was sent in his stead." She puffed her chest, proud of her new role as a nanny in this strange group, and unsuccessfully hiding her enthusiasm. *Babies are contagious,* she told herself.

"Are you sure this shop is even open?" Lucy gestured at the darkened inside. "Anyone have her social media?"

Grumbles abound.

"God no."

"Unfollowed"

Charlotte pulled out her phone and started scrolling. "Oh, I never delete anyone. She has to be here somewhere..."

"Did you see her husband is trying to make it as a video game streamer?"

"Good God. Has that man ever had a real job?"

"He doesn't have to work. He's Richard the Conqueror, Stephanie's prized and pampered pet."

"Jason told me he had a roster of every woman in his high school and convinced all but five to sleep with him. Said the rest were lesbians."

"I sure as hell didn't." said Emily.

"Lesbian." Said Stella.

"I kicked him in the balls when I was eleven. Didn't sleep with him." Said Isabella.

"Also, Lesbian. Did you lesbian together in high school?" Stella pressed. The others ignored.

"I'd love to know what dirt Stephanie's got on him to keep him around after all these years. She spent all of high school unpopular, no friends or boyfriend…then suddenly senior year she shows up with the guy who could--according to him--have *anyone*."

"Found her!" said Charlotte. "It says she's teaching a 'chakra alignment' class…whatever that is… until 8 pm, but she says the spots are almost sold out. She's probably busy tonight."

The group looked around the empty parking lot. A stray cow-print cat trotted by, howling in heat, and jumped into the dumpster behind the adjacent Chinese restaurant. All that was missing was a tumbleweed.

Isabella laughed. "Total bullshit. No one's here. Let's go inside, she's probably making friendship bracelets from glass beads to sell to unsuspecting teenagers as 'ethically sourced amethyst to strengthen their self-love and intuition'."

Only black candlelight lit the back room of Violet Visions Boutique. The candles were overstock from a Target post-Halloween clearance sale, then overstock again at her own store after she slightly melted the sides with a hair dryer, rolled them in loose smudge leaves, and tried to resell them for five dollars apiece. Surprisingly, not a big seller. They smelled wonderful, in her opinion. Maybe she'd try lavender next time, with crushed gemstones. She'd need to raise the price another dollar, of course. She lit another with a long match and hoped to deflect negative energies as she focused intently on the task at hand.

Two-ounce bags, razor blades, and a brick lay in front of her. She had an encounter with the police when she picked it up, but thankfully she wasn't searched--just a citation for trespassing.

She chiseled off a corner, and crushed the chunk in a mortar and pestle before meticulously chopping it with the razor blade until it was a fine powder. Then closing her eyes, and with her hands a few inches above the pile she prayed, "Oh Divine Goddess, please infuse this dust with protection and prosperity for the user. So be it."

Using a tiny spatula with a quartz crystal wire-wrapped on the end, she scooped the dust onto a scale, and then into the bags.

Rolling in her creaky office chair to her laptop, she printed a label:

*Brick Dust*

Brick dust is said to provide the user and their home with protection from evil or those who wish them harm. This particular brick is from a demolished bank built in 1869 and has the added benefit of prosperity energy. These energies have been clarified and amplified by a skilled High Priestess and Reiki Master.

2 ounces. $6.00

*Violet Visions Boutique*

Witch Bells tinkled on the knob as Gemma pushed open the door to Violet Visions Boutique. She'd only been there once before, and soon realized it wasn't what it was advertised to be. She'd expected a shop where she could browse tarot cards, sample incense, and connect with like-minded people living an alternative lifestyle. It was *so* hard to buy crystals online; they needed to be held and experienced. It's not just about whether it's citrine, amethyst, or kyanite. It's about whether the energy meshes with yours. Not to mention all the fakes out there. You need to see them in person.

Her first time at the shop, it had been crowded with groups of college freshman girls from Missouri State University, ogling crystals and leafing through love spell books. Stephanie had invited Gemma to explore her extensive collection of tarot cards. Admittedly, she had hundreds. Every deck imaginable published in the last twenty years filled a bookshelf the entire span of a wall. She even had the complete collection of Doreen Virtue's oracle decks--probably worth a fortune after she became Christian and pulled the rights to publish any of her work. However, the decks at Bohemian Betty Boutique were half the list price. Did Stephanie simply not understand the rarity of what was in her shop? Gemma passed on the Doreen Virtue decks--a little too "love and light" for someone covered in skull tattoos-- but bought *The Everyday Witch Tarot* for Trix, a perfect beginner deck, as a gift for their 16th birthday. Your first tarot deck must *always* be a gift. Tradition says if it's not, you don't truly have

The Sight. When she inspected the deck at home, she discovered it was fake. Instead of a guidebook, there was a slip of paper inside with a QR code, leading to a website with photocopies of hundreds of tarot guidebooks. The cards themselves were smaller than most tarot, and off-color. The box was flimsy. Gemma couldn't help but think of the enormous amount of work the creator had put into the original deck, only for it to be stolen and sold as this disgrace to the art of Tarot. The experience left a bad taste in her mouth, and she never returned to Violet Visions Boutique.

As the rest of the ladies entered the shop, most were immediately drawn to the crystal collection by the front door, expertly placed to entice visitors with shiny things and tempt them inside for further exploration. Emily inspected a handful of brightly colored crystals from a bowl. Gemma leaned into her ear and whispered, "It's fake. They're stained and painted glass or quartz. Don't buy anything here."

Emily slowly placed the "crystals" back in the ceramic bowl with a *tink*, and nodded with understanding.

"Let's check behind the desk for the map once Stephanie's distracted," Gemma said and then pretended to browse. It was around this point when the women realized they came to the store without much of a plan for what to do when they got there.

Charlotte tapped some chakra-themed windchimes with one hand and fiddled with her cross necklace with the other, looking incredibly uncomfortable. Gemma gestured for Charlotte to come over to where she stood at the incense.

"These are called smudge sticks." Gemma held up a fat bundle of herbs wrapped in white string. She held it under Charlotte's nose. She took a small sniff.

"It smells nice?"

"It's made from white sage, and sometimes other things like cedar, lavender, or rose petals. Smudge sticks help cleanse negative energy. This piece of wood here is called palo santo. We use that after the cleansing to bring in good energy. I'd like to smudge all our children...even yours. I know you're Christian, I don't want to offend you. I'm no exorcist but I know a thing or two about protecting energy. I figure it can't hurt." Gemma offered.

"I don't think Jesus would have a problem with that." Although Charlotte wasn't quite sure, she agreed, hoping if she was wrong God would forgive her ignorance.

"Ugh, I can't believe she's charging three dollars for each piece of palo santo." Gemma tossed a half dozen in a small shopping basket. "You can buy ten for five dollars online, but I need them now."

Stephanie emerged from the back room as she finished wrapping a white cloth around her head, the type worn by practitioners of kundalini yoga. What Stephanie didn't tell people is that she didn't actually practice kundalini yoga; its primary use was to cover a growing bald patch on the crown of her head. She fixed a welcoming smile on her face. "Ladies, good evening. Let me know if I can help you find anything. We have a collection of delicious vegan cupcakes in the refrigerator over there, baked fresh this morning. Just five dollars each…"

Emily peeked at Stephanie from behind a stand of watercolor greeting cards. "Thanks! Right now, we're just browsing." Then she turned around and silently mouthed to Gemma, "Five dollars!"

Gemma smirked, then made her way closer to the checkout counter to wait for her opportunity to look around for anything that might give them more information about the property the cave was on, if not the map itself.

Stella and Lucy skirted the edges of the store, casually looking at items in an effort to seem natural. Lucy found a knee-length, teal blue sweater with beautiful carved wooden buttons.

"Isn't that pretty?" said Stephanie from across the room. "It's one of my favorite pieces and our best-selling sweater."

Lucy rubbed the woven fabric in her hands. "It's so soft…and I've always thought teal was my color." She took the sweater from the rack and held it up to herself in the full-length mirror.

"Oh, it certainly is!" Stephanie stepped out from behind the counter and strode across the shop to assist Lucy. "And we have a large selection of handmade gemstone jewelry that would match perfectly!"

Emily and Gemma plunged behind the counter and quietly shuffled through documents and items below the register trying to find the map while Stephanie made her sales pitch.

Meanwhile, Stella scowled and scooted in between Stephanie and Lucy. She put an arm around Lucy, "Lulu? Are you sure you want to buy this? Don't you already have a closet full of sweaters?"

Stephanie smiled sweetly. "Well, what's one more then? It's on sale this week for only fifty dollars!"

Lucy gave Stella a confused glance but continued speaking to Stephanie. "Fifty? That's pretty reasonable for such a beautiful sweater."

Stella snatched the sweater from Lucy. "Lulu...I know it's only fifty dollars, but do you *really need it?*"

A crash came from the front of the store. Whether by accident or not, Charlotte knocked over a spinning display of novelty toilet paper with political figures' faces on it. "Oh no! I'm so sorry!"

Stephanie turned her attention to the mess, and Stella took the opportunity to pull Lucy out of earshot.

"What are you doing? You don't know that bitch." Stella demanded.

"What? I just want to buy this sweater..." Lucy was so confused at Stella's sudden anger with her that tears started to well in her eyes. "Why do I need to know her?"

Stella sensed she had been too aggressive and dialed it down a few degrees. "Listen...if you met her in the street would you just reach into your pretty little pink purse with your tiny little manicured hands and give her fifty dollars?"

Lucy stared at her trying to follow where this was going to no avail. "Uh, no?"

"That's right," Stella pointed a stubby finger in her face. "Because you don't know that bitch."

She took out her cell phone, checked to make sure Stephanie couldn't see them, and snapped a photo. "Watch this."

She tapped 'image search' and the exact sweater was listed at five different fast fashion websites for less than twelve dollars with free shipping.

"What! How can she do that?" Lucy exclaimed, unable to believe this woman nearly swindled her straight to her face.

Stella nodded, then whispered, "Listen to me *hermana*...most boutique shops are scams. Everything is priced three times what it is worth. If she was some mom you've known for ten years who's just hustling to try to put diapers on her baby--buy the sweater. But do it knowing you are just helping her with cash *indirectly*. It's charity." Stella could see clarity dawning on Lucy's face. "However, if you're looking for *value*, that's different. Take a picture and figure out where she got it from."

Lucy nodded in understanding and hung the sweater back on the rack, and then Stella pulled her in close. "As the people who run our households, we have to be wise stewards of our family's money and shit, right?" Her eyes narrow, "*Your* needs trump *hers*. You don't owe her anything. You. Don't. Know. That. Bitch."

Lucy didn't respond. She has a nearly five-million-dollar inheritance in her savings account and a cabin in the Ozark Mountains. Fifty dollars is nothing. Still, Stella was right. She doesn't know this bitch.

They joined the others at the front of the store. Gemma had three different types of sage, palo santo and a box of assorted colored candles placed at the register. "You girls doing a little seance? *Can I come?*" Stephanie grinned mischievously. The women give a dull laugh.

"It's for a blessing," explained Gemma. "A friend bought a new house with some bad vibes I'm trying to clear."

"I see." said Stephanie as she packed the items in a paper bag. Suddenly Lucy caught her eye. "Do you like that lamp better than you like the sweater, hun?"

Lucy jumped. Lost in her thoughts she had absentmindedly been swatting at the tassels of an upside-down pineapple lamp. A bowl sat underneath it full of business cards and pieces of paper with phone numbers. "Is this some kind of raffle?"

Stephanie held eye contact with Lucy just half a second longer than she was comfortable before saying, "Sure is...the winner gets invited to a very exclusive party. There's wine sampling and introductions to some of Springfield's most influential people. If you're new in town, or a new business owner, you should put your name and number in. It's a great way to meet people."

Lucy shrugged. "Hmm. Why not." She scribbled her name and number on some paper with a purple gel pen and tossed it in the bowl.

"Goodbye, ladies!" Stephanie said as they shuffled out the door. "Hope to see you soon!"

She didn't let up eye contact with Lucy until she left the shop.

As soon as the sliding door shut on the minivan, all the women began cackling--except for Stella and Lucy. Stella's face was bright red, as she turned around in the front passenger seat to yell at Lucy.

"Lulu, what the fuck is wrong with you? I just fucking stopped you from getting swindled by that snake and you fall for her shit again!"

"What! What did I do? I don't understand!" She pleaded.

Charlotte wiped tears of laughter from her eyes. "Don't you know what an upside-down pineapple is for?"

"I don't know...really tacky home decor?" she squeaked, knowing the truth she was about to hear was bad.

Charlotte took a deep breath and tried to keep a straight face. "Upside-down pineapples are how swingers let other swingers know they want to *get together*. You just told Stephanie you want to be invited to her and Richard's legendary swinger parties."

The girls were now howling with laughter, with the exception of Stella who scowled, rolled down the window, lit a cigarette, and watched stray cats climb in and out of the dumpster.

"She seemed friendly enough." Lucy said in her own defense.

"Oh yeah," Stella scoffed. "She'll be your friend...long enough to figure out your hustle. She'll see how you make your money, who you talk to, she'll even take notes on the things you're doing. Before you know it, she'll be wearing polka dot skirts and pearl necklaces, hosting tea parties in her English garden with the recipe for sleepy time tea that *you* gave her. I've known women like her. Don't tell her a damn thing about your life no matter how sweet she is it you."

Stella turned in her seat to make eye contact with Lucy. She blew smoke out both nostrils and looked like an angry Latino dragon. Lucy couldn't help but lean back ever so slightly, afraid of the heat from the fire that flicked in her eyes. "Friendly, but not your motherfucking friend. You don't know that bitch. I do."

"I thought you said you don't know Stephanie, Stella." Lucy replied.

She flicked her cigarette out the window. "I don't, but all *putas* are the same. All that changes is what they sell. Ass and titties, or candles and earrings. It's all the fucking same."

Silence filled the van, as the jest at Lucy's mistake changed into something darker.

"You need to stop being so naive, *munequita*. You're a cute-ass baby seal, and hoes like that are sharks." Stella continued to spew fire.

Lucy appeared at a loss at what to say, and Gemma broke the silence. "She's still young, Stella. You don't need to be so hard on her."

Lucy looked down at her 'pretty, pink, manicured hands' feeling like a child despite being in her late twenties.

"Fuck that!" Stella spat and turned once more to Lucy. "Lulu, I'm telling you exactly what I wish some jaded, fat bitch would have told me fifteen years ago. Not everyone is your friend. Most won't be. The sooner you accept that ninety nine percent of women are hiding a dagger in their Birkin bag to stab you in the back the first chance they get, the better off you will be."

Charlotte whispered to Isabella from the third-row seat, "I'm beginning to think this isn't about Stephanie…"

Rocky rolled her eyes. "Obviously, Charlie."

Gemma laid a spider-web tattooed hand on Stella's shoulder. "I don't have a dagger…or a Birkin bag…"

Stella took a deep breath, then grabbed her purse from the floor of the minivan and climbed out. "Well, it's been fun ladies, but I'm going to take a cab home. Let me know how things go with the demon cave and possessed kids and shit. I gotta go."

She slammed the door shut and speed walked as fast as her short legs could manage across the pothole-littered parking lot in the dark until one caught the heel of her ankle-high black boots. She fell face-first to the ground and didn't move.

"Oh my god!" Lucy scrambled for the handle to the sliding door of the van. It wouldn't open.

"Oh, sorry! Child safety locks!" Emily pushed the button for the automatic door opener. Slowly the door inched open, and as soon as it was wide enough for Lucy to squeeze through, she sprinted at Stella who lay knocked out cold on the asphalt.

Lucy rolled her over onto her back. "Stella! Oh no…wake up, wake up." She gently slapped her round cheeks.

"Ughh… *sana, sana, colita de rana…*" her eyes began to flutter.

Lucy breathed a sigh of relief. "I don't know what that means…do you know your name?"

"Estrella, in life…and on the pole."

They both gave small laughs, and Lucy helped her sit up. Emily pulled the van out of the parking spot and headed towards where Stella and Lucy sat on the ground.

"Stella…I just want to say," Lucy picked a piece of black asphalt out of Stella's forehead. "Thank you for looking out for me."

Stella coughed. "Sure, whatever kid. Alright *Munequita*, find my cigarettes."

Lucy scanned the ground and found several dirty needles on the ground, and then Stella's menthols ten feet away, apparently thrown from her hands on impact. She ran back just as the others were piling out of Emily's van. "I found your cigarettes, but first let's get you off the ground. It's really gross here."

"Stella, thank Goddess you're okay! You don't need to be walking around the city at night!" Gemma helped Lucy stand her up and walk her over to the front seat of the van.

Emily ran around from the driver's side with a pack of baby wipes. "Let me see your hands."

Stella obeyed like a dutiful child, and Emily picked small bits of gravel from her hands, and then cleaned them thoroughly with a baby wipe. "Now, give me your face."

Still dazed, Stella lifted her chin, and Emily thoroughly cleaned her forehead and nose, then smoothed her sleek black hair back into place. A lump the size of an egg was beginning to form "All done. Just as beautiful as ever."

Stella sat back as Emily reclined the chair. "Do you want to go to the hospital?"

"Fuck no," groaned Stella. "The emergency room is nothing but tweakers. I'm fine."

The rest of the women climbed into the van. "Where to now?" asked Emily as she buckled in and turned down the radio.

"I could eat." Announced Gemma.

"Me, too. But what's open right now?" asked Charlotte.

"Well, let's drive around and find out. I'm afraid if we stay in this parking lot much longer, Stephanie's going to come out and try to sell us something else." Scoffed Emily, as she turned onto one of the main streets of Springfield.

As they cruised down Glenstone Ave., most places to eat were closed except fast food.

"Hey Emily," said Isabella from the back, close to shouting so she could be heard. "Did you two find a map or anything?"

Emily shook her head no, but Gemma responded. "Nothing at all. It was all past due bills and tax receipts."

"Damn." Isabella sat back and crossed her arms. "Wait! Is that the Pineapple Whip truck?"

"I didn't know they opened already! Let's go." Said Emily. "Lucy, text Benny and tell him to meet us there."

Emily pulled into the furniture store parking lot that hosted the Pineapple Whip food truck. It was lit up by strings of patio lights and a neon sign of a hula dancer. After the women ordered their food, twenty minutes later Benny pulled up in his SUV, which now sported a shiny new bumper. "Mississippi Queen" riffed out the windows.

"Girls, what the hell is this? Please tell me we are not participating in a parking lot luau at eleven o'clock at night!" Benny approached the two picnic tables Isabella and Gemma pushed together.

"No, Benny…" Charlotte took a bite of the yellow nectar off her spoon and swallowed. "It's pineapple whip. Kind of like ice cream. Here's yours."

Benny took the cup and spoon from her hand and sat down. "Y'all are some weird ass hillbillies. You *do know* that the Ozarks is about the last place in the world that should be serving tropical drinks in the parking lot of Al's Discount Futons or whatever the fuck this is?"

"Oh my god, I haven't had one of these since I was a kid. It's so good. Why did I ever stop?" asked Isabella to herself in between bites.

"We all probably stopped about the time we started dieting in high school." Charlotte scraped the bottom of her cup with a spoon and was the first to finish.

Benny watched them all with curiosity and took a hesitant bite. "I guess it's alright...so is this pineapple ice cream an Ozark thing?"

"No, it's a Springfield thing. When Pineapple Whip opens, you know it's summer. The truck has been here every summer for almost fifty years." Explained Emma.

Rocky tossed her empty ice cream cup from ten feet away into the trash can. "Alright, back to business. How are we going to get the map? There's no way to ask Stephanie without it being suspicious. It has to be at her house..."

"I don't think any of us could pull off a drop-in for more than a few minutes without it being weird. We'd never be able to look around. Could we try to break in?" Gemma asked the group.

Isabella coughed. "As a law enforcement officer, I'm going to pretend you didn't say that. No, we are not breaking in."

"Oops..." Gemma grinned like the Cheshire Cat. "Sorry, Officer Rocky."

"Lieutenant."

Stella held one pineapple whip against the egg on her forehead and stabbed another with her spoon. "This shit is as thick as my thighs. Do you think if I turned it upside down it would stay in the cup like the Blasts at Dairy Queen?"

Everyone laughed as Stella turned the pineapple whip upside down and it stayed in the cup.

"Hey, look y'all—upside down pineapple whip!" joked Benny. "That must mean there's a swinger party nearby!"

Everyone stopped talking.

The pineapple whip dropped from Stella's cup and plopped with a splat on the warm pavement, but no one noticed.

They were all staring at Lucy with huge grins on their faces.

"...what?" asked Lucy. "Wait...no. NO! Oh, come on!"

# Chapter 14
## Ray-cism

*I know a guy* is not a sentence they expected to hear from Charlotte.

As the parents sat on wrought iron chairs drinking Lady Grey tea in Lucy's English cottage garden, Charlotte informed them in "another life" she was a meth dealer.

The hollyhocks and sweet peas gasped in shock.

Benny choked on a dry biscuit...or was it a cookie? "I'm sorry, what? Aren't you the woman who dragged my gay self into a Catholic church a few days ago to beg a bishop to exorcise our children?"

Charlotte set her jaw, and with conviction declared, "God has forgiven me, and I have lived a clean life since I gave Jesus Christ my heart and soul. I accept my difficult past as the path that led me to my soul's salvation."

"Okay, girl, calm down. I ain't judgin'." Benny dunked his cookie in the tea and tossed it whole into his mouth to avoid continuing the conversation.

Lucy proudly placed a steaming porcelain teapot in the center of the table.

Benny swallowed. "Darling, it is *84 degrees* outside, can you stop acting British just for today and make some damned sweet tea like a true American?" Emily and Gemma grinned, silently thinking the same.

She rolled her eyes and sat next to Charlotte. "So, this *guy*...how do you think he can help me?"

She squirmed in her seat as if the flames of hell were tickling her bottom. "He's a career criminal. If anyone can figure out how to raid a house without getting caught…it's him."

"I don't want to raid a house." Lucy protested. "I'd just feel more comfortable if there was some sort of plan for me to find this map at the party."

As those who knew Stephanie expected, Lucy received a text message the morning after she visited Bohemian Betty Boutique informing her she was selected to participate in their social event the following weekend. She gave Lucy their address and requested she bring a bottle of champagne.

"He'll know what to do." Charlotte nodded.

Stella sipped tea from a tiny China cup with her pinky in the air. "Am I to assume this is why Lieutenant Rocky was not invited to tea in Princess Lucy's lovely garden?"

Charlotte shrugged.

Benny sat his cup down on the table and began to stand, eager to swing by Bojangles and grab a gallon of the sweetest sweet tea money could buy. "Alright, let's go see him then."

Charlotte jumped up, evidently poked with Satan's pitchfork. "No!"

All eyes turned to her.

"Ray is…you can't go. Only Emily can go." Stammered Charlotte.

"Me? Why me?" laughed Emily. "I'm not going to the swinger party! I don't need to be there. Lucy's going with you, right?"

Charlotte shook her head aggressively. "Oh no, no, no. She's too pretty. And…clean."

"I'm clean!" protested Emily

"You are, by Ray's standards, normal. Not gay, a cop, a witch…or Mexican." Charlotte looked at them all apologetically. "He's one of those scary confederate flag-wavin' Ozarkers. If I'm going to get any help I have to meet him on his level."

Benny was the first to speak. "I get it Charlie…but are you two going to be okay?"

They looked worried for Charlotte and Emily rather than insulted, to which Charlotte was grateful. "Oh, I know how to handle him...but Emmy... why don't you leave your smartwatch and earrings here with Lucy? Also, don't take your phone out while we're there."

Emily's eyes were wide as she unstrapped her watch and handed it to Lucy. "I sure hope you find this map."


Charlotte drove halfway to Branson, up and down hills, around hairpin curves, and finally down into a densely forested valley where she turned off onto an unmarked dirt road...well, unmarked except by a post topped with the skull of a bull, and a "private property" sign. The deeply rutted road took an eternity to navigate in her low-riding van.

"How did you get clean, Charlie? You know, from drugs? I've heard it's nearly impossible to break an addiction to meth." Emily asked, gripping the ceiling handles as they bounced along.

"It's pretty simple actually. I overdosed, and Ray left me alone on a sidewalk to die...or not. He didn't want to get caught for possession, so he ran off. My now-husband, Brent, was working as an EMT while going to community college. He happened to be on his lunch break buying a slice of pizza at Kum and Go. Ray went in and told him where to find me. Brent not only saved my life, he went to his church and convinced them to help pay for my rehab...he paid half with his own savings."

Emily was stunned at such a selfless act. "Oh Charlotte, that's incredible of him. He didn't even know you at the time, right?"

Charlotte smiled as if lost in a sweet memory. "He said we he saw me lying on that sidewalk...dirty, in a pool of my own vomit and everything...God told him I would live, and that I would be his wife."

Emily smiled, always a sucker for real-life love stories.

"He's my knight in shining armor. He saved my life, and delivered me to Jesus Christ who saved my soul." Charlotte's eyes were misty.

Emily looked around the forest as they drove, littered with rusty old lawnmowers and piles of scrap metal. "What happened to Ray?"

Charlotte sighed as they approached a surprisingly sophisticated gate system with a camera and intercom on an electric swinging arm. "I saw him a few times after rehab in passing. He got clean from meth, but he did it by switching to other drugs. He got married, had a kid. His sister told me he was into wrestling or something. I suppose that's better than dealing drugs."

"Who's there?" a voice crackled over the intercom. "I see your van. I'm not in the market for Jesus or Jehovah. We follow the Old Ways here."

Charlotte got out of the van and stood in front of the camera. "It's Charlie, Ray. I need some help."

He didn't respond, but the gate swung open. Charlotte returned to the driver's seat and approached a steep driveway to the top of a hill. She pulled to the side and parked.

"I'm sorry, Emily. There's no way my van will make it up that hill, and even if it did, I'm not sure I'd be able to turn around if I remember Ray's place correctly. We'll have to walk." Charlotte shoved her purse under the seat and stuffed her phone and keys in her bra. Emily watched and did the same.

As they abandoned the van and climbed the muddy hill a herd of cats began to form behind them acting as escorts. Scrawny adolescents, weathered limping toms, and a litter of black fluffy-tailed kittens that looked like squirrels swarmed around them with a cacophony of mews, until the high-pitched rev of a small engine descended from the hill and they scattered into the bushes. A muddy UTV was driving towards them, swerving to avoid potholes and large tree roots.

Charlotte stopped walking. "Shit."

Emily raised an eyebrow, this being the first time she'd ever heard Charlotte swear. "...what's wrong?"

"It's my cousin, Twister." Charlotte crossed her arms. "I can't believe he's still hanging out with Ray."

Emily thought she caught a hint of betrayal in Charlotte's tone. "Why is he called Twister?"

They watched him hit the gas as he approached a small hill and send his UTV a foot off the ground before landing with a mechanical crunch. "You remember that EF-5 tornado in Joplin?"

"Of course...it's the one with multiple vortexes that leveled the city. I was part of a volunteer group that reunited lost pets with their owners…the ones that lived, anyway. " Emily watched him approach as cats scattered further into the forest and up trees.

"He was driving through Joplin after leaving the casino in Miami, Oklahoma. The tornado picked up his truck from I-44 and dropped him upside down two miles away in a Tractor Supply parking lot. Not only did he live to tell the tale…he still had his $4,000 winnings from the casino in his pocket. He was big into backyard wrestling at the time and messed up his shoulder pretty bad. Couldn't do it anymore. I'm not sure what he's doing now." Charlotte smoothed her shirt and steadied herself for a confrontation. "We lost touch years ago."

"Wow, he's fortunate. When I was helping with cleanup, I saw a chair impaled legs first into a stucco wall." Emily's eyes went dark at the memory, and she tried to shake it from her mind. To see entire neighborhoods leveled to nothing but a driveway and a pile of matchsticks is an image you don't forget.

Twister revved up as he approached the women, then slammed the brakes sliding sideways on a slick patch of clay. "High holy shit! I told Ray, there was no way in hell Charlie would show up at your doorstep. I had to see it with my own eyes! Cousin, it's been way too long."

Twister swung himself out of the UTV like a chimpanzee, and a scruffy, long-haired white and gray spotted Maine Coon hopped out from the cargo bay close on the heels of his Timberlands. He rushed Charlotte with a huge gap-toothed grin, wrapped her hard in a bear hug, picked her up, and shook her. "How's Grandma doing?"

"Put me down!" Charlotte tried to conceal a laugh and maintain composure as he placed her carefully on her feet, muscles bulging from his too-tight black t-shirt. "Grandma's fine…her Parkinsons is under control for now, but she really misses Grandpa. You should go see her, you know."

Twister looked at the feet. "She doesn't want to see a delinquent like me."

"Greg, you're thirty-seven. That no longer qualifies as a delinquent." Charlotte reminded him of his age that he tended to deny, and the white bread name he was given to remind him who he was before the persona of Twister took over.

"Charlie, come on. You know what I mean," he put a hand on her shoulder. "Grandma always wanted me to do something honorable like be a firefighter or some shit. I'm not even working right now. I can't show my face to her. Hey, who's your friend?"

Emily stuck out her hand and gave her most dazzling smile, the disarmingly sweet one she used for difficult patients. "Emily Sharp. Nice to meet you Twister...or do you prefer Greg?"

Clearly charmed, he slowly raised her hand to his mouth and gently kissed it. "Whatever you like, Emily. I couldn't help but notice you aren't wearing a wedding band."

"Twister!" Charlotte hit his hand off Emily's. "Knock it off! Take us up to see Ray."

He gave his cousin a mischievous grin. "You bring a beautiful woman with you and expect me not to show her appreciation? That would be rude." He opened the door to the UTV. "Ladies, your chariot awaits but sit in the back. Bjorn rides shotgun."

"Who's Bjorn?" Charlotte asked looking around at the empty forest.

"BJORN! Get over here!" He shouted as if he was commanding a platoon of soldiers.

*Me-ow-owow.* The fluffy Main Coon emerged from a cluster of tall ferns, gave a squeaky weak meow, and jumped in the driver's seat.

"Move over, you little motherfucker you know I'm driving." The cat obeyed without hesitation and sat in the passenger seat. "Excuse his pathetic meow. Little dumbass drank bleach water from a toilet when he was a kitten. Broke his fuckin' meower or something."

Emily gave Charlotte an amused smile. Despite Twister's rough exterior, there was something approachable about him that put her at ease. It wasn't hard to see Charlotte still had love for her cousin despite their estrangement and differing lifestyles.

They climbed the muddy driveway slowly, accounting for the weight of three people and Bjorn, who climbed onto Twister's lap. Twister drove one-handed to free the other for giving scritches. "So, Charlie, are you gonna tell me what you're doing here or what?"

She shook her head. "It's a long story. Let's wait till we see Ray."

He nodded and kept his eyes on the road. "Yes, ma'am."

At one point in time, Ray's house must have been a sight to behold atop this now-overgrown hill overlooking the valley. It was a Civil War era two-story farmhouse with a crooked wrap-around porch, peeling paint, and narrow windows with ripped screens where animals had torn through. An ancient maple tree stood in the front yard; scattered beneath it was a hodgepodge of lawn chairs and a scattering of crushed beer cans where visitors evidently enjoyed the shade. Despite the relentless Missouri heat, he didn't have air conditioning; every window in the house was open and some of them held dusty white box fans.

Ray stood shirtless behind a screen door watching them approach. His face was shadowed beneath a weathered gambler's cowboy hat. His white chest was turned orange by the setting sun and illuminated a tattoo of eight tridents radiating from the center: The Helm of Terror.

The UTV came to a stop and Charlotte reached for the handle. Twister stuck out his arm to stop her. "Hold on a sec."

Twister reached under Bjorn's seat and grabbed an orange and white spray can. "Where's the dogs, Ray?" His tone was accusatory.

"I put 'em up," he took a swig from a can of Coke. "On account of our visitors."

He tossed the can to the floor. "What about me? I'm a goddamn visitor! You're okay with them trying to rip my balls off every time I get out of my truck?"

"They're just doing what I trained 'em to do," A belch. "Besides, I gave you that orange spray. Keep usin' it and it'll train 'em eventually…"

Charlotte didn't remember Ray being this…sloppy. Memories are a funny thing, though. They're clouded with emotion and seen through the eyes of a person you aren't anymore and never will be again. It was hard to remember why she had stayed with him so long. She tried to put herself in the mindset of Old Charlotte. Free dope. A place to sleep. Someone to hold at night. The (false) sense of security "bad boys" tend to emanate. A monster to keep away other monsters. What she didn't understand then, is that all monsters will eat you eventually when having you around is no longer beneficial.

Isn't that why bad men love good women? So eager to please. Always finding new ways to make them stay. When the love isn't enough, you'll cook his favorite meal, give him a back rub, and ignore the texts from *the other woman*. Then you'll take a side job to feed his habits and give him any of your leftover cash. You'll pick up his dope in the parking lot of the old K-Mart on your way home from work because *he'll buy weed from 'The Blacks'…but he doesn't want to be seen talking to them.*

Then, when none of that is enough, and he starts growing distant, the Good Girl *may* start questioning her choices. You'll call up Mama on the phone and ask if you can stay the weekend. He sees you packing a bag and knows the Good Girl Gravy Train is about to derail…he always knew it would, but it's only supposed to happen after he changes tracks. Not her choice, his. Come here, baby. Do you want to get something to eat with me before you visit your Mama? How about a movie? Why don't you try this new stuff I just bought? Hey, when you pick up some more, ask the dealer for a little extra. My buddy Mike wants to try it, too. You know where he lives, right? Whatever the dealer charges, make Mike pay double. For delivery, you know. Then bring it to me.

The Good Girl almost always stays until the monster eats her up. If she survives, she'll spend the rest of her life healing from those wounds. If she's lucky, she'll meet a brave knight who isn't afraid of her scars. He knows the damage a Monster can do, and the pain they cause repulses him to the core. He'll learn where the scars are, even the ones you hide, and be gentle around them. He'll only ever kiss you in the places it hurts the most. When the Good Girl meets a Good Man, it doesn't matter what the monsters have done to either of them. Good People always heal each other. They know each other's weaknesses inside and out, not to exploit them, but to protect them. And when people feel safe, they grow. This is how Good People become great.

You will never be safe with a monster, even if he eats other monsters. A monster will always be a monster long after you brush his fur and teach him to behave. They will always be only once removed from *beast.*

Ray opened the creaky screen door and stepped onto the porch. "Whatchu doin' here, Charlie? I thought you damned me all to hell and never wanted to see me again."

She climbed out of the UTV, after Bjorn, of course. "I've forgiven you, Ray. I've asked God to do the same."

"I wouldn't've." another swig of Coke before he descended the chipped paint porch. "I deserve Hell for the shit I've done to you. Are you happy?"

He didn't ask *are you happy* in the sarcastic way it's often used. It was more like *did you find happiness despite me?*

Charlotte thought of her Quiverfull of children that she doted on like an eighteen-year work of art waiting to be unveiled to the world; the church community that supported her in the ways her family never did; and her husband who not only saved her life but made it one worth living. Despite everything going on with Oliver, she knew how blessed she was. "I have a wonderful life."

He gave a quick nod as if he was knocking a bubble of uncomfortable emotions back down to the dark place it usually hid. "Good." He stepped forward as if to hug her, then thinking better of it stuck out his hand. "What brings you to Hillbilly Hell then?"

Charlotte and Emily looked at each other, not sure where to begin. "It's kind of a long, strange story. I need your help."

Ray laughed from his belly "Me?" He looked over his shoulder for another person. "What the hell can a heathen like me do for an angel like you?"

Charlotte's face darkened and he took the hint.

"Alright, alright. I'll hear you out. I owe you that much, anyway." He gestured towards the big maple out front. "Let's *converse* over there, ladies. It's hot as hell, and my wife's not the best at keeping house. It smells like a mule's ass inside right now."

Twister set to work choosing the cleanest and most stable-looking lawn chairs for their guests as Ray settled in what was apparently his favorite judging by the neatly stacked pyramid of soda cans on the ground to the right and the coffee can full of cigarette butts to the left.

Twister gestured at a metal frame fold-out chair with woven red and white plastic "fabric" forming the seat. He smiled his big, goofy grin. "You can have this one right here, Emily. Next to me."

Emily shook her head in amusement and as she bent to sit Twister yelled. "Whoa! Hold on!"

He snatched the camo hat off his sweaty shaved head and furiously beat the lawn chair with it. "Goddamn black widow! Ray, that's the fourth one I've killed this week I think you got a nest or somethin' in this tree." He wiped the black and red spider carcass away with his bare hand. "All clear, darlin'."

Ray nodded knowingly, like a wise hillbilly sage. "Loki is sending us a message. You ladies aren't here to mate, are you?"

"It's dangerous business mating with a Black Widow." Twister nodded along. "The females kill and eat the smaller males."

Ray placed a cigarette in his mouth and spoke around it. "They symbolize protection from evil. Female empowerment. Connection. The weaving of fates."

Twister placed a hand on Emily's, which she immediately began removing a millimeter at a time. "Are you ladies in need of protection from evil?"

Emily froze and locked eyes with Charlotte who raised her eyebrows and decided to test the waters before presenting her own spiritual beliefs. "What's all this talk of Loki, guys? Aren't you Southern Baptist? I bet you're not letting the preacher see that symbol on your chest, Ray."

"I ain't Southern Baptist. My wife showed me and Twister a new perspective."

Twister nodded in agreement. That was when Charlotte noticed the symbol on top of his bald head-Vegvísir, the Viking Compass. She recognized it from a report Oliver did on an archaeological discovery in England. It is supposed to keep a Viking from losing their way in storms.

"We follow the Old Ways. The Nordic ways." Ray explained. "I want to live as a warrior and drink mead with the All Father when I die. Life ain't as black and white as Christianity makes it out to be. Heaven or Hell, Good or Bad. Odin understands that warriors are met with difficult decisions in battle. Sometimes mistakes are made." His eyes flicked away from Charlotte's.

The screen door on the porch slammed shut and a teenage boy, not much older than their own children, strode towards them. "Charlotte, this is my son, Magnus!"

"Dad, the puppies chewed a hole in the laundry room door and shit all over the living room." He said.

He was quiet for a minute as he decided what to do. "Alright. Don't let 'em outside right now, we have company. Mom will clean it up when she gets home from work. Go grab us some sodas, will ya? I'm assuming y'all aren't interested in Jim Beam."

"Soda's fine, thank you." Said Emily cheerily. Again, difficult patient voice.

"Yeah, I'm trying to quit drinking." Said Twister. "I'll take a Mountain Dew."

Ray threw his empty can at Twister's feet. "Man, you can bring your own drinks. I was talking to the ladies."

Twister scowled but didn't respond.

Charlotte wanted nothing more than to get this over with and go home, so she squared herself in front of Ray and said: "We need help stealing something."

Ray and Twister sat up with smirks on their faces. "So…what are we talking about, like a car? A ring? The Declaration of Independence?" Ray jested.

"A map. From someone's house." Said Charlotte.

Now Ray was grinning ear to ear. "Oh, you have got my every attention Ms. Charlotte! I can probably help you…but you're sure as shit gonna have to tell the tale!"

"Charlie," Twister scolded. "You're supposed to be keeping your nose clean. You've got kids now…and you don't need to be bringin' sweet Emily into your theft ring!"

Emily nearly snorted with laughter, and finally spoke up. "It's not a theft ring, Twister. We're having problems with our kids."

"You got kids?" he asked Emily.

"Yeah, a teenage daughter and a six-year-old girl."

"I mean…kids aren't necessarily a dealbreaker for me as long as their daddy is pulling his fair share of things." said Twister.

Emily's jaw dropped at the audacity of Twister, seemingly

envisioning their life together.

"Twister! It's high time you shut your mouth, cousin." Charlotte scolded him again. "She's a widow."

"…oh, sorry." He meant it.

Charlotte returned her focus to Ray. "A few weeks ago, our kids were arrested for trespassing out in the woods. We think they were exploring an old government cheese cave."

"Damn, I miss government cheese." Lamented Twister. "Best grilled cheese sandwich you'll ever have."

Charlotte shot daggers from her eyes at him, and he sat back in silence, taking the hint. "Ever since then…our kids have been acting strange. Moody. Mean. Violent. Making…bad choices. Things that are really out of the norm for them. Some even started using drugs."

Ray listened, non-judgmentally, and tapped his cigarette on the arm of his lawn chair. "You and I both know that drugs can change a kid's whole personality. Did they get into meth or something?"

She thought of Oliver, and his detox from an unknown substance. "No…we have reason to believe…this could be supernatural. Demonic, even."

"…the black widow." Whispered Twister.

Ray gave a small nod in his direction in acknowledgment. "My people don't believe in demons. What are you trying to say? That your kids are possessed? I ain't no exorcist."

"One of the kids… was too scared to go in this cave. He's having dreams about murdered women, but he's the only one who hasn't been acting differently. The dreams have him so messed up—" Charlotte lowered her voice "…he's in a mental institution."

"And what about your kid, Charlie?" asked Ray, watching his son exit the front door carrying three slippery Cokes and a Mountain Dew for Twister.

"He's locked in his room, detoxing from something. His father and I are taking turns watching him. He's violent and mean, he missed his AP exams. This is not how my kid behaves." Charlotte gratefully took the cold can from Magnus and tried not to make it obvious that she remembered him from church camp. She regretted she couldn't convince the others to let him stay all those years ago.

Ray looked at his son. "Alright, kid. Why don't you go on inside and do your homework?"

"…it's summer, Dad. I don't have school."

"Charlotte, why the hell did you just tell me your kid was taking exams?" Ray asked.

"Oliver's taking summer classes at the college." Said Charlotte.

Ray laughed. "Well shit, here I am thinking I'm being a bad daddy. No wonder your kid is pissed at you Charlotte! He's seventeen, he should be sowin' oats and floatin' on the river with his buddies!"

"No." Charlotte said firmly. "No, he should not."

"Git on out of here so the grownups can talk." Ray waved his hand at Magnus, who grabbed a pellet gun off the ground and walked off into the forest.

After Magnus was out of earshot, Ray said "So you're telling me your kid and his friends went into a cave and came out carryin' some kind of evil?" He didn't wait for a response; instead, he steepled his hands and turned to Twister. "What you think, comrade?"

"I think we don't believe in Satan." Twister pointed out.

"Maybe Dragur?"

"Did your kid see a zombie-looking creature, Emily? Reanimated dead?" Twister asked.

"Um, I don't think so…" Emily said. "One of the kids is dreaming about dead women though."

Both men said *hmm.*

"Could be run-of-the-mill ghosts…but it was a cave…prolly Dark Elves." Said Ray.

"Dökkálfar *are* mischievous little fucks." Twister scowled. "Their dark magic could be compared to demonic evil."

*Hmm*, they contemplated.

"Guys…" Charlotte said. "I don't exactly need your help figuring out what the entity is right now. The truth is, we don't know what happened in that cave because none of the kids can tell us. We don't know what we're dealing with. That's why we need to get into the cave and find out what is down there."

Both men raised their eyebrows.

"Ya'll can't be serious." Said Ray.

"Ya'll know better than to go cave crawling in the Ozarks," warned Twister. "you'll either find meth labs or get lost and never come out."

"That's why we're here…the kids had a map of this cave." She steadied herself. "The owner took it when the kids got arrested. We need to get it back."

"…I see." Ray puffed his cigarette.

"Emily," Twister said. "Are you and Charlie asking us to commit robbery for you?"

Emily raised her eyebrows at Charlotte. "Are we?"

"No!" she exclaimed. "…I don't think so?"

"I'm not one for committing felony crimes," Twister explained to Emily. "I mean, you're a fine lady and all, but even for love, I have to draw a line. I've managed to exist this long with no jail time except that one time I pissed in the fountain at the city square and they threw me in the drunk tank."

Emily continued ignoring his advances. "I'm not asking you to commit a robbery for me."

"Well then, do tell. What is it you think we can do for you Charlotte? I'm not exactly a man of many talents." Ray said.

Charlotte assembled her thoughts. "So, we have this friend that was invited to a party at the owner's house. I was wondering if you had anything that could maybe…relax…the other guests so this friend can search the house unnoticed."

*Hmm* they said.

"What kind of party is it?" asked Twister.

Emily smirked. "A swinger party."

Ray started hooting with laughter. "Oh, hot damn! Are you talking about Snake Oil Stephanie?"

Charlotte nodded.

Twister scowled. "Man, I hate those two. 'Rick the Dick' screwed my girl in high school."

Ray laughed again. "What girl didn't he screw?"

"Not me." Said Emily, indignant.

If possible, Twister became more smitten. "' Course not. You're too smart to fall for his shit, Emily."

Emily couldn't help letting a small smile escape. She was secretly proud of the fact she'd avoided being on his roster- not that Rick didn't try. Constantly. Men like that are always trying to fill a void inside themselves, and his was bigger than most.

"Alright, so just to recap," Ray took a sip of Coke. "Your kids are acting possessed by what you believe is a demon… so you want to steal a map to a cave and see what they got into. Your friend was invited to the property owner's swinger party, and you want my help incapacitatin' the partygoers so that she can find it. Is this correct?"

Said out loud, Charlotte realized how wild it sounded, but who was Ray to judge? "Sounds right."

"How fancy are we talking?" asked Twister. "Is this the type of place she could pull out a bag of magic mushrooms and it would be no big deal or…?"

"Pretty fancy." Said Emily. "They asked her to bring two bottles of 'good Champagne'."

Ray was deep in thought. Finally, he said: "Are you familiar with Pompey the Great?"

The women shook their heads *no*, but seemingly Twister was. He jumped up and clapped his hands. "Oh, hell yeah! Raymond, you are a genius!"

"Sit down and let me tell it to 'em." Ray gestured with his palms down to settle Twister, then he fixed his eyes somewhere in the distance. "Pompey was a general of the Roman Republic...you know who Julius Caesar is right?"

Charlotte rolled her eyes. "Of course I do, Ray. I apologize for not having the names of all his generals off the top of my head."

"No matter," Cigarette flick. "Nearly two thousand years ago during the Third Mithratic War, Pompey led an army up the coast of the Black Sea, chasing after the Persians." A sip of coke. "Now this Pompey fella was a scary motherfucker. He became a general when he was just a kid, and they called him *The Teenage Butcher*. He absolutely destroyed the Spartans, pirates, and kings. He was allies with Caesar, but eventually was a threat to him, too so Caesar tried to have him killed. He ran off to Egypt, but they did 'em in before he even stepped off the boat, on account of Julius bangin' their Queen. My point is...as I said, Pompey was a scary motherfucker."

Charlotte sighed with impatience, "It's great to see you've continued your education of the Roman Empire, Ray, but what does this have to do with my situation?"

"Charlie, just wait, he's gonna get to it." Twister grinned, eager for whatever came next.

Ray lowered his voice, "So here's the Persians, gettin' followed by Pompey's army up the coast, and they realize they can-*not* win in a fair fight. So, somebody gets this bright idea..."

"It's Mad Honey!" Twister squealed in delight.

"That's right." Ray nodded. "There's these flowers in the mountains in Turkey called *ro-do-dender-ons*. It's the only kind of flower that grows there. So when the bees make their hives way up in the mountain cliffs, their honey is made with pure, concentrated hallucinogenics...on account of this particular flower's pollen."

Twister was practically hopping with excitement, then stopped. "But you can't take too much. Or you'll shit yourself stupid. Maybe die."

"That's right." Ray nodded. "The Romans didn't know this...but the Persians did. So they come up on this village, and lay out a bunch of bread with honeycombs and mead made with the Mad Honey. Now if there's one thing I know about soldiers--and men in general--they are *always* hungry."

"Mmmhmm. That's right." Said Twister. "All that marchin'."

Another sip of Coke. "So, they set up the tables, knowing the Roman soldiers wouldn't be able to resist free food. The villagers got the hell out of dodge. The Persians hid and waited. Sure enough, here comes the Romans, and with no hesitation they stuff their faces with bread covered in honey, mead, and honeycombs. That's when the fun started."

"Ray, let me tell this part. PLEASE." Twister begged.

"Fine." Ray unbuttoned his pants, then lit another cigarette.

"The Roman soldiers were so disoriented they couldn't fight, and the Persians slaughtered them. Or they shit themselves to death." Said Twister. "That's why you can't take too much."

"I'm not taking any Mad Honey!" said Charlotte.

"Not you, woman!" Scoffed Ray. "The swingers. Put some in their champagne, and you could probably do whatever the hell you want. They won't remember a thing. It'll wear off in about a day. Plenty of time to do what you gotta do. I've got some in the house…a birthday gift from a buddy. Why don't you go grab it, Twister?"

"Why don't *you* go get it? I'm not your errand boy." Twister scowled.

"Because I'm entertaining these lovely guests and we need to discuss payment," Ray said.

Twister skulked off to the house.

"Can you believe this guy?" Ray threw his cigarette on the lawn in Twister's general direction. "Gettin' all high and mighty lately. He's salty at me for not being able to wrestle anymore. He used to be my manager. Now he's gotta get a real job. Talkin' about going to college. I told him *you are too goddamn old.* What he needs to do is find a good woman to take care of him. He's too picky though. Lookin' for true love and all that bullshit."

Emily didn't like Ray much and had a hard time imagining sweet, beautiful Charlotte with him.

"How much do you want? For the honey?" asked Charlotte, a little insulted he wouldn't do it as a favor for old time's sake.

He scratched his stubby salt and pepper beard. "For the honey? Fifty will do. For my expertise…that's a different story."

Ray always was a hustler, Charlotte thought. "What do you want?"

"Your vote." He pointed at Charlotte and Emily with his best smile.

"For…?" asked Emily.

"Mayor."

Charlotte stifled a laugh. "You're running for mayor?"

"Yup. Filed the papers yesterday. I may not have the education or experience of most, but I do understand the plights of the people in the Ozarks. Not the 'come-heres' from New York. I'm running for the every-man. The workin' poor of southwest Missouri." Ray sat up proudly in his seat. As someone who was probably poor, but definitely not working, the idea of him leading *anything* seemed absurd to Charlotte. Both women agreed to vote for him, despite living in a different district. Then Charlotte passed him a fifty from her bra just as Twister approached them with a bottle of honey and a slip of paper with his name and number on it.

"I'd love to take you out sometime, Em. We can go to the casino, maybe get a room or something." Twister pressed the small vial of honey and paper into her hand, as if it was already a done deal, then turned to Ray. "The dogs tore the hell out of your house. Those pitbull pups are out of control."

"They're fine! They're normal puppies, still learning is all." Ray shrugged him off.

"They're mean as badgers in a snake den, and ugly to boot." Twister held his ground.

The screen door slammed. Bam, bam, bam. Seven times, seven brown snouts pushed their way out of the house and ran wild around the yard, chasing screaming feral cats far and wide, up trees and inside hollow tree stumps.

That's when they all heard the unmistakably weak *meoowowow* and saw Bjorn scratching with all his might to climb up the hood of the UTV while a pit bull puppy dangled from his tail.

Twister's face turned purple with rage, and he sprinted with all his might to Bjorn's rescue, screaming obscenities at the unrelenting dog who was now starting the innate death shake all pit bulls instinctively know. Twister grabbed the dog around the stomach to pull him off…when suddenly he stopped fighting. Half of Bjorn's tail was in the dog's mouth. Twister's grip must have loosened in the shock of witnessing the cat's bloody stump. The dog wiggled free and ran into the forest with his souvenir.

"That's it, Ray. I'm done!" Twister pulled the shirt up over his head, scooped up Bjorn, and swaddled him in it like a newborn baby.

"Greg, calm down. I'll get rid of the dogs, I'll sell 'em half price." Ray was clamoring out of his chair looking for anything to use as a dog leash, and found a short bungee cord with a rusted hook. "I'll get 'em put up right now."

"No, I'm done with YOU. You don't respect me. You don't listen to me. And you sure as *hell* don't respect Bjorn!" Twister stomped to his rusty blue pickup with his whimpering cat and placed him gently in the passenger seat. Then he rushed to Ray, muscles pumping with rage, and raised a fist; Ray didn't move an inch. Instead, he held a face of stone and stared directly into his best friend's eyes.

"Do it. Do it, Greg. I know you've always wanted to." Ray pursed his lips.

Twister's chest heaved from adrenaline, and rather than swing his arm, he slowly uncurled his pointer finger and held it an inch from Ray's nose.

"I'm taking Bjorn. You don't deserve him. YOU NEVER DID."

Twister kicked up dust as he stomped to his truck, Ray following behind him.

"You can't take my cat!" Ray shouted. "He is my personal property!"

Twister stopped near the door to his truck, turned around, and shoved Ray hard enough to knock him back a few feet.

"First of all, Bjorn is not your property! He is a living being with feelings and he just had his goddamn tail ripped off! You don't take care of your shit! Because you don't know how to be a *real* man!" Twister shoved Ray again.

Ray took a step forward to challenge Twister. Twister also took a step forward until he was close enough the blast spittle in his face. "I. Am. Taking. BJORN!"

Two more cats jumped in Twister's truck. "…I'm taking Muppet and

Crisco, too!"

Charlotte and Emily stood stunned watching the event unfold. The strangeness of two middle-aged, tattooed men with shaved heads having a friendship breakup over a cat left them speechless.

Twister climbed into his truck, slammed the door, revved the engine then reversed down the driveway. Ray threw the bungee cord on the ground and stormed into the house.

Emily looked at the vial in her hand. "Well, I guess we'll just see ourselves out then."

# Chapter 15
## Mad Honey

Lucy smoothed the silky fabric of her black and white polka-dot, knee-length wiggle skirt. She checked her reflection in the storm door window, and carefully tucked the strap of her pushup bra under the shoulder of her sleeveless red top. The ladies called her The Bombshell which made her heart glow and her cheeks blush. She felt important, and after giving her grateful hugs, they showered her with promises of free drinks and "I owe you ones". The truth was, Lucy wanted so badly to be part of this group of parents, she would have done anything to be valuable to them. Including drugging a party of swingers and robbing their home.

She shifted the cloth shopping bag containing three bottles of the most expensive champagne at Brown Derby liquor store and rang the doorbell. Classical music chimed on the inside and voices lowered. Lucy looked closer at the cars parked in the driveway of the secluded home: all dark colors, dark windows, shiny rims. Expensive, but not flashy, cars with leather seats and all the options. Arkansas, Kansas, and Oklahoma plates. This was not some hillbilly Craigslist orgy. These were people with wealth.

*I am a person of wealth,* Lucy reminded herself. *I deserve to be here. I am not rejected-sad-girl, "crying on the bathroom floor Lucy" anymore.* She pulled up the elbow-length black silk gloves she wore to cover her scars. Her past wasn't something she felt like answering for to a house full of horny strangers. She refocused. *Find the map. Where could it be?* Benny and the ladies suggested looking in desks and file cabinets, maybe stacks of paper by the door, and bedside tables. First, she needed to make sure everyone drank the champagne. They all worried it wouldn't work. Lucy had no intention of sleeping with anyone tonight, so the backup plan was to climb out a bathroom window if necessary to escape. Stella was parked a mile down the road with Gemma, "ready to rumble" they said, Gemma with mace, Stella with an Irish shillelagh…for some reason.

Stephanie opened the door wearing a loose golden shimmery top and black leggings, with black wedge heels. Her hair was piled in a loose curly bun on her head, and she wore enormous false eyelashes that didn't suit her face. One had popped halfway loose from the adhesive and it looked like she had big spiders crawling out of her eyes. Eyes that swallowed Lucy up in one gulp.

"Oh. My. Goodness." Stephanie seemed to bathe in Lucy's essence. She wasn't the only one. Anyone within viewing distance of the front door had stopped mid-conversation to take her in. Middle-aged men in tailored suits with no tie and the top buttons of their shirts undone grinned like they were being served a sizzling steak at their favorite restaurant. "Lucy, you are gorgeous. Thank you so much for coming. No plus-one?"

Lucy turned on the charm. "I'm afraid it's just me, Stephanie. Lovely earrings, by the way."

Stephanie beamed. "Do you really like them? I made them myself. I'm thinking about putting some in the shop, but I'm afraid they may be a little too fancy for my customers."

Lucy gently touched Stephanie's arm. "You know, I own a shop too! It's less bohemian and more…classic. If you ever want to display at my shop just let me know!"

Hook, line, and sinker, Lucy netted Stephanie in a matter of minutes. "That's so generous of you. Small business owners need to support each other. Isn't that right Richard?"

The infamous Rick the Dick appeared from around the corner, summoned by his wife to receive his gift. He looked from Lucy to Stephanie with disbelief. "*This* is the woman you've been telling me about? Lucy, why haven't we met before?"

They shook hands. His were wide and strong like a carpenter's and they enveloped Lucy's tiny hands until they disappeared. He had muscles in the places that mattered to him, apparently his arms only. He wore a blue striped short-sleeved silk shirt in contrast to the rest of the suited-up men in the room, and a wool ivy cap on his head. He seemed charming, with a single dimple in his left cheek and curly hair poking out from under his hat--not at all what Lucy expected after the warnings from the other women.

"I've been keeping to myself the last few years," said Lucy. "I'm trying to get back in the game and network." She wasn't sure at what point this would transform from the guise of a networking event to hanky panky.

"Well thank you for coming to our event. You're a welcome addition." Richard led her into the large living room with cathedral ceilings. "Everyone, this lovely breath of fresh air is Lucy."

*"Look at that shiny unicorn."* Lucy overheard someone say.

The men's eyes grew wild as they greeted her one by one. Although their demeanor and faces remained stoic, she couldn't help but feel she was in a pen of bulls snorting and stomping, ready to challenge all the rest for the privilege of the mount. All, except one.

The last person to shake Lucy's hand was tall and slim, in a grey suit with a black striped tie. His hair was platinum blonde, shiny, and slicked back from his face. When he approached, he didn't offer his name, only lifted her hand to his lips, kissed it gently, and looked up at her with beautiful deep-set eyes-- one brown, one blue. Lucy felt an uncontrollable jolt through her body, and as quickly as he greeted her, he was gone again to mingle in a different room.

"What's this you have in the bag, sweetness?" Stephanie asked, already knowing the answer.

Lucy snapped out of her trance and smiled, "Three bottles of Armand de Brignac Ace of Spade."

As people of expensive tastes, the guests exclaimed in appreciation, fully aware of the quality and the eight hundred dollar per bottle price tag. Lucy had chosen it knowing no one would be able to resist at least a sample; and also for the golden color which could easily conceal the honey. Stephanie brought the bag to the kitchen as Richard led Lucy around the house.

"We appreciate a unicorn like yourself attending our party. It's almost entirely couples who swap around, but there are quite a few who would prefer an experience with only a third. I'm sure you sensed their eagerness." Richard explained as he casually led her out of the living room.

Lucy nodded politely. "So…what do I need to do, put my keys in a bowl or something?" Lucy had prepared a mock set just in case with the keys to her old apartment.

Richard laughed. "That's a myth, Lucy. At least mostly. Some people may do that, but here we follow standard swinging rules of consent. Women choose who they partner with, or not at all. It's entirely up to you what experiences you have tonight. Just say what you want or need, and if anyone disrespects you come to me or Stephanie and we will set it straight, okay?"

Again, Lucy struggled to apply the picture his old classmates painted with this reassuring and thoughtful man in front of her. "Okay, that sounds a lot better than a random partner."

He led her down a hallway. "The room we just left is our social room. There you can have a drink, chat and get to know people. If you don't leave the social room all night, that's fine. Each of *these* rooms is a playroom." Richard pointed to four different doors down a long hallway of his giant house. "Like I said, we follow standard rules: the Door Code is if the door is open you can watch from a distance and only participate if invited. If the door is closed it's "do not disturb".

Lucy nodded, afraid to admit to herself she found this whole experience utterly fascinating. "These rooms are bathrooms with showers and towels. That room over there is sundries--condoms, lube, toys, batteries. I think we even have some card games and dice in there...scarves, blindfolds. Honestly," Richard shrugged. "People leave stuff here all the time I don't know what you'll find in there. Probably a lot of fuzzy handcuffs."

Lucy managed a polite smile as they exited the hallway to another part of the home. Richard pointed out some sliding doors. "That leads outside to a hot tub and sauna. We clean it after every event so...ya know. And over there is the kitchen. We set out some snacks and extra booze. Let's go see if Stephanie hid your good stuff!"

They found Stephanie frantically rifling through drawers. "I can't believe I lost the corkscrew!"

Richard reached deep into his pocket and pulled out a red Swiss Army knife. "Don't worry honey, I've got it."

He pulled the corkscrew tool and with a pop, Richard had all three bottles open in a matter of minutes. If Lucy didn't act quickly, Stephanie was about to start pouring glasses before she had a chance to spike the champagne.

"Oh, Stephanie, you have a house full of guests. Why don't you let me fill the glasses for everyone? Back in college, I waited tables at a golf resort, this will be a piece of cake. I could bring that, too if you want." Lucy fake laughed and pointed to slices of angel food cake on a tray.

Richard and Stephanie laughed heartily, obviously smitten with Lucy the Kitten.

"You are *so* sweet, Lucy! I suppose if you insist…it is your champagne after all!" Stephanie pointed to a shelf under the island. "The glasses are under there. Oh, the guests are going to ADORE you!"

Richard stayed in the kitchen and continued to smile, giving Lucy a long look that said *dibs*. Lucy tried to ignore him by looking down under the island, slowly pulling out champagne glasses. When she finally peeked up he was gone. Breathing a sigh of relief, she pulled off her black gloves and reached inside her bra, deep under her left boob for the container of mad honey. When the girls gave it to her, she expected it to be shaped like a bear. Instead, it was a small glass spice jar the size of a bottle of pain reliever. She swirled it in the light. The honey was the color of red mud. She hoped it would blend well with the champagne.

"I haven't seen mad honey in a millennium." A smooth male voice with a British accent said behind her.

Lucy froze and lowered her hand to the counter, her heart thumping and her breath shallow. Click, click, click. His footsteps stopped at her side. It was the man with one blue eye.

"Go ahead, then. Don't let me stop you." He said nonchalantly. "You've got a room full of fifty-year-old men, they could use the aphrodisiac."

Unsure of what to do, she twisted off the lid with shaking hands. He watched her intensely. As she was about to pour into the first bottle of Armand de Brignac he said, "Hold on."

Lucy stopped, froze in mid-air, and watched as he grabbed two glasses and filled them to the brim. He smirked at her. Those eyes bored into her skull and made her feel like a mouse in a corner begging the cat to eat her, rather than trying to run away. "We don't need an aphrodisiac, do we Lucy?"

As he sipped and watched, she poured a third of the honey into the first bottle. It easily dissolved as she gently swirled it.

"Where'd you get those scars, Lucy?" the blue-eyed man asked.

Lucy had forgotten her gloves were off. "None of your business."

"True," he said. "I was simply allowing you an opportunity to share before I made any assumptions."

Lucy's cheeks blazed red. She turned her attention back to the task and poured another third of honey into the second bottle. She hoped this guy wasn't going to become a problem.

"I've heard mad honey can cause hallucinations...or worse...if you eat too much. But I'm sure you know what you're doing, don't you Lucy?" The blue-eyed man cocked his head in curiosity.

It was at that point Lucy realized no one ever told her how much to put in. It must have shown on her face because the man smirked in between sips.

After Lucy finished pouring the last bit of honey into the third bottle, the man sat down his own drink and began filling the guests' glasses. "You know," he said "there's a mushroom from Russia--*amanita muscaria*--it's a red toadstool with white spots, like the kind you'd see in a cartoon with fairies. If you consume it, you hallucinate for eight hours straight...either with euphoria or temporary insanity. Maybe you should have used that instead?"

Lucy felt like a worm was burrowing into her brain, seeking all her secrets. "Mushrooms are dangerous."

He nodded. "Yes, true. Amanita muscaria *must be boiled several times* before it's safe for consumption...otherwise, the user will meet a painful death." He nodded with a frown in mock sadness. "Still, I can't help but think you and I would have had a much more enjoyable time watching the guests temporarily insane than the literal shit show you're about to create, don't you think so, poppet?"

"What do you mean?" Lucy was told it would make the guests tired and confused, maybe hallucinate. "Mad honey's just an aphrodisiac."

He smiled mischievously. "I think I'm going to try the sauna. Let me know when the fun begins."

He slinked out of the room. Lucy found herself wondering who he was, how he made his money, and why he was here, then decided he was a puzzle she could solve later if necessary. She loaded two trays with champagne glasses and expertly hoisted them up, one on each hand. She hadn't lied about this part--she paid her way through college on the tips she earned at that country club and was damned good at her job. She exited the kitchen's swinging door to cheers from Stephanie and Richard's guests.

"There she is!"

"Finally, the good stuff! These cheap bastards brought Jim Beam."

The guests swarmed her; within minutes the trays were empty, and every single guest was sipping a drink. Phase one complete.

"Aren't having any sweetie?" Stephanie asked Lucy.

"Of course!" Lucy backed up. "I left it in the kitchen. Be right back!"

Lucy bolted into the kitchen, taking long deep breaths. She slammed back her unspiked champagne, which was delicious, and regretted not savoring it. As she sat on a stool, she looked around the room for anything that could possibly have the map. Nothing on the fridge magnets, so she started opening the kitchen drawers.

"What Midwesterner doesn't have a junk drawer?" Lucy asked herself out loud, finding nothing but carefully organized kitchen tools.

It had been ten minutes, and she realized she couldn't hide out much longer. The guests had begun getting louder.

"Lucy! Is there any more in there?" someone yelled.

She still had one full bottle. "Yup, one sec!"

Lucy grabbed the bottle and realized whoever had another glass would essentially be double-dosed. She scanned the "social room" with the bottle in hand. Who was the biggest? The most aggressive? The most likely to cause a problem?

Who did she most need to be out of commission?

Lucy made a b-line for Stephanie and Richard as she maneuvered around people holding out their glasses saying, "Lucy, Lucy, top me off!"

"I need to share with our lovely hosts first!" Lucy greeted them with her most dazzling smile and happily noticed both their glasses were empty; as she poured their second glass, she noticed their eyes were glazed over. "Drink up, friends."

Next, she made her rounds to the men. For a few, she tried to only give half glasses, but some insisted they be filled to the brim. Lucy acquiesced and worked the room until the bottle was empty.

After thirty minutes it was becoming clear the mad honey was taking effect. Belts and shoes were coming off, women were laughing and nuzzling the men's necks. Someone highjacked a Bluetooth speaker and began playing seventies rock. Richard and Stephanie were sunk deep into pillows on the loveseat. Lucy thought she heard Stephanie complain over the sound of Stix's "Renegade" that she had a stomachache but made no effort to move.

Lucy excused herself to the restroom to the few guests who would notice, but most seemed distracted: by the music, by their partner, or even by imaginary birds landing in their hair. She slipped from the "social room", and decided it was very unlikely the map would be in any of the "play rooms" or bathrooms. She tiptoed upstairs and began with the room furthest away, plotting that by the time people noticed her missing she would be close enough to the stairs she could pretend she was lost.

The first room was the primary bedroom which was surprisingly normal. Lucy half expected some sort of BDSM setup or another kink. Instead, the room was tidy and simple with an antique four-poster bed covered in a thick blue comforter. There was a small TV, a few dressers and bedside tables. On Stephanie's table was a purple pair of reading glasses and the classic self-help book "How to Make Friends and Influence People". Inside the drawer was a vibrator.

On Richard's side was a TV remote and a phone charger. In his drawer was a gun, six bullets, and a bag of chocolate-covered peanuts shoved in the back. No map.

"What are you looking for?"

Lucy turned around to see the blue-eyed man in nothing but a towel. His white-blond hair was wet with sweat.

"What are *you* looking for?" she snapped.

He laughed. "I was in the sauna. I'm looking for a place to take a shower. All the bathrooms are being used downstairs…can't imagine why."

Lucy squinted, afraid of what he meant.

"If you tell me what you're looking for, maybe I can help. I really don't want to go back downstairs." He said.

Lucy wanted to get out of there, out the front door, and bolt down the street to Stella's car; but she knew everyone was counting on her. She knew she was already in so deep she needed to see this through.

"Are you going to tell them?" Lucy asked.

"The real question is…why *shouldn't* I?" The blue-eyed man leaned against the door frame and crossed his arms.

Lucy had no intention of giving this man anything in return for his silence or help, but she blurted out. "I'm looking for a map."

A bigger smile. "A map of what, Lucy?"

"A cave."

"I see," he tapped his finger in contemplation. "You know, one of the rooms I looked in was an office. Maybe we should check there?"

Lucy rushed past him and into the hallway. "On the left." He said, casually strolling behind, still in a loosely secured towel.

She opened the door and was hit with the overpowering smells of old musty books. Unlike the rest of the home, which was minimalist and bright, this room had the curtains drawn and had the energy of a grumpy old man sitting in his own filth. The only items that weren't dusty were placed on the cherry-colored desk in the center of the room. On it were standard office items--a laptop, a cup of black pens, stacking paper sorters, and a coaster. The rest of the room could have passed for 150 years old.

Lucy was drawn to a glass gun cabinet. Inside were what appeared to be Civil War era pistols and rifles. The wall behind it was covered in framed photos from the 1800's, and thoughtfully displayed military regalia.

"Some interesting books here, wouldn't you say?" The blue-eyed man was dragging his finger across the spines of a shelf, leaving a trail in the dust.

"Stop touching things! They'll know someone was here." Still, her curiosity brought her to his side to read the titles of the books.

"*Moonchild…The Book of Thoth   Magick in Theory and Practice…Sex Magick.* Who's Aleister Crowley?" Lucy looked up from the shelves.

"An occultist." The man's gaze was on the wall behind her.

Lucy shrugged. "Well, that's not surprising. Stephanie does own one of those 'new age' shops."

"Of course, of course…" he said, almost sounding bored.

Lucy returned to the desk and began opening drawers. Again, nothing strange---scissors, phone bills, paper clips. No map.

As the man slowly wandered the room in his towel, Lucy frantically opened file cabinet drawers, and the downstairs guests grew loud. Some were screaming. Lucy heard a car door slam and tires squealing down the driveway. Her time was limited.

"Shit! Where else would someone keep a map? A dusty old office seems the most obvious place!"

The man nodded. "It most certainly does. I mean, they even have one framed on the wall behind you."

Lucy whipped around. Stained. Hand drawn. Titled "The Cheese Caves".

"Oh my God. That's it. It *has* to be it! Why is it framed?" Lucy reached to take it off the wall and paused.

"That *is* perplexing. Must have some sort of sentimental value, I'd assume. It's a shame you have to steal it." The man slowly spun a dusty globe.

"They're going to know! If I take it off the wall they'll notice." She froze with arms outstretched, trying to decide.

"Oh, he will notice." The blue-eyed man said. "…but will he know it was *you?*"

Lucy considered his words momentarily, then took the frame off the wall. She unclipped the back of the frame and removed the delicate map, gently folding it and placing it in her bra under her right boob, since the honey took up real estate on the left. She closed the back and put the frame back on the wall.

"There! They probably won't notice it's missing for a while." Lucy immediately switched to the next phase of the plan, escape.

"I imagine our hosts won't be missing much of anything besides a toilet for quite some time…" The blue-eyed man left the office and Lucy listened to his bare footsteps descend the stairs.

Lucy wasn't sure if the blue-eyed man could be trusted, but the moment she left the intense odor of the office…she understood he wasn't lying. The waft of sewage was being carried upstairs by the enormous ceiling fans. She hesitantly slinked towards the staircase and was greeted by groans--some of pleasure, some of agony. At the bottom of the stairs, Lucy stepped around an oblivious swapped couple feverishly kissing and licking each other's faces. She passed a shirtless man hiding behind a ficus tree screaming about giant flies. A woman with no shoes on rushed past her towards the front door, stopping to vomit in the umbrella holder on her way out. The social room was no longer social. Lucy and her mad honey had caused a full-service orgy amongst all those not puking, screaming, or fighting for a turn in the bathroom.

The smell was enough to make a lucid person faint, so she plugged her nose but briefly stood transfixed watching the pulsing mass of middle-aged bodies defiling the white carpet and good vibes of Stephanie and Robert's living room. Although, they didn't seem to mind, as they howled from the center of it all.

"I told you they wouldn't notice." The blue-eyed man put on his gray jacket over an untucked shirt. "Although, if I were you, I wouldn't stay too long. Once the euphoria wears off it's going to get messy in here…not enough bathrooms, you see."

He escorted Lucy to the front door, and they carefully stepped around the puddle of vomit that missed the umbrella holder. He held out his hand to help her down the steps to the driveway as if they had just left Prince Charming's ball. "I trust you have a ride waiting for you?"

Lucy nodded, still in shock by all she'd seen and confused by the feelings this strange-looking man welled up inside her.

He opened the door of his black Mercedes and took a moment to make himself comfortable on the oiled leather seats. He smiled at Lucy and raised an eyebrow.

"I hope the next time we meet, you bring mushrooms instead."

# Chapter 16
## Huckleberries

"I'm your huckleberry." Said Gemma.

Stella popped the last red gummy bear from the package in her mouth and looked over her shoulder at Emily who shrugged in confusion.

"What the hell does that mean, *hermana*?" Stella shook the bag and, not finding the color she wanted, tossed what was left to Gemma. "Is that a witch thing or a librarian thing?"

"It's a Southern thing. Haven't you heard the saying before?" Gemma cocked her head.

"No, I haven't." Stella crossed her arms. "Because Missouri isn't in the South, Gemma. Despite what my confederate flag-waving dipshit neighbors think, this is a Union state. I voted for Obama--twice--and they stole all our political signs. Now I let our dogs shit on their lawn."

Charlotte considered her most recent backwoods visit to Ray's compound. "I'm pretty sure the Ozarks thinks it's in the South. Arkansas bleeds over."

"Anyone who's been to Missouri knows the Arkansas state line is not where the Midwest ends. It's halfway through Missouri...Columbia maybe? Yeah, seems right." Emily snuggled deeper into Charlotte's overstuffed sofa. She desperately needed a nap after staying up until two am waiting for Esme to come home.

Everyone nodded in agreement.

"Anyway," Gemma reigned the conversation in. " 'I'm your huckleberry' means I'm the right person for the job. Going into the cave, I mean. You've all done so much to figure out what's going on with the kids. I should go… because I'm not afraid. I've made friends with the darkness."

Stella laughed with a snort. "Alright, Batman."

"You can't go down there alone. It's not safe." Emily pushed herself out of the sofa. "I'm going too."

"Well, I can't let you ladies have all the fun." Stella picked up a smudge stick from Charlotte's coffee table and sniffed it. "Batman, if you're the huckleberry, I'm your Robin."

The front door into Charlotte's living room burst open and overwhelmed the space with a cacophony of tossed shoes, backpacks, and children's laughter. The occasional "Hi Mom!" accompanied hugs from the littlest ones.

Charlotte stood up to stop the kids from leaving the room. "Hey guys, don't run off quite yet. How was co-op? Were you good for Mrs. Hansen?"

"Caleb fell asleep during Bible study."

"Yeah, well you farted."

"Did not! That was Jacob!"

Their mother looked at the door expectantly as she counted her chicks. Worry flooded her normally serene features. "Where's Oliver?"

"Dunno. He didn't leave with us."

"What?" Charlotte ran her hand through her dishwater blond hair as if trying to shake solutions loose from her mind.

"Yeah, he does that a lot." Said Rosilynn. "He never goes to Bible study. He told me he memorized the whole thing, so he doesn't have to go."

"He gets to play with his friends now." Gabriel spun a strand of his hair on his finger, and sweetly asked, "Mommy, if I memorize the entire Bible can I stop going to co-op and watch TV instead?"

Charlottle kneeled and pulled her young son in close enough to smell the graham crackers and peanut butter on his breath. "Sweet pea, what do you mean he gets to play with his friends?"

He shrugged. "Dunno. Two boys"

She looked over her son's shoulder at the women on the sofa. Furrowed eyebrows let her know they understood what this meant. Gemma nodded and rose to be introduced.

"Kids," Charlotte stood and smoothed the creases in her khaki pants. "I'd like you to meet my friend, Gemma."

Previously overlooked by the tiny tornadoes, Gemma waved a spider-webbed hand in their direction. "'sup?"

The children froze, transfixed, and absorbed every aspect of her aesthetic like sponges, from her purple and black shaggy bob cut to her mid-calf platform Doc Martens.

"Whoa," said Megan. "Are you a real-life witch?"

Charlotte coughed, but Gemma smiled sweetly. "I'm a *good* witch. Wicca is my religion, just like yours is Christianity."

After an uncomfortable silence, Caleb spoke. "The Bible says we're supposed to throw stones at you until you die."

"Caleb!" Charlotte squawked.

"Mommy, I don't want to do that."

"Me neither, her hair is cool and would get all bloody."

"I'll do it! I've been throwing stones at cans in the backyard, I've got good aim!"

"You've been throwing them at the goat. I saw you."

"Was not!"

Charlotte waved her hands in the air as if she were maneuvering airplanes. "Everyone sit down criss-cross-applesauce!" she snapped. "We are NOT stoning Gemma!"

"But Mom," Caleb squirmed into cross-legged position. "*Mrs. Hanson* says that the *Bible* says that we shouldn't suffer a witch to live."

Charlotte's cheeks flushed red as she avoided eye contact with Gemma. "Well…" she growled in frustration. "ignore that part!"

Her children gasped and sat in shocked silence.

"We can do that?" They whispered.

A low chuckle rumbled from Stella who watched the chaos unfold from Charlotte's husband's favorite recliner. "I know quite a few Christians who ignore a lot of things."

Emily smirked and sipped her coffee, entertained by this unfolding heathenous act.

"Gemma is my *friend*, and even though we have different beliefs about God, she's here to do a blessing on you."

"Do you mean like when Father Ezra puts water on our heads?" Tristan asked.

Charlotte cocked her head. "Sort of. Gemma is going to use smoke. Aren't you?"

Gemma cleared her throat and stood at attention. "Yes. So first I'll light this bundle of herbs on fire and then blow it out so it makes smoke." She held the smudge stick up for them to see while the mothers observed Gemma's sinful lesson.

"Ms. Gemma," Megan asked. "Is that pigweed, ragweed or Russian thistle? I have allergies."

Gemma laughed. "Um, no. It's white sage, from the desert."

Charlotte placed a hand on Megan's shoulder. "Sweetie, will you ask Ms. Stella and Ms. Emily's children to come inside?"

Little ears perked at the surprise news of young visitors. They wiggled and waited eagerly for Megan to return from the backyard with Emily's six-year-old daughter, Harper, and a slightly older bespectacled girl with gorgeously wild curls sprouting from two space buns on her head.

Stella immediately jumped up from the sofa, sloshing her coffee on her shirt. "Where's Xander?"

Megan smiled back cheerily. "Who's Xander?"

"Shit." Stella sat her coffee cup on the table. "Rosie, where is your brother?"

Rosie looked behind her and seemed surprised not to see him. "…he wanted to see the goat."

"Oh no," groaned Charlotte. "Not Bucky!"

Abandoning the smudging ceremony, Charlotte led Stella through her kitchen into a mudroom cluttered with garden gloves, sand toys, snow shovels… and a mountain of dirty muck books.

Charlotte dug through the heap and extracted two sets of rubber boots, tossing a child-sized pair of black boots printed with ladybugs to Stella. "Put these on. You won't make it twenty feet through my yard in those."

Stella looked down at her rhinestone-encrusted flip-flops, promptly kicked them off, and shoved her tiny bare feet into the ladybug boots.

The creaky old hinges of the screen door immediately summoned a free-range flock of ducks and chickens foraging beneath a large evergreen. "No!" Charlotte yelled. "Git! I'm not feeding you!"

Still, like a hoard of feathered zombies hungry for grains, they waddled and fluttered, trailing behind Charlotte as she led Stella to a small white barn enclosed in a pen.

"Bucky was supposed to be a pygmy goat. You know, those itty bitty ones. Worst thing they can do is give you a bruise on the shin." Charlotte explained. "A woman at the county fair sold him to us as a baby. Fun pet for the kids, right?"

Charlotte huffed as they b-lined for the barn. "Sure, I guess. Not *my* kids. They'd forget about it in a week and I'd end up taking care of it like I do their ugly ass iguana."

"Well, turns out he's a hundred-pound mutt that can't be trained. Well, not yet." Charlotte said as she unlatched the first of two fences. "He keeps charging at the kids, so Brent and I are trying to assert dominance."

"Are you telling me my child is in a pen with an angry goat?" Stella exhaled.

On cue, a piercing scream echoed across the yard, loud enough the scatter the following fowl in the opposite direction. Charlotte sprang into full rescue-mom mode, charged, and jumped the second white fence, landing on her feet with a squelch in the mud.

"Bucky! NO." She commanded the goat with a deep and powerful voice that contrasted with her usual soft-spoken nature.

For a moment, Stella was so taken aback she stopped walking and instinctively felt like she was a child being scolded by her own mother. She searched the pen for her son. Following the eyeline of the stamping goat, she found him barely recognizable covered head to toe in mud.

"Xander! Are you okay?" Stella yelled.

He groaned and propped himself up on his elbows. "*El cabro estupido me pego!*"

The goat held his position, transfixed on Xander as Charlotte prowled up to its side.

"You're the stupid one, *hijo!* You climbed in its territory." Stella scolded. "That's the same reason I don't swim in the ocean. It's where the sharks and jellyfishes live."

The boy started to cry. "I just wanted to touch his horns, Mom."

Charlotte slowly bent down at the oblivious goat's side.

"Well, now you touched the horns," Stella shouted. "Are you happy, Xander?"

In one quick swoop, Charlotte reached under the right side of goat and grabbed both his left legs firmly, one in each hand; then using her shoulder, she pushed him until he toppled on his side. The animal kicked in protest as Charlotte straddled it, flipped it on its back, then pinned one leg up by its head to prevent it from finding enough momentum to escape.

She grabbed a handful of mud and rubbed it on the goat's nose. "No, Bucky!"

Stella wiggled between the gap in the fence rails, then crab-walked through the mud to help her son, who looked like a churro dipped in chocolate.

"You're not getting in my truck like that." She surveyed the barn and found a garden hose with a sprayer attached to a wellhead. She lifted the lever and pointed the sprayer at Xander. "Alright, close your eyes."

Charlotte forced Bucky into submission enough that she was able to stand over the goat while holding it in place on its back with her feet. Every time it wriggled, Charlotte would yell "No!" loud enough to startle it. Stella peacefully hosed down her child as he whimpered from the cold blasts of well water.

"So, Charlie, does that method work on teenagers?" Stella asked.

Charlotte laughed. "Doubtful. You know I have a shower, right?"

"Nope. He gets the hose." Stella said. "Just like your goat, I want my kid to remember this experience."

She shook her head with a grin. "There's some towels in the barn by the sink."

Xander took that as his excusal from the hose and ran off to find a towel. Stella turned off the water and began wrapping the hose in a loop around her hand and elbow. She grinned, watching Charlotte wrangle the goat who had finally stopped squirming after fifteen minutes held still on its back. Seemingly accepting his fate, Bucky relaxed his head, and a long tongue lolled out of his mouth.

"I believe it now." Said Stella.

Charlotte laughed. "What?"

She stopped wrapping the hose. "The hillbilly thug formerly known as Charlie. I didn't see it under the quiet Catholic homeschool mom thing, but when you started yelling and flippin' that goat, it peeked out. You got a little bit of gangster in you."

"It's just a goat, Stella." She scoffed.

"You didn't see me jumping in there with that little devil-eyed monster…and the goat." Stella winked and hung up the hose. "Xander! Where are you?"

After Stella left to find her son, Charlotte released the goat, but Bucky didn't move.

She gently patted his face. "Get up big guy."

Bucky turned his head away from her.

"What? Are you mad at me?"

She patted his belly, pushed him on his side, and helped steady him on his feet. Indignant, he didn't acknowledge the help and trotted off to his lean-to.


After Charlotte and Stella washed up, they gathered the children outside for Gemma's ritual due to the dripping wet Xander and the strong smell of the sage that might require an explanation to Charlotte's husband. The children threw handfuls of cracked corn at the chickens while Gemma prepared for the smudging ceremony.

"Emily, can you cut open the smudge stick for me?" Gemma handed her a pair of scissors.

"Sure, but aren't you supposed to light the end and keep it bound? I imagine it's pretty messy otherwise." Emily snipped the cotton thread and began separating the bundle.

"Well, that's one way to smudge, but my husband says that's not the way they do it in his tribe. You take the sage leaves and roll it into a ball, like this." Gemma stripped the leaves from the small sticks and rubbed them together in her hands, whispering a quiet prayer as she went. "Here, Stella. You can do that part…about the size of a meatball."

Stella swept the loose smudge off the table into her hands and began rolling. "Whoa, whoa, whoa. Whose meatballs are we talking about? Because my man likes me to make his meatballs BIG and sauce-AY." Stella seductively rolled her body like a snake as she rubbed her hands above her head.

Charlotte gave Gemma a look that said *reel this in before the kids see.* "A gumball! Gumball size is fine." Said Gemma. "Here, put them in this cast iron pan. A lot of people use seashells, but Mika says to use this. It's firesafe and more practical."

Once the pan was full of smudge balls, Gemma separated herself from the group and knelt in the grass, placing it in front of her. She closed her eyes and slowed her breathing to a steady rhythm, then held her palms facing the sky as if receiving a gift.

*Divine Mother and Father please fill me with love and Light. Let it wash over me like a waterfall so that my cup overflows and I may bless those around me with your protection. Guardian angels, ancestors, and spirit guides- thank you for guiding me every moment of my life. Please protect me from any harm both physically and spiritually as I cleanse those in my presence today. So Mote it Be.*

Gemma lit a smudge ball with a match and waited for the flame to die out and smolder. She then placed her hands in the smoke, rotating them in circles as if washing them in water.

*May my hands be cleansed so they may do the work of Spirit with love.*

She then scooped the smoke with her hands, bringing it over her head three times.

*May my mind be pure and clear of negativity.*

Finally, she picked up a turkey feather and waved the smoke at her heart.

*May my heart be cleansed and always lead me to goodness and light even in the presence of evil and darkness*

Gemma opened her eyes to see frozen sets of tiny eyes staring in silence; curiosity being enough to halt the children's chaotic game of croquet through a pumpkin patch. Gemma rose and gestured for them to come over. They dropped their mallets, racing over with enthusiasm.

The six young children huddled around her as she assessed how best to proceed with the blessing. "Alright, I think this will work best if I do one at a time. Can you all get in line for me?"

Stella's children, Xander and Rosie, and Emily's daughter, Harper, immediately stood in a line in front of Gemma. Charlotte's four children didn't move and looked at each other in confusion.

Megan raised her hand. "Miss Gemma, what is *getting in line?*"

Charlotte jumped up from her plastic lawn chair. "Oh, goodness. Over here, kids, I'll show you. See how Rosie is standing behind Xander, and Harper behind Rosie? They form a *line* by doing so. It's a way of taking turns to get something done."

"Oh, okay, Mommy!" Her four quickly formed a line behind Harper.

Charlotte blushed apologetically. "Sorry, Gemma. Homeschooled kids don't generally need to get in line for things. They just recently learned about raising their hand to ask questions…"

Gemma laughed. "It's fine, I never thought about it that way!" She sat the cast iron pan, feather, and matches on the nearby toddler picnic table. "Okay kids, so like I explained earlier, I'm going to light this sage to make smoke and say a little prayer over you. It won't take long, and you can get back to playing. I even brought Traverse City Cherry ice cream for later! Just to double-check: moms, anyone allergic to sage?"

Emily and Charlotte shook their heads.

"Go for it, witch." Said Stella.

Megan's hand went up again. "Miss Gemma, since you are a witch, do you have a black cat?"

"Actually, yeah, I do. His name is Binx." Said Gemma.

"Just so you know I *am* allergic to cats." She shared.

Gemma smirked. "Well, I didn't bring Binx with me today, so I think you should be okay."

Satisfied, all eight children stood at attention in line.

"Xander, let's start with you," Gemma said.

"That's right," said Stella. "eat that frog, girl. Worst one first."

Cries erupted. "We're eating *frogs?* I don't want to eat frogs, mommy!"

Once again, Charlotte intervened. "You are not eating frogs. *Eat that frog* means to do the most difficult thing first."

"Wait a minute…" said Xander. "Why am I the frog?"

Gemma had already lit a new ball of smudge, and was blowing on it to encourage the smoke. She stood over Xander, who was sulking and scowling at his mother. In response, Stella stuck out her tongue. Gemma waved the smoke towards him with the feather, starting at his crown, and then down to his feet.

"Spirit, please cleanse this child of all negativity in the earthly realm or any other. May his angels, guides, and ancestors protect his mind, heart, body, and soul from evil. So mote it be."

She reached into her pocket and gave Xander an opaque white stick. "This is for you, Xander. It's a special crystal to put under your pillow--it will help protect you while you sleep."

With wide eyes, he held it up to the sun. "Whoa, that's so cool! Where'd you get it?"

"The crystal is called selenite. I dug it up myself at Oklahoma Salt Plains State Park. What you do is, dig a hole about a foot deep, pour some water on the sides and bottom of the hole, and the crystal will sparkle. After you dig it out you lay it in the sun to dry." Said Gemma.

Xander shoved it in his pocket. "Thanks, Gemma. Hey Mom, can we go digging for selenite?"

"I think since Gemma is an expert, she should take you," Stella said as she propped her feet up on a plastic riding horse with wheels.

After Gemma finished smudging and blessing the remaining children, she gave them all selenite as Emily passed out cherry ice cream. They chased chickens and whacked croquet balls with mallets to see who could hit the farthest.

"Ladies, I should smudge you as well. We also need to talk about our plan for tonight." Gemma stood in front of Charlotte with her smudge pan and wafted it over her body.

Charlotte coughed. "So when you say the prayer, can you say *Holy* Spirit, and maybe mention Jesus?"

She smiled. "Sure. *Holy* Spirit and Jesus Christ…please protect Charlotte from…sinful things and evil—

"Protect me from Satan," Charlotte stated.

"Right," Gemma continued. "And cleanse her heart, soul, mind, and body of all impurities in the Earthly realm or any other. Amen?"

"Amen." Charlotte nodded.

"Do either of you have prayer preferences?" Gemma asked the others.

"Nope, I'm not religious." Said Emily. "Is that an eagle feather?"

Gemma held it up to give her a closer look. "Nah, it's from a turkey. Most smudge feathers are. The only people legally allowed to possess eagle feathers are tribal medicine people and even they have to appeal for permission from the government. Other than poultry, it's illegal to possess any feathers in the United States, especially eagles. Even if you find one on the beach or something it's a $100,000 fine and a year in jail."

"No shit?" said Stella. "Well, come on over and bless me with Grandfather Turkey then."

As Gemma smudged Stella and Emily, they discussed their plans to explore the cave that evening, and the other parents.

As a law enforcement officer, Isabella previously urged them not to tell her any details she would be forced to divulge if they were caught but insisted they call her directly if they got into trouble. Isabella was still caring for her husband and son after what she called the "boxing accident", so Gemma gave her a blessed candle to burn in Theo's bedroom until Father Ezra could do more.

Benny's husband returned from Louisiana for a few weeks and quickly realized something had changed in the family dynamic. Assuming it was due to his extended absence, he insisted the entire family spend the next ten days together at a cabin in the Smokey Mountains of Gatlinburg, Tennessee. Gemma gave Benny an obsidian necklace for protection. Stella palmed him a small container of mace. Gemma then blessed the stuffed toy of Jesus that Father Ezra gave the twins, but was at a loss for how to help with Ashton; he was the most uncooperative and seemed to have the most severe spiritual attack of all the children. After consulting her husband, Mika, he gave Gemma a small leather pouch filled with the "four medicines" of tobacco, sweet grass, sage, and cedar to put under Ashton's bed.

Lucy hadn't returned phone calls or messages since the night of the swinger party. Since Benny hadn't needed a nanny with Christopher home, no one had spoken to her in weeks. Benny felt she needed a break after Stephanie and Richard's traumatizing orgy and promised the others he would attempt to break the ice with her after he returned from Tennessee.

To Gemma's amusement, her husband, Travis, devised a plan to keep a close eye on Trix by becoming a Furry himself. Gemma knew he often felt like the weak link in the thruple, and while she and Mika prepared for the smudging ceremony last weekend, he toiled away at the sewing machine, creating a very impressive full Fursuit of a cream-colored moth he called Moon Wing. Mika praised his natural talent for this sort of thing and encouraged him to develop it into a business…since the grilled cheese food truck didn't work out. *Thanks for bringing up yet another one of my failures in front of Gemma*, Travis thought. Travis managed to befriend enough local Furries online to get invited to the same Furmeet Trix regularly attended. Incognito he planned to ensure their child stayed out of trouble without setting off any teenagery alarms.

It was decided that Charlotte would stay home to keep in contact with everyone and host a sleepover for all their children, to her little homeschoolers' delight. By six that evening, Oliver still hadn't returned, and Charlotte's (oblivious) husband seemed relieved to leave the seemingly spontaneous sleepover of eight children under the age of ten to go searching for him.

As they prepared to leave, Charlotte fussed over the three women like a worried mother hen. "Do you have the map, Emily?"

"Yes, Mom." She patted a pink denim fanny pack. "Also have a flashlight and some bandaids. Water jug in the truck. We shouldn't be gone long enough to need much else."

Charlotte nodded. "What about you, Stella? Aren't you bringing anything?"

She reached into the interior pocket of her leather jacket and pulled out a flashlight shaped like a T-rex. She held it in front of Charlotte's face and pushed a button. The jaws opened wide making a weak and crackley *rawr…rr… rrr…r.*

"That's it?" Charlotte asked, averting her eyes from the light.

"What the hell else do I need? A sword? I'm already a level 40 Baddie. I'll be fine." Stella pocketed her dinosaur flashlight and crossed her arms in defiance.

"You absolutely cannot wear those shoes, Stella." Emily pressed.

Stella looked down at her rhinestone flip-flops, criticized for the second time that day. "Ugh! Fine." She stomped off to Charlotte's mud room and returned wearing the black ladybug boots. "I borrowed some of your husband's socks from the laundry basket. These boots make my feet sweaty."

Charlotte sighed. "Do all of you have your phones fully charged? Take pictures while you're in there if you can. Even if something doesn't make sense to you, Father Ezra may know what it is."

They nodded, waiting patiently for her to ask all her questions.

"Promise to text me when you get there and call when you get out. The kids will be fine but if I don't hear from you by dawn I'm calling Isabella, okay?"

"I'm sure we will only be gone a few hours. We don't plan on exploring further than what is safe or necessary." Reassured Emily.

Charlotte nodded tersely. "I hope you find something that will help us."

Gemma gave her a hug. "Me too. Be back soon."

"*Melatonin…*" whispered Stella on her way out the door, nodding at Xander who was jumping up and down on the sofa while shooting a Nerf gun at anyone who entered the room.


Stella slowed her SUV to a crawl as they approached the location off the farm road where Isabella said they could find the dirt trail into the woods. She turned the headlights as dim as possible, drove through the cornfield, and were quickly swallowed by the overgrown forest. They bounced along the same rutted path their children had followed and forded across the wet weather creek, now a foot deep. The bottom of Stella's vehicle scraped on a submerged field stone. She winced.

"I should have taken Mattie's work truck. How much farther?"

Emily never took her eyes off the map, trying to memorize every path and room of the cave. "Not much. Just around this turn."

The sun was barely more than a red smudge peeking through the dense trees as they approached the meadowed clearing. Black-Eyed Susans glowed as they reflected the little light that remained. Beyond the field, the limestone mound bulged from the earth.

"Over there by the hill. That must be the entrance. Mateo said there is a grate over it, right?" asked Emily.

Stella nodded. "Looks like a creepy ass version of the Poppy Fields in

*The Wizard of Oz."*

She turned off the engine, then locked their purses in the trunk, only taking what they could easily carry. Hesitantly, the women began walking towards the hill.

"Son of a –" Emily slapped at her ankle. "Damn mosquitoes."

"Hold on, I have bug spray." Gemma unclipped a tie-dye crossbody day pack and passed around a small can of deep-woods bug repellant.

"Thanks," said Emily as she gave it back. "What else did you bring? Honestly, I'm starting to feel a bit underprepared after seeing how desolate it is out here."

"Well, I have a couple of ritual candles and matches…a few tampons, cuz'…ya know. Pocket tissue. A bag of grapes—"

"What?" Stella raised an eyebrow in confusion.

"It's a healthy snack…" Gemma defended herself.

"Shouldn't you bring like protein and complex carbs and shit? Grapes are like…balls of water covered in foreskin." Stella said.

"Stella…you have a dinosaur flashlight. That's it." Gemma pointed out.

"Hmph." Stella contemplated. "Touché, Gemma. I'm sorry for judging your water balls covered in foreskin. What else is in there?"

She peeked in. "Not much…a Hello Kitty notebook, a pen, and Travis's Swiss Army knife. He doesn't know I took it."

They stood in silence for a moment and Emily finally asked, "So are we doing this, ladies?"

They began a slow, cautious trek through the field.

"The map says the entrance is by a Chinquapin Oak. I think that's it over there. Look at all the acorns." Emily pointed.

They reached it and immediately began scanning the ground, kicking away leaves and brush to find the grated entrance.

"Ouch!" Stella whined. "…found it."

She limped away as Gemma and Emily uncovered the entrance and pulled off the slatted metal door whose hinges had rusted off long ago. Gemma put on a headlamp, while the other two turned on their flashlights.

*rawr…rr…rrr…r.*

Stella's flashlight turned on, then went out.

*rawr…rr…rrr…r.*

On. Off.

*rawr…rr…rrr…r.*

"Are you fucking kidding me? The only way it stays on is if I hold the button down and the mouth is open. That's bullshit." Stella shoved it back in her pocket. "Forget it, I'll just follow you guys. I'll roar if I get lost."

Emily chuckled, and followed Gemma backwards, half crawling, down the slippery stone steps. After she reached level ground she shone her light up to the surface so Stella could find her way. They oriented themselves to the dark, then pulled the map from Emily's fanny pack.

"It looks like some sort of narrow passageway up ahead that opens up to a big chamber…then right, and past something called 'The Shakehole'." Said Emily.

"What's a shakehole? Is that like a sinkhole?" Gemma asked.

Stella and Emily shrugged.

The passageway was wide enough for Gemma and Emily to lead side by side, but it gradually became so narrow they all walked single file. This continued until they were all sideways and shimmying their way through.

"Uh…gang. We have a problem." Stella's voice echoed from behind.

Emily turned and shone the flashlight behind her. Stella's stout body was wedged between the weeping limestone walls twenty feet away. "Stella! Are you stuck?"

She wiggled and stepped back in the direction from which they came. "Well, not exactly. I can go back, but I can't go forward. For the first time in my life, my tits and ass have done me a disservice."

"What do we do?" Gemma whispered to Emily.

She stared at the wall as she thought for a moment, noticing for the first time hundreds of dated signatures spread across decades. Evidently, this cave had seen a lot of traffic. "Stella," Emily said. "The way I look at it, we only have two choices: we either all turn around…or you stay here until we return. Gemma and I can go check things out real quick and then we can all leave together."

Stella's normally lively features fell with defeat. "We've done so much to get here…and what Lucy went through to get the map, I wouldn't wish on anybody." She waved them on. "Go. I've got my dinosaur, I'll be fine. Worst-case scenario, if you two get ate by a demon, I think I can find my way back."

Emily nodded at her comrade. "We won't be long. Stay there."

Stella leaned against the wall, surrendering to the dark. She took her phone from her pocket and started playing Mahjong—it always calmed her down, and the phone gave her light.

Gemma and Emily continued crab-walking down the corridor. "I hate leaving her behind." Said Gemma.

"Me too…," said Emily. "But we have to find out what the kids were doing down here; this may be our only chance. It won't be long before Richard notices the map is missing from his office if he hasn't already."

Gemma nodded and then noticed the signatures on the wall. "Oh my Goddess, Em, look at the walls! They're covered in signatures!"

Gemma couldn't help but slow down as she fervently read the walls, scanning for a familiar name from Springfield's history. Emily bumped her with her hip more than once to get her to move along until suddenly, Gemma planted her feet and stopped dead.

Emily followed her eyes to the wall and read the signature aloud. "*Sam Clemens, March 9ᵗʰ, 1851*. Who's Sam Clemens? Gemma…are you okay?"

Gemma's hands shook as she patted her pockets, forgetting where she put her phone. Once found, she frantically punched her passcode and snapped ten photos in a row before turning to Emily. "Mark Twain. Sam Clemens is Mark Twain…he was in this cave. Wow. The historical significance of this is huge, Emily. Who else could have been here?"

"That's really amazing, but we have to remember why we're here…" Emily reminded her.

"Stella! Stella!" Gemma shouted down the corridor. "Mark Twain signed the wall!"

After a beat, she shouted back. "You think he was possessed by *el diablo*, too? Maybe he's some kind of dark wizard or something."

This snapped Gemma back into the mission. "Sorry…sorry." She whispered to Emily. "As a librarian, I'm just…it's incredibly cool."

"I get it." She said. "We're almost to the next chamber."


After ten minutes, they reached the end and entered a large, empty cavern.

"What's that?" Gemma pointed to what Emily thought was a boulder near her feet.

Emily shined her flashlight on it to reveal a tan colored tactical backpack, unzipped and opened. On the ground lay an uncapped black permanent marker. "Does that belong to Trix? It's not Esme's. It looks new, barely dusty or anything."

"No, it's not Trix's." Gemma's eyes were not on the backpack. They were on the wall.

"*Semper Revertemur.* That's Latin, right?" Emily asked.

Gemma nodded. "My Latin isn't the best, but I know *semper* means 'always'. You know, like how the Marines motto is *semper fi*- 'always faithful'."

Emily pulled out her phone and snapped a single photo before her screen turned black. "What the hell? My phone was fully charged before we left. It's dead."

Gemma checked hers, unable to hide a squeak as she said: "Mine too."

Emily zipped the large backpack shut and heaved it onto her back. "Let's make this quick. All we have to do is turn right, then past the shake hole is the storage room."

Stella had been comforted by Emily and Gemma's garbled chatter that echoed through the narrow pathway to where she waited for them to return. As it became further away, then silent, her anxiety rose a hundredfold. Her mind strayed, thinking about Mateo. Six-year-old Mateo, trapped alone in the dark for three days in a cistern. The monster named *parental guilt* pounded on the doors to her heart threatening to escape right when it was the last thing she needed.

She breathed rapidly, straining to look down the pathway, waiting for a beam from a flashlight. After thirty minutes she beat her high score on Mahjong, and it finally lost its soothing effect. Stella picked at her nail polish. Mumble rapped. Squirmed in her ladybug boots.

"Fuck this." Stella turned on the flashlight feature of her phone with one hand and reached around to expertly unhook her extra-support bra with the other. Standing on her tippy toes and lifting her breasts as high as she could, she managed to make it another ten feet down the cave passageway. Inch by inch, she maneuvered her body around the irregularities of the wall. Suck in the tummy, move a boob, duck, wiggle, tippy toes. She had been so engrossed in the process that she was shocked to eventually look up and see she had reached the end of the corridor.

She held up her phone to see where she was, and before the room was illuminated, her screen flickered and died, swallowing her in darkness.

"Oh, for fuck's sake! You've got to be kidding me," she grumbled, shoved the phone into her pocket, and exchanged it for the dinosaur flashlight.

*rawr...rr...rrr...r.*

Two paths. Down and right or up and left.

*Squeak. Squeak.*

Stella froze.

*rawr...rr...rrr...r.*

Using her T-rex, she followed the sound with her light. Above Stella, the ceiling began to thrum with movement. The air around her swirled, and quiet squeaks suddenly morphed into panicked, high-pitched squeals as startled bats dropped from their perches on the ceiling and fled deeper into the cave. Stella screamed hysterically as bats rushed past her, getting tangled in her long, dark hair as they escaped down the right-hand path.

Stella sprinted to the left.


They heard the scream just as they entered the Shake Hole Room.

"Oh, no. Stella!" Gemma exclaimed.

A cloud of bats erupted into the room. The women dropped to the ground and covered their heads as wailing bats fluttered and landed in crevices throughout the room. After ten minutes, the squeals turned once more to quiet squeaks. Gemma and Emily cautiously sat up.

"Well, at least we know it was just bats and not Stella," said Emily. "Hey, is that a shoe?"

They crawled over to a pile of rubble and pulled out a shiny black heel.

"No one would wear heels down here…" Gemma said.

They pointed their flashlights at the floor, looking for more clues as to why someone wearing three-inch heels was in a cave.

"Look at this. Very 1990's, eh?" Gemma held up a thick gold hoop earring.

Emily stood up and dusted off her pants. "Whoa, is that the shake hole?"

Water in the chamber dripped down the walls and jagged stalactites to the floor, where it dribbled steady streams from all directions to a depression in the ground. As they approached, they could see a large hole had been formed where the water had worn away a crack in the limestone, creating a pit.

"What do you think is down there?" asked Gemma, clearly making her own assumptions.

"Well…water for sure…but this looks an awful lot like Mateo's sketches, doesn't it?"

They exchanged an uneasy glance, then Gemma caught a glint of something on the wall behind Emily. "Hey! There's a lantern. It's got to be brighter than our flashlights. Maybe we can look down the hole."

They pulled the rusty lantern down and heard oil sloshing around inside. Gemma turned the knob and lit it with a match from her bag. They stood still, waiting for a reaction from the bats, who only momentarily protested, then quieted.

They crept as close as they could to the opening of the shake hole without risking slipping. Emily held out the lantern as far as she could. "I can't see a damned thing."

"I have an idea…what if you lay on your stomach and crawl out. I'll hold your feet just in case." Said Gemma.

Curiosity overrode all common sense, and Emily wiggled along the wet limestone as close to the hole as she could, holding the lantern outstretched in her hand.

"Hold on." Said Emily. "Unclip my fanny pack. It keeps getting caught underneath me."

Gemma squeezed the clip at Emily's waist and tugged to pull it free. Emily lifted one of her hips just as Gemma gave a firm tug, launching the bag from Gemma's hands to the opposite side of the shake hole. For ten agonizing seconds, it clung to the wet rock before finally succumbing to the slick surface. They listened as it landed with a splash in the water below.

"Sorry…" Gemma said through gritted teeth. "At least we know the hole has a bottom."

Emily was still on her stomach holding the lantern. "The map was in there."

Gemma lolled her head from side to side. "Let's just go. This whole thing was a terrible idea."

"No." said Emily. "Grab that branch over there. I'll hook the lamp on the end, dangle it over the hole and we'll peek in. We have to find out if this is what Mateo saw in his dream."

Gemma passed Emily the moss-covered branch with a convenient nub at the end to keep the lantern in place. They both crept on the stomach as close as they dared, the lamp hovering over the hole.

"Can you see anything?" Gemma asked.

"I can! Come here! I can see the water and stalagmites. It looks like people throw garbage down here or something." Emily's arm shook from holding the weight of the lantern with one hand.

Gemma wiggled up close next to Emily, soaking the front of her jeans in water pooling around them en route to its destination below. After a few moments, her eyes adjusted. She squinted and moved slightly closer.

"Emily…that's not garbage. Is that? It can't be…"

"Hurry up, Gemma. I can't hold this thing much longer."

"Look." Gemma pointed. "See that stalagmite right there? There're clothes or something stuck on it."

Emily gazed into the darkness below in silence, then suddenly began wiggling backward away from the hole.

"It's wearing the other shoe, Gemma."

She nodded frantically. "I know."

They squirmed away from the slippery shake hole, careful not to lose the lamp in the same way they lost the map.

After reaching a safe distance from the opening, they stood, both trembling.

"We have to get out of here *now*." Said Emily as she patted at her pockets. "Here, hold this so I can get my flashlight. We'll give Stella the lantern when we meet up with her."


Emily clicked on her flashlight. As the light illuminated the branch holding the lantern, Gemma's eyes grew wide and she dropped it to the ground. The lantern shattered on the damp limestone.


"That's not a branch, Emily." She whispered. "That's a femur."

# Chapter 17

## Cursed Purse Snacks

"**Y**our purse snacks suck." Said Stella, nursing the end of an applesauce pouch.

Slumped over the cool hood of Stella's SUV, Emily's chest heaved as she attempted to catch her breath after their long trek out of the cave. "Like you're one to talk, Stella. All you had was a pack of Mambas."

"First of all, the Mambas are mine, not the kids'." Stella squeezed the last bit from the pouch, then threw it in the back seat through the open window. "My heathens can wait until we get home to eat. But why cinnamon flavor, Emily? You couldn't get strawberry like everybody else?"

Emily lifted her head, dampened with sweat. "I bought the variety pack. Harper eats strawberry first. She doesn't like the cinnamon kind…which is why they're purse snacks."

Stella nodded in agreement. "Bottom of the purse is where bad snacks go to be forgotten…until some whiney ass kid wants to go to McDonald's after dance class and you're broke until payday."

Gemma pulled a hand out of her patchwork bohemian tote. "Trix is too old for snacks, but I have stuff I give my husbands while we're running errands. Let's see…one crushed apple cinnamon cereal bar—"

"Gemma! See, that's what I'm saying! No one likes cinnamon and here we are, just escaped a goddamn Satanic cave temple and this garbage is all we have to eat!" Stella snatched the cereal bar from Gemma's hands and threw it into the forest.

Emily was now drinking deeply from a tiny box of apple juice with a picture of Big Bird's face on it. "As I pointed out, Stella, you only contributed Mambas to our post-cave picnic."

"Hey!" Stella pointed a stubby finger at the pack of candy on the hood. "Those are the sour flavors! The only place I can find them is that run-down Kum n Go on Kansas Expressway."

Gemma continued digging. "I once saw a guy trade a rack of ribs for a bag of meth there in broad daylight."

"Yup. That's the one." Stella unwrapped the waxy paper off a piece of candy and popped the rectangular treasure in her mouth. "A little appreciation for my offering, please."

Gemma held up two red and white packages triumphantly in the air. "Behold! Chase's Cherry Mash!"

Emily plucked one from her hand, tore it open with her teeth and shoved it whole into her mouth. Gemma opened the other for herself and asked, "How long do you think we were down there?"

Stella kicked off the ladybug boots she borrowed from Charlotte and dumped out a pile of gravel she'd collected inside. "You know what kind of purse snacks my mother had? A single stick of Big Red covered in loose tobacco."

"Do you think that's why you hate cinnamon so much?" Gemma asked.

"Shit." Stella squinted. "You're right."

Barefoot, she climbed into the driver's seat and started the vehicle, immediately turning the high beams down to parking lights. The truck dinged and the dashboard flashed the time-- 12:45 am.

"Six hours? Our phones died after what, an hour? Charlotte is probably worried sick. Do you have a charger for Android?" Emily asked.

Stella stared at her blankly. "Are you kidding me? First cinnamon, now this. No. I do not have a charger for your peasant phone. I use an iPhone like every other person on the planet who also buys strawberry applesauce."

Emily turned to give Gemma a look in the back seat as if to say what's her fucking problem?

"Here, charge mine." Gemma passed up her iPhone. "Hey Stella, I found gummy bears in my bag do you want some?"

"Fuck yeah, I do. Only red ones though, they taste the best." She twisted her arm behind her with her hand out. Gemma dropped two red gummies in the palm.

"I'll take some gummy bears, too." Emily said, turning around.

Gemma shook her head no. She held up a little foil pouch indicating they were infused with cannabis.

Emily nodded in acknowledgement and still held out her hand. Gemma sighed and acquiesced.

"Two? That's it?" Stella complained. "Come on Gemma, you're not holding out on me are you?"

"Sorry about that…" Gemma said. "I gave Emily the last two."

Emily quickly popped them in her mouth.

"Whatever," Stella said as she made a wide turn with her vehicle and down the dark forest path to the cornfield.

As they bounced in their seats in silence, Stella was especially tight lipped, focusing intently on avoiding ruts and field stones.

Emily cleared her throat. "Uh, so, Stella…first I want to say I'm glad you made it out alright—".

"I don't want to talk about it." She said flatly.

Gemma pulled herself up toward the front seat. "But Stella, you need to tell us what you saw in there. We're all in this together."

"Hmph. Didn't seem like we were all in it together while I was screaming bloody murder and you didn't even come to check on me." Stella sniffed, holding back tears.

Gemma and Emily exchanged a look. If Stella is crying it must have been bad.

"We didn't know it was you." said Emily. "We thought it was bats screeching. We were dealing with our own situation in the Shakehole room…"

Gemma laid a spider-webbed hand on Stella's shoulder. "We would have been there in an instant if we thought you were hurt or scared."

Stella slowed the SUV as they exited the forest. "I wasn't scared. I don't get scared. I had bats in my hair." She turned on the high beams and revved across the fallow field, the SUV jumping slightly when it hit the asphalt. "Charlotte's house?"

"Yeah, yeah. We can talk about it there." Emily decided not to push Stella too far while she was in control of a motorized vehicle.


When they reached Charlotte's house, every porch light was on. She sat in a rocking chair smoking a cigarette and staring at the road. When she saw them pull in she sprang up and threw the cigarette, running barefoot to meet them, wincing from the jagged gravel.

Tears streamed down her face as she hugged each of them in turn. Then she held her gold cross in her hands and prayed, "Thank you, Lord, for guiding them home!"

"I'm pretty sure it was my flashlight, actually." Stella hit the button, opening the dinosaur's mouth. The light shone in Charlotte's face and it crackled *rawr -rr-rarr-rawrrrr* . The effects of Gemma's red gummy bears had dialed Stella down from a 10 to a 6.

Charlotte blinked and turned away. "Why don't we go inside so you can clean up. I'll make some coffee. All the kids are asleep upstairs."

As they walked past Charlotte's husband's Bonneville, Emily asked, "Charlie...did you guys find Oliver?"

She nodded tersely. "Brent found him passed out at a park. He's sleeping now but he found him with some other kids. One is Ray's kid, Magnus. Remember him?"

Emily's mouth dropped in surprise. "How did they even meet? They don't strike me as kids that would cross social circles."

"I don't know how they met, but I'm going to figure it out." Charlotte sighed. "Magnus actually took Brent to where Oliver was passed out. He promised not to call his parents. I don't know what to do."

Emily touched her arm gently. "I know." She felt the same way about

Esme.

After the women were washed up and exchanged their filthy clothes for borrowed leggings and t-shirts from Charlotte, they settled onto the sofas and covered themselves in beautifully crocheted afghans. Exhausted, they sipped their coffees while Charlotte loaded their clothes into the washer and brought out a heaping pile of nachos to share.

"I hope the Mexican food isn't on account of me. I'd be fine with a few cookies." Stella smirked.

Charlotte huffed. "Of course not. Saturdays are always for tacos and nachos. Just like Friday is for spaghetti or lasagna."

Stella expressed her appreciation by stuffing a chip loaded with guacamole into her mouth and nodding.

"So…" Charlotte pulled up a children's beanbag from the corner nestling herself into it like the mother hen she was. "Did you find anything?"

The three stared at each other, daring another to go first.

"Well, there is definitely some weird stuff going on down there." Said Gemma. "There are signatures all over the walls from people who've visited over the years. But on one of the walls someone wrote in a black marker *Semper Revertimur.*"

"*'We always come back'*? What is that supposed to mean?" asked Charlotte.

"You speak Latin?" asked Gemma in surprise.

Charlotte shrugged, "I guess I picked it up teaching scripture translations in homeschool."

As a librarian, Gemma found this genuinely admirable. And in this instance, useful.

"After that, we got separated," Emily interjected.

Charlotte's eyes grew wide with worry. "What?!"

Stella nodded and spoke through tortilla chips, dropping crumbs on her lap. "Yup. I was too fat to fit through the crevice." She swallowed. "And just so you ladies know, I actually did eventually make it through. It involved a lot of patience and wiggling, but I made it. Didn't see that Latin shit you were talking about though."

Realization dawned on Emily's face. "Wait. Stella did you go left or right at the fork after you made it through?"

She sat up and brushed the crumbs off her lap. "Well, the bats went right, so I went left. That's probably when you heard me screaming."

"Stella, you were supposed to go right at the fork."

"Well, I didn't." Stella snapped as her mood darkened a few measures. "Good thing, too. I don't think you realize how fucked up these people are."

Emily and Gemma's brows furrowed.

"I think we might…" said Gemma, remembering the human femur she used to carry a lantern, and the pit full of skeletons.

"Those kids got demons for sure. I don't need a Catholic bishop to tell me *shit*." Stella pointed a finger at Charlotte. "And you know what else…I don't think my Mattie is crazy. He didn't go into that cave. He didn't get infected with demons. He's got *the gift*. You know what I'm saying? Like a *curandero* or some shit. It woke up inside of him 'cuz his friends were in trouble."

After all the theories they entertained, Stella's wasn't totally dismissible.

"How do you know the kids—" Charlotte spoke barely above a whisper, afraid of the answer. "—have demons?"

Stella exhaled loudly from her nose. "I found their…Satanic temple worship room or *whateverthefuck*."

"What!" They shrieked.

Stella nodded. "They're probably doing sacrifices or something."

"Stella, you can't just assume stuff like that." Said Gemma, trying to keep her cool for Charlotte's sake who was now pale and hyperventilating. "Satanism doesn't necessarily mean they're sacrificing people, animals or anything else."

Emily held her breath waiting for Stella's response, knowing full well

Gemma had seen the same skeleton wearing a high heel shoe as she did.

"Well, I'm about ninety-nine percent sure." Stella reached deep into her bra and pulled out a faded burgundy colored wallet, embossed with roses and the brand name *Jean Paul Gaultier*. "I found this in a purse tossed in a corner. It's got ID in it from the 90's."

Gemma gulped. "Someone could have…lost their purse or something."

Stella nodded. "I thought so, too. Until I saw everything else down there."

*Frenzied bats squealed overhead as Stella crouched and scrambled in the opposite  direction of their destination. She followed the path as it elevated and the air became less dense. Any lingering bat squeaks echoed in what could only be a much larger chamber than the one Stella had previously entered. She curled into a ball, balancing on the balls of her feet and covering her head with her arms, waiting for the cloud of bats to dissipate.*

*After ten full minutes of silence, she unfurled herself like a fern into solid darkness. Drops of cold water steadily fell upon her skin, and the floor was slick underfoot. If any bats remained, they had grown silent and settled into nooks and crannies. Stella steadied herself and clicked on her t-rex flashlight, aiming it at the floor to avoid disturbing the rats with wings.*

*There was no response to the toy flashlight's roar , but the light illuminated red markings on the floor Stella didn't recognize as letters or numbers. There were enclosed withing a large circle, which she traced with her flashlight, stopping when she reached what she realized was the top point of a large pentagram. An iron clamp was fastened into the limestone floor. A quick sweep of the rest of the star shape revealed smaller clamps at each of the other four points. Head. Hands. Feet. Like some kind of medieval torture room,  she thought.*

*Upon further inspection she could see piles of wax, layered with different colors from various candles burned in the same place over time. Red-brown stains of various shades coated the floor like some sort of demented color-by-number, filling in the triangle spaces of the pentagram.*

*Stella's breath hastened. She wished she had taken her Catholic school studies more seriously. Were the markings something she should recognize? She checked her phone again, hoping to take a photo, but the screen stayed black. Lifting her flashlight from the floor to the walls, she found half-used candles and small effigies tucked into the natural irregularities of the cave walls—varying sizes of the same creature—a human female body with wings and a goat's head, sitting cross legged and pointing upward with two fingers. It looked vaguely familiar, maybe from a horror movie, but she couldn't quite pull it from memory.*

*Continuing the perimeter of the room, a dusty lump in a dark corner caught her attention. Reaching out, she brushed the dirt away to reveal a small, shiny, handbag; too fancy for someone to bring caving. It was something she would have taken with her on a date, or a junior high dance twenty-five years ago. Stella turned the gold clip and reached inside. Her nose was hit with the smell of perfume mixed with mildew. Her hands first touched a tube of red lipstick—barely used. At the very bottom of the bag were four quarters dated from the early nineties...and a burgundy wallet.*

*Stella's hands shook as she popped open the wallet, suddenly realizing this was more than just a bunch of teenagers dabbling in voodoo. This ran much deeper. What if...there was something much darker and more serious happening in this old cheese cave?*

*Forty-three dollars spotted with black mold. A Blockbuster movie card. A photo of a dog, grandparents, and a family vacation in what appeared to be Florida—parents, teenage girl, little brother. Library card. Driver's license.*

*Mariah Wilson1899 N. Clifton Ave., Springfield*

*D.O.B. May 11th, 1985.*

*Stella furrowed her brows. Eighty-five? That would mean she's my age. I don't know anyone by that name, but it sounded familiar. Mariah?*

*Mariah.*

*Mateo's drawing.*

*She stuffed the wallet in her bra and dropped the bag back on the floor. As she turned to leave, a small round figure caught her eye. Vastly different in shape and style from the goat headed idols, this one she recognized.*

*The rounded skull had oversized ears, meant to be held one in each hand while the user blew the whistle spouting from the top.*

*It was an Aztec Death Whistle.*

*Stella's cousin is an artist, and makes clay replications of Mexican artifacts to sell to tourists near the border in Texas. Creepy as hell, she brought one as a gift for Sophia on Christmas.*

*"At first archaeologists thought they were toys," she'd told us. "Then they realized they were actually used during ritual sacrifices to guide the victims on their journey to the afterlife. Gringos love it."*

*The conversation crashed through Stella's mind, puzzle pieces matching to create a much clearer picture of the situation.*

*These people had to be Satanists sacrificing women. But for what?*

*Could the kids really be possessed?*

*What about Mattie? He didn't go in the cave.*

*He wasn't crazy. He wasn't possessed. Something else was going on.*

*Stella stuffed the Aztec Death Whistle down her bra, under the boob opposite the wallet, and fled the room. Reaching the fork, she returned to the crevice and busied herself for thirty solid minutes wiggling through to the other side with no sight or sound of Gemma and Emily. She easily found the exit, and popped her head out of the entrance to the cave like a gopher. Not seeing them outside, she waited impatiently for their lights. Finally, after nearly an hour, she heard them frantically calling her name from below.*

*She turned on her flashlight. Rawr..raw.rraw…rawrrr*

*"Oh thank Goddess!" Gemma cried.*

*"Hurry up!" Stella snapped. "This place is fucked up, amigas."*

Charlotte snapped a picture of the driver's license with her phone. "I'm sending this to Isabella. Maybe she can find out who this person is. That's a good place to start."

"Can I see the Aztec Death Whistle, Stella?" Gemma asked.

Stella pulled it out of her bra, brushed off some lint and handed it over.

"You know, as a Wiccan, most people think I'm a Satanist. I've had to defend myself on their behalf more than once." Gemma inspected the mouthpiece, then decided not to blow it. "Satanists don't actually make sacrifices. They don't even believe in possession."

"Well, if that's not Satanism, what's with all the shackles and pentagrams?" asked Emily.

"Pseudo-Satanism? They're clearly worshipping Baphomet—that's the goat headed creature you described. It's supposed to symbolize balance, and is the main symbol of modern Satanism. Everything else is weird." Gemma shook her head. "The swinger parties make sense though."

"So, sex parties are Satanic?" Stella snarked.

"Well, Satanism is about balancing power. If you have too much sexual energy, there *are* rituals for that. They believe 'participants' can transmute the power into energy to fulfill their desires. Maybe Richard's sex parties are for rich people to blow off steam and feel more powerful? It's sex magick, basically. Wiccans do it too, but it's a little more love and light, I suppose. With a partner or friends. Not some kind of group freak-off."

Stella stood up and snatched the Aztec Death Whistle from Gemma's hand, then took her coat of the hook and slipped on her gemstone encrusted sandals.

"Wait, Stella, it's 2:30 in the morning, where are you going? Just sleep here until the kids wake up!" Charlotte pleaded.

Stella shook her head. "Nope. I'll be back for the kids in a few hours. I'm going to get Junior."

"You can't do that, Stella." Pointed out Emily. "Not without doctor approval."

"That is my *nino*. And he's not crazy. I don't need any 'doctor approval' to see my own child. I'm busting him out of the looney bin!"

"Go home, Mrs. Romero. Please don't make me call the police."

The office attendant stood on the opposite side of the glass door, refusing to open it.

"Go ahead!" Huffed Stella. "Call the police! I will tell them you are holding my young child hostage and won't release him to me. You'll be the one in trouble!"

The attendant sighed. "You signed an agreement, Mrs. Romero. We can't release him until his psychologist believes it is safe. You can visit Mateo tomorrow."

"No! I will see him right now. Mateo is not crazy! He's seeing ghosts and shit. He doesn't need to be here. He needs to be…well, I don't know where, but not here! Release him!" Stella's pounding palms dirtied the glass, which the attendant seemed to fixate on, knowing she'd be the one to have to clean it after this angry mother was gone.

The attendant picked up the phone from the wall and dialed an outside line. "Yes, this is the front desk at Willow Creek Hospital. I have an angry parent needing an escort off the property. Just the mother. Late thirties, Latino. Long hair. Short, chubby. Mmm hmm."

Stella scowled, turning purple-red with rage. "*Pinche pendejo.*"

Stella turned on her heel and flip-flop-stomped to her SUV, plotting a way to ram it through the front door and retrieve Mateo before the police arrived. By the time she unlocked the driver's side door, her angry tears had turned sad. She collapsed in the front seat, sobbing into the crook of her arm propped on the steering wheel.

*I've failed him in every way. I should have listened to him. I should have paid closer attention. I should have protected him. I didn't…and now he's a prisoner in a goddamn mental institution.*

*Should've. Would've. Could've. Story of my life.*

She reached inside the paper bag of fast food sitting on the passenger seat she'd bought for Mateo, and pulled out a stack of brown napkins. She dried her eyes, blew her nose and turned on the radio.

Stella then sat for fifteen minutes eating her son's chicken nuggets, plotting her next move, and watching as police searched the hospital grounds for an angry Latino mama bear attempting to free her cub.

# Chapter 18

## Three Rooster Luck

Benny woke to the sound of a rooster crowing.

He opened his eyes to a pitch black room, except for the dim glow of embers in the fireplace on the opposite side of the cabin. He tapped his smartwatch. 3:00 a.m. on the nose.

"People say a rooster crowing at night is bad luck."

Ash clicked on a lamp carved from a block of wood into the shape of a black bear. He observed Benny from an oversized leather recliner.

Benny's leg throbbed. The cast felt like it weighed five hundred pounds. "Yeah, well, it's a little late for that."

Ash pushed out the recliner's footrest and covered himself with a plaid sherpa-lined blanket. "Ironic, isn't it? To hear a rooster crowing in a cabin called 'The Crow's Nest'?"

Groggy from pain medication, lucidity crept slowly to Benny's brain. "What are you doing out here, Ash? Why aren't you in the loft?"

Ash shrugged. "I told Dad I'd watch you while he took the twins to dinner. They got back around nine."

Benny's skin crawled, but he didn't know why. "Wait…you heard the rooster, too? I thought I was dreaming."

Ash nodded.

"Hey, can you get me a glass of water?" Benny's mouth felt like cotton from the narcotics. What was a rooster doing way up here in the mountains?

Ash gestured at the table next to the leather sofa Benny had been sleeping on. There was a glass of water, bottle of medicine, his cell phone and the TV remote.

"Oh, right." He reached for the water, his hand slipping on the condensation collected on the outside of the glass. The glass tipped over, spilled water all over the table before smashing on the wood-plank floor. "Shit!"

Taking his time, Ash rose from the recliner and retrieved a dish towel from the kitchen, then began mopping up the water.

"You know," he said, "after dad got home, I went to the loft and tried to sleep. I tossed and turned. Just couldn't get comfortable in my bed, so I got up and tried flipping the mattress. And wouldn't you believe it…I found something of yours!"

Ash wadded up the dish towel and tossed it to the floor over the pile of glass, then reached in his pocket and pulled out the Native American medicine bag Gemma and Mika made. Benny's first day in Tennessee he hid it between Ash's mattress and boxspring while he was in the shower.

"Oh, that." Benny took it from Ash's hand gingerly. "The babies must have been playing with it. Just a little good luck charm from a friend."

Ash nodded, stone-faced. "I'm just surprised the twins made it up the stairs. Oh, by the way, you might check your phone. The remote, too. They got *soaked*. It would really suck to be all alone here in the cabin with a broken leg and nothing to do. No one to talk to. You'd have to read a book or something…I think there's a Bible in the drawer of that table if you're desperate."

Laughing nervously, Benny wiped his dripping phone on his t-shirt, quite certain it was toast. Ash held eye contact just a few minutes longer than felt comfortable before he turned to ascend the loft stairs.

"Ash…" Benny called him back, not knowing why, until the words dribbled from his mouth. "Why did you kill the roosters?"

"I thought you'd never ask." He said. "I did them a favor. I *thought* I did you one, too. Didn't you want them gone?"

"Well, *yes*," Benny sputtered, "but not like that. Not with such… brutality. Lucy and I were about to take them to live free-range at Rosewood

Farm. I'd found them a home."

"You know, Benjamin, I did those roosters a *kindness.*" His face mocked concern. "A quick death saved them from the curse of being a male in a matriarchal society where their only *use* is to *breed,* or to *feed* the two-legged 'gods' who bring the corn. Free-range or not, that's not *living.*"

This "justice warrior" rant was closer to normal Ashton behavior than Benny had heard in months—which was comforting—still, the context was weird.

"It wasn't your decision to make, Ashton. Those were *my* birds." Benny reminded his stepson.

He shrugged and smiled, climbed the stairs and disappeared into the cabin loft.


Maybe it was just the medication, but after his strange interaction with Ash, Benny was too spooked to sleep. He hobbled on his crutches to the kitchen where he found a small bag of dried rice in the cabinet. He burrowed his phone and the TV remote into the bag in a sad attempt to save his only connection to the outside world. Then he wandered around the cabin, trying to remember if he'd packed anything for the family that had internet capabilities.

He dug to the bottom of the twins' diaper bag, and sure enough, Christopher had snuck along the I-Pad Mini he sometimes used to entertain the twins when he was alone with them. Benny strictly forbade the use of technology for the twins until they were older, but he knew his husband sometimes struggled to manage both of them at the same time. Benny often looked the other way in exchange for an hour to himself or a much-needed nap.

The twins had video-called Lucy a few days ago, but she was still aloof with Benny. They'd barely had a private conversation since the swinger party at Stephanie and Richard's house. Ignoring the fact that it was nearly four a.m., Benny staggered to the back deck where the hot tub overlooked the Smoky Mountains and video-called her.

After three rings Lucy answered, looking more beautiful than should be legal for someone wearing foam curlers in her hair with no makeup on.

"Benny? What's going on? It's so early, are you okay?" she asked sleepily.

Benny saw Nolan roll over and look at the screen.

"Hi, Nolan, sweetie. Just checking in real quick with Lulu. Go back to sleep darlin'. You got lives to save in the morning." Benny gave Lucy a look that she understood to mean *get your ass out of bed*.

Benny watched the room spin on her end as she put on a robe, left the bedroom and shut the door behind her.

"Ben, why are you calling me so early?" Her tone was annoyed, but concerned.

"Girl, this child is insane!" Benny whisper-yelled into the tablet. "I am scared for my *life* right now. I think he cursed my ass, like some kind of evil warlock!"

Lucy yawned. "He's a teenager, Ben. All teenagers are dicks to varying degrees." She squinted. "Are those crutches?"

Benny pulled them into frame. "Yes, they most certainly are! I broke my goddamn leg on a stupid ass 'snow tubing simulation experience'. There were six-year-olds slidin' on down this big ol' hill, jumping off grinning and giggling at the end. I go down *one time*, flip the tube and fracture my tibia!"

"Oh, no! I'm so sorry that happened to you...," Said Lucy. "Are you coming home early?"

Benny sighed. "Oh, I don't know. This whole trip is so important to Christopher. I'm trying to tough it out, you know? You remember me telling you about all my bad luck lately?"

Lucy nodded. "Sure, 'Three Rooster Luck', right? Supposed to be only hens, and you get three roosters."

At this point Benny was raging like a storm in a teacup. "Do you want to know why I'm calling you on a child's tablet? A glass of water spilled on my phone! *And* the TV remote, so I can't use that either! Oh, and remember that medicine bag Gemma gave me to put under Ash's mattress? He found it. How the hell would he think to look under his mattress? Said he couldn't sleep! Yeah, I bet he couldn't! He's a damned warlock, Lucy!"

Lucy listened carefully, biting her lip then said, "I don't know about him being a warlock. I'm not really into supernatural stuff. Maybe you need a good luck charm to offset the bad? Don't they have those Appalachian backwoods mountain shamans in Tennessee? You could go talk to one of them."

He considered her advice. "You might be on to something. There are all sorts of weird shops downtown. I'll check them out tomorrow…or, well, I guess today." The sun was beginning to turn the sky pink on the horizon.

Lucy gave a sleepy smile. "Take care of yourself, Benny. Get some rest and let me know when you get home, okay?"

"Sure thing, Lulu. Bye."

Benny disconnected and searched the internet for Appalachian folk healers nearby. Finally, he settled on a place called *Granny Magic Apothecary.*

He dressed himself the best he could, accommodating his cast by wearing a loose pair of stereotypical cargo "dad shorts", then prepared eggs, pancakes and fresh fruit for breakfast.

As he flipped a tiny sand dollar pancake at the stove, the pattering of four tiny feet behind him as he cooked let him know the twins were awake. He never, ever, ever grew tired of seeing their sleepy, smiling faces in the morning. Balancing on one foot, he bent down and hugged them both close as they giggled and squealed from kisses. Benny buried his face in their uncombed hair and inhaled the comforting smell of baby shampoo. Those boys were the heartbeat of his day, and he spent every moment making sure they knew they were loved. They would *never* know the pain of rejection and indifference by their family as Benny had.

His mind flashed to Ashton, who hadn't come downstairs yet. Benny's heart softened. He wanted his stepson to feel accepted, loved and supported too. He wanted to be as close to Ash as he was the twins, even if he wasn't his biological parent. Before the cave, Ash was sometimes challenging—but never where family or friends were involved. School was a sore spot—mostly stress from the high expectations of Christopher. He was also known to get riled up over humanitarian causes or injustices, but it nothing unmanageable. Over the last year, Benny thought they had made progress getting to know each other. They even made plans to attend an upcoming blues festival and a road trip of college campus tours.

Yes, Ash had *always* been broody and a bit dark— sensitive soul with a warrior spirit. Not only was he brave enough to *see* the problems of the world, he had a passion and a willingness to change it, which Benny loved and admired. He'd pulled Ashton's birth chart before marrying Christopher; an Aquarius sun, moon and rising was not a personality to take into your home lightly. There would surely be drama; but as a Sagittarius, Benny felt confident he could handle it.

Ash's recent behavior was out of the norm.

He had never been creepy. Threatening. Callous. This all happened *after* the cave. Something had changed in his stepson, and as Benny poured scrambled eggs into a skillet for his family, Benny committed his heart to giving Ash the same grace he would give the twins if they were struggling.

He wondered if any of the other parents had made progress with their children or convinced the bishop of the Catholic church to help. For now, all the way in this isolated cabin in the mountains of Tennessee, he was on his own. Could demons be causing all his bad luck? Benny thought back to when it all started to worsen—the car accident with Emily, the rabbit biting off the tip of his toe, the roosters; but really, it started long before that.

For the last two years—since leaving New Orleans—life had been a constant stream of hard knocks. Benny realized he's probably just gotten so used to taking it on the chin that it barely fazed him until recently. Bad luck was now an expectation, and then reality. Delayed flights, identity theft, food poisoning. Last year he caught chicken pox even though he'd been vaccinated as a child. Just last month he had his wallet stolen, his email hacked, and packages pirated from his porch. If something could go wrong for him, it usually did. Now he just assumed the worst.

But if the bad luck wasn't because of Ash, what was it?

"Ben, you should not be up making breakfast!" Christopher pecked Benny on the lips and began pouring two cups of coffee. "But I will say, I'm glad to see you moving around. You were sleeping like the *dead* when we got home…had me a little worried."

Benny shook off a chill, and the thought that he was somehow in danger by being left in a vulnerable state with his stepson. "Hey, I was wondering if you could drive me into town after breakfast. There's a little trinket shop I want to check out."

"Yeah, sure." Said Christopher. "I'll pick up groceries while you're there and we can grill tonight."

"Sounds great. Good morning, Ashton." Said Benny, cautiously watching Ash enter the kitchen and pour a glass of orange juice. "Pancakes?"

"Nah. I'm going on a hike." He said.

"By yourself?" asked Christopher. "What about bears? And river hobos?"

"Dad. There's no river."

"Alright…well…" Christopher struggled to find reasons to not let his nearly adult son take a hike on a beautiful Saturday morning. "Bring supplies and extra water in case you get lost. Stay on the trail. We're going into town for a few hours."

"Mmkay. Can we have burgers tonight?" Ash asked.

"Sure, do you want the kind made with black beans and rice or the store-bought frozen soybean stuff?" Christopher asked.

"Beef is fine." Ash put his empty glass in the sink.

Christopher side-eye Benny. "So, you're not vegan anymore?"

"Nope."

Christopher laughed, but his eyes looked worried. "Well, at least groceries will be less complicated *and* expensive."

"Yeah."

Ash left the room as Christopher whispered to Benny. "What's that about?"

"He won't say." Huffed Benny.

"Weird." Said Christopher, and reaching the extent of his parental worry, stuffed his mouth with a toddler-sized chocolate chip pancake.


*Granny Magic Apothecary* was impossible to miss. Built into the side of a rolling hill, half the shop was perched on stilts. Customers climbed a set of rickety stairs to a slightly slanted wooden porch that was steadily sinking into the mountainside. The stairs, porch and door were all painted the same strange shade of blue-green, making it all appear shabbier in comparison to the gourmet gelato shop and a hand-carved furniture store it was sandwiched between.

Benny looked down at his cast. *Aren't all shops required to have a handicap accessible entrance?* This one most definitely *did not.* He propped himself against the rail of the porch with his right arm, tucked his crutches under left, and carefully hopped on one foot up each of the five steps. By the time he made it to the top, sweat was steadily dripping down his face, stinging his eyes. Benny had always been a "face sweat-er" and he hated it.

"You finally made it!" An old woman pushed open the screen door to invite him inside. "Next time, try using the accessible entrance 'round back. You get there from the alley. I'm surprised you didn't notice the sign. You were leaning on it."

Benny followed the direction of her knotted finger to the sign posted on the hand rail below. Of *course* he missed it. "Thanks. I'll do that." He tucked his crutches in his underarms and wobbled into the shop. Fans hit him in the face with musty air, and a display of handmade windchimes whipped and rang intermittently with every oscillation. Evidently, this old woman didn't use air conditioning despite Tennessee being notoriously hot and humid most of the year.

"Can I offer you a drink? It's on the house." She gave him a warm smile, accentuating the wrinkles on her weatherworn face. "I've got sweet tea or lemongrass water."

"Sweet tea, please." Benny gestured at a stool in the corner. "Is it okay if I sit down for a minute?"

"Go right on ahead, hunny. I'll be back with your drink."

Benny winced as he sat and shifted his leg out straight. He swatted at flies buzzing around his ear and wondered if coming here was a waste of time and energy. He should be at home, medicated, with his feet up.

The shop was dusty and made him slightly claustrophobic. Every wall was lined with old mason jars filled with doodads of all sorts—sticks, stones, seeds, bones and mysteriously murky liquids. Unlike most spiritual shops, there weren't many books, just a few old Bibles. Animal skins hung from the rafters; Benny could identify a raccoon, skunk and beaver. Others were so old and dusty with so many patches of fur missing he couldn't place them with certainty.

The old woman returned with a vintage McDonald's glass full of sweet tea and ice. Benny was pretty sure these were made with lead-tainted paint, but it was hot, so he gratefully drank it all in a few gulps. "Thanks, ma'am."

She nodded silently, waiting for Benny to introduce himself.

"Oh, sorry. My name is Ben. I'm on vacation from Missouri."

Again, she nodded. "I see. Well, I'm Mabel. This shop has been in my family for nearly a hundred and twenty-five years. They call us 'Granny Witches' in these parts, but really, we're just healers. We use the old ways to solve our health troubles…and sometimes a little bit of prayer. You looking to heal your leg, son?"

Benny looked down at his cast. "No…well, yes, but I think the doctors have that it covered. I'm actually here about my stepson."

"Alright. What ails him?" she dragged another worn, wooden stool close to Benny and sat down tenderly as her knees audibly cracked.

He took a deep breath. "It's not physical…I think it's…spiritual."

"I'm not a witchdoctor, nor some kind of voodoo priestess."

"I know, I'm just worried that he might have some kind of evil in him." Benny explained.

"You mean a *haint*?" Mabel asked.

He shook his head. "What's a haint?"

"A bad spirit. If they get in your home or heart they'll raise hell. *Your kid got a haint*?" She tilted her head to one side, and a long gray braid fell from her shoulder to her lap looking like a pile of rope.

"Maybe?" Benny leaned slightly back, away from her intense gaze.

She took the hint and pulled back. "You need to paint your porch."

"Paint my porch?"

"Yup. *Haint Blue*." She pointed outside to the soft blue-green colored porch. "It keeps the evil away."

"Alright, darlin'." He laughed. "I'll ask the HOA. Ashton might need a remedy that's a bit different though." Benny shifted in his seat; the ache intensified as the morning dose of pain medication wore off. "What if he's already infected with a haint? How do I get rid of it?"

The old woman pursed her lips in thought. "A Madstone might work. It's gonna cost you though. Only a few of 'em around here, so we share 'em."

Benny was becoming irritable and wondered if he was being toyed with. "Enlighten me. What's a Madstone?"

She scowled, sensing Benny's attitude shift. "It's found in the belly of a white-tailed deer. Grit, hair, fiber…all solidify into a white mass. You soak it in milk, and put it on the infected person. It'll draw out poisons from snakes, spiders and the rabies."

"My son hasn't foamed at the mouth yet. Not sure about rabies."

"He could have a sort of…rabies of the *spirit*. Soak the Madstone in milk, put it on your kid, it'll draw out the haint. *Maybe*." The old woman raised an overgrown eyebrow.

"How much?" asked Benny.

"Seven-fifty. Ain't many found round here. People don't check the deer bellies anymore like the old days." She said.

Benny sighed. "Yeah, that's a real shame. I'll take it. Seven-fifty."

Her eyes grew wide, surprised he didn't even attempt to haggle.

"Do you have anything to ward off bad luck?" He asked, growing tired as he fought off the pain in his leg.

"Yeah, *Haint Blue* paint. For the porch."

Benny steepled his fingers. "Alright. Do you have any recommendations for *good* luck?"

"Sure, a buckeye in your pocket." She smiled like it was the most normal thing in the world.

He stood from the stool. "Aww hell no. I am *not* putting a deer's eyeball in my pocket!"

Mabel laughed herself into a coughing fit as she went behind the checkout counter and pulled out a wooden bowl of horse chestnuts. "'Round here, we call 'em buckeyes. It's free." She winked and tossed one to Benny. He managed to lighten up for a moment and put it in his pocket.

Mabel then placed a small tin box on the counter, and opened it to reveal the Madstone. "We call 'em Madstones cuz we use em when people are going mad. Before doctors, or when us mountain folk couldn't afford 'em these stones were our only hope to keep our loved ones from succumbing to the poisons of the wild."

Benny removed the white stone from the box and held it like an egg in his palm. It was perfectly round and smooth, with swirls of cream throughout.

"That one there is extra powerful. It's from an *albino* deer. It saved my granddaddy from a black widow bite when I was a lil' one. Remember, ya gotta soak it in milk overnight and then leave it on your kid for a good long while for it to work. Sometimes it won't. Jesus has a say in these things, too, ya know?"

He nodded and placed it back in the tin, then pulled out his wallet and laid eight hundred-dollar bills on the counter. He stuffed the tin in his pocket. "Keep the change, Mabel. Use it to paint the porch *Haint Blue* again."

The heat and stuffiness of the shop was starting to give Benny a panic attack. He left Mable counting her crisp hundreds and hustled irritably down the stairs where Christopher sat waiting in their rental car playing a game on his phone. He looked up just as Benny reached the last step, and fumbled out of the car. The babies slapped the windows giggling and chanting "Da Da!" .

"Let me *help* you! Lord, I didn't know you went all the way up those steps. What were you *thinkin'* Benjamin?" He opened the passenger door and moved the seat all the way back.

After Benny was settled and sipping a bottle of water, Christopher loaded the crutches in the trunk nestled among the supplies needed for burgers and s'mores. They drove through winding and crowded streets to the edge of the tiny mountain town, following signs to the mountain resort where "The Crow's Nest" stood at the tippy top—the most private cabin in the resort with the best view, at Christopher's insistence.

Christopher turned into the entrance of the uphill drive and punched the code into the gate when they heard honking behind them. Red and blue lights flashed in the rearview mirror.

"What the hell?" Christopher rolled down his window and reached in his back pocket to pull out his wallet as a police officer exited his vehicle and approached.

"Sir, I cannot let you go up there right now." The man said before even reaching Christopher's window. "We need to keep the road clear for emergency personnel. There's a raging fire at one of the cabins." The officer was red faced and sweating. "We've been trying to get a bigger truck up there but it's too narrow. We don't know how far it will spread before we can get it contained. Are you staying here?"

Benny's heart dropped to his stomach.

Ash.

"Yes! We're at The Crow's Nest. My son is up there!" Christopher's voice cracked, obviously feeling the same sense of foreboding as Benny.

The officer's shoulder's fell. "I'm sorry to tell you, but that's the cabin on fire. I don't know where your son is, but I'll radio up top." The officer stood back and spoke into his walkie. "This is Officer Dunnam at the entrance, I have the people here that are staying in that cabin. Their kid was up there—hey, how old is he? What does he look like?"

Christopher was hyperventilating and gripping the steering wheel so tightly his knuckles were white. Benny leaned across him to answer the officer. "Seventeen, tall and thin. Half Asian-black hair, brown eyes, light skin. I think he was wearing a blue hoodie." *Dead eyes, possible demonic attachment, menacing aura.*

"—seventeen, half Asian, tall, blue hoodie."

Suddenly Benny's head was slammed backward into the seat as Christopher hit the gas and sped through the open gate towards the cabin.

"Chris, what are you doing?!" Benny shrieked.

"Ash is up there! We need to get him to safety. That cop has no idea what's going on, and I'm not waiting!" Christopher's eyes locked on the winding road as the car engine revved uphill.

The nearer they were to the cabin, the hazier the air became. Black smoke could be seen billowing overhead, and sirens wailed in the distance. When at last they mounted the summit and made it to the clearing, first responders and forestry staff stood back from the blaze as the roof caved in and the log cabin smoldered. Benny and Christopher jumped out of the car, leaving the twins inside with the air conditioner.

"Ashton!" screamed Christopher, running at full speed towards the cabin before any of the emergency workers could stop him.

"Chris, no!" Benny hopped on one foot attempting to catch his husband, but he was held back by a park ranger.

"It's not safe! The whole structure is collapsing, you *need to stay here.* Stay with your kids." The park ranger looked over his shoulder at the twins, fast asleep in the backseat. "Let us get him."

The emergency workers flanked the cabin at a safe distance, yelling for Christopher to get out.

*"Mark! The fire's out on the back patio now—propane tank!"*

"My stepson! Ashton! He might be in there! You need to find him, too!" Benny sobbed and searched with his eyes for any sign of his husband through the smoke.

"Everybody out, now!" shouted the ranger. "That tank's gonna blow."

The first responders dropped their extinguishers and fled for their trucks. "There'll be shrapnel, take cover!"

Benny limped back to the passenger seat of the car and slammed the door shut. As he turned to unbuckle the babies and put them on the floor, he was met face-to face with his muddy stepson, sitting in the driver's seat holding a hiking pack.

"Ashton?"

He raised an eyebrow, and looking from the fire to Benny asked, "What happened?"


Then they were consumed in a blast of smoke and light.

# Chapter 19
## Million Dollar Lucy

THE FIRST RULE OF SEDUCTION:

**Choose the Right Victim**

*"A target should be someone for whom you can fill a **void**."*

-Robert Greene, The Art of Seduction

Lucy peed on the stick, knowing those two pink lines were about to show themselves. She s had seen the signs her body was giving her—swollen breasts, mood changes, discharge. Ever so faint at first, five minutes later it was clear as day: it was finally *her time.*

She ran out of the bathroom in her underwear, calling out for Nolan and waving the stick in the air. He was piling luggage at the front door and waiting for a taxi.

"Two lines! We got two lines!" Lucy waved the plastic stick like a wand, grinning.

"Wait…is that…?" He asked, dropping his carry-on to the floor.

"I'm ovulating!" Lucy said. "The test says I'm ovulating!"

Nolan's face fell. "Oh…I thought…"

Lucy threw the stick across the room. "We need to have sex *right now.*"

"Lucy, I can't." he said. "I'll miss my plane. The cab will be here in like five minutes."

"That's enough time," Lucy laid on the checkered tile floor and spread her legs. "You can take me right here."

Nolan sighed. "Luce, come on. Not now."

Lucy crawled over to an apholstered accent chair and bent over, sticking her perky bottom up. "Is this easier? It would be really quick; I'll do that thing where I—"

"No," Nolan pulled her up patiently and hugged her tight. "Stop. I'm not doing it like this. Besides, we had sex last night. There's probably still a few of my guys waiting to greet your egg. Hell, they're probably throwing a parade in its honor."

He rubbed her back, knowing she'd started crying tears of petulance and frustration by the dampness on his t-shirt. "We're trying to make a human being, here." He reminded her. "I don't want to conceive our child via a quickie on my way out the door while you are bent over a chair and crying. I'll be back in a few weeks and we'll try again. A lot."

Lucy was one more "no" away from stomping her feet and throwing a tantrum. "I won't be ovulating then! Sex would be pointless!"

A cab honked in the driveway. Nolan kissed her on the forehead. "It would *not* be pointless, because we would be *making love* and I enjoy your company. *Especially* your naked company."

Lucy rolled her eyes with arms crossed, watching Nolan gather up his luggage. She seethed in pouty silence.

With his hand on the doorknob, he turned to his wife. "Luce, while I'm gone, there's something I want you to think about. Can we maybe chill out on the baby making stuff? You know, the tracking and the scheduled sex? Let's try simply living our lives. If we're blessed with a baby, I'll be grateful. If not… I'm grateful to have you."

Her arms fell to her sides as he rolled his luggage out the front door to the cab, on his way to fly to Colorado Springs. Nolan sometimes worked as a traveling nurse and was gone weeks at a time, but *why now?* Lucy slammed the front door shut just as Nolan blew her a kiss.

Lucy watched the cab drive off through the window, and immediately felt miserable about his absence, and their tiff. Instead of dolling herself up for the day, she threw on a pair of sweats and a t-shirt, then settled on the couch eating her secret shame—crunchy cheese curls—while Butterscotch licked her fingers.

"He's a *man*, Butters. He doesn't get it. He doesn't understand what it's like to be a woman whose body won't make a baby." She scratched behind his notched ear from his previous life as a gutter goblin. "I'm a failure. I have a *rotten womb*. I'll never be a mom."

She laid down and pulled the blankets over her head, sobbing into the throw pillow embroidered with Butterscotch's face. She stayed there feeling sorry for herself until the sun went down.

*Just like the good ol' days* she thought.

*At least back then I had fun sometimes. Nothing feels fun anymore.*

She tossed off her blanket and went to her bedroom closet. Nearly everything she owned was floral print or bright, cheery colors. She needed something that matched her mood, and found what every woman should have in her closet—her LBD.

A Little Black Dress should be simple, short and solid in color. A woman in a black dress is mysterious and has nothing to prove. She's confident enough in her own energy to draw a man's gaze from vibes alone. The LBD is reliable when nothing else is. A woman is always at home when she's in her Little Black Dress.

Lucy slipped it over her head, and it glided over her curves like a well-worn glove. She watched herself turn in the mirror. *I've still got it. I'm not Sad-Girl-DeLuLu anymore.* She pulled a small stepstool towards her and stepped up to reach into the darkest, farthest corner of her closet where she hid all the little treats she'd bought herself with her inheritance from Goldie—vintage jewelry, high end handbags and her still un-worn red-bottom shoes.

She pulled out the shoebox, a small jewelry box containing diamond studs and matching necklace, and a black Valentino rhinestone handbag. She ran her fingers across the "V" and sighed. There's no way she could ever wear any of this without Nolan—or anyone—questioning how she could afford it.

Lucy stepped down from the stool, cradling her treasures in her arms, then spread them out on the bed. She picked up a gorgeously shiny red-bottom heel—to wear that skinny stiletto took an amount of grace few women possess. Lucy shamelessly stuck her face in the shoe and inhaled. It smelled like…*money*. Power. Sex. She slipped it on her right foot and balanced effortlessly. Then the left. She piled her blonde hair on top of her head, making loose ringlets with her fingers; then she put on the glittering diamond earrings and necklace.

Twisting this way and that at her reflection, Lucy had to admit, she looked like a million dollars. Then she put the strap of the Valentino bag over her shoulder. *It's a shame to look this good and have nowhere to go.*

But where would "Million Dollar Lucy" go? What would be fun for her? Not the mall, or the bar. If she went to a club she'd be robbed, for sure. Frankly she felt too old at nearly thirty to find that sort of thing enjoyable. She wanted intelligent conversations, delicious drinks made with top-shelf spirits. Mostly, she wanted to be around interesting people.

Inferno Lounge.

She'd never been there personally, but overheard some well-to-do women shopping at Golden Era Boutique for vintage cocktail dresses. They had joked about trying to snag a rich husband so they could become tradwives. Lucy had rolled her eyes at that comment, but truthfully, tradwives were most of her clientele.

Lucy removed her wedding band and placed it on the dresser, trading it for the keys to Goldie's mint Mercedes-Benz, then dropped them in her Valentino bag. She moved her Victorian garnet engagement ring to another finger.

Tonight, she was the woman every man wanted, but none were good enough to have.

Beautiful, intelligent and independent—tonight, she was *Million Dollar Lucy.*

It turns out, Lucy discovered, that cigar lounges don't actually smell like cigars thanks to the high-powered air filtration systems they use, similar to casinos. What it *did* smell like was expensive cologne and *musk.* Lucy couldn't place it exactly, but she knew the last time she encountered it—Richard and Sarah's swinger party. And just like the party, she entered the lounge and was met with the hungry eyes of wolves in suits and ties.

"Ms. Murphey, since this is your first time at Inferno Lounge, allow me to show you around." The attendant gestured further inside, and Lucy couldn't help but notice his perfectly manicured fingers and the sparkling golden cufflinks on his jacket. *This is just the door man?* Inferno Lounge was already proving to be next level.

Lucy straightened her back. *Million Dollar Lucy doesn't need a man around her to feel confident.* "Fantastic," she purred, leaning forward to read the cursive on his nametag. "Thank you, Joseph."

Joseph blushed and cleared his throat as he pocketed the hundred-dollar bill she slipped him. "Right this way."

So many eyes took notice of the exchange The room briefly grew silent. Ties were straightened, seats adjusted, lint was picked off jackets. Even the barkeep wiped the already shining handcrafted wood bar top. Silently, the men were playing a game of 'dare'. Who would approach first? Who would be rejected by this mysteriously wealthy siren? More importantly, who would she *choose?*

As Lucy passed by an elderly woman in fur smoking a cigarillo at the bar, the woman exhaled and leaned forward to the barkeep. "Who's that? Is that William's daughter…or mistress, maybe?"

The barkeep discreetly shrugged and kept his eyes on the bar top until he was summoned by Joseph. "Ms. Murphey,—"

"Please, call me Lucy."

"As you wish." Said Joseph, dipping his head. "Lucy, this is our weekend bartender, Xavier. His creations are truly a work of art. He has an incredible gift of knowing the *perfect* drink for our patrons without them even asking. Mrs. Hampton, what did Xavier give you tonight?"

The old woman held up her glass to the amber light overhead. "Aww, hell…I don't even know. He makes it. I drink it."

"The Bee's Knees," said Xavier. "Circa 1921. Drumshanbo gin, lemon, honey."

Mrs. Hampton scoffed and drained the last of her cocktail. "Is it because I'm *old?* I will let you know, I was born in 1943, not 1921, *sir.*"

"No, it's because you're so sweet." Xavier turned on a bright smile, displaying perfectly straight white teeth Lucy was quite sure were expensive veneers.

The old woman grumbled and pulled a fifty dollar bill out of her wallet, then slid it across the counter and stumbled out of her chair. "See you next week."

Xavier chuckled as she left and addressed Lucy. "She's one of my regulars."

"She's what you'd call *old money*. Springfield royalty." Said Joseph, gesturing to the rest of the lounge. "You'll find a lot of influential people frequenting our lounge. We're very discreet and selective about our patrons, which is important to people of high standing in the community."

Lucy smiled. "So…I passed a test then?"

He pointed at her feet. "You can tell a lot about a person by their shoes."

A rumbling laugh rolled out behind them. "As if you'd have turned away a beautiful woman like her, even if she wasn't wearing designer heels?"

Peeking around Joseph's should, Lucy saw a large man with a friendly face puffing on a one-inch-thick cigar reading an Auto Trader magazine. It looked like a sausage, Lucy thought, as he tapped the ashes into a crystal tray. He winked at her beneath bushy eyebrows, then returned to reading.

The room was comfortably organized with leather chairs and sofas at perfect ninety degree angles, each group generously spaced from the others—assumably—for privacy. Small glass tables served as way stops throughout the room for empty glasses and cigar ashes. Two coasters, a box of matches and a crystal ashtray rested on each.

Joseph nodded politely in acknowledgment of the bushy-browed man, and said he was taking Lucy to the humidor. She had no idea what that was, but replied, "Wonderful!"

He led her to two floor-to-ceiling glass doors, which made a suction noise as he yanked them open. "The air inside the humidor is the perfect temperature and humidity to protect the integrity and quality of the cigars."

The room was filled with two stories of cedar shelving attached to the brick walls. The shelves displayed cigars in small cedar boxes, labeled by brand and then alphabetical.

"Feel free to sit wherever you feel comfortable in the lounge—except for this room. It is for purchasing *only*."

"Of course," said Lucy.

"There's a self-service checkout in the humidor if you wish to purchase any of our cigars. We sell our own brand, and practically every other fine brand in the world. If you have questions, probably ask any of our patrons would give their recommendations. Practically everyone here is a connoisseur of sorts."

Lucy nodded, but having never smoked a cigar in her life, had already planned on sticking to cocktails. "Thank you so much, Joseph. I'll take it from here so you can get back to screening people's shoes at the door."

He laughed at Lucy's light jab and gave a small nod. "Let me know if you need anything."

The shelves rose all the way to the ceiling; a wooden ladder on wheels led to a second level catwalk. Lucy considered how the large man reading the magazine, or some of the elderly patrons, managed to choose their cigars. Maybe they preferred the bottom shelves.

*Unlikely*, thought Lucy. All the best things are on the top shelf.

She changed her mind about sticking to cocktails, and assessed the ladder by giving it a shake. *Million Dollar Lucy would want the best cigar.*

She put her Valentino bag on the floor and kicked off her red-bottoms.

At first, she scaled the ladder with confidence, but as she neared the top she became nervous as the ladder wobbled. Hit with a sudden anxiety attack, she panted and tried to summon her courage by and focusing on the very top shelf. *Only the best. You're no bottom-shelf girl.*

"You know, they have someone who will do that for you."

The smooth English accent was unmistakable. She looked down and nearly fell off the quivering ladder which was quickly steadied by the man below.

"As much as I love this view, if you come down, I can get whatever you need."

Lucy's whole body trembled from a combination fear of heights and realization that she didn't even consider the possibility of encountering someone from Richard and Sarah's party at this place. Of *course* they would be here. It's exclusive, expensive and private.

As she reached the bottom, hands gently braced her hips. His slim arms were surprisingly strong, and he plucked her from the ladder like a daisy before her feet could touch the floor.

Lucy turned on him with not-quite mock offence. "Excuse *you*, sir!"

"You're welcome." A lopsided grin. His one blue eye sparkled as he confirmed his suspicion. "I knew it was you. Lucy the Unicorn."

Lucy fumed. "Don't call me that! I am *not* a unicorn!"

"If you say so. I see you made it home safely after the party. I don't think they suspect it was *you* at all." he said.

She put her hand over his mouth and looked around wildly.

The man locked eyes with hers and carefully removed her hand, grinning like the Cheshire Cat. "Excuse *you*, miss."

Lucy broke free of his gaze, stepped back and smoothed her dress. She slipped her heels back on. "I'd rather not talk about that night. Please leave me alone so I can have a drink."

He laughed. "Who drinks *alone*? That's rather sad, don't you think?"

"No, I don't think it's sad. I enjoy my own company." Lucy chose a random cigar off a shelf, picked up her bag and walked to the register.

The man moved in front of her, snatched the cigar from her hands before she could scan it and held it up to his nose. "No. Absolutely not. This cigar is repulsive. What are you looking for exactly anyway?"

Lucy deflated, accepting that she wouldn't be able to shake off the Brit easily. "I guess I'm looking for…the best?"

He raised an eyebrow. "I see. Is that why you're going to the very top?"

"Yes."

He placed the cigar back in its nest. "Let me tell you a secret, Ms. Lucy. The very best things are *never* at the top. The very best things are hidden. The top is the first place people look for quality…but really, the top is simply the place with the *highest cost*. It's in the ordinary, everyday places one will find that which is most *satisfying*."

The man reached into a bin next to the register labeled "Free with Every Purchase" and pulled out two cigars, passing one to her and pocketing the other. Lucy put it in her bag along with a pack of matches, unsure what else to do with it.

"So," said the blue-eyed man. "Are you still planning to have a drink by yourself??

"Of course." She stuck her nose in the air. *Million Dollar Lucy enjoys her own company above all others, especially a man's.*

"I see." He pocketed his cigar inside his jacket. "Well, just so you know, there are at least six gentlemen waiting for you to leave this humidor so they can approach you. You'll be busy all night rebutting suitors, I suspect. However, if you have a drink with me, I promise not to bother you much…and when you finish your drink you can leave without harassment."

He heaved the door open, gesturing her out and waited for her decision. Lucy could hear live piano music filling the lounge and easily imagined herself as a woman in the Roaring 20's, listening to jazz and having a cocktail amongst the city's elite. The blue-eyed man seemed interesting and considerate enough, and better than the alternative.

"Fine."

The man smiled—not at Lucy—but at the room of men, with a puffed chest and look of triumph.

The bartender, Xavier, barely had a glimpse of them approaching and took out two glasses from behind the counter. Before Lucy and the blue-eyed man were even settled in their seats, he was pouring alcohol into their glasses.

The blue-eyed man nudged Lucy, and gestured with his head across the room. Two different men, upon seeing Lucy no longer alone, smothered their cigars in an ashtray and left the lounge without a word.

"Told you. Despite the relaxed environment, you are in a lion's den. Would calling you a delicious little lamb be offensive?" The man pulled a bowl of pistachios and a napkin towards them. He cracked a shell and offered it to Lucy. She nodded in acceptance, and he tried to put it directly into her mouth.

She held out her hand. "Yes, I would find that offensive. Almost as offensive as you trying to feed me a nut like baby bird."

The man dropped it in her hand and began cracking his own. "Do tell, Lucy, what sort of prey would you be to these hungry lions?"

"I'm not prey."

"To them you are." Said the man. Xavier tapped a drink with his mixing spoon to signal he was done and pushed it towards the blue-eyed man. "You really should be more careful, Lucy."

Another *tink* and Xavier pushed a drink towards Lucy. It was plum colored, but smelled like whiskey. As she reached for it, the bartender wordlessly held up his finger for her to wait, then turned his back and busied himself placing items on a tray.

She returned her attention to the man. "You don't even know me. Maybe *I'm* the lion, and they're the sheep. Maybe I'm a damned *dragon* that can breathe fire and sleeps on a hoard of gold!"

Unperturbed, the man took a sip of his cocktail. "Well, I'd have to see it to believe it. The hoard of gold you sleep on, that is. And you're correct, I *don't* really know you. You don't know me either. Maybe I'm a dragon, too."

Xavier sat a tray in front of Lucy. He removed a wooden smoking top with a diamond shaped steel lid and placed it on top of her drink. He carefully removed the steel stopper and scooped a spoonful of dried lavender into the chamber. Then, using a culinary torch, lit the dried herb on fire. Lucy watched the flames rise and then smolder.

*He's right. Who the hell is this guy?*

The bartender replaced the stopper, and smoke flooded the glass in swirls. Lucy was momentarily mesmerized, until he removed the wooden lid from her glass.

"Tonight," proclaimed the bartender, "You are drinking 'Deep Purple'—Akashi plum whisky and honey, in a lavender smoked glass…" He squeezed a lemon slice. "With lemon and a butterfly pea flower." He dropped a tiny purple flower into the glass.

"It's beautiful." Lucy took a sip. "And delicious. May I ask why you chose this drink for me?"

In response, the bartender smirked.

"Lucy, you're not allowed to ask." Said the blue-eyed man. "It's against the rules." His normally mischievous face was stern.

The bartender smiled and dismissed himself to serve some local craft beers to two men carrying their suit jackets in their hands wearing loosened ties. Bleary-eyed, they seemed exhausted from whatever they'd been doing before they entered the lounge.

"…what is your name?" Lucy finally asked the blue-eyed man.

"I thought you'd never ask." His sly grin returned. "Tobias."

Lucy was silent for a moment. "Tobias…that's actually a really great name."

"Thanks. It was a gift from my parents." He sipped his own drink—dark amber, with red powder on the rim and garnished with a cucumber and lime. He grimaced. "Wow, *that* is jalapeno-infused something…with a chili powder rim."

Xavier laughed from the end of the bar.

"Can you at least tell me what it's called?" Tobias took a bite of the cucumber to calm his burning mouth.

"*El Diablo Suave*" he said. "The Smooth Devil."

Tobias chuckled. "Nice. Can you give me a lemon instead? I hate limes."

"I'm busy!" Xavier gestured at a group of women in their own LBD's who'd just entered the lounge in a cloud of expensive perfume. "Why don't you get it yourself?"

Tobias scoffed, and got out of his barstool. "Well, there goes *his* tip."

Lucy laughed and fidgeted with a napkin. She wondered if Nolan's plane had landed in Colorado Springs yet. She watched Tobias glide behind the bar, pulling out drawers and peeking in baskets. If she had met him before Nolan, this night would have been a dream come true. He was rich (although the source of which remained a mystery), well dressed in a gray slim-fit Armani suit. Blonde hair slicked to a point in the back. Was that a tattoo on his neck? Lucy couldn't make it out beneath his collar.

He popped up from behind the counter with a glass container of pre-cut lemons floating in lemon juice. "Here we are." Tobias plucked the lime from his rim, and used a fork to take a lemon from the container, then dropped it in his glass. He stirred exactly three times, clockwise. And stopped in the exact place he started. Lucy wondered if he had OCD. There had to be *something* up with this guy. He was too charming. Too handsome.

And those eyes were definitely *not* a flaw.

She felt she'd got her wish to talk to someone interesting, at least.

"What happened to your eye, Tobias? Why is one blue and the other brown? The pupil of the blue eye doesn't seem to adjust to the light. Were you injured?" Lucy asked.

He placed his fork on a napkin and locked his eyes with Lucy's. "Well, that's rather a personal question, don't you think? Do my eyes make you uncomfortable, Lucy?"

Lucy's face grew red with embarrassment. "What? No! No...I was just curious."

There was a heavy silence. "Let's just say it was *another* gift from my parents."

She squirmed under his gaze, and awkwardly sipped her drink. Tobias sensed this and shifted gears.

"Enough about me. I'm the bartender, after all. You're supposed to tell me *your* problems, not the other way 'round."

He British accent was more pronounced as he said that, and intentional or not, Lucy cracked a smile. "Where are you from?"

"That's a tricky question to answer. Does that mean 'Where was I born?', or, 'Where have I lived the longest?' or, 'What location influenced me to become the person I am the most?' or... 'Where do I consider *home?*' . Your *actual question* is the real question. And we're not here to talk about me, remember?" Tobias raised his eyebrows at her.

Her head swum from the man across the bar speaking to her in riddles. He was right. What did she want to know? Did it even matter? "Well, where were you born?"

"East End of London. I've worked hard to tame my Cockney accent, but it's still there." Tobias tilted his head to one side.

"Prove it." Said Lucy.

He laughed and loosened his black striped tie. "How 'bout we have a good ol' *rabbit and pork* 'bout your life, Lucy?" He returned to his posh accent. "That means *conversation*. What brings you to The Inferno this evening?"

Her eyes fell, and she swirled the butterfly pea flower with a straw. "I guess I just wanted to get out of the house. There was too much at home reminding me of my failures."

Nodding, Tobias leaned across the bar. "That's a common reason people are at Inferno. Whether it's a failed business deal or failed marriage...the wealthy come here to forget for an hour or two. One cannot reach great heights without risking an equally great decline. I'm sure you haven't done anything *nearly* as terrible as the others I've met."

Lucy's eyes misted. "That's the thing...I don't feel like I'm doing anything wrong *now*. I've turned my life around. I'm a good person! I feel like I'm being punished...by God...for things I've done in my past. I think God hates me."

Tobias placed two fingers under Lucy's chin and gently lifted her face to his. "I know what it's like to experience a...*fall from grace*. If God hates his creations, I would be at the top of his list. But I don't think God is willing to hate anyone...least of all, someone as sweet as you. Maybe he's just a little disappointed? Maybe you just need to try a little harder?"

"That's the thing!" Lucy pouted, "I'm doing everything I can! It's not working!"

There was a pregnant pause as Tobias assessed her, having clearly struck a nerve.

He reached into his glass of *El Diablo Suave* and plucked out his lemon, and held it in front of her face.

"You know what they say when life gives you lemons, Lucy?"

She nodded and rolled her eyes. She was tired of 'making lemonade' out of lemons.

Tobias shook his head, reading her mind. "When life gives you lemons...*put them in your drink*."

He dropped the lemon in her Deep Purple, then picked up her straw and began to stir.

Counter-clockwise. Three. Two. One.

The sun was just beginning to rise as Benny hobbled out his front door in a red silk kimono, leaning on one crutch with one hand and carrying a double grocery-bagged dirty diaper in the other. It was the blowout of the century thanks to little too much flaxseed in the twins' bedtime smoothies. The trash cart was at the curb and hadn't been dumped yet. There was *no way* he could let that diaper fester another week smelling up the can and attracting raccoons. It had to go out *now*.

He'd been managing it all by himself—the twins, the teenager, the household, doctors, food. Christopher had been bedridden for the last week as he recovered from second degree burns and lacerations due to the explosion at the cabin. After two days in the hospital, he had been stable enough to make the trip home, so Benny rented a van that allowed Christopher to recline in the back. Despite being a new driver, Ashton drove all the way from Tennessee to southwest Missouri by himself owing to Benny's broken leg. They had no other options.

He desperately needed Lucy's help with the twins. Benny, Christopher and the babies were sleeping in the family room since they couldn't make it upstairs. Ashton drove himself to summer school and took care of his own needs but rarely helped otherwise. He was never home. Benny had given up keeping tabs on him and nearly called Ashton's mother for help but Christopher refused. *The last thing he needs right now is that woman's influence*, he'd told Benny.

Benny had called and texted Lucy every day since the accident with no response. He refrained from knocking on her door so far, but he was getting desperate and considered visiting her today. He'd seen Nolan leave with luggage in a taxi yesterday and wondered if there was trouble in "tradwife paradise".

Benny traversed the stairs as fast as he could with crutches and a bag of dirty diapers—the trash truck always came at 5:30 a.m. on the dot or they'd be flooded with complaints by residents. He scampered barefoot across the cold, dewy law, his crutch making a trail of holes in the moist earth. He tossed the bag full of foul into the trash cart, and leaned against it for a moment to catch his breath. He heard Lucy's front door open and shut.

"It's five in the morning and that girl ain't got no poop covered child waking her up…" he mumbled to himself, hobbling towards her yard so he could peek over the hedges. Craning his neck over the bushes, he slipped in the wet lawn and tumbled, landing face down in the grass and bare ass up.

"Son of a bitch!" Benny groaned as pain shot up his leg. He rolled on his side, spitting dirt and grass from his mouth.

"Nice…*robe* you have there." Said a smooth English voice behind him.

Benny remembered he wasn't wearing anything under his robe. He quickly covered himself and attempted to stand. The strong hands of the stranger moved to help steady him on his feet.

The rising sun glowing behind him like an angel, Benny was faced the most gorgeous man he had ever seen in his life. He smelled like sandalwood, had *just enough* black stubble on his face to look both rugged and professional… and how in the world does someone get blessed with both a cleft chin *and* dimples? Benny's heart hammered. His mind wiped of all sense except infatuation as he croaked. "…thank you?"

A shiny black Mercedes pulled up to the curb in front of Lucy's house and tapped the horn. "That's my ride," the man gave a dimpled smile that would make a straight man's knees weak, "Cheerio."

Benny mumbled goodbye and made a small wave. As the man was about to climb into the backseat, he turned around and said, "Have a better morning, mate." He winked and closed the door.

It was too much to handle so early in the morning. Benny leaned against his crutch, flustered. What just happened?

Wait…why was he coming out of Lucy's house at the break of dawn?

Isn't Nolan gone?

Smelling drama, Benny slip-slided across his own lawn again, and trotted down the sidewalk as his wet feet slapped the cement leaving a strange trail of crutch-bottom and footprints. *At least Christopher will know where I went.* He dragged himself up Lucy's porch and opened the door without knocking.

"Good morning Ms. Lucy! Where the hell are you?" he said in a sing-songy voice as he entered the house. "You've got some explaining to do about that incredibly handsome stranger that just left your house in a sixty-thousand-dollar car…"

There was no response. Benny had only ever had tea with Lucy on the patio while the twins played, so he wasn't familiar with her house. He wandered around, peeking in doorways. A bathroom, office, linen closet…and then, an enormous nursery. It's contents put all the twins' belongings to shame. It was decked out ceiling to floor with every possible thing a baby could need for the first two years of their life—all high end, top of the line baby gear.

Benny knew Lucy wanted a baby, but until this moment he hadn't realized how badly. She had chosen a Peter Rabbit theme, and a large stuffed rabbit sat swaddled in a rocking chair by the window overlooking the English garden in her backyard. Benny and Christopher had done IVF three times with two different surrogates before they had a successful pregnancy. His heart broke for her.

His attitude softened and he gently closed the nursery room door, then tiptoed down the hallway. The last room must be hers and Nolan's.

A black Christian Louboutin heel lay sideways at the entrance of the door. "I didn't know this girl had redbottoms…*shit!*" Benny whispered to himself, following a trail that included a diamond earring, a Valentino bag (*I oughta beat her ass for throwing that on the floor*), then a hot pink bra and matching panties.

At the end of the trail, in the bed lay Lucy. Eyes closed, mouth open and arm hanging off the bed, her gentle snores told Benny she was alive at least. He shook her shoulder roughly. "Girl, get your ass up!"

Her eyes fluttered open. "What? Benny…what are you doing here?"

Benny balanced on one foot and crossed his arms. "I'll be asking the questions right now! And cover your beautiful titties when you talk to me. Good GOD, I wish I was as blessed as you!"

Panic flooded her face and she shot up, blond hair sticking up wildly and mascara smeared under her eyes. She wrapped herself up in her floral comforter and her eyes pleaded desperately with Benny. "Oh no…what happened?"

"Well, I can tell you what I *think* happened. Your husband is out of town and you slept with an unbelievably handsome British man!" Benny huffed. "While I do *not* condone adultery, I can't help but feel envious that *even when you misbehave* you continue to be so *Unbelievably Lucky Lucy*. Hashtag blessed. You make me absolutely SICK!"

Benny collapsed dramatically on her bed. "Look at me! Look at my broken-ass body! Look at the bags under my eyes! I haven't had a manicure in weeks. Now go on, *Lucky Lucy*. Tell me all about your sexual escapades with a mysterious stranger!"

Although she couldn't remember the act, it was clear what had happened. She knew she had slept with Tobias, all the evidence was clear. She had broken her marriage vows.

"I don't know…Nolan went to Colorado for work. I was feeling sad, I guess, so I went to a cigar bar…" Lucy stammered.

"You went to The Inferno? They let you in?!" Benny threw one of Lucy's pillows across the room. "You have GOT to be kidding me. I hate you. Continue."

Her mouth felt like cotton and her head swam. This wasn't an ordinary hangover. "I think he did something to my drink."

The spilling of this tea was too much for Benny. He held his chest. "Girl, I am so sorry that happened to you, but seriously why would a man like *that* need to spike a drink? I damn near sucked his dick on the front lawn after a ten second conversation."

"Wait," said Lucy. "You saw him?"

Benny nodded. "Sure did. I was taking out the trash and fell on my ass in the lawn. He helped me up, then left in a Mercedes. He winked at me. Just sayin'. I think he would've spiked my drink if given the right situation."

"What about Nolan? …I love him so much, I would never cheat on him! He's going to leave me!" Lucy sobbed.

Benny pulled her hands from her face. "Look at me Lulu. *Look at me!* I'm going to tell you what you are going to do. You are going to get your ass up. Take a shower. Change the sheets. And then…you are going to pretend this never happened."

"What! I can't live with myself knowing I cheated on Nolan!" she squeaked.

"Can you live without Nolan?" Benny asked.

She sniffed. "No."

Benny nodded. "Exactly. If you want to keep Nolan and your pretty little tradwife life, you will erase this memory from your mind. And never, EVER, go back to The Inferno Lounge *without also taking me* because I've always wanted to see the inside…and it's not safe for your beautiful self to go out alone. Understand?"

"Yes." Lucy wiped her eyes on the back of her arm. "You won't tell Nolan?"

He raised an eyebrow. "Oh, I won't tell Nolan…as long as you get your ass over to my house and do the goddamn dishes."

# Chapter 20

## Ghosted

A distressed old woman snapped her fingers in front of Esme's face. "Hey! Are you okay? What's your name?"

Esme blinked, momentarily aware she was in unfamiliar surroundings: a small living room with brown velvety furniture covered in plastic—the kind from the 1990's you always seem to find in second-hand furniture stores, usually printed with herds of deer, mountains or pioneer wagons crossing the plains. These had wagons. Every flat surface of the room held knickknacks and photos—those, too, seemed frozen in time. Kewpie figures, porcelain dolls, decorative plates. There were also photos of a young woman arranged by age from infancy to late teens.

"Where am I?" Esme started hyperventilating, sucking in the sickly sweet smell from bowls of potpourri.

"Well, my name's Betty. I'm not sure what you're doing here, but I think you need help." The woman rubbed Esme's shoulders to comfort her. "Before I go and get the cops involved, would you rather I call someone to come get you? Do you have a phone?"

*A phone? Yes. I have a phone in my bag.* Why did that feel like such a strange thought?

Esme opened the small purse sitting on her lap, and handed her cellphone to the woman without a word.

"Passcode, dear?"

Esme fixated on the photos, eyes flicking back and forth. *A passcode?*

"Alright then…" Betty held the phone in front of Esme's face, which unlocked the screen. "Who should I call?"

Esme closed her eyes and rocked back and forth.

The woman sighed and opened the contacts. "This one says 'Mom'. I'm calling her, alright?"

Esme nodded in agreement, but it felt forced, like she had to pull herself up from beneath a wave in the ocean. *Mom. Emily. Please come get me. I don't know where I am...who I am.* Her thoughts raced, but her mouth couldn't move. Esme hugged her knees and rocked, feeling like a prisoner in her own body.

Twenty minutes later, Emily pounded on the screen door of Betty's home. "Esme! Esme, where are you?"

"Come on in, she's right here." Said Betty, ushering Emily into the living room. Relieved to finally have the confused child off her hands she collapsed into her rocking chair. "Esme, is it? That's a pretty name." She took a sip of her now-cold coffee. "Look, there's your mom, honey."

Emily swept into the room, wrapping her arms around her daughter, burying her face in her chest. "Esme...what are you doing here?"

"I don't know," Esme sounded groggy. "I just felt like I needed to be somewhere, so I got in the car and drove. I kept thinking I was driving home. I stopped out front and went inside."

Betty nodded, "Yep. That girl was standin' on my porch and I about fainted. She looks so much like my daughter, I let her right in."

Emily furrowed her brows. "Esme, why did you come here?"

"I told you; I was driving home." She said.

"...but we live on the other side of Springfield. We've never lived over here," emphasized Emily.

"What do you mean?" Esme seemed confused. "I was born here. It's the only home I've ever known."

Emily looked over at Betty, who had stopped rocking in her chair. "Do want me to call an ambulance?"

"No, I can—" Emily stopped, as her eyes caught the last row of photos of a young woman in her teens. "—who is that?"

Betty slowly looked over her shoulder. "That's my daughter. Did you know her? She'd be about your age? Her name is Mariah."

Mariah.

The sketch.

The wallet.

*No. It can't be.*

"I…I think I might have known her…" Emily stood up and tried to pull Esme to her feet, but she wouldn't budge.

"Mom! Mom, help!" said Esme, but she wasn't looking at Emily; she was pleading with Betty. "He wasn't a good guy. He hurt me, and now I'm in the dark. Please come get me. I can't find the light!"

Betty's eyes were wide. "I'm not your mother, Esme."

"You are. You are. Please, I want to get back to you and Ruthie. Is Ruthie okay? Where is she?" Esme had tears in her eyes. She was reaching for Betty as Emily held her back.

Her voice shook. "…Ruthie…is Mariah's little sister. She's married and lives in Orlando."

"He said we were going out to dinner at Benovicci's…" Esme sobbed.

"Benovicci's?" asked Betty. "That place has been closed at least fifteen years."

Emily shook her daughter's shoulders. "Ez, stop it! Stand up, we need to go home."

"That's what I'm saying!" said Esme. "I want to go home! I want to be with my mom and sister, but I'm trapped! We all are…"

"Esme…I'm your mother. Harper is at school…" Emily's hands shook as she moved Esme's hair out of her face. Her daughter's features, though the same, were somehow different. Maybe it was the way she pursed her lips, or slouched slightly. Esme almost felt like a stranger.

"What about Dad?" Esme asked Betty.

Emily cupped her daughter's chin and turned it towards her. "Esme, your father is dead. You know that. He's been gone nearly a decade."

"No...not her dad. Mine." Esme pulled away from Emily, crawling across the carpet to Betty's feet. "Mom, get Daddy. He can help bring me home. Tell him to bring his shotgun."

Betty scrambled out of her chair, frightened. "What is this? Some sort of cruel prank? My husband took off with some thirty-year old gold digger eight years ago."

"Daddy wouldn't do that!" Esme rose from the floor in anger.

Emily grabbed her daughter by the sleeve and yanked her away from the old women standing in front of the childhood photos of Mariah. "Betty," Emily asked, trembling. "Is your last name Wilson?"

"Yes, but who are *you*?" Betty was alarmed and inching her way towards her cell phone in the kitchen.

"What street is this again?" Emily already knew the answer.

"...Clifton Avenue."

Emily shook Esme's shoulder. "Let's go, *right now*. Betty, I'm so sorry to bother you. I think I *did* go to school with your daughter. Remind me again, what happened to her?"

"Honey, she's been missing for twenty-five years. She was supposed to go on a date one night, and never made it to his place," Betty was trying to keep her cool and not overreact. The teenage girl seemed sweet enough...just a bit tetched. "It's been so long...we expect the worst."

The room spun, and Emily wobbled backwards towards the door, feeling the blood rush from her face as her heart thumped harder.

Mateo's drawings. Bones. Wallet.

*What is going on with my daughter?* Thought Emily. "Oh, my goodness. I'm so sorry. I don't think that's the same Mariah I knew."

Emily pushed her daughter outside. Now unblinking and unresponsive, she appeared catatonic. "Thank you so much for helping my daughter. I'll send someone to pick up her car within a few hours."

Betty appeared equally confused and skeptical. "Alright...but how'd she know my other daughter's name, Ruthie?"

Emily shrugged. "Oh, she gets in these strange stupors and says all sorts of things, I wouldn't read into it. Okay, bye-bye now!" She dragged her daughter down the steps to where she had parked in the street, then forced her into the backseat.

Hands shaking, the keys jingled as she started the van. *What do I do? Where do I take her? To a church or a hospital? Maybe she just needs rest. Is she on drugs like Oliver?*

Emily peered in the rearview mirror and watched as Esme opened a piece of gum, popped it into her mouth and smiled. It was unnerving.

"Put your seatbelt on, Esme."


She giggled. "Esme's taking a nap. I'm Laurie. Can we go to *my* house next?"

# Chapter 21

# Lovecraftian Horrors

I t was just a fishhook.

Trix winced, unwrapping the bandage from their hand. The wound had been festering for weeks ever since Trix pricked it climbing on the bridge. They started with antibiotic cream and a bandage, but it reddened and swelled more each day. Red lines now spiderwebbed from the small point of origin in her palm all the way up to her elbow like a horrific tattoo. How could all this happen from getting stuck on a rusty fishhook?

Trix knew they should have told their parents. *How did that happen? Why didn't you tell us?* Blah, blah, blah. Trix felt they had better things to do than spend the afternoon at the doctor's office. Ragekitten, Shrox, and Direpaw were waiting for Trix at the Furmeet. The Furries accepted her in every way; Furmeets were the only place they could relax and be themselves. It amazed Trix how much easier it was to connect with people while wearing her rabbit Fursuit. They didn't feel judged or self-conscious.

Sweat drenched Trix's hair and they weren't even in their Fursuit yet. They flipped the fan switch inside the suit and it hummed to life. *There's no way I could wear this thing without it today.*

A horn honked out front and Trix saw Ragekitten waving from her little orange Fiat. Her real name was Michelle. She was a year older than Trix—18—but still lived with her parents while she attended college. They texted each other almost constantly, except during their nightly phone call. Even though they weren't official, it's what Trix wanted more than anything. They'd never felt this way about anyone before. Tonight, Trix planned to make a move and kiss her. They knew it would make or break their relationship, but Trix was done wondering: did Ragekitten feel the same?

Eric watched from behind the sheer kitchen curtain as Trix tossed their costume in the back of the Fiat, then quickly gathered his own. He'd toiled over his Fursuit for two weeks, maxing out his credit cards at the craft store and hand sewing the wings every night while watching reruns of *The Trailer Park Boys*. He'd finally been accepted into the private online Furry group after he sent photos of his work, and this was the first Furmeet he was invited to. Eric didn't know if Trix was going, so he loitered by the front door for the last hour to see if she caught a ride with anyone.

After the orange clown-car was out of sight, he rushed to the driveway, swinging open the door of his small pickup, and then, pausing in appreciation of his work, gingerly laid his costume in the passenger seat, buckling in the headpiece for good measure. Although this whole "Fursuit thing" started as simply a disguise to keep an eye on his stepdaughter, Eric had never been more proud of a creation in his life. Even his best-selling jalapeno-popper grilled cheese sandwich didn't fill him with as much satisfaction as his artistic Fursuit interpretation of a Large Tolype Moth; dark metallic scales. Furry white and gray body with tinsel throughout. Six legs with itty bitty grippy-grabbers on the ends. Brown, drooping antennae made with artificial grasses. Shiny black mesh eyes. It was beautiful. It was a magnificent work of art.

His truck rumbled and died after the first try. "Oh, come on! Not now…" He tried again and the pickup buzzed but didn't turn over. Gemma and Mika had already left for work. His only option was…the food truck.

Eric hated that truck but couldn't find a buyer willing to pay enough to cover the loan he had taken out to buy it. The loan was his first mistake. Never finance *anything* when you're just starting out in the mobile food business. Every time he saw it in the driveway, covered in pollen and birdshit, he was reminded how he'd failed at yet another financial venture. He always fucked up anything good. That's why it was only a matter of time before Gemma dumped him. The newest husband, Mika, was the whole package wrapped up in a hand-beaded Native American bow. Eric felt like a bag of flaming dog shit left by her front door. She didn't need a loser like him getting in the way anymore.

*No*, Eric reminded himself. *There is a reason she chose me.*

He'd promised Gemma he would try to replace his negative thoughts with positive ones. "Thoughts become things." She'd said. She also said I have potential. *If a woman like her can believe in a dumpster fire like me, I owe it to her to at least* try.

He growled as he grabbed his Furry gear and swapped vehicles. The door to the food truck creaked loudly as he opened it. The leather seat burned his ass as he sat down, and the interior still smelled like bacon and onions. It reminded him of the first time he ever looked inside, so full of optimism and hope. Being in here now brought a confusing mix of joyful nostalgia and heartbreak. Eric knew it was his fault. He's never been good with money, and hated negotiating with vendors. He blew through his startup funds in six months, letting the cost of food and gas get away from him. Eric didn't use social media to advertise where he was parked either. By the time he figured out his mistakes it was too late. He was broke and *Melted Magic* closed its windows for good. He'd prayed and burned prosperity candles every day before work—just like Gemma instructed—but nothing helped. His dreams were over before he even had a chance to get his footing.

Melted Magic Food Truck reliably roared to life, but Eric sat for ten minutes wiping bird shit off the windshield with washer fluid just so he could see where he was going. He knew he would be late to his first Furmeet, but he needed to make sure Trix was alright. He wanted his stepdaughter to have a shot at a good life, and to stay away from the wrong sorts of people. Even though she wasn't biologically his he'd practically raised her since she was a toddler after Gemma's boyfriend ran off to live in Florida. Eric and Gemma had been best friends since high school, and their relationship happened naturally. Things just flowed. First the kid, then moving in together, marriage. Before he knew it, fifteen years had gone by. He loved Trix unconditionally, and he loved Gemma so much that he'd agreed to a polyamorous relationship if that's what it took to keep them both in his life.

Gemma had been the only one dating in the open relationship. Eric didn't *want* anyone else. Then she met Mika and things got all serious. They wanted to get "spiritually married" and live as a thruple. Although Gemma never said it, Eric knew his options were either agree or move out. There's no way he could compete with Mika: He was all bronze and tall with shiny black hair down to his waist. He worked as a visiting professor of Native American history across the Midwest, so he was all *smart* and shit. He even had a 401k. In contrast, Eric wouldn't have graduated high school if Gemma hadn't written his English essays senior year. It's no wonder she loves Mika so much, and Eric hated to admit it, but he really admired the guy. Secretly, he wanted his respect and approval. But more than anything he wanted to be worthy of Gemma.

Trix's ride long gone, Eric followed the directions to the Furmeet on his phone. It led to an old Victorian home in the central part of town. It was one of those "up and coming" neighborhoods where every other house was lovingly renovated by some bored retired couple with too much money. The houses that weren't had been in families for decades or were rentals to groups of college students. In both cases, the houses were the same: chipped paint, shabby lawn, plastic over drafty windows. The Furmeet was at one of those.

The only parking spot big enough for the food truck happened to be directly in front of the house. Eric hoped Trix would be too busy to notice, and planned to leave the gathering before she did. His plan was to pop in and assess the situation, then leave before getting too involved… unless he needed to.

Eric climbed in the back of the truck to change into his moth suit. He was actually kind of glad he brough the truck because he realized he didn't know where he was supposed to change when he got there. Was he just supposed to drive over in his suit? What did everyone else do if this was a place to hide your identity? Eric realized he had a lot to learn if he was going to blend in. Before placing on his headpiece, he fluffed his wings and looked at himself in the distorted reflection on the steel cabinets.

*I look so fucking cool.*

He put the headpiece on. Inside, he was Trix's loser stepdad. Outside, he was *Nocturne*, the Large Tolype Moth.

As Nocturne shambled out of the truck he heard audible gasps behind him. He turned to see a fox carrying a party size bag of nacho chips and a red panda with a 2-liter bottle of root beer under each arm standing behind him.

"Are you the new person?" asked the red panda. "Dude, your Fursuit is dope."

"Where'd you get it?" asked the fox.

Eric cleared his throat.

"I made it myself." Said Nocturne. Without waiting for a response, he glided to the front door. Nocturne didn't need their approval, but he certainly had it.

The door opened before he had a chance to answer. It was a kangaroo. "Hey, you must be Nocturne! I'm Scooter. This is my place." He waved Nocturne inside. "I have the biggest house out of everyone so it's usually where we have mini-meetups. Everybody! We have a new person. This is Nocturne!"

Nocturne waved from the entryway. "Hello."

Muffled hellos and compliments on his costume could be heard beneath headpieces. Furries were lounging on sofas and an alligator sat at a piano. The fox and red panda scooched around Nocturne and dropped their offerings of chips and soda on a plastic fold out table littered with the remains of cookies and cheese trays.

"Sorry, I forgot to bring a snack." Said Nocturne. He didn't see Trix's rabbit Fursuit in the crowd.

The kangaroo patted Nocturne's shoulder, respectfully avoiding his handcrafted wings. "No big deal, bro. Just bring a little extra next week."

Next week. Nocturne hadn't thought about making this a regular thing. Would he need to? "Okay, sure."

Nocturne was smart enough to not make feet for his Fursuit. He just wore a pair of white sneakers. He had seen how much Trix struggled with theirs, and it was cumbersome enough to manage his moth wings. He spotted Trix's rabbit feet near the slightly crumbling fireplace. *Well, at least they are here.* Nocturne cautiously entered, not sure what he was supposed to be doing.

"So…" he said to Scooter. "Is this everybody or do people hang out other places too?"

If Scooter emoted, Nocturne couldn't tell. "Nah, there are more of us. Some people out back. A few went upstairs, but…uh…I wouldn't go there. In the basement we have some boardgames set up, but that's for people who are cool with their real identity being known. Kinda hard to play games with gloves and a headpiece, ya know?"

"Okay," said Nocturne. "Cool."

Where would Trix want to hang out? He hoped it wasn't upstairs. He wandered through the kitchen to the back door, saying hello to a squirrel, a German Shepard and a tabby cat as he went.

The backyard was small but fenced in. A tire swing hung from an old oak tree where a rabbit was pushing a white cat. Trix.

The cat waved, and jumped off the swing. "New guy! Welcome. What's your name?"

They high fived as she approached. "Nocturne."

"Great name. It fits. I'm Ragekitten, a bit of an O.G. around here. Let me know if you have any questions." She said, hands on hips.

"...and you are?" Nocturne asked Trix, who cautiously approached.

"Trix."

They used their real name. Interesting. Nocturne lowered his voice slightly to disguise it. "Nice to meet you, Trix."

After an awkward silence, Nocturne decided Trix was okay for the time being, and it would be weird to interrupt what kind of seemed like a romantic thing. Did Trix have a Furry girlfriend? That would explain the sudden deep dive into Furry culture. It eased his mind tremendously. He'd done plenty of weird shit in the name of love. Like polygamy. "Alright, well, I'm gonna head down to the basement and check that out...so...see ya."

The rabbit and the cat waved goodbye and returned to the swing, swapping places so that now Ragekitten was pushing Trix.

Nocturne relaxed, feeling confident Trix was only into the Furry stuff to impress this Ragekitten girl. Even if they were genuinely interested in it for other reasons, it didn't seem so bad. Everyone Nocturne had met seemed welcoming and nice. *Different*, but not weird. He went back inside the house and wandered around, following the sound of lo-fi beats into the dimly lit basement.

A pile of gloves, headpieces and a few overly-bushy tails lay at the bottom of the stairs where Nocturne left his own. At one table, he watched a partially costumed rat rolling D-20's behind a cardboard screen while another rat chewed on its pink tail in suspense. An eagle doodled on his character sheet. A wolf texted with a scowl on his face. They were intensely focused on their already-established RPG, so his eyes moved on.

On the floor were a few teenagers playing a trading card game—probably Pokemon or something. Meh, too young. That would be weird. A bald guy around his age sat alone on a folding chair assembling a puzzle on a TV tray. In between placing pieces, he picked his nose and neurotically sipped his energy drink like a hummingbird at a feeder. Nope.

In the corner of the basement, illuminated by a desk lamp, a moose—or deer?—leaned over a wooden wire-spool table, his chin propped on his hand, considering the game in front of him. He seemed to be building a battlefield, and miniatures were dived into groups in front of him. Nocturne ran a quick assessment. He had a few tattoos on his neck and knuckles, but his hair and beard were neatly trimmed into one of those retro styles with closely trimmed sides and a poof on top. This bro had a curly mustache. Cool, but not *too* cool. He *was* dressed as a moose, after all.

Approaching quietly so as to not startle him, Nocturne cleared his throat. "Hey, man. What are you playing?"

He looked up from the game and gave a welcoming smile. "Hey! You must be the moth guy everybody is talking about. Those wings look so *real*." The moose came up to him for a closer look, but never touched the handiwork. Nocturne knew it was a gesture of respect not to give scritches or touch another person's costume without permission. Fursuits were expensive and laborsome to create, not to be subjected to unnecessary wear…or so he read online.

"Thanks," said Nocturne. "I'll have to show you the headpiece sometime. I spent like three days on the antennae. I'm Eri—Nocturne."

"Cool." They shook hands. "I'm Icewind."

"So, are you a moose…or…?" Nocturne asked.

Icewind laughed. "Nah, man. I'm a reindeer. I really love Icelandic folklore and animals. I've been trying to find someone to help me make a Fur-bearing Trout suit, but they always end up looking like some kind of Lovecraftian horror. That's why I was checking out your wings. It's all wispy like the hairs on a Shaggy Trout. You do commissions?"

Nocturne became flustered. "Me? No, I'm new to all this."

"Hmm." Said Icewind. "Coulda fooled me. You want to help me set up terrain? I can teach you how to play."

Nocturne felt like he was in second grade again, meeting another kid who liked the Power Rangers. *Be cool, Eric.* "Sure."

Icewind spent the next hour explaining the rules of Warhammer to Nocturne. He was patient and funny, and a super interesting dude.

Nocturne was almost certain they were going to be best friends.

"So, what do you do for a living?" asked Nocturne. "Wait, am I allowed to ask that?"

He chuckled. "Well, it depends on the person, but I'm an open book. I'm an accountant. Pretty lame, I know, but it pays the bills. My parents own a few restaurants and side businesses, so I help them out. Have you heard of The Inferno Cigar Lounge?"

It was Nocturne's turn to laugh. "Yeah, but I've most definitely *not* been inside. I don't own a suit."

Icewind smiled sympathetically. "Don't feel bad, my parents own it and I've never been inside. I just run the books. They also own a few barbershops, tattoo parlors, Chinese buffets. They're always on my ass to help them make sure the books look clean for the IRS. I do shit like this— Warhammer, Furries, cycling—to blow off steam, ya know?"

Nocturne nodded. He couldn't help but feel a bit deflated. This guy was probably well off and had a *real* job. He wouldn't hang out with me.

"So, Moth Man, what do *you* do for a living?" Icewind asked.

He stammered, his mouth opening and closing like an Icelandic Fur-Bearing Trout caught on land, when someone shouted down the stairs.

"Hey guys, there's a grilled cheese food truck parked outside if anybody's hungry!"

"Oh, cool." Said the Furries.

"Yeah, I could eat."

Nocturne ran to the stairs. "No! No, no. It's not open. *That's my truck.* My restaurant is closed."

Disappointment flooded the room.

"Well, where do you usually park? Maybe we could stop by sometime." Asked the rat.

"Nowhere…" said Nocturne. "I'm out of business."

"Dang, that sucks." Said the wolf. "I've heard most food trucks fail in the first six months."

Melted Magic lasted four. "Yeah. I suppose that's true."

Icewind coughed, sensing Nocturne's embarrassment. "Hey, Nocturne. Let's get back to our game."

Nocturne hung his head and returned to the box of miniatures he was unpacking. An awkward silence filled the air.

"You know," said Icewind, carefully choosing his words, "I know a thing or two about the restaurant business. You want to tell me what happened? Maybe I can offer some insight."

Nocturne squirmed under the scrutiny of someone whose family clearly knew how to succeed in every way he had failed.

*Be inspired by people who are doing better than you, not intimidated.* Gemma had once told him. *Learn from them rather than resent them.*

"Well, I'll tell you what I did right first." Nocturne managed a small smile. "I make a damned good grilled cheese sandwich. Everybody loved my stuff, and the food truck was the coolest job I ever had. I loved meeting knew people and giving them a few minutes of happiness on their lunch break, ya know?"

Icewind nodded. "That's awesome, man. Everyone should love what they do."

"Like the way you love being an accountant?" Nocturne prodded.

"I fucking hate being an accountant." He scowled, momentarily lost in his own head.

Sensing he should back off, Nocturne turned the conversation back to himself. "Yeah, well, it's an important job anyway. Wish I had an accountant...that's what happened to me. I didn't keep track of my shit. Didn't ask for better deals from suppliers. I blew through all my seed money in a few months."

"Hey, maybe we should run your grilled cheese food truck together." Icewind laughed.

Then he didn't.

They stopped assembling the game and exchanged small grins.

"Do you want to come see it?" asked Nocturne.

"Your food truck?" replied Icewind.

"Yeah." Nocturne glowed.

Icewind dropped his game pieces. "Fuck yeah I do."


The two men dressed in their full Fursuits to go upstairs where it was required to be in complete Fursona. Nocturne straightened Icewind's antlers.

"If I come see your food truck...I need you to do me a favor," asked the reindeer.

Nocturne held out his arms, still learning to emote in his costume. "Okay, what is it?"

"Consider making me a Fur-bearing Trout suit. I'll pay you, of course. I'm tired of everyone thinking I'm a moose."

"Bro, I don't even know what that animal *is*." Said Nocturne.

"Okay, so it's this fish called the *Lodsilunger*. There's been reports of sightings since the 1600's but it *could* be extinct. It's got this wispy fur on it, kind of like your moth or a baby chick, but you can only see the fur when it's in the water. It's inedible to every animal. Totally poisonous. In Iceland, they used to find people dead along the river, the remains of the fish still on their fork. The folklore it that it is the creation of demons and giants, meant to kill off the human race." Icewind rambled.

"Um…okay…well, are their any drawings of this or anything—" Nocturne was interrupted.

"Somebody call an ambulance!" a voice yelled from upstairs. He recognized it as Ragekitten.

Trix.

Eric threw down his headpiece and climbed the basement stairs two at a time. One of his wings caught on the doorknob at the top and ripped off. He found Ragekitten with her headpiece and mittens off. Tears streaked her cheeks.

"Where's Trix?" Eric demanded.

Ragekitten's brows furrowed in confusion. Why did the new guy care?

"I'm their step-dad." He explained.

Deciding that questions could wait, Ragekitten gave a nod and led Eric to the backyard where Trix lay on the ground. Their face was red and sweaty, but their eyes were open. Eric ran and collapsed on his knees, covering the legs of his white moth suit in grass stains and dirt.

"Trix!" he patted their cheeks. Their eyes fluttered as they turned to him. "Trix, what's wrong?"

"Eric?" they stammered.

"What's wrong, Trix?" he pleaded. "Tell me what's wrong so I can help you?"

"I saw them." Trix mumbled. "*Shadow people.* The voices telling me to die. I finally saw them."

Eric touched their forehead. Trix was on fire. "Ragekitten, what happened?"

She sat at Trix's head, stroking their hair. "Trix started rambling about shadows, then fainted and fell off the swing. They've been really quiet today; I think they might be sick."

Eric nodded, summoning every ounce of courage within him to be the dutiful father under complete control of himself and the situation, but inside he was spooked as hell. Gemma had explained everything that was happening with the other kids who went in the cave. They believed Trix was okay because of all the spiritual protections from Gemma. They wanted to believe Trix was just being a little weird with the Furry stuff. Every time they left the house, Gemma and Mika blessed their bedroom with sage and holy water, and put fresh medicine bags under their bed…just in case.

"Let's get Trix to my truck. I'll call Gemma."

# Chapter 22

## Possession with Intent
## to
## Deliver Us from Evil

# My Knight to Your Bishop. Checkmate.

Isabella hated patrolling Commercial Street. It was the oldest street in the city and had fallen into disrepair; first, the businesses left, then the seedy sort of people claimed it as their territory, pushing anyone decent out. Fast forward twenty years and the cheap real estate is purchased by developers and gentrified into coffee shops and art studios. None of them lasted long. Commercial Street's reputation as a place of "sin" was ingrained in the minds of Springfield's residents, whether they found that appealing or not. The riffraff had called this street home for fifty years and wouldn't leave without a fight.

Isabella wasn't bothered by sex workers, drug dealers, or tweakers—she'd grown up around that sort of thing in the north-central part of the city not far from here. It didn't scare her. David had trained her well—maybe even better than the academy where she had graduated with honors. The other officers in her unit would never admit it, but she could read a situation better than any of them. She had good instincts, honed from a young age to help her survive a life around unpredictable and sometimes violent people. She could talk the angriest person down…with the exception of *her own goddamn son.*

Mostly, she hated Commercial Street because she was afraid of seeing her mother. Finding her *alive* would probably be a worse situation than finding her dead. Overdoses were most of her calls on this side of town and she had grown numb to it. Her mom's death would be a welcome finality and relief. It had been twenty-five years since they'd seen each other, and although the pain of her abusive childhood was now a dull ache, Isabella knew if she ever saw her again it would bring it all back. She'd purposely avoided exposing herself to any information about her mother and had no idea if she still lived in Springfield—or lived, period. She'd once parked next to her biological aunt at a pharmacy, and instead of saying hello, Isabella sat for twenty minutes waiting for her leave. Her aunt looked like a brunette version of her mother, only older. So did Isabella. She didn't want to risk being recognized by her estranged relative.

Dispatch called with a report from the owner of a small café who lives in a loft above his business. They reported a black car parked in the alley behind the building, with a known prostitute in the passenger seat. The resident was requesting they be asked to leave. *Should be easy enough* thought Isabella. Sometimes "tricks" cheap out and do business in a car rather than pay for an hourly hotel. Isabella's favorite pastime was ruining a prostitute's night— probably because they reminded her of her mother.

The vehicle was easy enough to find It was barely obscured from the road and, sure enough, the car was *rockin'*. The lights were on in the upstairs loft and a man in the window waved as the patrol car approached, pointing down below. Isabella didn't turn on the lights or siren of her cruiser, preferring to surprise them in the act. She wanted there to be no confusion about why they were together in the alley when she issued a ticket.

Isabella quietly opened the door of her cruiser and left the door slightly ajar. This probably wouldn't take long. She approached the dark-tinted driver's side window and knocked with her flashlight. She wondered if Red Robin was still open so she could get a milkshake on her lunch break.

"Roll down the window. Then put your hands on the steering wheel."

The rocking immediately ceased. The passenger honked the horn on the way out of the driver's seat which made the officer jump. Adrenaline caused her hand to impulsively drift to the gun on her hip. She took a deep breath to relax, and forced herself to smile as as the window went down.

"License and registration, please." She told the driver. "Oh, hey, Cambodia! Didn't I just ticket you last night for indecent exposure?"

"*Pfft.*" Cambodia wiped her mouth with the back of her hand and turned to look out the window. She mumbled something like *fuckin' pig bitch* under her breath, which Isabella ignored. She'd been called much worse during her law enforcement career. That insult was completely lacking in creativity by comparison.

The man handed over his ID, registration, and insurance, and the Lieutenant's flashlight caught the shine of a ring on the man's hand: large, gold, and set with an amethyst.

She looked at the driver's license and it took every ounce of self-control she had to suppress a laugh.

"I always thought Episcopalian rings were worn on the right hand. Why did you move it? Is that what you two are doing out here? Was Cambodia kissing your ring, Bishop Vincent?" Isabella shined the light in his face. His pupils were wide and wild. "You've got a little something under your nose... yeah, right there...looks like powder."

Bishop Vincent stammered and wiped at his face. "I'm sorry, officer...do I know you?"

Isabella ignored the question and instead addressed the sex worker. "Cambodia, I will let you go this *one time* if you leave *right now* and promise to never do business in this alleyway again."

She reached for the door handle, then turned back, her eyes flicking from the officer to the bishop.

"You're not getting paid, Cambodia. Get the fuck out of here before I bring you in." commanded Isabella.

The bishop waited with his hands on the steering wheel, staring straight ahead while the click, click, click of Cambodia's heels grew fainter as she trotted down the sidewalk.

"I can leave, too, officer. I'll never come back here, I promise." He said.

Isabella squatted so she was level with the holy man as they spoke. "Do you remember me, Bishop Vincent?"

He shook his head frantically. "No, I don't. Like I said I could just—"

"What's in that plastic bag on your dashboard? I only ask because it looks a whole lot like cocaine. You being a man of God and all, I hate to assume the worst. Maybe it's just a little powdered sugar you sprinkle over the communion wafers to make them more palatable for the kids in your diocese. You know, kids like Oliver Gladstone?" Lieutenant Kentworth waited for the Bishop to process the clue as to who she was.

"...you were with Charlotte Gladstone. You were asking me to do an exorcism."

Isabella nodded. "That's right. And you said, if I recall, that all we needed was prayer because our kids *were probably on drugs.*"

The irony was not lost on the bishop. *God certainly has a sense of humor.* "What do you want?" He asked flatly.

"I want you and Father Lucas to do an exorcism on our kids." Her face was stone cold and threatening.

Isabella wasn't religious, but she barely recognized her son anymore and she was desperate. They'd tested him for drugs at the hospital after Big Hefty hit him in the head with a fire extinguisher, and it came back clean. Not even steroids. Hefty was so mad about El Hacon being in a coma that Theo was banned from the gym for life. He was surly and mean to everyone…even the person he loved the most: his grandfather. It broke Isabella's heart to see the rift between Theo and David. Tyler was still recovering from a broken jaw, and none of them knew what to do about Theo's anger. If Charlotte felt there could be some sort of demon attached to her son, Isabella didn't see the harm in trying a blessing.

"And if I don't do the blessing?" Bishop Vincent asked, testing the extent of his Godly authority.

Isabella took out her cell phone and snapped a picture of the bishop in his car, disheveled and wide-eyed with a bag of cocaine on the dashboard. "Well, I'm sure your church would love to see this photo, for one. Also, I can arrest you right now for soliciting a prostitute and possession of cocaine. Missouri cocaine laws charge the sale or possession of any amount of cocaine as a felony, which can result in a seven-year maximum prison sentence. Minimum of one year."

Isabella had barely finished speaking before Bishop Vincent was nodding his head in agreement. "I'll do it! I'll do it…I'll do an exorcism."

# The Sins of the Father are Visited Upon the Children

**H**e was fired.

There was no other explanation for why Bishop Vincent would invite him to his office so suddenly and with such urgency. Father Lucas knew he probably pushed too hard for an intervention on behalf of the children, but he also felt their condition was serious. Bishop Vincent had a duty to take his concern seriously, and it was insulting and irresponsible to ignore his request with such blatant disregard of possession symptoms right in front of his face. The angry outbursts, killing animals, promiscuity, Mateo's nightmares and drawings—all of which after entering a cave where others are known to have disappeared, like the Lost Boys of Boliver who went missing in that same cave system back in the fifties. He'd seen the same sort of behavior displayed by oppression victims before, when he lived in Italy. He sympathized with the parents. He knew how it felt to have someone you care about under the control of a spirit entity. It's the same kind of powerlessness you feel when you witness a birth, a death, or a miracle. It's the helplessness you feel when you realize that *all* life is largely in God's hands…and sometimes Satan's. We have free will, certainly, but Father Lucas always seemed to question *how much*. If most things are fated, why should humans bother trying? Are we all just pawns in a cosmic game of chess?

It wasn't like him to be pessimistic, but he couldn't help but question his career path while practicing his faith under the thumb of Bishop Vincent. Father Lucas's church was small, and received very little help maintaining the property. Being in the older, north side of Springfield, most of his patrons were low income—what they could contribute financially was limited. The tradesmen in the church helped keep the place from falling apart—plumbers, painters, pest controllers—but they couldn't afford a new roof, carpeting or appliances for the church kitchen. Father Lucas also desperately wanted to create a program to help the patrons of his church in emergencies like utility shutoffs or house fires. For some reason, Bishop Vincent seemed to have it out for him. A visiting nun once suggested it's because he saw Father Lucas as competition, with the potential to replace him if he slipped up.

Whatever the case may be, it was unfair, which made his choice to become a priest all the more unfulfilling. It didn't help that he saw Emily for the first time in fifteen years. Now he was wondering what his life would have been like if he'd stayed working at The Black Sheep Tavern and finished college. He'd been studying archaeology, but his parents grew tired of paying for what they considered a "useless degree". He took a job as a bartender to pay his own way. Unfortunately, working at Emily and Mark's bar didn't cover tuition, even with big tips and a decent wage. He felt so guilty for leaving them short staffed. Their place was really starting to take off and they treated him well, but he needed to get out of Springfield and away from Emily.

Emily never knew the way Father Lucas felt while they worked closing shift, him at the bar and her waiting tables. She was married to Mark and never did anything suggestive in any way, so I suppose it was considered a one-sided crush. Emily was everything a man could want—smart, funny, hardworking, and a great mother to Esme who was just a toddler at the time. She was also beautiful. Seeing her again at nearly forty still took his breath away. He'd played it cool when he saw her for the first time in fifteen years at the church, but he recognized her right away. The only difference in Emily was a small streak of gray hair, and a hint of sadness in her eyes that she tried to hide with her eternally-warm smile. At first, Father Lucas assumed it was over the trouble with her daughter, but soon realized it was likely over the loss of Mark.

Mark was one of the best men Father Lucas had ever met. He matched Emily in wit and work ethic like no other. They were a true power couple, and there was no way The Black Sheep Tavern would fail as long as it was in their hands. Besides losing her husband, it must have devastated Emily to lose her business. Guilt crept up again when he realized Mark had been diagnosed with cancer just a few months after he'd left. Mark had gone into remission, but it came back again ten years later. Father Lucas almost wished he would have stayed to help them, but knew deep down it was for the best he didn't. Emily never knew he'd came close to attempting to kissing her one night in the storage room, turning his head at last second knowing he was about to do something he'd regret. He was too tempted being around Emily five days a week. He needed to leave. Catalina was just a convenient excuse to go.

He'd met Catalina the same night he'd tried to kiss Emily, and in a vulnerable mental space, latched on to her energy. She was an exchange student at Missouri State from Italy, and she was about to return home. Her American friends had reserved the bar to throw her a farewell party. She was fun and beautiful, and thought Lucas was cute. They'd spent a few hours drinking wine together after the party ended. She jokingly invited him to stay at her place in Italy, but when Lucas said yes, she didn't back out of her offer. They went back to his place, and after fooling around, he bought a plane ticket and packed a few bags. They flew out together in the morning.

Catalina was no Emily, but she was light-hearted and pretty with a good heart. She took Lucas to all the typical tourist traps that summer—the buildings of Rome, the Amalfi Coast with its turquoise waters and lemon groves, and the museums of Matera. As an anthropology major he found this ancient city fascinating. Lucas was having the time of his life, until one weekend they returned to Catalina's apartment to find a man sitting at her kitchen table.

Lucas spoke almost no Italian, but it was clear this was no ordinary intruder. They knew each other, and the way the man tried to pull Catalina close to him with tears in his eyes told Lucas they knew each other *intimately*. She'd resisted, gesturing to Lucas and crying. Not knowing what to do, Lucas quietly left and waited in the courtyard until thirty minutes later a door slammed and the man stormed down the street. Catalina had explained it was her former lover, whom she hadn't spoken to in a year. Apparently, he'd been waiting for her to return the entire time and was devastated to hear she'd brought home an American man and was walking around holding hands with him for all the world to see. Her ex was humiliated and heartbroken. Catalina assured Lucas that she'd officially cut it off for good and he wouldn't be an issue anymore. They'd continued their tour of Italy with a visit to the beaches of Sicily, until a week later Catalina began acting strange.

Looking back now, the signs of black magic of some sort were clear. Catalina was having nightmares of being chased by someone trying to kill her. The next night, that man's face was Lucas's. She awoke screaming and scratching at him as he tried to comfort her, her long pink nails leaving a wound along his jawline. The scar remains to this day, and every time he looks in the mirror, he's reminded of her.

After that night, Catalina stopped sleeping completely, so they decided to leave Sicily to relax at home for a few weeks before embarking on an adventure into France to visit The Louve.

Although she did sleep that night, it was fitful. She rolled around, punching Lucas in her sleep while mumbling about "the dark man". When the sun finally rose, he left the bedroom to make a pot of coffee and was stunned to find all of Catalina's carefully tended houseplants—looked after by the landlord while she traveled, and healthy the night previously---were now brown and limp. Her cat scampered out from behind an armchair, hissed at Lucas, then jumped onto a window sill, pawing at the glass to be let out. He obliged, and watched the frightened animal bolt across the courtyard so fast his hind legs kicked up wildly behind him. A gust of wind blew in through the window, blowing dirt into his eyes and knocking over the wilted plants.

Then he heard the growling.

She appeared to be asleep, so Lucas tiptoed to the bedside quietly. As she reached her head, her eyes flew open and locked on him in a rage. Her pupils were dilated, and her eye sockets were sunken and dark. Her usually golden skin was sallow and sickly with sweat. "Cataina," Lucas said. "what's wrong?"

"*You*," she growled. "*You* are wrong. You must die."

Catalina reached for Lucas and grabbed him by the throat with both hands, using a strength he didn't think possible from this petite Italian woman. He felt his throat closed shut by her grip and he struggled to pull her arms apart, then threw her on the bed. Lucas ran from the apartment to find help, and pounded on the door to the only person he'd met who spoke English: Catalina's landlord.

"*Buongiorno*, handsome American boy!" The bubbly, round woman said, unraveling foam curlers from her heavily colored, bright red hair. "Do you not have plungers for the toilets in America? Surely Catalina can show you how they work."

"Catalina's sick...I think." Lucas stammered, not knowing how to explain what he was experiencing. "Can you come look at her, Evangeline?"

Evangeline frowned, but sensing Lucas's urgency, agreed with a nod. "She probably just drank too much wine last night, but I'll check her."

When Lucas opened the door, Evangeline scowled at the sight of the dead houseplants. "What did you two do to the beautiful plants?! I've cared for them like my own children for the last year!"

Lucas held up her hand to stop her. "There is a lot of weird things happening. They were alive last night...I found them dead like that this morning."

She gave him a sideways assessment, then moved past him to the bedroom. She gasped and took a step back in the doorway, then approached cautiously. Catalina was sitting up in bed, but unnervingly straight as if she were tied to a board. Her mouth was open as she panted like a feral dog, drool dripping from the corners of her mouth. She hissed at Evangeline, whose demeanor quickly turned serious.

"When did this start?" she demanded.

"Well, about a week ago she started having nightmare and couldn't sleep. She started getting violent when I'd wake her up." Lucas explained.

"Is that what happened to your face?" she asked, knowing the answer.

He nodded. "We came home so she could rest, and she rolled around and talked in her sleep all night...kicked and punched me too. When I woke up, the cat was acting weird and all the plants were dead. And Catalina...well, she growled at me, and said she wanted me dead."

Evangeline took a deep breath, and led him by the crook of the arm out of the bedroom, shutting the door behind them. She went into the kitchen and made Lucas a tiny cup of espresso. "Tell me, American boy, did anyone come to visit recently? Perhaps a man about *this* tall...mustache...black, curly hair?"

"Yes, actually. Catalina said it was her ex, but that they were done." He said.

She nodded. "*Catlina* is done. Alessandro is not."

Lucas's heart began to race, and he nervously sipped the espresso. What is this old woman telling him?

"That man—Catalina's boyfriend—is Romani. You don't piss off the Roma, or you'll get the *malocchio*—evil eye." She said.

Lucas nearly choked on the hot liquid. "Wait, are you trying to tell me Catalina has a gypsy curse? Come on, that's ridiculous."

"Is it?" Evangeline cocked her head to the side. "My mother was a *benandati*. You don't find many practitioners anymore. They're usually born with a caul on their face. *Benandati* means "good walker". They can leave their bodies in sleep and fight evil *nello spirito*. I suppose you could call them good witches that serve God to protect their communities. My mother always said 'plants and animals will know evil before you do.' Sick pets, dead plants are one of the first signs of *malocchio*."

Lucas instinctively picked up a broom to start cleaning up the dirt cast across the floor. "So, what, this Alessandro cursed Catalina? Wouldn't she have bad luck or something? She's acting like she's possessed."

Evangeline pursed her lips. "Exactly."

"Wait, you said she was cursed. Now you say she's possessed?" Lucas was getting nervous, but found all of it hard to believe.

"If I had to guess, Catalina—and probably you—were *malocchioed* by her scorned lover. He probably doesn't have the juice to send an evil entity to kill you, but he most certainly has family that could." Evangeline turned on the gas stove and lit a cigarette. "I can't help you with that, American boy."

Catalina had evolved from growling to cackling maniacally. "Maybe we should just call an ambulance. She's probably just having an episode from stress or something."

Evangeline scoffed. "If you take her to the hospital, they'll throw her in the looney bin for sure. That's not what she needs."

"Okay, what does she need then?" Lucas was growing impatient as Catalina became more feral, spitting and snarling in the other room.

She stumped out her cigarette in a dirty cereal bowl. "You know that big Catholic church on the corner? Go there and tell them what you've seen. Tell them the daughter of the *benandati* sent you."


Lucas rode Catalina's pink bicycle three blocks away to Chiesa di San Michele Arcangelo. *The Church of Archangel Michael.* Lucas's grandmother had given him an amulet of his image for his high school graduation. She told him to ask St. Michael to help him be brave should he encounter evil in his life. He wished he had the amulet at the moment, and instead, sent a silent prayer to the angel asking for guidance and protection.

He was welcomed into the church by a nun that only spoke Italian. When he tried to say he wanted to speak to a priest, he made a cross on his chest and prayer hands, but she led him to a confession booth. Lucas went inside, figuring he could at least speak to the priest this way. He hadn't been to confession since childhood and felt awkward in the stuffy closet.

"Uh, forgive me Father, for I have sinned, and I need your help. Wait... do you speak English?" said Lucas.

"Yes, I speak English my son. I spent many summers in Florida, much like you are probably spending your summer in Italy." The priest laughed. "Perhaps you should try learning Italian."

Lucas cleared his throat. "Father, I need your help. I met this girl and she's sick or something. I came to Italy with her from America."

"I see. Why did you leave America, young man?" the Priest asked, not recognizing Lucas's urgency.

Without thinking, Lucas responded. "I needed a fresh start. I needed a different perspective on life and to accept the things that I couldn't have."

The priest was quiet for a moment. "These things you say you could not have, would it have been sinful?"

"Yes." Lucus replied barely above a whisper. "Another man's wife."

"I see. It's admirable of you to recognize this as wrong." The priest replied. "Many men let their impulses guide them rather than sense or sanctity."

Lucas snapped out of his own head and back to the task at hand. "Father, I'm not here to confess my sins. I'm here to get help for someone else, a woman named Catalina. I was sent here by someone who wants me to tell you she is the daughter of the *benandati*. She thinks Catalina is posssed or cursed and wants you to see her."

"Are you referring to the old woman named Eva?"

"Yes. She's Catalina's landlord." Lucas was already standing and exiting the confession booth.

The other side creaked open. "Well, if Eva says she needs help, she's doing the work of the Lord. Lead the way, young man."


When Lucas and the Father reached Catalina's apartment, they could hear her howling from inside. Lucas opened the door and led the Father to the bedroom where Evangeline was using a towel to tie one of Catalina's hands to the bedframe.

"About time! Look what the hellion did to my face!" Evangeline turned her head to reveal four pink jagged scratches from temple to chin. Near her jawline droplets of blood were forming.

Grabbing another towel, Lucas wrestled Catalina's other hand away from her body and secured it tightly to the bedpost. "Maybe we really should call an ambulance."

The priest shook his head. "She doesn't need medicine. I've seen this before. Only God can help her now." He handed a Bible to Evangeline. "Pray over me, sister."

She nodded and began flipping through the pages, stopped and began whispering an inaudible prayer.

The priest carefully sat at Catalina's feet and laid a gentle hand on her leg. The woman yowled as if she had been touched with a hot iron.

"Catalina, I want you to listen to me now. You must fight to be free of this Evil. I will help you but you must also try to help yourself. Do you understand?"

Catalina spit at him.

"You must reach for the Light of the Lord. Remember the Peace and freedom of resting in his love."

She choked out a guttural, menacing laugh. "She's long gone, Holy Man. It was easy, too. Kind of like *her.*"

Lucas's face grew hot with anger, but at who or what, he didn't know. This was from Catalina's mouth, but it was not her words.

"Have I said something *wrong* boy?" Catalina's eyes darted to Lucas. "Did you think you were special because this beautiful woman took an interest in you? She was going to dump you as soon as your money ran out, you know. Just like she did with Alessandro."

Lucas shrank back to the wall. *Could that be true?*

The priest caught his attention and shook his head. "Ignore anything the demon says. It preys on fear and pain."

Evangeline looked up from the Bible. "So, it is *lo spirito malign?*"

"Keep praying." He said, then turned back to Catalina. "Who are you?"

Catalina laughed.

"Are you a Being of Darkness?"

Catalina nodded and smiled without taking her eyes off the priest.

"Who sent you?"

She growled. "The gypsy."

"And what are you supposed to be doing to your victim?"

"First, I kill *him* while he sleeps," Catalina pointed at Lucas. "Then I kill the woman and get to keep the soul for my Master's army. He will be pleased."

The priest laughed at the demon. "I see. However, you must be very weak because both of them are still alive. *You* are the one trapped in that human form. It must be very uncomfortable."

Catalina's face softened with shock, then confusion. Then, the priest splashed a small vial of hold water in her face. She screamed in agony.

"In the name of Jesus Christ, I command you to leave this body at once!" The priest barked.

"Fuck you!" Catalina responded. "You cannot command me to do anything!"

The priest laughed in Catalina's face. "Oh, so you are free to come and go as you please? You are trapped within this woman until you accomplish what you've been asked to do by the Gypsy, then? You will let a lowly, weak human command you to stay within a body you didn't ask to be in?"

Catalina pulled herself back and settled down. "I'm am not under the command of mortals. I can leave whenever I want."

"I don't believe you, demon. You must be very low in the hierarchy of the Dark One's army. That's why you were given such a weak woman…and you can't even break her, can you?"

"I don't need this woman. I can leave whenever I want, Priest!" growled Catalina.

The priest stood above Catalina and leaned over her face. "Then show me, Demon."

Catalina grimaced and twisted in her restraints, then gradually relaxed into her pillows with closed eyed. They all watched with bated breath, concluding she was now asleep. The priest, Evangeline and Lucas released a collective exhale.

"Demons…especially lower-level ones…are incredibly easy to manipulate." The priest dabbed the sweat off his brow with the sleeve of his robe. "I believe it has left, but keep an eye on her overnight. When she is able to walk, she must come to confession and pray every day to keep herself spiritually strong. We will do a blessing every day for a month, and she must live a clean and holy life or it could enter her again. Do you know how to pray, son?"

"Uh, kind of?" he reached for his neck where the amulet of Saint Michael used to be, remembering it was packed away in his parent's basement. "Just read from the book, right?"

The priest stared at him sternly. "Wrong. You must ask God and the Angels to help protect you and Catalina and to keep evil away from you both. It is more important for you to have conviction in your words than to say them exactly as the Bible does. Do you understand?"

Lucas nodded. "I can do that. I'll pray over her all day and night until she's better."

"Good." The priest reached in his pocket, and pulled out a string of wooden rosary beads. "These will help."


Lucas spent the day in bed next to Catalina, reading the Bible from page one. She slept deeply, and although he could see her eyes moving rapidly beneath her lids, she didn't move or speak. He became swallowed up in the words of the Bible, and for the first time in his life they were meaningful. Every thirty minutes like clockwork, he prayed over Catalina's sleeping form and asked for God to protect her from evil and to heal her body, mind and soul. Just past midnight, barely able to keep his eyes open, he set aside the Bible and climbed under the blankets with Catalina.

He awoke to birds chirping and a soft orange glow through the window. His body was covered in goosebumps as he realized the bed had been stripped bare and he was no longer under blankets. Catalina was gone.

Lucas shot out of bed and checked to bathroom and found it empty. One of the blankets lay in the hallway. The kitchen was empty. No coffee had been made or food cooked. He flung open the apartment door and ran down two flights of stairs barefoot and wearing nothing but boxers, shouting her name. He hoped she was in the courtyard feeding the birds as she sometimes did, or visiting Evangeline. He reached the courtyard and found only Catalina's cat, stretched out on the smooth stones of the walking path. It didn't hiss this time. It stood up and meowed, rubbing its body on Lucas's bare feet as he circled the courtyard checking the patios of ground-level apartments where Catalina sometimes visited with her neighbors.

Then he heard the scream.

Behind him stood Evangeline. One of her hands covered her mouth. The other pointed up at the building.

Above him was Catalina's lifeless form, hanging by a bedsheet tied to her neck and the other to the balcony rail.


After Catalina's death, Lucas knew he should have gone straight home but he stayed in Italy frozen by fear, confusion and grief. He realized he wasn't necessarily grieving Catalina—he'd barely known her. Her suicide was tragic and traumatic, but now that he's older he looks back with understanding that he was really grieving the loss of his innocence. He had now experienced firsthand the destructive powers of true evil. If evil is lurking everywhere, how could he live and love without fear again? In his crisis of faith, he spent so much time at the Catholic church asking the priests and nuns these questions, they invited him to live there in exchange for helping with maintenance. Eventually, they invited him to the priesthood.

After several years shadowing Padre Pio to blessings, meetings, sermons and even a few exorcisms, Lucas's parents convinced him to return home. Padre Pio also encouraged him to leave, assuring him the God was calling him to serve as a leader to the people of his homeland.

Father Lucas returned to Springfield, and began serving under Bishop Vincent in an impoverished area of Springfield. "The Working Poor" is what the bishop had called them. Bishop Vincent felt that Father Lucas, as a younger priest, would have the stamina to keep up with a community of families with a big need for guidance. Father Lucas figured out pretty quickly that what he meant is they needed a younger priest who was capable of doing repairs to an old church belonging to patrons with little money to support it.

Not that is mattered anymore, since he was about to be fired. Father Lucas wondered if he should return to Italy. Or maybe move to another state. Utah? No, people are mostly Mormon there. Maine? Too cold.


"Father Lucas, thank you for seeing me on such short notice." Bishop Vincent sat stiffly in his office chair, nervously clicking a silver pen.

Father Lucas sat across from him, steadying himself for the blow. "Of course, Bishop. I'm here to serve you—and God—in whichever ways you need."

The bishop coughed. "Yes, well, I'd like to speak to you about the people who visited us requesting an exorcism a few weeks ago."

"Bishop Vincent—about that—I would like to apologize for springing it on you so suddenly, but—" Father Lucas blurted out before being interrupted by his superior.

Bishop Vincent held up his hand to stop him from speaking. "I've had a change of heart."

Father Lucas sat stunned. *He wasn't getting fired?*

"I would like to do a blessing, and if warranted, a minor exorcism on the children. I would like you to organize it and assist me in this work. When it is prepared, tell me when and where to meet you." Said the bishop.

"Oh! Of course!" said Father Lucas. "Forgive me for asking—you were so against it—what made you change your mind?"

Bishop Vincent squirmed in his seat, looking down at his hands. He stopped clicking the pen.

"Deuteronomy 29:29…'The secret things belong to the Lord our God, but the things that are revealed belong to us and to our children forever, that we may do all the words of this law.'"

# Hellhound On My Trail

"*Hola, Padre.*" Stella opened the hatch of her SUV as Father Lucas locked his vehicle parked behind hers. "So, how'd you manage to convince the bishop to exorcise our little hellions?"

He stuffed his hands in his pockets. "I didn't. Honestly, I don't know what changed his mind, but I'm glad he did." Father Lucas peeked around Stella looking for her son, instead finding a full sized poodle wearing a bow tie and smelling like cologne. "Where's Mateo?"

She sighed. "Still in Willow Creek. I tried to bust 'em out so they banned me from visitation for a few weeks. Mateo Sr. has to go alone." She guided the poodle out of her SUV to Emily's front lawn. "Doesn't matter. Mattie's not possessed and doesn't need an exorcism. He's some kind of *brujo*. I think he should keep that shit, you know? We need every advantage we can get in life, am I right *amigo*?"

Father Lucas sidestepped both the statement about her son being a witchdoctor and the poodle urinating on the grass. "So, if you don't mind me asking, why are you here then…with a dog?"

Stella sniffed, inflating herself with *machismo*. "I mean, they're not my kids so I don't really care… but…I was in the area, you know, picking Bandito up from the groomer. Fuckin' high maintenance ass poodles. Anyway, I guess I'm invested in this whole demon drama and want to see how it all plays out. Maybe I can help or something. I'm Catholic, too, you know?"

Father Lucas smirked. "Oh really? If you don't have a church, you're welcome to attend mine this Sunday."

Stella jumped. "What? Oh, yeah, yeah. I'll do that. Come on, Bandito."

Stella slinked away with her dog and walked the perimeter of Emily's front yard while Father Lucas unloaded his supplies of holy water, crosses and restraints from the trunk of his car. When Charlotte called to say the exorcism would be at Emily's house, he knew exactly where to go.

He'd only visited a few times to pick up his paycheck many years ago, but there wasn't much about Emily he could forget. He wondered if she recognized him yet. He was much younger then, and they probably had dozens of employees at The Black Sheep Tavern since. Still, he couldn't help but feel a little hurt Emily didn't remember him. Maybe it was just limerence, but Father Lucas thought there had been a spark of something between them, even if it was just friendship.

He walked past Stella who side-eyed him from a distance, afraid he'd invite her to church again, and knocked on Emily's door. He took a deep breath and repeated his vows to himself: *celibacy…obedience to the bishop…a life of simplicity…prayer.* He was determined to treat Emily as he would any other distressed parent.

The door opened. "Lucas…BRENTWOOD. You used to bartend for me! I'm still kicking myself for not recognizing you. A little gray hair, but your eyes haven't changed a bit. I must have been distracted by the whole priest getup!" Emily welcomed Father Lucas into her home and gave him a hug.

Father Lucas's heart beat like a freight train as he wrapped his arms around her in return. She smelled like lavender soap, and was just as beautiful as the first day he met her. *Chastity…obedience…poverty…prayer.*

He pulled away. "Well, it's Father Lucas now…but yes, I was your bartender in my former life."

She smiled, taking in the vision of her old friend she hadn't realized was sitting right next to her during their meeting at the church. "Well, you look great, Father Lucas. We'll have to catch up sometime outside of all this. I'm sure there's a story behind your sudden interest in the priesthood." Emily leaned around him and waved Stella and Bandito into the house.

"Yes," said Father Lucas, setting his bags in the floor. "I would love that."

"I can't thank you and the bishop enough for coming. Things are getting really weird with Esme. I found her at another person's house practically catatonic. *Then* she said she was the woman's missing—and presumed dead—daughter!" Emily sank into herself. "I'm at a loss. Every day she says she's someone else. It's like she has multiple personalities."

Father Lucas became troubled. "That doesn't exactly sound like demonic possession…at least not the ones I've experienced or studied."

Emily nodded. "I know. Gemma thinks she knows what it is. She should be here soon."

Bandito jumped up on Emily's sofa, stretched out and closed his eyes.

"Is it okay if he's inside? I mean, he's cleaner than I am right now." Stella tossed her purse on the table and sipped on her large iced coffee overflowing with whipped cream and chocolate drizzle.

"Sure. Ziggy is out back so we don't have to worry about them fighting or anything. She's an old lady and gets grumpy around other dogs." Emily warned.

"Cool. Bandito's a lover, not a fighter. He won't start any trouble. Will you, you pansy-ass pampered pooch?" Stella spoke the last sentence in a baby voice, sending Bandito's tail wagging wildly despite his supine body and closed eyes.

Emily led Father Lucas to a guest bedroom to set up a holy space to do the blessings, then returned to the dining room to set out snack trays and sodas for the rest of the guests expected to arrive that afternoon.

"Don't forget the Deviled Eggs." Said Stella, deadpan.

"What? I didn't—" Emily rolled her eyes when she caught on to the joke. "Nice one, Stella."

"It's a gift." She smiled. "So, what's with you and the preacher man? You know each other or something?"

Emily straightened the sodas into neat rows. "My husband and I used to own a bar, and he was one of our bartenders. Nice guy, but one day he just up and left with some Italian girl and moved to Europe. I had no idea he was back in the States, let alone a Catholic priest. I didn't recognize him the first time we saw him at the church."

"He's handsome." Stella gnawed on a baby carrot. "Are priests allowed to fuck? I mean, when I was stripping, I saw them all the time...but that doesn't mean they're supposed to be doing that shit. Father Lucas seems like a guy who takes his job seriously. Can he date and kiss or whatever?"

Emily's cheeks flamed red. "I, uh, don't know...you'll have to ask him." Emily was suddenly curious herself, but had no intention of asking Father Lucas.

The front door to Emily's house flung open, startling Bandito who jumped up and barked at the intruder. Gemma stopped dead still as the dog approached with a low growl. Her arms overflowed with various sized boxes. Candles and a small gem-encrusted sword hilt stuck out of tote bag on her shoulder. "Whoa, hey there puppo…I'm Gemma."

Bandito stopped growling and approached her carefully. He walked around her, sniffing in a circle, then once satisfied, walked away, returning to his nap on the sofa.

"Bandito! You little shit, this is not your house. Stop being territorial!" Stella pointed at the dog. "*Lo siento*, Gemma. Let me help you with that."

Gemma didn't argue. They were heavy and she passed off most of the boxes to Stella. "Emily. I've been doing research and talking to my psychic friends. I think I know what's wrong with Esme, and it's not demons. It's ghosts."

"Ghosts?" Emily took the tote from Gemma and gave her a bottle of water, pre-opened out of habit as if she were a young child. "You think she picked up ghosts in the cave?"

Gemma perched on a barstool and took a sip of water. "I do. I think all those women Mateo drew in his sketchbook…the skeletons we saw in the cave…these people were murdered. Esme is getting jumped by their ghosts!"

"So, she's not possessed?" Emily confirmed.

"Well," Emily tilted her head side to side, "not by a demon. She's possessed by spirits. They must find something energetically compatible with Esme which made it easy for them to align. Maybe age."

Emily relaxed. "That's good news, isn't it? Ghosts have to be easier to exorcise than demons, right?"

"I hesitate to say *easy*, but it's something I should be able to do rather than a Catholic priest. I'll see what I can pick up with Reiki. We can try to ask them to leave, first." Said Gemma.

"Ask them to leave?" scoffed Stella. "What are you, the bouncer at a strip club? Why the hell would the dead girl ghosts listen to you, *mamacita?"*

Normally nonplussed, Gemma appeared insulted. "I am a powerful energy-worker, Stella."

"Give me a break, Gemma. You can't just woo-woo all over Emily's kid with your Big Spirit Energy. You could end up possessed yourself. What qualifies you to extract ghosts? Shouldn't we just leave it to the priests?" Stella prodded.

"Not all spiritual attachments are the same. You need different methods and talents for each one. Demons need a priest. Curses, a witch. Ghosts, a medium. I am a certified Reiki Master; I can find the attachments…figure out what they are…and mend the soul so it can't get back in. Depending on how deep the ghosts are enmeshed, we may be able to extract them. Then I can do my healing work, and Esme should be fine with daily meditation and yoga. A vegan diet can't hurt, also." Gemma explained.

Emily shrugged. "It's worth a try. Esme is in her room. What do we need to do?"

Gemma pointed to one of the boxes. "I need the new white candle, the mirror, the box of chakra stones…and that kyanite. It's for my protection. I've already meditated and I'm ready to go. Now there's one more thing…and this is very important—after we've started, no matter what, don't touch Esme. Jumpers spread through physical contact."

Emily and Stella nodded in agreement.

Bandito leapt from the couch and ran to the door barking. *Then* the doorbell rang.

Emily welcomed Bishop Vincent into her home, thanking him so profusely he seemed embarrassed. He mumbled something about how he's *simply doing the work God wants him to do*, and asked for Father Lucas. Emily led the bishop to the room where he was setting up for the blessing and found him ringing a small bell and reciting a prayer in Latin. The bishop entered, quickly shutting the door behind him, owing to the relentless barking of Bandito who had followed him from the front door to the guest room and was now digging at the door.

Stella grabbed his leash and hooked him on the collar. "Wow, he really doesn't like the bishop. He's not usually like this. I'm sorry Emily; I'll put him out back with Ziggy."

"Thanks. Meet us in Esme's room down the hall when you're done." Said Emily.

While Stella wrangled Bandito, Gemma and Emily carried their supplies to Esme's room and gently rapped on her door. "Ez, can I come in and speak with you? I have a few friends with me."

"Uh, okay. Whatever." Esme said. Her mother opened the door before waiting for permission.

"This is Gemma, and Stella will be here in a minute. We were wondering if we could talk to you about the voices you've been hearing." Said Emily.

Esme crossed her arms, appearing embarrassed. "Wow, Mom. Thanks for telling my private business to strangers."

"I'm not exactly a stranger…," said Gemma. "We haven't met yet, but I'm Trix's mom."

She looked up at Gemma and assessed her. "You two look alike."

Gemma smiled as Esme relaxed. "I get that a lot. The other woman with us is Mateo's mom, she'll be here in a minute. The reason we are here is because all of you have been acting pretty weird since you went in the cave. Do you agree?"

The girl looked out her bedroom window to avoid eye contact. "I guess. I haven't really talked to any of them since. I got into a fight with Mateo… that's about it. Is Trix doing okay?"

Gemma sighed. "Do you know what a Furry is?"

"Hola amigas!" Stella entered the bedroom and closed the door behind her. She dumped out a crate of Esme's stuffed animals, flipped it over and sat down. "Are we ready to pow-wow? Did you woo-woo yet?"

"Woo woo?" asked Esme.

Gemma reached into her pocket and extracted seven colored stones. "Esme, I am an energy healer. Each of these stones represents an energy center in your body. If you would oblige me, I'd like to do a Reiki scan of your body to find out if you picked anything up while you were in that cave."

"Really? That sounds weird. What do mean by 'scan'?" The teenager appeared cautiously curious.

Gemma cleared her throat. "Okay, so you won't have to do anything except lie down. I won't even touch you except to lay these stones on your chakras. I'll hold my hands a few inches above your body and assess the condition of your energy centers, once I know what we're dealing with, we can figure out a way to help you."

"So, what, you're some kind of psychic?" smirked Esme. "Mom, you really must be desperate."

"Yes, actually. I am desperate." Emily scowled at her daughter for being rude.

"It's okay, Emily. Esme, I understand the skepticism. I'd hesitate to call myself a psychic." Explained Gemma. "I can't predict the future or talk to God. My gift is for interpreting and manipulating energies in the human—or animal—body. I'm also a witch. A good witch. Well, unless I *need* to be a bad witch…but that doesn't happen very often."

Esme sat silently in thought for a moment, then laid back on the bed, folding her arms on her chest like a corpse. "Go ahead with the stones then."

Before going to work on the stones, Gemma handed Stella her trusty Hello Kitty notebook and pen. "I need you to take notes of the important things I say or anything else you notice. I don't always remember what I channel."

"You got it, girl." Stella clicked the pen, crossed her legs to prop up the notebook and positioned her hand at the ready.

"Emily, you can help hand me supplies while I work. Kind of like when you become a nurse." Instructed Gemma. "For now, just light that candle while I do the scan."

Gemma placed the stones delicately on Esme's body: a red stone at her feet, an orange stone on her pelvis, a yellow stone on her navel, a green stone over her heart, a blue stone in the cavity of her throat, a purple stone on her forehead, and a large white quartz positioned on the pillow so it touched the crown of her head.

"There we go." Gemma stood back and assessed her work. "Oh, and just so you guys know…Isabella is supposed to be bringing a list of all the women who went missing within fifty miles during the nineties. Thought we could look over it later."

"I brought Mattie's sketchbook." Added Stella.

"Can we get this over with, please?" Esme asked impatiently.

Gemma looked up and closed her eyes. She held her hands out at her sides, palms up, as if she were catching raindrops. After a few moments, she slowly brought her hands together, appearing to hold an invisible basketball. She pushed her hands together, and then pulled them apart, stretching the energetic tendrils. Pushing her hands together one last time, she rubbed her palms together briskly, then opened her eyes and approached Esme.

"Close your eyes." She whispered to Esme. Gemma then held her hands over the crown of her head.

"Oh wow…her crown chakra is wide open! I've never seen that before." Gemma remarked. Stella scribbled.

"What does that mean?" asked Emily.

"It's the door to the soul. It's how energy gets in and out. During reiki we can open it to pull bad energy out and replace it with Light…but for Esme this is the equivalent of sleeping with your door wide open when you live in the Belmont neighborhood of Detroit."

"Why the fuck would anyone live in Detroit?" said Stella.

Gemma continued moving her hands across Esme's body. "Spirits are free to come and go as they please. And they definitely are. Her aura feels like Swiss cheese. Do you feel tired and drained a lot Esme?"

"Pretty much always." She confirmed. "Except for the times I don't remember."

"They're just burrowing like worms, eating her energy and leaving tunnels. They're probably influencing her to do things that would build up her soul energy so they can utilize it…risky behavior, food, sex, gambling. There are healthy ways to build energy too—meditation, love, sleep, exercise, joy. But the first ways I mentioned are cheap and easy. A Twinkie for the soul, if you will."

"I would kill for a Twinkie right now." Said Stella as she doodled a picture of a Twinkie and wrote 'For Stella's Soul' above it. "I'm on a diet. Boo."

Gemma stepped back, propping her hand under her chin in contemplation. "All of her chakras are sputtering and spinning in the wrong direction. Her aura is full of holes and her crown is blown open. What little I can see of her soul is blotchy with black and green. It's negativity left behind from others…a sickliness. It's the worst I've ever seen, but I think we can fix it. I just need to make sure the ghosts are out of her before I do the Soul Mending."

She collected the stones off Esme's body, then helped her sit up. "Esme…sweetie, I'd like to practice something else with you, okay. Emily, please hand me that mirror."

Esme's eyes grew wide as Gemma took it in her hands, and the witch noticed. "You see things in mirrors, don't you?"

Her eyes welled up with tears as she nodded. "It's not my face. And it changes all the time."

"It's okay." Said Gemma. "I'm going to hold this mirror up to your face and I want you to describe what you see."

The girl closed her eyes and shook her head. "Please, no. Mom, don't make me do this."

Emily knelt beside the bed and held her hand. "I trust that Gemma will do everything she can to help you. We *all* want you to go back to being your normal, happy self. Just tell us what you see."

Gemma slowly lifted the mirror in front of Esme. Esme's breath rattled as she exhaled and opened her eyes. Gemma jumped. She didn't see the reflection in the mirror, but for a moment one of Esme's eyes flashed and one turned black. "Did you guys see that?"

Emily shook her head no and kept her eyes on her daughter. Stella leaned in close and scribbled in the notebook.

"I have blue eyes. And really big hair…it's like light brown with those big bangs…you know, with the teasing and hairspray." Said Esme, dazed. "She's a little bit older than me, and wearing a white sweater."

Stella stopped writing. "White girl, then? You have any beauty marks, scars, braces?"

"No," said Esme. "There are more girls waiting…four more, I think. To jump me."

The mothers sat in contemplative silence. Then Gemma grabbed Esme's arm.

"I command all of you to leave this girl and enter my body. Tell us what you want. I will help you, and guide you to the Light, but you *must* leave this child!"

"Gemma, no!" said Emily. "We don't know what will happen!"

"It's the only way! We have to do a transfer. I'm strong enough to hold them. Take the mirror! I can feel them rolling around in her aura…once the transfer happens, get as much information as you can." Gemma closed her eyes, taking rhythmic breaths. "Esme, it's going to be okay. Let them pass through you into me…then I want you to leave the room. Go outside under a tree and meditate. Imagine yourself drenched a waterfall of light. Let it pour into a tiny door in the top of your head. Then imagine yourself closing the door and locking it. Do you understand?"

Her eyes were wide and scared, but she agreed. "I can feel them moving. It feels like cold water pouring through my body."

"That's it, Esme. Let them go." Gemma whispered.

Esme hunched over holding Gemma's hand. Gemma sat frozen on the bed with her eyes closed yet swirling in her sockets. Her breathing turned to a pant.

Emily pulled her daughter off the bed by the shoulders. "Go outside. Go right now."

She obeyed, stumbling over her own feet as she looked back at Gemma before shutting the door behind her.

Gemma was now breathing so hard she was nearly convulsing.

"This is some freaky shit." Said Stella, moving to sit next to Gemma while transcribing.

Emily positioned the mirror in front of Gemma's face.

"Open your eyes." Said Emily.

Gemma's eyes flew open. "Ow," she held her hand to her left temple. "It hurts so bad…"

"You're safe, Gemma. That's not you, it's someone else. What's your name?" said Emily

"Mariah." Said Gemma in a voice that was notably higher and with a slight southern twang native Ozarkers tended to have. "I can't feel my legs…my back…I think it's broken."

Emily felt goosebumps forming on her arms. "How did that happen?"

"I fell…no, he dropped me. In a hole…he seemed like such a nice guy. I had no idea he was so *evil*. He's done this before and he's going to do it again. You have to stop him. Please, for my mom. Tell my mom where I am."

"Where are you?" Emily asked. She already knew the answer.

"A cave." Said Gemma.

Stella's hands were shaking, and she dropped the pen, watching as it rolled to the floor.

"Is anyone with you? Any other women he's hurt?" asked Emily.

"Yes," said Gemma. "Four more…oh no…*no*…not them. No, no, no. Why did you bring them? They're going to do it again. Even if you catch him, another will take his place."

The doorbell rang.

Gemma scratched at her face and cried. "No! NO! No! We were finally free and you brought them here to torture us, didn't you?!"

Emily grabbed Gemma's hands from her face as the witch rolled around on the bed roaring like a lion. "Gemma! Gemma, listen to me! Set them free! Take them to the Light, like you said!"

"*Semper revertimur!*" she wailed.

With Emily occupied restraining Gemma, Stella took the initiative and grabbed the tourmaline pendant on a silver chain around Gemma's neck, snapping it off with one quick movement. Then she started swinging it back and forth in front of Gemma's face and spoke to her calmly.

"Hola, Mamacita…it's your friend Estrella…I want you to look over here baby…that's right, follow the stone…back and forth, back and forth… good…" she spoke low and gently, just loud enough for Gemma to hear. Gemma had stopped writhing on the bed and Emily released her grip.

Gemma sat up once more, eyes transfixed on the swinging necklace in front of her face. "Follow the stone and listen to my voice, Gemma." Said Stella. "I'm going to count back from three, and when I get to one, you're going to do whatever I tell you to do, because you trust me, don't you? Back and forth, back and forth…that's right…deep breaths…three…two…one."

Gemma sat still, and Stella stopped swinging the necklace. "The first thing I'd like you to do is to ask your angels or Goddess or grandma to come to you and protect you, comprende? Nod yes when it's done."

Gemma nodded.

"Now, I want you to ask them to help you bring these murdered women to Heaven…or wherever witches think souls go." Instructed Stella.

"Summerland." Gemma mumbled.

"Sure, Summerland. Help them get there, okay. When they've left, I want you to nod again."

Gemma closed her eyes, and although she was breathing deeply it was more peaceful, and a small smile formed on her lips. After a few moments she nodded, and when she opened her eyes, tears fell down her cheeks.

"Good. Now, I want you to close that door in your head that you told Esme about. Then you lock that motherfucker with a deadbolt. Don't let those girls back in, okay?"

Gemma closed her eyes again, then nodded.

"Now, it's time for you wake up. You are safe with me and Emily, so don't be afraid. I'm going to count back from three, and when I get to one… wake up. Three…two…one." Stella said.

Gemma's eyes fluttered and she touched her wet cheeks. "Angels…I saw angels. They took the girls."

There was a light rap on the bedroom door and it slowly creaked open as Isabella peeked her head in. "Hey guys, what are you doing in here? I brought Theo…he's out back with Esme. Oh, and I have that list of missing women from the nineties you wanted."

# Litany of the Saints

"**D**o I even want to know how—or why—you know how to hypnotize people?" asked Emily.

Stella raised an eyebrow. "I wasn't always the upstanding citizen you see before you. It started out as a joke between me and my best friend. When we first started stripping, guys would test us by getting handsy during lap dances and we were coming up with ways to get them to stop. One night I used one of my tassels on a guy, and it worked. And *wouldn't you know it*, when the lap dance was done, he had such a good time he opened his wallet and gave me everything in it. Made enough money stripping after a couple of years, and I didn't need to do it anymore. My friend…now that's a different story. She's got a voice like nails on a chalkboard. She chose to sleep her way to the top."

"Wait a minute," said Isabella. "Did you work at Big Hefty's club?"

"Yup, that's the one. You seen my titties before?" asked Stella.

"Well…technically, yes, the first time we met." Laughed Isabella. "But not at the club. Big Hefty owns my boxing gym. He's trained three generations of Kentworths. Oh my God…*a voice like nails on a chalkboard*. Your friend is Hefty's fiancé, Perfect Storm, isn't she?"

Stella scoffed and crossed her arms. "*Ex* best friend. And her name's not Perfect Storm. It's Gretchen. As in get-me-retchin'-over-that-stank-ass-pu—"

"Anyway!" interjected Gemma, "Thank you so much for helping me, Stella. You're a really talented hypnotist, and I'm so grateful you thought to do that. Maybe we should check in with the bishop to see if he's ready for Theo. Will you come help me?"

Stella grumbled, but followed Gemma to talk to the priests, leaving Isabella and Emily alone.

"So, does Theo know why he's here? I know Benny's having a hard time figuring out how to get Ash to come. Charlotte can't even *find* Oliver, I'm not sure she will show." Emily peeked out the window at Esme. She sat cross-legged under the tree, just as Gemma told her to. Theo walked around the yard awkwardly, keeping his distance from her. He picked up a dirty tennis ball and threw it to Ziggy. She lifted her head from her spot in the shade, watched it land nearby, then laid back down, stretching out her furry white body until she looked like a polar-bear skin rug.

"Well, I told Theo if he ran errands with me, I would take him to lunch at Jose Loco's for fajitas and Jarritos. Boys are like dogs…offer them food and they'll go anywhere." Laughed Isabella.

Emily smiled. "I wouldn't know, both mine are girls. They need to know the 'why' behind everything!"

Soft steps approached behind them. "Lieutenant Kentworth, I'd like to speak to you before we begin…about your son."

Bishop Vincent stood patiently with his hands clasped behind his back. He gestured to the sofa where Father Lucas, Stella and Gemma were already waiting. After everyone was settled, he took the floor.

"I'd like to speak to you without the children around to explain some of the process before we begin. First—we simply can't have everyone in the room. I am responsible for protecting the souls in the vicinity of the potentially possessed child, and that's where I need to focus my attention."

The parents nodded in agreement and allowed him to continue.

"Do any of you know what a demon truly *is*, or what they are capable of?" the bishop asked.

"I went to church as a kid," said Stella. "Demons are fallen angels, right? They didn't want to obey God and got kicked out or some shit?"

The holy man gave a slight sneer at Stella's vulgarity. "That is *correct*. Catholics believe that in the beginning of all things, God created the angels—each with their own particular gifts—to guide mankind during their time on Earth. For example, there are angels who encourage chastity or generosity. Like humans, angels are also given free will. This means both humans and angels are able to chart their own course without God's intervention…even if it wasn't the plan God made for them. God's plan always creates the highest and best outcome, and will always lead back to Him. The soul that follows God's plan will always be blessed. The angel Lucifer was the highest level of Cherub, meant to be a guardian and to praise God's greatness at His side. He was an angel of beauty, perfection and wisdom. He became jealous of God's love of humanity, and believed he was better suited to manage them than God. He rebelled against his creator, and convinced a third of the other angels to do the same. God's punishment was to cast Lucifer and the angels out of heaven, and strip them of their beauty and some of their power. Lucifer became Satan, and the fallen angels became demons."

Although cast out of heaven as a punishment, Satan still believed he could overthrow God. The mission of Satan and his demons is to destroy anything that brings glory to God—especially His greatest creation, mankind. Despite losing most of God's blessings, these fallen angels are still powerful, especially Satan. They still maintain the gifts they were given at Creation. Angels of chastity become Fallen Angels of Lust. Angels of Generosity become Fallen Angels of Greed. And just like the angels of heaven, the demons of hell have a hierarchy with Satan as the most powerful of the Fallen Ones. They all fear punishment from their superiors, but God is still the most powerful of *all* beings. Even Satan fears God and knows that on the Day of Judgement he will burn in a lake of fire."

"It's his own damn fault." Stella said. "So, what, Satan and the demons are trying to taint our kids' souls? Why? It's not like a teenager has much influence in the world. Why not go for someone like the president or Brad Pitt?"

This time Father Lucas spoke. "It is my belief that your children wandered into a place of great evil, and the demons seized an opportunity to use them as pawns to create *even greater* evil. By themselves, your children have little influence compared to someone like Adolf Hitler. They are a tiny pebble thrown into a pond, but the ripples project out into ways we will probably never understand. I believe demons want to control your children. Teenagers are excellent targets. They are emotional and insecure, often uncertain of who they are as individuals. They are the ideal candidate for demonic possession."

"That said…" continued Bishop Vincent. "We cannot be certain your children are possessed until we begin the ritual. It is still possible there are medical or psychological issues creating their behavior—"

Isabella coughed to remind the bishop of their agreement.

"—*but* I will do an initial blessing *regardless*. If your children *are* under the control of a dark force entity, there are varying degrees of influence. As I've explained, there are different types and levels of demons as well. It's important that all of us approach this ritual with an open mind to *all* possibilities for the best outcome of the children." Said the bishop.

"And a warning," said Father Lucas, remembering some of his own experiences in Italy. "If a demon shows itself, as a layman, *do not engage*. Don't speak to it. Don't respond to anything it says in an attempt to bait you. Pray for yourself, your child and the priests. Exorcising demons requires a deep and powerful faith to perform safely and correctly. And no matter what happens, remember this: our souls belong to God. In that way, demons are limited. They can only influence mankind to do things to themselves that dishonor God and cause harm to those in their circle. Although demons can tempt us to do harm, ultimately, we decide to indulge or not."

The parents had grown quiet. None of them were particularly religious and hadn't fully understood the role of demons previously.

"So," said Isabella. "What are you going to do first? I'm concerned Theo won't cooperate."

In priestly stereotype, he steepled his fingers. "Father Lucas and I will first speak to Theo about any strange symptoms he's experiencing. Then, together we will perform a *quite lengthy* prayer over Theo called 'The Litany of the Saints". If there is a demonic entity present, it will likely show itself at that time. If it does…we will continue with a Minor Exorcism ritual. During this ritual I will provoke the demon and cast it out in the name of Jesus Christ. There is no way to predict a demon's behavior once we reach that point, so be prepared for anything." Concluded Bishop Vincent. "Are there any questions?"

"Wait, so you're saying the only person who can get rid of a demon is a Catholic priest?" asked Stella. "What did people do *before* Catholicism? Were demons just running wild, *padre*?"

"That's an excellent question…and the answer is similar to the question *'Why are so few exorcisms performed now?'*. It's no secret the Christian faith is losing followers. That doesn't mean there aren't demons. People are simply undiagnosed or misdiagnosed. Or perhaps, influenced to do self-destructive acts such as drug abuse. We focus on the addiction, but not the moral depravity that caused it. What people *lack* is spiritual guidance more than anything. Before the time of Christ, and the development of Christianity, humanity was *absolutely brutal* to each other. No matter your faith, from an historical perspective Christianity is responsible for a much more peaceful and kinder world. Christians were the first to create hospitals, orphanages and feed the hungry. Before Christianity, it was believed to was best to let the sick, orphaned and poor die. Monasteries were the first libraries, and precursor to modern universities. Even the concepts of government—freedom, liberty, justice—are based on the laws on God, laid out in the Bible. Christianity even changed the way we view the economy. Christianity honors all work, even that which is done with one's hands; Jesus himself was a carpenter. Ancient Romans despised physical labor and reserved it for whom they viewed as the lowliest of all men. And despite what most people believe, the earliest Christian churches were founded on nonviolence and took a pacifist stance on conflict, in honor of Jesus's sacrifice on the cross. As with any faith, greed, fear and power has often used Christianity as a mask for diabolical acts."

"…wow. I *really* should have paid more attention in church." Said Stella.

Father Lucas smiled at her. "It's not too late to learn, Stella. The children will need weekly blessing after today, so it's a great way to build the habit of going to church."

"What? No, *my* kid is *not* possessed. I told you that. He's a prophet or some shit." Said Stella.

The bishop raised a fuzzy gray eyebrow at Stella, and thinking it was better not to respond, turned to Isabella. "Lieutenant, would you like to bring Theo inside now? Emily, Gemma, Stella…for your safety it's best you stay here. We will let you know if we need assistance. Please pray, meditate, or at the very least, think Godly thoughts."

Gemma gave a sigh of relief, sinking back into the sofa, exhausted from the spirit transfer. Her skin was pale, and her eyes sunken behind her horn-rimmed glasses.

Isabella called Theo inside, and he approached the door slowly like a wild animal sensing a trap. After he was inside, Isabella slipped between Theo and the door and locked it.

"Teddy…I need you to speak to someone." Said Isabella, as the priests entered the room.

The bishop cautiously approached Theo. "Hello, Theodore. My name is Bishop Vincent, and this is Father Lucas. We'd like to speak with you for a bit in another room." He gestured down the hallway with a dramatic swoop of his robed arm.

Theo stood frozen and everyone in the room held their breath, knowing full well that he was capable of violence that nearly killed a man. "Mom…what is this?"

Isabella moved in between the priests and Theo, instinctively putting herself between a potential threat and the innocent as she would in uniform. "These men would like to speak to you about your experience in the cave. It's not just you—they are speaking to your friends, too. We think all of you could benefit from a blessing. It's worth a shot, isn't it? You haven't been feeling like yourself lately, right? Don't you want to start competing again?"

He blinked, and deflated slightly under his mother's will. For her to be asking him to talk to a priest meant she was desperate. Isabella was not a religious woman and often said she felt God abandoned her in hell as a child and that she could never quite forgive Him for that.

Theo surrendered. "Fine…so are we actually going to Jose Loco's for dinner or was that a lie?"

"No, Teddy, it was not a lie. We can even get cheesecake if you want."

Satisfied with her response, he followed the men and Isabella to the impromptu blessing room Father Lucas created in Emily's spare room. The smell of frankincense wafted out the doorway, and inside a large white candle was lit next to an open and bookmarked Bible. Another book lay closed on the bed, a red woven cover, with gold writing in Italian. *De Exorcismis et Supplicationibus quibusdam.* Theo pushed it away from him to the far end of the bed and sat down.

Isabella picked it up to make room for herself as the priests took the other two chairs positioned in front of Theo. She passed it to Father Lucas. "*Libreria Editrice Vaticana?* Is that…the library of the Vatican?"

He placed the book gently on his lap. "Publisher, actually. The Roman Catholic Church has its own publisher for official documents and reference books."

Theo squirmed on the bed trying to get comfortable. "Can I have something to drink? Is that water over there for me?" He pointed at a bottle of water on the dresser next to the priest's bags of supplies.

"That's ho—" said Father Lucas.

"…absolutely for you, Theo." Interjected the bishop.

Father Lucas passed the water to Theo. It looked comically small in his enormous hands, and the priests waited with baited breath as he took a sip.

Theo made a face. "Gross. Is this alkaline water or something? It tastes super weird. Bleh." He gave the bottle to Isabella, who turned it in her hands and didn't see anything strange about it.

The bishop didn't answer. "Theo, I'd like to ask you a few questions about how you've been feeling since that night you went in the cave. What is the last thing you remember?"

He glanced sideways at his mom. "...come on man, are you trying to get me in more trouble with my parents than I already am?"

Isabella laid her hand on Theo's. "You're not going to be in trouble. I just want you to feel better, okay?"

He scowled suspiciously. Okay...the last thing I remember is that we were getting ready to leave. We didn't find any cheese...well, actually we did but it was dusty and gross. I found an old gun from the Civil War. I really wanted to show Dad—" he turned to his mother. "It was so cool, a Le Mat Revolver."

"Wow, really?" asked Father Lucas. "What kind of grip?"

"Ivory!" said Theo.

"No way. Do you still have it?"

Theo's excitement dissipated. "No...I don't know where it is. Right after that, Esme and Ash were complaining about feeling creeped out so we started to leave. Then all our flashlights went out."

"I see," said Bishop Vincent. "So, if you were deep in this cave with no lights, how did you get out?"

He scratched at his throat, leaving red welts. Isabella recognized fear on her son's usually unshakable face. "I have no idea. After that, the next thing I remember was Mom yelling at me to get away from Mateo. He was bloody on the ground...and there was blood on my hands. I don't even know why I hurt him."

Father Lucas fidgeted with the placeholder ribbon on *De Exorcismis et Supplicationibus quibusdam.* "Your mom told us about what happened with your boxing opponent recently. Do you remember hurting him?"

"Sort of..." explained Theo. "I remember just...getting so *angry*, and thinking about how Big Heavy is probably going to replace me with Falcon. I got mad at Dad, too...I don't *ever* get mad at him. I went at The Falcon without thinking. I knew I was fighting dirty, but I couldn't stop myself. Then when Hefty hit me with the fire extinguisher, it all went dark...but I heard a voice in my head saying some weird stuff..."

The priests looked at each other.

"What did it say, Theo?" said Isabella through a shaking voice. Her mouth was a think line.

"I dunno, something about being a good fighter and the swoop of a falcon." Theo shrugged. "It's hard to remember."

"The voice *quoted Sun-tzu*?" asked Father Lucas.

"Who's that?" asked Theo.

"*The quality of a decision is like the well-timed swoop of a falcon, which enables it to strike and destroy its victim. Therefore, the good fighter will be terrible in his onset, and prompt in his decision.*" Father Lucas recited.

"Yeah, yeah!" Theo pointed enthusiastically. "That's it! I don't know what it means though."

"...it means a warrior should maintain his composure and strike at the opportune moment to destroy their enemy." Said Father Lucas, knowing that Theo's rabbit punch to the skull of El Hacon had put him in a coma, and probably left him paralyzed.

The bishop redirected the conversation. "Theo, since your time in the cave, have you experienced any physical symptoms other than blacking out?"

"Well, headaches, but I did get gonged in the head by a 400-pound ex-boxer with a fire extinguisher." Theo tapped his right temple.

"His doctor says he's fine." Isabella interjected.

"...also. some back pain, like *right here.*" Theo twisted his muscley arm around to point at his lower back.

"*A gateway.*" Father Lucas whispered. The bishop nodded in agreement.

The priests both stood. "Theo, we would like to perform a blessing on you."

Theo shrugged. "Like I said, it's whatever. I'm just doing what my mom wants right now. I messed up big time and my parents have me by the balls."

Father Lucas chuckled, and Bishop Vincent took the bottle of holy water from Isabella that Theo had been drinking. He poured a small amount in his hand and anointed Theo's forehead with a cross.

He tried to move away. "Hey, stop it. I told you that stuff is gross. It smells bad and I don't want it on me."

"It's only blessed water, Theo." The bishop said calmly.

Theo grew tense. "I don't believe you. It smells like matches."

Father Lucas pulled one of the chairs to the opposite side of the room. "Isabella, please sit over here."

As she stood, she noticed her son looking agitated. She wanted to believe it was because he just wanted it over with, but she hesitated to be out of range in case he needed to be restrained.

As if not wanted to waste a moment, Bishop Vincent immediately held up a silver cross in front of Theo and began reciting The Litany of the Saints.

"Lord, have mercy on us."

"Lord, have mercy on us." Repeated Father Lucas.

"Christ, have mercy on us." Said the bishop.

"Christ, have mercy on us." Father Lucas echoed.

The holy men continued reciting The Litany of the Saints, invoking the Holy Trinity, Holy Mary, and then the angels.

Theo huffed, and he looked towards the door. "How long is this going to take?" He attempted to interrupt the bishop, but he continued.

"St. John the Baptist,"

"Pray for us."

"St. Joseph,"

"Pray for us."

"All ye holy Patriarchs and Prophets,"

"Pray for us."

After twenty minutes of prayer, Theo knocked the priests hand that was holding the cross, away from his face and stood to leave. "Seriously, I'm done. This is stupid."

Bishop Vincent stuttered, but increased his pace as he invoked the Apostles. Father Lucas followed.

"St. Peter,

Pray for us.

St. Paul,

Pray for us.

St. Andrew,

Pray for us."

The hair on Isabella's neck stood up as she watched Theo rise from the bed, her carefully tuned instincts as a law enforcement officer—and his mother—were triggered. "Sit down, Theodore." She commanded.

Theo ignored her and reached for the doorknob. Isabella slapped his hand away. Theo snapped his head towards her, "I'm done with this bullshit. I'll walk home."

His mother stood. "Like hell you will. *Sit down* and let them finish."

When The Litany had reached the invocation of the Holy Martyrs, Father Lucas flicked a small amount of holy water at Theo with each *pray for us*. As a droplet hit the young boxer's cheek, he turned and rushed the man. Theo grabbed the bottle from Father Lucas, crushed it in his enormous hand, and threw it across the room.

"For the *third fucking time* stop putting your fucking swamp water on me. It smells like a bog. This whole room smells like a dumpster." Theo bellowed.

The bishop continued with the prayer, now invoking the Holy Bishops and Confessors.

Father Lucas held his ground and locked eyes with Theo. "Pray for us."

Theo laughed. "Look at you, Father Dipshit. You think you're tough, huh? You're not scared, since you have the blessing of…who are we on now, Bishop?"

He continued to follow Theo to where he stood menacingly breathing over Father Lucas like a bull. He held the cross in front of him. "Saint Benedict,"

"Pray for us." Father Lucas growled in Theo's face.

The teenager smirked. "Saint *Benedict*, eh? Didn't he make the rules for how a monk should live? There's an interesting story about him that might help you, Father…"

Isabella grabbed Theo's arm. "Stop it. You don't know anything about Saint Benedict. Go sit down, *now.*"

"All ye holy Priests and Levites," continued Bishop Vincent.

"*Pray. For. Us.*" Father Lucas said to Theo, almost daring the demon to show himself.

"Saint Benedict *knew* he was a hypocrite." Said Theo. "He laid out all these strict rules for the monks to live by so they could honor god, but he struggled with one—*chastity*. One day the Saint was alone in a field, and a blackbird began to flutter in front of his face. Bishop, stop me if you've heard this one—"

"St. Mary Magdalene," he replied.

"Pray for us." Whispered Father Lucas. The irony of the rumored lover of Jesus being summoned at this moment was not lost on him.

"—this bird was so close to his face, he could have grabbed it and *crushed it in his hand.*" Theo put his hand in front of the father's face and slowly closed his fist. "But he didn't. He did the sign of the cross, and the bird flew away. Temptation never ends though, does it Father?" Theo smiled. "Even if the bird flies away, or if you run away, sin follows. Be *ever vigilant*! Right, Bishop?"

"St. Lucy,"

"Pray for us."

Despite a cool exterior, Isabella had begun to panic. *This was not her son speaking.* Theo had never been to church; in school the closest he ever got to learning about the Saints was a medieval history class which he only passed because his father is a history teacher and tutored him every weekend. Isabella knew her Theo was out of her reach, locked away somewhere inside this beast that scratched at the door of her son's eyes. *Could demons be real?* She'd been agnostic her entire life, and was being forced to consider something she never had before. When faced with uncertain situations, her brain defaulted into police officer mode. She didn't know how to exorcise a demon, but she *did* know her son was a threat to the priests and himself. She scanned the room in an attempt to create a plan to control the situation.

That's when she saw Father Lucas's bag wide open on the cherrywood dresser.

Inside the only items he hadn't removed were two leather wrist restraints embossed with the holy cross. She inched her way towards it as Theo—or the demon—continued his monologue.

"Saint Benedict was suddenly flooded with thoughts of a beautiful woman he'd seen in the nearby village every day, a woman he secretly fantasized about. This urge was suddenly so strong that he found himself leaving the monastery to speak to her. On the way, he stepped on a briar and pierced his foot. This pain made him stop and think...*what am I doing? Why would I give up my life of godliness to go fuck some woman I barely know?*" Theo leaned forward and whispered in Father Lucas's ear. "*Especially when she probably doesn't even want me.*"

"Pray for us." Said Father Lucas through gritted teeth. His cheeks were red and beads of sweat formed on his brow, fighting every male urge within him to punch the teenager in the face.

"So, you know what Saint Benedict did? He looked down at his foot and saw the ground was covered in a patch of nettles and briar. This monk then took off all his clothes and rolled around in the thorns and stinging nettles until he was covered in welts and his own blood, thereby purging himself of sin." Theo chuckled and slapped a hand on Bishop Vincent's shoulder, who nearly collapsed under the weight. "You know what they don't tell you in church? This crazy motherfucker *did not stop* until he completely mangled his dick. That's right. He mangled his dick just to bring glory to God!"

"From all evil, O Lord!" Bishop Vincent now raised his voice.

"Deliver us!" pleaded the father.

Theo turned back to Father Lucas. "What would *you* do to bring glory to God, Lucas? Would you mangle your dick? Wait, wait, wait…don't answer…this is my favorite part…"

"From anger, and hatred, and every evil will!" said the bishop.

This time Isabella joined in. "Deliver us!"

Theo looked at his mother with feigned surprise. "Are we having a sing along now? I'll get the next part…FROM FORNICATION!" He pointed at Father Lucas, smiling. "Your turn."

"Deliver us."

Theo nodded in approval at Father Lucas, but his eyes flicked to the silver cross the bishop now held less than a foot away from Theo's ear. "There's a lot you could learn from Saint Benedict, Lucas."

"From plague, famine and war, from everlasting death!" Bishop Vincent shouted.

"Deliver us!" Isabella and Father Lucas responded, both voices trembling as Theo's chest heaved and threatened violence.

"Maybe all you need, Lucas…" although Theo spoke the father, he had turned his head to stare daggers into Bishop Vincent's eyes as he relentlessly continued The Litany of the Saints.

Then, in one quick swipe, he grabbed the bishop's hand that held the silver cross up to his face. "Maybe all you need…to bring glory to God…is a little *pain.*"

They heard the crack before they saw the bishop's pinky finger gruesomely sticking out to sideways. The bishop himself stared blankly at his hand for ten seconds before screaming in agony and dropping the cross.

*The quality of a decision is like the well-timed swoop of a falcon…*

For some reason, in that moment those words jingled around in Isabella's mind, louder than any other thought.

*Do it now.*

Isabella quickly reached into Father Lucas's bag and swiped one of the restraints. She grabbed Theo's forearm, twisting it around his back as she would putting cuffs on a criminal. She wrapped the leather strap around his wrist and fed it through the loop. Theo didn't resist; instead, he laughed at the bishop yowling in pain on the floor.

Tears welled in Bishop Vincent's as he looked up at Father Lucas. "Continue the rite. Do it!" He turned to Isabella. "Restrain him *now* while you still can. *It's going to get worse.*"

Father Lucas snatched up the small leather prayer book Bishop Vincent had dropped on the floor and immediately resumed the prayer.

"We sinners, that Thou wouldst spare us," Father Lucas read, as Theo laughed maniacally and Isabella struggled to restrain his other arm.

Bishop Vincent sat hunched on the floor cradling his hand. Sweat slid down his temples, but he managed to groan. "We beseech Thee, hear us!"

Isabella and Father Lucas pushed Theo to the bed and forced him to sit down, the entire time Father Lucas recited prayer and the bishop responded with *we beseech Thee, hear us.*

Despite Isabella practically dangling from his shoulders, Theo didn't resist being manhandled. He didn't cooperate either. It was as if the 17 year old could do nothing except hold on, and keep taking the demon's punches until the round was over. Isabella took one of Theo's long arms and fastened it to the bed frame. Father Lucas stopped praying briefly and tied the other side.

"That Thou wouldst deliver our souls, and the souls of our brethren, relations, and benefactors, from eternal damnation." Said Father Lucas

"We beseech Thee, hear us!" The bishop and Isabella said in unison.

Theo stopped laughing. His mother, who stood in front of him clasping his shoulders the size of boulders, saw a flash in his eyes. For a moment, something changed.

"Mom?" Theo asked, looking dazed.

Isabella longed to reach inside his head and pull out the evil. "Fight, Theo! Don't let it win."

"Lamb of God, who takes away the sins of the world,"

"*Spare us, O Lord!*"

"Christ, have mercy,"

"*Christ, have mercy!*"

"Lord, have mercy,"

"*Lord, have mercy!*"

And finally, in unison, Father Lucas and Bishop Vincent said, "And lead us not into temptation, *but deliver us from evil.*"

Once more, Theo's face changed to a sneer. Isabella released her son's shoulders and took a step back.

A loud *thump* hit the window, triggering the guardian senses of Emily's Great Pyrenees. From across the yard, her deep bark could be heard approaching the house as the black bird fluttered and beat its head into the window.

"Is that a crow?" said Isabella.

"Isabella, would you please get Emily to look at the bishop's hand?" asked Father Lucas as he picked up the red book emblazoned with the emblem of The Vatican, and feverishly flipped through pages.

After six attempts to break the glass, at last the bird fell to the ground.

No longer meditating, Esme could be heard outside. *"Leave it! Ziggy, drop that right now! I'll get the hose!"*

Isabella abruptly opened the door to get help and ran face first into Stella. Emily stood behind her.

"What is going on in there, *amiga*? You need us to say some prayers or something?" asked Stella as she cautiously peered over Isabella's shoulder into the room.

"Emily, I think Theo broke the bishop's finger." Isabella moved aside to let Emily in, and Stella slid in behind.

Emily knelt at the bishop's side, and he held up his hand with the pinky pointing out at an odd angle.

"Bishop…I'm not a doctor, but that looks dislocated." Emily's eyes were wide, and Stella gasped audibly behind her.

"Oh yeah, my kid did that playing basketball. You gonna pop it back in place, Emily?" asked Stella.

"…I've never done it before…but I know how." Said Emily.

"I mean *I've done it before* but my kid's hand is all fucked up. I probably should have went to urgent care." Said Stella.

The bishop pleaded with Emily. "Do it. *You* do it." He side-eyed Stella.

Theo watched them from the bed where his extremities were tied down. He looked like a lion that had just been captured. Isabella didn't take her eyes off him for a second.

"Are you sure you don't want me to take you to the hospital?" Emily asked.

"There is no time. The Beast has shown himself and Father Lucas cannot do it alone." Bishop Vincent held out his mangled hand to her.

"Come on, Emily. Help *el obispo* out." Stella encouraged. "The guy's in agony! Just grab it real tight and yank. Then put it back where it goes."

Emily gently took the bishop's hand and felt for the base of the dislocated bone. The bishop winced, but held steady as Emily tugged and moved it to where she believed it should be.

The bishop's chest heaved, but he said nothing as Emily worked, nodding at her in gratitude as she helped him up. Bishop Vincent was intensely focused on Theo, but kept his distance.

"Stella, Emily, now you need to get out of here. It's not safe." Isabella said, her instinct to protect and serve still applied despite a supernatural threat.

They reluctantly left, and after the door shut, the men's faces turned grim.

"Isabella," said Father Lucas. "I'm sure you've realized what needs done here. Theo needs an exorcism. Are you ready?"

"I wrestle meth-heads for a living. If there's any career that can prepare someone to handle demonic possession, it's law enforcement." Isabella responded. "So, what do you need me to do? Hold a cross or something?"

Bishop took *De Exorcismis et Supplicationibus quibusdam* from Father Lucas. "Isabella, I think the best thing you can do right now is what you do best: observe. If there is anything we need to be aware of, tell us. Otherwise, keep out of his reach."

She nodded and as her son carefully watched each person as they spoke.

The bishop began the minor exorcism by holding up his cross. "I call upon God and the Angels of Light to be with us now. Archangel Michael, protector of mankind, please watch over us now." He now turned to address Theo. "As an emissary of God, I command you to answer me: how do you identify?"

Theo laughed. "I think you got the wrong kid, bishop. She—I mean *they*—will be here soon, though. That kid was a *real* weak one. We broke Bellatrix like glowstick…won't be long before the light fades. I'm not sure if she'll make our team though…I think her meatsuit is going to expire before she's had long enough to *marinate.*"

"Answer me! How do you identify?" commanded Bishop Vincent.

"*He-slash-him.* Lowercase 'h'." Theo taunted.

"In the name of Christ almighty, tell me…what are you?" asked the bishop for a third time.

Theo's head rolled. He scowled and looked up from under his brows. "I am Astaroth, being of Darkness."

"Whom do you serve?" asked the bishop.

"I serve myself!" Astaroth spat.

The bishop moved closer, and Astaroth's eye twitched. "All demons serve another. No demon is free to do as they wish; you are all enslaved to a master! Whom do you serve?"

"Asmodeus…" he growled.

"What are the terms of your contract?" asked the bishop.

Theo tugged at his restraints. Just a test. "There are no terms. He is a King; I am a Duke. I do as he says."

"And what does he say to do?"

"*Find a body to possess. Break the soul. Use it as the King commands.* I really lucked out with this one, don't you think?" Asmodeus gestured with his head at Theo's arms. "I mean, he's *huge*, and my job is to protect the rest of them. This guy's not too smart either. Real easy win, for me."

Isabella fumed and took a step forward, then stopped, remembering this was still her son's body, and locked away inside was his mind and soul.

Astaroth grinned with amusement. "Whatcha gonna do, Lieutenant? *Hit me*? You haven't done that in what, eighteen years? Hardly seems like a fair fight." Said Astaroth.

Father Lucas splashed holy water on Theo's face. "The only fight you'll be having is with Jesus Christ. In the name of the Lord, I command you to leave this child!"

Theo flinched. "Don't push me, Father *Benedict.*"

The bishop plunged into prayer:

"O Eternal God, Who has redeemed the race of men from the captivity of the devil, deliver Thy servant, Theodore Kentworth, from all the workings of unclean spirits. Command the evil and impure spirits and demons to depart from the soul and body of Theodore, your servant, and not to remain nor hide in him. Let them be banished from this the creation of Thy hands in Thine own holy name and that of Thine only begotten Son and of Thy life-creating Spirit, so that, after being cleansed from all demonic influence, he may live holy, godly, justly and righteously and may be counted worthy to receive the Holy Mysteries of Thine only-begotten Son and our God with Whom Thou art blessed and glorified together with the all holy and good and life-creating Spirit now and ever and unto the ages of ages. Amen."

*Amen* said the father and Isabella. *Amen* said Stella and Emily from beyond the door.

"It doesn't matter!" Astaroth cursed. "I'll be back. We'll *all* be back. *Asmodeus* will make sure of it."

"Theo, listen to me…" Isabella pleaded to her son. "Fight like it's a championship title. Kick that demon out of your body and take your life back!"

Theo spat in her face.

"The Lord rebukes thee, devil!" Bishop Vincent continued, looking pale and shaken. "He Who calls forth the water of the sea and pours it upon the face of all the earth. Lord of Hosts is His name. O devil: Fourth Prayer the Lord rebukes thee!"

The priests continued taunting the devil and invoking the Lord through prayer, reciting the Catholic Rites of Exorcism, while splashing holy water and presenting the cross. Theo appeared increasingly uncomfortable, pulling at the restraints and attempting to stand, cursing God and Jesus and the priests until becoming so irritated he kicked at the men with his free legs.

"Stop! Stop..." Astaroth whined. *"The others will be here soon enough,* and they will finish you off! *Nos semper revertemur!* There will always be another man to use."

Theo exhaled deeply, his body seeming to cave in upon itself. His muscled and restrained arms dangled without resistance. The same window the crow flew into earlier rattled as if a bomb went off down the street, and the room grew silent.

Isabella cautiously approached her son. His eyes were closed. She placed a hand on his knee, and pushed his blonde, curly hair out of his face. "Teddy?"

He sniffed and began to sob. Isabella removed his restraints and he sat up.

"I'm sorry, Mom." Head hanging, tears dripped down his nose and landed on his lap. "I don't know why I did it. Why I hurt him...and Dad. I don't know how I'll ever make it right to *any* of them."

Father Lucas placed the cross and Bible he was holding on the bed next to Theo and sat next to him. "Theo... it's going to be very important that you come to see me every week to receive a blessing for at least six months. If you'd like, we can talk about ways you can make things right with the people you've hurt...and with God."

He sniffed, wiped his nose on his sleeve and nodded in agreement. Then he stood, and reached for Isabella, wrapping her in a hug so tightly she nearly disappeared in his arms.

"Let's go home." She said, wiping away her own tears.

"...but you promised me fajitas." Theo pouted.

Isabella laughed, relieved that Theo was already showing signs of his old self again.

"You're right, Teddy. Fajitas and Jarritos."

# Shadow People

"**Y**ou must have the wrong house. We didn't order any food." Emily said to the girl on her porch wearing half a cat suit. *Melted Magic* food truck was stopped in the street.

"Is Gemma here?" the girl exhaled fast as if she'd been running.

Gemma, who'd been dozing off on the couch while waiting for Benny and Ash, sat up and peeked at the door. "I'm Gemma. Who are you?"

"I'm Melanie, Trix's friend. Something is wrong with her. Eric said you were here. Do you want us to bring her in?" She asked.

In response, Gemma jumped up and flew past Emily out the door to the truck parked in the street. Eric saw her coming and opened the side door.

Like Melanie, Eric was half-dressed in his Fursuit, wings torn and soft white fur soiled green and brown with dirt.

The sight of him took Gemma by surprise, and she stopped momentarily. "You know what…I'm not even going to ask." She climbed into the odorous truck, where Trix lay sprawled out on their back. Trix's head lolled side to side. They whimpered for their mother.

"Mom…mom, I'm scared. They want to take me with them." Trix cried.

"Who, baby? Who wants to take you?" Gemma looked at her child, whose cheeks were bright red and hair was matted with sweat.

"The Shadows…they're like vultures. They want me to die…so they can tear me apart and eat me…" Trix sobbed. "…but the other ones won't let me go."

Gemma's skin crawled. After ghosts and demons, now she knew anything was possible. "Who won't let you go? What other ones?" she whispered.

Trix opened and closed their dry mouth like they were trying to drink air. "They have six huge white wings…with eyes all over them."

Gemma smoothed back Trix's turquoise hair. "No, honey, that's just Eric. He's dressed like a moth."

Hurried steps approached behind her. "Actually, Gemma, what she's just described is the Seraphim." Father Lucas did the sign of the cross in front of him.

Eric, who had been silent until this point, looked nervously from the priest to Gemma. He spoke to his wife from the side of his mouth. "Sweetie...I didn't realize the *friend* you are visiting is a Catholic priest...*maybe we should talk about that later?*"

"The Seraphim are God's most powerful angels." Said Father Lucas as he climbed inside the truck. He pulled a vial of holy water from his pocket and made the cross on Trix's forehead. "They purify thoughts so that mankind can see the holiness of God within them. Gemma, Trix is burning up with a fever."

Trix's eyes rolled around in their head, then landed on Father Lucas. Trix smiled. "They said you'll help me. Your light is bright, like theirs."

"Trix, my name is Father Lucas. Can you tell me what happened to you?" He sat the Bible on her stomach and it shook and her breath trembled.

"The voices—the same ones that led us out of the cave—they keep talking to me. They tell me I'm ugly and wrong...an abomination against God." Trix's voice shook.

His face grew stern. "Don't listen to them. Listen to me. God loves all of his creations, and he must especially love *you* if he's sent the Seraphim to be by your side and protect you."

"The Shadows tell me to kill myself," Trix whispered. "They say when I die they'll be my new family."

Gemma's eyes began to well with tears. "They *will not.* That is a lie. You have a family here! And you have friends that love you. The shadows aren't real!"

As if on command, the sun moved behind a cloud, and the inside of the food truck grew dark. Gemma swore she felt hot breath on her neck, yet the air around her seemed to drop ten degrees as if stepping into a walk-in refrigerator.

The priest must have felt it, too. They locked eyes.

"Trix isn't possessed," he said. "But she's definitely *oppressed.* They're breaking her down mentally and physically so they can take control."

A small voice spoke up from the darkest corner of the food truck, where Melanie had stationed herself out of the way. "Did you guys hear that? It sounded like...growling."

Bare feet slapped down the sidewalk as Emily and Stella realized something was wrong, running outside without shoes. Emily threw herself into the food truck like she was practicing to be an EMT. She quickly took in the scene. "What's wrong with Trix?"

"She's seeing shadows...and angels...and thinks she's dying..." Gemma was distraught and focused on the wrong things.

"She's burning up, Emily." Pointed out Father Lucas. "I think she's also sick."

Emily laid her palm on Trix's forehead and gently touched their cheeks as they dipped in and out of consciousness. "They absolutely have a fever. We need to get this costume off right now, and get to a hospital."

Father Lucas and Emily rolled Trix on their side as Ragekitten showed Gemma how to remove the rabbit suit. Once the gloves were off, and the costume peeled off their sweaty body from shoulder to feet, they rolled Trix onto their back once more.

Emily gasped in horror. "I have never seen sepsis that bad," said Emily. She'd done rotations at a retirement home during her nurse's aide training and sepsis was a common occurrence in the elderly, but usually caught before it spread too far.

"Dang..." chirped in Stella from the sidewalk. "It looks like some kind of purple spider web wrapped around her arm."

Father Lucas scrambled out of the food truck and Emily followed.

"Gemma," said Emily. "Trix must have a wound on their hand that got infected. All those reddish lines going up their arm means they're septic. If the infection reaches the organs...well, it's bad news. Drive the truck to the hospital immediately. It'll be faster than waiting for an ambulance."

Gemma's hands were shaking as she put her rolled-up sweater under Trix's head while Eric and Ragekitten climbed up front. As Gemma shut the door to the food truck, she caught Emily's worried expression and their hearts locked together in a comradery as only two mothers in the trenches of childrearing could know.

"...thank you." said Gemma.

Emily gave her a small smile, knowing hours earlier she had helped save Esme. "No, Gemma. Thank *you*."

# Boo-ray

"**A**re you aware that Stella's ugly ass poodle is scrumping a polar bear on your back deck in front of the priest and Baby Jesus and all the world to see?" asked Benny.

"What?!" Emily ran to the back door.

"Don't worry, Em." Said Stella. "She's old, right?"

Emily pounded on the glass of the sliding door to break them up, knowing full well it was too late. "She's eleven...which is ancient for a Great Pyrenees."

"Exactly," Stella reassured. "She's already been through doggy menopause. Let the old girl have her fun. She's keeping Bandito busy."

Benny helped himself to a Diet Coke. "It didn't cross your mind to have him neutered?"

Stella shrugged. "I've been busy." Her eyes caught Ash's, who leaned against the wall with his arms crossed. "'Sup, kid? I'm Mateo's mom."

"Is he here?" Ash asked.

Stella shook her head. "Nope. He's in the looney bin for a few more weeks. I tried to bust him out for the occasion but they gave me the ol' *boot-with-no-laces*."

Ash seemed at a loss. "Uh, okay. Where's Esme? Shouldn't we be having birthday cake or something?"

"Today's not my birthday..." Esme appeared from her room. She turned to her mom. "Is he possessed, too?"

Ash's arms stiffened at his sides and he looked ready to bolt. "Benny, what is this?"

Benny passed his stepson a soda. "It's no big deal, Ash. Don't you want to be *hashtag blessed*? All of your friends are doing it."

"Except Oliver." Stella pointed out.

"Where's Oliver?" Esme asked, concerned.

The adults looked at each other, unsure what to tell her.

"He's missing…," said Emily. "Have either of you heard from him?"

"Not since the cave." Said Esme.

Ash began walking to the door. "I'm leaving. I don't need a blessing."

Benny ran in front of him and held out his arms. "Yes, you do. It will only take a few minutes. Please sit down."

Ash fumed, staring down his stepfather. The tension in the room thickened. Stella stood up from the sofa, preparing for a teenage rumble, as Emily approached Benny's side as a show of parental solidarity.

"Lord, have mercy on us." Bishop Vincent could be heard walking down the hallway of Emily's home.

"Lord, have mercy on us." Said Emily and Stella.

The bishop appeared in the room with a prayer book in one hand, and the other wrapped in a bandage. "Christ, have mercy on us."

"Christ, have mercy on us." Emily, Stella, and Father Lucas echoed.

Benny squinted at them, confused, then he caught the twitches in Ash's face as he scowled at the holy men. It triggered some primal fear response in his mind as if he was in a small room with a lion. His stomach flopped.

"Christ, have mercy on us, I guess..." stammered Benny. He hadn't yet been told about Theo's exorcism or Trix's condition.

Father Lucas held a bottle of holy water in his hand. "Ashton, we have no doubt that you are under the influence of a dark force entity. Please sit down so we can help you."

The teenager glared, but obeyed and sat on an oversized accent chair. "Fine. What now?"

"God the Father of Heaven," said the bishop.

"Have Mercy on us." Said the others in unison.

Ash scowled in suspicion. "Holy shit, Benny. Did you join a cult? Is this a cult? Do I need to call Dad?"

"I did not join a *cult*, child. Just sit still, dammit." Said Benny, watching Father Lucas attempt to make a cross on Ash's forehead with a finger dipped in holy water.

Ash slapped the father's hand away. "Stop it. I don't want that."

"Holy Mary, Mother of God," Bishop Vincent continued.

Father Lucas forced his hand through Ash's flailing arms to bless his forehead. "Pray for us."

Ash shoved Father Lucas off of him, and he stumbled to the floor.

Distraught and embarrassed, Benny attempted to help the priest to his feet. "Ashton, how could you?! He is a man of the cloth!"

Father Lucas stood quickly and pulled a silver cross from his pocket. "I'm fine, Ben. Prepare yourself for worse than this."

"What do you mean?" asked Benny, raising an eyebrow.

*"Tu penses vraiment que ces prêtres peuvent m'faire disparaître?"* said Ash, in perfect Cajun French.

The blood froze in Benny's body, and by reflex he replied. *"Qu'est-ce que tu as dit, hein?"*. *What did you say?*

Ash laughed. "The Devil may have gone down to Georgia, but he has a summer home in the swamps of New Orleans. For those unfamiliar with Cajun-speak, I said, *'Do you really think these priests can banish me?'*"

Bishop Vincent stopped praying. "Identify yourself."

"Certainly." Ash crossed his legs, sitting in his chair as if it were a throne. *"Môsieur* Asmodeus. Or, if you like, King Asmodeus."

Emily's knees gave out and she squeaked. "Did you see that?"

Stella caught her under the arms. "See what, amiga? Jesus...use your legs..."

Ash chuckled. "Tell me, woman, have you witnessed death? If so, it's possible for you to witness my true form."

Emily collapsed to the floor. "I don't want to! I don't want to see it!"

The bishop stepped over Emily and held a cross to Ash's face. "Asmodeus, King of Demons, by the power of the Lord I command you to leave this child at once!"

He smirked. "Or else, what? Are you trying to *bribe* me, Bishop Vincent? Kind of like how that cop bribed you to be here after she caught you shoving coke up your nose while a prostitute sucked your dick?"

Ashton mimed giving a blowjob, using his tongue to push out the side of his cheek.

The others all turned to stare at the bishop whose face had turned scarlet.

Father Lucas looked like he was about to be sick. "Bishop...is this true?"

Bishop Vincent opened and closed his mouth, then settled on pursing his lips. He dropped the cross to the floor.

"Well... that explains a lot." Said Stella.

Bishop Vincent turned to Father Lucas and whispered. "I can't help you now. I'm compromised. For a dark entity of this level, you need someone...pure. I'm sorry." He lifted his robes and swept out of the house, slamming the door on his way out.

Satisfied, Ash placed his hands on his lap and grinned while the adults stared at each other in stunned silence.

Stella reached down in front of Ash and picked up the silver cross, then passed it to Father Lucas. "Looks like it's just you, Padre."

He took it hesitantly, then turned the cold metal effigy over in his hands. *There's no way I can do this on my own.*

*You're right.* Asmodeus said.

*Get out of my head!* Father Lucas thought.

*Make me, and I will.* Asmodeus replied.

Father Lucas cleared his throat, then stumbled and fumbled through the red book of exorcism prayers. "Let us pray...God of power, who promised us the Holy Spirit through Jesus your Son, we prayed to you for these catechumens, who present themselves before you."

Ash scowled. "Really? The Prayer of Minor Exorcism? Practically an insult to a King, don't you think?"

Flustered, Father Lucas flipped through his book as the parents grew anxious. Finally, Benny spoke.

"What do you want? What could you possibly need with a 17-year-old boy who can't even operate a dishwasher?"

"Have you learned nothing from the patterns of mankind?" Asmodeus rested his elbow on the armchair. "Evil only needs a *useful tool* to achieve its means. A person with the right access is more important than someone with intelligence or wisdom. Actually, it's preferred. Those with mental discipline are *much* more difficult to manipulate." He turned his attention to Father Lucas. "Not impossible, though."

He held up the cross. "In the name of Jesus Christ, I command you to leave this child at once."

The cross grew so hot in Father Lucas's hands that he winced in pain and dropped it.

The demon laughed. "Please, Father. Enough is enough. You cannot *force* me to leave. Especially on your own. How about we make a deal instead?"

"No," Father Lucas replied immediately. "Even if you win in a game against the devil, you lose."

Ash tapped his finger on the chair. Ziggy and Bandit barked ferociously at the door as the trees bent from gusting wind. "I said a *deal*, not a game. Would you *like* to play a game? Would that make it more fair to you?"

"No!" shouted Father Lucas.

"What game?" asked Stella looking genuinely interested. "What are the terms?"

Ash smiled. "*Elección del jugador.* Player's choice. Winner gets Ashton's soul."

"And if we lose?" asked Stella.

"Obviously, I get yours as well, *Mamacita*." Ash raised his eyebrows.

Without hesitation, Stella pulled up the coffee table. "Emily, get me some cards. We're playing Blackjack."

This brought Benny out of stunned silence. "What? Like Hell you are! You are *not gambling your soul* for my good-for-nothing stepson's. Go sit your big ass down, Stella!"

Benny pulled up a chair to the coffee table in front of Ash. "Emily, do you have cards and poker chips?"

She nodded. "Are you sure you want to do this?"

Benny scoffed. "I'm gay—apparently I'm going to hell anyway."

"Benny, I'm begging you not to do this. You *will not* win." Pleaded Father Lucas.

Benny waved him away. "I've been playing Bourre since I was old enough to count. If I can win any game, that's the one."

"Bourre it is." Said Ash, who opened a pack of cards Emily sat on the table and began shuffling them in the air dramatically like a magician.

"…what's Bourre?" asked Emily as she handed Benny a dusty wooden box of poker chips she extracted from a hallway closet.

"It's like Cajun spades. It's a trick-taking game they play out on the oil rigs. Most of us grew up playing with our grandmamas. I paid my rent more than a few times thanks to winning a pot of Bourre." Said Benny as he unpacked tokens.

"Listen to me. It won't be enough. It doesn't matter how good you are, Asmodeus will be better. Demons are tricksters." Father Lucas begged.

Ash spread his hands out wide, and feigned offence. "I'm right here. I can hear you, you know."

"Father, I appreciate your concern but it appears you have reached the limits of your usefulness in this situation." Said Benny. "Maybe there's some sort of prayer to baby Jesus to give me a good hand or something? Maybe spritz me in the face with some holy water? Don't get my hair…I just colored it."

Father Lucas looked defeated, which pleased Asmodeus who grinned ear to ear.

"Alright, Benjamin." Said Asmodeus. "To avoid any claims of cheating, how about *you* deal?"

Benny took the deck from Asmodeus's hands. "Fine." He riffle-shuffled and passed out five cards to each of them.

Before Benny could pick up his cards, Asmodeus reached across the table and slapped his hand on top of Benny's. "Now wait just a second…" Ash spoke with a Cajun accent.

Benny scowled. "You saw me deal. I didn't cheat."

The corner of Ash's mouth rose. "No, you didn't. The problem is your offering. It's no good."

"My offering?" Said Benny. "You mean my soul?"

Ash nodded slowly. "It's already spoken for."

All eyes were on Benny. "What in the hell are you talking about, *my soul is spoken for?*"

Asmodeus ignored the question. "The game has already been chosen. Someone must play in your stead. Someone whose soul is free to give." The Demon King sat back and steepled his fingers, waiting for Benny to decide.

"I have no idea who spoke for my soul, but ain't nobody here in this room who knows how to play Bourre except me! And they sure as hell won't give you their soul." Benny looked around frantically.

"The wheel is already turning. Decide what to do now, or concede your stepson to me forever." Asmodeus said.

"I'll do it." Father Lucas swept up the cards. "Winner gets Ash's soul."

"Unless you lose." Asmodeus pointed out.

"…then you get mine." Said Father Lucas. He fanned open his cards and assessed them cluelessly.

"You do not have a damn clue what you're doing, Father!" Benny waved his hands around. "For fuck's sake. Can I at least coach him?"

Asmodeus nodded. "I'm feeling generous today. Why not?"

Benny nodded and began passing out chips.

"There's one more thing you seem to have forgotten, Benjamin." The demon said.

Afraid to ask, he said, "…what's that?"

"Bourre must be played with at least three players." Asmodeus said. "What ever shall we do?"

Stella and Emily exchanged glances

"What are the terms for me?" said Stella. "Am I putting my soul up, too? I'm pretty sure I'm not spoken for but I was a stripper for like ten years so I'm probably already going to hell. You know what I'm saying *Mosier* Diablo?"

"Well, as Benjamin should already know, only one person can win a round of Bourre—which is five hands." Said Asmodeus. "The person with the most tricks in a round wins. If you cannot play any tricks in a round you are considered Bourre and must pay the penalty equal to the pot. This means that one person will win Ash's soul at the end of the round. What happens to the other participant? What is the currency with which we gamble, friends?"

"I've got like twenty-three dollars in my wallet. You take credit cards?" Stella suggested.

Asmodeus ignored her. "How about *years of your life*? The winner takes the pot…and Ash's soul. Whatever chips you have left at the end of the round you get to keep. They equal years of your life. How many shall we wager? Twenty-five seems fair, don't you think?"

"I guess," Stella shrugged. "We all gotta go sometime, right?"

Asmodeus held out his hand to Benny. "Five chips, please."

Benny counted them out hesitantly, watching Stella carefully. "You sure you wanna do this, girl?"

"Yup." Stella was stone-faced. "Memento Mori. I'd rather go out early 'cuz I played cards with a demon than emphysema or whatever my mom had."

Benny nodded and dropped five chips into the demon's palm. Asmodeus formed them into a neat stack between his thumb and first finger and blew. The smell of sulfur filled the room.

"Stella, are you ready to accept your chips and the terms of our agreement?" he asked.

She held out her hand. "Let's do this shit."

As the five chips dropped, she was surprised by the weight and her hand fell to the table. The chips, previously blue, were now black. One side was embossed with the image of a skull mounted on top of an hourglass. The other, five tally marks.

"Father, are you ready to accept your chips and the terms of our agreement?" Asmodeus sneered.

"God is the only One who can give or take life away." He said.

Asmodeus slid a stack of chips from Benny's pile and gathered it in his hand. "Are you saying you no longer wish to participate, and I win by default?"

Father Lucas frowned but held out his palm. "I agree to your terms."

The demon held the chips to his lips and unleashed his sulfur breath until they turned the color of soot, then dropped them into the priest's open hand. Father Lucas barely acknowledged the transaction and set them aside.

"Each of your chips is worth five years, totaling twenty-five." Said Asmodeus. "Although we are ultimately playing for Ash's soul, we will *all* wager chips. For every chip you win, you will gain five years of life. For every chip you lose, you will pay five years of life. Understood?"

Father Lucas and Stella mumbled their agreement.

Benny counted out five chips for Asmodeus and began to teach the rules of Bourre. "Alright. First thing y'all need to do is ante. Put in one chip."

"Five years of your life." The demon reminded them.

"Dealer—that's you, Father—deal five cards to each of you—no, don't deal to yourself first give that to Stella—alright. Now, Father, flip your fifth card over. That's the trump suit." Instructed Benny.

The Father flipped over the six of spades.

"Spades is the trump suit. Put that card back in your hand. The goal is to win at least one trick, otherwise you're *Bourré*. That means 'drunk' in French… in this game, it means you have to pay into the pot however much is already in there." Explained Benny.

"So, if Father Lucas here doesn't take any tricks during this hand, he has to put in chips equal to the ante?" asked Stella.

Benny nodded. "Yup, three chips."

"Fifteen years." Said Asmodeus.

"Right…" Benny frowned, then continued. "You win the trick by playing the highest card in the leading suit. If you can't play the leading suit, you wanna play a trump card—in this hand it's spades. Hey demon, how many hands we playin'?" Benny asked.

"Three."

"Hmph. That's not a lot. Alright. Stella, you're left of the dealer so you pick the leading suit. It doesn't have to be trump…save that shit until you need it." Said Benny.

Stella placed the queen of hearts in front of her.

"Good. Aces are high, by the way." Said Benny. "Now y'all need to decide if you're gonna pass or play. If you play, you can trade in your cards to try for a better hand."

"*No, you may not.*" Said Asmodeus. "We're playing by the rules of Hell's Casino…down there, you must *always* play the hand you're given. No trades. No one may pass."

"Oh, I see, you're making up your own rules, now? How is that fair?" Benny was indignant. "You sound like my Cajun grandmama."

"You chose the game, but I choose the rules." Said the demon.

"I told you," Father Lucas said. "Demons will always stack the deck against you."

"Well, *pardon me.*" Sneered Asmodeus. "I do believe *you* are the one who shuffled."

Benny crossed his arms and scowled. "It's your turn, then."

Asmodeus considered his hand, then played the king of spades with a menacing grin.

"You don't have a heart?" Benny asked is disbelief.

"Oh, I'm afraid God took that away when he kicked me out of heaven."

Asmodeus feigned sadness.

"Cry me a fuckin' river…" Benny mumbled. "Alright, Father, here's the deal: Stella is leading with hearts. If you have a heart, you gotta play it. If you don't have a heart—like the demon—you have to play a trump suit; spades. He played a king…so…"

Father Lucas nodded curtly, and placed a card from the back of his hand on the table: Ace of Spades.

Benny whooped. "Thank you, sweet baby Jesus! That is *literally* the only card that could have won."

Stella and Father Luca grinned. The round continued until Father Lucas had won two in a row, Stella two, and the final trick to Asmodeus. He said nothing and pushed the pot of winnings towards the priest.

"Alright, everyone took at least one trick so no one is Bourré, but Father wins the round. Stella, you ready to deal for round two?" Benny asked, noticing her eyes follow the chips Father Lucas stacked in front of him. He'd gained ten years; Stella had lost five.

She nodded, anted another five years, and collected the cards. Stella shuffled the deck then dealt five to each player, flipping over the last to reveal the trump suit: diamonds.

The demon in an Ash suit led the hand with a 7 of diamonds. Father Lucas played the jack of diamonds; Stella played the ten of diamonds.

"Father takes the first trick." Said Benny.

The round continued with Asmodeus taking the second, Father Lucas taking the third, and Asmodeus the fourth.

"Two to two," said Benny. "Whoever wins the fifth trick takes the round."

What he didn't consider, was the possibility that Stella could win the fifth hand.

"Well, shit." Said Benny.

Stella was confused. "Well, what happens now? They tied…do they split the pot?"

Benny sighed. "No. It carries over to the last round. Ante again; demon deals."

The demon dealt and flipped the trump suit: clubs.

After Asmodeus won the first hand, Father Lucas won two. The players were intensely focused, but Benny struggled to maintain his elation. He ran into the kitchen where Emily was pouring herself a shot of bourbon. Benny snatched the shot glass from her hands and swigged it down. "Girl, I think we're gonna win. Oh shit, I'm not supposed to drink while I'm on pain meds, right?"

Emily took the glass back with a scowl and poured another shot. "I just saw *a demon's true form.* I think we've got bigger problems right now, Benny."

"You're right," Benny ran back to the game, just as Asmodeus laid down his card.

Father Lucas sat back in his chair. "I won. Three out of five…I win!"

"Hold on, hold on…" Benny seemed relieved, but hesitant. "The game's not over yet. You have to play out the last hand."

Asmodeus's eyes twinkled. "That is correct. Everyone, please play your last card."

Father Lucas laid down the two of hearts with little thought. Stella played her last card—an eight of clubs, from the trump suit, and Asmodeus laid his last—the queen of clubs.

"I win the last trick." Said Asmodeus.

Father Lucas stood up. "Yes, but you lost the game. By the terms of our agreement, you must leave Ashton's body immediately!"

Asmodeus waved his finger. "Father, will you please allow me a moment to conclude the rest of my business? Congratulations, by the way. You've extended your life by, what, forty years?"

Father Lucas's face grew pale, and his eyes flicked towards Stella.

Asmodeus shook his head. "Even though you had us in a clinch that last round, and won Ashton's soul, there is still the matter of Ms. Estrella. You see, she didn't take a single trick that hand, which means she is Bourée. Why don't you remind them what that means, Benjamin?"

"...wait. No! Father Lucas won! That's the end of the game!" Benny cried.

"You know as well as I do that *it is not*." Said Asmodeus.

Benny began to hyperventilate and steadied himself against a chair "Bourée means...anybody who doesn't win a trick during a hand will have to match the amount of chips in the pot." Said Benny.

"Wait," Stella counted. "It's a double pot because of the tie...there's six chips in there. That's thirty years. I don't even have that many chips left!"

Asmodeus picked at his nails. "Yes, it was quite *kind* of me to cap it at twenty-five, don't you think? You're welcome."

"I don't want her chips!" said Father Lucas. "Can I just give them back to her?"

"You *know* it doesn't work like that." Asmodeus turned to Stella. "You're what, nearly forty? You might be able to see your kids grow up. You *are* a smoker though..."

Stella picked up a handful of the black chips and threw them across the room. "Fuck you!"

Asmodeus laughed. "Such drama. My terms were clear, Estrella."

"Please," Father Lucas pleaded. "I don't want her twenty-five years. Take mine. How about I give you my chips instead? Just let Stella go. She has kids!"

"No." Asmodeus smiled.

A switch flipped in Father Lucas. "Why the *fuck* not?!"

The room fell silent in shock at the priest's outburst.

Asmodeus stood from his chair so he was face to face with Father Lucas. His eyes were black and the air in the room felt thick. He waved his hand and the chips disappeared.

"You know what..." Asmodeus said. "I may be able to offer you a deal after all, Father Lucas."

The priest was still unable to reign in his temper. The thought of Stella losing twenty-five years of her life with her children filled him with righteous rage. He resisted the urge to spit in Asmodeus's face and tell him to shove the deal up his ass.

"What sort of deal?" he asked through gritted teeth.

"Well, I was thinking maybe you could offer me something *else*. Not *years*. Stella could keep her time, you can keep yours and Ashton can keep his soul. I'll just move along to someone new…" Asmodeus took a step back from Father Lucas.

"What do you want?" asked Father Lucas.

"I want that which you value most: *your special connection to God.*" Said Asmodeus. "Give up the priesthood, and I will call it an even trade."

Without a second thought, Father Lucas unbuttoned his white collar, removed it, and tossed it on the table, scattering cards to the floor.


"I'll do it."

# Chapter 23

## Oliver and Company

Charlotte pushed the boy using the full force of her weight into an ice machine outside the Kum & Go convenience store. "Tell me where my son is before I shove that vape up your ass!"

"Whoa, chill out lady. Isn't your family all churchy and shit? I don't think Jesus would approve of that." Said Scott.

"Where is he?" she growled. Her husband stood back, watching for trouble and swatting at moths attracted to the fluorescent parking lot lights above their heads. He knew better than to get in the way of *Charlie*.

"Even if I told you where I last saw him—ouch!" Scott flinched as Charlotte twisted the collar of his shirt until it tightened around his throat. "It's not like you can just walk in there or something. You'll get killed."

Charlotte relaxed her grip. "Fine, take me there. Tell them I just want to get my son."

The boy's eyes bugged out of his head. "What? No way! I can't…I owe them money. All thanks to Oliver, I might add! He kept sayin' he'd pay me and never did."

"Pay you for what?" she snarled, afraid of the answer.

The boy blinked rapidly. "…you seriously don't know?"

Charlotte let him go, but her teeth were bared like a rabid dog.

Scott knew he was cornered. "Look, I'll tell you where I last saw him but like I said you can't just go in there. Your best bet is to talk to Glitter."

"Who's Glitter?" Charlotte demanded.

The boy nodded with his head across the parking lot where an unaccompanied pink Jeep was parked. Pink and purple rubber ducks littered the dashboard. The steering wheel cover was encrusted with rhinestones, and the leather seats were embroidered in gold with the word 'Glitter'.

"She's inside buying smokes, but she's the one to ask about your kid." He said. "She's the Trap House Queen. I'm not saying she has a heart of gold or anything, but she might let you in. I know for sure the others won't."

Brent approached slowly. "You're saying Oliver's in a trap house?"

The boy shrugged. "Sorry, man. He got lost down the rabbit hole I guess."

A rattling car pulled up next to them and tapped the horn twice. "That's my grandma, I gotta go." Said Scott. "Spaghetti night."

As Scott's grandmother pulled out, the only woman who could possibly be named Glitter exited the convenience store. She clutched a plastic shopping bag in one pink-clawed hand and a small gold pet carrier in the other. Charlotte caught a glimpse of curly white fur inside. The woman balanced her too-skinny frame on four-inch platform shoes by trotted in itty bitty baby steps. She wore black leather pants and a loose gold sequined tank top, barely held in place by her dramatically augmented chest.

Charlotte took a deep breath and looked up at the gloomy, light pollution-filled sky. *God, please show me the way to get my son back.*

"Brent…go back to the van, I need to handle this alone. Woman to woman, okay?" said Charlotte.

"Are you sure? I don't know what a Trap House Queen is, but it doesn't seem safe for you to go alone." Brent fiddled his keys in worry.

Charlotte reached deep into the well of experiences she had in another life, long before she found Jesus and became a mother, to a time so long ago it only seemed to exist in her nightmares. "I've known her type. She's basically the 'lady' of the drug den. Runs errands. Keeps the cogs moving. Knows everything that's happening but pretends she doesn't…just let me talk to her."

He conceded and went to the van while Charlotte sprinted across the parking lot to catch the woman before she left. She strategically slowed right before reaching the Jeep. In that life, people don't appreciate an ambush.

From a safe distance away, Charlotte said. "Excuse me! Are you Glitter?"

She rolled her eyes and buckled her dog into the passenger seat with the care a mother would a child. "I don't have anything on me, get a hold of Fezzik if you're looking to buy."

Then Glitter turned around and expertly evaluated the picture of Charlotte—neat ponytail, button-up floral shirt—ironed. Knee length khaki shorts and practical sneakers with smudges of mud from chasing the chickens out of her tomato garden before she left. Gold cross around her neck. Her tone changed to defensiveness. "If you're looking to save my soul, I already sold it to the highest bidder."

Charlotte cautiously approached, maintaining a respectful distance. "I'm sorry to bother you, but I'm looking for my son."

Glitter shook her head and fastened her seatbelt. "Nope. I don't know nothin'. Don't see nothin'."

"I'm not looking to cause trouble for you, I only want to get help for my son. We've been looking for him for weeks. His name's Oliver." Charlotte slowly closed the distance between them. "Please, he's only seventeen."

Glitter sat in the driver's seat, reached into the shopping bag and pulled out an energy drink. She cracked it open and took a sip. "Blonde kid?"

"Yes! That's him!" At least now Charlotte had confirmation he was at Glitter's house.

"Sweet kid. Taught me how to convert US measurements to metric on the scales. Saved my ass." Said Glitter.

Charlotte fought back tears. "He's such a smart boy. He speaks three languages and wants to go to college abroad."

Glitter turned off her Jeep. "Yeah, once upon a time I did too. I wanted to be a ballerina in France and shit. I feel bad for my parents, you know? From the time I was like five years old they dumped all that money into dance school, competitions, and wardrobe. Then I met Mazi. Fast money is addictive, you know?"

"I do know." Charlotte nodded. "I used to be where you are."

She smirked. "And now your little boy is following in your footsteps, isn't he? I bet you did everything right, too. I bet you loved him, gave him everything you didn't have, and anything he could have wanted. I bet he went to church every Sunday." Glitter pointed at Charlotte's necklace. "It doesn't fuckin' matter. If the Devil wants you, *he'll get you.*"

"I don't believe that. I was saved by Jesus." Said Charlotte. "Let me help my son, please. Glitter…please tell me where my son is."

After another long sip of her energy drink. "Fuck it. I'm tired of babysitting anyway. Get in the backseat. *And don't tell a motherfuckin' soul what you see.* I've got a picture of your kid's ID on my phone as collateral. I know where you live, you understand?"

She nodded frantically and fumbled with the door handle. Charlotte had barely sat down before Glitter put the Jeep in drive and whipped out of the parking lot onto the highway.

Glitter drove to the northwest part of town where the houses were old and rent was cheap. Most of the residents in these neighborhoods were immigrants and other people who wanted to keep a low profile and with under-the-table deals with landlords looking to avoid paying rental property taxes. Nestled behind a cluster of evergreens, Glitter's house had a bigger lot than most and could barely be seen from the road. She drove her Jeep across the lawn to a back door and parked. The window panels of the old house audibly shook and the ground rumbled from a nearby train. The blast of the horn was so loud that Glitter and Charlotte sat without speaking until it passed.

As the last cart clanged in the distance, Glitter turned in her seat to address Charlotte. "So, you lucked out. It's the weekend and the boys are out running errands *if you get what I'm saying*…it's just me and a few of the girls here. Still, I don't trust them bitches."

Charlotte remembered that feeling.

"What I want you to do is call your husband I saw sittin' in that minivan and tell him to park in the street. Don't come down the driveway. You're gonna have to walk Oliver out on your own. Try to stay in the shadows under the trees…Mazi's got cameras. I don't think he'll do anything about your kid leaving but you never know." Glitter unbuckled her dog from the seat and climbed out. "I'll be right back."

Charlotte took out her phone and saw eleven missed calls from Brent. She texted him her location, telling him she had Oliver and to park in the street. He responded with a thumb's up emoji, meaning he was probably already driving. Charlotte climbed out of the Jeep and paced by the back door, chewing on her lip.

Finally, she heard thumps of footsteps from inside.

"Come on, kid. *Use your legs.*" Glitter complained from behind the door.

When it opened, she saw a thin boy with sunken eyes and gray skin that barely resembled her son. His hair was greasy and his clothes were stained. He wasn't wearing shoes.

Charlotte rushed forward and tore him from Glitter's arms, nearly collapsing under his dead weight. Oliver's eyes were barely open and he smelled like he hadn't showered in weeks, yet Charlotte choked back sobs and hugged him close.

"Mom...what are you doing here?" Oliver managed to mumble.

Glitter waved them on. "Hug later, get the fuck out of here before they figure out I brought a square to the house."

Oliver put his arm over his mother's shoulders and tried to stand, but instead keeled over and vomited in the gravel driveway.

"Oh shit, hold on." Glitter disappeared behind the door. "You're taking the other one, too."

Charlotte rubbed Oliver's back as he continued heaving what looked like SpaghettiOs onto his feet. "What do you mean *the other one?*"

Glitter's hands shoved another skinny body out of the back door, then slammed it shut and clicked the deadbolt.

"Um...hi Mrs. Gladstone."

There, looking just as worse for wear, but slightly more aware than Oliver, was Magnus—the boy she tried to save at church camp years ago, and the son of the man who left her for dead on the sidewalk.

# Chapter 24

## Lesser of Two Evils

"I think I'm possessed." Said Lucy, leading Benny, Gemma and Emily to her living room without a greeting.

"I'm fine, Lulu, thanks for asking…" Stella stared daggers at her.

Lucy collapsed on her burgundy velvet sofa and cradled her embroidered pillow of Goose. "You're right. I haven't talked to any of you in so long. I know I've been a terrible friend. How are the kids?"

"Mattie's still at Willow Creek. They're giving him stuff to help him sleep and anxiety meds. Won't let him come home yet though." Stella shrugged.

Gemma began unpacking a wooden box that held her blessed candles and chakra stones. "Trix is in the hospital. Apparently, they got a fishhook stuck in their hand at some point and it got infected. Trix is on antibiotics and oxygen in the ICU. The doctors are monitoring for kidney failure."

Lucy gently touched Gemma's arm. "I'm so sorry…really. I'm going to send Trix some flowers today."

"Thanks…alright, so you want me to do a scan of your aura to see if there are any dark energies attached?" Gemma asked as she cradled a palm full of smooth stones, each of a different color corresponding to the seven chakras.

Lucy laid back on the couch and propped her feet up on the arm. "I don't know what else could be wrong. I've been *so* mean to Nolan. Can't eat, can't sleep. I'm always tired."

Gemma began positioning the stones on Lucy's body. "I see. I mean, I wouldn't be surprised if you picked up some bad energy at that swinger party. Stephanie and Richard are into some really weird stuff. That says a lot coming from me." She laughed.

Benny and Stella had disappeared from view. From the kitchen, glasses tinked and dished rattled. The door to the refrigerator opened and closed.

"What are you looking for?" Lucy asked from the couch.

"Something to drink that isn't served on a doily. Girl, you did not make sweet tea just for me, did you?" Benny exclaimed.

"I sure did. Two whole cups of sugar and everything. It's absolutely disgusting. I'm sure you'll love it." Lucy grinned.

A pour. A slurp. "Just like grandma's. Perfect. You use Luzanne's tea?"

"Lulu, do you have any salami?" yelled Stella.

"Bleh, no. Lately, I just can't stand the smell. All I can keep down is yogurt." Said Lucy.

Gemma rubbed her hands together to create energetic friction, pulling them apart as if she were stretching taffy. She then held them over the crown of Lucy's head to begin scanning her body. "Your chakras seem pretty active…a few broken heart-strings, but we all have those. I'll send some energy there. A few dark blotches. You've been depressed, you said?"

"Yeah. For no reason. Things are pretty good, I guess." Said Lucy.

"You need to get out of the house, *muneca*." Stella said as she sat cross-legged on a floor cushion with a heaping plate of green grapes in her lap. "We should go line dancing."

Gemma laughed. "Stella, I thought you said grapes are just 'balls of water covered in foreskin'."

"I stand by that statement. However, Miss Lucy only has boring stuff in her fridge. Next time I visit I'll pack a lunch." She tossed a grape in her mouth. "Hey, aren't you gonna ask Benny about *his* kid?" Stella smirked.

"Lord, the poor woman already thinks she's possessed, I don't want to drop that bomb on her right now." Benny sipped his tea, watching Gemma create invisible sigils in the air, then push them towards Lucy's energy centers.

She sprang up from the sofa and the stones fell to the floor. "Why? What happened?"

Stella pounced to deliver the news. "Benny's kid was possessed by one of the Kings of Hell. He spoke Cajun French and we played boo-ray. I almost lost twenty-five years of my life but Father Lucas gave up his priesthood for me. He's a cool guy. The priest, that is. Asmodeus is a dick." Stella shoved a handful of grapes into her mouth and looked like a squirrel gathering acorns.

Benny sighed. "Thanks for easing her in to that information, Stella."

"All that actually happened?" asked Lucy in disbelief. "What about Ash?"

Benny shrugged. "He seems fine. Lucas took off his collar and put it on the table, then Ash just kind of blinked and looked around confused…and that was that. We went home and he's been his normal self."

"I think I'm gonna be sick." Said Lucy.

"Girl, calm down. You ain't got no demon." Reassured Benny.

Gemma collected her stones off the carpet. "I'm not really seeing anything in your aura. It's healthier than most people's, actually. Your sacral chakra is especially active."

Lucy shoved her way past Gemma and bolted down the hallway. They heard her vomiting in the toilet.

"Are you thinking what I'm thinking?" Gemma asked Stella.

"Duh." Another grape. "I knew as soon as I saw her. Her face is fat."

Benny slowly sat his drink down on the end table. He gave a weak smile. "Come on now, girls. You don't think she's…"

Stella put down her bowl. "Damn, Benny. You're white as a ghost. You're not the father, are you?" She winked and stood up.

"No! Of course not! It's just a surprise is all." Benny laughed, his mind preoccupied counting back weeks since Nolan was out of town.

"I mean, not really. Babies are all she ever talks about," said Gemma.

"Can I tell her?" asked Stella, giddy with delight. She didn't wait for an answer and ran off to the bathroom.


Lucy's head hung in the sparkling clean toilet where her groans echoed in her ears. She felt careful hands pull her hair back and tie it in a scrunchie, then heard running water from the bathroom faucet.

"Lulu. Take this and wipe your face." Stella handed her a cold wet washcloth.

She wiped tears, snot, and drool off her face. "Do you think Father Lucas could bless me even if he's not a priest anymore?"

"Nah. I'm pretty sure that demon took all his God-juice." Stella started digging through cabinets and drawers. "Besides, we don't need him anyway."

Lucy lifted her head. "What do you mean?"

"I've seen this kind of evil before. It's the kind of evil that can only come from one place…" Stella found what she was looking for and passed it to Lucy. "A woman's ovaries."

Lucy held the box in her hand dumbfounded. "A pregnancy test?"

"You know, for someone who's been trying to have a baby since forever, you'd think you'd recognize the signs of pregnancy right away," Stella smirked.

"But…but…Nolan was gone while I was ovulating." Lucy stammered.

Stella squinted. "Are you and Benny bangin'?"

"No!" said Lucy.

"For the last time, Stella, I am one hundred percent gay!" Benny from the living room. "AND married."

"You've never introduced me to your husband *or* invited me to your home *Benjamin,* so I don't believe you!" Stella shouted back.

Lucy shoved Stella out of the bathroom. "Will you get out so I can pee?"

"*Real* friends pee in front of each other. Y'all are fake friends! I don't trust none of you hoes." Stella shouted from the other side of the door.

Lucy opened the package and peed on the stick while listening to Benny promise to have Stella over for dinner to meet Christopher. Stella demanded an exact date and time within the next week.

She sat the test on the counter, washed her hands and set a timer for ten minutes on her phone, then opened her fertility tracking calendar. She was ovulating the week Nolan was in Colorado. They'd slept together the night before he left. She didn't know for sure what happened with Tobias, but the evidence was pretty clear to both her and Benny. She's wanted to be pregnant so badly... but what if it wasn't Nolan's child?

The door cracked open. "Cover up your lil' Lucy coochie, I'm comin' in, girl."

Benny wiggled his way in, elbowing Stella away from the door and locking it behind him. He looked down at the test. A faded pink line was already visible. "How long has it been?"

"Five minutes." Lucy was still looking at her calendar.

Benny knelt in front of her and took the phone from her hands. "This moment is going to change your life forever. Having a baby is what you want, right?"

Lucy nodded. Her blotchy red cheeks were streaked with tears.

"Then my advice to you now is the same as it was *then*: keep your mouth shut. Live your life. Be happy. Love your baby. You understand?" said Benny.

She wouldn't look at him.

"Lulu! Listen to me. This wasn't your fault. You don't *have* to keep this baby, but there is still a chance it's Nolan's. I'm here for you no matter what you want to do." Benny smoothed back the hair from her sweaty forehead. "Nothing that happens will leave this room. We can tell Stella and Gemma the test was negative. Pretend to have a ghost living inside you and they won't know the difference."

Lucy picked up the test to check it: two bright pink lines indicating—finally, after all this time—she was pregnant. "I don't know if I'll have another chance. It took so long this time."

"I know how you feel, Lucy. Christopher and I did just about everything but sell our souls for the twins to be born." He said.

She tossed the test in the trash can. "I'm keeping it."

Benny smiled and gave her a tight hug. "Well then...congratulations, Lil' Momma Lulu."

Stella pounded on the door. "I heard happiness! Open up!"

As soon as the door unlocked, Gemma and Stella enveloped Lucy and Benny in a group hug.

"I'm so happy for you, Lucy!" said Gemma. "Have you considered a natural childbirth? I have a friend who is a doula. She does waterbirths where they bring the pool to your house and everything."

"Are you kidding me, *hermana*?" Stella was practically offended on Lucy's behalf. "Why would you want her to suffer? Get out of here with that hippy shit. Childbirth is the worst pain imaginable, Lucy. You'll be in so much pain you pass out in between contractions. Get the epidural. No need to be a hero if modern medicine exists."

Benny's face was muffled in Stella's chest, but he managed to come up for air. "Can we stop hugging and leave the bathroom, please? It smells like vomit in here. Gemma, hit the fan. What's that perfume over there?"

"Chanel Number Five." Said Gemma.

"Of course that's what you wear. What's that cheap shit on the back of the toilet? Spray that. Cucumber melon, Jesus Christ what is this 1997?" said Benny.

"It was a gift." Said Lucy.

"I was a Vanilla Fields girl myself." said Stella.

"Ya'll remember Michael Jordan cologne?" asked Benny.

"I only remember the 'smells like' version from the dollar store my cheap-ass high school boyfriend wore. Smelled like gasoline." Said Stella.


That afternoon, they made brunch together and ate on Lucy's patio to celebrate her pregnancy. They texted all the other to share her good news and within minutes started a group chat to coordinate a baby shower. Lucy knew there was only a fifty percent chance Nolan was the father, but she tried to convince her mind and heart he *one hundred percent was*. It was her dream to have the husband, the white picket fence, and the kids—she almost had it all. That night when Nolan returned from work, she almost told him the news, but stopped herself

Maybe I should wait until I know for sure, she thought.

Lucy chose to be happy. She had everything she ever wanted. She knew her husband would be thrilled to become a father. She scheduled her first checkup and immediately started making lists of baby names. During the day, she was chipper and excited, busy curating the closet full of baby clothes, making lists, and researching obstetricians. Yet in her sleep, the night with Tobias came back to her. A flash of clothes here or there. Laughing, kissing, biting. She'd see images of his face floating above her—one blue eye, one brown. It tormented her. She wanted to confront him. To find out what happened. She wanted him to know she was pregnant.

The most obvious place to search for him was The Inferno Cigar Lounge. She dressed in a modest, yet colorful, suit dress, afraid they wouldn't recognize her in street clothes. They were only open in the evenings, so she waited until six p.m. and approached the door attendant, Joseph. He pretended not to recognize her.

"Welcome to Inferno Lounge, do you have a reservation?" he asked rather coldly.

Lucy plastered on a smile. "Hi Joseph, don't you remember me? I'm Lucy."

"Do you have a reservation, miss?" he asked overly-politely.

"Well, no. I didn't need one last time. I'm just looking for someone. His name is Tobias." She explained.

The attendant didn't move from in front of the door. "I'm sorry, I am unable to disclose any information about our guests."

She grew frustrated a bit faster than usual. "Will you let me in then, so I can look for him myself?"

"I'm sorry, but the lounge is full," Joseph said.

Lucy gestured around the empty street. "It's six p.m. There's no one here!"

He shook his head *no* and stared off into the distance, eyes glazed over, signaling the end of their conversation. Lucy stormed back to her Mercedes and fumed.

Did Tobias blacklist her from the lounge? Who the hell was this guy? There were only two people who might have the answer: Richard and Sarah.

According to Tobias, they hadn't suspected her of stealing the map or spiking their drinks. Maybe she could ask them where he lives, or get his phone number. The only time Lucy had been to their house was for the party, and Stella drove. She pawed through her purse and found the business card with their address on it and entered it into the GPS in her car. It was only a ten-minute drive, so it was worth a shot to find out.

Their home looked less menacing in the daylight. Carefully tended landscaping, birdfeeders, windchimes. They even had a small koi pond near the front door which Lucy missed during her first visit. It was actually a very inviting abode.

Her heels clicked on the cobblestone as she approached the door. She wondered if they had cameras to announce her arrival. She rang the doorbell, and classical music chimed from all angles of the house. After a few minutes, Richard opened the door barefoot with wet hair and wearing a beach towel.

"Lucy! What a surprise! I haven't seen you since the party—can't say I blame you. Must have been bad oysters or something." Richard smiled apologetically. "Come on in. Sorry it took me so long to get to the door. I was swimming in the pool and Sarah's away at some yoga retreat. She's getting certified to teach Kundalini yoga. Have you tried it?"

"No, I can't say I've given any kind of yoga a fair shake." Said Lucy.

Richard removed the towel from his waist to reveal a green speedo, then used it to dry his hair. "Kundalini is this…powerful life force that lives at the base of your spine, coiled up like a snake. If you awaken it, you can use to energy to reach your fullest spiritual potential."

Lucy cocked her head, curious. "How do you awaken it?"

"Meditation, breathwork, yoga, chanting…but for some people it happens spontaneously after a life-changing event. Can I offer you a drink?" He poured himself a double of Kentucky Bourbon.

"No, thank you." Said Lucy.

He smiled and took a sip. "There's nothing quite like a kundalini awakening. It changes your entire perspective on life. Everything suddenly makes sense, even the things that *don't*. It's this overwhelming sense of oneness, like you're plugged in directly to a higher power."

"That sounds nice," Lucy was becoming uncomfortable with Richard's lack of clothing and blatant disregard for the purpose of her visit she had yet to reveal.

Richard nodded. "It's more than nice. It's superhuman. Not everyone can handle the fire, though. It makes some people lose their minds. For others, they get just a *taste* and become overwhelmed or scared of the power. Kundalini awakening is not for faint of heart. It's for people willing to rise above the trivialities of everyday living to see the grander picture, the great plan The Source of All Things has for us." He gestured dramatically with his glass. Lucy wondered if he'd already been drinking before her arrival.

"I see…" Lucy tried to pivot the conversation. "Well, if Sarah starts teaching classes, I'd love to check them out. Who couldn't use a little extra life force?" She forced a polite laugh.

"We all could." Richard switched from drinking bourbon to drinking in Lucy. "And what do I owe the pleasure of your visit, lovely unicorn? Are you inquiring about our next event? I'm afraid it may be a month or two before our guests recover from the last one's excitement."

Lucy nervously fidgeted with the button on her shirt sleeve. "Actually, I was wondering if you could help me get in touch with one of your guests— Tobias. He's a tall, blonde English guy. He loaned me his jacket at the party and I'd like to return it to him."

Richard nearly scowled, and Lucy thought she caught his eye twitch. "Oh, I wouldn't worry about that. He's probably already replaced it."

"I know, I'd just like to thank him properly is all." Lucy pressed.

He put down his drink and strode towards Lucy who still stood a few yards from the door. She thought of forgetting the entire thing and running away.

"Lucy, my beautiful unicorn, you understand that one of rules of these engagements is that *there shall be no socializing outside the events to preserve the privacy of our participants*," Richard said as if he were reciting the U.S. Constitution.

She shifted uncomfortably. Richard noticed, relaxed his shoulders,  and directed her to the sitting room. "Are you feeling alright? You look a little pale. Why don't you sit down a moment?"

Her stomach was starting to cramp. Lucy didn't have morning sickness, she had morning, noon, and night sickness. She hadn't eaten in a few hours. Her empty stomach rumbled from subsisting on only a single yogurt every few hours for the last week. "Sorry, I just feel a bit off today."

Lucy sat in a striped armchair, and Richard pulled up the footrest to sit directly in front of her. Despite still being in a speedo, he opened his legs and rested his elbows on his knees, crouching close, steepling his pointer fingers under his chin. He observed Lucy from under his eyebrows patronizingly. "Tell me, how much do you actually *know* about Tobias?"

It took every ounce of self-control for Lucy to look him in the eyes rather than glance down to see if his balls managed to escape their prison. "Not much, like I said, I just wanted to return his coat. He seemed like a nice guy, and I—"

"Want to get to know him better?" Richard said flatly. "They always do. The pretty ones, that is. I used to be like him, especially in high school. Girls were throwing themselves at me. Then, as you get older, if you're not wealthy… well, women are less interested in middle-aged men with mid-grade careers and a little bit too much around the middle." Richard looked down at his stomach and slapped it. He wasn't fat, but he didn't have etched abs either. "I guess I'm past my prime."

Not knowing what to say, she spat out, "Do you have his phone number or email or any other way to contact him…"

"You know, guys like Tobias will *bleed a woman dry*. They'll take and take until she's nothing but a pale whisp." Richard laid an unwelcome hand on her knee. "You deserve so much better, Lucy."

Lucy wanted to run. She reached for her handbag. "So, do you know where he lives or works or anything so I can stop by and give him his jacket? If not, I better get going." Lucy knew he wasn't going to tell her, but she was attempting to keep the conversation from getting any weirder as she pushed for the exit.

Richard caught her wrist and pulled her back in the chair. "Lucy. Please."

Her eyes grew wide with fear. Richard noticed, so he smiled his dazzling, dimpled best.

"Of course. I have a number for him and the address to his office upstairs in my desk. Why don't you wait right here while I go get it?"

Lucy exhaled deeply as he stood from the ottoman, leaving a wet butt-print in the fabric, and padded barefoot upstairs. She wondered if she should just leave without Tobias's number.

What did he mean by Tobias bleeding a woman dry? It seems like he has his own money, and seemed perfectly gentlemanly. Not codependent or clingy at all.

Lucy thought it almost seemed as if Richard was jealous of Tobias. But why?

Richard's footsteps approached from behind the armchair. "As requested, I have Tobias's phone number and address right here."

He reached around the back of her chair and held the white paper in front of her face.

It was blank.

Lucy turned her head to ask if this was some kind of joke, and using his other arm, held her against the back of the chair. Richard then brought the paper closer to Lucy, and in one rough movement used it to cover her nose and mouth.

That was when she realized it wasn't a blank piece of paper. It was a white cloth.


Why did it smell like nail polish?

# Chapter 25

## Dirty Dick

I've always been a little sadistic.

I remember when I was eight years old, my older sister used to collect tree frogs in a huge pickle jar. She poked holes in the lid for air and filled it with branches. It's kind of a weird hobby for a girl, but she's a biologist now so I guess it makes sense. Anyway, she loved those things, always feeding them bugs and giving them fresh leaves. She kept them outside on the back porch so they could stay warm in the sun. That summer, it was all she ever talked about. She gave them all names and personalities. Then she'd spend hours sketching their pictures in a Lisa Frank notebook. I don't know why, but her joy over those stupid frogs drove me nuts.

That was when I realized I have an uncontrollable urge to destroy things that people love.

Beauty, love, order…repulse me. Now that I'm older I understand that "normal" people enjoy these things, so typically I allow them to exist around me. I'm more careful about choosing moments to indulge my impulses. But as a child of a weak-willed single mother, I had free reign to do whatever the hell I pleased. I took every opportunity I could to cause pain to others. And I quickly learned that the most satisfying pain to inflict was not physical (although I wasn't opposed to that as well). I found the deepest enjoyment in inflicting *emotional* pain. It lasts longer, you see. It festers, it breeds, and it bleeds into other areas of the person's life. Then it affects the people around them. Physical pain is dropping a pebble in a pond–in a few moments the ripples are gone. Emotional pain is like dropping a cinder block. I *really* enjoy the splash.

Every now and then, when I'm tired of listening to my mother whine about how her "family is torn apart", and cry about how she "doesn't understand why Abigail won't come around" and "she's missed her grandchildren growing up"…I just close my eyes and remember the look of utter terror, disgust and heartbreak on my sister's face when she walked out to porch and found me squeezing each and every frog until their guts popped out of their mouths.

Like a puzzle piece sliding into place, that was the magical moment when I knew my life purpose: to make women cry. It felt almost…sacred. To me, it was satisfying in a way that one only experiences when they are fully on the path A Higher Power has laid out for them. Which higher power I serve is probably clear.

The frogs were kind of a last straw for my sister, I guess, especially since my mother never really did anything about my behavior. *His dad was doing coke when I got pregnant* or *It's because of the divorce* is what she said to other people who questioned my tendency towards cruelty. Blame someone else, usually my father's genetics. With my sister though, my mother always blamed *her*.

*He's just a little boy, get over it.*

*Go find more frogs.*

*Why'd you leave them outside where he could reach them?*

I could tell something broke in Abigail. She was fifteen years old at the time, old enough to begin to see the cracks in my mother's reasoning. Old enough for her female intuition to tell her what a rare few pick up on—I'm rotten to the core.

She "gray-rocked" me. Apparently, that's a psychology term for "being so uninteresting to an antagonistic person that they move on from you to obtain a better target". The goal is to not react, not give them access to your emotions. I laugh when I think about it. Gray-rocking doesn't work on me, especially if you've already shown me you *do care* about literally anything. Abigail spent nearly all her teenage years out of the house, or at her friends' places. When she was home, she locked herself in her room. At least she tried to. I would kick and kick at her door until it popped open or came off the hinges. I'd enter triumphantly, grinning maniacally. She'd be standing there with fists raised ready to fight and say "What do you want?!"

I'd just smile and say "Nothing. I just wanted you to know I could get in if I wanted to."

She signed up for the U.S. Navy as soon as she turned eighteen, despite the fact that we were just attacked during 9/11 and war was inevitable. Can you believe that? I fucked up my sister so much that she would rather be on an active-duty warship than be on the same continent as me. She deployed right after high school graduation in May, and completely cut contact with my mother and I. We'd gotten word she'd become a nurse, married, and had a few kids. She eventually went back to college to become a biologist— my mom Googled her and found her research published in some scientific journals online. She built quite a life for herself despite my abuse and my mother's incompetent weakness. Yes, Abigail was my first victim. She was eventually able to sniff out the sociopath in me and eventually got away…but did she *really*? Because of me, she doesn't have a family. No connections to parents or relatives. Her children don't have grandparents, aunts, uncles, cousins. That must be lonely. Because of me, she's forced to live an incredibly private life—no social media, no internet footprint except a faceless entry in a scientific journal that no one except my desperate mother would read. I'm sure she's been to therapy. I'm sure she has to explain why she doesn't have a family to everyone she meets. I'm *pretty sure* I'm still living rent-free in her head, squeezing the life out of her pet frogs and stealing her peace in her nightmares. I'm still winning, even if she doesn't speak to my mother and me anymore.

Abigail saw who I was, but didn't have a choice but to live with me. Some women are luckier and don't get in very deep with me before some inner danger guage starts whirling and guides them in another direction. Instinctually, I think *all women who are honest with themselves* know there's something dark and twisted inside me. Women have incredible intuition, but most ignore it because they secretly enjoy the danger. The small voice inside them says, "This is a bad guy, stop talking to him." But the louder voice says, "Your life is so boring, wouldn't a little bit of danger be fun? How bad could he be?" As they say, girls just wanna have fun. It's true, mostly. Maybe 90 percent of the time, I can pluck my target from the Tree of Life as easily as low-hanging fruit…but every now and then I meet one who knows better. My sister was one. I haven't figured out which Lucy is. I suppose it doesn't matter. It's too late now.

Just like my sister, I'm a bit of a scientist. Over the years I've been experimenting to find the best ways to torture a person.

There are three types of women in my eyes:

1. Smart women who see me for who I am and flee.

2. Victims.

3. Tools.

My mother was my first Tool. Maybe I reminded her of my father who left her, or HER father who left her, but *that woman* would do anything to please me and keep me from leaving her life. Nothing I ever did was *that bad*. Why was everyone so hard on me? My sister is just a moody bitch. My teacher must have it out for me because of my last name. My doctor is just an old quack. "Boys will be boys," she'd say. My mother always gave me what I wanted.

How I felt about her was…well, nothing. I nothing'ed her. How do you feel about a pen you use to write your grocery list? Certainly not love. No, the only thing I love is another person's suffering.

In high school, I found that you catch more flies with honey than vinegar. I became less outwardly aggressive. My first targets were those too weak to fight back; then I worked my way up to more challenging targets. It was a satisfying game of cat and mouse. There were rumors I had a roster of women I'd slept with in high school, and my goal was to sleep with every woman on campus before graduation. It was true, and with the exception of a handful, I conquered Central High. My buddies called me "King Richard the Conqueror". What people *didn't know* was I had another roster of women who filled another desire. My Black Book.

Really, none of this would have been possible without Stephanie. She was my second Tool. Sure, there were plenty of women I used over the years— minor Tools if you will, sort of like a pair of nail clippers: to buy booze and cigarettes when I was underage, to buy me a drink or lunch in the cafeteria, to do my homework…but Stephanie was a machete. She helped with the darker things. Honestly, she wouldn't have been my first choice—she's not exactly arm candy as frumpy, balding, and basic as she is—but she locked me down with her usefulness and unending loyalty. After she found me on her family's property with my third girl the summer before our senior year, I knew I had to make her an offer she couldn't refuse to make her stay silent. It wasn't difficult. I promised to take her to prom; she countered with me being her boyfriend. I agreed, but only if she helped me clean up the blood.

Not exactly a fairy tale coupling, but it works for us. Fellas—find yourself a woman who'll eat chips and salsa in bed at night while watching your favorite show, and the next morning help you bury a body. Or throw it in a pit. That's the secret to our successful twenty-year marriage. Flexibility and variety. Sex parties also help keep things interesting

Stephanie is supremely perceptive when it comes to people. She knows exactly how a person can be utilized, whether for influence in the community or for a little fun at our parties. She can read people like a book. Once in a while, she'll even bring me home a juicy mouse to play with–although I prefer to catch my own. Lucy was a mouse that walked into her trap and ate the cheese. She's so clueless that even after Tobias freed her leg from the trap, she still came back for another nibble.

Fucking Tobias. He always snares the best ones before I've had a chance. Not this time. He's nowhere around to spoil it for me. He never sticks around after the parties for the rituals like the rest. I don't think he really participates in the sex either, at least not in the rooms I've been in. I'm too afraid to ask the others. They all insist he's invited to every event whether he shows or not. He doesn't come to them all, but when the richest and most powerful people in the Ozarks tell you to accommodate someone, you do it. Well, Stephanie and I do. In the grand scheme of things, we're a couple of nobodies. Maybe that's why our parties are so popular. There are no eyes on us, and so few people know about the cave and the power that pulses within.

Tobias knows what we're doing even if he acts like he doesn't. He's so fucking arrogant. I tell him over and over again my name is *Richard*, but he insists on calling me Dick. Stephanie says to let it go because he's British and that's how they shorten the name. Personally, I think, like everyone else, she doesn't want to step on his toes. He's just being an asshole. I wish I knew what he's got on everyone. He acts as if he doesn't need money, power, or influence. Are you fucking kidding me? Everyone wants that. He turns his nose at Crowley's teachings. While we're building energy with sex magick, he's in the sauna drinking all the expensive wine. Just sitting around judging us, probably. Then, he'll usually leave with a woman…and 9 times of 10, it's the one Stephanie invited for me. He does that shit on purpose. I swear he's got it out for me. If he was a woman, I'd have thrown him in the Honey Hole years ago.

Maybe, like my sister's tree frogs, I can get to him another way. How would he feel watching me squeeze the life out of Lucy's gorgeous body? Would he turn the other way as I turned her inside out? I'm not sure. It's obvious she's interested in him, but he must not have taken her home the night of the party… otherwise, she wouldn't be here. They never come back after they've been with Tobias.

Lucy groaned, her head lolled to one side. Her eyes flew open as she regained consciousness. She tried to stand but was held in place by the ropes I used to tie her to my office chair.

"Well, you woke up much faster than I thought you would." I smiled. "I'll be with you in just a minute, darling. I need to make a phone call."

I sat on my desk in front of her, cell phone to my ear and holding eye contact. She flung herself against her restraints fruitlessly. I've been at this thing for 25 years. She's not going anywhere. She screamed herself hoarse through the ball gag while I sharpened each of the pencils on my desk methodically with a manual sharpener, placing them on my desk from longest to shortest.

"Quiet down, please. It's ringing." I scolded. "Tobias, hello…It's Richard. No, *Richard*."

She managed to kick me in the shin. I snapped the pencil I held in my hand in half and threw it across the room. I should have tied her ankles. Lucy stopped screaming, briefly. A whisper of fear passed across her eyes. Delicious.

"So at our last event, we weren't able to complete the ritual because of the whole food poisoning incident, and I—"

Lucy wailed for help through the ball gag, drool bubbling and dripping from the corners of her mouth like a cornered feral cat.

I muted the phone. "Will you *please* be quiet! We haven't even *started* yet and you're carrying on like a banshee."

She screamed louder and tugged at the ropes that tied her wrists to the arms of the chair.

Unmute. Continue sharpening pencils. "—as I was saying, We weren't able to complete the ritual and–lucky enough for us–the Chosen showed right up at my door. I figure we should probably take advantage of this opportunity the Gods have given us."

I heard water dripping and looked down to see Lucy had pissed herself all over the chair. Damnit. I'd just broken that one in, and it's so hard to find a good office chair.

I rolled my eyes and returned to the call. "What? Oh, yeah, that's her. She's restrained but came out of the chloroform a lot faster than I expected. She's a tiny bit mad about it. Aren't you, Lucy?"

Her screams grew shrill and it pierced right into my skull. Ugh. "Yeah, Lucy. The tall blond tradwife-looking one. Yup. It's funny, she was actually here looking for you for some reason."

"Tobias!" she howled.

Something about hearing her scream his name flipped a switch in me. I swept up a handful of newly sharped pencils, and with one quick movement stabbed the bundle into the top of her hand.

There's this beautiful moment of silence between the act that causes severe injury and their brain's registration of pain that is *so* satisfying. Lucy stared in disbelief at her hand, with little pools of blood already beginning to form around the tips of a dozen or so pencils buried deep in her hand. Her wide eyes searched mine.

"Why aren't you screaming anymore, Lucy? Doesn't that hurt?"

Her body shook violently.

I wrapped my hands around the pencils as if I were going to pull them out. Instead, I snapped it sideways, tearing at the thin flesh on the top of her pale, moisturized hand, and leaving pieces of lead inside.

Finally, Lucy wailed.

I picked up the phone again. "Sorry about that, Tobias. What were you saying?"

"What do you mean you don't want to come to the ritual? I thought you were interested in Lucy?" I gave her an exaggerated wink that she didn't notice as she writhed in pain.

"I'm sorry, I can't hear you, Tobias. She's screaming *so* loud right now. Did you just say you don't even *like* her?"

He didn't really say that. I don't know *what* he said because this *cow* knew she was on her way to the slaughterhouse and She. Was. Mooing.

"Hold on one sec, Toby."

If he calls me Dick, I'll call him Toby.

I pulled the bottle of chloroform from my pocket and soaked a dustcloth from my bookshelf. There's no way I could get anything done with her acting like this.

She shook her head no violently, and although she screamed, no words came out as she finally made herself mute. I suppose at this point I didn't need to, but I held the rag over her nose and held it in place for ten seconds until she was out again.

I sighed and returned to my phone call. "Okay, I'm back. No, of course I didn't kill her. I'm waiting for everyone else. Are you coming?"

He asked if we were having a party beforehand. I said no, Sarah's out of town and usually handles that sort of thing, so BYOB. I called everyone else, and with all of them being "busy, important people" they requested the ritual be the following night. Tobias made me promise not to kill her until then. Whatever. I don't know why he thinks I have to obey him.

What could I do with her for twenty-four hours that didn't kill her?


The possibilities were endless.

# Chapter 26

## The Great Escape

The Harvest Moon glowed orange, just barely above the horizon. People screamed as chainsaws revved in the distance. It was warm and dry for an October in Missouri, and the crispy cornstalks scratched against each other in the night breeze. Six-year-old Mateo's stomach flip-flopped with fear and excitement. He's been waiting all week for their visit to Rosewood Farm's annual pumpkin festival. He'd begged his parents relentlessly through hay rides, a pumpkin patch, and the petting zoo until—finally—his mother agreed to let him go through the haunted corn maze when it opened at dusk.

"Fine, but you have to stay with Dad. Don't run off or next year you'll only be doing the little kid maze with the normal clowns and arrows on the ground telling you where to go. You understand Mateenio?" Stella raised her eyebrows at her son.

"*Si*, Mama." He jumped up and down with joy. "Thank you, thank you!"

"Remember, the chainsaws don't have chains on them. They won't hurt you, understand?" said Stella.

He grabbed his father's hand and tugged him toward the entrance. Mateo Sr. planted his feet while his son yanked with all his might. "Estrella, are you sure you're going to be alright? You're so close to your due date I wish we'd have stayed home."

Stella cradled her giant belly and gracelessly squatted down on a straw bale. "I'll be fine. Mattie loves all this spooky shit. Halloween's important to him. Now, why don't you just hand over your red velvet funnel cake, so I can keep it safe for you while you're gone."

He gave it over without hesitation but grumbled. "Aww man...I waited in line for twenty minutes for that, baby."

Stella grinned as she ripped off a chunk and stuffed it in her mouth. "I appreciate you so much, Papi. Your daughter does, too."

"Come *on* Dad!" Mateo complained.

Mateo Sr. bent down and kissed Stella on the forehead, then gave her beachball-belly a light pat.

"Luf ew! Be good Mateenio!" said Stella through a full mouth as her husband and son ran off to catch the next group of visitors being admitted into the maze.

Mateo jumped up and down in his new-but-now-filthy light-up Spongebob sneakers, giggling every time he heard the group before them screaming in the distance. Every few minutes a set of headlights could be seen in the distance, and a horn honked as visitors passed a rusty farm truck. When it was their turn to enter, Mateo Sr. passed the tickets to his son to give the attendant.

"He might be a little young for some of the stuff in there…" the zombie whispered to Mateo Sr, not sure if she should take the tickets from the little boy's hand.

Overhearing, Mateo chimed in. "I'm not scared of anything! Ever! My favorite animal is a bat. I'm not afraid of the dark. AND. I've watched 'Shaun of the Dead' like four times. I can handle it, right Dad?"

He sighed but nodded. "You sure can, kid. Just stay close to me, remember?"

Mateo nodded. "I have my light-up shoes on so you can find me!"

His father laughed. "I can barely see the lights through all that dirt. Alright, let's do this thing. Don't tell your mom if I scream okay? Clowns creep me out."

"Promise." Said Mateo, displaying a grin with one missing front tooth and another halfway out that seemed way too big for his mouth. He stuck out his pinky.

After they hooked pinkies in a pinky-promise, they followed the trail into the maze, with the rest of the group long out of sight.

Mateo and his father laughed as they passed crawling zombies reaching for their legs, vampires rising out of coffins, and the Grim Reaper swinging a plastic scythe. It grew darker and quieter at every fork in the maze, as they chose paths leading further and further from the group.

"Hey kid, I think we better turn around." Mateo Sr. carried his son on his shoulders to get a better vantage point.

Mateo pointed in the distance. "No way, Dad! Don't you hear that oinking? There's a guy in a pig mask on top of a school bus up ahead. Put me down! I'll show you."

"Alright, just a little bit farther though. If we stay out much longer, by the time we get back your mom will be holding your baby sister." Mateo Sr. lifted his son up and over his head. The little boy's legs were kicking in motion before they even touched the ground.

Mateo ran ahead about twenty feet, came to a crossroad, and stopped, looking right and left.

"Son, slow down. Stay right there until I catch up." Mateo Sr. started trotting, knowing—much like his mother—Junior did not have a lot of patience.

"This way, dad!" Mateo shouted, turning right and disappearing.

Mateo Sr. began a full sprint. "Mattie, stop! It's this way! That doesn't seem like part of the maze."

Mateo heard his father approaching closer so ran further ahead in his excitement. He'd never been inside a school bus—his mom always drove him to kindergarten. He'd definitely never been inside one with a murderous pig-face man.

The orange moon blazed, and as Mateo stood mesmerized, he realized it was the only light around him. The snorts and screams from the haunted school bus seemed more distant now, not closer. Where was Dad?

He stomped his sneakers, but the blue and white lights were barely visible under the muck they'd collected in the field. "Dad? I'm over here!"

He listened and stomped his feet like he was in a marching band. Why couldn't Dad find me? He pretended to be a moth and followed the light of the moon to guide his way. All he saw in front of him was corn twice his height. Skritch, scratch, skritch. Distant shouting. Was that him?

Mateo turned and bolted towards his father's frantic calls until something grabbed both his feet and slammed him face-first into the dirt. He screamed hysterically, certain a crawler zombie had been stalking him all night and was about to make a meal of his leg. Then he realized he wasn't being held– he was stuck. Mateo wiggled his foot and, snapping freed of the Velcro, he pulled it out—but his brand new light-up Spongebob shoe was gone. How was that possible?

He yanked his other foot with all his six-year-old strength until suddenly the ground beneath him began to creak and crack. "What the heck?"

The buried cover of the old cistern began to cave in as Mateo scrambled away to the edge, grasping at brittle corn stalk as he fell, effectively concealing his new prison.

He fell ten feet into a dark hole and landed with a splash into an additional foot of slimy black water. He gasped when his back slammed against the floor of the cistern, and filled his lungs with filth. He had enough sense to stand up, then vomited, coughed, and gagged the water from his lungs. Only the tiniest pinprick of light shone through the cornstalks and into the pit. The cistern was a type of darkness he'd never known before. The kind where it didn't matter if your eyes were open or shut. The black stayed the same. Except for the moon. Tiny, tiny moon. It's where he focused his attention when he needed to ignore the squeaks of field mice or the spiders crawling in his hair.

He knew the night had passed when it grew warmer in the cistern and the cornstalks above him were illuminated around the edges as if someone were holding a flashlight behind them.

Something was happening to his ears. They had started to ache, and soon the mouse squeaks grew muffled. Mateo thought they had left. At least he didn't have that to worry about.

Mateo was hungry and thirsty but knew better than to drink the water. He leaned against the wall of the cistern, screaming for help until his voice grew hoarse. When the moon poked through again, the coughing started. By morning his ears pounded in agony and he was hacking up blobs of phlegm and spitting it into the swampwater around him. He phased through shivers and sweat and before he knew it he was sitting submerged in the water nearly to his chin, too weak to stand. How long had he been down here? Why didn't his parents look for him? At six years old, Mateo hadn't thought about death much, but all living creatures seem to have a sense of the end. He thanked his friend– the moon–and closed his eyes knowing he wouldn't open them again.

"*Yelp, yelp yelp, yelp!*" A cornstalk fell from above and into the water, splashing Mateo awake. Dirt fell on his head. He looked up and saw the silhouette of two floppy ears, curly hair, and a pointy nose.

"Bandito?" he mumbled in confusion. "Are you dead, too?"

"*Yelp! Yelp!*"

"*Bandito, what is it? Oh my God! Mateo? Are you down there?!*"

"Mom?" he asked.

"*Hold on! We're coming! Sophia, go get Mattie! Call the police!*"

A baby cried.

The sun shone. Goodbye moon.

He was lifted into the air. Higher and higher, all the wetness dripping off him ten feet below.

Now he's twenty feet above.

His hands are shackled together. He's hanging by his wrists from a hook in the stone ceiling. His shoulders throb in agony, and his right arm is covered in dried blood that collects in his blond hair and feels sticky in his armpit. Below, a man taunts him.

"*Picture yourself in a boat on a river…with tangerine trees and marmalade skies…*" the man sang. "That *does* sound better than where you are right now, doesn't it Lucy?"

Looking down below, all his features seemed blurred. All Mateo could focus on was his eyes. Black and calm, like the sky before a tornado—that moment before it rips everything in its path apart. The moment when the birds stop singing.

Mateo's stomach flopped. That was the look of real evil, not the kind that wears a pig mask and stomps on the roof of an old school bus. Actual evil is felt in the bones, not seen.

Lucy?

Who am I? Where am I?

Through the woman's eyes, he looked around to see candles lit at each point of a pentagram painted onto a stone floor. Limestone everywhere. Symbols carved into stalagmites. *This is The Cheese Cave.*

Lucy…Not the most common name. Isn't that one of mom's friends?

The sun shone.

Mateo was once again lifted

Then dropped

Face first on the cold, tan-speckled tile.

"Get up, asshole. It's your turn to use the shower."

Mateo rolled on his back, his head and nose throbbing from the drop. "Jesus Christ, you didn't need to flip my mattress to wake me up." He groaned.

"I didn't do *shit*, homie." Said his roommate, Tate. "You better not go telling people that. I'm hoping to get my own room soon, on account of good behavior. Your crazy ass rolled out of bed on your own. You talked all goddamn night again, too."

"…sorry about that." Mateo pushed the hair out of his eyes. "Bad dreams I guess."

"Whatever. Nutcase." Tate scoffed as he threw his purposely-thin and unsuffocateable pillow around while making his bed.

Mateo started doing the same before the orderly returned. "Bro, you can't call me nuts. You're here too. We are both literally here because we're crazy."

"Bitch, I ain't crazy. I'm addicted to vaping and my grandma is tired of me stealing from her purse. It was rehab or homeless." He said.

The orderly returned and pushed open the curtain to the shower room.

"Alright, Mateo, your turn to shower. You have to leave the curtain open. I'll be sitting right out here to make sure you're safe."

Mateo grumbled and grabbed a towel and sweatpants off the shelf near his bed. " I keep telling you guys, I'm not suicidal."

"Doesn't matter what you say. It's protocol." The orderly sat in a folding chair just outside the shower room he shared with his roommate, and opened a magazine.

Mateo held out his hand for the orderly to give him a disposable hygiene pack with a toothbrush, toothpaste, floss, and deodorant– all of which required to be returned to the staff at the end of the shower. "Fine…but can he leave the room at least?"

"What you worried about Mateo?" laughed Tate. "Newsflash, we've both seen each other's dicks already because we have to shit with the door open. I'm not scared of your anaconda, son, cuz' you ain't *got* none." Laughed Tate.

"My dick is plenty big enough!" Mateo shouted.

Girls giggled from the common area. *Why did I have to be in a co-ed crazy bin? Girls make every bad situation worse. Nothing but drama.*

Mateo sulked as he showered, scrubbing his body with the tiny sliver of soap and tablespoon of shampoo he was given. His coarse curly hair had transformed into a wild and frizzy mop during his time at Willow Creek Hospital. His mom always bought him the stuff in the purple bottle, and the conditioning spray for curly hair. Mateo never even had to ask; like magic, he always had special shampoo and clean towels in his bathroom. It's stupid the things he missed being in a place like this, where a bar of soap could be carved into a weapon to hurt yourself or someone else.

Unconciously, he had been scrubbing his right arm nearly raw. The memory of the dream came back to him. Mateo flexed his fingers open and closed. For some reason, he was surprised that the tendons in his hand responded to his brain's request. Lucy…

A face—beautiful and expertly painted—passing him in the hallway with an expression of pity. He remembered her for the way she dressed. What were they called? Those women who bake bread and dress like it's the 1950's? His mom had mentioned going to a "networking party" with Lucy. Could this woman really be in the cave, like all the others in his dreams?

Is it happening *now?*

This dream felt as real and traumatizing as the others. A pit in his stomach told him it was true. Every fiber of his being told him this Lucy person—whether it was the same friend of his mom's or not—was being held against her will. He had to talk to his mom, or maybe the police.

Mateo stepped out of the shower, and as he dried himself off, inquired to the shower attendant. "Hey Paul..how much longer do you think I'll be in here? You know…how long do other kids like me stay?"

"You know I can't tell you that, Mateo. That's up to your psych team." Paul said, turning the page in his magazine and acting bored in hopes Mateo would drop it.

"I know," Mateo pulled on his drawstring-less sweatpants. "I mean, in general…how long do people stay?"

Paul sighed and held out a trash can to Mateo. "You probably have a couple more weeks. They need to make sure you're not a danger to others or yourself, that you're on the right medication, and that you will have the right care after discharge."

Mateo dropped his soap sliver, an empty paper cup that held his shampoo, and toothbrush into the can. "Is there any way I can get out early?"

Paul chuckled and collected Mateo's towel and dirty clothes. "You could always climb the fence."

Mateo forced a laugh and slipped on his mom's pink clogs. Those shoes were the envy of every girl in the place. Most kids only had grippy socks to wear, even outside. From what Mateo gathered, a lot of the kids here came from troubled homes. Their parents were just glad for them to be someone else's problem–they didn't give a fuck what their kids wore in here. Most relied on the donation bin of "safe-for-crazies" gray sweatsuits.

The intercom crackled. "Alright, patients. It's the moment you've all been waiting for…*breakfast.* Today's menu is pancake and sausage on a stick, fruit cup, and whole milk. For our vegetarians, breakfast is—"

"Oatmeal…" the patients groaned in unison.

"—after breakfast, you may enjoy the courtyard for fresh air and exercise. Today the attendants are bringing out kickballs."

Tate shoved Mateo out of his way as he left their room to get in line. "Damn Mateo, get your ass in gear. Might ask the doc about switching up your meds, man. You're all spacey."

Mateo followed his roommate to the common area and stood in line behind the same group of "gigglers" who'd overheard Mateo defending the size of his penis.

"Hi Mattie," said one of the girls.

"Hey…" He didn't make eye contact. Vanessa had made it clear she had a thing for him and shadowed him everywhere. Unlike most of the other patients, Mateo wasn't interested in a mental institution romance.

"*Estoy seguro de que tu pene es más que adecuado.*" Vanessa grinned mischievously. She was the only other Latino on the floor and sexually harassed him endlessly in Spanish.

"*Callete!*" Mateo whispered-yelled, looking around to see if anyone overheard and understood.

Vanessa swooped to his side and grabbed his hand in hers. "Will you sit by me today, Mattie?"

He pulled his hand away as the line began to move. Truthfully, Mateo didn't care where he sat. The food was trash and he barely ate anyway. He must have lost at least ten pounds since he'd been admitted. Vanessa mistook his silence as approval and glowed in glee.

In the cafeteria he was handed a small tray of two pancake-and-sausages (without the stick), a sad-looking cup of canned fruit cocktail (his unfortunate serving lacked even one maraschino cherry), a plastic spork, and a small red and white carton of milk. He sat down at the table closest to the courtyard exit. It wasn't long before Vanessa followed him, shooing her friends away to a different table as she approached.

Mateo took a bite of his pancake-and-sausage-not-on-a-stick. It was hard and chewy on the edges as if it had been microwaved too long. Damn, they couldn't even be bothered to bake them? He dropped it to his plate dramatically and opened his milk carton. Vanessa watched him longingly, guzzling his surly sad-boy vibe like lemonade on a hot day…or a carton of whole milk in a mental hospital.

"Why are you here, Mateo?" she asked dreamily.

He sniffed the milk. "My parents think I'm destined to become a serial killer."

Undeterred, Vanessa continued. "Why?" She hadn't touched her food since sitting down.

"I have nightmares of women being murdered, and I draw their pictures." Accepting the milk's level of freshness, Mateo began guzzling the container. It dripped down the sides of his mouth.

Vanessa handed him a paper napkin. "Why? I mean…why do you think you dream of women being murdered?"

Mateo dropped the empty carton on his tray. "I dunno. I think I'm psychic or something, and they're actually murdered. Just not by me."

Her eyes grew wide in wonder. "No shit! That is *so* cool! My *abuela* reads tarot cards and she's psychic as fuck. She knew when all the women in my family were pregnant before they did! The 'gift' is supposed to skip generations, so I guess I'm just waiting for it to kick in or something…"

"Cool." Mateo poked through his fruit cup with the spork, double-checking he didn't miss any cherries before dumping it in the trash.

"Don't you want to know why *I'm* here, Mateo?" she asked sweetly.

"Sure," Mateo said, disinterested. "Man, I would *kill* for an energy drink right now."

Vanessa laughed with just a hint of unease at his word choice. "…yeah, me too. Anyway. I'm here because I was making videos and selling nudes of myself online for money. When my parents found out, they flipped. I told my mom to chill out, it's not like I'm meeting them in person, you know? Besides, how did she think I helped her pay the electricity bill last month? Come on, she knows damn well I didn't get that much birthday money. *Mi familia es muy barrato.*"

Mateo managed a laugh. "Yeah, I get it. Well, I'm gonna go outside now."

"Me too!" Vanessa snatched Mateo's tray from his hands. "I'll take care of your trash for you."

"…thanks." Mateo turned from her and exited the cafeteria. *Why is she so in to me? Maybe she's just lonely or something in this place.*

He looked around him and assessed the fence. Closely spaced vertical steel bars to seven feet, then another three feet of chainlink. Mateo knew he could climb over the chainlink, but climbing up high enough past the vertical bars would require a boost to reach a good place for a grip.

Everything in the yard was permanently affixed to the ground besides the kickballs. *Could he balance on a kickball to get out, kind of like a seal?* Even if he managed before the attendants saw, it probably wasn't high enough.

"Wow, it's a really nice day, isn't it Mattie?" Vanessa grabbed Mateo's hand.

"No touching, Vanessa!" yelled Paul from across the yard.

She grumbled. *"Lo siento, Paulie!"*

"It's Mr. Paul, Vanessa." He reminded her.

Vanessa turned her back on him and crossed her arms, facing Mateo. "Whatever…" she grumbled. "I can't wait to get out of this place. Hey, do you want to hang out after we leave?"

"Sure." He approached the fence and touched the vertical bars to figure out if his feet could get a grip. They were slick silver steel, and possibly oiled.

"Get away from the fence, Mateo!" yelled Paul.

He snapped his hand back. *"Lo siento,* Mr. Paul."

"That guy is such a dick." Said Vanessa. "What *are* you doing, anyway?"

"I'm going to escape." Said Mateo. He knew his mother was trying to get him out, and doubted she would be mad. He could probably call her from wherever and she'd pick him up.

Vanessa's eyes scaled the fence. "Seriously? How are you going to get out? That's too high."

"I thought maybe you could help me." Mateo gave her the smallest of a charming smile, just enough to crack any sense of reserve.

The girl's cheeks flushed red. "Oh, well…how could I do that?"

"You could give me a little boost up, you know? I just need to be able to reach the chainlink and I can pull myself up and over." Cool as a cucumber, Mateo put on a false bravado.

"What about Paul? He's watching us like a hawk." Vanessa pointed out.

"Hmm…" he looked around the courtyard. The Gigglers were also watching them like hawks. "What about your friends? Maybe they could create a distraction."

A moment of sanity snapped into Vanessa's brain. "Wait, wait, wait…I may be young, but if there's one thing I learned from making videos is that you should never do anything for a man for free. What do *I* get out of it?"

Mateo held out his empty hands. "I mean…come on, I don't have any money."

She pointed at his feet. "Give me your pink shoes."

He looked down at her grass-stained, floppy grippy socks, then kicked off his mother's clogs. "No problem."

Vanessa didn't put them on; she continued scowling at him with her arms crossed. "…and one more thing."

"Sure, anything!" Everything in Mateo's soul was telling him he needed to get out of this place.

"I want your phone number," Vanessa smirked.

Mateo groaned internally. *This girl is relentless.* "I don't have a pencil or paper."

Vanessa pulled the dirty socks off her feet and gave them to Mateo. She placed her tiny feet into the pink clogs like Cinderella into a glass slipper and glided across the courtyard to The Gigglers for a brief conversation. Then, she disappeared into the cafeteria.

*Does this mean she's helping me?*

Now barefoot without the clogs, Mateo put on Vanessa's socks. Even clean, wearing other people's socks always feels weird. These were warm and moist with body heat and dew. It was better than nothing, he thought. On the other side of the fence he would have to cross through a field before reaching a newly built cookie-cutter suburb where he hoped to find a way home. He needed something on his feet.

Vanessa returned with a coloring book and crayons, and gestured for him to sit next to her in the grass under the watchful gaze of Paul. She opened the coloring book to an activity page with tic-tac-toe and handed him a blue crayon. "Write down your phone number."

Mateo obeyed and began scribbling his cousin's number.

"Your *real* number," said Vanessa, reading his mind. "Or I will find you on my own."

Mateo scratched out his cousin Julio's number. "If you can find me on your own why do you need my number?"

She raised her overly-plucked eyebrows at him. "Do you want my help or not?"

Mateo wrote his real number at the bottom of the page and handed her back the crayon.

Vanessa nodded, then waved at The Gigglers. Like flipping a switch, they started screaming at each other about some guy named Gavin, and shoved each other until they dramatically collapsed to the ground and rolled around on top of each other. Paul and two other attendants from inside the cafeteria rushed to break the feral girls apart.

"Now's your chance. Let's go!" Vanessa tossed the coloring book and jumped up, running to the fence.

Mateo followed, unable to believe how quickly Vanessa had manipulated her surroundings to get everything she wanted. He was surprised to find himself impressed with the girl he had been shunning for nearly a month. He ran and grabbed the verticle bars, trying to hoist himself up as high as possible.

"No! Not there, idiot! Once you get over the fence, you'll land in a bunch of blackberry vines. Come over here where it's clear." Vanessa crouched down and made a hammock with her hands. "Hurry up, I'll boost you."

Mateo rushed over, and standing in front of her placed his hands on her shoulder and his foot into her intertwined hands.

She planted her feet firmly and clenched her muscles. "Three...two... ONE!"

Vanessa heaved upward with all her might as Mateo leaped and grabbed for the ledge where the steel bar frame met the chainlink. He dangled and nearly lost his grip until Vanessa cradled both his buttcheeks in her hands and pushed up. He strengthened his grasp and used his grippy socks to climb the vertical bars.

Once he made it past the bars, scaling the chainlink was easy; every time he skipped school he would climb the five-foot fence and land with the stealth of a cat on the other side. This was higher. Although he was up and over the other side in a matter of minutes, it was a seven-foot drop from the top of the bars.

"Hurry up, Mateo! Turn around! Don't fall backwards! Bend your knees!" Vanessa coached.

He followed her suggestions, and landed—albeit gracelessly—on a mat of pine needles. Unfortunately, without the benefit of a drawstring on his pants, they fell to his ankles and prevented him from immediately running off.

"Shit!" he pulled up his pants as Vanessa watched helplessly from the other side, stifling a laugh.

"Jesus…come on Mateo, you're gonna get us both in trouble!" She scolded.

He held his pants up and began to run towards the suburb in the distance, but stopped and turned around. "Hey…thanks, Vanessa."

She blew him a kiss, then picked up the coloring book and went inside.


It would be obvious to any onlookers that Mateo had escaped from Willow Creek. The sweatpants. Canary yellow grippy socks. Wild hair. Wide eyes. Fortunately, it was 11 a.m. on a Tuesday. Most people in Creekbed Estates were at work, daycare, or school.

The first row of houses he reached were the newest, unfinished, and empty. He entered a yard through one of the unlocked back gates and immediately searched for a water spigot. He guzzled water from the side of the house as he caught his breath and considered his options. Where the hell was he? They threw him in an ambulance and drove for twenty minutes. He was in some new suburb outside Springfield, but what town?

The first thing person he needed to try was his mother. She might be pissed…but maybe not. Either way, she'd come get him. He peeked into the house. It was bare bones and empty. No one had home phone lines anymore. He snuck around the side of the brick house, hiding behind a newly planted bush, looking for a person who might let him use their phone. Even if someone left a phone inside their car, it's not like he could unlock it. The pool attached to the community center had a sign hanging up saying it was closed for maintenance, so there was no one around. Mateo waited for a car to pass and then bolted like a rabbit from the bushes to the building.

The door—normally requiring a code to open—was propped open with a doorstop presumably while maintenance crews went in and out. Mateo slipped inside and was greeted by the welcome blast of air conditioning.

Televisions could be heard from the gym, as well as the rhythmic thumps of someone running on a treadmill. He passed that room and instead tried the knob on a door labeled *office*. He jiggled it, and finding it unlocked he opened it slowly. He was prepared to feign ignorance if someone was inside, but it was empty. The only lights were a few dots of red and green glowing from a desktop computer and wifi box.

Mateo entered, and locked the door behind him, and turned on a lamp. He opened a mini-fridge in the corner and found a lone Diet Coke and half a turkey sandwich. He ate the food in two bites, sat down in the office chair, and cracked the Coke. On the desk sat a standard office phone with multiple lines. A sticky pad taped to the desk said: 0 for Manager. 3 for Maintenance. 4 for Security. 9 for Outside Line.

Mateo pressed "9", the dialed his mom's number.

He didn't expect her to answer an unknown number, but he left a voicemail.

"It's Junior. I got out, but *do not* call me back on this number. I need you to pick me up. If you get a call from a weird number today, just answer it. It's me. Also…don't call the hospital. They don't know I'm gone. Sorry."

Who else did he know that could drive? Whose number did he have memorized?

Theo.

He was the first of the group to get a cell phone when they were eleven. He dialed Theo from a landline for three more years before he had his own cell. He knew his number by heart.

After three rings he answered. Mateo hadn't heard his voice since the night at the cave.

"…hello?" Theo said with hesitation.

"Don't hang up. It's Mateo." He said.

"…where are you calling me from? My mom said you were in a mental hospital." Said Theo.

*Word travels fast, apparently.* "Well, I was…I'm not anymore. I escaped."

"Are you sure that's a good idea? Don't they need to give you an okay or something?" Theo asked.

Mateo sighed. "Look, I'm not crazy. I think there's something…cursed or haunted about the cave. I've been having all these weird dreams—"

"I believe you." Said Theo.

Mateo was prepared for more of a fight. "What? Really?"

"Yeah…I've seen stuff too." Said Theo.

He breathed a sigh of relief. He hadn't convinced himself fully that he wasn't losing his mind. "Okay, well, look…we can talk about this later but right now I need help. I need you to pick me up."

"I had a concussion. I'm not supposed to drive." Said Theo.

Mateo begged. "Come on, man. There's no one else. I'm in some gated community right outside Willow Creek Hospital. Do you know where that is?"

"No. Hold on, let me check Maps." Theo's end grew quiet, and after a few minutes he returned. "Shit, Mattie, that's like a thirty-minute drive from me."

"Please, Theo. I think somebody might be hurt. I had a dream last night that was just…so real. Please…you owe me." Mateo played the last card he had, guilt. "You punched me in the face, remember?"

"Fine." Theo sighed. "Where exactly *are* you?"

Forty minutes later, Theo's grandfather's ancient pickup rumbled just past the gated entrance to Creekbed Estate. Mateo jumped out from his hiding spot in the ditch and threw himself across the old cracked leather seats. He was taken aback by how thin and somber his normally hulking and good-natured friend looked. "Dang, you look like shit, Theo."

"Nice hair, Mateo." Theo pointed at his friend's feet. "Cool socks, can I borrow them sometime?"

"Grippy socks must be earned. Never given." Mateo smiled, unable to hide the relief he felt at seeing a familiar face.

Theo slapped him on the shoulder. "I missed you, man."

"I missed you, too." Mateo pushed Theo's hand off his shoulder. "Just promise to keep your hands to yourself...I have a whole new respect for your boxing opponents."

Theo grimaced. Mateo didn't know about The Falcon. "Yeah...I'm really sorry about that Mattie. That wasn't me. I mean, *I don't remember doing it.*"

Mateo took in the sickly image of his formerly vital friend. "I believe you...I forgive you, man."

Theo nodded and stuffed down his emotions, straightening his gaze on the road in front of them. "Cool. So where am I taking you?"

"Home." Said Mateo. "I need to get some stuff."


"Isn't it kind of weird we've known each other so long, and I've never been to your house?" Asked Theo, as he scratched behind Bandito's ears.

Mateo rummaged through the refrigerator, opening random storage containers to see what leftovers he could raid. "Empanadas! Heck yeah!" He took the lid off the container and popped it into the microwave. "Yeah, it *is* weird. I guess all of us never really wanted to hang out at our houses is why. It never came up. It's not that I didn't want you over or anything."

"Same." Bandito licked Theo's chin. "You know, you can come over to my place any time you want."

"Cool. You, too." Mateo took two plates out of the cabinet. "You want some, right?"

"Got ketchup?" Theo asked.

"Yeah, but don't let my mom catch you putting that on her food. She considers it an insult." Mateo put three empanadas on each plate, then opened the fridge and handed Theo a bottle of ketchup. Then he took out the last empanada from the container and gave to Bandito, who grabbed it greedily from his hand.

"You know," said Theo, watching Bandito gulp down his food even faster than Mateo was, "for some reason I only ever thought of poodles as girls."

"Everybody does." Said Mateo through a full mouth. "That's why Mom got him the bow-tie collar."

"Makes sense." Theo squirted a swirly mountain of ketchup on his food, then sprinkled it with salt and pepper.

Mateo shook his head in condemnation. "Shameful. My mother's empanadas are a work of art. Come with me, I need to get some supplies."

They took their food with them to the back of the house, Bandito hot on their heels, to a door with a sign of a bumblebee wearing a crown. Across one of the stripes said: Office of the Queen Bee.

Stella's office was where she managed Mateo Sr.'s work projects, as well as their home and family life. But mostly, it was the place she kept all the shit she didn't want her kids to break. The walls were lined with various awards they had earned in school—spelling bee's, track and field, honor roll—but also awards from Stella's former career—a golden high heel with the title of "Pole Princess", two crossing poles that signified the "Double Trouble" award to Star and Storm, and then a hand-painted mug that said *I Love You Mom* with a picture of the moon and stars from Mateo's younger sister.

One of the walls, however, looked like something you'd find in a museum. "Holy shit, why does your mom have an armoury?" asked Theo.

"She likes weird stuff. My dad sometimes does handyman work for people who don't have a lot of money…they'll give him antiques and stuff. He does it cuz' he knows Mom's into it. Her favorite is that Irish Sheleligh over there. It's like 400 years old. Got a loaded head, filled with lead." Said Mateo.

"Hey, kind of like you, Mattie." Theo laughed, and then something caught his eye on the floor. "Isn't that Oliver's backpack? Why does your mom have it?"

Mateo picked it up and put it on the desk. "Honestly, I don't know. Maybe she thought it was mine." He unzipped it and looked inside. "Why is there a bone in here?"

Theo took it from Mateo's hand. "Oh yeah! I forgot about that! All the cheese down there was gross but we found some other cool stuff. Esme thought this might be part of a mammoth jaw. Oh my god…wait…please, please, please…let it be in here…"

Theo rummaged through the bag, and jumped up and down with glee when he reached the bottom, shaking the objects on the wall. Stella's trophies inched dangerously close to the edge of the shelves. When he pulled out a pistol, Mateo took a step back.

"You guys found a *gun*?" Mateo exclaimed.

Theo laid it gently on the desk to fully admire the piece. "Not just any gun, Mateo. This is a ivory-gripped Le Mat. A Grapeshot Revolver."

Mateo shrugged. "This means nothing to me."

"Uncultured swine." Theo gasped dramatically. "It's from the Civil War era…mid 1800's. Super rare. It's got two barrels—one for ball shot and another for a shotgun load. Super deadly…but kind of unpredictable. Could blow your arm off. Anyway, collectors would pay a shit ton for it. My dad would probably sell a kidney for one."

"So you're saying…if we sell this, we would have enough money to go to the Set it Off concert?" said Mateo. So much had happened over the last few months, he almost forgot how it started.

"As much as it pains me to do so…if we sold this gun, we could go to *ten* concerts." His eyes gleamed and he looked like Smeagal with the One Ring.

For a moment, a small fountain of joy sprang from the well in Mateo's heart, reminding him that he was still a teenager. He thought about all the fun he and his friends would have traveling to the big city, watching their favorite band perform all night, and then enjoying the legendary midwestern cuisine of St. Louis. Maybe they would even go down to the lesser-known Graffitti Wall down by the river and take photos for the 'gram.

*Would his friends even want to go?* They've all changed so much in so little time. Even Theo, though *better*, wasn't fully himself yet. There was more important stuff to think about now.

"Listen, Theo…the reason I ran away from the hospital is because I had a dream last night…of a woman being hurt…and I think it's happening *right now*." Mateo picked up the revolver and put it back in the bag.

"Is that why you were in the hospital?" asked Theo. "You dream of stuff?"

Mateo nodded. "It's worse…it's like I become them, and see through their eyes."

"Oh, you mean like remote viewing? I watched a movie about that once, where a psychic goes inside someone's body and can see what they're doing." Said Theo.

"Wait…what I'm doing is a *thing*?" said Mateo.

Theo started inspecting the artifacts mounted on Stella's wall. "It must be, right? Why else would they make a movie about it? Hey, what's that thing?" Theo pointed to a clay sculpture of a human head with oversized ears and a mouthpiece sticking out of the top. "It gives me the creeps."

Mateo moved closer and took it from the shelf. "I dunno…I've never seen it before. You think it's some kind of instrument?"

"Blow in it," Theo said. "let's find out."

Mateo took a deep breath and blew hard into the mouthpiece. A loud wail like a screaming man bounced off the walls of the tiny room. Theo instinctively covered his ears while Bandito barked and ran around in a circle wildly, looking for a place to hide.

After he stopped blowing, he looked at Theo wide-eyed. "Damn, that thing is loud."

"It sounds like a death wail." Said Theo.

Mateo put it in the bag and pointed at the wall. "Hand me that bow and quiver of arrows."

Theo did as he was asked, and handed the weapon over hesitantly. "Are we going hunting, or…?"

"I need to find out if there really is a woman down in the Cheese Cave." Said Mateo as he adjusted the strap on the quiver to fit his body.

"Wait a minute. If you think someone's down in the cave, why not just call the police? I can call my mom right now. She won't judge you." The worry was evident in Theo's voice.

"I can't tell the police. What if I'm wrong? They'll lock me up in a mental institution and throw away the key. I need to prove to myself I'm not crazy." Said Mateo.

"Mattie, you *are* crazy. You're claustrophobic and anxious. You like creepy shit but are afraid of the dark. And that's *cool* bro. We've all got issues, and we live with 'em. You don't need to prove you're sane to anyone, even yourself."

Mateo thought about what Theo was saying. "Maybe you're right. But if the dreams are right, and there's someone down there being tortured by a psychopath, I couldn't live with myself. And what about all those other women I've dreamt about? What if they're down there, too? Or what's left of them anyway…"

Theo hugged himself and rubbed his arms like he was cold. "I'm worried something bad is going to happen to you…like the rest of us."

Mateo scoffed. "I can't get any worse than I already am, right?"

Theo locked eyes with Mateo and his face grew stern. "You'd be surprised."

"I'm going," Mateo replied.

Theo nodded but looked down at the ground.

"We need to hurry up. You can use my mom's shillelagh. It's too heavy for me." Mateo searched the drawers of Stella's desk and found two purple flashlights and a package of sour Mambas which he packed in Oliver's bag.

"I can't go with you, Mattie." Said Theo. "That place did something to me. I almost killed somebody."

"Stop it, Theo. You punched me in the face and knocked me out. You didn't *almost kill me.*" Mateo zipped the bag shut and hoisted it on his back.

"Not you…someone else. I put a guy in a coma. If he ever comes out of it, he won't walk again." The shame Theo felt was palpable.

Mateo was stunned. "Sorry…I…I didn't know."

"I'll drive you, but I won't go inside. I can't." Theo's eyes were red as he spoke and threatened tears,

Mateo knew what this meant. He'd have to go alone. "That's okay. I can do it. I just need to grab a few more things from my room."

Theo waited with Bandito in the living room while Mateo changed his clothes into his favorite devil-horned hoodie, a thick pair of jeans, and combat boots. He grabbed the rosary off his bedpost and slipped it over his head, then shoved his cloud of wirey hair into a black beanie. Bandito used his nose to push open the door and jumped up on Mateo's bed. He started barking.

"It's just a hat, stupid. Calm down." Mateo sprayed deodorant under his arms to help tame his urge to jump in the shower after a day of hiding in bushes. He didn't have time to waste showering.

Mateo went out to meet Theo in the living room, and Bandito followed nearly underfoot, barking and growling.

"What's his problem?" asked Theo.

"Maybe the hat? I dunno. Dogs are dumb." Mateo opened the front door, and Bandito wiggled between their legs, jumped over all three of the porch steps, and bounced and scratched his way up the bumper of Theo's grandpa's truck and into the bed.

"Oh man…he messed up the paint…" Theo rushed to the rear of the truck and ran his finger across four deep scratches down to the primer. "I guess I could say it was a shopping cart or something…Grandpa's gonna kill me."

"Bandito! Get out of there! Go inside!" Mateo yelled from the porch, holding the door open.

"rrrr RUFF!" the dog replied, shaking his shaggy head.

"Now, Bandito!" Mateo commanded.

Bandito growled.

"You want me to grab him?" asked Theo.

Mateo shrugged. "Sure. He normally listens, I guess he's decided to be a dick today."

Theo stepped up on the bumper and into the bed of the truck. Bandito stood in fight stance, growling at Mateo as Theo approached him from behind with his hands out.

As Theo closed in on Bandito's curly midsection, the dog whipped around and bit Theo on the hand. He leaped over the side of the truck bed cradling his hand. "Son of a bitch! He bit me."

"Lemme see." Mateo inspected his hand—four puncture wounds from Bandito's canine teeth wept blood.

"Jesus, Bandito..." he scolded his snarling dog. "I'm sorry dude, I don't know what to do."

Theo grumbled, mumbling something about a fire extinguisher, and pressed his t-shirt against his hand to slow the bleeding.


Approaching Bandito slowly, Mateo tossed the backpack, Osage bow, and quiver into the bed of the truck with his dog. He stopped growling and laid down.

"Well...I guess Bandito's coming with us."

# Chapter 27

# Lucy in the Sky with Diamonds

*Picture yourself in a boat on a river*

*With tangerine trees and marmalade skies*

Did you take your medicine, Lucy?

You're so hard to handle.

I've only had to drug someone once before, and that was a man. He was bigger than me.

You're a little wildcat, Lucy. You know, there's actually a few down here. Sometimes I see their prints or evidence of their kills.

Hell, they probably think the same about me.

Anyway, the last time I drugged somebody was with heroin, not LSD. Since he was bigger than me, I had to use the chloroform *first*. Then I just let Big H do its work…doesn't take much for someone clean. Their body's not used to it. I don't usually kill men; it's just not as fun for me, you know? But I had to. He caught me with one of my girls. My wife gave me the okay even though he's her brother. She said, *he knows the rules…always call before coming over*. He made his choice and suffered the consequences.

You know a little bit about that, don't you Lucy?

Should've called first. Ahh, well, even if you called I can't say the outcome would have been any different. I had you tagged in my mind since the moment we met. I knew if I saw you again I would do anything to keep you.

It was your name that inspired me this evening…a lyric kept repeating in my head *Lucy in the sky, with diamonds*…it bugged me so much that I called up Stephanie. I said babe, I've got Lucy over here for playtime, what is that song that goes *Lucy in the sky with diamonds*? She knew right away. Can you believe it, it's The Beatles? I'm more of a grunge rock guy myself. She was a little upset with me at first because I'm playing without her, but *she knows how I am*. If I get the itch, I gotta scratch it.

So some people think that Lucy in the Sky with Diamonds is a code for LSD, because the song is total nonsense. The Beatles, of course, deny this...but come on. "Rocking horse people eating marshmallow pies"? What does that even mean?

I told Stephanie you were giving me a hard time so she suggested I check The Stash. I practically have a pharmacy back at the house, little leftovers, and gifts from our guests. Sure enough, way in the back was some LSD. How do you feel, Lucy? I'm not sure how it works on pain. That hand looks like it stings a bit.

So the chorus is just the same thing, over and over. *Lucy in the sky with diamonds*. So I thought it might be fun to put you in the sky. Lucy, wake up, or you'll miss the fun. Come on, now, my little *girl with kaleidoscope eyes*. I'm gonna take off this tape now so you can sing along with me. Are you ready? I'm going to tell you the rules of the game.

There you go...*gross*, did you throw up in your mouth? No, no, no... shh...no screaming or you'll scare the bats. We'll save that fun for later. First, we are going to play a game I call "Lucy in the Sky with Diamonds". How this works is I'm going to put these shackles on your wrists, then tie a rope around the center chain, and hoist you up in the air using that pully system. You'll be hanging, oh, twenty feet or so above me. That pulley's an old relic from when this place was being mined...I've used it with my girls a few times. I'm getting older and my back's not as good as it used to be, so I save it for the really special ones, like you.

So what we're going to do is, I'll sing one line of the song, and then you sing the next. Do you know *Lucy in the Sky with Diamonds* by The Beatles? No? Are you sure? I thought I didn't know the song either, but it turns out *I did know it* just from hearing it on the radio or whatever. Maybe it will come back to you as we play the game. For your sake, I hope it does. See, for every line you don't know, I get to throw a "diamond" at you. Down here, there aren't any diamonds, but there's certainly a lot of chunks of limestone, so I'm going to use those. Sound good? Are you ready? Up we go...

Is that clamp too tight on your wrist? Yeah, I bet that does hurt since you're already injured. Don't worry, pretty soon all the blood will rush downward and you probably won't feel anything. What do I know? I've never done LSD. You tell me. Do you still feel pain, Lucy? What did you say? Was that a yes? Hmm, that's a shame. Alright, let's get started. I already sang you this part, so I'm giving you a freebie…

*Picture yourself in a boat on a river…*

Sing louder, Lucy, I can't hear you. I've got my diamond picked out and everything. It's a big one.

…that's correct! Tangerine trees and marmalade skies! My turn.

*Somebody calls you, you answer quite slowly…*

Did you say you don't know? Too bad.

Ouch, right in the thigh. That's gonna leave a nasty bruise. You have great legs, by the way, Lucy. The correct lyric was *a girl with kaleidoscope eyes.*

*Cellophane flowers of yellow and green…*

Come on, Lucy! You aren't even trying! *Towering over your head.* I'll give you a pass on that one.

*Look for the girl with the sun in her eyes…*

Yes, yes! *And she's gone.* This next part is easy. *Lucy in the Sky with Diamonds.*

Now you.

*Lucy in the sky with diamonds!*

Next verse. My turn.

*Follow her down to a bridge by a fountain…*

That's incorrect, Lucy. It's the other way around. *Rocking horse people and marshmallow pies.*

Incoming! Wow, think I broke a rib with that one! Hopefully, you can still sing.

*Everyone smiles as you drift past the flowers…*

No? You don't have anything? The correct lyric is *that grow so incredibly high.*

Well, shit. I clipped her in the head. I should've aimed for the stomach…I'm losing her.

"Lucy, wake up."

Lucy's eyes fluttered. Well, one did. The other was swollen and crusted over with blood. Her shoulders ached so badly she wondered if they were dislocated.

"Does that asshole ever shut up? If he's gonna kill you, get it over with. He just likes to hear himself talk. Typical narcissist."

"Goldie?" Lucy choked out a sob. "Are you taking me to heaven?"

"I wish. I haven't quite made it there myself yet for some reason. I've just been following you around."

From Lucy's vantage point, she couldn't find Richard anywhere below. She twisted her body to look behind her. Her chest crunched with the movement. She moaned in pain.

"After you passed out, he got bored and went home. I think he's eating dinner. You've probably got an hour or two before he comes back."

"Goldie…" Lucy slurred through a fat lip. "Where are you? I can't see you."

"Of course you can't see me, I'm dead! I guess that wallup to the noggin makes it so you can hear me at least. So tell me, girl, do you want to get out of here or not?"

She looked down at the twenty-foot drop. "How? Even if I get my hands free, I may not survive the fall."

"True," said Goldie. "When you fall, you may die…but if you live—even if you're hurt—there's potential to survive another day and possibly escape. One thing I can tell you for certain is this: if you stay where you are now, you'll be tortured another day or two before they kill you. Then you'll have plenty of new friends to keep you company as a ghost."

"…are there a lot, Goldie?" Lucy asked, afraid of the answer.

"There are *dozens*. And you won't be the last. If you get out of here, you can stop him…and give the rest justice."

"I'm scared." Lucy cried.

"I know, baby. You *should* be scared. You gotta do it anyway."

Lucy sniffed. "…how?"

"I see you are wearing that beautiful ring I left to Nolan. Have you figured out its secret yet?"

Lucy tried to look up at her hands. They were white like the hands of a corpse. She could still feel the weight of the garnet ring on her finger. "What secret? It's Victorian, that's all I know."

"That is a Victorian *bracelet* ring. There's an itty bitty clasp on the back of the centerpiece. I want you to take off the ring, and open it into a bracelet."

Lucy twisted her hands closer together and wiggled it off the ring finger of her left hand. The problem was, only the thumb and first finger of her right hand were working. She held the ring carefully between the two fingers. "What's wrong with my hand? Why won't my fingers work?"

"Oh honey…he severed your tendons when he stabbed you with those pencils. Don't worry about it. You still have two good fingers on that hand and can get the rest fixed later. Now go ahead and open it. Flip that clasp."

Lucy held the ring still with the two good fingers of her left hand while using her right to flip the clasp. She pulled the ring apart and it unfolded accordian-style into a series of thin, interlocking circles.

"The metal is very delicate…try your best to twist it into a pick shape to see if we can get at this janky old lock. Don't worry about damaging it, Lucy. Nolan wants you alive more than he wants that ring, you understand?"

Tears streaming down her face, Lucy nodded as Goldie read her mind. She twisted the metal and it gave way with little effort. She watched as the garnet and enamel centerpiece broke off and fell into oblivion. Somehow she managed to finagle a toothpick-shaped piece from the rest.

"Good. Now these old locks are real easy to pick. Just wiggle it around until you find the lever and push up."

She immediately stuck the pick in the lock of her manacle when Goldie stopped her.

"Hold on, hold on…just a minute. When you fall, try to land on your right side, okay?"

"But what about my right hand? It's all mangled." Lucy asked.

"I know, sweetie. But your ribs are broken on the left side and could puncture your organs. You understand?"

Lucy took a deep breath as if it were her last. Without much effort, she found the internal lever, pushed it, and with a click, her right arm was free. Her left wrist screamed in agony as the entirety of her body weight swung from one point. Quickly she used her two working fingers to pick at the cuff of her right hand.

She found it, pushed the lever, and closed her eyes.

# Chapter 28

## The Brave Banditos

"If you're not out in a few hours, I'm calling my mom. Got it? I don't care if we get in trouble." Said Theo.

Mateo readjusted Oliver's tactical bag and the quiver of arrows on his back. He wasn't quite sure what to do with the bow and dangled it clumsily at his side.

"Got it." Said Mateo. His voice was shaking.

"Do you even know how to use that thing?" Theo pointed at the bow.

"I mean…I'm more proficient in profanities as an offensive attack, but I've messed around with it in the yard before. I've shot really close the the bullseye a few times."

"I think you're better off with Osage Oranges than an Osage bow. Didn't you learn anything playing Dungeons & Dragons? You need something for close combat in a cave. Bows are for long-range attacks." Theo teased in an attempt to ease Mateo's anxiety.

"My mom's shillalegh's too heavy." Mateo shrugged.

"Weakling." Theo laughed. "When you get out of there, we need to start hitting the gym together, okay? I can whip your skinny ass into shape in 3 months."

"Yeah, right." Mateo looked down at Bandito, who stared up at him lovingly, his tongue lolled out to the side as he panted. "Damn, I didn't bring any water for Bandito. All I have are energy drinks."

"A killer like him doesn't need water," Theo laughed and reached under the driver's seat, pulling out a gallon of water. "I got you. The truck leaks radiator fluid sometimes and I've gotta fill it up with water to make it home."

Mateo put the half-full gallon of water in his bag. "Thanks, man. See you in a few."

"Don't get possessed." Theo waved as Mateo trekked through the field towards the cave entrance. "Have a good day at school, son!"

"Thanks, Dad!" Mateo laughed, and for a moment his heart felt light. As he turned away from his friend and was swallowed by the waist-high weeds, it didn't take long to remember why he was there– someone could be in danger. Reality fell like a boulder on his shoulders. If he actually was "remote viewing", Mateo was about to walk into a lion's den.

He reached the limestone hill and pulled aside the rusty grate. He wasn't worried about getting lost—he'd looked at it so often he had it memorized. Mateo tried to draw it again from memory, then gave a detailed copy of the route he planned to take to Theo. The problem was Mateo had no idea what he was looking for. He was literally and figuratively wandering in the dark.

"It's your last chance, Bandito. You can go back to the truck if you want to." Mateo said to his companion.

In response, the dog descended into the cave ahead of him. "Hold on, Bandito. You need a light."

Mateo pulled out a headlamp on an elastic band he'd found in Oliver's bag, clicked it on, and fastened it around Bandito's neck like a collar. "There you go. Now you can see where you're going."

He put on a headlamp and also turned on his mom's purple flashlight. As descended the stone steps, all things considered, he was doing alright. He kept reminding himself that if Lucy was down here, she was in worse shape than he was–he was the only person who could help her.

The two Xanax he took before leaving the house also helped.

The first landmark they reached in the cave was the signature wall. Theo told him all about it, and how they found the signature of Jesse James. Mateo was a much smaller frame than Theo and navigated it easily. He didn't stop to read the signatures and at the end, the corridor branched off left and right. Theo told him to watch out for bats. He turned off his headlamp and aimed it at the floor. His flashlight caught black writing on the wall.

*Sempre Revertum.*

Isn't that the U.S. Marine motto?

Mateo listened quietly for any disturbance among the bats, but they squeaked peacefully. Still, Bandito's ears perked. He stood frozen at attention facing the lefthand path.

"Bandito…don't do it. We're going right, not left. It's just a rat or something." Mateo wished he'd brought a leash.

Of course, Bandito darted left.

Mateo followed close behind, watching as Bandito's headlamp climbed upwards to an elevated portion of the cave. "Bandito! Stop!"

Finally, Bandito stopped, but this time Mateo also heard what his dog did: singing.

*Lucy…in the skyyy…with diamonds…Lucy in the sky with diamonds…*over and over the same six words repeated.

Was it her?

Bandito continued down the corridor, and Mateo fully surrendered to the dog's lead. At first, he appeared to be using only his sense of sound to guide him, but now Bandito was also sniffing the ground. He was definitely on the scent of something, and the singing was becoming more clear. Bandito and Mateo slowed as they turned a corner and were met by the soft glow of candlelight flickered on the walls. Mateo couldn't help but be surprised by how bright a single candle could be in a completely darkened room.

"*Lucy in the sky with diamonds…Lucy…Lucy in the sky…with diamonds…*" a small form sang weakly from the ground.

Bandito approached cautiously, illuminating a bloody mass of blond hair with his headlamp collar.

It was her.

Mateo's hands shook as he lifted his flashlight towards her.

If Lucy's here, that means his dreams are real. So are the murdered women.

And the killer.

The hair on the back of his neck stood up, but he snapped back to reality and rushed to Bandito's side where he carefully licked at the woman's face.

"Goldie…Goldie, who's this? Why is there a dog?"

Mateo moved into her line of sight and pushed back her hair so she could see him. She had a bloody egg on her head and her eye was swollen shut. "Are you Lucy?"

"Yes…that's me…I am *Lucy in the Sky…with Diamonds.*" She mumbled.

"My name is Mateo. I'm going to help you." He shone his flashlight on her busted up body. Her right arm was underneath her and twisted at an unnatural angle.

"Mateo…hey, *I know you…* are you Stella's boy? You look just like her…she has *way* better hair though…" Lucy tried to sit up, but couldn't manage to get the right leverage to move off her side with a bent and broken arm trapped beneath her.

Mateo pulled her up and held her stead as she sat upright. There's no way he could make her walk yet. His flashlight caught the rope attached to the wall, and he followed it up to the ceiling with his light until it reached the pully and dangling manacles. "Oh my God…did you fall from all the way up there?"

"I set myself free. Otherwise, he's going to kill me. He's probably going to sacrifice me to Satan…or Aleistar Crowley. *Tobias wouldn't help me.* Goldie did though." Lucy was in a daze of LSD and trauma.

"I don't know who any of those people are…well, except Satan. So this man, the man who did this to you, where is he now?" Mateo asked as he opened his backpack.

"He'll be back soon. Goldie says we need to leave. She says *I need to get my ass up off the ground right now."* Said Lucy attempting to stand.

The woman shivered in the 50-degree cave. She probably hadn't eaten or drank in days, and was clearly under the influence of some sort of sedative. Mateo took off his hoodie and gently put it over Lucy's head. He helped her feed the arm that wasn't broken through a sleeve and left the other loose. Then he took off his beanie and put it on her head.

"Thank you, Mateo. It is a little cold in here." Lucy wobbled but was now able to hold herself up in a sitting position without support.

Mateo reached in his bag and cracked open two energy drinks. He passed one to Lucy whose hand shook violently and splashed as she attempted to hold it to her mouth.

"Let me help." Mateo took the drink from her and held it to her lips. As soon as the orange liquid touched her tongue, she began to swallow greedily until the entire can was empty.

"Do you have any food?" She asked, exasperated.

"My mom's tamales. They're a little spicy though. Well, 'white people' spicy." Mateo unwrapped one from its corn husk wrapper and held it up while she ate it like a baby bird.

"Give me the other one." She said.

Mateo unwrapped it and handed it to her. This time Lucy fed herself.

Bandito sniffed at the corn husk wrapper on the ground, licked it, and sneezed from the spice. He began casing the rest of the room, stopped, and fixated on something.

Lucy gestured for Mateo's other energy drink, which he gave to her before crawling over to where Bandito sniffed, fixated on the ground.

"What'd you find Bandito?" Mateo shone his light at the ground and it bounced on something purplish red and shiny. "Looks like some kind of jewelry."

Lucy belched, trying not to throw up from the sudden intake of spicy food and energy drinks. "Is it my ring?...oh my God, my ring...bring it here, please...oh thank you, thank you..." Lucy cried as Mateo handed it to her, and she put it in the pouch of his hoodie. Suddenly Lucy froze.

"...what's wrong?" asked Mateo.

"He's coming...Goldie says he's coming. We have to go. There's no way out of this room. She says we have to go the way you came in." Lucy pushed with all her might to her feet but continued to collapse. "Something's wrong...I think...I think my hip is broken." She seemed to resign to her end. "Go. Just go on without me, and tell the police! I'll be gone before they get here...but at least he won't do it again."

"Absolutely not," said Mateo. "No way am I leaving you here to die with that monster. I'll carry you as far as I can…and if we meet him, well…I'll deal with it." Mateo reached down and pulled Lucy to her feet but she was completely dead weight. Maybe he could go back and convince Theo to help carry her out.

*"Newspaper taxis appear on the shore, waiting to take you away. Climb in the back with your head in the clouds and you're gone…"*

Bandito made a low growl at the cavern entrance.

"Goldie says he's almost here…" Lucy whispered in his ear. "Put me down, Mateo. You have to fight, or he'll kill you too."

*He'll kill you, too.*

He sat Lucy down gently and picked up his bow. He removed an arrow from the quiver and prepared to notch it in the string. Then his eyes caught a glimpse of the Aztec Death Whistle in his bag.

"Lucy, I have an idea…I'm going to try to scare him off." Mateo dropped the bow to the ground and readied himself to blow the whistle. Lucy watched him through sad eyes that seemed to surrender not only her fate but Mateo's as well.

He took a breath, filling his lungs as deeply as he could, and blew hard into the whistle. A deafening cacophony of ghost wails screamed and echoed through the chamber.

The singing stopped.

*What the hell?* The man said.

Bandito growled and rushed off into the dark.

"Bandito, no!" Mateo yelled.

Bandito's growls grew muffled as he descended into the cave towards Richard. Mateo ran back to his supplies, reattached his headlamp, and notched his bow.

*Fucking mountain lions.*

A click.

A gunshot.

A yelp.

"No!" Mateo cried into the darkness.

*A dog?*

*Hey! Who's back there? The ritual's not until tomorrow!*

"I'm going to kill you!" Mateo screamed, wiping angry tears of grief from his eyes and charging into the dark.

A hand grabbed the back of his shirt and yanked him back. "No, you're not."

Mateo froze.

"You're going to turn around, go back to Lucy, and let me handle it. Do you understand?"

Mateo couldn't help but obey the voice's commands. He dropped the bow.

Two steady hands turned Mateo around into the pitch black until his headlamp illuminated the face of a blonde-haired man he'd never met before.

A man with one blue eye and one brown.

# Chapter 29

## The Devil Wears a Suit and Tie

"Good evening, Dick."

"You don't strike me as a poodle sort of guy, Toby." Richard holstered his gun and wiped the gunpowder from his hands onto his pants.

"It's *doctor*, actually," Tobias stalked towards Richard, hands behind his back to conceal a twelve-inch ancient ritual athame.

"Doctor Tobias?" Richard sneered.

Tobias stopped at an eight-foot distance. Most people can't lunge farther than that. Shooting is another matter. He noticed Richard was now standing *enguard*.

"Doctor Tobias Vale."

Richard clocked that Tobias was hiding his hands. He leaned against the cave wall in an attempt to seem casual, but his eyes bounced wildly around the room calculating the ways Tobias posed a threat. "And what exactly are you a doctor *of?*"

"Psychology." Tobias gave a lopsided grin. "Would you like to book a session, Dick?"

Richard flinched at the use of that nickname. "I don't need a shrink."

"The woman you had hanging from the ceiling might argue otherwise." Tobias gestured behind him to the ritual room.

"That?" Richard laughed. "That's just a bit of fun before the ritual. Are you coming this time? Lucy seems to have an interest in you."

"I don't need to beg heaven and hell for money and power. I have plenty already." Tobias tightened his grip on the golden hilt. "No need to sacrifice beautiful women on my behalf."

Richard's eye twitched. "Then why are you here, *Doctor Vale*?"

"I'm here for something much more important than money or power, Dick." Tobias cocked his head, almost in a challenge. "I'm here for revenge."

"Revenge?" Richard forced a laugh, but his hand floated near the pistol at his side. "You can't be here to avenge *Lucy*? You know as well as I do that women like her are a dime a dozen if you can afford to keep them happy. I don't *like* you because you're an arrogant British twat, but what did I ever do to you worthy of revenge?"

"*You*? You are nothing to me. What dragon could die from the bite of a snake?" Tobias took a step forward, closing the distance between them. "I don't need revenge against you, Dick. You could spit in my face right now, and frankly, I wouldn't give a fuck."

Richard struggled to conceal the fear bubbling up inside him. "Okay, well…I'm the only one here, so…"

"You're not, though." Tobias took another step forward and watched Richard squirm and fight against his basic human instinct to flee a creature with hidden claws and fangs. "What about those voices in your head, Dick? Are you sad they don't talk to you anymore? Have they moved on to someone stronger…someone *younger* perhaps? Is that why you kill all those women? Are you trying to make Big Demon Daddy happy so he'll give you special mojo again?"

Even in the dim light of the lamp, Tobias could see Richard's face had grown pale. The poodle lay at his feet, its spongy white fur now absorbed in red. "I don't know what you're talking about."

"Yes, you do. You were Chosen, decades ago. And now you're not. Tale as old as time." Tobias showed his knife. "You're an old dog now. An old dog who sold his soul to an owner that no longer has a use for him."

Richard pulled out his gun, but his shaking hands dropped it. "Are you…*him*?"

"Oh, no, not at all. In this era, I am merely the psychologist for men like you. I let them vent and give generic advice. I keep their secrets, and in exchange, they give me enough money to live comfortably and *access* to all the people and places I need." Tobias moved forward.

Richard moved back.

"What do you want from me? I don't have money…or access to anything! I'm a nobody!" Richard defended himself.

"That's where you're wrong, Dick." Tobias held the athame up so it was level with Richard's face. "You have access."

"To what?!" Richard yelled.

"Big Daddy Demon…Asmodeus." Tobias leaped towards Richard, slicing his face.

Richard screamed, and ran through the corridor towards the cave exit, using his hands to feel the walls and guide his way. "Why kill me?" he pleaded. "I can show you the ritual rooms…give you access to ancient books…help you summon him yourself! You don't need me!"

There was a finger snap, and Tobias appeared in front of Richard, his outstretched hand holding a ball of light. "You're right, Dick. I don't have to kill *you*. I could use any of his followers, but the fact is…*I just don't like you.*"

He plunged the athame into Richard's chest, and he collapsed to the ground. Tobias stood above him, watching blankly as he groaned and gurgled the blood in his mouth. "Dick, I'm going to leave that athame in place for now because as soon as I remove it, you're going to bleed out. I'd like you awake for this next part. Do you have a knife on you I could borrow, old chap?"

Richard coughed and blood spattered all over his own face.

"Alright, then. I'll get it myself."

Tobias patted Richard's pockets and pulled out a red Swiss Army Knife. "Which tool to use…whoops, that's a can opener…corkscrew. Hey, do you sharpen your knives? I hope so. I think I need to make quick work of this. You're almost dead, and I want you to suffer at least a *little* longer for what you've done to Lucy."

Richard cried and groaned, reaching for the athame.

Tobias slapped his hand away. "Don't do that! I told! If you take that out, you'll be dead in ten seconds."

Richard reached for the knife again.

Tobias smiled. "Oh, I see. You *want* to die." Tobias opened the pocket knife to the largest blade. "That's too bad. You've got maybe five or ten more minutes at least. Ol' Raf told me I need *three things* from one of his followers: a gallbladder, a liver, and a heart. You *do* have a heart, don't you? At least from an anatomical perspective?"

Richard screamed.

Tobias stabbed the pocket knife into Richard's stomach. "Well, I guess I'll start with the gallbladder, then we'll move a little bit next door and get the liver. I'll save the heart for last…probably have to use the athame for that…this pocket knife is about as dull as your wife. Seriously, man. What do you see in her?"

Richard's screams echoed through the corridor and into the ritual chamber where Lucy lay collapsed on the floor. Mateo stood at the entrance with his bow drawn.

"What's happening, Mateo?" asked Lucy.

"Some guy…he told me to go back…and now the man that hurt you… that's him screaming…" Mateo's voice quivered.

"Who was the guy? What did he look like?" Lucy tried to sit up.

"Tall…blonde…two different colored eyes." Mateo's eyes never left the entrance. He didn't know what to expect around that corner except his dead dog.

"Tobias…" Lucy whispered. "He came to help me."


Twenty minutes passed before the screaming stopped, and quick footsteps approached.

Mateo planted his feet and pulled back the arrow. "Stop right there or you'll get an arrow in your eye!"

"Oh will I?" A voice from behind him whispered in his ear.

Mateo jumped and the arrow dropped to the ground.

The man's cold laughter filled the room. "Put down your weapon, boy. Not that you know how to use it. You've got the wrong foot forward."

"Get away from her!" Mateo shouted, re-notching his arrow and pulling it back.

Lucy sat up as Tobias approached her. "It's okay Mateo...he won't hurt me. I think..."

Slowly, Mateo lowered his bow. *Did this guy just apparate?*

"I'm afraid I can't stay long, Lucy. I have a package about to expire. However, I will help you and your young hero find the exit." Tobias effortlessly lifted Lucy, then drew a symbol in the air with his hand. "Why don't you get one side and I'll get the other?"

"One of her arms is broken pretty badly. There's no way to hold her under her shoulders without hurting her." Said Mateo.

"I see. She'll have to be carried out like a baby then. You seem like a strong young man, why don't you carry Lucy and I'll get your gear?" Tobias held out his hand for the backpack.

"Come on man, you know I'm not strong enough to carry Lucy. I can barely pick up my little brother. You're twice my size, why can't you do it?" pointed out Mateo.

A light burst from Tobias's palm, revealing the fullness of his interaction with Richard. He was covered head to toe in blood and black liquid.

"As you can see, I am a bit of a mess right now." Tobias raised his eyebrows at Mateo, who–though shocked by the blood—was completely mesmerized by the ball of light hovering in his hand. "Besides, you may find that she is significantly lighter than previously."

Mateo squinted. "What do you mean?"

"You're asking a man who just summoned light to his hand how he could make something less heavy than it actually is?" Tobias made a fist and they were once again surrounded by dim candlelight and Mateo's headlamp.

Mateo gave his bag, bow, and quiver to Tobias, then carefully picked up Lucy like a bag of potatoes. She wrapped her uninjured arm around his neck and slipped in and out of consciousness as they left the ritual room.

"Your deodorant smells nice Mateo." Said Lucy.

"Thanks."

As they carefully traversed the corridor, Tobias cleared his throat to get his attention. "I would suggest averting your eyes as we round the bend. Lucy, now would be a great time to take a nap."

He waved his hand in front of her eyes, and she drifted off peacefully in Mateo's arms just as bloody footprints turned to puddles, then puddles to piles of flesh.

"I'm afraid to say your dog has passed…he's up ahead." Tobias kept his tone emotionless.

Mateo chose not to look down. Although he died a hero, he didn't want to remember Bandito's death. He wanted to remember his oldest friend at his best: shamelessly snoring upside down on the sofa, balls to the wind. He only regretted he wasn't brave enough to bring Bandito's body home for Mom to bury properly.

They reached the end of the corridor, and Mateo recognized the signature wall. It was difficult, but he was able to squirm sideways with Lucy in his arms, holding her like a hotdog in front of him. To Mateo, she seemed even lighter than before and he wondered if Tobias had something to do with it.

What is this guy? Must be some kind of magician or wizard. A demon with good tendencies? A murderous angel? A vampire? Theories filled his mind until he reached the cave entrance and his thoughts were interrupted by the flicker of red and blue police lights. Voices argued in the distance.

"I think the police are here. It may not be a good idea for you to—"

Mateo turned to see his belongings in a pile on the floor, and Tobias gone without a trace.


Isabella and Theo didn't notice Mateo emerging from the earth with Lucy.

"You put a tracker on my phone? That's a huge invasion of my privacy, Mom!" Theo shouted.

"A good thing I did! Do you know how dangerous it is for you to be out here?" She rebutted.

"I'm helping Mateo!" said Theo.

"Bullshit!" Isabella scolded. "He's in Willow Creek!"

"I'm right here." Mateo huffed. "Call an ambulance...please..."

Lucy's full weight returned. He collapsed to his knees and laid Lucy gently on the ground.

"What the...Lucy? Oh my God! Lucy! What happened to you?" Isabella fell to her side and checked her pulse.

"She's alive, just asleep."

"Theo! Get on my radio and call for an ambulance! Bring back the first aid kit from the trunk!" She began inspecting Lucy's injuries with a grimace.

"Did you carry her out of there all by yourself?" Isabella stared in shock at Mateo.

He looked back across the empty field and decided it was best not to mention Tobias.

"Yeah, I guess I did," Mateo said.

Isabella had tears in her eyes, overwhelmed by the trauma inflicted on her friend. "Mateo, these are the worst injuries I've ever seen in my law enforcement career...what happened to her?"

Mateo looked up at the moon. "You're gonna need a lot of police, Lieutenant Kentworth."

Theo sat the first aid kit on the ground next to his mother and looked around the field.

"Mattie...where's Bandito?"

# Chapter 30

## Recovery

Stella placed a heavy wooden box in Mateo's hands. The lid was hand-carved with roses, and painted on the front were the words *Bandito, Forever in Our Hearts.*

"I chose the roses because the little shithead was always digging mine up," Stella sniffed and pretended to look out the window. "I painted his name myself…got some new paint markers, you know…just wanted to try them out…"

"Mom…how did you get him back? I thought he was part of the crime scene or whatever?" Mateo didn't expect the box of ashes to feel so heavy.

"Theo's mom. She went right in there with a body bag and carried him out herself. Told the detectives to kiss her ass or whatever. Said it's the least that could be done for you," Stella wiped her eyes on her sleeve. "Anyway, I figure you should have him…if you want. You two have been through a lot together."

Mateo nodded. "Thanks, Mom."

Stella sat down on his bed. "She's awake, you know. A few of us are going down to the hospital to see her. She's been asking about you."

"I don't want to go yet," Mateo said. "I'm not ready. I'm still really messed up about Bandito, and it seems stupid to feel that way after everything Lucy went through. He's just a dog."

She put an arm over his shoulder and pulled him in close. "Pain is pain, Mattie. It doesn't do anyone any good to compare hurts. Take however long you need. Lucy will understand."

"Tell her I said hi, though…and I'm glad she's awake." Mateo set Bandito's ashes on his nightstand where his sketchbook used to be.

"I will. Be back in a bit."

A horn honked in the driveway. "That's Charlotte. Gotta go."

"Hey, uh…tell Oliver I hope he gets better soon. So we can hang out again," said Mateo.

Stella smiled. "Will do, kid."


Charlotte and Stella's drive to Springfield General Hospital was quiet. All of the parents were exhausted and overwhelmed by the experiences of their children, and Lucy's trauma.

"You know, I wish I would've gone to that swinger party instead of Lucy." Stella seethed. "If that guy tried to kidnap me, I'd kick his balls so hard they'd pop out his ears."

"Don't place guilt where it doesn't belong. This was the work of an evil man, under the influence of Satan. There's nothing you could have done to change that. Only God can." Charlotte preached.

"Maybe I should become an exorcist. I'll eradicate all the evil *sonsabitches* from the Earth." Stella spat.

"You can't. First of all, you have to be a priest. You barely qualify as Catholic. Not only that, you're a woman. Only men are allowed to become exorcists." Charlotte pointed out.

"Says who? That's some bullshit right there. Wouldn't God want me to be able to exorcise demons from my own children? Isn't that my right as their parent?" Stella ranted.

"Well, I think the idea is that it's for the layman's safety…" said Charlotte. "You need to have an exceptionally deep faith in God to command a demon out of a person or place. Also, most exorcists don't have families, friends, or even pets. Demons will use everything around an exorcist to break them down They'll hurt everything they love."

Stella scoffed. "Well, I guess that makes sense. Can I smoke in here?"

"No!" Charlotte put on the window lock. "Don't even try it!"

"Come on! They don't let you smoke on the hospital campus." Stella complained. "We'll be there hours."

"Too bad. Maybe you should quit." Charlotte pointed out.

"Damn, Charlie. You act like quitting smoking is as easy as quitting meth or something." The two women looked at each other and busted up laughing.

"Maybe I'll get some patches or whatever…hanging out with you is turning me into a square. Will you unlock the window, please?"

Charlotte scowled but hit the button.

Stella reached into her purse, took out her pack of cigarettes… and threw them out the window.

"Happy?"

"Actually, no. You just littered."

"Are you serious right now? I'm trying to be a better fucking person and you're giving me a hard time." Stella whined.


They were still bickering in the parking garage, up the elevator to the fifth floor, and all the way to the end of the hallway to the recovery ward. Stella excused herself to the ladies' room as Charlotte checked in to visit Oliver.

"You ever figure out your demon situation, Charlie? Or was it just drugs like I said?"

Charlotte turned around to see Ray sitting in the waiting room eating potato chips and watching a gameshow on the television. She sighed. *Of course he was here.*

Surrendering to the fates forcing their paths to cross once more, Charlotte sat down next to him. "It was both. I suppose demons influenced him to try the drugs…it's called demonic oppression. It's how they break someone down so they can be possessed."

"Hmm. I think I've been demonically oppressed more than a few times in my life. You think I might need an exorcism?" Ray tossed a chip in his mouth.

"Couldn't hurt." Charlotte gave a small smile. "You seen the news? The stuff about the cave?"

"Oh yeah, that shit's unbelievable. How many bodies they pull out so far? Five?" he sipped his free waiting room coffee from a foam cup.

"Actually, eleven. They've only identified five." Charlotte caught Stella's attention as she exited the bathroom, and she took the hint: this was not a conversation she would want to be part of.

Stella busied herself putting dollar bills into vending machines and picking snacks at random.

"Wait a minute…" Ray said, connecting the dots. "Is that the cave your kids went into?"

Charlotte nodded. "It's even worse than they said on the news. The place was basically some kind of Satanic temple or something. They did ritualist sacrifices and everything…the woman that escaped, Lucy…well, she's a friend of mine. We're going to see her after we visit Oliver."

"That's wild. So what's ya'll do to get rid of the demons?" Ray was enthralled in the conversation.

Charlotte didn't realize how much better she would feel spilling her guts to a neutral party. "Well, one of the kids was being oppressed–they're in therapy and recovering from sepsis. Released today, actually. Another needed a "spirit release"…basically, her body was haunted by a bunch of ghosts. Two others needed exorcisms. One of them even broke a bishop's finger."

Ray was beside himself. "No shit…I can't wait to tell Twi–…" He fell silent and turned his attention back to the gameshow.

"You guys still not speaking?" Charlotte asked.

He absentmindedly wiped crumbs off the small end table to the floor. "The asshole even unfriended me on social media," said Ray. "I was gonna send him a message and tell him I got rid of all the puppies but he had me blocked."

"I'm sorry to hear that," said Charlotte. "I hope you guys can work things out."

"Me too…" Ray was momentarily distracted by Stella. "Why is that lady buying so much candy? Those vending machines are a rip-off. She's better off walking across the street to Kum n Go."

"Stella," Charlotte gestured her over. "I want you to meet Ray."

Stella dumped her snacks into a pile on an empty chair, then stuck out her hand to shake Ray's. "Is this…ex-boyfriend, Ray?" Stella raised an eyebrow.

"The very same…" said Charlotte.

Ray laughed. "Nice to meet you, Stella. Why do I feel like my reputation precedes me?"

"Cuz it kind of does, *amigo…*"

Ray looked uncomfortable and changed the subject. "So Charlie…how's Oliver? Does he need an exorcism too?"

"Well, Oliver needs rehab…and lots of prayers. Probably not an exorcism." Charlotte sighed. "And Magnus? How's he?"

Ray scratched his beard. "Ugh, this kid. He really got into the wrong crowd. Probably my own damn fault for not giving him enough attention and whatnot. He probably needs rehab and prayer too. At least prayer is free…not so sure we'll be able to make rehab happen."

"I think most insurance will pay for rehab, Ray." Said Charlotte.

He gave her a sad smile. "Yeah, well, the wife and I are the 'cash under the table' sort of folks. We don't have health insurance."

Charlotte closed her eyes and connected to her heart. This man had not only put her through hell, but his failures as a parent tainted his son…who then tainted hers. If Oliver hadn't met Magnus, he wouldn't be in the addiction recovery ward right now. He'd be on his way to Spain for the summer.

Was that true, though? If it hadn't been Magnus, maybe it would have been someone else. Maybe God put Magnus in her path to teach her compassion, and to help her not-quite-healed heart find forgiveness towards Ray.

"I'd like to pay for Magnus to go to rehab." Said Charlotte.

Stella choked on a cheese puff.

"Charlie…you can't do that for us." Ray was taken aback. "It just ain't right after everything I've done to you, and my son getting yours in trouble."

"I believe it is *exactly* what I need to do," said Charlie. "If you want to make things right with me, be a good dad and stop the cycle of addiction. Get Magnus the help he needs so he can live a good life. Please, Ray. Let me do this for your son."

A nurse pushed open the heavy door to the addiction ward and stuck out her head. "Magnus's family! He's ready to see you now."

Flustered, Ray stood up and gathered his chips and coffee, splashing some on his pants. "Charlie…thank you. I'd like to take you up on your offer to help Magnus…and I hope you and I can be friends again. Eventually."

Charlotte stood and gave him a hug. She reached into her purse and pulled out a business card. "That's my number. I have a little side business cleaning offices after hours. Call me and we can work out the details, okay?"

Ray tipped his cowboy hat at her and nodded goodbye to Stella, then disappeared behind the door with the nurse.

"You are one good-ass person, Charlotte Gladstone." Said Stella in awe. "I bet you made Jesus all kinds of proud."

"Thank you…but I didn't do it for Jesus. I did it for *me*."


While Charlotte visited Oliver, Stella decided to go to the intensive care unit to see if she could catch Lucy alone. The curtains were drawn around Lucy's bed when she entered, but the room was flooded with balloons, flowers, cards, and stuffed animals. As Stella waited for the doctor to finish treating Lucy, she read the tags. They were from old friends and in-laws, but most were from complete strangers who saw her story on the news. Some were from the families of victims that had been identified…and some that hadn't been identified yet, but most likely would be. She found a small vase of rainbow-dyed daisies—it was from Mateo. He must have used his own money.

"Who's out there?" Lucy croaked from behind the curtain.

"Well, normally I'd say *The Baddest Bitch Who Ever Lived*…but I think you stole my title," said Stella.

"Come back here, I want you to see something," said Lucy.

Stella pulled back the curtain to see Lucy with her gown pulled up over her badly bruised torso. A doctor sat on a stool near a portable ultrasound machine and was moving the wand around her jellied belly.

"Can you believe it, Stella?" Lucy glowed behind her battered face.

"After everything that happened!"

The doctor was smiling. "Now you've still got another month or so before you're in the clear…but from my perspective, everything looks good. That's a steady, strong heartbeat."

Stella burst into tears. This young woman, tortured and left for dead, still wanted nothing more than to be a mother. "Oh, Lulu…I'm so happy for you. That's great news." She wrapped Lucy in a hug, cradling her head in her bosom.

"Ouch…Stella let go," Lucy laughed. "Come sit down."

The doctor wiped the jelly off Lucy's stomach and left with the nurse, so the two of them were alone.

"This is the first time there's been less than five people in here at a time," said Lucy.

Stella pulled the white cotton hospital blanket up to Lucy's neck and tucked them underneath her body to seal in the heat. "What can I say, *Muneca*? I know how to clear a room."

"Stella, stop fussing over me…I'm fine," Lucy swatted at her hand.

She scowled. "Don't you tell me what to do. I'll fuss if I want to."

Lucy laughed, soaking in the love and thunder of Stella's presence.

"So…what did Nolan say when you told him about the baby?" Stella asked.

Lucy bit her lip. "I haven't told him yet. I wanted to make sure, you know? He's grieving enough right now over what's happened to me. I didn't want him to hurt even more."

Stella reached for Lucy's hand, then remembered it was heavily bandaged. "How did surgery go?"

"Pretty good, but it's hard to tell until I've healed. I'll need a lot of physical therapy to be able to do fine motor things like cross-stitching," said Lucy.

"You just need to pick up a more brutish hobby. Maybe Isabella could teach you how to box," Stella laughed.

The curtain swished back. "Nah, she's got too pretty a face for that. Maybe martial arts?"

Isabella was dressed in uniform and held a small black notebook in her hand. It was obvious this was more than a friendly visit.

"Hi Isabella…I didn't think I'd see you until later with everyone else," said Lucy.

Isabella put a "share size" chocolate bar on Lucy's bedside table. "I brought you some candy…that's the good stuff right there."

"Hell yeah, it is. You get the one with almonds?" asked Stella.

"No, toffee."

"Oh, hell yeah," Stella nodded in approval.

Isabella settled on the doctor's stool. "I'm here a little early because Theo wanted to say hi to Trix. They're supposed to be released today. Also, there have been some updates on the case I thought Stella might need to know…I hoped to find you here."

"Well, Mattie told the police everything he saw. When Lucy woke up she confirmed it," Stella said.

"I know…it has to do with your brother-in-law," said Isabella. "Can we talk in the hallway?"

Stella's face flamed red. "I knew it! I knew Jason didn't overdose! That sick motherfucker killed him?!"

Isabella grabbed her by the arm. "Hallway! Now!"

Lucy had shrunk back into her pillow and grown silent. Stella canned her rage for a moment and fought back angry tears. Isabella pushed her out of the room and shut the door behind her.

She let Stella seethe in anger for a few moments before continuing. "What I'm about to tell you will be very upsetting, Stella. I need you to understand that Lucy is the one who told me…and at the time, she had no idea he was connected to you in any way." Said Isabella.

"Not only did they *kill* him, Isabella, they destroyed my sister's life! They took her house and everything they owned together because they weren't technically married. She's living in a goddamn hotel and can barely make ends meet!" Stella kicked the concrete wall.

"I know, Stella…I know. Calm down a minute, okay? The good news is, Stephanie confessed. Your sister may be able to sue her. Hell, maybe she will just settle out of court. That psychopath is going to be thrown in prison for *life* and has no heirs. The property is all going to the state, including the cave," said Isabella.

"Why did they do it?" Stella sniffed. "How?"

"Apparently Jason caught Richard with one of the girls…Richard used chloroform on him, then gave him a hot shot. Stephanie helped cover it up," Isabella explained. "There was so much evidence of her involvement in the other murders…then if you add Lucy's testimony…her lawyers told her to plead guilty. No jury will ever find her innocent."

"Fuckin' Snake Oil Stephanie. If you've met one, you've met them all. I told Lucy to stay away from her! Why did she go back, Isabella? Did she tell you?" Stella whispered-yelled.

Isabella shrugged. "I guess she borrowed something from someone at the party and went to drop it off. That's when Richard drugged her."

"I warned her so many times…" Stella said.

Isabella touched Stella's arm. "I know. You didn't fail Lucy…she just found herself in a vulnerable position, and Richard is a master manipulator. He's been devastating women his entire life. He even tried to get *me* during high school, but I got away. That shit keeps me up at night. Honestly, Richard deserved the end he got."

Stella stopped crying. "…what end?"

"Well…when we found his body it was missing the gallbladder, liver, and heart. The coroner thinks he was tortured," Isabella whispered. "Don't tell anyone I told you…"

"Mattie couldn't do that," said Stella.

"Of course not," said Isabella. "Mateo and Lucy said someone else was there…someone from their cult or whatever it is. They did it. No one's sure why though. This whole thing goes deeper than Richard and Stephanie."

"Mateo didn't tell me someone else was there," Stella pursed her lips.

Isabella shrugged. "Both their statements align with the evidence."

"Did you girls already go in without me?" Benny hollered from down the hallway. "Now you're makin' me look like some kind of asshole arriving late to the party!"

A nurse stepped in front of him and asked him to quiet down. He apologized and sashayed towards Stella and Isabella carrying a stuffed duck and a balloon.

"I thought y'all said four o'clock? Ash wanted me to drop him off at your place to see Mateo," Benny whispered.

"It's fine, Benny. I'm here early to talk to Stella. Why don't you go say hi to Lucy?" suggested Isabella.

"Pfft." Benny crossed his arms. "Well hello to you, too, Officer Rocky."

"Hello, Benny." Isabella gave him an exaggerated smile.

Benny smiled back, then took a deep breath. "My god y'all. I'm so nervous. I haven't seen her yet. My heart just breaks at the thought of what that monster did to my beautiful fake-wife. I*s it bad?*' he whispered.

Stella's eyes grew wide and gave a quick nod. "Put your big girl pants on. Don't let her see you upset."

"Got it," Benny straightened his back and preemptively plastered a smile across his face before diving into the room, leaving the other two to converse.

He flowed into the room to her bedside. "Well hello, Miss Lucy!...oh my God...holy shit." Ben dropped the duck onto a table littered with gifts. "You poor, sweet thing..."

"Calm down, Benny...they've got me medicated. I can't feel most of it," she said.

Benny sat on the bed next to her, with his hand to his mouth. "Did...*did the baby make it?*"

Lucy smiled.

"Oh, hunny...that's a miracle." He laid his hand gently on her leg. "You know, the twins really miss you. Whenever you're up to it, let me know and I'll bring them by."

Lucy smiled. "I will. How's Liam? Did his tooth finally come in?"

"YES, thank *God*. He's finally sleeping through the night again," said Benny.

Stella and Isabella came in with Gemma who held a potted plant.

"Hi Gemma!" said Lucy.

"Hello, Warrior Woman! I brought you a bamboo plant…you know, for good energy." Gemma smiled and placed on the window sill.

"Oh, that reminds me, I brought a duck," said Benny.

"I brought a candy bar," said Isabella

"I brought myself," Said Stella. "Guess I won!"

"Knock, knock! I have another flower delivery for you dear!" said a woman in the doorway wearing an apron from a local flower shop. "This is a big one, so your friends might want to clear some space while I get my cart."

Gemma and Isabella started clearing a table, piling gifts in a corner of the room.

"I'll go get the flowers," said Benny.

He returned a few moments barely peeking over to top of an enormous banana-leaf basket overflowing with sunflowers, purple gladiolus, cream-colored roses, and ferns the size of palm fronds.

"Oh my goodness! Let me help you!" Gemma grabbed one side, and they guided it to a table where the flowers spilled over the edges like a waterfall. "This is absolutely stunning!"

Lucy wiggled up in the bed, eager to get another look. "Benny, read the card. Who's it from?"

He unclipped the little pink card from a plastic stake, and read it silently to himself first.

*Get well soon, Lucy in the Sky With Diamonds.*

*The baby needs you.*

*Your friend,*

*Tobias*

Benny thought his heart stopped beating.

"Well?" said Stella. "Who's it from, Benny?"

He shoved the card in his pocket. "Sorry y'all, I forgot. It's from Christopher and the twins! They wanted to choose their own flowers for you, Lulu. I didn't expect them to go so overboard, but, you know...*you deserve it*!"

Lucy smiled. "That's so sweet...it must have cost a fortune."

"I bet it did..." said Benny.

Mateo still wasn't used to listening for a doorbell. Coco and Beemo weren't as concerned about visitors as Bandito was. They gave a few quick barks to announce Ash's arrival and then went back to sleep.

Mateo opened the door. "Ash...I didn't know you were stopping by. Come on in."

Ash stuffed his hands in his pockets. "Yeah, Benny wanted to go to the hospital. I don't like that sort of thing...so I told him to drop me off here and pick me up later. Is that cool?"

Mateo perked up. "Of course! I don't think you've ever been to my house before."

"I know, isn't that weird? We always meet up at other places." Ash looked around the room at family photos on the wall. He laughed at one of a gap-toothed Mateo wearing Mickey Mouse ears at Disneyland.

"It's funny, Theo said the same thing," said Mateo. "Did you hear Trix is being discharged today?"

"Yeah. Gonna be a while before we see Oliver though. He's going to rehab," said Ash. "Ez seems a lot better. She's back at work...gave me extra onion rings today."

"Maybe we could get the gang back together and start playing Magic again," Mateo said, hopeful for a fresh start with his friends.

"Sounds good to me," Ash picked up Mateo's sister's tuxedo cat, and hoisted her on his shoulder where she perched like a parrot.

Mateo laughed. "What the heck? Tippy's never done that before."

"Yeah, I dunno. Cats really like me now for some reason. You have anything to drink?" Ash asked, already walking into the kitchen.

Mateo followed and opened the fridge, grabbing a few sodas and a bag of chips. "Wanna play some video games?"

"Hell yeah, I do. Hey, Mattie…" said Ash, as he removed the cat from his shoulder and sat it on the ground.

"Yeah?" said Mateo.

"I'm glad you're okay."

# Chapter 31

## The Lemon Ladies

"Those are the ugliest fucking puppies I have ever seen, Emily."

Stella watched Esme and Mateo throw tennis balls to six long-legged, white, curly-haired Pyredoodles. Their eleven-year-old mother lay exhausted under the shade of a pear tree, grateful for the break.

Emily didn't deny they were ugly. "They have allergy-friendly coats."

"Yeah, but they're goofy as hell. Look at that one—it's got this big ass square head with a pointy poodle nose." Stella popped a piece of nicotine gum in her mouth and grimaced at the taste.

The dog saw Stella pointing and ran towards her.

"No, go away! I did not call you over here to me *perrito*," Stella moved away and it followed, sniffing at her freshly painted toes. "Don't you mess up my pedicure!"

The puppy looked up at her, wagging its tail, then licked her toes. Stella giggled reflexively.

"Stop, that tickles!" She ran around Emily with the puppy close behind her.

Emily laughed. "So do you want one or not?"

Mateo held a pot-bellied Pyredoodle mutant up to the sun like Simba. "I want this one, Mom!"

Stella rolled her eyes and pushed away the toe-licker with her foot. "Well, I guess Mateo wants that one."

"*Yip! Yip!*" The puppy at Stella's feet demanded her attention. Finally, she bent over and picked it up so they were nose to nose.

"What's your problem, dog?" She asked.

It belched.

"You got a real attitude, don't you? You look like some kind of baby seal or something."

They stared into each other's souls for a moment, considering one another.

Stella put the puppy in a football hold under one arm. "I'll take this one, too."

Emily laughed and scratched under the puppy's chin. It jumped in surprise as Harper slammed the sliding door shut. Stella put it down and threw a squeaky toy.

Harper's hurried footsteps thumped on the deck. "Mom! Mom! You've got mail from the school! Open it!"

Emily's heart sank. Didn't the interviewer say she'd get a letter in the mail if she wasn't accepted? She put on a smile for Harper's sake and took the letter from her eager hands. "Alright, alright. Just remember, Harper, I can always try again next semester if I'm not admitted this time."

"Just *open* it, Mom!"

Stella was now busy with Mateo throwing tennis balls to the herd of puppies. Emily quickly opened the letter before anyone saw and asked questions. She pulled out a thick piece of brownish paper.

"Wait…" said Harper. "Is that my *drawing*?"

Emily unfolded the letter to find the coloring page Harper had made during her nursing school interview. It was Emily as Cinderella, but in a nurse's uniform. Now—drawn in red ink—Cinderella was holding a letter that said *Accepted*.

Harper snatched the drawing from her mother for a closer look, as Emily read the enclosed letter.

*Ms. Sharp,*

*We are pleased to inform you that you have been selected to attend our nursing school program. Please check your email for further information, class times, and uniform requirements...*

Harper ran to the backyard where her sister was scooping dog doo. She showed her the drawing, and Esme clapped and jumped.

"Congrats, Mom!" she yelled through cupped hands.

Stella dropped the tennis ball she was throwing and trotted over.

"You got in?" she asked with a grin.

"I got in." Emily hugged the letter to her chest.

"You know what that means, don't you?" Stella rubbed her hands together with glee.

"It's time to celebrate?" said Emily.

Stella nodded. "That's right. Do you have a blender?"


Charlotte was on her way to Emily's house for the impromptu celebration of her good news. She didn't have time to make a dish to share, so she stopped at a warehouse store and bought a party-size tray of cookies and a case of hard lemonade. After getting to her van, Charlotte realized–if previous get-togethers were any indication–Benny will likely bring five different types of crackers and nothing to put on them. She went back inside and purchased a 2-pound block of cheese and a container of chicken salad. Then she saw laundry detergent on sale and a cute pair of running shoes. She taste-tested a new flavor of popcorn. Then bought a slice of pizza and a drink at the café.

By the time she left the store, she was already thirty minutes late. She turned on the van, and her Bluetooth blasted with phone notifications.

*Eight messages from Brent.*

*First message: Charlie I have a flat tire. Pick me up.*

*Second Message: I'm at the bowling alley.*

*Third Message: Where are you? I called a tow truck.*

*Fourth Message. Charlie, why is your phone off?*

"End messages!" Charlie yelled in frustration. "Give me directions to the bowling alley."

*Giving directions to bowling alley.*

"Text Emily," Said Charlotte.

*Texting Emily Sharp. What do you want to say?*

"Running late. Husband got a flat tire. I bought cheese for Benny's crackers."

*Message sent.*


Charlotte found Brent sitting on the curb at the bowling alley chewing his fingernails. Evidently the car had already been towed, and the bowling alley closed, so he was the only person in the parking lot. He jumped up when he saw her and climbed into the passenger seat, tossing the box of sneakers and block of cheese in the backseat. He sat the hard lemonade on his lap.

"I was getting worried! I almost called a cab, then I saw your location headed this way. You going to a party or something? What's with the cookies and lemonade?" Brent buckled his seatbelt.

"Just a little get-together at Emily's. She was accepted into nursing school," Charlotte pulled out of the parking lot towards their home.

"Wow, that's great! Tell her I said congratulations," he said.

"I will."

"You know, Charlie…I'm really glad you found some friends outside of the homeschool groups and church. It's good to have things for yourself rather than the family sometimes. You, know, like me with my bowling team." Brent opened the cookie tray and took out one of each kind. "Man, I'm starving. Am I making dinner tonight then?"

"Just tell the kids it's a freezer food night. There's all kinds of burritos and stuff in the deep freezer." Charlotte could always gauge Brent's stress levels by the number of cookies he ate. When Oliver was missing he could clear a pack of Oreos in a day. Tonight the kids could give him a break and eat chicken nuggets.

"Sounds good to me," he shoved a chocolate chunk cookie in his mouth.

"How was the game? Did you win?" Charlotte asked.

He shook his head and gulped. "Nope."

*One new message.*

"That's probably Emily. Read message."

*From: Unknown Number*

*First Message: Hey there Demon Ladies. It's Ray. I've got a friend with a real big problem in his basement. Some spooky shit down there. I told him I knew some girls who might be able to take care of that sort of thing. Since I'm trying to look out for you, I told him you wouldn't do it for free. He says he's got a freezer full of venison to trade. All I ask for is half, as a finder's fee. Text me back.*

"Demon Ladies? What's that about?" Brent shook crumbs out of his beard.

Charlotte searched her mind frantically for an explanation that would make sense to her husband. "Ray's a client for my office cleaning business. He must be talking about a referral."

"A freezer full of venison as payment for cleaning someone's basement, and this Ray guy wants half? I'd be rethinking that arrangement!" Brent laughed.

Charlotte giggled nervously. "I know, right? We'll work something else out."

"We?" Brent asked.

"Uh, yeah. I'm expanding. The girls and I started working together… sharing clients, you know…to accommodate our busy parenting schedules…. and whatnot…" Charlotte trailed off.

"And you're called The Demon Ladies?" he teased, taking a bite of a rainbow candy cookie this time.

"No…of course not!" said Charlotte. Her eyes landed on the drinks in her husband's lap.

Charlotte smiled.

"It must have been a typo. Our cleaning company is called *The Lemon Ladies.*"

# Author's Notes

When I first entertained the idea of *The Lemon Ladies*, I had recently returned from hiking The Adirondack Mountains in Upstate New York and planned for the characters to embark on a *Blair Witch*-style camping trip rather than a haunted cave expedition. The story would have focused on Esme and Emily rather than Mateo and Stella. A couple of things happened to change the trajectory of *The Lemon Ladies* series; now, I can't imagine it any other way.

Writers often encounter people in real life who are *characters*. For me, when I meet a "character", I scribble on an index card what I find interesting about them and save it in a shoe box. Good or bad, these are personalities so rich (to me, anyway) that their essence deserves to be in print. After experiencing a "Stella and Mateo" situation in the wilds of life, I knew they had to be in *The Lemon Ladies*. I found their parent-child dynamic fascinating and wondered what it would be like to have this mother as a "mom friend". *What was her story?* I added her to my box of characters, but I couldn't get her out of my head. The idea of Stella hijacked my brain for weeks, blending with some of my own traits (mostly my deadpan humor. I am not a retired stripper.). I often tell readers that Stella is an amplified version of my 40-year-old self, whereas Lucy is my 20-year-old self. It's no coincidence that Stella is so protective of Lucy.

I don't write chapters in order (weird, I know), so even before I fully formed the plot for *The Lemon Ladies*, I wrote Stella's introduction chapter. I laughed so hard as I wrote it, remembering my absolutely ridiculous encounter with the real-life stranger who inspired her...I just *knew* I couldn't help but make her the *estrella* of the show. The next chapter I wrote was Benny's. Then Isabella's. One by one, Stella and Mateo's friends appeared on the pages. As the cast came to life, the camping trip setting just didn't feel right. I started considering other possibilities.

At the time, I wanted to install a bat house on my property and was obsessed with learning about bats of the Midwest. During my research I came across a story about Mark Twain Cave in Hannibal, Missouri. As much as I love St. Louis, I never seemed to make it a few hours north to see the cave. I ventured down an internet rabbit hole of its history to plan a visit, and I felt like The Muses were whispering in my ear. Fascinating and spooky, the story of Mark

Twain Cave was perfect for *The Lemon Ladies*.

In Missouri, there are over 6,500 discovered caves. The Mark Twain Cave system is one of the largest, spanning a total of 6.5 known miles. It was discovered by a hunter in the early 1800's, and purchased by "mad doctor" and grave robber, **Joseph Nash McDowell, in 1840 as a place to perform experiments on human corpses.** One of the many rumored ghosts in Mark Twain Cave is that of his young daughter, Amanda. After Amanda died from pneumonia at the age of 14, Dr. McDowell became convinced that he could commune with the dead, so he filled a container with alcohol and placed her body inside to preserve it. He then hung it from the ceiling of the cave so he could continue to speak to her.

The children of Hannibal were known to sneak into the cave to witness the spectacle of the dead girl floating in a glass tube, and eventually their parents caught on. Two years after Amanda's death, the citizens of Hannibal stormed the cave to remove the girl's corpse and give her a proper burial.

Beyond his medical experiments, Dr. McDowell was also a known supporter of the Confederacy—Missouri was a Union state—and was said to have a massive stash of weapons hidden away in the cave for Confederate soldiers to use during the Civil War. One of those rebels was none other than the **legendary outlaw Jesse James**. After the war, it's believed he used his knowledge of the cave to hide out there after an 1867 train robbery in Kansas City. **His signature can still be found on the cave walls.**

The cave remained known only to locals for over seventy-five years. The 19th century author **Mark Twain** often explored this cave system as a child and included it in *"The Adventures of Tom Sawyer"*; after the book was published in 1876, the cave was so famous it became a tourist attraction, and McDowell Cave was renamed Mark Twain Cave. It's rumored he once stared into a pit within the cave and saw a demon, inspiring the death scene of Injun Joe in *Huckleberry Finn*. After decades of searching nearly 250,000 signatures on the cave walls, Mark Twain's given name—Samuel Clemens—was finally found in 2019.

It would be another hundred years before this cave system became a source of worldwide news. While building a new highway (Route 79), construction crews were using dynamite to blast through the hillsides and accidentally exposed new entrances into the cave. Despite being grounded by their parents for visiting the construction site previously, three boys—Billy Hoag (10), Joey Hoag (13) and Craig Dowell (14)—were last seen entering the cave with shovels and flashlights on March 10th, 1967. They never returned home.

Rescue teams including spelunkers, The National Guard and even psychics searched the cave system and nearby river for ten days before ending the search without a single piece of evidence indicating their survival. Spelunkers from all over the world have continued to search for the boys' remains for nearly sixty years, but the **"Lost Boys of Hannibal"** case is no closer to being solved than the day they disappeared. They were likely killed in a tunnel collapse; other possibilities are that they drowned in a flood, were victims of a kidnapping, or simply became so lost in the labyrinthian cave system they were never found. **It's one of Missouri's most frustrating missing persons cases and most likely will never be solved.**

I've barely scraped the surface of these stories, so I encourage you to do your own research if anything piques your interest. And, yes, the cheese caves are real. Check those out, too.

I look forward to covering other Missouri legends throughout *The Lemon Ladies* series including The St. Louis Witch, The Devil's Chair, Zombie Road, Missouri State Penitentiary and the ghosts of Route 66.

I hope you had as much fun reading *The Lemon Ladies* as I did writing it. For me, it was an absolute joy. I hope this series becomes one of your favorites.

Email me at amyquillenwrites@gmail.com to let me know which characters or folklore you want to read about!

The series will continue with a little "side-quest" to Benny's hometown of New Orleans, Louisiana, where he discovers the source of all his bad mojo.

Y'all ready for a little voodoo?


Thanks for reading,

*Amy*